THE PENGUIN CLASSICS

FOUNDER EDITOR (1944–64): E. V. RIEU

HENRI MARIE BEYLE, known through his writings as Stendhal, was born in Grenoble in 1783 and educated there at the École Centrale. A cousin offered him a post in the Ministry of War, and from 1800 onwards he followed Napoleon's campaigns in Italy, Germany, Russia and Austria. In between wars, he spent his time in Paris drawing-rooms and theatres.

After the fall of Napoleon, he retired to Italy, adopted his pseudonym, and started to write books on Italian painting, Haydn and Mozart, and travels in Italy. In 1821 the Austrian police expelled him from the country, and returning to Paris he finished his book *De l'Amour*. This was followed by *Racine et Shakespeare*, a defence of romantic literature. *Le Rouge et le Noir* was his second novel, and he also produced or began three others, including *La Chartreuse de Parme*, none of which was received with any great understanding during his lifetime.

Beyle was appointed Consul at Civita Vecchia after the 1830 revolution, but his health deteriorated and six years later he was back in Paris and beginning a life of Napoleon. In 1841 he was once again recalled for reasons of illness, and in the following year he suffered a fatal stroke. Various autobiographical works, his *Journal*, his *Souvenirs de l'Egotisme* and *La Vie de Henri Brulard*, were published later, as his fame grew.

MARGARET SHAW was born in 1890 and took a B.A. degree by correspondence course from London University before going up to St Hugh's College, Oxford, to gain a 'first' in languages. She was at the Sorbonne when the First World War broke out, and returned to teach in Bradford, but she later went back to Paris and spent a long time there. She did research on Laurence Sterne, and published a book about his 'Letter to Eliza'. She became a tutor at St Hugh's, and taught in Repton in the Second World War. She translated two other books, Stendhal's *The Charterhouse of Parma* and the *Chronicles of the Crusades* of Joinville and Villehardouin, for the Penguin Classics, and had begun on another when she died in 1963.

STENDHAL

SCARLET AND BLACK

A CHRONICLE
OF THE NINETEENTH CENTURY·

TRANSLATED
AND WITH AN INTRODUCTION BY
MARGARET R. B. SHAW

PENGUIN BOOKS

Penguin Books Ltd, Harmondsworth, Middlesex, England
Penguin Books, 40 West 23rd Street, New York, New York 10010, U.S.A.
Penguin Books Australia Ltd, Ringwood, Victoria, Australia
Penguin Books Canada Ltd, 2801 John Street, Markham, Ontario, Canada L3R 1B4
Penguin Books (N.Z.) Ltd, 182–190 Wairau Road, Auckland 10, New Zealand

—

This translation first published 1953
Reprinted 1955, 1957, 1961, 1962, 1964, 1965, 1967, 1969, 1971, 1972, 1974, 1975,
1976, 1977, 1978, 1979, 1981, 1982, 1983, 1984

—

—

Made and printed in Great Britain by
Hazell Watson & Viney Limited,
Member of the BPCC Group,
Aylesbury, Bucks
Set in Linotype Juliana

CONTENTS

PART TWO

INTRODUCTION

WHEN *Scarlet and Black* was published round about November 1830, France had just passed through a second revolution. The novel, begun towards the end of 1828 and finished during the summer of 1830, has a certain historical interest, for in Stendhal's picture of life in the provinces and in Paris we are constantly meeting traces of the clash between Royalists and Liberals that was to lead to the 'glorious days' of July 1830 and the abdication of Charles X in favour of a 'citizen king'. The France of Stendhal's novel is a country in which the differences between Liberals, upholding Republican principles of freedom of thought and freedom of the press, and Ultra-Royalists (Ultras for short), supporting Charles X in his attempt to regain the absolute powers of a king under the *Ancien Régime*, are already too wide for hope of settlement. It is a country, too, in which the Church has taken sides in the conflict and, by proclaiming the 'alliance of throne and altar', has intensified the ill-will amongst men of opposite views.

The author of *Scarlet and Black* was a Liberal, a Bonapartist moreover and a freethinker, and he has on that account been accused, by certain critics, of undue bias. The picture, however, that he gives us of France in 1825–30 is in the main corroborated by outside evidence; and his sympathetic portraits of the Ultra-Royalist Marquis de la Mole and of the two priests, Father Pirard and Father Chélan, go far to clear him of the charge of being an extremist. We can therefore take it for granted that he gives us as fair a view of the times as can be expected of a man who is living through the experiences he describes and has not had an opportunity of setting them in perspective.

It is not, however, as an historical novel that *Scarlet and Black* is of most interest to us, but as a work which is at one and the same time a novel of manners and a novel of character, written by a man who is more of a psychologist than a party politician, a creative artist rather than a chronicler of events.

For the plot of his story Stendhal takes an incident of the police-courts which he found in certain numbers of the *Gazette des Tribunaux* of December 1827. Antoine Berthet, handsome, intelligent, and ambitious, but the son of a blacksmith, was anxious to rise in the world. Helped by the curé of his village, he obtained a post as tutor in a well-to-do middle-class family in Grenoble, but was dismissed before the end of a year. He entered a seminary at Belley, but at the end of two years was asked to leave; he obtained admission to the seminary at Grenoble, but at the end of a month was told he was unfitted to become a priest. Desperate and penniless, he began to write insulting letters to his former employer's wife, Madame Michoud, whereupon her husband, fearing an open scandal, found him another post in a M. Cordon's family. He was very soon dismissed, and began writing letters to M. Michoud, threatening to kill his wife. M. Michoud found him a post in another family. A few weeks later, Berthet suddenly appeared in church during Mass, and fired two shots at Madame Michoud. At his trial he pleaded provocation. He had wanted (he said) to atone for his fault and become a 'virtuous priest', but confession of it to the Rector of the seminary had only resulted in expulsion. He had tried to behave decently in M. Cordon's house, but his employer, influenced by a letter from Madame Michoud, and disliking Mademoiselle Cordon's friendly attitude towards him, had driven him out. Acting on a sudden impulse, he had revenged himself on the woman whom he believed to be the cause of all his misfortunes. Many people, moved by Berthet's defence and seeing him as the unfortunate victim of people in a superior station, had tried to help him obtain a reprieve, but in spite of their efforts he was executed.

Readers of *Scarlet and Black* will recognize here the groundwork of Stendhal's novel, but they will recognize no less in the book itself the genius of a writer whose imagination enlarges and transforms this sordid incident into a masterpiece of fiction on the grand scale. Grand? The style of the novel hardly seems to warrant this description. Here are no fine phrases, no heroics, no broad sweeps of imaginative writing, but a story simply told in the language men use in talking to each other by the fireside or across the dinner-table. Yet the novel is grand in its scope and in its purpose. A 'chronicle of the nineteenth century' Stendhal calls it. And a chronicle it is, though, as I have already suggested, of men and manners rather than of constitutions and kings. True, we find references to the Charter and government by two Chambers, to plots against the monarchy and counter-measures against the Republicans, to censorship of the press and to the constant fear of a new revolution that made the Royalist see 'a Jacobin behind every hedge'; we meet also, amongst the characters of the novel, Royalists and Liberals, Gallicans and Ultramontanists, Jesuits and Jansenists; but all the time our attention is drawn not so much to what is happening in the field of history as to the effect of current events on the lives and behaviour of ordinary people. The subterfuges and intrigues of local politics, the scramble for posts and peerages and decorations, the hypocrisy and greed for power of certain clerics, the indignation of upright men against the 'ills of church and society', the exasperation of moderate minds with the unreasoning bitterness of extremists, the backward-looking dreams of Royalists and Liberals alike – all these together form what Stendhal called his 'mirror of life', reflecting, as it 'journeys down the highway', the 'blue of the skies and the mire in the road below'; all these add up to a grand indictment of a society in which wealth and rank are preferred to personal merit, and energy is 'frittered away in a round of little social duties'.

Rightly a 'mirror': the action of the story passes through a series of scenes reflecting the life of the times in various settings – a little town in the provinces, a country house with an orchard and a garden, a seminary, a nobleman's house in Paris, the assizes in Besançon – in which conversation and soliloquy supply the main comment, and every detail is chosen to give back the mood of a character or a picture of manners. Yet a mirror, rather than a painting, reflecting, as it passes, stray gestures, odd, but revealing, images of life in drawing-rooms, fragmentary glimpses of landscape. On the mountain path up which Julien climbs, the quiet and coolness under the trees, the high, bare rocks, the sparrow-hawk taking flight, are needed as a contrast to the chatter at M. de Rênal's dinner-table, and the irritation of a life in which Julien has no freedom to be himself. They reflect naturally the colour of his mood. At the Hôtel de la Mole, the heavy gilding, the 'imposing' eight-foot mirrors, are characteristic of a society outwardly splendid and inwardly dull. We know at once that individuality will be stifled here; we can forecast what Julien's reactions will be when once this splendour has ceased to awe him. Critics who have blamed Stendhal for the inadequacy and banality of his descriptions overlook the fact that these are part of the structure of his novel, and not decoration, as so many more beautiful descriptions are.

In this way Stendhal links up the people of his novels with their background. But there is a further link. The three chief characters of *Scarlet and Black* are all dissatisfied with their environment, and out of their dissatisfaction springs the story. If Madame de Rênal had not been married to a boorish husband and had not felt out of sympathy with provincial ways; if Mathilde had not compared, to their disadvantage, the young men in her mother's drawing-room with a sixteenth-century ancestor; if the one had not found an 'elective affinity' between herself and her children's tutor, and the other not thought to discover in her father's secretary the energy and enterprise lacking in the young nobles around her; if Julien's wounded pride had not sought satisfaction in seducing the wife of a man of superior rank to his own, or in being preferred to the young Marquis who wished to marry Mathilde – there would have been no final catastrophe. And then, what remains of the book?

We may admire the neatness of structure in this novel, the art with which Stendhal develops his theme of conflict between society and the individual, leading smoothly on from one episode to another and setting off a darker passage by contrast with a lighter one (as, for instance, where Julien forgets his ambitions to go chasing butterflies in the orchard, or M. de Moirod takes a header off his horse plumb into a mud-puddle); we may praise him for a psychological insight rarer in his day than in ours, for his recognition, in particular, of contradictions that distinguish the live human being from the type; or we may follow certain critics in calling his art artifice, his neatness mechanical, his story of Julien Sorel little more than an amplification of the 'Beylist' maxim that the energy to will and to put will into action, is the highest mark of a 'superior being', even if it leads to crime.

All depends on our interpretation of Julien's character, and in particular of the motives behind his attempt on Madame de Rênal's life. The point turns on whether Julien, in full possession of his senses, believes he is committing an act that 'releases him from laws that bind the common herd', or whether, driven out of his mind by the shock of reading Madame de Rênal's letter, he is hardly conscious of what he is doing.

We must turn to the novel to see how Stendhal develops the character of his hero. He shows him, if I read the book rightly, as a young man of strong emotions but little discretion, who has adopted a code of hypocrisy, not because deception comes naturally to him, but because, from his all-too-little experience of the world, it seems to him the only method by which a man of humble birth can make his way. By choice he would have worn a soldier's *scarlet* tunic – like so many young men of his time he looks back with regret to the days of the Grand Army and takes Napoleon for his hero. Now, by force of circumstances, a priest's *black* cassock seems his only alternative. So he is launched on a course of action in which he has to suppress his real feelings, and we are not surprised to see that when they do find outlet they do so with excessive violence. Faced with an emergency, he almost always loses his head, and that, I believe, is what Stendhal meant us to understand in the particular incident of the shooting.

This view is supported by Stendhal's account of Julien's state of mind after reading the letter – he cannot think, he cannot hold a pencil to write, he can scarcely make the gunmaker understand what he wants. It is confirmed by a passage after the event, in which we are told that Julien recovered from 'the state of semi-insanity and nervous irritation in which he had been since leaving Paris' only on learning that Madame de Rênal was alive, and then his first feeling was 'remorse' for his crime. 'Mon petit Julien', as Mathilde calls him, is not only too impulsive to make a good hypocrite, but, even more certainly, not ruthless enough to be an earlier edition of Nietzsche's Superman. In short, if I interpret Stendhal rightly, it is not by his crime but by his repentance, and above all by his quiet acceptance of death as the expiation of guilt, not as the world but as his own conscience sees it, that Julien Sorel stands above the 'common herd' as Stendhal's 'superior being'.

Contradictions in the character of the man who was both Beyle and Stendhal are a tempting subject, but I will not let myself digress. My purpose here is to disentangle the reflective mood of the artist from the many bursts of temper that led the man to make wild statements, many of his 'Beylist' maxims being, in my opinion, among the wildest. That is why, in the paragraphs that follow, I do not quote Stendhal's oft-quoted but misleading comparison of his own style to that of the *Code Civil*.

At the time of its publication the book aroused unfavourable criticisms from Romantics, who found it lacking in beauty, and Classicists, who thought it vulgar and flat. Stendhal was piqued by their want of appreciation, but he would not allow that it was warranted. In a pamphlet entitled *Racine et Shakespeare* he had given reasons for his choice of style. When writing of 'everyday events', he maintained, a nineteenth-century author should use the style of current conversation as more natural, and therefore a truer expression of thought and feeling, than the 'rhetoric', however poetical, of more violent, if more heroic, ages. This choice was justified provided – it is an important proviso – there was 'fire' in the writing. It did not trouble Stendhal that it was an innovation for an author of a serious work of fiction to use a colloquial style; indeed, he was proud to be an innovator. 'I shall be understood in 1880,' he told his critics. His prophecy came true.

Unlike the men of 1830, we can judge this style on its merits. It is the form best suited to 'mirror' a civilized society in which emotions are by custom decently veiled in half-tones and under-statements, clichés and generalizations acceptable to the group. Its very plainness has advantages. No 'purple patches' break the unity of form and content. None the less, it is the medium which a writer as sensitive and skilled as Stendhal can use to suggest, behind the apparent decorum, emotions common to all human beings whether they belong to a sophisticated age or no. We hear, for example, M. de Rênal's heavy self-importance, Father Pirard's irritability, Mathilde's petulance, Julien's 'fire'. In the narrative the tale goes quietly forward, but even here a quickening of the movement or a stronger emphasis in the phrase mark those passages where emotion come more nearly to the surface.

Stendhal makes very little use of slang, and, where he uses it, either underlines the expression or refers to it as 'vulgar'. His style remains pre-eminently the style of *polite* conversation. He was, it is true, a realist, admired and recognized as a pioneer by later realists of the nineteenth century, but his manner is very different from theirs. A writer should be, he said, 'romantic in his ideas, but classical in his style', a principle he follows in this novel, which is, in fact, a highly romantic story, narrated with the measure and the reticence of the best French classics. We see this more particularly in episodes where less urbane realists might find opportunity for sensational writing – in Julien's attempt on Madame de Rênal's life, in the scene of his execution, and, above all, in that final chapter where Mathilde mourns over her dead lover's head. Here the restrained simplicity of Stendhal's treat-ment illustrates the finer possibilities of colloquial style.

In my translation of this novel I have tried to keep the plain-ness and 'good manners' of the original. I have used modern English, not only because that is the aim of this series, but be-cause, with this particular writer, it corresponds best to his idea of 'current conversation'. I have therefore avoided archaisms such as 'egad', albeit', 'thee', and 'thou' in intimate conversations (already out of date in 1830), and the use of 'will not', 'cannot', etc., where contracted forms are more natural – all of which I find in an earlier translation. In the matter of titles, I have used M.,

Madame, Mademoiselle, and kept the French form with the particle *de* (Comte de Caylus, but Count Altamira); I have left the worldly Abbé de Frilair untranslated, but have given parish priests and others the customary title of 'Father'. I have consulted friends who know more about such matters than myself on the right equivalents for terms relating to the Church and the Law, and have used the *Dictionnaire de l'Académie* of the period, side by side with a modern dictionary, to check my renderings. Although I am not sure that I have always caught the exact shade of meaning – in certain contexts alternative renderings would have been equally appropriate – I think I can claim that my translation is a more exact reproduction of the original than any previous one.

If I had space there are many things I would like to speak of: the personality of the author as reflected in his book, the experiences that influenced the development of his genius and coloured his picture of society, the writers – Shakespeare in particular – behind his conception of a tragic story, the sensationalist philosophers – Helvétius, Condillac, Destutt de Tracy – from whom he derived his reading of human nature, his own peculiar theories on the 'crystallization' of love. I would like to refer more fully to the real people on whom he based many of his characters – the unsympathetic father, the mother whose gentleness and 'gaiety' are reflected in Madame de Rênal, the disdainful Méthilde Dembowski who is the original of Mathilde de la Mole. I would like, above all, to point out the many resemblances between Stendhal and his hero that made it possible for him to say : 'Julien is myself'.

But all these, though they help to place the novel in its context and give it more value as a 'human document', are not essential to the appreciation of it as a work of art, nor to the enjoyment of it as a good story. I have therefore contented myself with a brief biographical note on Stendhal and his writings, and have limited this Introduction to a consideration of qualities in the book itself. Readers of *Scarlet and Black* may not agree with all my findings, but I hope these are provocative enough to make them form their own opinions. I hope, above all, they will enjoy reading this novel as much as I have enjoyed translating it.

BIOGRAPHICAL NOTE

HENRI MARIE BEYLE, the son of a lawyer at Grenoble, was born on 23 January 1783. His family were in comfortable circumstances, but, from the time of his mother's death when he was seven, the boy was unhappy at home. He was educated by private tutors until he was thirteen, and then went to the École Centrale at Grenoble. In 1799 he was offered a post at the Ministry of War by his cousin, Pierre Daru. From 1800 onwards he took part in most of Napoleon's various campaigns : in Italy, as a second lieutenant in the 6th Dragoons and aide-de-camp to General Michoud; in Germany (1806) with a junior post in the commissariat; in Russia (1812); in Austria (1813). In between he spent most of his time in Paris, frequenting drawing-rooms and theatres. When the Allies invaded France he was helping to organize defence on the south-east frontier, and after the fall of Napoleon (1814) he retired to Italy and, taking the pseudonym of STENDHAL, began to write. His first works were a history of Italian painting, the lives of Haydn and Mozart, and a book of travels, *Rome, Naples et Florence* (1817), in which his keen curiosity about men and manners begins to show itself. Expelled from Italy in 1821 by the Austrian police, he returned to Paris, where he finished *De l'Amour* (1822), a semi-didactic, semi-autobiographical dissertation on love. He was friendly with a small group of writers including Mérimée and Paul-Louis Courier, but his works were not popular. In *Racine et Shakespeare* (1822 and 1825) he defended the Romantics against attacks from their Classical opponents, but at the same time defined his own ideas of style in terms that showed him more of a realist than a romantic. His first novel, *Armance*, with the sub-title, 'a few scenes from a Paris drawing-room in 1827', marked the beginning of his campaign against society, continued with greater force and subtlety three years later in *Le Rouge et le Noir* (the *Scarlet and Black* of this edition). After the Revolution of July 1830, he was appointed Consul at Civita Vecchia. Here he began another novel, *Lucien Leuwen*, but left it unfinished. From 1836 to 1839 he was on prolonged 'sick leave' in Paris, during which time he began a life of Napoleon, wrote *Les Mémoires d'un Touriste*, and completed two more novels – *La Chartreuse de Parme*, which like *Le Rouge et le Noir* ranks as one of his greatest works, and *L'Abbesse de Castro*. He went on writing after his return to Civita Vecchia, but found his isolation in that city deadening to his mind. He suffered from gout and fits of giddiness, and then in 1841 a slight stroke caused him to ask to be recalled to Paris. On 15 March 1842 he had another stroke, and yet another, this time fatal, on 23 March. He left many unpublished works, among them his *Journal*, the *Souvenirs d'Égotisme*, and *La Vie de Henri Brulard*, all autobiographical writings giving a record of his experiences from earliest childhood, from which is gathered much of what we know about the man himself, his likes and dislikes, his many unhappy love affairs, his unfulfilled ambitions. The dates of publication of these many works (from 1855 onwards) mark the growing esteem of his countrymen for a writer whose chief misfortune was to have been a realist in an age of Romantics.

NOTES ON BACKGROUND

ALLUSIONS to the historical background of the times form part of Stendhal's picture of manners. Some of these are self-explanatory. I will only attempt to set in their context those that need explanation, just as allusions in a modern novel of manners to 'appeasement', the Atlantic Charter, Marshall Aid, etc., will need it a hundred years from now. I have grouped my comments, for convenience of reference, under three headings.

The State and Society

At the time of the Restoration Louis XVIII's government had defined the terms of a new constitution for France in the Charter of 1814. This was an attempt to conciliate both Liberals and Royalists, but it did not please the Ultras, who wanted a return to the *Ancien Régime*, nor the left-wing Liberals, who wanted a Republic. In Stendhal's picture of life in Ultra-Royalist drawing-rooms there is little explicit reference to the Charter, but full relief is given to the hatred of the nobles for the system of government it defined. Stendhal himself, who was a Liberal but no democrat, mentions (p. 164) as a 'great misfortune of governments voted into power . . . and a country that has a Charter' the freedom given to 'fools' to shape public opinion. This and other passages in the book support the view that his attack on society was levelled rather against the 'mediocrities' who dictated its tone than against a particular brand of politics.

It was, however, levelled against certain tyrannies of the
government in power, and so far may be construed as an attack
against the Ultras. The Charter had guaranteed freedom of
thought and, within limits, freedom of the press. But this agreement had been broken by a Ministry of Ultras at the end of Louis
XVIII's reign, and censorship had grown more severe under
Charles X (1824–30). The book contains passing references to
measures taken against editors and writers: the imprisonment of
the poet Béranger (p. 307) for his verses on Napoleon, and of
Fontan and Magalon (p. 335), editors of a Liberal periodical, condemned to five years in jail for publishing a 'seditious' pamphlet.
An allusion to Liberal risings in 1821–2 against this censorship
and other contraventions of the Charter is found in the mention
of Colonel Caron (p. 335), who was shot as a *suspected* leader of
the rebels. (The circumstances of his arrest and trial have points
in common with the Dreyfus case.) These, in their immediate context, illustrate reactions in Julien's own mind, but taken in con-
junction with Stendhal's account of the persecution of Falcoz (pp.
141–2), who was, in real life, his friend Falcon, a bookseller at
Grenoble, they are further evidence for the author's case against
society. We may note that well before 1830 not only moderate
Liberals, but moderate Royalists as well, were roused to protest
at infringements of the Charter.

The Church

Stendhal gives a dark enough picture of the Church of his day;
his allegations, however, are supported by Catholic evidence. The
alliance of '*throne and altar*', a natural, but unfortunate, result of
sufferings experienced by nobles and clergy alike during the Revolution, became under Charles X the instrument of a kind of holy
war against 'atheist' Liberals. (Many of them, as it happened,
were devout Catholics.) *Congrégations*, or societies of prominent
laymen established under the direction of the clergy in many of
the larger towns, though formed ostensibly in the interests of
religion, acted as a kind of secret police in the interests of the
Ultras. *Missions* (p. 156), largely composed of Jesuit priests, paid
annual visits to the chief towns in the provinces, preaching the
'true faith' and the 'right political doctrines'.

The Jesuits, who had been expelled from France in 1757, returned in full force with the Restoration. They were zealous sup-

porters of absolute monarchy, and their influence was great in the *Congrégations*. The Jansenists formed a small minority of the clergy, distinguished by their unorthodox views on certain points of doctrine, the puritanical austerity of their lives, and their refusal to mix religion with politics. They were particularly hated by the Jesuits, whose quarrel with them had begun when Jansen published his *Augustinus* (1640) attacking Jesuit doctrine and methods. Stendhal accepts the popular identification of Jesuit with hypocrite, and represents the two upright priests in his book as Jansenists.

There are references in this book to the two main parties in the French Church in 1830 – the Ultramontanists and the Gallicans. The former accepted the absolute authority of the Pope in all matters of religion and recognized his infallibility; the latter, clinging to their independence, accepted the supremacy of the Pope in questions of dogma, but would not admit the infallibility of his judgements nor his right to dictate on matters of Church government or to interfere with the 'old Gallican usages' as defined by Bossuet in the seventeenth century. These differences lie behind the exchange of words (p. 390) between the Ultramontanist Cardinal and another member of the secret meeting ('Ah ! Rome ! Rome !' 'Yes, sir,' the Cardinal answered proudly ... 'the Clergy, guided by Rome, etc. ...'). They explain Father Pirard's astonishment (p. 187) on hearing Julien quote Joseph de Maistre's *Du Pape* (an Ultramontanist document) in place of 'maxims of the old Gallican Church'. These may seem old, remote quarrels, but we need to know something about them to enter into the minds of people in the book.

A last small point : the clergy and their 'woodlands'. Before the Revolution the Church in France drew most of its wealth from large tracts of forest land. At the Restoration the clergy hoped to have these lands restored, but they were retained by the Crown. Reference to this, their greatest grievance, is made at the secret meeting (p. 391).

The Law

There are a few points to note in the account of Julien's trial. A Public Prosecutor, as in Scotland, conducts the case against the accused. The Jury can reach a verdict by a majority vote. By the Penal Code of that time an attempt at murder, even though it did not result in death, was punishable by death; Julien's sentence is therefore perfectly legal. His best defence would have been to plead provocation, but he has a finer sense of honour than

Antoine Berthet. By rashly admitting to 'malice aforethought', he gives the jury no option but to find him guilty; and he himself admits his sentence is just.

This being so, on what grounds could he appeal? Stendhal leaves this vague; possibly he meant us to understand a petition for reprieve, on the grounds of his youth. I have not attempted, however, to alter the original.

The machinery of appeals – or petitions – differs slightly from ours. In France there are a number of district courts of appeal to which application is made in the first instance through the *procureur-général* of the district. There is no exact equivalent for this office in English. It is certainly not Attorney-General, which the dictionary gives as the only meaning. As chief legal officer of a district he corresponds in some way to the American District Attorney, and although this is a rough-and-ready translation, I have adopted it.

M. R. B. S.

This translation follows the text of the first edition of
Le Rouge et le Noir
as published by Levavasseur, Paris, 1831

PART ONE

Truth – Truth in all her rugged harshness
DANTON

CHAPTER 1 : *A Little Town*

> Put thousands together
> Less bad,
> But the cage less gay.
>
> HOBBES

THE little town of Verrières is one of the prettiest in Franche-Comté. Its white houses, with their red-tiled, pointed roofs, stretch out along the side of a hill where clumps of chestnut-trees thrust sturdily upwards at each little bend. Down in the valley the river Doubs flows by, some hundreds of feet below fortifications which were built centuries ago by the Spaniards, but have long since fallen into decay. High above the town, and protecting it on its northern side, rise the jagged peaks of Verra, a branch of the Jura mountains, whose crest is covered with snow from the moment the October cold sets in.

A torrent, rushing down from the mountain-side before flinging itself into the Doubs, sets a number of saw-mills busily whirring. This industry is not an important one, but it gives the people it employs, whose tastes are rather those of simple country-folk than of townsmen, the chance to make a fairly comfortable living. The town, however, does not draw its wealth from these mills, but from the manufacture of the printed fabrics known as Mulhouse linens. This is the source of that prosperity which, from the time of Napoleon's downfall, has enabled the people of Verrières to remodel the frontages of nearly every house in the town.

No one can enter Verrières without being deafened by the clatter of a monstrous and horrible machine. Twenty heavy hammers, attached to a wheel which is worked by the waters of the torrent, come pounding downwards with a din that makes the cobbles tremble, swing up into the air again, and turn out an incredible number of nails every day. But what most amazes any traveller making his way into the heart of the mountains dividing France from Switzerland is to find that the very rough task of placing the little bits of iron beneath these hammers is handled by pretty, fresh, rosy-cheeked young women.

If a stranger to the town inquired who owned the enormous machine which deafened everyone coming up the High Street, someone or other would be sure to tell him, in the drawling speech of the district: 'Why! it belongs to his Worship the Mayor'. If he lingered for a moment in that street which climbs upwards to the mountain from the banks of the Doubs, a hundred to one he would see a tall man making his way along it, a rather self-important individual and seemingly preoccupied with business matters.

As he passes, everyone promptly raises his hat. His hair is growing grey, his clothes are grey, too; the lapel of his coat is studded with decorations. He has a broad forehead and an aquiline nose, and his features, on the whole, are fairly regular. He affects the solemn pose which petty officials consider in keeping with their position, but, in spite of this, his face has that kind of charm which is still to be seen in men of forty-eight or fifty.

Yet, all the same, a visitor from the larger world of Paris would quickly note, and be repelled by, something about the man that marks him as not only self-sufficient but singularly limited and lacking in initiative, and would realize, in the end, that such a person's energies are all concentrated in making other men pay him what they owe, while putting off to the very latest date the payment of his debts to others.

Such a man, in short, is M. de Rênal, the Mayor of Verrières, who walks with slow and pompous step across the road and disappears inside the municipal buildings. Should the visitor continue his stroll, he would see, some fifty yards farther up the street, a rather fine-looking house and, through the iron railing that comes close up to it, catch a glimpse of an impressively extensive garden. Beyond this, in the distance, the Burgundian hills appear on the horizon, shaping it into a line that seems expressly designed to charm the eye. So spacious is this view that anyone seeing it forgets a town where petty financial interests poison the air, and in which he has begun to feel stifled.

This fine house, now nearly finished, in all the freshness of its new-hewn stone, belongs, as a visitor would be told, to Monsieur de Rênal, and has been built for him out of profits made by manufacturing nails. His family, so it is said, is of Spanish origin, an ancient line established in Franche-Comté a long time before this province was conquered by Louis XIV.

Since 1815 he has felt some embarrassment at having to own his connexion with business; that is the year in which he became Mayor of Verrières. The walls supporting the terraces of his magnificent garden, extending tier upon tier to the banks of the Doubs, are, like his house, the reward of his skill in the iron trade.

You must not expect to find, in the manufacturing towns of France, such beautiful landscape gardens as adorn the outskirts of Nuremberg, Frankfort, and Leipzig and other German centres of industry. In Franche-Comté, the more walls a man builds and the more his property bristles with stones laid one above the other, the more highly he is respected by his neighbours.

M. de Rênal's garden, with its full complement of walls, is all the more admired for his having bought, at almost their worth of weight in gold, some of the little bits of land on which it is laid out. On the very spot where the fourth terrace wall is now being constructed, a saw-mill formerly stood. The new mill, occupying a prominent position about five hundred yards farther down the Doubs, doubtless attracted your attention as you entered the town. You could not have failed to notice the name of its owner, Sorel, standing out in enormous letters on a board which looms above the roof.

In spite of his pride, the Mayor had to approach that hard-headed, obstinate old peasant, Sorel, time and again; he had to pay him a good round sum in golden louis before Sorel would agree to move his mill to another site. As for the stream that worked the mill, it was the property of the town, but M. de Rênal, thanks to his contact with influential friends in Paris, managed to get it turned out of its course, a favour which he obtained after the elections of 182–.

The Mayor gave Sorel four acres in exchange for one. The new site of the mill, some five hundred yards farther down the Doubs, was a much more convenient one for a sawyer's business, but Sorel senior, as he has been called since he became rich, was shrewd enough to take advantage of his neighbour's impatient greed for land by extracting from him the sum of 6,000 francs over and above all that he had gained by the exchange.

This transaction, it is true, was sharply commented on by the wiseacres of the district. Then, one Sunday, four years ago, as he was coming back from church in his mayor's robes, M. de Rênal caught a glimpse of old Sorel in the distance, accompanied by his sons, and noticed that he was smiling as he glanced at his neighbour. All at once, the meaning of that smile was bitterly clear to the Mayor, and from that moment he realized that he might have concluded a much better bargain.

To win public esteem in Verrières, it is essential, while building walls, not to adopt any sort of plan imported from Italy by the stonemasons passing every spring through the Jura gorges on their

way to Paris. Such an innovation would brand the builder of walls
for ever as a rebel against accepted convention, and damn him
without hope of redemption in the eyes of those prudent and sagacious persons who assess a man's reputation in Franche-Comté.

To tell the truth, these same worthy people exercise here the
most irritatingly despotic control. And that is why, for one who
has lived in that great republic men call Paris, life in these little
towns is insupportable. The tyranny of public opinion – and what
sort of opinion! – governs in these out-of-the-way corners of
France every whit as foolishly as in the backwaters of a small
American town.

CHAPTER 2 : A *Mayor*

Prestige! Why, sir, is that nothing? A thing
that fools revere, and children gape at, that
rich men envy and wise men scorn.

BARNAVE

FORTUNATELY for M. de Rênal's reputation as an administrator, a huge supporting wall was urgently needed for a public
promenade that ran along the side of the hill a hundred feet or so
above the Doubs, and from which could be seen a landscape as
lovely as any in France. Every spring the driving rain ploughed up
the path, hollowing out deep ravines and making it practically
impossible for anyone to walk there. This disadvantage, which
affected everyone, placed M. de Rênal in the happy necessity of
winning immortal fame for his administration by building a wall
some twenty feet high and about two hundred and fifty feet long.

As for the parapet to this wall, about which M. de Rênal had to
make three journeys to Paris – the Home Secretary of that date
having declared himself bitterly opposed to any scheme for im-
proving the promenade – this parapet rises now a good four feet
above the ground, and is being topped, at this very moment, with
solid slabs of granite, as if in defiance of all Ministers, past and
present.

How many times, with my thoughts on Paris balls and festivities just left behind, have I leant breast-high against those mas-
sive stones of a pleasant shade of grey inclining to blue, to gaze at
the valley of the Doubs. Over on its western slopes five or six
more valleys wind back into the mountains, in each of which the
eye picks out a number of little streams tumbling down from one
cascade to another, to fall at last into the river. The sun strikes
hot in these mountains, but even when its light is shining full
upon them, here, on this terrace, magnificent plane trees protect
the traveller and his dreams.

The rapid growth of these trees when first planted, and the
blue-green tint of their handsome foliage, comes from the good,
rich soil which the Mayor ordered to be put behind his huge supporting wall; for, in spite of opposition from the Town Council,
Monsieur de Rênal made the promenade some six feet wider than
before. (Although he is on the extreme Right, and I am a Liberal,
I applaud him for it. It gave him reason for believing, as did M.

Valenod, the successful Superintendent of the workhouse at
Verrières, that this terrace could challenge comparison with the
famous terrace of Saint-Germain-en-Laye.)

I, for my part, find only one thing amiss with the Cours de la
Fidélité – its name can be read on the marble tablets the Mayor
had affixed to the wall in fifteen to twenty places, an act for which
he received yet another decoration – only one thing with which
I have a fault to find, and that is the ruthless way in which the
local authority cuts and clips its plane-trees. They would ask for
nothing better than to keep those noble outlines with which we
see them in England, instead of looking, with their low, crushed,
rounded tops, like the most plebeian of kitchen-garden plants. But
the will of a despotic Mayor is not to be gainsaid, and, twice a
year, all the trees belonging to the commune are lopped without
mercy. The Liberals of the neighbourhood assert, though doubtless they exaggerate, that the gardener employed by the Town
Council has pruned them more drastically ever since M. Maslon
acquired the habit of annexing the profits from this clipping. This
young cleric had been sent from Besançon a few years before to
keep an eye on Father Chélan and other parish priests in the district.

An old army surgeon, a veteran of the Italian campaign, who
had come to live in Verrières after he had retired from the army,
and who, according to the Mayor, had been in his day both a Jacobin and a Bonapartist, ventured on one occasion to complain to
the Mayor himself of the way in which these trees were periodic-
ally mutilated.

'I like shade,' M. de Rênal answered coldly, in a tone of proud
aloofness nicely suited to conversation with a surgeon who was a
member of the Legion of Honour, 'and I have my trees cut to provide shade. What else a tree is made for, I can't imagine, especially
when, unlike the useful walnut, it doesn't bring in money.'

Bringing in money – that is the magic phrase determining everything in Verrières; by itself alone it represents the usual subject for
thought of more than three-quarters of its population. Bringing in
money is the decisive reason for everything in this little town you
thought so pretty. A stranger to it, on his first arrival there, enchanted by the cool, deep valleys that surround it, imagines its inhabitants are sensitive to beauty. They speak all too frequently of
the beauty of the town and its environment; nobody can deny
that they set a high value on it; but that is only because this
beauty attracts visitors, whose money makes the innkeepers rich,

while they, in their turn, by paying tax on commodities from outside, increase the revenue of the town.

One fine autumn day M. de Rênal was taking a walk along the Cours de la Fidélité with his wife on his arm. As he listened to her husband, who was talking to her with a serious expression on his face, she was anxiously following the movements of three little boys. The eldest of them, who seemed to be about eleven years old, kept running up too close to the parapet, and looked as if he were going to climb up on top. Each time he attempted it, a gentle voice called out his name, Adolphe, and each time the child gave up his ambitious enterprise. Madame de Rênal was about thirty, but she was still a rather pretty woman.

'This fine gentleman from Paris,' M. de Rênal was saying angrily, with his cheeks even paler than usual, 'may well come to regret what he's done. I'm not without some friends at the Château. . . .'

But although I may be proposing to talk to you on the provinces for a good two hundred pages, I will not be so inhuman as to subject you to the lengthy, subtle meanderings of provincial conversation.

This gentleman from Paris, whom the Mayor found so hateful, was no other than a certain M. Appert, who had managed to find his way, a couple of days before, not only into the prison and the workhouse, but also into the hospital run on a voluntary basis by the Mayor and the leading landowners of the district.

'But what harm can this gentleman from Paris do you?' said Madame de Rênal timidly. 'After all, you're so conscientious in the way you administer the funds allotted for poor relief.'

'He's only coming to lay the blame on someone. And then he'll have articles put in all the Liberal papers.'

'But, my dear, you never read them.'

'Even if I don't, there's plenty of people who talk to me about this revolutionary stuff. All that kind of thing's very upsetting, and *prevents us from doing good*. Anyhow, for my part, I'll never forgive the curé.'

CHAPTER 3 : *Poor Relief*

> An upright, undesigning priest is God's
> providence in a village.   FLEURY

I SHOULD inform you that the parish priest of Verrières, an old
man of eighty, but thanks to the mountain air as hale and
strong-willed as ever, had the right to visit the prison, the hospital,
and even the workhouse at any hour of the day or night. M.
Appert, having wisely timed his arrival in a little town full of
curiosity, reached Verrières at precisely six o'clock in the morning and went straight to the curé's house.

As he read the letter written to him by the Marquis de la Mole,
a peer of the realm and the richest landowner in the province,
Father Chélan grew thoughtful.

'I'm an old man,' he said at last under his breath, as if to himself, 'and the people here love me. . . . They wouldn't dare !' Then
he turned to his visitor, his eyes, in spite of his age, aglow with
the sacred fire that reveals delight in doing a fine though slightly
dangerous action.

'Come with me, sir,' he said, 'but pray be good enough not to
pass an opinion on anything you see when the gaoler's present,
and be particularly careful in front of the workhouse attendants.'

M. Appert realized he was dealing with a kindly, generous-
hearted man. He followed the old curé, visited the prison, the hospital, and the workhouse and asked many questions, but in spite
of certain curious replies, he did not allow himself to utter the
least unfavourable comment.

This visit lasted several hours. The curé invited M. Appert to
dinner, but the latter made out that he had letters to write; he did
not wish to compromise his brave companion any further. Towards three o'clock the two men went to finish their tour of the
workhouse, and then came back to the prison. There, at the
entrance, they found the gaoler, a tall giant of a fellow over six
foot high and bow-legged, whose mean face had grown hideous
from terror.

'Oh, sir !' he said to the curé as soon as he saw him. 'Isn't that
gentleman I see with you there M. Appert?'

'What does that matter?' replied the priest.

'Well, sir,' the gaoler explained, 'it's only that yesterday I received the strictest orders – and a gendarme galloped all through

the night to bring them – that I wasn't to let M. Appert enter the prison.'

'This traveller, whom you see here, M. Noiroud, is M. Appert, right enough. But you recognize, don't you, that I have the right to enter this prison at any hour of the day or night, and to bring with me anyone I choose?'

'Yes, your reverence,' said the gaoler under his breath, hanging his head like a bulldog that unwillingly obeys only for fear of the stick. 'But, your reverence, I've a wife and children, and if anyone tells on me I'll lose my place. I've nothing but this job to live on.'

'I should be just as sorry to lose mine,' the kind old priest went on, in a voice that grew more and more distressed.

'But what a difference!' replied the gaoler quickly. 'Your reverence, as everyone knows, has a private income of eight hundred livres or more, and a nice bit of land on the sunny side of the valley. . . .'

Such are the facts which, commented upon and exaggerated in twenty different ways, had for two days past been stirring up every kind of hateful passion in the little town of Verrières, and were at this moment serving as text for M. de Rênal's little discussion with his wife.

That morning, accompanied by M. Valenod, the Superintendent of the workhouse, M. de Rênal had gone to the curé's house to express his very keen dissatisfaction. Father Chélan had no patron to protect him; he understood all that their words implied.

'Well, gentlemen,' he said, 'so I shall be the third parish priest aged eighty to be deprived of his living in this neighbourhood. I have lived here for fifty-six years. I have christened nearly all the inhabitants of this town, and almost every day I marry young people whose grandfathers I married many years ago. Verrières is my family. But I said to myself, when I met this stranger, this man who comes from Paris may be a Liberal – there are only too many of them about. But what harm can he do to our poor or our prisoners?'

At this the Mayor's reproaches, and still more those of the Superintendent of the workhouse, increased in vehemence, until at last the old priest exclaimed in a trembling voice : 'Well, then, gentlemen, deprive me of my living if you will, I shall, none the less, remain in the district. As everyone knows, I've inherited a small property that brings me in 800 livres. I can live on that income. I make no dishonest profits in my sort of work,' he said pointedly, 'and that, perhaps, is why I am not so frightened when people talk of taking it from me.'

M. de Rênal was usually on very good terms with his wife, but on her timid repetition of the question : 'What harm can this gentleman from Paris do to the prisoners?' he was on the verge of losing his temper with her, when she uttered a cry. The second of her sons had just climbed up on to the parapet of the terrace wall and was running along it, though this wall was more than twenty feet above the vineyard on the farther side. Madame de Rênal was afraid to say anything to her son, lest she should frighten him and make him fall. After a little time the child, who was laughing with pride at his own daring feat, looked back at his mother, and seeing how pale she was, jumped down on to the promenade and ran up to her. He was given a good scolding.

This little incident altered the course of the conversation.

'I have absolutely made up my mind,' said M. de Rênal, 'to take young Sorel, the sawyer's son, into my house. He will look after the children; they're beginning to be too much of a handful for us. The young man's a priest, or as good as one, knows Latin well, and will get the children on with their work, for he has a very determined character, or so the curé says. I shall give him three hundred francs and his board.

'I had some doubts,' the Mayor went on, 'about his morals; for he was very much a favourite with that old army surgeon who came and planted himself on the Sorel family on the pretext that he was a cousin of theirs. For all I know, the man might well have been a spy of the Liberal party, though he said our mountain air was good for his asthma. But there's no proof of that. He served in all that fellow *Buonaparte*'s Italian campaigns, and even, so it's said, once voted against the Empire. This Liberal taught young Sorel Latin, and left him the considerable number of books he had brought to the house. So I'd never have dreamt of bringing in this carpenter's son to live with the children if the curé hadn't told me, just the day before the incident which broke up our friendship for good and all, that the boy has been studying theology for the past three years. So he can't be a Liberal — and he does know Latin.'

M. de Rênal glanced shrewdly at his wife and went on : 'This arrangement suits me in more ways than one. That fellow Valenod is putting on airs because he's just bought two fine Norman horses for his carriage. But he hasn't a tutor for his children.'

'He might very well take this one from us.'

'Then you do approve of my plan?' said M. de Rênal, thanking his wife with a smile for the excellent idea she had just had. 'All right, then, it's settled.'

'Good gracious, my dear,' said his wife. 'How quickly you make up your mind!'

'That's because I'm a man of character, and the curé saw very well I was. But don't let's make a secret of it; this place is swarming with Liberals. Those linen manufacturers, now – they're all envious of me, I'm certain of it. All right! I'll be rather glad for them to see M. de Rênal's children going by, out for a walk in the charge of their tutor. That'll impress people. My grandfather often used to tell me how, when he was young, he had a tutor. It may cost me three hundred francs, but that's one of the things that must be classed as necessary expenses for upholding our position in society.'

This sudden decision left Madame de Rênal wondering. She was a tall woman with a very good figure, and had been the belle of the district, as they say in these mountains. A Parisian's eye would have noted at once a certain natural simplicity in her manner and a youthfulness in all her ways and gestures. Her innocent, eager, and utterly unconscious grace might even have aroused in him ideas of mildly sensuous delight, though had Madame de Rênal realized the nature of her success, she would have been sadly embarrassed. There was no place in this heart for either coquetry or affectation. The wealthy M. Valenod had once, according to current rumour, attempted to make love to her, but with little success; and this had only added to her reputation as a woman of outstanding virtue. For M. Valenod, a tall, muscular young man, with a florid complexion and imposing jet-black whiskers, was one of those vulgar, bold, and boisterous creatures who pass as handsome men in the provinces.

As a matter of fact, Madame de Rênal, who was very shy and apparently very temperamental, found M. Valenod's loud voice and restless, bustling ways intensely irritating. The distaste she felt for all that Verrières called enjoyment had gained for her the reputation of being proud of her high birth. She was quite unaware of this, and was only too glad when fewer people began to call at her house, and called less often. The married women of her acquaintance, let us make no secret of it, put her down as dull and stupid because she had no schemes for getting round her husband, and so let the finest opportunities slip past of buying fashionable

hats from Besançon or Paris. But she herself never found any
cause for complaint, provided she was left alone to wander in her
own beautiful garden.

Madame de Rênal, indeed, had a simple, childlike nature. She
would never have ventured to sit in judgement on her husband,
nor to admit that she found him boring. She believed, though she
did not put her thoughts into words, that no husband and wife
had ever had pleasanter relations. She felt drawn to M. de Rênal
most of all when he talked to her of his plans for their children,
the eldest of whom, he had decided, would go into the army,
while the second would become a judge, and the third a priest. In
short, she found M. de Rênal much less boring than any other
man of her acquaintance.

She had reasonable grounds for such wifely sentiments. For the
Mayor of Verrières had gained some reputation as a man of wit
and good breeding on the strength of a handful of amusing stories
passed on to him by his uncle. Old Captain de Rênal had served as
an infantry officer, before the Revolution, in the Duke of Orleans'
regiment, and later, coming to Paris, had been a guest at receptions in the Palais-Royal where he had met Madame de Montesson,
the famous Madame de Genlis, and M. Ducrest, the inventor, who
was one of the Duke's household. These people make an all too
frequent appearance in M. de Rênal's anecdotes, though by degrees
the memory of things so delicate to relate had become a wearisome task for him, and for some time past he had reserved the
repetition of stories concerning the house of Orleans for important
occasions. As he was always very courteous, except when money
was the subject of conversation, he was still considered, and not
without reason, to be the most distinguished and aristocratic person in Verrières.

CHAPTER 4 : Father and Son

And will it be my fault if things are so?
MACHIAVELLI

M Y wife certainly has a good head on her shoulders, said the
Mayor of Verrières to himself as he went down the hill to
old Sorel's saw-mill at six o'clock the following morning. Although
I may have said as much to her, to maintain my rightful superiority, it really hadn't occurred to me that if I don't take this young
abbé Sorel, who, so they say, has a marvellous knowledge of
Latin, that restless busybody, the Superintendent of the workhouse, might easily get the same idea and snatch him from
me. How smugly he'd talk of his children's tutor ! . . . But,
by the way, once I've got hold of this tutor will he wear a
cassock?

M. de Rênal was absorbed in this question when, some distance
away, he saw a peasant, a man about six feet tall, who had apparently been very busy ever since dawn measuring some pieces
of timber lying by the side of the Doubs, on the towing-path. The
peasant did not look any too pleased to see the Mayor approaching; for these logs were blocking the path, and it was an offence
against the by-laws to have them lying there.

Old Sorel, for it was he, was greatly suprised and even more
deeply gratified at the extraordinary offer M. de Rênal made him
on behalf of his son. None the less, he listened to it with that air
of glum dissatisfaction and indifference with which the inhabitants of these mountains can so cleverly cover up their shrewdness. Slaves at the time of the Spanish domination, their faces
still preserve something of the look that characterizes the Egyptian
peasant.

Sorel's answer was at first nothing more than a lengthy recital
of every formula of respect he knew by heart. All the time he was
repeating these empty phrases, with an awkward grin that emphasized the sly and almost knavish expression natural to his
face, the old peasant's active mind was trying to discover what
reason could induce a man of such importance to take this good-
for-nothing son of his into his house. He was extremely dissatisfied with Julien, and yet it was for him that M. de Rênal was
offering the unhoped-for salary of 300 francs a year, together with
board, and even clothing. This last stipulation which Sorel had

been clever enough to put forward quite suddenly, had been granted with equal promptness by M. de Rênal.

The Mayor was impressed by such a demand. Since Sorel is not overwhelmed and delighted by my offer, it's clear, he said to himself, he's had an offer from some other quarter. And from whom, if not from M. Valenod? All in vain M. de Rênal urged Sorel to settle the matter on the spot; the wily old peasant's mind was obstinately set against it. He wished, so he said, to ask his son's opinion, as if, in the provinces, a father with money would consult a penniless son, except as a matter of form.

A water saw-mill consists of a large open shed at the river's edge, with a framework of timber resting on four stout wooden pillars to support the roof. In the middle of the shed, some nine or ten feet above the ground, a saw can be seen moving up and down, whilst a very simple mechanical device propels a log of wood towards it. A wheel, turned round by the action of the water, sets both parts of this dual mechanism in motion : the part that controls the upward and downward movement of the saw and that which gently pushes the log of wood towards the saw to be split up into planks.

As he approached his workshop, old Sorel called out to Julien in a stentorian voice; but no one answered. He could see only his elder sons, gigantic fellows armed with heavy axes with which they were squaring the pine trunks before carrying them to the saw. Intent on following exactly the black mark traced on the log, from which each blow chipped off enormous shavings, they did not hear their father's voice. Sorel went on towards the shed, and as he entered looked in vain for Julien at the place where he should have been beside the saw. He caught sight of him five or six feet higher up, astride one of the beams in the roof. Instead of keeping a watchful eye on the general movement of the machine, Julien was busy reading. Nothing could have seemed more objectionable to old Sorel. He could have forgiven Julien his slender frame, so little adapted to heavy labour and so unlike the build of his elder brothers; but this mad craze for reading was hateful to him. He himself could not read.

He called out to Julien two or three times; but all in vain. The lad's absorption in his book prevented him, far more than the noise of the saw, from hearing his father's terrifying voice. In the end, in spite of his age, Sorel jumped nimbly up on to the tree trunk in process of being sawn, and from the trunk to the crossbeam supporting the roof. A violent blow sent the book in Julien's hand flying down into the river; another blow, as violent as the first, and this time aimed at his head, made the boy lose his balance. He was on the point of tumbling twelve or fifteen feet down, right into the levers of the moving machine below him, where he would have been pounded to bits, when his father's left hand caught him and held him back as he was falling.

'So, you lazy scamp! You'll always be reading those damned books, will you, when you're set to watch the saw? Read them, if you will, in the evening, when you go and waste your time at the curé's.'

Although stunned by the violence of the blow and streaming with blood, Julien took up his post of duty beside the saw. There were tears in his eyes, but these came less from physical pain than for the loss of his beloved book.

'Get down, you young brute, I want a word with you.' Once again the noise of the machine prevented Julien from hearing this order. His father, who was down on the ground again and did not want the trouble of climbing up on to the machine a second time, went and fetched a long pole used for knocking down walnuts, and struck him with it on the shoulder.

Julien had hardly reached the ground before his father began driving him brusquely along in front of him, hustling him on towards the house. God knows what he's going to do to me, the boy thought to himself. As he passed by, he looked sadly into the river where his book had fallen; it was the best loved of all his books – the *Mémorial de Saint-Hélène*.

His cheeks were flushed, his eyes downcast. He was a short lad, about eighteen or nineteen years of age, with irregular, but delicately cut features and an aquiline nose. His large black eyes, which in calmer moments revealed a thoughtful, fiery spirit, were at that moment alive with the most savage hate. His dark auburn hair, growing down over his forehead, made it seem low, and gave him, in moments of anger, a rather forbidding, ill-natured air. Of all the innumerable varieties of the human countenance none perhaps has been distinguished by such striking individuality. His trim, slender figure gave more promise of agility than of strength. The thoughtful expression and the extreme pallor of his face had from his early childhood made his father think he had not long to live, or would live only to be a burden to his family. An object of scorn to everyone at home, he hated both his brothers and his father. In Sunday sports on the public square he was always beaten.

It was only a short time back, in fact rather less than a year, that his handsome face had begun to make some of the young women speak of him in friendly terms. Despised by everyone as a weakling, Julien had worshipped that old army surgeon who had dared one day to speak to the Mayor on the subject of the plane-trees. This surgeon would sometimes pay old Sorel for a day of his son's time, and would teach him Latin and history, or at least all the history he knew, that is to say the Italian campaign of 1796. When he died, he left Julien his cross of the Legion of Honour, his arrears of half-pay, and thirty or forty books, the most treasured of which had just somersaulted into the communal stream, turned out of its course by the Mayor's influence.

Julien had hardly entered the house before he felt his father's powerful hand on his shoulder, making him stop still. He trembled, expecting further blows.

'Answer me now, without lying!' The old peasant's voice boomed harshly in Julien's ears, while his father's hand swung him round as a child's hand turns a toy soldier to the rightabout. Julien's big, black eyes, brimming with tears, found themselves confronting the old carpenter's little grey ones, which seemed as if they were trying to read right down into the depths of his soul.

CHAPTER 5 : *Negotiations*

Delay sets everything to rights.   ENNIUS

'ANSWER me now without lying – if you can, you miserable bookworm! How'd you get to know Madame de Rênal? When have you spoken to her?'

'I've never spoken to her,' Julien replied. 'I've never seen this lady except in church.'

'But you've looked at her, haven't you, you impudent rascal?'

'Never! You know that when I'm in church I see no one but God himself,' added Julien, with a faintly hypocritical air, well adapted, in his opinion, to ward off further blows.

'There's something behind it, anyhow,' the crafty old peasant replied, and stopped speaking for a minute. 'But I'll never get anything out of you, you damned hypocrite. Anyhow, I'm going to be rid of you, and my saw will only go all the better for it. You've managed to get round the curé or someone else who's got you a fine situation. Go along and pack up your bundle, and I'll take you over to M. de Rênal's where you'll be his children's tutor.'

'What shall I get for that?'

'Your keep, your clothes, and three hundred francs in wages.'

'I don't wish to be a servant.'

'Blockhead! Who's talking of making a servant of you? D'you think I'd want a son of mine to become a servant?'

'But whom should I have my meals with?'

Old Sorel was taken aback by this question. Feeling that if he spoke he might say something unwise, he flew into a rage with Julien, heaping insults on him and accusing him of being a useless mouth to feed, and then left him to go and consult his other sons.

A short time after Julien saw them, each leaning on his axe and talking things over. After watching them for some little time and seeing he could guess nothing of what they were saying, Julien went and took up his place on the other side of the saw, to avoid being taken by surprise. He wanted to think over these unexpected tidings which were about to change his lot, but he felt incapable of acting wisely. His imagination was completely absorbed in picturing to himself what he would see in M. de Rênal's fine house.

I must give all this up, he said to himself, rather than let myself be reduced to eating with the servants. My father would like to force me to it. I'd rather die. I've fifteen francs and eight sous put by; I'll run away tonight. In two days' time, if I stick to bypaths where there's no fear of meeting any gendarmes, I'll be in Besançon. There I'll enlist as a soldier, or, if need be, get across into Switzerland. But then it's good-bye to all hopes of advancement, to that grand profession of the priesthood which leads to everything.

This horror of eating with servants was not a natural instinct with Julien. He would have done far harder things to make his way in the world. He drew his repugnance from Rousseau's *Confessions*, the only book that had helped his imagination to form a picture of society. This work, together with a collection of bulletins of the Grand Army and the *Mémorial de Saint-Hélène*, comprised his manual of conduct. He would have let himself be slain in defence of these three works. He put no faith in any other. As the old army surgeon had once remarked, he looked on all other books in the world as so many lying documents, written by fraudulent knaves for their own advancement.

Along with a fiery temperament, Julien had one of those amazing memories so frequently found in combination with dullness. To gain the old priest Chélan's favour, for he clearly saw that his future depended on him, he had learnt the New Testament in Latin off by heart. He also knew the whole of M. de Maistre's work on the Pope, and believed the one as little as the other.

As if by mutual agreement, Sorel and his son avoided speaking to each other that day. Towards evening, Julien went to the curé's house for his lesson in theology, but did not consider it wise to tell him anything about the strange offer made to his father. It may be a trap, he said to himself. I must make it look as if I'd forgotten it.

Early the next morning M. de Rênal sent for old Sorel. The latter, after keeping him waiting for an hour or two, finally arrived, uttering a hundred excuses as soon as he reached the door, interspersed with as many bowings and scrapings. By running through all sorts of objections one after the other, Sorel managed to understand that his son would have his meals with the master and mistress of the house, and on days when they had company would take them alone with the children in a separate room. Becoming more and more inclined to raise difficulties as he became aware of the Mayor's very genuine eagerness, and being, more-over, full of amazement and mistrust, Sorel asked to see the room where his son would sleep. It was a large apartment very nicely furnished; into it, however, the servants were already moving the three children's beds.

The sight of this came like a sudden flash of light to the old peasant's mind. There and then he boldly demanded to see the suit his son would be given. M. de Rênal opened his bureau and took out a hundred francs.

'You can go with this money to M. Durand, the clothier, and order him a black suit.'

'And even if I take him away from you,' said the peasant, sud-denly forgetting his obsequious manners, 'he'll keep this black suit?'

'Certainly.'

'Oh well!' said Sorel in drawling tones, 'then there's nothing else left for us to agree upon except the money you'll give him.'

'What!' cried M. de Rênal indignantly, 'we agreed upon that yesterday. I'm giving him three hundred francs. It's a lot of money, I think. Perhaps too much.'

'That's what you offered, and I don't deny it,' said old Sorel speaking still more slowly. Then, by a stroke of genius which will astonish only those who are unacquainted with the peasants of Franche-Comté, he continued, looking hard at Monsieur de Rênal: 'We can get something better elsewhere.'

On hearing these words, the Mayor's face fell. He recovered himself, however, and after a skilfully conducted conversation lasting two good hours, in which not a single word was uttered without design, peasant cunning prevailed against the cunning of the rich man, who does not depend upon it for his livelihood. All the numerous articles governing Julien's new way of life were duly settled. Not only was his salary fixed at four hundred francs, but these were to be paid in advance on the first of each month.

'Very well!' said M. de Rênal, 'I'll hand him over thirty-five francs.'

'To make a round sum of it,' said the peasant in a wheedling tone of voice, 'a rich and generous man like his Worship the Mayor could very well go to thirty-six francs.'

'All right!' said M. de Rênal. 'But that's an end to it.'

This time anger lent firmness to his voice. The peasant saw he must leave off trying to press the matter further. Then, in his turn, M. de Rênal made some progress. Not on any account would he consent to hand over the first month's thirty-six francs to old Sorel, who was very eager to accept it for his son. It had occurred to M. de Rênal that he would be obliged to give his wife an account of the part he had played in the course of these negotiations.

'Give me back the hundred francs I gave you,' he said with a touch of temper. 'M. Durand owes me some money. I'll go myself with your son and order the black cloth.'

After this vigorous action, Sorel prudently returned to respectful forms of address. These compliments took up a good quarter of an hour. Finally, seeing that he had decidedly nothing more to gain by them, he took his leave, rounding off his last bow with the words: 'I'll send my son round to your château.' That was how people under the Mayor's jurisdiction spoke of his house when they wished to please him.

When he got back to his workshop Sorel hunted vainly for his son. Suspicious of what might happen, Julien had left the house in the middle of the night. He wanted to put his books and his cross of the Legion of Honour in a place of safety, and had taken them all away with him to the house of a young timber merchant, a friend of his, called Fouqué, who lived on the slopes of the high mountain overlooking Verrières.

When he reappeared his father called out to him. 'You damned lazy rascal!' he said, 'God knows if you'll ever be honourable enough to pay me back all the cost of your food I've been advancing to you for these many years past! Take your beastly rags and be off with you to the Mayor's.'

Astonished at not being beaten, Julien made a hurried departure; but he was hardly out of his father's sight before he slackened his pace. He judged that it would be of service to his hypocrisy to go and say a prayer in church.

Does the term *hypocrisy* surprise you? The soul of this young peasant had had a long, long way to travel before he happened upon so horrible a word.

In his earliest childhood he had been violently attracted to the military profession by the sight of certain dragoons of the 6th Regiment returning from Italy, in long white cloaks, and helmets with long black plumes of horsehair on their heads, whom he had seen tying up their horses to the iron-barred window of his father's house. Later on, he had listened, entranced, to tales of battles at the bridge of Lodi, at Arcola and Rivoli, told him by the old army surgeon, and had seen the old man's eyes flash as he glanced at his cross.

But when Julien was fourteen, they were beginning to build a church at Verrières, one that could be termed magnificent for so small a town. There were four marble columns, the sight of which particularly impressed him; they became famous throughout the district on account of the deadly enmity they aroused between the justice of the peace and a young cleric, sent from Besançon, who was thought to be a Jesuit spy. The justice of the peace was on the verge of losing his post, or at least that was the common opinion. Had he not dared to disagree with a priest who went to Besançon nearly every fortnight where, so people said, he saw his Lordship the Bishop?

In the midst of all this the justice of the peace, who was the father of a large family, passed several sentences which were apparently unjust. They were all of them given against inhabitants of the town who read the *Constitutionnel*. The clerical party exulted. It is true it was only a question of fines amounting to three or five francs; but one of these fines had to be paid by a nailmaker who was Julien's godfather. In his anger this man exclaimed: 'What a change of front! And to think that, for more than twenty years, this justice of the peace was thought to be such an honest fellow!' By that time Julien's friend the army surgeon was dead.

All at once Julien stopped talking about Napoleon. He announced his plan of becoming a priest, and was constantly to be seen in his father's sawmill, busy committing to memory a Latin Bible which the curé had lent him. This good old man, marvelling at his progress, gave up whole evenings to teaching him theology; and in his company Julien made show of none but pious sentiments. Who would have guessed that his girlish face, so pale and so gentle, concealed an unshakeable determination to undergo a thousand deaths rather than fail to achieve success?

For Julien, achieving success meant first and foremost getting away from Verrières. He loathed the place in which he had been born; his imagination was frozen stiff by everything he saw there. From his earliest childhood, he had experienced moments of ecstatic excitement. Then it was that he revelled in dreams of being one day introduced to beautiful Parisian women, whose attention he would manage to attract by some remarkable feat or other. Why should he not be loved by one of them, just as Bonaparte, when still poor, had been loved by that distinguished lady, Madame de Beauharnais? For many years past Julien had not let, perhaps, a single hour go by without telling himself that Bonaparte, an unknown, penniless lieutenant, had made himself master of the world with his sword. The thought of this consoled him in the midst of misfortunes which, to him, were serious ones, and added to whatever joys came his way.

The building of the church and the incident of the sentences passed by the magistrate enlightened him in a flash. An idea that came into his head drove him almost crazy for several weeks on end, and finally took possession of him with all the force of an idea that a highly emotional nature believes it has discovered for itself.

When Bonaparte, he thought, made people talk about him, France lived in fear of invasion. Military ability was an essential need, and it became the fashion. Today we see priests only forty years old with stipends of a hundred thousand francs – that is to say, three times as much as any of Napoleon's famous major-generals. These priests must have people who back them up. Look at that justice of the peace, for instance, such a decent fellow and such an honourable man up till now, and so old, too, committing a dishonourable action for fear of displeasing a young cleric of thirty. I must become a priest.

Once, in the midst of his new-found piety, when Julien had already spent two years studying theology, he was betrayed by a sudden uprush of the fire devouring him within. It was at M. Chélan's house, at a dinner the good curé gave for his clerical colleagues, to whom he introduced the boy as a prodigy of learning, that Julien took it into his head to utter immoderate praise of Napoleon. He strapped his right arm to his chest, pretending that he had dislocated it in moving the trunk of a pine-tree, and kept it for two months in this uncomfortable position. After enduring such corporal punishment, Julien forgave himself. Such was the young man of eighteen, though of such frail appearance that one would have thought him seventeen at the most, who was at this moment entering the magnificent church of Verrières with a little bundle under his arm.

He found it dark and deserted. In celebration of a feast of the Church, all the windows of the building were curtained with crimson cloth, producing, as the rays of the sun filtered through, a dazzling effect of light at once impressive and profoundly religious in character. Julien gave a sudden start. All by himself in the church, he went and sat down in what appeared to be the finest pew. M. de Rênal's coat-of-arms was on it.

On the ledge of the *prie-dieu*, Julien noticed a scrap of paper, with printing on it, lying there flat as if it were meant to be read. He cast a glance at it and saw the following words: *Details of the execution and last moments of Louis Jenrel, executed at Besançon on* ...

The paper was torn. On the other side were the first words of a line which read: *The first step* ...

Who could have put this paper there? thought Julien. Poor wretch! he added with a sigh, his name ends just like mine ... and he crumpled up the paper.

As he was leaving, Julien fancied he saw some blood near the holy water stoup. It was some of the holy water that had been spilt, and which looked like blood in the reflection of the red curtains covering the windows.

Julien ended up by feeling ashamed of his secret terror. Am I a coward, after all? he said to himself. *To arms!*

This phrase, so frequently recurring in the old surgeon's tales of battle, had heroic associations for Julien. He sprang to his feet and marched quickly off towards M. de Rênal's house. But in spite of all his fine resolutions he was seized with a shyness he could not overcome the moment he saw it twenty feet in front of him. The wrought iron gate stood open; it seemed to him magnificently imposing. Nevertheless, he must needs go in.

Julien was not the only one whose heart was troubled by his arrival in this House. Madame de Rênal's excessive shyness made her feel upset at the thought of this stranger who, by virtue of his functions, would be constantly interposing himself between her and her childdren. She was accustomed to having her sons sleeping in her room. That morning she had shed many tears on seeing their little beds being carried off into the rooms assigned to the tutor. She had pleaded in vain with her husband to let the bed belonging to her youngest boy, Stanislas-Xavier, be brought back into her room.

Feminine sensibility was developed to an excessive degree in Madame de Rênal. She drew for herself the most disagreeable picture of a coarse, unkempt individual whose duty it would be to scold her children, simply and solely because he knew Latin, a barbarous language on account of which her children would be whipped.

CHAPTER 6 : *Boredom*

> I no longer know what I am,
> Nor what I am doing.
>
> MOZART

MADAME DE RÊNAL was coming out of the french window leading from the drawing-room into the garden, with the graceful ease and liveliness natural to her when no man's eyes were on her, when, just by the front door, she noticed a young peasant, still almost a child, whose face was extremely pale and bore the mark of recent tears. He was wearing a spotlessly white shirt and carried under his arm a very clean and tidy jacket of purple rateen.

This young peasant had such a fair complexion and his eyes were so gentle that Madame de Rênal's somewhat romantic nature made her at first imagine it might be some young woman in disguise who had come to ask a favour of the Mayor. She pitied the poor young thing, standing unable to move in front of the door, and evidently not daring to lift a hand to pull the bell. Madame de Rênal went up to him, her mind for the moment distracted from the bitter grief the tutor's arrival caused her. Julien, whose face was turned towards the door, did not see her approaching. He started when a gentle voice said close to his ear : 'What brings you here, my boy?'

Julien turned round sharply and, struck by the very gracious look on Madame de Rênal's face, partly forgot his shyness. Very soon, astonished by her beauty, he forgot everything, even why he had come. Madame de Rênal had to repeat her question.

'I've come here as tutor, madam,' he said to her at last, utterly ashamed of the tears he was doing his best to wipe away.

Madame de Rênal was left speechless. They stood very close together, looking at each other. Julien had never met anyone so well-dressed, especially a woman with such a dazzlingly beautiful complexion, who had spoken to him gently. Madame de Rênal gazed at the large, round teardrops, halted in their passage down this young peasant's cheeks, which had been at first so pale and were now so pink. Very soon she began to laugh, with all a girl's irresponsible gaiety. She was laughing at herself, finding it impossible to comprehend the full extent of her happiness. What!

was that the tutor she had pictured to herself as a shabby, slovenly priest, who would come to scold and beat her children !

'What, sir,' she said at last, 'so you know Latin?'

The term 'sir' astonished Julien so much that he paused to reflect a moment.

'Yes, madam,' he said shyly.

Madame de Rênal was so happy that she ventured to say to Julien : 'You won't scold these poor children too much, will you?'

'I scold them !' said Julien in amazement. 'And why !'

'You'll be kind to them, won't you, sir?' she added after a short silence, in a voice that every moment became more charged with emotion. 'You promise me that?'

Hearing himself a second time addressed as 'sir', quite seriously too, and by such a well-dressed lady, was far and away beyond all Julien's expectations. In every castle in Spain his youthful fancy had constructed, he had told himself that no real lady would ever deign to speak to him unless he was wearing a handsome uniform. As for Madame de Rênal, she was completely taken in by the beauty of Julien's complexion, his big, dark eyes and his fine head of hair, which was more than usually curly from his having just plunged it into the basin of the public fountain to freshen himself up. To her great joy she discovered something of a young girl's timidity about this tutor fate had forced upon her, and whose harsh ways and unprepossessing manner she had so much dreaded for her children's sake. The contrast between what she had feared and what her eyes now saw was a thing of great import to someone of Madame de Rênal's peace-loving nature. Recovering at last from her surprise, she was amazed to find herself standing like this at the door of her house with a young man practically in his shirt-sleeves, and so very close beside him too.

'Shall we go in, sir?' she said to him in some embarrassment.

Never in all her life had Madame de Rênal been so deeply moved by such a wholly pleasurable sensation; never had so gracious a sight succeeded more disquieting fears. Her pretty children, then, to whom she had shown such a tender care, were not to fall into the hands of a dirty, disagreeable priest.

Almost before she had entered the hall, she turned round towards Julien, who was timidly following her. His look of astonishment at the sight of so fine a house was an added grace in Madame de Rênal's eyes. She could not believe those eyes; it seemed to her that a tutor should certainly be wearing a black suit.

'But is it really true, sir,' she said, stopping once again, in deadly

fear of having made a mistake, so happy was she in what she believed, 'do you really know Latin?'

Her words offended Julien's pride and broke the spell that had
held him for the last quarter of an hour.

'Yes, madam,' he answered, endeavouring to appear cold, 'I
know Latin as well as his reverence the curé does, and he's even
sometimes been good enough to say that I know it better.'

It seemed to Madame de Rênal that Julien was looking very disagreeable. He had stopped a few feet away from her. She went up
to him and said in a half-whisper: 'You won't whip my children
during the first few days, will you, even if they don't know their
lessons?'

Such a gentle and almost suppliant tone of voice, coming from
such a beautiful lady, made Julien instantly forget what he owed
to his reputation as a Latin scholar. Madame de Rênal's face was
close to his, he smelt the fragrance of a woman's summer dress,
a very astonishing experience for a humble peasant. He grew very
red and, sighing, said to her in a faltering voice: 'Don't be afraid,
madam, I'll obey all your wishes.'

It was only at that moment, when her anxiety on her children's
account was completely dispelled, that Madame de Rênal was
struck by Julien's extraordinary good looks. His bashful manner
and the almost feminine contour of his features did not appear in
any way ridiculous to a woman who was herself extremely shy.
The virile strength that is commonly considered essential to
manly beauty would only have made her feel frightened.

'How old are you, sir?' she asked Julien.

'I'll be nineteen soon.'

'My eldest boy is eleven,' Madame de Rênal went on, completely reassured. 'He'll be almost a companion for you. You'll be
able to reason with him. Once when his father tried to beat him,
the child was ill for a whole week, and yet it was only a very
slight whipping.'

How different from me, thought Julien. Only yesterday my
father beat me. How lucky these rich people are!

Madame de Rênal had already begun to conceive the finest
shades of what was passing in the tutor's mind. She interpreted
this fleeting mood of melancholy as shyness and was anxious to
give him courage.

'What is your name, sir?' she said, in such a sweetly gracious
tone of voice that Julien felt all its charm without quite knowing
why.

'My name is Julien Sorel, madam. I find myself trembling all over on entering a strange house for the first time in my life. I've need of your protection and for you to forgive me many things in the first few days. I've never been to school – I was too poor. I've never talked to any other men except my cousin, the army surgeon, and M. Chélan, our curé. He will give you a good account of me. My brothers have beaten me continually – if they speak ill of me, please don't believe them. And forgive me my mistakes, madam. I'll never intend any ill.'

During this rather long harangue Julien was gaining confidence as he studied Madame de Rênal. Such is the effect of perfect grace when it is a natural characteristic, especially when the person it adorns is quite unconscious of possessing such a quality. Julien, who was a very good judge of feminine beauty, would have sworn at that moment that she was no more than twenty. There and then the bold idea of kissing her hand came into his mind; but he quickly took fright at the thought. A moment later he was saying to himself: It would be cowardly of me not to perform an action which may be of service to me, and lessen the disdain this fine lady probably feels for a humble workman only just snatched from his saw-mill. Possibly Julien was a little encouraged by the words 'good-looking boy' he had heard repeatedly on the lips of a number of young women every Sunday for the past six months.

All the while this debate was going on inside him, Madame de Rênal had been addressing a few words of advice to him on the way he should begin to handle her children. The violent constraint he was putting on himself brought back the pallor to Julen's cheeks. He said stiffly: 'I'll never beat your children, madam. Before God, I swear it.'

As he uttered these words, he ventured to take hold of Madame de Rênal's hand and carry it to his lips. She was astonished at this gesture and, on second thoughts, shocked. As the weather was very hot, her arm was quite bare under her shawl, and Julien's action in carrying it to his lips had completely uncovered it. A second or two later she reproached herself, feeling she had not shown her indignation as quickly as she should.

Hearing someone talking, M. de Rênal came out of his study and said to Julien, in the same paternal and majestic manner he was wont to adopt when officiating at a wedding in the town hall : 'I simply must have a word with you before the children see you.'

He ushered Julien into a room and made his wife stay with

them, although she was anxious to leave them alone. After shutting the door, M. de Rênal solemnly sat down.

'The curé tells me you are steady and well-behaved. Everyone here will treat you with respect, and if I myself am satisfied with you, I will help to settle you later on in a little business of your own. I do not wish you to see anything more of your friends or your relations – their ways of life would not suit my children. Here are thirty-six francs for your first month's salary, but I insist on your giving me your word that you will not hand over a single sou of this money to your father.'

M. de Rênal's encounter with the old man still rankled; he had been sharper than himself over this business.

'Now, sir – for I've given orders to everyone here to call you sir – and you will feel the advantage of being received into a gentleman's house – Now, sir, it is unfitting for my children to see you in a jacket. Have the servants seen him?' M. de Rênal asked his wife.

'No, my dear,' she answered, looking extremely thoughtful.

'So much the better. Just put this on,' he said to the astonished youth, handing him over a frock-coat of his own. 'And now we'll go and see M. Durand, the clothier.'

When M. de Rênal returned home an hour later with the new tutor clothed from head to foot in black, he found his wife sitting where he had left her. She felt her mind set at rest by Julien's presence; studying him closely, she forgot to be afraid of him. As for Julien, he had no thoughts to spare for her. For all his lack of confidence in destiny and in mankind, his heart at this moment was like a child's. Years had passed, so it seemed to him, since that moment, three hours before, when he had stood trembling in the church. He noted Madame de Rênal's coldly distant manner, and gathered she was angry with him for having dared to kiss her hand. But the feelings of pride awakened in him by contact with clothes so different from those he was accustomed to wear, made him so beside himself with joy, and yet so anxious to hide the joy he felt, that there was something fantastically brusque in all his movements. Madame de Rênal gazed at him with astonished eyes.

'Behave yourself more gravely, sir,' M. de Rênal warned him, 'if you wish my children and my servants to respect you.'

'I'm so ill at ease in these clothes, sir,' Julien replied. 'A poor peasant like myself never wears anything but a jacket. If you'll give me leave, sir, I'll go and shut myself up in my room.'

'What do you think of our new acquisition?' M. de Rênal asked his wife.

Instinctively, yet certainly without being conscious of it, Madame de Rênal concealed the truth from her husband.

'I'm not so delighted with this young peasant as you are,' she said. 'Your kindness will make him cheeky, and you'll be obliged to dismiss him before the month's out.'

'All right, then; we'll dismiss him. It'll cost me a hundred francs, maybe, but Verrières will have got used to seeing M. de Rênal's children with a tutor. I shouldn't have achieved this aim if I'd left Julien in his workman's clothes. When I dismiss him, I'll keep, of course, the black suit I've just ordered at the clothier's, and leave him nothing but the one I've just found ready-made at the tailor's and made him put on.'

The hour that Julien spent in his room seemed only a minute to Madame de Rênal. The children, informed of their new tutor's arrival, overwhelmed their mother with questions. Finally Julien made his appearance, an altogether different man. It would have been incorrect to say he was grave: he was gravity incarnate. He was introduced to the children, and spoke to them in a way that astonished M. de Rênal.

'I am here, young gentlemen,' he said, in conclusion, 'to teach you Latin. You know what it means to say your lesson. Here is the Holy Bible,' he went on, showing them a tiny volume in 32mo, bound in black. 'It is more especially the life of Our Lord Jesus Christ, that is to say that part that is called the New Testament. I shall often ask you to recite your lessons, now hear me recite mine.'

The eldest child, Adolphe, had taken the book. 'Open it where you like,' continued Julien, 'and give me the first word of a paragraph. I will recite this Holy Book, which guides every man's conduct, word for word from memory until you stop me.'

Adolphe opened the book, read out a word, and Julien recited the whole page with as much ease as if he had been speaking in French. M. de Rênal cast a triumphant glance at his wife. The children, seeing their parents' astonishment, gazed wide-eyed at the scene. A servant came to the drawing-room door, still Julien went on reciting Latin. The servant stood at first stockstill and then disappeared. Soon Madame de Rênal's maid and the cook came and stood by the door. By then Adolphe had already opened the book in eight different places, and Julien was still reciting it with the same facility.

'Bless my soul !' cried the cook, a good-natured and very pious young woman. 'What a pretty little priest !'

M. de Rênal's self-respect was slightly hurt. Far from thinking of putting the tutor to the test, he was racking his brains for a few Latin phrases, and managed at length to quote a line from Horace. Julien knew no Latin except what was in the Bible. He answered, frowning : 'The sacred ministry to which I have dedicated myself forbids me to read so profane a poet.'

M. de Rênal went on to quote a number of lines he alleged to be from Horace. He explained who Horace was to the children; but the children, awestruck, paid hardly any attention to what he was saying. They were gazing at Julien.

As the servants were still gathered round the door, Julien felt it incumbent on him to prolong the test. 'Master Stanislas-Xavier,' he said to the youngest child, 'you must also choose a passage for me from the Holy Book.'

Little Stanislas, bursting with pride, read out the first word of a paragraph more or less correctly, and Julien repeated the whole page. To complete M. de Rênal's triumph, both M. Valenod, the possessor of those fine Norman horses, and M. Charcot de Maugiron, the sub-prefect of the district, came in as Julien was reciting. This incident earned for Julien the right to be called 'sir', which even the servants did not dare dispute.

That evening everyone in Verrières flocked to M. de Rênal's house to see this marvel. Julien kept them all at a distance by the sullen manner of his replies. His fame spread so rapidly that a few days later M. de Rênal, fearing someone would snatch him away, proposed to Julien that they should sign a two years' contract.

'No, sir,' Julien answered coldly. 'If you should wish to dismiss me, I'd have to go. An agreement which binds me without in any way committing you is not on equal terms, and I refuse to make it.'

Julien managed to handle things so well that, less than a month after his arrival, M. de Rênal himself respected him. And as the curé was on bad terms with both M. de Rênal and M. Valenod, there was no one to give away Julien's former passion for Napoleon; he himself only mentioned Napoleon's name with horror.

> They know not how to touch the heart save
> by wounding it.   MODERN AUTHOR

THE children adored him; he, for his part, had no love to give them – his mind was elsewhere. Nothing the little urchins could do ever made him lose his patience. Cold, just, impassive, and none the less loved, because his coming had in some way driven boredom from the house, he made a very good tutor. For himself, he felt nothing but loathing and abhorrence of the distinguished company into which he had been admitted, though, in truth, at the bottom end of the table, which may perhaps explain his abhorrence and his loathing. There were certain ceremonious dinners at which he found great difficulty in holding back his hatred of everything around him. Once, on the occasion of the feast of Saint-Louis, when M. Valenod was holding forth, he was on the verge of giving himself away. He rushed off into the garden, on the pretext that he had to see to the children.

How they sing the praises of honest dealing, he exclaimed to himself. You'd think it was the one and only virtue. And yet, what servile respect they pay to a man who has obviously doubled – and tripled – his fortune since the money allotted for poor relief was given him to handle ! I wouldn't mind betting he even makes something out of the funds reserved for the foundlings – unhappy children whose misery is even more sacred than that of other people ! Ah ! the brutes ! the brutes ! And I, too, am a sort of foundling, hated as I am by my father, my brothers, and my whole family.

A few days before this feast of Saint-Louis, as he was walking all alone and reading his breviary out loud in a little wood, known as the Belvedere, which looks down on to the Cours de Fidélité, Julien had unsuccessfully tried to avoid a meeting with his brothers, whom he had caught sight of in the distance, coming towards him down a lonely path. The jealousy of these two rough working-men had been so provoked by their brother's fine black suit, his extremely neat appearance, and the open contempt he showed them that they had thrashed him soundly and left him fainting and covered with blood.

Madame de Rênal, out for a walk with M. Valenod and the sub-prefect, happened to come to this little wood, and seeing

Julien lying full length on the ground, had believed him dead. The shock this gave her was so great that it aroused M. Valenod's jealousy.

He was too quick to take alarm. Julien found Madame de Rênal very beautiful, but he hated her for her beauty, seeing in it the first reef on which his career had nearly foundered. He spoke to her as little as possible, in the hope of forgetting the ecstasy that had moved him, on the very first day, to kiss her hand.

Madame de Rênal's maid, Elisa, had not failed to fall in love with the young tutor, and often spoke of him to her mistress. Mademoiselle Elisa's love for him had earned for Julien the hatred of one of the footmen. He heard the man say to her one day : 'You won't speak to me any more since that greasy tutor came to this house.' Julien did not deserve such an insult, but a handsome young man's instinctive vanity led him to pay more attention than ever to his personal appearance. M. Valenod's hatred of him grew greater too. He openly stated that so much foppishness was unbecoming in a young priest. Though Julien wore no cassock, his clothes were otherwise such as a priest might wear.

Madame de Rênal, noticing that Julien was speaking to Elisa more often than usual, found out that these conversations were occasioned by the poor condition of his meagre wardrobe. He had so little linen that he was obliged to have it washed very frequently outside the house, and Elisa was useful to him in such little concerns. Madame de Rênal was touched by an extreme of poverty she had not in the least suspected. She longed to make him a present or two, but did not dare to do so. The opposition in her mind was the first painful sensation she had felt on Julien's account. Up till then the name of Julien had been for her a synonym for pure and wholly platonic delight. Tormented by the thought of his poverty, she spoke to her husband of making him a present of some linen.

'What an absurd idea !' he replied. 'What ! give presents to a man with whom we're perfectly satisfied, and who serves us well ? If he began to neglect his personal appearance, then would be the time to encourage his zeal.'

Madame de Rênal felt humiliated by this way of looking at things, though she would have taken no notice of it before Julien's arrival. She never observed the extreme, but unassuming, neatness of this young abbé's dress without asking herself : How can the poor boy manage it ? Gradually she began to feel pity for all Julien's shortcomings, instead of being shocked by them.

Madame de Rênal was one of those women to be met with in the provinces whom you may very well consider merely silly in the first fortnight of making their acquaintance. She had not the least experience of life, and did not trouble to make conversation. Endowed with a sensitive and proudly fastidious disposition, the instinct for happiness natural to all human beings inclined her, most of the time, to pay no attention at all to the actions of those coarse, insensitive individuals amongst whom her lot was accidentally cast.

Had she had any sort of education, her spontaneity and the lively turn of her mind would have attracted attention. But as she was an heiress, she had been brought up amongst nuns absorbed in passionate adoration of the Sacred Heart and bitter hatred of all Frenchmen who were enemies of the Jesuits. Madame de Rênal had possessed enough good sense to forget, as something quite absurd, everything she had been taught in the convent; but she had put nothing else in its place and had ended up by knowing nothing at all.

Compliments and attentions paid to her, as heiress to a great fortune, at too early an age, and a decided leaning towards intense religious devotion, had made her something of an introvert. While outwardly behaving with the most perfect compliance and with a complete surrender of her will that every husband in Verrières quoted as an example to his wife, and that gave M. de Rênal cause to exult, the usual conduct of her inner life was governed by the dictates of a high-souled nature. Many a princess quoted for her pride pays infinitely more attention to what her gentlemen-in-waiting are doing around her than this very sweet-tempered and seemingly humble-minded woman paid to anything her husband said or did. Up to the time of Julien's arrival, she had really paid attention to no one but her children. Their little illnesses, their griefs, their childish joys absorbed all the power of feeling in one whose soul, her whole life long, had never adored anyone but God, and that when she was at the Convent of the Sacred Heart in Besançon.

Although she did not deign to say so to anyone, if one of her children had a feverish attack it reduced her to almost the same state of mind as if the child were dead. Confidences on troubles of this sort which her need to open her heart had prompted her to make to her husband in the first years of her marriage had been constantly greeted by a rude burst of laughter, a shrug of the shoulders, or some trite quotation concerning the folly of the

female sex. Pleasantries of this kind, especially when they touched
on her children's illnesses, were like the twisting of a dagger in
Madame de Rênal's heart. This was what she found in place of
the obsequious, honeyed compliments of the Jesuit convent where
she had passed her youth. She was educated in the school of
sorrow. Too proud to mention griefs of such a kind, even to her
friend, Madame Derville, she pictured to herself all men as being
like her husband, like M. Valenod, or the sub-prefect Charcot de
Maugiron. Boorishness, brutish insensibility to all that did not
concern either money, questions of precedence, or decorations;
blind hatred of any argument opposed to their own point of view
– these seemed to her as natural to this sex as the wearing of high
boots or felt hats. After many long years, Madame de Rênal had
not yet grown accustomed to these moneyed folk amongst whom
she had to live.

Hence the success of the young peasant, Julien. She found a
sweet pleasure, bright with all the charm of novelty, in the sympathetic affinities of this proud and noble nature. Madame de
Rênal had soon forgiven him his utter ignorance, which was indeed one grace the more, and his uncultured ways, which she
managed to correct. She found him worth listening to, even when
talking of the most everyday matters, even when their conversation was about a poor dog run over by a peasant's cart as it was
crossing the road. The sight of this suffering had drawn the usual
loud burst of laughter from her husband, while Julien's finely
arched black eyebrows, so she noticed, had contracted into a
frown. Gradually she came to think that nobility of soul and
human kindness were nowhere to be found save in this young
abbé. For him alone, she felt all the sympathy – and even admiration – which such virtues arouse in generous hearts.

In Paris, the nature of Madame de Rênal's attitude towards
Julien would have very quickly become plain – but in Paris, love
is an offspring of the novels. In three or four such novels, or even
in a couplet or two of the kind of song they sing at the *Gymnase*,
the young tutor and his shy mistress would have found a clear
explanation of their relations with each other. Novels would have
traced out a part for them to play, given them a model to imitate.
And sooner or later, though without any pleasure and possibly
with reluctance, Julien's vanity would have compelled him to
follow this model.

In some little town in the department of Aveyron or the
Pyrenees the fiery heat of the climate might have rendered the

smallest incident decisive. Under our more gloomy skies, a young man without money, ambitious only because his sensitive heart creates a need for some of those pleasures money can supply, finds himself every day in the company of a genuinely virtuous woman of thirty, absorbed in her children and in no way concerned to model her conduct on novels. Everything moves slowly; everything happens gradually in the provinces – everything is more natural there.

Many a time, as she thought of the young tutor's poverty, Madame de Rênal was moved to tears. One day Julien surprised her openly weeping.

'Why, madam, has anything happened to distress you?'

'No, my dear boy,' she answered. 'Call the children, and we'll go for a walk.'

She took his arm and clung to it in a way that Julien thought strange. It was the first time she had called him 'dear boy'. Towards the end of the walk Julien noticed that she was blushing deeply. She began to walk more slowly.

'You will have been told,' she said without looking at him, 'that I am the sole heiress of a very wealthy aunt who lives in Besançon. She's always loading me with presents. ... My sons are getting on well with their work ... so surprisingly well ... that I'd like you to accept a little present as a token of my gratitude. It's only a few louis to buy you some linen. But ...' she added, blushing still more deeply. Then she stopped.

'Well, madam?' said Julien.

'There's no need,' she continued, looking down on the ground, 'to mention this to my husband.'

'I may be a man of low birth, madam, but I am not base,' replied Julien, stopping and drawing himself up to his full height, his eyes bright with anger. 'That's something to which you haven't given enough thought. I should be less than a lackey if I put myself in the position of concealing from M. de Rênal anything whatever relative to my wages.'

Madame de Rênal was dumbfounded.

'His Worship the Mayor,' Julien continued, 'has given me five times thirty-six francs since I came to live in his house. I am prepared to show my account book to M. de Rênal, or to anybody in the world, even to M. Valenod who hates me.'

After this outburst Madame de Rênal was left pale and trembling, and the walk ended without either of them being able to find a pretext for resuming their conversation.

Julien's proud heart found it more and more impossible to feel any love for Madame de Rênal; she, for her part, admired and respected him for having scolded her. Under pretext of making amends for the humiliation she had unwillingly caused him, she allowed herself to show him the most affectionate attentions, a novel mode of behaviour which kept her happy for a whole week. It had the effect of partially allaying Julien's anger, but he was far from seeing in it anything in the least like a personal inclination. There you are! he said to himself. That's just like the rich. They humiliate you and then imagine they can put everything to rights with a few monkey tricks!

In spite of all her resolves on the matter, Madame de Rênal's heart was too full, and as yet too innocent, for her not to tell her husband of the offer she had made to Julien and the way it had been rejected.

'What!' said M. de Rênal, highly annoyed, 'how could you tolerate a refusal from a *servant*!'

As Madame de Rênal protested against his use of this term, he added: 'I'm speaking, madam, like his Highness the late Prince de Condé presenting his chamberlains to his wife. "All people of this sort", he told her, "are our servants." I once read you the passage from Besenval's *Memoirs*, an essential work on all that concerns question of precedence. Anyone living in your house who's not a gentleman by birth and receives a salary is a servant. I'll say a word or two to Master Julien, and give him a hundred francs.'

'Ah! my dear,' said Madame de Rênal trembling. 'Please don't let it be in front of the servants!'

'Yes, they might be jealous — and with reason,' said her husband as he went off thinking what a large amount of money it was.

Madame de Rênal sank into a chair, almost fainting with distress. He's going to humiliate Julien, and it will be all my fault! She felt horrified with her husband and, hiding her face in her hands, she promised herself she would never again confide in him.

When she met Julien again she was trembling all over; there was such a tightness in her chest that she could scarcely manage to utter a single word. In her embarrassment she caught hold of both his hands and shook them.

'Well, my dear boy!' she said at length. 'Are you pleased with my husband?'

'Why shouldn't I be?' replied Julien, with a bitter smile. 'He's given me a hundred francs.'

Madame de Rênal looked at him in a hesitating kind of way. 'Give me your arm,' she said at last with a note of courage in her voice that Julien had never heard before.

She was brave enough to venture right inside the bookseller's in Verrières, in spite of the man's frightful reputation as a Liberal. There she chose ten louis' worth of books and gave them to her sons, insisting that each of them should write his name in the books that fell to his share at once, before leaving the shop. While Madame de Rênal was feeling happy about the kind of amends she had been bold enough to make to Julien, the latter was feeling amazed at the number of books he saw in the shop. Never before had he dared to enter so worldly a place; his heart was beating fast. So far from having any thought of trying to guess what was going on in Madame de Rênal's heart, he was absorbed in pondering by what means a young student of theology could get hold of some of these books for himself. At last he hit on the idea that it would be possible, with a little skilful persuasion, to make M. de Rênal think that a history of famous gentlemen who were natives of the province should be set as the subject of one of the children's essays.

After working on this idea for a month, Julien saw the success of his plan; so much so, indeed, that shortly after, in talking to M. de Rênal, he ventured to suggest something far more difficult for the noble Mayor. It amounted to contributing to a Liberal's bank account by becoming a subscriber to his library. M. de Rênal certainly agreed it would be a good thing to give his eldest son a first-hand acquaintance with various books he would hear mentioned in the course of conversation at the *École Militaire*; but Julien found the Mayor obstinately resolved to go no farther. He suspected some hidden reason for this, but could not guess what it was.

'I've been thinking, sir,' he said to him one day, 'that it would be highly unsuitable for the name of a respectable gentleman like a Rênal to appear on the ledger of a low-class bookseller.' M. de Rênal's face grew brighter. 'It would also,' continued Julien, in a humbler tone of voice, 'be a bad mark against a poor student of theology if his name were to be discovered one day on the ledger of a bookseller who lends out books. The Liberals might accuse me of having asked for the most scandalous works – who knows they wouldn't even go so far as to enter the titles of such indecent publications against my name.' But Julien was getting off the track. He noticed the Mayor was beginning to look moody and ill-at-ease again, and stopped talking. I've got my man, he said to himself.

A few days later, in M. de Rênal's presence, the eldest son asked Julien about a book which was advertised in the *Quotidienne*. 'To avoid giving the Jacobins any cause to exult,' the young tutor remarked, 'yet to provide me with material for answering Master Adolphe's questions, you might, sir, allow the least important of your servants to take out a subscription at the bookseller's.'

'That's not a bad idea,' said M. de Rênal, obviously extremely delighted.

'All the same,' added Julien with the grave and almost melancholy expression so becoming to certain people when they see the successful realization of things they have most constantly desired, 'you would have to make this servant understand that he mustn't take out any kind of novel. Once such dangerous works get into the house they might corrupt Madam's maids – and even the servant himself.'

'You're forgetting political pamphlets,' M. de Rênal added haughtily, in his desire to hide his admiration for the skilful compromise his children's tutor had discovered.

Julien's life was made up in this way of a series of little negotiations, the success of which occupied his mind far more than the marked feeling of preference Madame de Rênal had for him, and which, had he only wanted to, he could have read in her heart.

In the Mayor's house he found himself once again in the same psychological situation as that in which he had been his whole life through. There, as in his father's house, he felt a profound contempt for all the people with whom he lived, and was hated by them. Every day, as he listened to accounts the sub-prefect, M. Valenod, and other friends of the family gave of things that had recently happened under their eyes, he saw how little their ideas corresponded with reality.

If any action seemed to him worthy of admiration, that was precisely the one that drew unfavourable comments from the people around him. His inner reaction was always : What brutes! or What fools ! The funny thing about it was that, with all his pride, he frequently did not understand a thing of what they were talking about.

His whole life long he had never spoken frankly to anyone except the old army surgeon, and what few ideas he had related only to Bonaparte's Italian campaigns or to questions of surgery. His youthful courage revelled in detailed accounts of the most painful operations. I wouldn't have flinched, he would say to himself.

The first time Madame de Rênal attempted to talk to him about things that had nothing to do with the children, he began speaking about surgical operations. She turned pale and begged him to stop.

Apart from such matters, Julien knew positively nothing. And so, while he spent his days in Madame de Rênal's company, the most curious silence fell between them whenever they found themselves alone together. In the drawing-room, whatever humility there might be in his manner, she read in his eyes a sense of his intellectual superiority over everyone who came to see her. If she found herself for a moment alone with him, she noticed his visible embarrassment. This made her uneasy, for, with a woman's intuition, she realized that this embarrassment contained not a trace of tender feeling.

Influenced by some notion or other he had picked up from accounts of good society as the old army surgeon had seen it, Julien felt humiliated whenever silence fell in a place where he found himself in a woman's company, just as if this silence had been his own particular fault. This sensation was a hundred times more painful in a *tête-à-tête* conversation. His imagination, crammed with the most exaggerated – and the most romantic – notions of what a man should say when he finds himself alone with a woman, suggested to him in his agitation none but the most unsuitable ideas. His mind soared free into the upper air, and yet he could not manage to break a silence which he felt intensely humiliating. Thus, in long walks which he took with Madame de Rênal and the children, the severe expression on his face was intensified by his most cruel anguish.

He was frightfully contemptuous of himself. If he happened unluckily to force himself to speak, he only managed to say the most ridiculous things. As a final touch to his misery, he was conscious of his own absurdity and took an exaggerated view of it. What he did not see, however, was the expression of his eyes, which were so fine, and bore witness to so ardent a spirit, that, as clever actors do, they sometimes imparted a delightful meaning to things that had no meaning at all. Madame de Rênal noticed that when he was alone with her he never happened to say anything worth listening to, except when some unforeseen occurrence took his mind off himself and he left off thinking of how to make pretty compliments. As the friends who came to her house did not spoil her by putting forward new and brilliant ideas, she joyfully welcomed Julien's flashes of intelligence.

Ever since Napoleon's downfall, provincial usage has rigorously banned all manifestations of gallantry. Everyone is afraid of being turned out of his post. Scoundrels seek the support of the Jesuit party, and hypocrisy has made enormous strides, even among the educated classes. Boredom is twice as great as ever, and no pleasures remain save farming and reading.

Madame de Rênal, the wealthy heiress to a pious aunt, and married at sixteen years of age to a gentleman of good family, had never in all her life experienced anything in the least like love. At most, the worthy curé, M. Chélan, her confessor, had spoken to her of love in reference to M. Valenod's pursuit of her, and then had painted such a revolting picture of it that the word itself meant nothing to her but the vilest debauchery. She counted as exceptional, or even as something altogether contrary to nature, that love she had read of in the very small number of novels chance had put in her way. Thanks to this ignorance, Madame de Rênal, perfectly happy and unceasingly preoccupied with thoughts of Julien, was very far from addressing the least little reproach to herself.

CHAPTER 8 : *Minor Incidents*

> Then there were sighs, the deeper for suppression,
> And stolen glances, sweeter for the theft,
> And burning blushes, though for no transgression.
> *Don Juan*, i. 74

THE angelic sweetness of Madame de Rênal's temper, for which she had both her own character and her present state of happiness to thank, was only in some slight degree ruffled when she happened to think of her maid Elisa. This young woman, coming into some money, went to the curé Chélan to make her confession and told him of her design to marry Julien. The curé was delighted at his friend's good fortune; but he was intensely surprised when Julien resolutely declared that he could not possibly think of accepting Mademoiselle Elisa's offer.

'Examine well what is going on within your heart, my son,' said the curé, frowning. 'If it's your vocation alone that makes you scorn the offer of a more than sufficient fortune, then I congratulate you. I've been priest of the parish of Verrières for more than fifty-six years; none the less, to all appearances I'm going to have my living taken from me. This grieves me, and yet I have a private income of eight hundred livres. I'm confiding this detail to you so that you will have no illusions about what awaits you in the priesthood. If you are thinking of paying court to those in authority, then your everlasting damnation is assured. You may get on in the world, but you'll have to do things which will harm the poor and needy. You'll have to flatter the sub-prefect, the Mayor, and, in short, any man of importance, and make yourself the servant of his passions. This way of behaviour, which the world calls *savoir-vivre*, may possibly, for a layman, be not entirely incompatible with salvation. But in our calling, a man has to choose between success in this world or the next – there is no middle way. Go away, my dear boy; think it over and come back in three days' time to give me your definite answer. It grieves me to think that deep down in your character I can see a darkly burning fire which hardly suggests to me the moderation and complete renunciation of all earthly benefits necessary in a priest. As far as your mind is concerned I have very good hopes for your future, but allow me to say,' the good priest added with tears in his eyes, 'that I tremble for your salvation should you enter the priesthood.'

Julien was ashamed of the emotion he felt. For the first time in his life he found himself loved. Weeping for joy, he went away to hide his tears in the spreading woods above Verrières.

What's the reason, he said to himself at last, that I find myself in such a state? I feel I could give my life a hundred times over for this good priest, and yet he's just proved to me I'm an utter fool. He's the man above all others whom I should deceive, and yet he guesses what I am. This secret fire he speaks of is my plan to make my way. He believes me unworthy to be a priest, at the very moment too when I was imagining that my sacrifice of fifty louis a year would give him the highest opinion of my piety and my real vocation. In future, Julien went on thinking, I'll only count on those qualities in my character I've put to the test. Who would have told me I'd find pleasure in tears? Or feel drawn to a man who proves to me I'm no better than a fool?

Three days later Julien hit upon the excuse with which he should have provided himself on the very first day. This excuse was a slander – but what of that? He confessed to the curé, though with much hesitation, that a reason he could not possibly explain, since it would injure a third party, had turned him at first against the proposed marriage. This amounted to an imputation against Elisa's conduct. M. Chélan observed a certain worldly enthusiasm in his manner, very different from that which should have inspired a young candidate for the priesthood.

'Choose rather, my dear boy,' he said to him again, 'to be a respectable, well-educated country farmer than a priest without a vocation.'

As far as words were concerned, Julien made a very good answer to this fresh attempt to dissuade him. He found the exact expressions a fervent young theological student would have used; but the tone of his voice as he uttered these words and the ill-concealed gleam in his eyes made M. Chélan feel alarmed.

We must not forecast too gloomy a future for Julien. He was discovering for himself – and correctly too – the language of cunning and cautious hypocrisy. That is not bad for a boy of his age. As for his manner and his gestures, he was living in the midst of country folk; he had had no chance of seeing the best models. Later on in his life, no sooner was he given the opportunity of coming in contact with these men of the world than his gestures became as worthy of admiration as his language.

Madame de Rênal was surprised that her maid's newly acquired fortune did not make the girl any happier. She remarked that the maid was constantly going to see the curé and coming back with tears in her eyes. Finally Elisa spoke of the marriage to her mistress.

Madame de Rênal believed herself to be ill. A kind of feverish excitement kept her from sleeping; she was only really alive at times when either her maid or Julien was there right under her eyes. She could think of nothing but these two and the happiness they would find in their home. The poverty of this little house, in which they would have to exist on fifty louis a year, was painted in the rosiest colours in her imagination. Julien might very well become a lawyer at Bray, a place some six miles distant from Verrières, where the sub-prefect lived. In that case she would see him now and then.

She honestly believed she was going out of her mind. She told her husband so, and finally became really ill. That evening, as her maid was waiting on her, she noticed the girl was crying. At that moment she was loathing Elisa and had just spoken sharply to her. She asked the girl's pardon, but Elisa's tears fell twice as fast. She said that if her mistress would allow it, she would tell her all her troubles.

'Please do,' said Madame de Rênal.

'Well, madam, he's refused me. Some wicked people have told him bad tales about me, and he believes them.'

'Who's refused you?' asked Madame de Rênal, hardly able to breathe.

'Who else but M. Julien, madam,' the maid answered, sobbing. 'His reverence hasn't been able to get him to change his mind. For his reverence thinks he oughtn't to refuse a decent, respectable girl just because she's been a chambermaid. After all, M. Julien's father is only a carpenter. And how did he earn his own living, either, before he came to Madam's house?'

Madame de Rênal was no longer listening – excess of joy had almost made her lose her reason. She got the girl to assure her several times over that Julien had given a definite refusal and of such a kind as gave him no chance of returning to a wiser decision.

'I'll make one last attempt,' she said to her maid. 'I'll speak to M. Julien myself.'

The next morning after lunch Madame de Rênal allowed herself the exquisite pleasure of pleading her rival's cause and of hearing, for an hour on end, Elisa's hand and fortune repeatedly rejected.

Gradually Julien left off making stilted replies and finally countered Madame de Rênal's sensible arguments with spirit and intelligence. Unable to resist the joy which, after so many hopeless days, swept like a torrent in flood through all her being, she fell into a dead faint. When she had recovered consciousness and was comfortably settled in her own room, she sent everyone away. She was deeply amazed. Can it be that I'm in love with Julien? she said to herself at length.

This discovery which, at any other moment but this, would have left her plunged in remorse and deep distress of mind, seemed now to her as some strange spectacle to which she was indifferent. Her heart, exhausted by all she had just gone through, had no more feeling left in it to minister to passion.

She tried to work, but fell into a deep slumber. On waking, she was not so alarmed as she should have been. She was too happy to be able to look on the dark side of things. By nature artless and innocent, this good provincial lady had never racked her mind in the attempt to extract a grain of emotion from any new shade of feeling or new degree of unhappiness. Entirely taken up, before Julien's arrival, with the host of duties that fall to the lot of a good wife and mother who lives far away from Paris, Madame de Rênal regarded passion as we regard lotteries – certain disappointment and a happiness only sought for by fools.

The dinner bell rang. Madame de Rênal blushed deeply on hearing Julien's voice as he brought the children in. Since falling in love she had become a trifle more cunning, and complained of a frightful headache to account for her red cheeks.

'That's like all you women,' said M. de Rênal roaring with laughter. 'Such little machines are always in need of repair.'

Although accustomed to jests of this kind, Madame de Rênal was set on edge by his tone. To take her mind off it, she glanced at Julien's face. Had he been the ugliest man on earth, he would have pleased her at that moment.

As soon as the first fine days of spring came round, M. de Rênal, careful to model his way of living on the manners of the court, installed himself at Vergy, a village made famous by Gabrielle's tragic adventure. A few hundred feet away from the very picturesque ruins of the Gothic church was an old château belonging to M. de Rênal, with four towers, and a garden laid out like the Tuileries gardens, with a goodly number of flower-beds bordered with box and avenues of chestnut-trees clipped twice a year. A field close by, planted with apple-trees, provided a place in which to walk. Nine or ten fine walnut-trees stood at the bottom of the orchard, their enormous leafy branches rising to a height of maybe eighty feet.

'Every single one of those blessed walnuts,' M. de Rênal would say to his wife whenever she admired them, 'costs me half an acre's crop. No wheat can grow under their shade.'

The sight of this landscape affected Madame de Rênal as if it were new to her; she was even ecstatic in her admiration. The feeling that inspired her made her energetic and enterprising. The morning after their arrival in Vergy, M. de Rênal having gone back to town on business connected with his office as mayor, she engaged workmen at her own expense. Julien had given her the idea of making a little gravel path to go round the orchard and under the tall walnut-trees, so making it possible for the children to walk there in the morning without getting their shoes wet with dew. This scheme was begun and completed less than twenty-four hours after it was planned. Madame de Rênal spent the whole day very gaily helping Julien direct the workmen.

When the Mayor of Verrières came back from town he was greatly surprised to find the path completed. His arrival was also a surprise to Madame de Rênal, who had forgotten his existence. For the next two months he spoke with some show of temper of the bold way in which so important an improvement had been made, and without consulting him, either; but Madame de Rênal had had it carried out at her own expense, and that was some little consolation.

She spent her days running about with the children in the orchard chasing butterflies. They had made big nets of transparent gauze in which they caught the unfortunate *Lepidoptera*, a barbarous name for them Madame de Rênal had learnt from Julien. For she had sent to Besançon for Godart's fine work, and Julien had told her of the poor creatures' curious habits. They stuck these butterflies mercilessly on pins inside a large cardboard show-case which Julien had also made.

Madame de Rênal and Julien had at last a subject for conversation; he was no longer exposed to the frightful torment occasioned by moments of silence. They talked to each other unceasingly and with extreme animation, but always about very innocent things. This active life, full of occupations and gaiety, was to everyone's taste except Mademoiselle Elisa's, who found herself worn out with work. Not even at carnival time, she would say to herself, when there's a ball in Verrières, has madam taken such pains over what's she wearing. She changes her dresses two or three times a day.

As it is not our intention to give a flattering picture of anyone we will not deny that Madame de Rênal, who had a marvellous skin, had her dresses made in such a way that it left her arms and neck and shoulders very much uncovered. She had a very good figure, and this way of dressing suited her divinely. 'You've never *looked so young*, madam,' so her friends from Verrières would say to her when they came to dine at Vergy. (This is a current compliment in the district.)

Strangely enough, though we may be little inclined to believe it, Madame de Rênal had no deliberate intention in all the trouble she took. She found a pleasure in it, and without thinking of it as anything else, she employed whatever time she did not spend chasing butterflies with Julien and the children in making dresses for herself with Elisa. Her only expedition to Verrières was occasioned by her desire to buy some new summer gowns that had just arrived from Mulhouse.

She came back to Vergy with a young woman who was some sort of relation. Since her marriage Madame de Rênal had gradually become very friendly with this Madame Derville, a former schoolfellow of hers at the Convent of the Sacred Heart.

Madame Derville found much to laugh at in what she called her cousin's queer, fantastic notions. 'I'd never have thought of that on my own,' she would say. When she was with her husband these odd fancies of hers – which would have passed for flashes of wit in Paris – embarrassed Madame de Rênal as much as if they were mere stupidity; but Madame Derville's presence gave her courage. At first her voice had been shy as she told of her thoughts; but when these two friends had been for a long time alone together Madame de Rênal's intelligence grew lively and a long solitary morning would pass like a moment, leaving both of them in an extremely merry mood. On this visit, the shrewd Madame Derville found her friend much less gay and very much happier.

As for Julien, he had lived like a veritable child since coming to stay in the country, as happy running after butterflies as his pupils themselves. After a life of so much restraint and clever scheming, now that he found himself alone, out of sight of other men and instinctively unafraid of Madame de Rênal, he aban-

doned himself to the joy of being alive, which people of his age
feel so keenly, amongst the loveliest mountains in the world.

From the moment of Madame Derville's arrival she seemed to
Julien to be his friend. He hastened to show her the view that
could be seen from the end of the new path under the great
walnut-trees : it equalled indeed, if it did not surpass, the most
wonderful views that Switzerland and the Italian lakes can offer.
By climbing the steep slope that begins a few feet farther on, you
come very soon to great precipices fringed by woods of oak-trees,
pushing their way forwards till they almost overhang the river.
It was to the summit of these rocks, falling sheer down to the
water, that Julien, happy and free and, what was even more, king
of his castle, led these two friends, revelling in their wonder at
so sublime a sight. 'For me,' said Madame Derville, 'it's like
Mozart's music.'

Julien's pleasure in the country-side around Verrières had been
spoilt for him by his brothers' jealousy and the presence of a cross,
tyrannical father. At Vergy no such bitter memories confronted
him; for the first time in his life he found no enemies. Whenever
M. de Rênal was in town, a thing that frequently happened, he
could venture to read. Soon, instead of reading at night, and even
then having to be careful to hide his lamp under an upturned
flower-pot, he could abandon himself to slumber. In the daytime,
in intervals between lessons with the children, he would come
and sit amongst these rocks with the book that was his sole
manual of conduct and the subject of his rapturous dreams. In its
pages he found at one and the same time happiness, ecstasy, and
comfort in moments of discouragement.

Certain of Napoleon's remarks about women, together with
one or two of his disquisitions on the merits of novels fashionable
in his reign, gave Julien then, for the very first time, a few ideas
that any other young man of his age would have thought of
long before.

Days of intensest summer heat came round. They made it a
custom to spend the evenings under an enormous lime-tree a
few feet away from the house. It was very dark indeed out there.
One evening, as Julien was making lively conversation, full of
delight in the pleasure of his own eloquence in the presence of
ladies, he happened, in gesticulating, to touch Madame de Rênal's
hand as it lay on the back of one of those painted wooden
chairs that are found in gardens.

This hand was very quickly withdrawn; but Julien felt it his *duty* to manage things so that this hand should not be withdrawn when he touched it. The idea of a duty to be carried out, and of making himself ridiculous or rather being made to feel his inferiority if he failed, banished at once every thought of pleasure from his heart.

CHAPTER 9 : *An Evening in the Country*

M. Guérin's Dido, a charming sketch !
STROMBECQ

JULIEN looked at Madame de Rênal in a very curious way when he met her the next morning; he was taking stock of her as of an enemy he had to fight. His glances, so unlike those of the previous evening, drove Madame de Rênal distracted. She had been kind to him, and he seemed to be annoyed; she could not take her eyes away from his.

Madame Derville's presence gave Julien a chance to talk less and to give more thought to what he had in mind. His sole concern throughout the day was to fortify himself by reading that inspired book which helped to brace his courage. He cut the children's lessons much shorter, and then, when Madame de Rênal's presence made him once more wholly intent on thoughts of what his self-esteem demanded, he made up his mind that she absolutely must allow her hand to remain in his that evening.

The sun as it set and brought the decisive moment nearer made Julien's heart beat strangely. Night fell. He noticed, with a sense of joy that lifted a huge weight off his chest, that the evening would be very dark. The sky, laden with heavy clouds driven across it by a sultry wind, seemed to announce a storm. The two women prolonged their walk until very late – all that they did that evening seemed to Julien very strange. They were revelling in this kind of weather which, for certain delicately sensitive minds, seems to increase the joy of loving.

At last they were all seated, Madame de Rênal next to Julien and Madame Derville beside her friend. His mind preoccupied with what he was about to attempt, Julien could find nothing to say. Conversation languished.

Shall I tremble and feel as miserable as this when I have to fight my first duel ? said Julien to himself, too mistrustful of himself and other people to be unaware of his own state of mind. In such a moment of mortal anguish any kind of danger would have seemed to him preferable to this. How many times did he not find himself hoping some business would intervene, obliging Madame de Rênal to leave the garden and go indoors ! The violent constraint he was forced to exercise was too great to keep his voice from faltering. Soon Madame de Rênal's voice was trembling too, though Julien did not notice it. Duty was waging too terrible a fight with shyness for him to be in a state to notice anything outside himself.

The clock on the house had just struck a quarter to ten, and still he had not dared to do anything. Indignant with his own cowardice Julien said to himself: The moment ten o'clock strikes, I'll carry out what I've been promising myself the whole day long to do this evening, or else I'll go upstairs to my room and blow my brains out.

After a few last moments of anxious waiting, during which Julien was as if beside himself from excess of emotion, the clock immediately above his head struck ten. Each stroke of its fatal chiming echoed in his breast, making it quiver as if by a physical shock.

At last, as the final stroke of ten was still resounding, he stretched out his hand and took hold of Madame de Rênal's, which was instantly withdrawn. Without knowing very well what he was doing, Julien seized hold of it a second time. Although deeply moved himself, he was struck by the icy coldness of the hand he was clasping. He pressed it convulsively. She made a last attempt to snatch it from him, but in the end this hand remained in his.

His heart was overflowing with happiness, not from any love for Madame de Rênal, but because a frightful state of torment was at an end. To keep Madame Derville from suspecting anything, he felt obliged to begin talking. His voice at that moment was sonorous and strong. Madame de Rênal's voice, on the contrary, betrayed so much emotion that her friend thought she had been taken ill and suggested going indoors. Julien realized his danger. If Madame de Rênal, he thought, goes back into the drawing-room, I shall find myself in the same frightful position in which I've been all day. I've held this hand too short a time for it to count as an advantage won.

As Madame Derville renewed her suggestion of going back into the drawing-room, Julien tightly squeezed the hand relinquished to him. Madame de Rênal, who was already getting up from her chair, sat down again and said in the faintest tones: 'I really do feel a little ill, but the fresh air does me good.'

These words confirmed Julien's happiness, which was at the moment extreme. He began to talk, he forgot all affectation and pretence, and showed himself the most agreeable of men to the two women who were listening to him. All the same, there was still some slight lack of courage underlying his new-found eloquence. He was in deadly fear lest Madame Derville, growing impatient with the wind now beginning to blow more violently as a forerunner of the storm, would want to go indoors, and then he would be left alone with Madame de Rênal. He had somehow had that blind sort of courage that is sufficient for action, but he felt it quite out of his power to make the simplest remark to her. However mild her reproaches, he was bound to be defeated, and the advantage he had won would be entirely wiped out.

Luckily for him, that evening, the vigorous, moving tone of his conversation had found favour for him with Madame Derville, who had often found him a trifle dull, with something of a child's shy clumsiness in his ways. As for Madame de Rênal, with her hand in Julien's clasp, she was thinking of nothing at all; it was enough for her to be alive. The hours spent under this tall lime-tree, which according to local tradition had been planted by Charles the Bold, were for her a time of happiness. She listened with keen delight to the moaning of the wind in the thick foliage of the lime and the noise of scattered raindrops beginning to fall through on to its lowest leaves.

Julien did not remark a circumstance that might well have re-assured him. As Madame de Rênal rose to help her cousin pick up a pot of flowers the wind had just overturned at their feet, she had to withdraw her hand. But she had hardly sat down again before she let him take it in his once more, almost without any trouble and as if it were something agreed upon between them.

Midnight had struck a long time since; they had to leave the garden at last and separate for the night. Madame de Rênal transported by the joy of loving, had so little experience of such things that she hardly reproached herself at all. Happiness kept her from sleeping. Julien slept like a log, completely worn out by the battles that timidity and pride had been waging all day long in his heart.

He was woken up at five the next morning; and, what would have been a cruel disappointment to Madame de Rênal had she known of it, he hardly gave her a thought. He had done his *duty*, and an *heroic duty*, too. Filled with happiness at the thought, he locked himself in his room and abandoned himself with an entirely new delight to reading of his hero's exploits.

By the time the bell rang for lunch he had quite forgotten, in reading the bulletins of the Grand Army, every advantage he had gained the evening before. As he went down to the drawing-room he remarked in an airy way to himself: I must tell this woman that I love her.

In place of the glances full of passion he had expected to find, he encountered the grim features of M. de Rênal, who had returned from Verrières two hours before and did not hide his annoyance with Julien for spending the morning without troubling himself about the children. Nothing could have been more hideous than this important gentleman when he was in a temper and felt at liberty to show it.

Every bitter word her husband uttered pierced Madame de Rênal's heart. As for Julien, he was so lost in ecstasy, so preoccupied still with the great things that had been happening for several hours under his eyes, that he could scarcely bring his attention down to the point of listening to the harsh remarks that M. de Rênal was addressing to him. He said to him at last, rather curtly: 'I was unwell.'

The tone of this reply would have stung a much less touchy man than the Mayor of Verrières, who had some idea of answering Julien by dismissing him on the spot. He was only restrained by the thought of a maxim he had adopted – that in matters of business one should never act too hastily.

This young idiot, he reminded himself very soon, has made a kind of reputation for himself in this house. That fellow Valenod may take him himself, or he'll marry Elisa. In either case, in his heart he may think he's made a fool of me.

In spite of these sensible reflexions, M. de Rênal's annoyance found vent, none the less, in a string of scurrilous epithets which gradually irritated Julien. Madame de Rênal was almost dissolved in tears. Lunch had hardly ended when she asked Julien to give her his arm and take her for a walk. She clung to his arm in a friendly way, but to all that she said Julien could only mutter in reply: 'That's like the rich all are.'

M. de Rênal was walking quite close to them; his presence made Julien feel angrier still. Suddenly he noticed that Madame de Rênal was leaning on his arm in a most significant way. This action of hers horrified him; he pushed her away from him with some violence and freed his arm.

Fortunately M. de Rênal did not see this fresh piece of impertinence, which was only noticed by Madame Derville. Her friend burst into tears. M. de Rênal was at this moment engaged in throwing stones to chase away a little peasant girl who had ventured where she had no right, and was cutting across a corner of the orchard.

'M. Julien,' said Madame Derville hurriedly, 'for goodness' sake, control yourself. Remember that we all have moments of temper.'

Julien looked at her coldly with eyes that expressed the most supreme contempt. His glance astonished Madame Derville, and would have astonished her very much more if she had guessed what it really expressed; she would have read there something like a vague hope of the most frightful revenge. There is no doubt that men like Robespierre are created by such moments of humiliation.

'That Julien of yours is very violent,' Madame Derville whispered to her friend, 'he frightens me.'

'He has a right to be angry,' her friend replied. 'After the amazing progress the children have made with him, what does it matter if he spends one morning without speaking to them? Men are hard, you must agree.'

For the first time in her life Madame de Rênal felt a kind of desire for vengeance on her husband. The bitter hatred of the rich now filling Julien's heart was on the verge of showing itself in a violent outburst. Luckily M. de Rênal summoned his gardener and stayed with him busily engaged in stopping up the forbidden way with hawthorn twigs. Julien did not say a single word in reply to all the friendly attentions shown him during the rest of the walk. M. de Rênal had hardly left them before the two friends declared they felt tired and asked him to give each of them an arm.

Julien's haughty pallor and his stubborn, sulky expression formed a striking contrast to the women on either side of him, whose extreme distress was marked by the redness of their cheeks and the look of embarrassment on both their faces. He was full of contempt for these women and for all tender sentiments too.

What! he said to himself, not even five hundred francs a year to help me finish my studies! Ah! how I'd send him about his business!

Engrossed in such stern thoughts, the little he condescended to understand of the kindly words the two friends addressed to him offended him as something void of meaning, silly, weak – in short, *feminine*.

Speaking for speaking's sake and endeavouring to keep the

conversation alive, Madame de Rênal happened to remark that her husband had returned from Verrières because he had just purchased some maize straw from one of his farmers. (In these parts maize straw is used to fill palliasses.)

'My husband won't be coming to join us again,' added Madame de Rênal. 'He'll be busy with his valet and the gardener getting all the palliasses in the house refilled. This morning he's had every bed on the first floor stuffed with straw and now he's on the second.'

The colour fled from Julien's cheeks. He glanced in a strange sort of way at Madame de Rênal, and, quickening his pace, managed somehow to draw her aside. Madame Derville let them go.

'Help to save my life,' he said to Madame de Rênal. 'You're the only one who can, for the valet, as you know, is my deadly enemy. I must confess to you, madame, that I've someone's portrait. I've hidden it in the palliasse on my bed.'

At these words Madame de Rênal in her turn grew pale.

'You're the only person, madam, who can go into my bedroom at this moment. Put your hand – but don't let anyone see you – into the corner of the palliasse nearest the window. You'll find a little shiny black cardboard box there.'

'It contains a portrait?' said Madame de Rênal, hardly able to hold herself upright.

Julien noticed her evident discomposure and took advantage of it.

'I've a second favour to ask you, madam. I must beg you not to look at this portrait. It's my secret.'

'A secret!' echoed Madame de Rênal in the faintest voice.

But although she had been brought up amongst people proud of their wealth and alive to money interests only, love had already made a place in her heart for generous feelings. Cruelly wounded, yet in tones that spoke of the purest self-devotion, Madame de Rênal asked Julien all the questions necessary for her to carry out her errand properly.

'So it's a little round box,' she said to him as she was moving away, 'of black cardboard and very shiny.'

'Yes, madam,' Julien answered in that callous tone danger brings out in men.

She went up to the second floor of the château, as pale as if she were going to her death. To crown her anguish she felt as if she were about to faint; but Julien's need of help gave her strength.

I must have that box, she said to herself, and began to quicken her pace.

She could hear her husband talking to the valet right inside Julien's room. Luckily they moved off into the room occupied by the children. She lifted up the mattress and thrust her hand so violently into the palliasse that she took some skin off her finger. But although very sensitive to such trifling kinds of pain, she was not conscious of this one, for almost at the same instant she felt the shiny surface of the box. She seized it and rushed away.

Hardly was she free from fear of being surprised by her husband than the horror this box aroused in her made her really feel ready to faint. So Julien is in love, she thought, and I'm holding here the portrait of the woman he loves!

Seated on a chair in the antechamber of these rooms, Madame de Rênal fell a prey to all the horrors of jealousy. Her utter lack of experience served her again at this moment — amazement tempered her grief. Julien came in, and seizing hold of the box without a word of thanks, without even saying anything at all, ran off with it into his room, where he struck a light and immediately burnt it up. He was pale and completely overcome; he exaggerated the extent of the danger to which he had just been exposed.

The portrait of Napoleon, he said to himself with a toss of the head, found hidden in the room of a man who's made such a profession of hating the usurper! And found by M. de Rênal who's so much of an Ultra and so annoyed with me! And as a crowning act of folly, some lines in my own writing on the white cardboard on the back of the portrait! And every one of these loving effusions dated! Some of them the day before yesterday! All my reputation ruined, destroyed in a single instant! he added, as he watched the box burning. And my reputation is all I have, it's my whole life . . . and yet, good heavens, what a life!

An hour later, fatigue and self-pity made him inclined for tenderness. When he met Madame de Rênal he took her hand and kissed it with more sincerity than he had ever done. She blushed for joy and almost at the same moment repulsed Julien's advances in her jealous anger. Julien's pride, so lately wounded, made him stupid on this occasion. In Madame de Rênal he saw merely a rich woman, he scornfully let go of her hand, and turned away. He went and walked in the garden, lost in thought; soon a bitter smile appeared on his lips.

I'm walking here, quite calmly, like a man who's master of his time! I'm not troubling about the children; I'm laying myself open to humiliating remarks from M. de Rênal and he'll have reason for them. He rushed off to the children's room. The caresses of the youngest boy, whom he was very fond of, somewhat soothed his agonizing grief. This little fellow doesn't despise me yet, thought Julien. But soon he reproached himself for this lessening of his pain as if it were a further weakness. These children fondle me, he said to himself, as they would fondle a young greyhound bought the day before.

CHAPTER 10 : *High Heart and Low Estate*

> But passion most dissembles, yet betrays,
> Even by its darkness; as the blackest sky
> Foretells the heaviest tempest.
>
> *Don Juan*

I N his progress through all the rooms one after the other, M. de Rênal came back into the children's room with his servants, who were carrying the palliasses. The sudden entrance of this man was just the last straw for Julien. Paler, and more sullen than usual, he rushed up to him. M. de Rênal stood still and looked at his servants.

'Sir,' said Julien, 'do you believe your children would have made the same progress with any other tutor but myself? If your answer is no,' he went on without giving M. de Rênal time to reply, 'how dare you complain that I neglect them?'

M. de Rênal, barely recovered from his fright, concluded from the strange tone this young peasant was taking with him that he had some advantageous offer in his pocket and was intending to leave him.

Julien's anger mounted as he spoke. 'I can live without help from you, sir,' he added.

'I am really very sorry to see you so upset,' said M. de Rênal, stammering slightly over his words. The servants were ten feet or so away, busy making the beds.

'That's not what I want, sir,' continued Julien, beside himself with rage. 'Just think of the shameful things you said to me, and in front of ladies, too !'

M. de Rênal understood only too clearly what Julien was demanding, and his mind was torn in two by a painful struggle. Julien, really mad with anger, happened to exclaim : 'I know where to go, sir, when I leave your house.'

At this remark M. de Rênal had a vision of Julien installed in M. Valenod's house. 'Very well, sir,' he said at last with a sigh, looking as if he had called in the surgeon for the most painful operation, 'I grant what you ask. Reckoning from the day after tomorrow, which is the first of the month, I'll give you a monthly salary of fifty francs.'

Julien stood there thunderstruck, seized with a desire to laugh. All his anger had vanished. I didn't despise the brute enough, he thought. It's no doubt the greatest apology such a base mind can offer.

The children, who had listened to this scene with open mouth, ran out into the garden to tell their mother that M. Julien was very angry, but he was going to have fifty francs a month.

Out of habit, Julien followed them, without even glancing at M. de Rênal, whom he left feeling extremely sore.

That's a hundred and sixty francs M. Valenod's cost me, the Mayor was thinking. I really must have a few straight words with him about his contract for supplies to the orphanage.

A moment later Julien stood once again face to face with the Mayor. 'I have to consult M. Chélan on a matter of conscience,' he said. 'I have the honour to inform you that I shall be absent for a few hours.'

'Why, my dear Julien,' said M. de Rênal, and his laughter rang false, 'stay away the whole day, if you like, and the next day too, my good friend. Take the gardener's horse for the ride into Verrières.'

There he goes, said M. de Rênal to himself, to give Valenod his answer. He's made me no promises, but it's best to let the young man's head cool down a little.

Julien got away quickly and took the road upwards towards the great woods through which one can go from Vergy to Verrières. He did not want to arrive too soon at M. Chélan's. Far from wishing to involve himself in another hypocritical scene, he felt the need of looking clearly into his own heart, of giving a hearing to the host of emotions which were agitating him.

I've won a battle, he said to himself as soon as he found himself alone in the woods and far away from other men's eyes. I've really won a battle!

This reflexion painted the whole situation for him in rosy colours, and restored some of his peace of mind. So here I am, he thought, with a salary of fifty francs a month. M. de Rênal must have been in a fine state of fright. But what about?

Meditation on what might have frightened the fortunate and influential man against whom but an hour ago he had been boiling with anger set his mind completely at rest. For a moment he was almost sensitive to the enchanting beauty of the woods through which he was walking. Huge, naked boulders had fallen long ago from the mountain down into the middle of the forest. Tall beeches, towering almost as high as the rocks, gave with their shade an exquisite freshness to places only three feet away from where the sun would have made it impossible to linger.

Julien stopped for a moment to take breath in the shade of these great rocks, and then continued his climb. Soon, after following a narrow, faintly marked track used only by goatherds, he found himself on top of an enormous boulder where he was very sure of being right away from all other men. This physical situation brought a smile to his face – it represented the situation he ardently desired to reach in the moral sphere. The pure air of these lofty mountains filled his heart with serenity, and even joy. The Mayor of Verrières was still indeed the representative, in his eyes, of all rich and insolent men on earth, but Julien could feel that, for all the violence of its manifestation, the hatred which had recently disturbed him had nothing personal in it. If he stopped seeing M. de Rênal he would have forgotten him in a week, himself, his country house, his dogs, his children, and all his household. I forced him, he thought, though I don't know how, to make the greatest sacrifice. What, more than fifty crowns a year! A moment before I had got myself out of the most frightful danger. That's two victories in a single day. There's no merit in the second – I must try to guess how and why it happened. But tomorrow's time enough for such tedious researches.

Standing on top of the great rock, Julien looked at the sky aflame in the August sun. The cicadas were chirruping in the meadow below the rock; when they ceased, all around him was silence. At his feet stretched twenty leagues of country. Now and then he caught sight of a sparrow-hawk, taking off from the high rocks above his head, and silently tracing huge circles in its flight. Mechanically, Julien's eyes followed the bird of prey. He was struck by its powerful, tranquil movements; he envied such energy, he envied such isolation.

This was Napoleon's destiny – would it one day be his?

> Yet Julia's very coldness still was kind,
> And tremulously gentle her small hand
> Withdrew itself from his, but left behind
> A little pressure, thrilling and so bland
> And slight, so very slight, that, to the mind,
> 'Twas but a doubt.
>
> *Don Juan*

JULIEN had, however, to put in an appearance in Verrières. As he was leaving the curé's house, by some lucky chance he met M. Valenod, whom he hastened to inform of the increase in his salary.

On his return to Vergy Julien did not go down into the garden until nightfall. His mind was worn out with the very many powerful emotions that had excited him during the day. What shall I say to them? he thought, remembering the ladies. He was far from realizing that his mood was precisely fitted to comprehend those trivial matters which are usually the sole interest of women. Julien had often seemed incomprehensible to Madame Derville and even to her friend while he in his turn had only half understood all they had said to him. This was an effect of the violence, and, if I may venture to say so, the grandeur of those passionate impulses which convulsed this ambitious youngster's mind. With a being so extraordinary, almost every day was stormy weather.

As he came into the garden that evening, Julien was in a mood to be interested in the ideas of the two pretty cousins. They were waiting for him impatiently. He took his usual place beside Madame de Rênal. Soon it grew very dark. He tried to take hold of a white hand he had for a long time observed very close to him, resting on the back of a chair. There was some little hesitation, but in the end this hand was withdrawn in a manner that showed some annoyance. Julien was feeling inclined to let matters rest and go on chatting gaily, when he heard M. de Rênal approaching.

That morning's brutal insults were still ringing in Julien's ears. Wouldn't it, he thought, be a way of showing my little respect for this individual so overloaded with wealth if I took possession of his wife's hand in his very presence. Yes, I'll do it – I, whom he's treated so contemptuously.

From that moment the tranquillity so little akin to his nature rapidly disappeared. He could think of nothing else but his anxious longing for Madame de Rênal to consent to his holding her hand.

M. de Rênal was angrily talking politics. Two or three of the manufacturers in Verrières were on the way to becoming decidedly richer than himself, and intended to work against him in the elections. Madame Derville listened to him talking. Julien, irritated by the conversation, brought his chair closer up to Madame de Rênal's, all his movements concealed by the darkness. He ventured to put his hand down very close to the lovely arm that her dress left uncovered. He was agitated, he could no longer control his thoughts; he put his cheek close to this lovely arm and ventured to touch it with his lips.

Madame de Rênal shuddered. Her husband was only four feet away. She hurriedly gave Julien her hand and at the same time pushed him a little away from her. While M. de Rênal continued his abuse of people of no account and of Jacobins who grow rich, Julien was covering the hand left in his with passionate kisses, or which seemed such to Madame de Rênal. Yet the poor woman had had proof on that fatal day that the man she adored, though without admitting it to herself, was in love with someone else! All the time Julien had been away she had been a prey to intense unhappiness, and this had made her think.

What! she said to herself. Can I love him, feel love for him? Can I, a married woman, have fallen in love? Yet, she thought, I've never felt for my husband such a dark, secret passion as this which makes it impossible for me to put Julien out of my mind. After all, he's really only a boy who looks on me with respect. This is merely a passing folly. What does it matter to my husband what feelings I have for this young man? M. de Rênal would merely be bored by my conversations with Julien on things of the imagination. He himself thinks only of his business. I take nothing away from him to give to Julien.

There was no hypocrisy here to sully the purity of an innocent mind led astray by a passion never experienced before. She deceived herself, but all unknowingly, and yet some instinct of virtue in her took alarm. Such were the inner conflicts troubling her when Julien appeared in the garden. She heard him speak and almost at the same time saw him sit down beside her. Her heart was as it were carried away by this enchanting happiness that for a fortnight past had more amazed than charmed her. Everything came as a surprise to her. All the same, after a moment or two she said to herself: Is Julien's mere presence enough to blot out all his faults? She felt afraid – that was the moment at which she withdrew her hand.

His passionate kisses, unlike any she had ever received before, made her forget on the spot that he might be in love with another woman. Soon he was no longer guilty in her eyes. Relief from the stinging pain born of suspicion, and the presence of a happiness of which she had not even dreamed, aroused an ecstasy of love in her, a wild, unreasoning joy.

That evening was a delightful one for everyone except the Mayor of Verrières, who could not forget his money-grubbing manufacturers. Julien's mind was no longer on his dark ambitions, nor on the projects he found so difficult to carry out. For the first time in his life he was drawn away by the power of beauty. Lost in vague, sweet dreams to which he was by temperament a stranger, gently pressing a hand that delighted him by its perfect loveliness, he listened half unconsciously to the rustle of the leaves in the lime-tree as the soft night-wind stirred them, and the distant barking of dogs from the mill beside the Doubs.

Yet this emotion was one of pleasure, not of passion. When he got back to his own room again, his thoughts were all of one kind of happiness, that of taking up his own favourite book once more. When one is twenty, ideas of the outside world and the effect one can have on it take precedence over everything else.

Soon, however, he put down his book. Reflecting on Napoleon's victories had made him aware of some new feature in his own. Yes, he said to himself, I've won a battle. I must press home my advantage; I must crush the pride of this arrogant gentleman while he's in retreat. That's true Napoleonic strategy. I must ask for three days' holiday to go and see my friend Fouqué. If he refuses, I'll take a high hand with him, and he'll give in.

Madame de Rênal could not get a wink of sleep. Unable to keep her mind from dwelling on her feeling of happiness when Julien had covered her hand with burning kisses, it seemed to her she had not lived until that moment.

Suddenly the dreadful word – *adultery* – confronted her. All the most disgusting associations lent by debauchery of the lowest kind to the idea of love on its physical side rose up in her imagination, filling it with thoughts that strove to sully the heavenly pure and tender image she had made of Julien, and of the bliss of loving him. The future took on terrible colours. She saw herself a thing of scorn.

It was a fearful moment; her soul had penetrated into unknown regions. The previous evening she had enjoyed a happiness such as she had never experienced before, now she was suddenly plunged in agonizing grief. She had had no idea anyone could suffer so cruelly, it drove her frantic. For a minute she thought of confessing to her husband her fear of being in love with Julien. She would at least have had his name on her lips. Luckily she remembered a piece of advice her aunt had given her long ago, on the eve of her wedding, concerning the danger of confiding in a husband who is, after all, one's lord and master. She wrung her hands in excess of grief.

She was drawn this way and that, haphazard, by contradictory and painful images of her situation. Now she was afraid of not being loved, now the dreadful thought of her sin tormented her, as if, the next morning, she were to be exhibited in the pillory, in the public square in Verrières, with a placard setting forth her adultery for all the people of the town to read.

Madame de Rênal had not the slightest experience of life. Even had she been fully awake she would not have been aware of any interval between being guilty in the sight of God and of finding herself subjected in public to the most boisterous manifestations of popular scorn.

Whenever the dreadful idea of adultery, and all the disgrace that, in her opinion, this crime entailed, left her any peace of mind, and she began to think of the sweet delight of living innocently with Julien as in the past, she found herself haunted by the horrible thought of Julien's love for another woman. She could still see his pallor when he feared to lose her portrait or to compromise her by letting it be seen. For the very first time she had surprised a look of fear on a face ordinarily so calm and noble. He had never shown such emotion on her own or her children's account. This grief on top of other griefs reached the highest pitch of sorrow the human soul can possibly be asked to bear. Without knowing what she did, Madame de Rênal uttered a cry that woke her maid. She suddenly saw a gleam of light beside her bed and recognized Elisa.

'Are you the one he loves?' she cried in her delirious frenzy.

The maid, amazed at the shocking state of distress in which she found her mistress, fortunately failed to remark this singular question. Madame de Rênal realized her imprudence. 'I'm fever-ish,' she said, 'and a trifle light-headed I think. Stay with me, please.'

Completely awakened by the need for self-control, she found herself less unhappy; reason resumed the sway of which a half-waking state had deprived it. To escape from her maid's staring eyes she ordered her to read the paper to her, and it was listen-ing to the monotonous sound of Elisa's voice as she read a long article from the *Quotidienne*, that Madame de Rênal formed the virtuous resolution of treating Julien with absolute frigidity when she next met him.

CHAPTER 12 : A Journey

Elegant persons are to be found in Paris; the
provinces may possibly contain people of
character.
SIÉYÈS

BY five o'clock the next morning, before Madame de Rênal
had made her appearance, Julien had obtained three days'
leave of absence. Contrary to his expectations, he found himself
eager to see her again; his mind was filled with thoughts of her
lovely hand. He went down into the garden, where he had to
wait a long time before Madame de Rênal came down. Had Julien
only been in love with her he would have seen her standing
behind her half-closed shutters on the first floor, gazing at him
with her forehead pressed against the window-pane. At length,
in spite of her resolutions, she decided to appear in the garden.
The liveliest colours replaced her usual pallor. This simple-minded
woman was obviously troubled; a feeling of embarrassment and
even of anger marred the habitual deep serenity of her expression,
as if far removed from all trivial concerns of life, that gave such
a charm to her heavenly face.

Julien came forward eagerly to meet her, admiring those lovely
arms exposed to view beneath the shawl flung hastily over them.
The fresh morning air seemed to increase the dazzling beauty
of a complexion which the night's turmoil only rendered more
sensitive to every impression. This modest, appealing beauty, yet
instinct with thoughts one does not find amongst the
lower classes, seemed to Julien to reveal some quality of her mind he
had never appreciated before. Wholly absorbed in admiration of
charms that astonished his eager eyes, Julien was not thinking at
all of the friendly welcome he might expect to receive. He was
all the more amazed at the icy coldness she endeavoured to show
him, behind which he even thought to discern an intention to
put him in his place.

The smile of pleasure died on his lips; he called to mind the
rank he occupied in society, above all in the eyes of a rich and
noble heiress. In a moment nothing showed on his face but
arrogant disdain and anger directed against himself. He felt
violently resentful for having let himself delay his departure for
more than an hour only to meet with such a humiliating reception.

Only a fool, he said to himself, loses his temper with other people. A stone falls, doesn't it, because of its weight? Must I always be a child? When shall I acquire the sensible habit of selling just so much of my soul to people of this sort as their money warrants? If I wish to be respected by them and by myself, I must show them that, while I barter my poverty for their wealth, my soul is a thousand leagues out of reach of their insolence, in a sphere too high for their petty marks of favour or contempt to affect it.

All the while such feelings came crowding one on top of the other into the young tutor's mind his mobile face was gradually assuming an expression of fierce and wounded pride. Madame de Rênal was intensely disturbed to see it. The virtuous frigidity she had tried to show in her greeting of him gave place to a look of interest, and an interest quickened by all her surprise at the sudden change she had just observed. The empty phrases people use to each other in the morning on one's state of health, the beauty of the day, etc., dried simultaneously on both their lips. Julien, whose judgement was not disturbed by any sort of passion, soon found a way of impressing on Madame de Rênal how little he considered himself on any terms of friendship with her. Saying nothing to her about the short journey he was going to make, he bowed to her and went off.

As she watched him go, her mind appalled by the sudden disdain she had read in his glance, which the evening before had been so friendly, her eldest son came running up from the bottom of the garden and flinging his arms round her said, 'We've got a holiday. M. Julien's going away on a journey.'

At these words, Madame de Rênal felt a deathly chill come over her. Her virtue had made her unhappy, her weakness made her unhappier still.

Her imagination was completely taken up with this new turn of affairs. She was swept away, far beyond the wise resolves she owed to the terrible night she had just experienced. It was no longer a question of resisting so pleasing a lover, but of losing him for ever.

She had to appear at lunch. As a climax to her anguish Madame Derville and M. de Rênal talked of nothing but Julien's departure. The Mayor of Verrières had noticed something unusual in the determined way in which he had asked for leave of absence.

There's no doubt, he thought, this young peasant has an offer from someone up his sleeve. But whoever it is, even if it's M. Valenod, he'll be rather put off by the sum of six hundred francs to which he'll now have to raise his yearly disbursements. Yesterday at Verrières he'll have asked for three days' delay to think it over. And this very morning, to get out of giving me a definite answer, my little gentleman skips off to the mountains. Fancy being obliged to make terms with a miserable working-man who chooses to be insolent. That's what we've come to in these days!

Since my husband, thought Madame de Rênal, who's no idea how deeply he's wounded Julien, thinks he's going to leave us, – what must I think? Ah! it's all settled!

To be free at least to cry as she would without having to answer Madame Derville's questions, she said she had a frightful headache and went to bed.

'That's just like a woman!' M. de Rênal remarked once more. 'There's always something out of gear in these complicated machines.' And he went off chuckling.

While Madame de Rênal was suffering all the cruellest anguish that springs from a terrible passion such as that in which chance had entangled her, Julien was gaily pursuing his way amidst the most beautiful landscapes mountain scenery can offer. He had to cross the great chain of hills to the north of Vergy. The path he followed, rising gradually through extensive beech woods, twists and turns in unending zigzags up the slope of the high mountain framing the northern side of the valley of the Doubs. Soon the traveller's gaze, passing over the less lofty hillside bounding the river bed on the south, reached as far as the fertile plains of Beaujolais and Burgundy. However insensitive the mind of this ambitious youth might have been to this type of beauty, he could not help stopping from time to time to look at so vast and imposing a sight.

At last he reached the summit of the great mountain, close to which he had to pass to arrive, by way of this short-cut, at the isolated valley where his friend Fouqué, the young timber merchant, lived. Julien was not at all in a hurry to see him, nor any other human being. Hiding, like a bird of prey, among the bare rocks crowning the great mountain, he could see from a long way off any man who might be approaching.

He discovered a little cave in the almost vertical slope of one of the rocks, and going towards it had soon settled down in this retreat. Here, he said to himself, his eyes alight with joy, no man can come to harm me. He was seized with the idea of indulging

in the pleasure of writing down his thoughts, a thing so dangerous for him to do elsewhere. A squarish stone did duty as a desk.
His pen flew on; he had no eyes for anything around him. At last
he noticed that the sun was setting behind the distant mountains
of Beaujolais.

Why shouldn't I spend the night here, he asked himself. I've
got some bread – and *I'm free!* At the sound of this magnificent
word his spirit soared aloft; even with his friend Fouqué his habit
of hypocrisy did not allow him to be free. His head supported on
his hands, Julien remained inside this cave, happier than he had
ever been in his life, excited by dreams and by the joy of being
free.

Without being consciously aware of it, Julien saw the last rays
of twilight fade out utterly one by one. Encircled by the boundless
dark his mind was lost in contemplation of all he fancied he would
one day meet in Paris. First of all it would be a woman much more
beautiful and with a far more lofty spirit than he had ever been
able to discover in the provinces. He would love her passionately
and she would return his love. If he were separated from her for
a moment, it would only be to cover himself with glory and earn
the right to even deeper affection.

Even supposing we grant him an imagination such as Julien's,
a young man brought up amidst the sad realities of Parisian
society would at this point have been aroused from his romantic
dreams by the chill hand of irony. High feats would have faded
into nothing along with the hope of ever accomplishing them, to
give place to the well-known truism : 'Who leaves his mistress
runs the risk, alas ! of being deceived by her two or three times a
day.' The young peasant saw nothing between himself and the
highest feats of heroism save lack of opportunity.

But darkest night had taken the place of day, and he still had
two leagues to go before dropping down to the hamlet where
Fouqué was living. Before leaving the little cave Julien lit a fire
and carefully burnt everything he had written.

He astonished his friend very much by knocking on his door at
one o'clock in the morning. He found Fouqué busy making up his
accounts. He was a tall young man, rather clumsily built, with
heavy, strongly pronounced features, a nose of infinite length,
and a good deal of kindliness underneath his forbidding appearance.

'Have you had a row with M. de Rênal, to arrive like this unexpectedly at my house?'

Julien gave him, but with suitable adjustments, an account of what had happened on the previous day.

'Stay here with me,' said Fouqué. 'I see you know M. de Rênal, the sub-prefect Maugiron, and the curé M. Chélan. You understand the ins and outs of their characters; you're in a position to act in the matter of contracts. You've a better head for figures than I have – you can keep my accounts. I rake in a lot of money in my line of business. The impossibility of doing everything myself and the fear of coming up against a rogue in any man I take as a partner prevent me every day from taking on really good things. Not a month back I gave Michaud over at Saint-Amand the chance of making six thousand francs – and I hadn't even seen him for six years, and just happened to run into him at the sale at Pontarlier. Why shouldn't you have earned that six thousand francs yourself, or at any rate three thousand of it? For if only I'd had you with me that day, I'd have bid for that lot of wood, and everyone would have quickly let me have it. So do say you'll be my partner.'

This offer put Julien in a bad temper; it interfered with his fantastic dreams. All the time they were having supper which, like Homer's heroes, the two friends cooked for themselves – for Fouqué lived alone – the latter was giving Julien an account of his profits and proving to him how many advantages his timber business afforded. Fouqué had the highest opinion of Julien's character and intelligence.

When Julien was at last alone within the deal walls of his little room, he said to himself : I can make a few thousand francs here, it's true, and be in a better position when I go back to being a soldier or a priest, according to the profession that's fashionable in France. The little nest-egg I'll have saved will relieve me of all worry about ways and means. Living alone in this mountain I'll have got rid of some of my frightful ignorance of so many things that interest these men of the world. But Fouqué's given up all idea of getting married and keeps on telling me that he's miserable living alone. It's obvious that if he takes on a partner without any money to invest in his business it's in the hope of securing a lifelong companion.

Can I deceive my friend? cried Julien moodily. This being, for whom hypocrisy and an utter lack of fellow-feeling were ordinary means of salvation, could not for this once tolerate the idea of the least want of delicate consideration for a man who loved him.

But all of a sudden Julien felt happy again – he had found a reason for refusing. What! shall I abjectly throw away seven or eight years of my life! And thus reach twenty-eight! But at that age Bonaparte had performed his greatest deeds! Even supposing I earned some money in a hole-and-corner sort of way, running from one timber sale to another and getting on the right side of a few rascally nobodies, who can tell me if I'd keep alight within me the sacred fire by which men make themselves a name?

The following morning Julien gave a very cool and collected answer to the worthy Fouqué, who had looked on the matter as settled, telling him that his vocation for the sacred ministry did not allow him to accept his offer. Fouqué could not get over his amazement.

'But are you considering,' he said to him time and again, 'that I'd make you my partner or, if you prefer it, give you four thousand francs a year? And you want to go back to M. de Rênal, who has as little respect for you as the mud under his feet! When you've two hundred *louis* right there in front of you, what's to prevent you entering a seminary! I'll tell you more – I'll undertake to get you the best living in the district. For,' added Fouqué, lowering his voice, 'I supply M. le—, M. le—, and M.— with firewood. I let them have real good oak of the finest quality, and they pay me for it as if it were plain deal – but never was money better placed.'

Nothing could prevail against Julien's vocation. Fouqué ended up by thinking him a little wrong in the head. On the third day, very early in the morning, Julien left his friend, to spend the day amongst the rocks on the great mountain. He found his little cave again, but no longer with the same peace of mind – his friend's offer had taken it from him. Like Hercules, he found himself balanced, not between vice and virtue, but between the settled mediocrity of a secure and comfortable existence and all the heroic dreams of youth. I've no real strength of character, so it seems, he said to himself. I'm not the stuff of which great men are made, since I'm afraid lest eight years spent in earning my daily bread might rob me of that sublime energy by means of which outstanding deeds are done.

CHAPTER 13 : Open-work Stockings

A novel is a mirror passing down a road.
SAINT-RÉAL

As Julien came in sight of the picturesque ruins of the old church at Vergy, he realized that for two days past he had not once thought of Madame de Rênal. As I was leaving the other day this woman reminded me of the infinite distance between us. She treated me as a working-man's son. Doubtless she wished to show me how she regretted having let me hold her hand the evening before. Yet what a pretty hand it is! What charm, what noble dignity in that woman's expression!

The possibility of making a fortune in Fouqué's business lent a certain ease to Julien's cogitations. They were no longer so frequently marred by irritability, nor by a stinging sense of his poverty and low estate in the eyes of the world. Placed as it were on a lofty promontory, he could judge and, so to speak, look down alike on extremes of poverty and the comfortable circumstances he still called wealth. He was far from forming a philosophical estimate of his position, but he was clear-sighted enough to feel himself a *different man* after his little trip into the mountains.

He was struck by the extreme agitation with which Madame de Rênal listened to the short account of his journey she had asked him to give her.

Fouqué had had his plans for marriage and his own unhappy love-affairs; conversation between the two friends had been full of long confidences on such matters. After finding happiness too soon, Fouqué had discovered he was not his mistress's only love. All these tales had astonished Julien and had taught him many new things. His solitary life, all taken up with fancies and suspicions, had kept him apart from everything that might have given him insight.

Life for Madame de Rênal during his absence had been nothing but a succession of varied torments, all of them unbearable. She was really and truly ill.

'Now mind,' said Madame Derville as she saw Julien arriving, 'you don't go out into the garden in your poor state of health. The damp air would make your trouble worse.'

Madame Derville was surprised to see that her friend, who was always being scolded by her husband because of the extremely plain way in which she dressed, had just bought herself some open-work stockings and some charming little slippers that had recently come from Paris. For the past three days Madame de Rênal's sole distraction had been getting Elisa to cut out and make for her with all possible speed a summer dress of a thin and very pretty material which was much in the fashion. They had only just been able to finish this gown a few minutes after Julien's arrival. Madame de Rênal put it on at once.

Madame Derville had no further doubts. Realizing what all the curious symptoms of her friend's illness implied, she said to herself: The poor woman's in love!

She saw her speaking to Julien. Pallor followed hard on the deepest blushes. Anxiety was depicted in her eyes as they gazed intently into the young tutor's. Madame de Rênal was expecting every moment that he would explain his intentions and declare whether he was going to leave the house or stay there. Julien had no idea of saying anything on this subject: the thought had not even entered his mind. After a terrible struggle, Madame de Rênal ventured at length to say to him in a trembling voice in which all her passion found utterance: 'Are you meaning to leave your pupils to take a place elsewhere?'

Julien was struck by the hesitation in her voice and the look in her eyes. This woman loves me, he said to himself. But after this passing moment of weakness for which her pride reproaches her, and as soon as she no longer fears I'm going, she'll be just as proud as ever. This view of their respective positions passed swift as lightning through Julien's mind. He answered, hesitatingly, 'It would grieve me very much to leave children who are so delightful and so *well-born*, but it might be necessary. One has duties also towards oneself.'

As he pronounced the words 'so *well-born*' (it was one of those aristocratic expressions Julien had recently picked up) he was dominated by a feeling of the deepest antipathy. In this woman's eyes, he said to himself, I, at any rate, am not well-born.

As Madame de Rênal listened to him, filled with admiration for his intelligence and his good looks, the possibility of his leaving them, which he had allowed her to suspect, pierced her to the heart. All her friends from Verrières who had come to dinner at Vergy in Julien's absence had, as it were, vied with each other in complimenting her on the wonderful man her husband had been lucky enough to unearth. It was not that they had any understanding of the progress the children had made. The fact of his knowing the Bible off by heart, and in Latin moreover, had left the inhabitants of Verrières in the grip of an admiration which, maybe, will last for quite a century.

Julien, who never spoke to anyone, had no idea of all this. If Madame de Rênal had had the least presence of mind, she would have congratulated him on the reputation he had won, and, with Julien's pride once set at ease, he would have been sweet and agreeable with her, all the more because he found her new dress charming.

Pleased herself with her pretty frock and with what Julien said to her about it, Madame de Rênal had attempted to take a walk round the garden; but soon she confessed she was not in a fit state for walking. She had taken the traveller's arm, but far from gaining added strength from this, her contact with his arm deprived her of it altogether.

Night had fallen. They had scarcely sat down before Julien, making use of his old privilege, ventured to touch this pretty arm with his lips and take hold of her hand. He was thinking of Fouqué's bold behaviour with his mistresses, and not of Madame de Rênal – the term 'well-born' still made his heart feel heavy. His hand was pressed, but that gave him no kind of pleasure. Far from being proud of – or at least grateful for – the feelings Madame de Rênal betrayed that evening by all too unmistakable signs, her beauty, her grace, and her innocent freshness found him almost insensitive. Purity of heart and the absence of every hateful passion undoubtedly prolong the duration of youth. It is the expression of the face that ages first with the majority of pretty women.

Julien was in a sulky mood for the whole of the evening. Up till now his anger had been directed only against fortune and against society; but ever since Fouqué had offered him an ignoble way of becoming comfortably off, he had been out of temper with himself. Lost in his thoughts, though from time to time addressing a word or two to the ladies, Julien ended up, quite unconsciously, by letting go of Madame de Rênal's hand. This action drove the poor woman distracted – she saw in it the revelation of her fate.

Had she been sure of Julien's affection, her virtue might have given her the strength to resist him. Trembling at the thought of losing him for ever, her passion led her so far astray as to make her once again take Julien's hand, which, in his absence of mind, he had left resting on the back of a chair. Her action roused this ambitious youth from his musings. He could have wished to have as witnesses all those proud nobles who had stared at him at dinner with such patronizing smiles as he sat at the bottom end of the table with the children. This woman cannot despise me any longer, he said to himself; in that case, I ought to respond to her beauty. I owe it to myself to become her lover. Such an idea would not have occurred to him before he had listened to his friend's naïve confidences.

The sudden decision he had just taken made a pleasant distraction. I absolutely must have one of these women, he said to himself. He realized that he would have preferred to make love to Madame Derville. It was not that he found her more likeable, but that she had always known him as a tutor honoured for his learning, and not, as he had appeared to Madame de Rênal, as a simple carpenter with a rateen jacket folded under his arm. It was precisely as the young workman, blushing to the roots of his hair and hesitating at the door of the house without daring to ring the bell, that Madame de Rênal had the most charming picture of him.

On continuing to review the position, Julien saw that he must not think of making a conquest of Madame Derville, who was probably aware of the inclination Madame de Rênal showed for him. Obliged to bring his mind back to the latter, Julien said to himself, What do I know of this woman's character? Only this — before I went away, I took hold of her hand and she withdrew it; today I withdraw my hand and she takes hold of it and presses it. There's a fine opportunity of paying her back all the contempt she has felt for me. Heaven knows how many lovers she's had! Possibly she only decides to favour me because it's so easy for us to meet.

Such, alas! is the result of over-civilization. At twenty, a young man's heart, provided he has had a little education, is a thousand miles away from that easy nonchalance without which love is often nothing but the most tedious of duties.

I owe it to myself all the more to succeed with this woman, Julien's petty vanity went on arguing, since, if I make my way in the world and someone casts up in my face my humble occupation as tutor, I can let it be understood that love drove me into this position.

Once again Julien withdrew his hand from Madame de Rênal's, then took hold of her hand again and pressed it. As they were going back into the drawing-room towards midnight, Madame de Rênal said to him in a whisper: 'Are you leaving us, are you going away?'

Sighing, Julien replied: 'I really must go away, for I love you passionately. That's a sin ... and what a sin, too, for a young priest!'

Madame de Rênal leant upon his arm, and with so much abandonment that her cheek could feel the warmth of his.

It was a very different night for these two people. Madame de Rênal was in an exalted mood, carried out of herself by pleasureable sensations on the loftiest moral plane. A coquettish girl who falls in love at an early age grows accustomed to the disturbances love causes; when she reaches the true age of passion, the charm of novelty is lacking. As Madame de Rênal had never read any novels, every shade of her happiness was new to her. No saddening truth came to freeze her gladness, not even the spectre of the future. She saw herself as happy ten years ahead as she was at that moment. Even the thought of virtue and of the fidelity she had vowed to M. de Rênal, which had troubled her some days before, presented itself to her in vain. She dismissed such ideas as she would an importunate guest. I'll never grant Julien any favours, Madame de Rênal told herself. We'll go on living in the future as we've been living for the past month. He'll be just a friend.

CHAPTER 14 : A Pair of Scissors

> A young girl of sixteen had a rosebud complexion – and she put on rouge. POLIDORI

As for Julien, Fouqué's offer had in point of fact robbed him of every vestige of happiness. He could not make up his mind either way.

Alas ! he sighed. Maybe I'm lacking in character. I'd have made a poor kind of soldier for Napoleon. But at least, he added, my little intrigue with the mistress of the house will serve to take my mind off things for a moment.

Happily for him, even in such a minor quandary, the innermost feelings of his heart corresponded little with his flippancy of tone. He was frightened by Madame de Rênal in her pretty frock, which seemed in his eyes the advance guard of Paris. His pride would not allow him to leave anything to chance or the inspiration of the moment. Guiding himself by Fouqué's confidences and the little he had read of love in his Bible, he drew up a closely detailed plan of campaign; and as, though he did not admit it, he was much disturbed in his mind, he set the plan down in writing.

The following morning Madame de Rênal was alone with him for a moment in the drawing-room.

'Haven't you any other name except Julien?' she asked him.

Our hero did not know what to reply to so flattering a question. Such a circumstance had not been anticipated in his plan. But for his stupidity in making one, Julien's quick intelligence would have served him well – surprise would only have made his observations all the livelier.

He answered awkwardly and believed himself more awkward than he really was. Madame de Rênal very quickly forgave him for this, putting it down to his charming candour, though an air of candour, in truth, was in her eyes precisely what was lacking in this man whom everyone thought so talented.

'I feel very suspicious of that young tutor of yours,' Madame Derville would sometimes say to her friend. 'He seems to me to be always turning things over in his mind and never doing anything without some ulterior motive. He's a sly sort of fellow.'

Julien was left with a sense of deep humiliation at his ill-luck in not having known how to answer Madame de Rênal. A man of my sort, he thought, owes it to himself to retrieve his failure.

Taking advantage of the moment when they were going from one room into the other, he thought it his duty to give Madame de Rênal a kiss.

Nothing could have been more unprepared, nothing less agreeable both to himself and to her, nothing more rash. They only just missed being seen. Madame de Rênal thought he had taken leave of his senses. She was frightened, and even more than that — she was shocked. This silly act of his reminded her of M. Valenod.

What would happen to me, she said to herself, if I were left alone with him? All her virtue returning with the eclipse of love, she took care to keep one of her children with her all the time.

It was a weary day for Julien. He spent the whole of it in clumsy attempts to carry out his plan of seduction. He never once looked at Madame de Rênal without making his glance convey a question. All the same he was not so foolish as to be unaware that his efforts to appear agreeable, and, still more, to charm her fancy, were meeting with no success.

Madame de Rênal could not get over her surprise at finding him at once so awkwardly shy and yet so bold. It's the bashfulness of a scholar in love! she said to herself at last with inexpressible delight. Could it be possible my rival never loved him!

After lunch, Madame de Rênal went back into the drawing-room to meet M. Charcot de Maugiron, who was paying her a visit. She was working at a little tapestry frame raised a good way from the floor, with Madame Derville beside her. While she was in that position and in full daylight, our hero thought fit to thrust his boot out and touch Madame de Rênal's pretty foot, just at the moment the gallant sub-prefect's eyes were attracted to the silk stocking and the neat little slipper from Paris.

Madame de Rênal was terrified. She let fall her scissors, her ball of wool, and her needles, and Julien's gesture could thus pass for a clumsy attempt to prevent the fall of the scissors as he saw them slipping down to the floor. Luckily these little scissors, made of Sheffield steel from England, were broken, and Madame de Rênal was profuse in her regrets that Julien had not been nearer at hand.

'You saw them falling before I did, and might have prevented it,' she said, 'instead of which you only succeeded in kicking me violently in your zeal.'

All this deceived the sub-prefect, but not Madame Derville. This good-looking young fellow has very queer manners, she thought. Notions of breeding one gets in a provincial capital are no excuse for mistakes of this sort. Madame de Rênal found a moment to say to Julien: 'I must order you to be careful.'

Julien realized his blunder, and it made him cross. He pondered for a long time whether to take offence at the words: '*I must order you.*' She might say to me 'I order it', he thought, if it were something to do with the children's education; but in responding to my love, she implies equality. There's no love without *equality* ... and his mind went wandering off in quest of commonplaces with equality as their theme. He repeated angrily to himself a line of Corneille Madame Derville had taught him a few days before:

Love makes equalities, it does not seek them.

In his obstinate endeavour to play the part of a Don Juan, he who had never had a mistress in his life, Julien behaved like an utter fool for the rest of the day. He had only one sensible idea – annoyed with himself and with Madame de Rênal, he saw with dread the approach of evening, when he would be sitting in the garden beside her, in the darkness. He told M. de Rênal he was going to Verrières to see the curé, and leaving the house after dinner, he did not return until late that night.

At Verrières, Julien found M. Chélan busy moving house. He had been deprived of his living at last and M. Maslon was coming in his stead. As Julien helped the good curé, he was seized with the idea of writing to Fouqué and telling him that while the irresistible call he had felt to the sacred ministry had at first prevented him from accepting his kind offer, he had just seen such an instance of injustice that it might be more advantageous to his welfare for him not to take orders. Julien congratulated himself on his cunning in taking advantage of the curé's dismissal to leave a door open so that he could fall back on a business career if, in his country, sad and sober caution prevailed over heroism.

Love is in Latin writ *Amor*.
It spelleth Death to mortal men,
And mordant Care, that goeth before,
With Mourning, Grief and Weeping sore,
Deceit and Sin, and then, perforce,
The bitter sting of vain Remorse –
For Time doth not return again.
Blason d'Amour

HAD Julien had a little of the shrewdness with which he so gratuitously credited himself, he might have found cause for congratulation the next morning on the effect produced by his journey to Verrières. Absence had caused all his blunders to be forgotten. That day again, he was rather sulky. As evening approached, an absurd idea came into his head which he communicated, with unusual recklessness, to Madame de Rênal.

They had scarcely sat down in the garden when Julien, without waiting for it to be sufficiently dark, put his mouth close up to Madame de Rênal's ear, and at the risk of compromising her terribly, said to her : 'Madam, tonight at two I will come to your room. There's something I must say to you.'

Julien was trembling lest his request should be granted. The part of seducer weighed so heavily on his mind that, if he could have followed his inclinations, he would have retired to his room for several days and never seen these ladies again. He realized that by yesterday's over-cunning behaviour he had ruined all the fine promises of the previous day, and did not really know what saint to invoke for aid.

There was genuine indignation, not in the least exaggerated, in the way Madame de Rênal answered the insolent declaration Julien had dared to make. He thought he could discern a note of scorn in her brief reply. Certainly this answer, spoken very low, contained the words, 'You ought to be ashamed.'

Giving as his excuse that he wanted a word with the children, he went off into their room. On his return he sat down next to Madame Derville and a long way away from Madame de Rênal, thus avoiding all possibility of taking her hand. Their conversation took a serious turn, and Julien acquitted himself well, except for occasional moments of silence in which he was racking his brains. Why can't I devise some clever manoeuvre, he thought, and force Madame de Rênal to show me those unmistakable marks of affection which only three days ago made me believe she was mine!

Julien was extremely upset by the almost desperate state into which he had got his affairs, and yet nothing would have embarrassed him more than success. When they parted company that night, his pessimism convinced him he had won Madame Derville's contempt, and was probably on little better terms with Madame de Rênal.

Feeling terribly cross and intensely humiliated, Julien was unable to sleep. His mind was miles away from the idea of giving up all plans and all pretences and living from day to day in Madame de Rênal's company, contented as a child with the happiness each day would bring.

His brain grew wearied with devising subtle tactics, only to find them absurd a moment later. In short, he was feeling utterly miserable, when the clock outside the château struck two.

Its noise aroused him as the crowing of the cock had aroused Saint Peter, and he knew the hour of his hardest enterprise had come. He had not given his insolent proposal another thought from the time of making it – it had been so ill-received!

I told her I'd go to her room at two, he said to himself as he got out of bed. I may be as inexperienced and as boorish as one would expect of a peasant's son – Madame Derville made me realize it plainly enough – but at least I won't be weak.

Julien had reason to congratulate himself on his courage; never before had he imposed such harsh constraint on himself. As he opened his door, he was trembling so much that his knees were giving way under him, and he was obliged to lean up against the wall.

He had taken off his shoes. He went and listened at M. de Rênal's door. He could hear him snoring. The sound distressed him, for now he had no longer any pretext for not going to her room. But, what, good heavens! would he do when he got there? He had no plans, and even if he had any, he felt so agitated that he would have been incapable of keeping to them.

In the end, suffering a thousand times more than if he had been going to his death, he turned into the little corridor leading to Madame de Rênal's room. With trembling hand he opened the door, making a frightful noise as he did so.

It was light in there; a lamp was burning just below the mantelpiece. He had not expected this fresh mishap. Seeing him enter, Madame de Rênal jumped out of bed. 'Wretch!' she exclaimed. For a moment all was confusion. Julien forgot his useless plans and became his natural self once more; failure to please so charming a woman seemed to him the greatest misfortune that could happen. All the reply he gave to her reproaches was to fling himself at her feet, his arms clasped round her knees. As she went on speaking to him with the utmost harshness, he burst into tears.

When Julien left Madame de Rênal's room a few hours later, it might be said, to adopt the language of novels, that he had nothing further left to wish for. He was, in truth, indebted to the love he had inspired and to the unexpected impression produced on him by her seductive charms for a victory to which all his unskilful cunning would never have led him.

Yet, even at the most sweetly blissful moments a victim of his own queer pride, he still aspired to play the part of a man accustomed to subduing women to his will, and made incredibly determined efforts to spoil what was lovable in himself. When he might have been attentive to the transports he aroused, and the remorse that only served to heighten their eager ecstasy, he kept the idea of a *duty to himself* unceasingly before his eyes. He was afraid of feeling terrible regret and of making himself for ever ridiculous if he departed from the model of perfection he had resolved to follow. In a word, what made Julien a superior being was the very thing that prevented him from enjoying this happiness right in front of his eyes. He was like a sixteen-year-old girl with charming colouring who is silly enough to put on rouge when going to a ball.

Frightened to death by Julien's sudden appearance, Madame de Rênal soon fell a victim to the cruellest apprehensions. Julien's tears and his despair disturbed her acutely; so much so, that, even when she had nothing left to refuse him, she pushed him away from her in a fit of genuine indignation, and a moment after flung herself into his arms. There was no apparent design in all this line of conduct. She believed herself lost beyond hope of redemption and sought, by loading Julien with the most eager caresses, to shut her eyes to the vision of hell. Nothing, in short, would have been lacking to our hero's happiness, not even the ardent response of the woman he had just seduced, had he but been able to enjoy it. The transports that, in spite of herself, excited her were not brought to an end by Julien's departure, nor were her struggles with the remorse that tore her in two.

Good heavens! Is being happy, is being loved no more than that? were Julien's first thoughts when he got back to his room. He was in that state of amazement and tumultuous agitation into which man's spirit sinks on obtaining what it has so long desired. The heart, grown used to desiring, finds nothing more to desire, but has as yet no memories. Like a soldier returning from parade Julien was busily absorbed in reviewing every detail of his conduct. Have I been wanting in anything I owe to myself? Have I played my part well?

And what a part! That of a man accustomed to success in his dealings with women.

He turned his lips to hers, and with a sigh
Called back the tangles of her wandering hair.
Don Juan, i. 170

HAPPILY for Julien's pride, Madame de Rênal had been too greatly disturbed and surprised to realize the stupidity of the man who all in a moment had become everything in the world to her.

As she was begging him to go, for she saw that day was beginning to break, she exclaimed : 'Good Heavens ! If my husband has heard any sound, I'm lost !'

'Would you regret your life?' said Julien, who had found time to think out a few set phrases and called to mind this one.

'Ah ! very much at this moment, but I shouldn't regret having known you.'

Julien felt it behoved his dignity to return to his room in broad daylight and without taking any precautions.

The constant care he gave to his least actions, with the foolish idea of appearing a man of experience, had only one advantage – when he saw Madame de Rênal again, at lunch, his behaviour was a masterpiece of prudence.

As for her, she could not look at him without blushing deeply and could not exist for a minute without looking. She became conscious of her agitation, which she only increased by her efforts to hide it. Julien only once raised his eyes to look at her. Soon, remarking that this single glance was not repeated, she grew alarmed. Can it be he doesn't love me any longer? she thought. I'm very old for him, alas ! I'm ten years older than he is.

As they were going out of the dining-room into the garden, she pressed Julien's hand. In the surprise occasioned by such a singular mark of love, Julien gazed at her passionately – she had seemed very lovely to him at breakfast, and although he had kept his eyes lowered, he had spent the time considering all the aspects of her beauty one by one. Madame de Rênal was comforted by this glance. It did not wholly relieve her anxiety, but this anxiety almost wholly relieved her of remorse on her husband's account.

All the time they were having lunch, this husband had noticed nothing; but such was not the case with Madame Derville, who thought Madame de Rênal was on the point of yielding to temptation. The whole of that day her friendship, bold and caustic of tongue, spared Madame de Rênal not a single hint intended to paint for her in the most hideous colours the risk she was running.

Madame de Rênal was consumed with longing to be alone with Julien – she wanted to ask him if he still loved her. In spite of the unchangeable sweetness of her character, she was several times on the point of making her friend understand how very much she was in the way.

In the garden that evening Madame Derville managed things so well that she found herself sitting between Madame de Rênal and Julien. It was therefore impossible for Madame de Rênal, whose imagination had been dwelling with delight on the pleasant prospect of pressing Julien's hand and raising it to her lips, to say even a single word to him.

This disappointment increased her agitation. There was one thing she regretted bitterly – she had scolded Julien so severely for his rashness in coming to see her the night before that she trembled lest he should not come that night. She left the garden early and retired to her room; but unable to control her impatience, she went and listened with her ear close to Julien's door. In spite of the anxiety and the passion that consumed her she did not dare to go into his room. This action of hers seemed to her the very most degrading thing anyone could do – they have a saying on this subject in the provinces.

The servants had not all gone to bed. Discretion finally obliged her to return to her room. Two hours of waiting seemed two centuries of torment.

Julien, however, was too faithful to what he called his duty to fail in carrying out in every detail what he had set himself to do. As one o'clock was striking, he slipped quietly out of his room, and having made sure that the master of the house was asleep, went to visit Madame de Rênal. He found more happiness in his mistress's company on this occasion, for he was thinking less continually of the part he had to play, and had both eyes to see and ears to hear.

What Madame de Rênal said to him about her age gave him some degree of confidence. 'Alas!' she exclaimed. 'I'm ten years older than you. How can you love me?' She said this several times, rather pointlessly, and merely because the thought was weighing on her mind. Julien could not understand her unhappiness, but he saw it was very real, and almost lost his fear of appearing ridiculous.

The foolish notion that he was regarded as an inferior type of lover because of his humble birth vanished also. In proportion as Julien's raptures reassured his timid mistress some of her happiness came back to her, and with it the power to form an opinion of her lover. Fortunately, he showed, on this occasion, almost none of the stiff self-consciousness that had made their meeting of the previous night a victory and not a pleasure. Had she seen any sign of his playing a part, this woeful discovery might have destroyed all her happiness for ever, since it might have seemed to her nothing but the sad effect of the disproportion in their ages. For although Madame de Rênal had never given a thought to theories of love, difference in age, next to difference in fortune, is one of the chief commonplaces on which provincials exercise their wit every time the question of love crops up.

A very few days later, Julien, having recovered all the fiery enthusiasm natural at his age, was desperately in love. I must admit she's angelically kind, he thought. – And no one could be lovelier.

He had almost entirely lost sight of his idea of playing a part. In a moment of open-hearted expansion, he even confessed to her all his fears and anxieties, a confidence which brought to its height the passion he inspired. So I've never had any more fortunate rival, thought Madame de Rênal in an ecstasy of joy. She ventured to question him about the portrait which had given him such concern. Julien swore to her that it was the portrait of a man.

When Madame de Rênal felt sufficiently self-composed to think the matter over, she could not recover from her surprise to find such happiness existed – or that she should ever have doubted its existence.

Ah! she said to herself, if I'd only known Julien ten years ago, when I still could pass for a pretty woman!

Such thoughts were very far from Julien's mind. His love was still another name for ambition. It meant for him the joy of possessing so beautiful a woman, when he himself was a poor, unhappy creature whom men despised. His acts of adoration, and his rapture at the sight of his mistress's charms, ended by reassuring Madame de Rênal on the question of the difference in their ages. Had she possessed a little of that practical knowledge of the world which in the most civilized countries a woman of thirty has had at her disposal for a number of years already, she might have trembled for the duration of a love which apparently only existed on surprise and the transports of gratified self-esteem.

There were moments when, forgetting his ambitions, Julien revelled in admiring even Madame de Rênal's hats, even her dresses. He could never tire of the pleasure of inhaling their fragrance. He would open her mirror-fronted wardrobe and remain there for hours at a time admiring the beauty and the orderly arrangement of everything in it. His mistress, as she leant against him, would gaze at him; but he himself would be gazing at jewels and finery such as fill the coffers of a bride on the eve of her wedding.

And I might have married a man like this! Madame de Rênal would sometimes think. What an eager, fiery creature! How thrilling life with him would be!

As for Julien, he had never come so close as this to these terrifying weapons from a woman's armoury. It's impossible, he would think, for Paris to have anything finer! At such moments he found no obstacle to his happiness. The sincerity of his admiration, joined with his mistress's overwhelming delight in his love, often made him forget those futile theories which had made him so stiff and so little short of ridiculous in the first moments of their liaison. There were times when, for all his accustomed hypocrisy, he found it extremely sweet to confess to this great lady who admired him his ignorance of a thousand and one little social usages. It seemed to him as if his mistress's rank raised him above his own degree.

Madame de Rênal, for her part, took a most exquisitely virtuous pleasure in thus instructing in innumerable little ways a young man so talented, whom everyone regarded as certain to go very far one day. Even the sub-prefect and M. Valenod could not help admiring him; they seemed to her less stupid on that account. As for Madame Derville, she was far from inclined to express such views. Full of despair at what she imagined she guessed, and seeing that wise counsels were becoming distasteful to a woman who had quite simply lost her head, she left Vergy without giving an explanation, for which, indeed, no one cared to ask. Madame de Rênal shed a few tears over this, but soon it seemed to her that her happiness was all the greater for it, since this departure left her almost all day long alone with her lover.

Julien gave himself up to his mistress's sweet company all the more readily because, every time he was left too long alone, Fouqué's unlucky offer still came to trouble his mind. There were moments in the first days of this new life when he, who never before had loved, or been loved by anyone, found so exquisite a pleasure in being sincere that he was on the point of confessing to Madame de Rênal the ambition that up till then had been the very essence of his life. He would have liked to have been able to consult her about the strange temptation Fouqué's offer put in his way. But a certain little incident made candour impossible.

CHAPTER 17 : *The Mayor's Chief Deputy*

> O, how this spring of love resembleth
> The uncertain glory of an April day;
> Which now shows all the beauty of the sun
> And by and by a cloud takes all away!
> SHAKESPEARE

HE was sitting beside his mistress one evening at the far end of the orchard, away from all intruders, deep in dreams. Will such sweet moments, he mused, last for ever? His mind was entirely taken up with the difficulty of choosing a profession, and he was deploring that most unhappy crisis which puts an end to the childhood and spoils the early manhood of young people of small means.

'Ah!' he cried aloud, 'Napoleon was most certainly a man sent from God for the youth of France! Who will take his place? What will those unlucky wretches do without him, even those who are better off than I am, and who have just the few crowns necessary for a good education but not enough either to buy themselves a substitute to escape conscription or to succeed in a career! Whatever we do,' he added sighing deeply, 'the memory of such disaster will for ever prevent us from being happy!'

All at once he noticed that Madame de Rênal was frowning. Her face took on a look of cold disdain; such a way of thinking seemed to her only fit for menials. Brought up knowing that she was very wealthy, it seemed natural to her to take for granted that Julien was the same. She loved him a thousand times more than life itself, and had absolutely no interest in money.

Julien was far from guessing her thoughts, but her frown brought him down to earth again. He had enough presence of mind to choose his words carefully and to let this noble lady, sitting so close beside him on the grassy bank, understand that his recent remarks were quoted from things he had heard during his visit to his friend the timber merchant, and were the arguments of men without religion.

'Well, don't have anything more to do with people of that sort,' said Madame de Rênal, still with the icy look that had suddenly replaced a look of keenest affection.

Her frown, or rather his regrets for his rashness, gave the first check to illusions that were sweeping Julien away. She is kind and sweet, he said to himself, she has a keen affection for me, but she has been brought up in the enemy's camp. People of this sort are bound to be particularly afraid of all that class of men of spirit who, after receiving a good education, have not money enough to embark on a career. What would become of these nobles if we were given a chance to fight them with equal weapons? Were I, for instance, Mayor of Verrières, and as well-intentioned and honest as M. de Rênal really is underneath, how quickly I'd get rid of M. Maslon, M. Valenod, and all their dishonest practices! How justice would triumph in Verrières! It isn't their ability that would hinder me. They never do anything but muddle along.

That day Julien's happiness was near to becoming a lasting one, but our hero fell short of daring to be sincere. He would have had the courage to engage in battle if only he had done so *there and then*. Madame de Rênal had been taken aback by Julien's remarks, for the men of her acquaintance were always saying that the existence of young men of the lower classes with education above their rank made Robespierre's return particularly likely. Her manner remained cold for rather a long time; Julien thought this coldness decidedly marked. In point of fact the fear of having indirectly said something disagreeable to him followed hard on her keen dislike of his ill-chosen remarks. The unhappiness this caused her was vividly reflected in a face that was so pure and so ingenuous whenever she was happy and away from people who bothered her.

Julien no longer dared abandon himself to his dreams. In a calmer frame of mind and less in love, he found it unwise to go and visit Madame de Rênal in her own room. It was better for her to come to his. If a servant saw her moving about the house, a score of different pretexts might explain her movements.

This arrangement, however, had its own disadvantages. Julien had received from Fouqué certain books which he, as a student of theology could never have asked for at a bookseller's. He only dared to open them at night, and would often have been very glad not to have been interrupted by a visit which would have made reading an impossibility, had he been expecting it such a short while back as the day before the little scene in the orchard.

He was indebted to Madame de Rênal for an altogether new understanding of these books. He had ventured to ask her questions about countless little details, an ignorance of which would have put any young man born outside the best circles completely at a loss, whatever natural intelligence he might be presumed to have.

This education through love, given him by a woman with very little learning, was a stroke of luck for Julien, for it enabled him to get a direct impression of society as it is today. His mind was not befogged by accounts of what it was once upon a time, two thousand years, or even only sixty years ago, in the days of Voltaire and Louis XV. To his inexpressible delight, a veil fell from before his eyes; he understood at last the kind of things going on in Verrières.

The foreground was occupied by very complicated intrigues which had been on foot for two years past in the prefect's office in Besançon, and were backed by letters from Paris written by all the most eminent people. The question involved was the appointment of M. de Moirod, the staunchest upholder of religion in the district, as principal, and not second, deputy to the Mayor of Verrières. He had as chief rival a very wealthy manufacturer who absolutely had to be relegated to the position of second deputy.

Julien understood at last certain hints he had overheard when high society in the district came to dinner at M. de Rênal's house. This privileged circle was getting profoundly busy over this choosing of the Mayor's deputy, though the rest of the town, and the Liberals in particular, had not even a suspicion of such a possibility. What made the affair important, as everyone knows, was that the east side of the High Street in Verrières was due to be set back some nine feet or more, since this street had become a public highway.

Now if M. de Moirod, the owner of three houses on the list of those to be set back, happened to become deputy Mayor and, in due course of time, Mayor (supposing M. de Rênal were elected to the Chamber of Deputies) he would keep his eyes shut and it would be possible to make certain little adjustments to the houses jutting out into the public highway, and so keep them standing there for another hundred years. In spite of M. de Moirod's eminent piety and his recognized integrity one could be sure he would be *easy to handle*, for his family was a large one. Nine out of the houses to be set back belonged to the best people in Verrières.

In Julien's eyes, this intrigue seemed very much more important than the history of the battle of Fontenoy, a name which he saw for the very first time in one of the books that Fouqué had sent him. There were things that Julien had found very surprising since the time when, five years back, he began to go to the curé's house in the evenings; but, discretion and humility of mind being the first qualities required in a student of theology, he had always found it impossible to ask any questions.

Madame de Rênal was giving orders one day to her husband's valet, Julien's enemy.

'But, madam, today's the last Friday of the month,' the man replied with a curious expression on his face.

'All right then, you can go,' said Madame de Rênal.

'Well!' said Julien, 'so he's going off to that old place for storing hay which was once a church and has recently been reconsecrated. But what do they really do there? That's one of the mysteries I've never been able to fathom.'

'It's a very sound institution, but a very strange one, too,' replied Madame de Rênal. 'Women aren't admitted, and all I know of it is that everyone there is on familiar terms. This servant, for instance, will come across M. Valenod there, and that man who's so proud, and so stupid, will take no offence if Jean addresses him as an intimate friend, and will answer him in a similar way. If you're really anxious to know what goes on there, I'll ask M. de Maugiron and M. Valenod for details. We pay twenty francs for each servant, and all to prevent their cutting our throats one day.'

Time flew rapidly by. The remembrance of his mistress's charms kept Julien's mind clear of dark ambition. The necessity, since they belonged to opposite parties, of saying nothing to her on sad or serious topics increased, without his suspecting it, the happiness he owed her and her empire over him.

At times when the presence of intelligent children obliged them to restrict their talk to the language of cold and sober sense, Julien, gazing at her with eyes alight with love, would listen to her explaining the ways of the world to him. Often, in the midst of telling him some cunning instance of chicanery concerning the making of a road, or getting some contract for supplies, Madame de Rênal's mind would wander wildly off the subject, and Julien would have to scold her for allowing herself the same little intimate gestures with him as with her children. For there were days when she would delude herself with thinking that she loved him as if he were her child.

Had she not constantly to answer his artless questions on a thousand things of which no fifteen-year-old child of good family is ignorant, only to admire him, a moment later, as her master?

She was even alarmed by his genius; every day she seemed more clearly to discern a future great man in this young abbé. She saw him Pope, she saw him, like Richelieu, chief minister of France. 'Shall I live long enough, my dear,' she would say to him, 'to see you in all your glory? There's room for a great man. Both King and Church have need of him.'

> Are you good for nothing but to be cast aside like carrion, a people without a soul, and with no blood left in your veins?
> *The Bishop's address in Saint Clement's Chapel*

AT ten o'clock on the evening of the third of September, the whole of Verrières was aroused from sleep by the galloping of a mounted gendarme up the High Street. He brought news that the King of — was arriving the following Sunday, and it was already Tuesday. The prefect authorized, or rather commanded, the formation of a guard of honour; there had to be the greatest possible display of pomp and ceremony. An express messenger was sent post-haste to Vergy. M. de Rênal returned to Verrières that night and found the whole town in a flutter of excitement. Everyone had his own claims to importance; people with the most time on their hands hired balconies from which to view His Majesty's entry into the town.

Who would command the guard of honour? M. de Rênal saw at once how important it was, in the interests of the properties which were to be moved back, for M. de Moirod to take command. That might give him some title to the post of deputy mayor. No one had any fault to find with M. de Moirod's piety, it was beyond all comparison – but he had never been astride a horse in his life. He was a man of thirty-six, a timid sort of individual in every way, who was equally alarmed at the prospect of falls and of being made to look ridiculous.

On the stroke of five that morning the Mayor sent for him.

'You see, sir,' he said, 'I am asking for your advice as if you already held the office all decent people would like you to have. In this unhappy town the factories are thriving; men of the Liberal party become millionaires and aspire to power; they are capable of turning anything into a weapon. Let us consider the interests of the King and the monarchy in general, and above all the interests of Holy Church. To whom do you think, sir, we might entrust the command of our guard of honour?'

In spite of his frightful fear of horses, M. de Moirod finally accepted this honour as a call to martyrdom. 'I shall know how to behave in a fitting manner,' he told the Mayor. By now there was scarcely time to furbish up the uniforms which had done service seven years before when a prince of the blood royal passed through Verrières.

At seven o'clock Madame de Rênal arrived from Vergy with Julien and the children. She found her drawing-room full of ladies of the Liberal party who were holding forth on the union of Liberals and Royalists, and had come to beg her to persuade her husband to grant their men-folk places in the guard of honour. One of them alleged that if her husband were not chosen his grief would drive him into bankruptcy. Madame de Rênal dismissed all these people very promptly. She seemed to be very much pre-occupied.

Julien was surprised and even more annoyed that she should make a mystery of what was disturbing her. It's just as I foresaw, he thought bitterly. Her love is eclipsed by the joy of welcoming a king to her house. All this fuss and bustle dazzles her. She'll be in love with me afresh as soon as her head's no longer bothered with all these class notions. What was a surprising thing, he loved her all the more for this.

Upholsterers and decorators began to invade the house. He watched for a long time, but in vain, for a chance of saying a word to her. At last he met her coming out of his room, carrying one of his coats. They were alone. He was anxious to speak to her but she refused to listen to him and hurried away. I'm an utter fool to love such a woman, he thought. Ambition makes her as crazy as her husband.

She was even crazier. One of her dearest wishes, which she had never confessed to Julien for fear of offending him, was to see him throw off, if only for a day, the sombre black he wore. With a cunning really to be wondered at in so ingenuous a woman she first of all got M. de Moirod, and then the sub-prefect, M. de Maugiron, to agree to Julien's appointment as one of the guard of honour in preference to some five or six young men who were sons of very well-to-do manufacturers, and at least two of whom were noted for their exemplary piety.

M. Valenod, who was counting on lending his carriage to the prettiest women in the town and thus gaining admiration for his fine Norman horses, agreed to give one of them to Julien, the man he most detested. All the guards of honour, however, either possessed or had borrowed one of those handsome sky-blue coats with colonel's epaulettes in silver which had made such a fine show seven years before. Madame de Rênal wanted to have a new coat made, and only four days were left in which to send to

Besançon and have the uniform returned, complete with sword
and hat, etc. – in short all that goes to make a guard of honour.
For the most curious thing about the whole affair was that she
thought it unwise to have Julien's clothes made in Verrières. She
wanted to surprise him, and the whole town as well.

This business of the guard of honour and of everything that
public opinion called for having been settled, the Mayor had to
turn his mind to arranging a grand religious ceremony. The King
did not wish to pass through Verrières without going to visit
the famous relics of Saint Clement, which are kept at Bray-le-
Haut, a short three miles from the town. It was thought desirable
to have a good concourse of clergy present, and this was a most
difficult thing to arrange, for M. Maslon wished at all costs to
avoid including M. Chélan. In vain M. de Rênal represented to
him that this would be unwise. The Marquis de la Mole, whose
ancestors had for so long been governors of the province, and
who had been chosen to accompany the King of —, had known
M. Chélan for thirty years. He would certainly ask for news of
him as soon as he arrived in Verrières, and, if he found him under
a cloud, he was just the sort of man to go and seek him out in the
little house to which he had retired, accompanied by as large a
following as he could command. What a slap in the face that
would be !

'I shall be discredited both here and in Besançon,' said M.
Maslon, 'if he appears amongst my clergy. A Jansenist ! Good
heavens !'

'Whatever you may say, my dear abbé,' M. de Rênal replied,
'I'll not expose the Town Council of Verrières to receiving a snub
from M. de la Mole. You don't know him. When he's at court his
opinions are sane and level-headed; but down here, in the provinces, he's a man with a caustic tongue, fond of poking fun at
everything and only out to make people feel embarrassed. He's
quite capable, merely for his own amusement, of covering us with
ridicule in the eyes of the Liberals.'

It was not until the night between Saturday and Sunday, and
after three days' parleying, that Father Maslon's pride gave way
before the Mayor's fears, which had turned to courage. A letter
full of honeyed phrases had to be written to M. Chélan, inviting
him, if his advanced age and infirmities permitted, to be present
at the ceremony of the relics at Bray-le-Haut. M. Chélan asked for
and obtained a letter of invitation for Julien, who was to accompany him in the capacity of sub-deacon.

Early on Sunday morning, thousands of peasants, coming in from the neighbouring mountains, thronged the streets of Verrières. The sun was at its brightest. At last, towards three o'clock, the whole of this crowd was in commotion; a great bonfire, signalling the King's entry into the territory of the Department, could be seen on top of a rock two leagues out of Verrières. Immediately the sound of all the bells and reiterated volleys from an old Spanish cannon belonging to the town marked its rejoicing over this great event. Half the population clambered up on to the roofs. All the women appeared on the balconies. The guard of honour began to move into line. Their brilliant uniforms were admired; everyone recognized a relation or a friend. People were laughing at the terrified M. de Moirod, with his cautious hand getting ready every minute to clutch at his saddle-bow.

One thing they noticed, however, which put all else out of mind. The first rider in the ninth row was a very slender, very handsome young man whom, to begin with, nobody recognized. Soon a cry of indignation from some, astonished silence on the part of others, announced a general sensation. In this young man, mounted on one of M. Valenod's Norman horses, people recognized young Sorel, the carpenter's son.

Everyone cried out upon the Mayor, especially the Liberals. What ! just because this young workman dressed up as a priest was tutor to his brats, had he had the cheek to appoint him a guard of honour, to the prejudice of M. — and M. —, the wealthy manufacturers ! 'These gentlemen,' a banker's wife remarked, 'should really administer a snub to this insolent upstart from the gutter.' 'He's a slippery customer, and he wears a sword,' her neighbour replied. 'He'd be quite treacherous enough to slash their faces with it.'

The remarks of upper-class persons were more dangerous. The ladies wondered if this striking lack of taste originated only from the Mayor. People in general justly credited him with contempt for humble birth.

All the while he was exciting so many remarks, Julien himself was feeling the happiest of men. By nature bold and enterprising, he sat his horse rather better than most of the other young men of this mountain town. He could read in the women's eyes that they were talking about him.

His epaulettes, being new, glittered more brightly. Every moment his horse reared up; his joy was at its height. His happiness knew no bounds when, just as he passed beneath the ancient ramparts, the noise of the tiny cannon made his horse jump out of line. By great good luck he did not fall off, and from that moment he felt himself a hero. He was Napoleon's orderly officer leading the charge against a battery.

There was one other person who was happier than he. First of all, looking out of one of the Town Hall windows, she had seen him pass by and then, getting into her carriage and quickly making a wide detour, had arrived in time to shudder with fright when his horse bore him out of line. Finally, with her carriage passing at full gallop through another gate to the town, she had managed to come out once more on the route by which the King would pass, and had been able to follow twenty paces behind the guard of honour, in the midst of a glorious cloud of dust.

Ten thousand peasants shouted: 'Long live the King!' as the Mayor had the honour of haranguing His Majesty. An hour later, when the King, having listened to all the speeches, was about to enter the town, the diminutive cannon began once again to let off volley after volley. This occasioned an accident, not to the gunners, who had given proof of their skill at Leipzig and Montmirail, but to M. de Moirod, whose horse deposited him full and fairly on top of the one and only puddle on the highway, thereby creating a scandal, for he had to be fished out before the King's carriage could pass.

His Majesty stepped down from his carriage in front of the new church, adorned that day with all its crimson hangings. The King had to dine and then get back into his carriage to go and worship at the shrine containing the famous relics of Saint Clement. He had hardly reached the church before Julien was galloping back to M. de Rênal's house.

There he took off his fine sky-blue coat, his epaulettes, and his sword, sighing as he laid them by, and put on his shabby little black suit again. He mounted his horse once more and in a very short space of time reached Bray-le-Haut, which stands on the summit of a very stately hill. Enthusiasm multiplies these peasants, Julien reflected. It's impossible to move in Verrières, yet there are more than ten thousand of them here around this ancient abbey.

Left half in ruins by republican vandalism, the building had been magnificently restored since the Restoration, and there was talk of miracles happening there. Julien joined Father Chélan, who scolded him severely as he handed him a cassock and a surplice. Julien put them on at once and followed M. Chélan, who was going to present himself to the young Bishop of Agde. He was the Marquis de la Mole's nephew, who had been recently appointed to this office and whose duty it was to exhibit the relics to the King. The bishop, however, could not be found.

All the clergy were getting impatient. They were awaiting their superior in the gloomy Gothic cloister of the ancient abbey. Four-and-twenty parish priests had been assembled here to represent the former chapter of Bray-le-Haut which, before 1789, had numbered four-and-twenty canons. After lamenting the Bishop's youth for a good three-quarters of an hour, the priests considered it would be fitting for the Dean to seek out his Lordship and warn him that the King was about to arrive, and the moment had come for them to assemble in the chancel.

M. Chélan had been chosen Dean on account of his great age. In spite of the annoyance he had shown with Julien, he signed to the young man to accompany him. Julien looked very well in his surplice. By some means or other employed by clerics at their toilet, he had made his handsome curls severely straight; through some oversight, however, which made M. Chélan twice as angry as before, a guard of honour's spurs were visible beneath the long folds of his cassock.

When they arrived at the Bishop's suite of rooms, tall footmen tricked out in braided livery could scarcely condescend to inform the old priest that His Lordship was not to be seen. They laughed at him when he tried to explain that in his capacity as Dean of the Noble Chapter of Bray-le-Haut it was his privilege to be admitted at all hours to the presence of the officiating bishop.

Julien's haughty temper took offence at the insolence of these lackeys. He took it on himself to go through all the dormitories of this ancient abbey, rattling at every door he met. A very small one opened as he tried it, and he found himself inside a cell, surrounded by all his Lordship's servants, dressed in black with chains hung round their necks.

He seemed in such a hurry that these persons thought the Bishop must have sent for him, and they let him pass. He took a few steps forward and found himself in a huge and extremely gloomy hall of Gothic architecture, completely panelled in dark oak. With one exception, all the pointed arches of the windows had been bricked up. Nothing disguised the coarseness of this masonry, which contrasted pitifully with the magnificence of the ancient woodwork. The two longer sides of this hall, famed among Burgundian antiquaries, and which Duke Charles the Bold had

had built round about 1470 in expiation for some sin or other, were furnished with richly carved wooden stalls. All the mysteries of the Apocalypse were to be seen figured there, in wood of varying shades.

This melancholy grandeur, though disfigured by the sight of bare bricks and plaster still in its first whiteness, affected Julien greatly. He stood there, motionless and silent. At the far end of the hall, close to the only window through which daylight could penetrate, he saw a portable mahogany mirror. A young man in a purple cassock and a surplice trimmed with lace, but with his head completely bare, was standing three feet away from the mirror. The piece of furniture seemed strange in such a place, and had doubtless been brought there from the town.

Julien thought the young man looked annoyed. With his right hand raised, he was gravely describing gestures of benediction in front of the mirror. What can it all mean? thought Julien. Is it some primary ritual this young priest's performing? Perhaps he's the Bishop's secretary. ... And he'll be as insolent as those lackeys. ... Good heavens! what does it matter! I might as well have a try.

He stepped forward, covering the whole length of the hall rather slowly, and keeping the single window in his line of vision while he looked at this man who went on making gestures of benediction, slowly but in an unending series, and without pausing a moment to rest.

As Julien drew nearer he could distinguish his cross expression more clearly. The rich quality of the lace-trimmed surplice brought him involuntarily to a standstill a few steps away from the imposing mirror.

It's my duty to say something, he told himself at last; but the beauty of the hall had impressed him, and he was already feeling ruffled in anticipation of the harsh remarks that would be addressed to him.

The young man saw him in the long looking-glass and turned round. Suddenly losing his cross expression, he said to Julien in the gentlest possible tone: 'Well, sir, has it at last been put in order?'

Julien stood there dumbfounded. As the young man turned round towards him, he saw the episcopal cross on his breast – it was the young Bishop of Agde. How young he is, thought Julien. Six or eight years older than I am, at the most! ... And he felt ashamed of his spurs.

'Your Lordship,' he answered shyly, 'I am sent by M. Chélan, the Dean of the chapter.'

'Oh yes! he's been strongly recommended to me,' the Bishop remarked in such polite tones that Julien was even more enchanted. 'But I must really beg your pardon, sir. I took you for the man who was to bring me back my mitre. It was carelessly packed for me in Paris, and the silver stuff is badly damaged towards the top. It will create a very bad impression,' the young Bishop added sadly, 'and I'm still kept waiting for it!'

'If your Lordship will allow me, I'll go and fetch your Lordship's mitre.'

Julien's handsome eyes produced their usual effect.

'Very well, sir, go and fetch it,' the Bishop replied in a charmingly polite tone of voice. 'I really must have it at once. I'm deeply distressed at keeping these gentlemen of the chapter waiting.'

As Julien reached the middle of the hall, he turned to look back at the Bishop and saw he was going on with his benedictions. What can it mean? Julien wondered. No doubt it's some form of procedure the Church prescribes as a necessary preparation for the coming ceremony.

As he got to the cell where the menservants were waiting, he saw the mitre in their hands. Yielding against their will to Julien's look of authority, these gentlemen handed over his Lordship's mitre.

He felt proud to be bearing it. As he came down the length of the hall, he walked slowly, carrying it with respect. He found the Bishop sitting in front of the glass; but from time to time his right hand, tired though it was, continued to be raised in blessing.

Julien helped him put on his mitre. The Bishop gave his head a shake.

'Ah! it will keep on,' he said to Julien, looking pleased. 'Now would you mind going a little way away?'

The Bishop walked quickly to the centre of the hall, and coming back towards the mirror with measured steps, resumed his vexed expression and gravely gave more benedictions.

Julien stood motionless in amazement; he was tempted to find some explanation but did not dare. The Bishop stopped, and looking at him with an air that suddenly ceased to be grave, said to him: 'What do you think of my mitre, sir? Is it on all right?'

'Quite right, my Lord.'

'It isn't too far back? That would look rather silly. But it mustn't be worn down over the eyes, either, like an officer's cap.'

'I think it looks very well indeed.'

'The King of — is accustomed to clergy of very venerable years and doubtless very grave. I wouldn't like, particularly because of my age, to appear too deficient in gravity.'

The Bishop began to walk to and fro again, once more describing benedictions.

It's quite clear, thought Julien, daring at last to understand, that he's practising giving the blessing.

A few moments later the Bishop said, 'I'm ready now. Go and warn the Dean and the clergy of the chapter.'

Very soon, M. Chélan and the most aged priests came in through a very large door, magnificently carved, which Julien had not noticed. This time, however, he remained in his proper place at the extreme rear and could only catch sight of the Bishop above the shoulders of the clergy who came crowding hurriedly through the door.

The Bishop moved slowly down the hall. When he reached the threshold, the clergy formed in procession. After a brief moment's confusion, the procession moved forward, intoning a psalm. The Bishop came last, between M. Chélan and another extremely aged priest. Julien crept up quite close to the Bishop, as attendant on M. Chélan. They passed down the long corridors of the Abbey of Bray-le-Haut which were dark and damp in spite of the brilliant sunlight, and came at last to the cloister porch.

Julien was struck dumb with amazement and admiration at so splendid a ceremony. His ambition, awakened once more by the Bishop's youth, contended with this prelate's delicacy of feeling and exquisite politeness for mastery of his heart. Such politeness was very different from M. de Rênal's, even on his best days. The nearer one rises towards the highest ranks of society, thought Julien, the more one finds such charming manners.

They entered the church through a side door. Suddenly a terrifying noise re-echoed all along its vaulted roof; Julien thought it would come tumbling down in ruins. It was the little cannon again which had just arrived, drawn by eight horses at a gallop, and had no sooner arrived than, touched off by the Leipzig gunners, it started firing five volleys a minute, as if the Prussians were lined up in front.

But this marvellous noise no longer made any impression on

Julien. He was not dreaming of Napoleon any more, nor of military glory. So young, and yet Bishop of Agde? he was thinking. But where is Agde? And how much money does it bring in? Two or three thousand francs a year, perhaps?

His Lordship's lackeys appeared with a gorgeous canopy. M. Chélan took hold of one of the poles, but in reality Julien held it up. The Bishop took up his position beneath it. He had actually made himself look old — our hero's admiration was unbounded. What can't one do, if one has the skill? he thought.

The King made his entry. Julien was lucky enough to have a very close view of him. The Bishop delivered an unctuous address, not forgetting a little trace of agitation very flattering to His Majesty. We will not linger over the description of the ceremony at Bray-le-Haut, which filled the columns of every newspaper in the Department for a fortnight. Julien learnt from the Bishop's address that the King was a descendant of Charles the Bold.

Later on, it was one of Julien's functions to check the accounts of the money this ceremony had cost. M. de la Mole, having obtained a bishopric for his nephew, had wished to pay him the compliment of bearing all the expenses. The ceremony at Bray-le-Haut alone amounted to three thousand eight hundred francs.

After the Bishop's address and the King's reply, His Majesty took up his place under the canopy, and then knelt down very devoutly on a cushion near the altar. There were stalls round the chancel raised by two steps above the level of the pavement. Julien sat on the bottom step at M. Chélan's feet, almost as if he were a cardinal's train-bearer seated near his master in the Sistine Chapel at Rome. There were a *Te Deum*, surging waves of incense, unending volleys from muskets and artillery; the peasants were drunk with joy and religious fervour. Such a day undoes the work of a hundred issues of Jacobin newspapers.

Julien was six feet away from the King, who was wholeheartedly deep in prayer. He noticed for the first time a little man with a keen, intelligent expression who was wearing a coat that had scarcely any embroidered trimmings; but over this very simple coat he wore a sky-blue ribbon. He was nearer the King than many other nobles, whose coats were so thickly embroidered with gold that, as Julien put it, you could not see the cloth. He learnt a few moments later that this was M. de la Mole. He thought his manner haughty and even insolent.

This marquis wouldn't be so polite as my handsome little bishop, he reflected. Ah! how gentle and wise men become in the clerical profession! But the King came to see the relics and I don't see any relics here. Where can Saint Clement be?

A young cleric seated next to him informed him that the venerable relics were kept high up in the building in a *chapelle ardente*. What is a *chapelle ardente*? thought Julien. But he did not like to ask for an explanation of this term and only became more attentive.

On the occasion of the visit of a reigning monarch etiquette demands that the canons do not accompany the Bishop. But as he began to move towards the *chapelle ardente* the Bishop called to M. Chélan. Julien ventured to follow him.

After climbing up a very long flight of steps they came to a door which was extremely tiny, but had a lavishly gilded Gothic framework that looked as if it had been painted the day before.

On their knees in front of this door were twenty-four young women belonging to the most distinguished families in Verrières. Before opening this door, the Bishop fell on his knees in the midst of these twenty-four young women, who were all of them very pretty. All the time he was praying aloud it seemed as if nothing could sate their admiration of his fine lace-trimmed vestments, his kind and gracious ways, his sweet, young face. What was left of his reason forsook our hero as he gazed on this scene.

Suddenly the door opened. The little chapel seemed as if ablaze with light. Innumerable candles ranged in rows of eight, with bouquets of flowers between them, were to be seen on the altar. A sweet smell of purest incense escaped in whirling clouds through the sanctuary door. The newly gilded chapel was very small but its roof was very high. The young women could not restrain a cry of admiration. No one had been allowed to enter the little antechapel except the twenty-four young women, the two priests, and Julien.

Soon the King arrived, followed only by M. de la Mole and the chief chamberlain. The guards themselves remained outside, presenting arms.

His Majesty sank, or rather flung himself on to the *prie-dieu*. It was only then that Julien, pressed close against the gilded door, was able to see, under the bare arm of one of the young women, the charming statue of Saint Clement in the garb of a young Roman soldier, concealed beneath the altarpiece. He had a large wound in his throat, from which blood seemed to be flowing. The artist had surpassed himself. The languid eyes, although half-shut, were full of grace; a budding moustache adorned his charming mouth, with lips half-closed yet seeming still to move in prayer. The young woman next to Julien shed hot tears at the sight, and one of her tears fell on Julien's hand.

After a moment of prayer in the deepest silence, broken only by the distant sound of bells from all the villages for ten leagues round, the Bishop of Agde asked the King's permission to speak. He concluded a very moving little address in words which were all the more telling for their simplicity.

'Never forget, young Christian maidens,' he said, 'that you have seen one of the greatest kings of the earth on his knees before the servants of the almighty and terrible God. These servants, though weak and persecuted and done to death in this world, as you can see by the still bleeding wound of Saint Clement, are triumphant in heaven. You will forever remember this day, will you not, young Christian maidens, and hold in hatred the ungodly man? And be for ever faithful to this God who is so great and terrible, yet so kind?'

At these words the Bishop rose to his feet with an air of one in authority.

'Do you promise me this?' he asked, with arms outstretched as a man inspired.

'We promise,' said the young women, bursting into tears.

'In the name of the most terrible God,' continued the Bishop in deeply sonorous tones, 'I accept your promise.' And the ceremony was over.

The King himself was in tears. A very long time elapsed before Julien had sufficient self-command to ask in what place this saint's bones, sent from Rome to Philip the Good, Duke of Burgundy, had been laid. He was told that they lay concealed inside the lovely wax image.

His Majesty graciously permitted the young women who had been with him in the chapel to wear a red ribbon embroidered with the words: HATRED OF THE UNGODLY — PERPETUAL ADORATION OF GOD.

M. de la Mole ordered ten thousand bottles of wine for distribution among the peasants. That evening at Verrières the Liberals discovered reasons for illuminating their houses a hundred times more brilliantly than the Royalists. Before leaving the town the King paid a visit to M. de Moirod.

> The curiously comical aspect of everyday
> events conceals from us the very real suffering
> caused by our passions.   BARNAVE

WHILE he was helping to put the usual furniture back into its place in the room that M. de la Mole had occupied, Julien came upon a very thick slip of paper folded in four. At the bottom of the first page he read the words: To his Excellency the Marquis de la Mole, peer of the realm, Knight of the King's Orders, etc., etc.

It was a petition written in coarse handwriting like a cook's and read as follows:

My Lord Marquis,

All my life I have been a man of religious principles. I was under bombardment in Lyons at the time of the siege, in '93, of execrable memory. I am a communicant, I attend Mass every Sunday in my parish church. I have never failed in my Easter obligations, even in '93, of execrable memory. My cook – before the Revolution I had a household of servants – serves up fish every Friday. I am generally respected in Verrières, and I venture to assert that this respect is deserved. In processions I take my place under the canopy beside his reverence the Curé and his worship the Mayor. On great occasions I carry a large wax candle purchased at my own expense. You will find documentary proofs of all this at the Treasury in Paris. I ask his Lordship the Marquis to give me charge of the lottery bureau in Verrières, which cannot fail to fall vacant soon, one way or another, since the man who has the post is seriously ill and votes, besides, for the wrong party in the elections, etc.

(Signed) *De Cholin.*

In the margin of this petition was a note signed by M. de Moirod, the first line of which was: 'I had the honour of speaking to you yesterday about the very deserving man who makes this request, etc.'

So, thought Julien, even this idiot Cholin shows me the road I ought to follow.

A week after the King had passed through Verrières, all that

remained of the countless lies, the senseless constructions put on
this or that, the ridiculous discussions, etc., etc., on the subject
of the King, the Bishop, the Marquis de la Mole, the ten
thousand bottles of wine, and poor somersaulting Moirod – he
had not left the house for a month in the hope of receiving a
decoration – was the extreme impropriety of pushing Julien
Sorel, the carpenter's son, so unceremoniously into the guard of
honour. You should have heard what the wealthy manufacturers
of printed linens, who morning, noon, and night would talk
themselves hoarse in the cafés preaching equality, had to say on
the subject. That proud, disdainful woman Madame de Rênal was
at the bottom of this outrageous occurrence. And why? That
young abbé Sorel's handsome eyes and rosy cheeks said all that
was necessary.

A short while after their return to Vergy the youngest of the
children, Stanislas-Xavier, had an attack of fever. Madame de
Rênal was immediately seized with frightful remorse. For the
first time she showed some consistency in blaming herself for her
love. She seemed to realize, as by a miracle, the enormity of the
offence into which she had let herself be drawn. Although by
nature deeply religious, she had not, up till that moment, reflected on the greatness of her crime in the eyes of God.

Long ago, at the Convent of the Sacred Heart, she had loved
God with passionate devotion; in the present circumstances, she
had as great a fear of him. The inward conflict that tore her in
two was all the more terrible because there was nothing rational
in her fear. Julien found that the least attempt to reason with
her, far from soothing her mind, only made her irritated – she
saw in such arguments the language of the devil. Yet, since
Julien himself was very fond of little Stanislas, he had the better
right to talk to her of his illness, which soon took on a serious
turn. Then Madame de Rênal's incessant remorse became so great
that it even made her unable to sleep. She never broke her fiercely
sullen silence. Had she opened her mouth it would have been to
confess her crime before God and man.

'I earnestly implore you,' Julien would say the moment they
found themselves alone, 'not to say anything to anyone. Let me
be the only confidant of your distress. If you still love me, say
nothing. No words of yours can take Stanislas' fever away.'

His consoling words, however, had no effect. He did not know
that Madame de Rênal had got the idea in her head that, in
order to appease the wrath of a jealous God, she must either hate

Julien or see her son die. It was the feeling that she could not hate her lover that made her so unhappy.

'You must go away from me,' she said to him one day. 'In heaven's name, leave this house. It's your presence here that's killing my son. God is punishing me,' she added under her breath. 'And he is just. I adore him for his justice. My crime is a fearful one, yet I went on living without a sense of remorse! That was the first sign God had forsaken me; I deserve to be doubly punished.'

Julien was deeply moved. He could see in this neither hypocrisy nor overstatement. She thinks she will kill her son by loving me, he thought, and yet the poor woman loves me more than she loves her son. That – I cannot possibly doubt it – is the real nature of the remorse that's killing her. There's nobility of feeling. But how can I have inspired such a love as this – I who am so poor, so ill-bred, so ignorant, and sometimes so grossly ill-mannered?

One night the child's fever was at its worst. About two o'clock in the morning M. de Rênal came to see him. The child, consumed by fever, was very flushed and did not recognize his father. Suddenly Madame de Rênal flung herself at her husband's feet; Julien saw that she was about to tell him all and ruin herself for ever. Fortunately M. de Rênal was annoyed by her extraordinary behaviour.

'Good-bye! I'm going,' he said as he turned to go away.

'No! listen to me!' cried his wife on her knees in front of him, trying to keep him from going. 'You must know the whole truth. It's I who am killing my son. I gave him life and now I'm taking it away. Heaven is punishing me. In the sight of God I am guilty of murder. I must ruin and humiliate myself – maybe the Lord will be appeased by my sacrifice.'

If M. de Rênal had been a man with imagination, he would have known all.

'Romantic fancy!' he exclaimed as he walked away from his wife who was trying to embrace his knees. 'Mere romantic fancy, that's all it is. Julien,' he added, 'see that the doctor's sent for as soon as it's daylight.' And he went back to bed. Madame de Rênal sank to her knees half-fainting. As Julien tried to come to her aid she pushed him away with convulsive gestures. Julien stood there amazed.

So that's what adultery means! he said to himself.... Could it be possible that these deceitful priests ... are right? That they

who commit so many sins themselves are privileged to know the
true theory of sin? What a grotesque idea! ...

For twenty minutes after M. de Rênal had gone to his room,
Julien watched the woman he loved, lying motionless and almost
unconscious, her head resting on the child's little bed. There's a
woman whose nature is of the very highest reduced to depths of
misery all on account of knowing me. Time's going by very fast.
What can I do to help her? I must make up my mind somehow.
It's no longer a question of my own interests. – What do I care
for men and the silly fuss they make? What can I do for her?
... Leave her? But then I leave her to suffer the most frightful
anguish alone. This automaton she has for a husband is more
of a hindrance than a help. He'll say something harsh to her,
merely because he's a coarse-minded brute. She may go mad,
fling herself out of the window....

If I leave her, if I don't still keep an eye on her, she'll confess
everything to him. He might, who knows, create a public
scandal, in spite of that inheritance of hers he expects to get.
Good heavens! she may even tell that foul brute, Father Maslon,
who's making the illness of a six-year-old boy a pretext for never
stirring from the house – not without some design, either. In her
sorrow she forgets what she knows of the man – she only sees the
priest.

'You must go away, my dear,' said Madame de Rênal suddenly,
opening her eyes.

'I'd give my life a thousand times over,' Julien answered, 'if I
could find out how to help you. I've never been so deeply in love
with you, dearest angel, or, rather, from this very moment I've
begun to adore you as you deserve. What will become of me
when I'm far away from you, knowing, too, that I'm the cause
of your unhappiness! But don't let's talk of what I shall suffer.
I'll go away – yes, I'll go away, my love. But if I leave you, if I'm
no longer there to watch over you, to come continually between
you and your husband – you'll tell him everything, you'll ruin
yourself. You must consider it, he'll drive you ignominiously out
of this house. All Verrières, all Besançon will be talking of this
scandal. Everyone will be against you. You'll never recover from
the shame of it....'

'That's what I ask for,' she cried, rising to her feet. 'I shall
suffer – and so much the better.'

'But by this abominable scandal you will ruin him, too!'

'But I shame my own self, fling my own self into the mud.

And maybe by doing this I'll save my son. Such a humiliation, and in the sight of all, is possibly a kind of public penance. So far as my weak heart can judge, isn't that the greatest sacrifice I can make to God? ... Maybe he'll do me the grace to accept my shame and leave me my son. Show me another and more painful sacrifice, and I'll run to make it.'

'Let me punish myself. I too am guilty. Would you have me shut myself up with the Trappists? The austerity of such a life might possibly appease your God. Ah, heavens! Why can't I take Stanislas' illness upon myself....'

'Ah! you love him!' cried Madame de Rênal, getting up and flinging herself into his arms, only to push him away in horror almost immediately.

Then she fell on her knees again. 'I believe you, yes, I believe you!' she went on. 'Oh my only friend! why couldn't you have been Stanislas' father! Then it wouldn't be a horrible sin to love you better than your own son.'

'Will you let me stay and from now on love you only as a brother? That is the only reasonable atonement. It might appease the wrath of the Most High.'

'What about me?' she cried, 'What about me? Could I love you as one loves a brother? Is it in my power to love you that way?'

Julien burst into tears. 'I will obey you, dearest,' he said to her, falling at her feet. 'Yes, I'll obey you, whatever you order. That's all that's left for me to do. My mind is struck with blindness – I can't see which way to decide. If I leave you, you'll tell your husband all – you'll ruin yourself and him as well. He'll never be elected as Deputy after a scandal like this. If I stay, you'll believe me the cause of your son's death, you'll die of grief. Would you like to try the effect of my going away? If you wish it, I'll punish myself for our fault by leaving you for a week. I'll go and spend it in any place of retreat you choose – at the Abbey of Bray-le-Haut, for instance. But swear to me you'll confess nothing to your husband in my absence. Consider that I can never return if you speak.'

She promised him this and he went away; but after two days she called him back.

'I find it impossible to keep my oath if you're not with me. If you're not constantly at hand with your eyes commanding me to keep silence, I shall speak to my husband. Every single hour of my hateful life seems to me as long as a day.'

Heaven took pity at last on this unhappy mother. By slow degrees Stanislas' life ceased to be in danger. But the ice was broken; reason had made her conscious of the whole extent of her sin, and she could not settle calmly down again. She still suffered pangs of remorse, and of such a kind as were natural for so sincere a heart. Her life was both heaven and hell – hell for her when Julien was out of her sight and heaven when she was at his feet.

'I don't delude myself any longer,' she would say to him, even in moments when she dared abandon herself to his love. 'I'm lost – lost beyond all hope of redemption. You are young, I seduced you and you yielded. Heaven may pardon you – but I am lost. I know it by a very certain sign. I'm frightened – who wouldn't be frightened at the sight of hell? But all said and done I don't repent. I'd commit my fault afresh if it were still to be committed. Only let heaven not punish me here and now through my children, and I'll have more than I deserve. But you, at least, Julien,' she would at other times exclaim, 'are you happy? Do you find, dearest, that I love you enough?'

As for Julien, with his particular need for love that was based on sacrifice, he found that neither suspicions nor wounded pride could withstand the sight of so great and so unmistakable a sacrifice every moment renewed. He adored Madame de Rênal. It doesn't matter that she's noble and I'm a workman's son – she loves me! She doesn't look on me as one of her lackeys doing duty as a lover. Once this fear was removed, Julien plunged into all love's wild delight and all its fatal uncertainty.

'At least,' she would exclaim whenever she saw him doubting her love, 'let me make you really happy in the few days left to us to spend together! Let's make haste – tomorrow, perhaps, I shall be no longer yours. If heaven should strike at me through my children it would be all in vain my trying to live for nothing but to love you – or shutting my eyes to the fact it's my crime that kills them. I'd not be able to survive such a blow. Even if I wished to, I couldn't – I'd go mad. Ah! if I could only take your sin on my shoulders, as you so generously offered to take Stanislas' fever!'

The nature of the feeling uniting Julien and his mistress was transformed by this great moral crisis. His love was no longer merely made up of admiration for her beauty and pride of possession. From that time onwards there was a much higher quality in their happiness; the flame that consumed them both was more intense; the ecstasy they experienced full of frenzy. In the eyes of the world their happiness would have seemed all the greater. But they no longer found in it the sweet serenity, the unclouded bliss, the facile joy of those first days of their love, when Madame de Rênal's only fear was lest Julien should not love her enough. At times, indeed, this happiness assumed the character of a crime.

In the happiest and most seemingly tranquil moments, Madame de Rênal, clutching nervously at Julien's hand, would cry, 'Ah, heavens! I see hell before me. What dreadful torments! Yet I've well deserved them.' And she would clasp him closely, clinging to him as ivy clings to the wall.

Julien would try in vain to calm this troubled spirit. She would take his hand and cover it with kisses; then, falling back into sombre musings, cry out, 'Hell itself would be a mercy for me. I'd still have a few days left on earth to spend with him. But hell, here and now, in this world – in the death of my children. . . . Though, maybe, at such a price my crime will be pardoned. . . . Ah, Almighty God! Do not grant me pardon at such a price. These poor children have done nothing to offend thee. I alone am guilty – I love a man who is not my husband.'

Then Julien would see her next arrive at moments of apparent calm. She would make an effort to control herself – she had no wish to poison the life of the man she loved. In the midst of such alternations of love, remorse, and pleasure the days passed swift as lightning for them. Julien lost the habit of thinking.

Mademoiselle Elisa went to Verrières to attend to some trifling legal business which concerned her. There she found M. Valenod incensed with Julien, and as she hated the tutor she talked a good deal to him about this man.

'You'd get me into disgrace, sir, if I told you the truth,' she said one day to M. Valenod. 'You masters are all hand in glove with each other when it comes to important matters. . . . We poor servants are never pardoned for speaking out about certain things. . . .'

After these commonplaces, which M. Valenod's impatient curiosity cleverly cut short, he learnt certain things that were very mortifying to his vanity.

This woman, the most distinguished of any in the district, whom for six years he had surrounded with so many little attentions, and that, unfortunately, in the sight of and to the knowledge of everybody, this woman, who was so proud, who had so many times made him blush by her disdain, had just taken a young workman, disguised as a tutor, for her lover. And, to let nothing be wanting to make the Superintendent of the work-house completely vexed and humiliated, this lover was adored by Madame de Rênal. 'Moreover,' as the maid said with a sigh, 'M. Julien didn't put himself out at all to win her, he wasn't any less stand-offish than usual on madam's account.'

Elisa had not felt sure about this until they were in the country, but she thought it dated from a very much longer way back. 'No doubt it's because of that,' she added spitefully, 'that some time ago M. Julien refused to marry me. And there was I, like a silly, going and talking it over with Madame de Rênal and begging her to speak to the tutor!'

That very evening M. de Rênal received from the town, along with his daily paper, a lengthy anonymous letter informing him in the fullest detail of what was going on in his house. Julien saw him grow pale as he read this letter, written on bluish-grey paper, and cast very nasty glances at him. The Mayor did not recover from his agitation for the whole of that evening; in vain Julien tried to court his favour by asking him for an account of the genealogies of the noblest families in Burgundy.

CHAPTER 20 : *Anonymous Letters*

> Do not give dalliance
> Too much the rein; the strongest oaths are straw
> To the fire i' the blood.   *The Tempest*

As they were leaving the drawing-room towards midnight, Julien had time to say to his mistress, 'Don't let's meet to-night, your husband suspects something. I could swear this long epistle he was reading and sighing over is an anonymous letter.'

Luckily, Julien locked himself into his room, for Madame de Rênal got the crazy idea that his warning was merely a pretext for not seeing her. She lost her head completely and came to his door at the usual hour. Julien, hearing a noise in the corridor, immediately blew out his light. Someone was trying to open his door – Was it Madame de Rênal, or was it a jealous husband?

Early the next morning the cook, who had taken Julien under her wing, brought him a book on the cover of which he read the following, written in Italian: *Guardate alla pagina 130.* Shuddering at this imprudence, Julien turned to page 130 and found pinned to it the following letter, written in haste and wet with tears, and without the least attention to spelling. Ordinarily Madame de Rênal spelt very correctly. This detail touched him, and made him half forget her frightful rashness.

So you didn't wish to see me tonight, my dear? [the letter ran] *There are moments when I believe I have never yet read deep down into your heart. I'm frightened by the way you look at me. I'm frightened of you. Good God! does it mean you've never loved me? If so, may my husband discover our love and keep me for ever a prisoner, in the country, far away from my children. Maybe God wills it so. I'll soon be dead – but you'll be a monster.*

Don't you love me? Have I tired you with my foolish ways, my remorse – you godless man? Do you want to ruin me? I'm giving you an easy way to do it. Go and show this letter to everyone in Verrières, or rather show it only to M. Valenod. Tell him I love you – but no, don't utter such a blasphemy. Tell him I adore you; that life only began for me the day I saw you; that in the maddest moments of my youth I never even dreamed of such happiness as I owe to you; that I've sacrificed my life for you –

that for you I'm sacrificing my soul. You know that I sacrifice much more for you.

But does such a man understand what sacrifice means? Tell him – tell him just to vex him – that I defy all evil-minded people; that there's only one sort of unhappiness in the world for me any longer – and that's to see the one man who holds me to life change towards me! How happy I would be to lose my life, to offer it up as a sacrifice and be no longer afraid for my children!

Don't have any doubts about it, my dearest love, if there is an anonymous letter it comes from that hateful creature who for six years has pursued me with his loud, coarse voice, with tales of his jumps on horseback, his fatuous gallantries, his endless summing up of all his advantages.

Is there really an anonymous letter? That's what I wanted to talk over with you, you unkind man. But no, you've acted wisely. Clasping you in my arms, for the last time perhaps, I could never have discussed it coldly and calmly as I do now, being alone. From now on, it won't be so easy to come by our happiness! Will that vex you? Yes, maybe, on days when you haven't received some interesting book from M. Fouqué. I've made my sacrifice – tomorrow, whether or no there is an anonymous letter, I'll tell my husband I've received one too, and that we must make it easy for you to go at once, and find some decent pretext for sending you back to your family without delay.

Alas! my love, we'll have to be separated for a fortnight, or perhaps a month! Yes, I'm being fair to you – you'll suffer as much as I shall. But after all, it's the only way of defending ourselves against the effect of this anonymous letter. It's not the first my husband's received, nor about me, either. Alas! how they used to make me laugh!

The whole aim of my conduct will be to make my husband believe this letter comes from M. Valenod. If you leave the house, don't fail to stay in Verrières. I'll manage things so that my husband gets the idea of spending a fortnight there, just to prove to all stupid people there's no coldness between himself and me. Once you're in Verrières, get on friendly terms with everyone, even the Liberals. I know all their ladies will be anxious to look you up.

Don't go and lose your temper with M. Valenod, nor cut off his ears, as one day you said you would, but be on the contrary as charming as possible to him. The one essential thing is to have it generally believed in Verrières that you're entering that fellow

Valenod's house, or someone else's, to look after the children's education.

Now that's a thing my husband will never allow. Even supposing he had to make up his mind to accept it, well, at least you'd be in Verrières, and I'd see you now and then. My children too, who're so fond of you, would come and see you. Heavens above! I feel I love my children all the more because they love you. What remorse that gives me! How is all this going to end? ... I'm wandering from the point. ... Anyhow, you understand how you should behave. Be gentle, be polite, and don't show any contempt towards these vulgar persons. — I ask it on my knees; they're going to decide our fate. Don't doubt it for a moment, my husband's behaviour towards you will conform to what public opinion prescribes.

I look to you to provide me with this anonymous letter. Arm yourself with patience — and a pair of scissors. Cut the words you'll see here out of a book, and then stick them with paste on the piece of bluish-grey paper I enclose with this. I got it from M. Valenod. You must expect your room to be searched, so burn the book you've damaged. If you don't find the words ready made for you, be patient and make them up letter by letter. To spare you trouble I've made the anonymous letter rather too short. Alas! if you've ceased to love me, as I fear you have, how long you must find this letter of mine!

The anonymous letter read as follows:

Madam,

I know all about your little goings-on; the people, moreover, whose interest it is to stop them have been informed about them. Out of what remains of my friendship for you, I advise you to break completely with this young peasant. If you are wise enough to do this, your husband will believe the warning he has received is a hoax, and we will leave him in his error. Reflect that I know your secret. Tremble for yourself, unhappy woman. From now on you will have to treat me properly.

Julien went back to what Madame de Rênal had written.

As soon as you've finished sticking on the words that make up this letter (did you recognize M. Valenod's style of talking?) go out of the house at once. I'll come to meet you. ... I'll go into

*the village and come back looking greatly upset – I shall certainly
be feeling extremely so. Heavens! what risks I'm running, and
all because you thought you guessed there was an anonymous
letter. Finally, with a very troubled expression, I shall give my
husband the letter, which will have been handed to me by someone I don't know. As for yourself, you must go for a walk with
the children – and don't come back until it's time for dinner.*

*You can see the tower of the dovecote from the top of the rocks.
If this little affair of ours is going well, I'll put a white handkerchief up there. In the contrary event, there'll be nothing.*

*Won't your heart, you thankless creature, help you to find out
some way of telling me you love me before you set out on this
walk? Whatever happens, you can be sure of one thing – I
shouldn't live a day after our final separation. Ah, wicked
mother! – there are two words, my dear Julien, that have no
meaning for me. I can't feel them – I can think of no one but you
at this moment. I only wrote them so that you should not reproach me. Now that I see myself on the point of losing you,
what's the good of pretending? Yes! let my heart appear horrible
to you, but let me not lie to the man I adore! I've already practised too much deception in my life. All right, then, I forgive
you if you don't love me any longer. I haven't time to read over
my letter. It seems but a small thing in my eyes to pay with my
life for the happy days so recently passed in your arms. You
know that I'll have to pay even more dearly for them.*

> Alas, our frailty is the cause, not we;
> For such as we are made of, such we be.
> *Twelfth Night*

FOR an hour on end Julien took a childlike pleasure in collecting and arranging words. As he was coming out of his room he ran into the children and their mother. She took the letter from him with such simplicity and courage that he was frightened at her calm.

'Is the paste dry enough?' she asked him.

Is this the woman driven so mad by remorse? he thought.

What plans has she got in her head at this moment? He was too proud to ask her, but never, perhaps, had he found her more attractive.

'If this turns out badly,' she added with the same cool composure, 'they'll take everything I've got. Bury this box I'm giving you, somewhere up in the mountains. One day it may be my sole resource.'

She handed him a red morocco case, of the kind in which glass is usually kept, filled with gold and a few diamonds.

'Go off now,' she said.

She kissed the children, the youngest one twice. Julien stood there without moving. She walked quickly away from him, without giving him a glance.

From the moment of opening the letter, M. de Rênal's existence had been one of frightful torment. He had not been so painfully excited since 1816, when he had all but fought a duel. To do him justice, the prospect of being hit by a bullet would have made him less unhappy. He scanned the letter up and down. Isn't that a woman's writing? he said to himself. If so, what woman can have written it? He ran over in his mind all the women he knew in Verrières without being able to fix his suspicions on any one of them. Could a man have dictated this letter? And who is this man? The same uncertainty here. He was envied, and no doubt hated, by most of those he knew. I must ask my wife, he said out of habit, getting up from the armchair into which he had sunk.

Good God! he cried, almost before he was on his feet. He beat his brow, ejaculating. Why, she's the person I should mistrust

the most – the one who's my enemy at this moment. Anger
brought tears to his eyes.

By just compensation for that hardness of heart which is all
the provinces take for wisdom, the two men M. de Rênal most
feared at this moment were his two most intimate friends.

After these, he thought, I can count on some ten or so who
are possibly friends of mine. He considered them one by one,
weighing them up in turn, to find what degree of comfort he
might get from each. Every one of them, he exclaimed, yes, every
one will be intensely gratified by my frightful misadventure. As
luck would have it, he was not without grounds for thinking
people envied him. In addition to the magnificent house he had
in town, and which the King of — had for all time honoured by
sleeping in it, he had made his country house at Vergy into a
very fine place indeed. The front was painted white and the
windows were furnished with handsome green shutters. The idea
of this magnificence consoled him for a moment. The fact is that
this château could be seen from three or four leagues away, to
the great detriment of all those country houses or would-be
châteaux of the neighbourhood, which were left with the humble
grey hue that time had given them.

M. de Rênal could count on the tears and the sympathy of one
of his friends, who was churchwarden of the parish, but the man
was an utter idiot who shed tears on every occasion. This man,
however, was his only standby.

What unhappiness can be compared to mine? Or what loneliness either? he cried in his rage. Can it be, this truly pitiable
man said to himself, that in my misfortune I haven't one friend
I can ask for advice? For I'm losing my reason, I know I am. Ah,
Falcoz! Ah, Ducros! he ejaculated. These were the names of
two friends of his childhood whom he had estranged by his
arrogant conduct in 1814.

They were not of noble birth and he had wished to abandon
the terms of equality on which they had lived since their boyhood. One of them, Falcoz, an intelligent and courageous man,
who owned a newspaper shop in Verrières, had bought a print-
ing-house in the capital of the Department and started his own
newspaper. The *Congrégation* had made up their minds to ruin
him; his newspaper had been condemned, his printer's licence
withdrawn. In these sad circumstances he had ventured to write
to M. de Rênal for the first time in ten years. The Mayor of
Verrières thought it incumbent on him to answer like an ancient

Roman: 'If the king's chief minister paid me the honour of consulting me, I would say to him: "Ruin all the printers in the province without pity and make printing a monopoly like tobacco".'

This letter to an intimate friend, which at the time had aroused universal admiration in Verrières, was now recalled with horror by M. de Rênal. Who would have told me that, for all my rank, my wealth, and my decorations, I should one day regret having written it? In such transports of anger, now directed against himself, now against everybody around him, M. de Rênal passed a terrible night. Fortunately it did not occur to him to spy on his wife.

I've grown used to Louise, he said to himself. She knows all my concerns. Even if tomorrow I were free to marry again I couldn't find anyone to take her place. Then he found satisfaction in the idea that his wife was innocent. Such a way of looking at things did not oblige him to make a firm stand, and suited him much better. How many wives haven't we seen slandered!

But, good heavens! he suddenly exclaimed, as he paced excitedly up and down, shall I allow her to make a fool of me with her lover, just as if I were a man of no importance, a mere miserable ragamuffin? Must everyone in Verrières chuckle over my obliging disposition? What was there they didn't say about Charmier, the most notoriously deceived husband of any in the district? Isn't there a smile on everyone's lips whenever they mention him? He's a good lawyer, but who talks of his eloquence? 'Ah! Charmier!' they say, 'Bernard's Charmier,' — designating him thus by the name of the man who holds him up to shame.

Thank heaven I have no daughter, said M. de Rênal to himself at other moments. So the way I intend to punish the mother won't do any harm to my children's prospects. I can surprise this young peasant with my wife and kill them both. In such a case this tragic character of my story may perhaps remove any chance of ridicule; he followed it up in every detail. The Penal Code is on my side and, whatever happens, my friends among the *Congrégation* and on the jury will come to my rescue. He examined his hunting knife. It was very keen, but the thought of blood frightened him.

I could thrash this impudent tutor and send him packing. But what a scandal then in Verrières and throughout the Department! After Falcoz' paper had been condemned, and its chief editor let out of prison, I helped to get him out of a job which was worth six hundred francs. I've heard say this wretched scribbler has dared to show himself in Besançon; he can disparage me so skilfully and in such a way that I'd never be able to bring him to trial. Bring him to trial! ... why, the impudent rascal will discover countless ways of insinuating that he's told the truth. A man of good family, who maintains his rank as I do, is hated by all the common sort. I shall see myself in those dreadful Paris papers. God! what a catastrophe! to see the ancient name of Rênal dragged in the mud and made a laughing-stock! ... If I ever travel, I shall have to change my name. Heavens! give up a name from which I derive all my reputation and my power. What crowning misery!

If I don't kill my wife, but drive her out of my house in disgrace, she has her aunt in Besançon who'll immediately hand her over all her fortune. My wife will be off to Paris with Julien; people in Verrières will know about it, and they'll still take me for a man who's been fooled.

By now the pallid glow of his lamp made this unhappy man aware that day was beginning to appear. He went out into the garden to get a little fresh air. He had almost made up his mind at this moment to create no scandal, and more especially because he was thinking of how his good friends in Verrières would be overjoyed by such a thing.

The walk in the garden made him a little calmer. No, he exclaimed, I won't get rid of my wife, she's too useful to me. He was horrified as he pictured what his house would be without her. His only relation was the Marquise de R—, a stupid, ill-natured old woman.

An extremely sensible notion occurred to him, but carrying it out would ask for much greater strength of character than the poor man possessed. If I keep my wife, he said to himself, I know that one day or other in a fit of impatience with her I'll reproach her with her fault. She's proud, we'll break with each other, and all this will happen before she inherits anything from her aunt. How people will laugh at me then! My wife loves her children, everything will come to them in the end. But as for me, I'll be the talk of Verrières. 'What!' they'll say, 'why, he couldn't even be revenged on his wife!' Wouldn't it be better for me to rest content with suspicions and not try to find out the truth? But then I tie my hands and can't reproach her with anything afterwards.

A moment later, M. de Rênal, once more in the grip of his wounded vanity, was doggedly striving to recall every device he had heard tell of at the Casino or Gentlemen's Club in Verrières whenever some witty, talkative fellow interrupted play at the billiard-table to make merry at the expense of some deceived husband or other. How cruel, at this moment, such pleasantries appeared!

Good God! why isn't my wife dead! he thought. Then I'd be entirely safe from ridicule. Why aren't I a widower? I'd go and spend six months in the best company in Paris.

After the momentary happiness this thought of being a widower brought him, his imagination reverted to means of making sure of the truth. Should he scatter at midnight, when everyone was asleep, a thin layer of something or other in front of Julien's door? In daylight, the next morning, he would see the print of footsteps.

But that way's no good! he suddenly cried in rage. That bitch Elisa would see it, and soon the whole world would know I was jealous.

In one of the other stories told at the Casino a husband had made sure of his misfortune by sticking a hair with a bit of wax as a seal on both his wife's door and her lover's. After so many hours of hesitation, this way of getting informed of his position seemed to him decidedly the best, and he was thinking how to put it into practice when at a bend in the garden path he came upon this wife he had been wishing to see dead.

She was coming back from the village, where she had been to hear Mass in the church. A tradition, which in the opinion of coolly critical minds is of doubtful truth, but which she herself believed, claims that the little church in use today was once the chapel of the castle belonging to the Lord of the manor of Vergy. This idea had been haunting Madame de Rênal's mind all the time she had thought to spend praying in church. Constantly before her eyes was a picture of her husband killing Julien as if by accident while out hunting, and later on, in the evening, giving her his heart to eat.

My fate depends, she said to herself, on what he's going to think while he's listening to me. After this decisive quarter of an hour, I may perhaps find no further chance of speaking to him. He's not one of those wise people ruled by reason. In that case I might, with the help of my own feeble reason, foresee what he would do or say. He will decide the fate of both of us; that's in his power.

But what fate depends on my own skill, on my own cleverness in guiding the ideas of this odd, capricious creature, blinded by anger and prevented from seeing half of what's in front of him. Good heavens! I've need of ingenuity and presence of mind, but where can I find them?

She recovered her composure as if by magic when, on coming into the garden, she saw her husband some way away. His rumpled hair and clothes all in disorder told of a sleepless night. She handed him a letter folded up but with the seal broken. He looked at his wife without opening it, a gleam of madness in his eyes.

'Just look at this revolting thing,' she said to him. 'An ugly-looking fellow, who claims to know you and to be under some debt of gratitude to you, handed it to me as I was passing by the solicitor's garden. There's one thing I must ask, and that is for you to send M. Julien back to his family, and without delay.' Madame de Rênal hastened to utter these words, though perhaps a trifle prematurely, just to free herself from the fearful prospect of having to say them.

She was thrilled with joy to see the delight she gave her husband. She knew from the way in which he stared at her that Julien's guess was right. Instead of grieving over such a real misfortune, she said to herself: What genius! What perfect skill in handling the situation! and for a young man with so little experience, too! Where can't he hope to arrive in the course of time? Alas! his success will make him forget me then.

This little impulse of admiration for the man she adored completely restored her composure. She congratulated herself on the steps she was taking. I've not shown myself unworthy of Julien, she told herself, in secret, sweet delight.

Without saying a word, for fear of committing himself, M. de Rênal scanned this second anonymous letter, composed, as the reader may remember, of printed words gummed on to blue-grey paper. Someone's still trying to make a fool of me in every way he can, thought M. de Rênal, utterly worn out with fatigue.

Still more fresh insults to look into, and always on my wife's account! Hardly restrained by the thought of the Besançon inheritance, he was on the verge of hurling the coarsest abuse at her. The need of taking it out of someone or something devoured him; he crumpled up the paper on which this second letter was written and began to stride up and down. He felt he had to get away from his wife; yet a few seconds later he came back to her considerably calmed down.

'We'll have to make up our minds to dismiss Julien,' she said to him straight away. 'After all, he's only a workman's son. You can give him a few crowns as compensation — besides he's a clever lad and will easily find a place somewhere or other — with M. Valenod, for instance, or with the sub-prefect, M. de Maugiron — they've both got children. So you won't do him any harm. ...'

'Spoken just like the silly woman you are,' exclaimed M. de Rênal in a terrifying voice. 'What common sense can one expect from a woman? None of you ever pay attention to what's reasonable — how should you know anything then? Your happy-go-lucky, idle minds give you nothing to do but chase after butterflies, like the feeble creatures you are, and whom we're unlucky enough to have in the midst of our families. ...'

Madame de Rênal let him go on talking, and he talked for a very long time, *digesting his anger*, as they say in those parts.

'Sir,' she replied at last, 'I'm speaking as a woman whose honour has been outraged — that is to say she's been attacked in all she holds most precious.'

Throughout the whole of this painful conversation, on which the chance of her living under the same roof with Julien depended, Madame de Rênal's composure was unshaken. She hunted for the ideas she thought most apt to guide her husband, blinded by his rage. She had remained unmoved by all the insulting references he had made to her — she did not listen to them: all her thoughts at that moment were of Julien. Will he be pleased with me? she was wondering.

At last she spoke to him. 'This young peasant,' she said, 'whom we've overwhelmed with kind attentions and even presents, may possibly be innocent — he's none the less the occasion of the first open insult I've received. ... When I read this revolting document, sir, I promised myself that either he or I would leave the house.'

'Do you wish to create a scandal and bring dishonour both on me and yourself? You'll make a fine stir among the people in Verrières.'

'That's very true — you're generally envied for the prosperous state you yourself, your family, and the town have reached through your wise administration. Very well then. ... I'll get Julien to ask you for a month's leave to go and stay with that timber merchant in the mountains who's such a suitable friend for this young working-man.'

'Kindly refrain from doing anything,' replied M. de Rênal, fairly calmly. 'What I demand above all is for you not to speak to him. There'd be some anger in your words, which would make him on bad terms with me. You know how touchy that young gentleman is.'

'That young gentleman has no tact,' answered Madame de Rênal. 'He may be a scholar – you're the best judge of that – but underneath he's nothing but real peasant; after all, for my part, I've never had any opinion of him since his refusal to marry Elisa, which would have meant a safe income for him, merely on the pretext that she sometimes visited M. Valenod on the sly.'

'Ah!' said M. de Rênal, raising his eyebrows to an almost exaggerated degree. 'What, did Julien tell you that?'

'No, not exactly. He always spoke to me of the vocation which attracts him to the sacred ministry – but, believe me, the first vocation of all such humble folk is earning their bread. He let me understand pretty clearly that these secret visits were not unknown to him.'

'But I didn't know of them myself!' exclaimed M. de Rênal once more completely furious and stressing his words. 'Things go on in my house and I know nothing about them. What! has there been anything between Elisa and Valenod?'

'Well, it's ancient history, my dear,' said Madame de Rênal, 'and possibly nothing wrong took place. It was at the time when your good friend Valenod would not have been annoyed at people in Verrières thinking a nice little love affair – quite platonic of course – was developing between him and me.'

'I once thought there was something of the sort myself,' said M. de Rênal angrily pummelling his head with his fist as he advanced from one discovery to another. 'And you didn't say anything to me about it?'

'Was it necessary to stir up trouble between two friends just because our dear Superintendent's vanity was a little puffed up? What woman is there in our circle of friends to whom he hasn't addressed a few witty letters with even perhaps a little gallantry in them?'

'Then he wrote to you?'

'He writes a great deal.'

'Show me these letters at once, I command it.' M. de Rênal made himself appear a good six feet taller.

'I'll take good care not to,' was her answer, delivered with a gentleness that came near to indifference. 'I'll show you them one of these days when you're in a better frame of mind.'

'This very instant, damn it !' cried M. de Rênal, drunk with rage and yet at the same time happier than he had been for the past twelve hours.

'Will you swear to me,' said Madame de Rênal very gravely, 'never to quarrel with the Superintendent of the workhouse over these letters ?'

'Quarrel or no quarrel, I can take the orphanage away from him. But,' he went on in a furious temper, 'I want those letters at once – where are they ?'

'In the drawer of my writing-table, but I certainly won't give you the key.'

'I can break it open,' he cried, running off towards his wife's room.

Using an iron bar, he actually broke open a valuable figured mahogany writing-table, which he had often polished with the tail of his coat if he thought he saw any spot on it.

Meanwhile Madame de Rênal had run up the hundred and twenty steps of the dovecote and was tying a white handkerchief by its corner to one of the bars in the window. She felt herself the happiest of women as she gazed with tears in her eyes towards the great woods on the mountain-side. There's no doubt, she said to herself, that Julien's waiting under one of those tufted beeches to receive this happy signal. For a long time she listened carefully, then cursed the monotonous cry of the cicadas and the singing of the birds. But for this seasonable noise a shout of joy coming to her from the towering rocks might have reached her where she stood. Her eye gazed greedily at the huge slope of dark green ver-dure, smooth as a meadow, formed by the tree-tops. Why hasn't he the intelligence, she said to herself with deep and tender emotion, to think of some signal to tell me his happiness equals mine ? She did not come down from the dovecote until she began to get afraid her husband would come to look for her there.

She found him in a furious rage. He was scanning M. Valenod's anodyne phrases, which were little used to being read with so much feeling.

Seizing a moment when her husband's ejaculations allowed her a chance of being heard, Madame de Rênal said to him : 'I keep coming back to the same idea – Julien must go away on his travels. However much skill he may have in Latin, he's nothing after all but a boorish and often tactless peasant. Every day, with the idea he's being polite, he pays me the most extravagant and tasteless compliments which he learns by heart from some novel or other. . . .'

'But he never reads any,' M. de Rênal exclaimed. 'I've made sure of that. D'you think I'm the sort of master of a house who's blind to everything and doesn't know what's going on in his own home?'

'Well, if he doesn't read these ridiculous compliments anywhere, he invents them, and that makes him even worse. He must have adopted the same tone with me in Verrières . . . and without looking any further, he must have spoken to me like that in front of Elisa, which is much the same as if he had spoken when M. Valenod was present.'

'Ah!' cried M. de Rênal, making the table and the room both shake with one of the biggest thumps a fist has ever given, 'the printed anonymous letter and the letters Valenod wrote are all of them on the same kind of paper.'

At last! . . . thought Madame de Rênal. She made a show of being struck with amazement at this discovery and, not feeling enough courage to add a single word more, went and sat down on the divan a good way away at the far end of the drawing-room.

From that moment the battle was won. She had great difficulty in preventing M. de Rênal from going off to have a word with the supposed author of the anonymous letter.

'How is it,' she said, 'you don't feel it would be the most utter blunder to pick a quarrel with M. Valenod without sufficient proof? People envy you, sir, but where does the fault lie? With your outstanding ability. Your wise administration, the good taste of your house, the dowry I brought you, and above all the considerable inheritance we can expect from my good aunt – though its importance is immensely exaggerated – all these have made you the first man in Verrières.'

'You're forgetting my birth,' remarked M. de Rênal, smiling slightly.

'You're one of the most distinguished gentlemen in the province,' Madame de Rênal hastened to reply. 'If the King were free to give birth its due, you would doubtless have your place in the House of Peers and elsewhere. And yet, just when you are in such a splendid position as this, you want to give envious people something to talk about.'

'To speak to M. Valenod about his letter,' she went on, 'would

be to proclaim in Verrières and indeed in Besançon and throughout the province that this young commoner, admitted, perhaps
rashly, to share the family life of *a Rênal*, has found out a way of
abusing his privilege. Even supposing these letters you've just
discovered could prove that I returned M. Valenod's love, then you
should kill me – I'd have deserved it a hundred times over – but
you should never show any anger towards him. Just think how
all our neighbours are only waiting for a pretext to take their revenge on you for being superior to them. Think how in 1816 you
helped to make certain arrests. There was that man who had taken
refuge on his roof. . . .'

'I can only think you have neither regard nor friendship for
me,' cried M. de Rênal with all the bitterness such a memory
aroused. 'And I didn't get made a peer ! . . .'

'And I am thinking, my dear,' replied Madame de Rênal smiling,
'that I shall be richer than you, that I've been your companion
twelve years, and for all these reasons, I ought to be given a voice
in your affairs, especially in the affair that happened today. If
you prefer M. Julien to me,' she added with ill-concealed annoyance, 'I'm quite prepared to go and spend a winter with my aunt.'

These words were aptly chosen. There was in them the firmness that seeks to clothe itself in politeness. They made up M. de
Rênal's mind for him, although, as is the habit of the provinces,
he still went on talking for a considerable time, going back over
all his arguments again. At length two hours of useless babbling
wore out the strength of a man who had suffered a fit of anger
for a whole night through, and he settled on the line of conduct he was going to pursue with M. Valenod, with Julien, and
Elisa.

Once or twice, in the course of this tremendous scene, Madame
de Rênal was nearly moved to feel some sympathy for the very
real unhappiness of this man who for twelve years past had been
her friend and companion. But genuine passion is a selfish thing.
She was, besides, expecting every moment to hear him acknow-
ledge his receipt of the anonymous letter of the day before – but
this acknowledgement did not come. To have her sense of security
complete Madame de Rênal needed to know what ideas might have
been put into the mind of the man on whom her fate depended.
For, in the provinces, husbands control public opinion. A husband
who complains merely covers himself with ridicule, a thing that
is growing every day less dangerous in France. His wife, on the
other hand, supposing he gives her no money, sinks to the status

of a working-woman at fifteen sous a day, and, even so, the kind-
liest people have scruples about employing her.

An odalisque in a Turkish harem must at all hazards love her
husband – he is all-powerful: she has no hope of depriving him
of his authority by a series of little artful tricks. Her master's
vengeance is terrible, bloody, but soldier-like and generous – a
dagger thrust ends all. When a nineteenth-century husband strikes
down his wife, he uses the weapon of public scorn; he bars every
drawing-room door against her.

On her return to the house Madame de Rênal was sharply
aroused to a sense of danger. She was shocked by the disorder in
which she found her room. The locks of all her pretty little boxes
had been broken open; several blocks of the parquet floor had been
prised up. He would have had no pity on me! she said to herself.
Fancy spoiling this parquet of coloured wood in such a way when
he was so fond of it! Why, if one of his children comes in here
in wet shoes, he gets red with anger. And now it's spoilt for good
and all! The sight of such violence at once drove out of her mind
the last of those reproaches she had been addressing to herself
over her too rapid victory.

A little while before the bell rang for dinner, Julien came back
with the children. At dessert, after the servants had gone,
Madame de Rênal said to him very curtly: 'You have expressed
a wish to go and spend a fortnight in Verrières. M. Rênal is willing to give you leave. You can go when you like, but so that the
children shall not waste their time, their exercises will be sent to
you every day for you to correct.'

'I shall certainly not allow you more than a week,' added M.
de Rênal in very acid tones.

Julien read in his face the distress of a man who is suffering
great torment.

'He hasn't yet made up his mind,' he said to his mistress during
a moment when they were alone in the drawing-room. Madame
de Rênal told him briefly of all she had done since that morning.

'I'll give you the details tonight,' she added, laughing.

A woman's perversity! thought Julien. What pleasure, what
natural inclination prompts them to deceive us? 'I find you at
one and the same time clear-sighted and yet blinded by your love,'
he said to her with a touch of coldness. 'Your behaviour today has
been wonderful – but is it wise for us to try and see each other
tonight? This house is riddled with enemies – think how passionately Elisa hates me.'

'This hatred is very much like the passionate indifference you seem to feel for me.'

'Even if I were indifferent, I must save you from the danger into which I've plunged you. If by chance M. de Rênal speaks to Elisa a word from her might tell him all. Why shouldn't he hide himself, fully armed, close to my room? . . .'

'What! not even courage!' said Madame de Rênal with the haughty disdain of a noblewoman by birth.

'I'll never lower myself to discuss my courage,' Julien said coldly. 'That's a contemptible thing to do. Let the world judge me by my actions. But,' he added, taking hold of her hand, 'you haven't the least idea how deeply I'm attached to you, and what joy it is to me to be able to say good-bye to you before this cruel parting.'

Speech has been given to man to hide his thoughts
R. P. MALAGRIDA

JULIEN had hardly reached Verrières before he began to reproach himself for his injustice towards Madame de Rênal. I'd
have despised her as a mere silly little woman if, through weakness, she had failed to bring off her scene with M. de Rênal ! She
handles it like a diplomat – and here am I sympathizing with the
man she's beaten, and my enemy, too. There's some vulgar sort
of pettiness in this. ... My vanity's offended, all because M. de
Rênal is a man. Multitudinous and illustrious brotherhood to
which I have the honour to belong – behold in me an utter ass !

On being deprived of his living and driven out of his house,
M. Chélan had refused the accommodation which the most highly
respected Liberals in the neighbourhood had vied with each other
in offering. The two rooms he had taken were cluttered up with
his books. In his desire to show Verrières what a true priest really
was, Julien went and fetched a dozen pinewood planks from his
father's workshop and carried them himself on his back up the
whole length of the High Street. He borrowed some tools from an
old associate of his and had soon constructed some sort of bookcase in which he arranged M. Chélan's books.

'I thought the vanities of this world had corrupted you,' the
old priest said to him with tears of joy. 'Here's something which
redeems the childish folly of that brilliant guard of honour's uniform which won you so many enemies.'

M. de Rênal had ordered Julien to stay at his house. Nobody
had any suspicion of what had happened. The third day after his
arrival, Julien saw no less a personage than M. de Maugiron
coming right upstairs to his room. It was not, however, until after
he had listened for two long hours to insipid chatter and lengthy
lamentations on the wickedness of men, the little honesty amongst
people entrusted with the administration of public funds, the
dangers threatening this unhappy country, France, etc., etc., that
Julien finally saw the purpose of his visit beginning to poke
through.

They had already reached the staircase landing and the poor
half-disgraced tutor was escorting the future prefect of some fortunate Department to the door with suitable respect, when the

latter was pleased to interest himself in Julien's welfare, to praise his moderation in money matters, etc., etc. Finally, M. de Maugiron, clasping Julien in his arms in the most fatherly fashion, proposed to him that he should leave M. de Rênal and take a post in the house of a public official who had children needing education and who, like King Philip, gave thanks to God, not so much for giving them to him but for permitting them to be born in a neighbourhood where Julien lived. Their tutor would enjoy a salary of eight hundred francs, payable, not by the month – that was never a gentleman's way – but on a quarterly basis and always in advance.

Julien, who for the past hour and a half had been wearily waiting for an opportunity to speak, now took his turn at talking. His reply was perfect, and, into the bargain, as long-winded as a pastoral charge. It left everything to be understood, while stating nothing clearly. It expressed at one and the same time respect for M. de Rênal, deep esteem for the people of Verrières, and gratitude towards the illustrious sub-prefect. This individual, astonished at finding someone possessing more Jesuitical subtlety than himself, tried in vain to get some precise statement out of him. Julien, thrilled at this, and seizing the chance to exercise his powers, began his answer all over again in different terms. Never had any minister eloquent of speech, and wishing to utilize that end of the session when Parliament seems inclined to wake up, said fewer things in a greater number of words.

Hardly had M. de Maugiron left the house before Julien burst out in a wild fit of laughter. To turn his Jesuitical humour to advantage, he wrote a letter nine pages long to M. de Rênal, in which he gave him an account of all that had been said to him, and humbly asked his advice. This rascal, by the way, thought Julien, hasn't given me the name of the person who makes this offer ! It must be M. Valenod, who sees the effect of his anonymous letter evident in my exile at Verrières.

His epistle despatched, Julien left the house to seek advice of M. Chélan, feeling happy as a hunter who at six o'clock in the morning on a fine autumn day comes out upon a plain full of game. Before he could reach the good priest's lodgings, heaven, as if wishing to provide him with occasions for rejoicing, threw M. Valenod in his way. Julien made no attempt to hide from him that his heart was torn in two. A poor lad of his sort really ought to devote himself to the vocation heaven had inspired in his heart, but vocation was not everything in this base world. To work worthily in the Lord's vineyard and not be entirely unworthy of so many learned fellow labourers, education was an essential; so, too, was spending two very costly years in the seminary at Besançon. Consequently it was becoming absolutely indispensable to save money, which was much easier on a salary of eight hundred francs payable quarterly than on six hundred francs which got eaten up from month to month. On the other hand, did not heaven, by finding him a situation looking after the young Rênals, and above all by inspiring him with a particular affection for them, seem to indicate to him that it was not fitting to leave off educating them and undertake another man's children?

Julien reached such a pitch of perfection in rhetoric of the sort that has taken the place of the swiftness of action seen at the time of the Empire that he ended by getting bored himself with the sound of his own words. On coming back to the house he found one of M. Valenod's footmen, in full livery, who had made the round of the town in search of him with a note inviting him to dinner that very day.

Julien had never visited this man's house; only a few days back he had been thinking of nothing but how to trounce him soundly without letting himself in for a police court case. Although the note showed that dinner was not till one o'clock, Julien thought it more respectful to present himself in the Superintendent's study at half past twelve. He found M. Valenod parading his importance in the midst of a mass of portfolios. Neither his thick, black side-whiskers, nor his enormously abundant crop of hair, his smoking-cap awry on the top of his head, his huge pipe, his embroidered slippers, nor the thick gold chains that trailed in every direction across his chest, nor all the apparatus of a provincial man of business, who fancies himself a ladies' man, made any sort of impression on Julien. His mind was only all the more on the cudgelling he owed him.

He begged the honour of being introduced to Madame Valenod; she was busy dressing and could not receive him. By the way of compensation he enjoyed the advantage of being present while the Superintendent dressed. They then went on into Madame Valenod's room, where she introduced her children to him with tears in her eyes. This lady, one of the most important in Verrières, had a coarse, heavy face like a man's on which she had been putting rouge in honour of this grand ceremony. She gave a full display of maternal pathos.

Julien thought of Madame de Rênal. With his suspicious nature he was hardly ever sensitive to any memories save those evoked by contrast, and then he was so deeply affected that he was moved to tears. This propensity of his was intensified by the appearance of the Superintendent's house. He was shown over the whole place. Everything in it was new and sumptuous; he was told what each piece of furniture had cost. None the less Julien found something sordid about it all, something that smelt of stolen money. Everybody in it, down to the servants themselves, seemed to be putting up a bold front as if to ward off scorn.

The inspector of taxes, the excise officer, the chief constable, and two or three other public officials arrived with their wives. They were followed by a few wealthy members of the Liberal party. Dinner was served. Julien, who already was feeling ill-disposed towards it all, happened to reflect that on the other side of the dining-room wall some wretched men were held in confinement, men from whose ration of meat, perhaps, had been filched the wherewithal to buy all this tasteless luxury with which they were trying to dazzle him.

At this very moment, perhaps, they're hungry, he thought. His throat felt constricted; it was impossible for him to eat, almost impossible to speak. Things were much worse a quarter of an hour later. At rare intervals they had been hearing a snatch or two of a popular song – a rather vulgar one, it must be confessed – which one of the prisoners was singing. M. Valenod glanced at one of his servants. The man disappeared and soon after there was no further sound of singing.

A footman, at that moment, was offering Julien some Rhine wine in a green glass. Madame Valenod had been careful to draw his attention to the fact that this wine cost nine francs a bottle in the market. With his glass in his hand Julien remarked to M. Valenod, 'They're not singing that low song any more.'

'By Jove! I should think not!' M. Valenod answered triumphantly. 'I've had the beggars reduced to silence.'

These words were too much for Julien – he had the manners but not as yet the mentality of his present position. In spite of all his frequent practice of hypocrisy, he felt a big tear stealing down his cheek.

He tried to conceal it behind the green glass, but it was utterly impossible for him to do justice to the good Rhine wine. *Stop him singing*: he kept on saying to himself. O God, how canst thou suffer this!

Fortunately no one remarked his ill-bred emotion. The inspec-

tor of taxes had struck up a royalist song. During the rollicking
refrain, sung by everyone in chorus, Julien's conscience was telling him: There you see the filthy riches you'll acquire – and
you'll not have them save on such conditions and in company like
this! Possibly you'll get a post worth twenty thousand francs,
but then, while you are gorging yourself with meat, you'll have
to stop some wretched prisoner singing; you'll give dinners with
the money you've stolen from his miserable pittance – and while
you dine he'll be unhappier still! Oh, Napoleon; how sweet it
was in your day to climb to fortune through the risks of battle! –
but to add so meanly to some poor fellow's misery! . . .

I must say the weakness Julien gives proof of in this soliloquy
gives me a poor opinion of him. He would be a worthy colleague
of those kid-glove conspirators, who aspire to change all the ways
and habits of a great country while not wishing to bewail the
least little scratch.

Julien was violently reminded of the part he had to play. He
had not been invited to dine in such distinguished company merely to dream and not say a word.

A retired manufacturer of printed linens who was a correspond-
ing member of the Academy of Besançon and of that of Uzès
spoke to him from the other end of the table, and asked him if
what was commonly said about his amazing progress in the study
of the New Testament was really true.

Immediately deep silence reigned; as if by magic a New Testament turned up in the hands of the learned member of the two
academies. On Julien's replying, half a sentence in Latin picked at
random was read to him. He began to recite: his memory was
perfect, and this wonderful feat was admired with all the noisy
exuberance that attends the close of dinner. Julien glanced at the
beaming faces of the ladies – several of them were not bad-looking.
He noticed in particular the wife of the tuneful inspector of taxes.

'I'm really ashamed,' he said, looking at her, 'of speaking so
long in Latin in front of these ladies. If M. Robineau' (this was
the name of the member of two academies) 'will kindly read out
any sentence in Latin he happens on, I will attempt an impromptu
translation.' This second trial of strength covered him with glory.

There were several Liberals in the company, wealthy men, but
happy fathers of children qualified to hold scholarships, and who
on account of this had suddenly become converted since the last
religious mission. In spite of this clever political move, M. de
Rênal had never been willing to invite them to his house. These

worthy people, therefore, who only knew Julien by repute and
from seeing him on horseback on the day of the King of —'s entry,
were loudest in their admiration of him. When will these idiots,
thought Julien, get weary of all this Biblical phraseology, none of
which they understand? But on the contrary the very quaintness
of the style amused them and made them laugh. Julien, however,
grew tired.

He solemnly rose to his feet as six o'clock was striking and
mentioned a chapter of Liguori's new work on theology which he .
had to learn to repeat to M. Chélan on the following day. 'For
my business,' he added, pleasantly polite, 'is making others say
their lessons and saying my own.'

Everybody laughed a great deal; everybody admired him. This
type of wit is the right thing in Verrières. Julien was already on
his feet; everyone else rose too, in defiance of etiquette – such is
the power of genius. Madame Valenod detained him for a further
quarter of an hour; he really had to hear the children recite their
catechism. They made the queerest muddles, but only Julien
noticed them. He took good care not to point them out. What
ignorance of the first principles of religion ! he thought. He bowed
to Madame Valenod at last, thinking to make his escape – but he
had to endure one of La Fontaine's fables.

'This author is really very immoral,' Julien remarked to
Madame Valenod. 'There's a certain one of his fables about a M.
Jean Chouart in which he dares to shed ridicule on everything
most worthy of veneration. The best commentators have sharply
reproved him for this.'

Before he left, Julien received four or five invitations to dinner.
'This young man confers honour on our Department,' cried in
chorus all the guests he had made so merry. They even went on
to talk of a yearly grant of money voted out of the communal
funds to enable him to continue his studies in Paris.

While the whole dining-room was ringing with this rash pro-
ject, Julien had skipped nimbly away towards the carriage entrance. Ah ! the swine ! the vulgar swine ! he ejaculated three or
four times in succession under his breath as he gave himself up
to the pleasure of breathing in fresh air.

He who for so long had taken such offence at the disdainful
smiles and haughty airs of superiority he found behind all the
courtesy shown him in M. de Rênal's house was now, at this
moment, an aristocrat through and through. He could not help
being conscious of the extreme difference. Even if, he said to him-

self as he was going away, one overlooks the fact that it's a question of money stolen from poor, imprisoned wretches, and what's more of preventing them singing – did it ever occur to M. de Rênal to tell his guests the price of each bottle of wine he offers them? And there's this M. Valenod who can't start reckoning up his properties – a subject by the way that's always cropping up – can't even mention his house, his estates, etc., in his wife's presence without saying to her, 'Your house', or 'Your estates'.

In the course of the recent dinner this lady, who was apparently so sensitive to the pleasures of ownership, had made a frightful scene with one of her servants who had broken a wineglass and *ruined one of her sets*: and the servant had answered back in the rudest possible way.

What a collection of people! thought Julien. Even supposing they gave me the half of what they steal, I wouldn't want to live with them. One fine day I'd betray myself; I shouldn't be able to keep myself from expressing the disdain they make me feel.

All the same, in deference to Madam de Rênal's orders, he was forced to put in an appearance at several dinners of a similar kind. Julien became all the rage; his guard of honour's uniform was forgiven him, or rather this imprudent act was the real cause of his success. Soon there was talk of nothing in Verrières but the question of who would be the winner in the fight to get hold of this learned young man – M. de Rênal or the Superintendent of the workhouse.

These two gentlemen, together with M. Maslon, made up a triumvirate which for a number of years had tyrannized over the town. People were envious of the Mayor, the Liberals bore him a grudge; but all said and done he was of noble birth and made for a superior position, while M. Valenod's father had not left him so much as six hundred francs a year. The town had had to pass from pitying him for the shabby apple-green coat everyone had seen him wearing when he was young, to envying him his Norman horses, his gold chains, the clothes he ordered from Paris, and all his present wealth.

Amid the surging torrent of a world completely new to him, Julien believed he had discovered one honest man. He was a mathematician called Gros, who was reputed to be a Jacobin. Julien, who had made up his mind never to say anything but what he himself felt to be untrue, was obliged to rest content with expressing nothing more than suspicions regarding M. Gros.

Fat parcels of exercises were being forwarded to him from

Vergy. He was advised to go and see his father frequently and complied with this sad necessity. In short, his reputation was fairly on the mend when, one morning, he was surprised to find himself awakened by two hands placed over his eyes.

It was Madame de Rênal, who had journeyed into town, and running upstairs four steps at a time, had left her children busy with a pet rabbit they had brought with them, and reached Julien's room a few minutes before they did. This was a moment of delight, but a very brief one; by the time they arrived with the rabbit, which they wanted to show their friend, Madame de Rênal had vanished.

Julien gave them all a hearty welcome, including the rabbit. It seemed to him he had found his family again; he felt he loved these children, that it was pleasant to chatter with them. He was astonished by the gentle tone of their voices, by the unassuming nobility of their little ways; he felt the need of washing his imagination clean of all those vulgar ways of behaviour, all those disagreeable thoughts surrounding him as he breathed the air of Verrières. It was always the fear of being in need, always luxury and misery at loggerheads with each other. The people with whom he dined would tell him, in reference to their roast beef or mutton, confidential details that humiliated them and sickened anyone who listened.

'You people of good birth, you have the right to be proud,' he said to Madame de Rênal. And he went on to tell her of the dinners forced upon him.

'So you're all the fashion then!' she said, laughing heartily as she thought of Madame Valenod feeling obliged to use rouge every time she expected Julien. 'I believe she has designs on your heart,' she added.

Lunch was a delightful meal. The children's presence, although outwardly a restriction, actually added to the general merriment. The poor youngsters did not know how to show their joy at seeing Julien again. The servants had not failed to tell them that he was being offered two hundred to educate the little Valenods.

In the middle of lunch, Stanislas-Xavier, still pale from his serious illness, suddenly asked his mother how much his silver table set and the cup from which he drank were worth.

'Why do you ask?'

'I want to sell them and give the money to M. Julien, so that he won't be *diddled* by staying with us.'

Julien embraced him with tears in his eyes. His mother was

quite dissolved in tears as Julien, who had taken Stanislas on his knee, explained to him that he ought not to use the world *diddle*, which was servants' language. Seeing the pleasure he was giving Madame de Rênal, he tried to explain, by picturesque examples, what it really meant to be taken in by someone.

'I understand,' said Stanislas at last. 'It's the crow who's so silly he drops his cheese, and the fox who was flattering him picks it up.'

Madame de Rênal, beside herself with joy, covered her children with kisses, which she could not do without leaning slightly against Julien.

All at once the door opened – and there was M. de Rênal. His face, with its look of severe displeasure, contrasted strangely with the gentle gaiety his presence drove away. Madame de Rênal grew pale; she felt incapable of denying anything whatsoever. Julien burst out speaking and began to tell M. de Rênal in a very loud tone of voice about the silver goblet Stanislas wanted to sell. He was certain the story would be ill-received.

To begin with M. de Rênal frowned, as was his excellent habit at the mere name of silver. 'Any mention of this metal,' he was wont to say, 'is always a prelude to some charge on my purse.' But here there was more than money interests; there was something that increased his suspicions. The air of happiness animating his family in his absence was not calculated to put matters right with a man who was dominated by so ticklish a vanity.

As his wife was telling him with pride of the very graceful, ingenious way in which Julien gave the children new ideas, he interrupted her. 'Yes, yes! I know, he makes me seem hateful to my children. It's very easy for him to be a hundred times more pleasant to them than myself, who am, after all, their lord and master. Everything in this country tends to cast odium on *lawful* authority. Poor France!'

Madame de Rênal did not stop to examine every shade in her husband's greeting. She had just faintly grasped the possibility of spending a whole day in Julien's company. Having a host of things to buy in the town, she declared she had absolutely set her mind on having midday dinner at the tavern; and, no matter what her husband could say or do, she stood by her plan. The children were overjoyed at the mere name of *tavern*, which modern prudery pronounces with such great pleasure.

M. de Rênal left his wife in the first draper's shop she entered, to go and pay some visits. He came back again more morose than in the morning, convinced that the whole town was talking of Julien and himself, though no one, in truth, had as yet allowed him to have any suspicion of the offensive side of public gossip. Those things that had been repeated to the Mayor bore only on the question of whether Julien would stay with him for six hundred francs or accept the eight hundred offered him by the Superintendent of the workhouse.

This same Superintendent, meeting M. de Rênal in public, had given him the cold shoulder. Such behaviour on his part was not void of cunning: there are very few thoughtless acts in the provinces, where people so rarely feel emotion that they thrust their feelings down below the surface.

M. Valenod was what a hundred leagues away from Paris would be known as a *bounder*; in other words a type of man who is by nature impudent and vulgar. His triumphant career, from 1815 onwards, had made such fine natural tendencies more marked. He governed Verrières, so to speak, under orders from M. de Rênal, but as he was much more active, blushed at nothing, had a finger in everyone's pie, was always on the go, writing, talking, overlooking snubs, and advancing no claims to personal importance, he had ended up by gaining equal repute with the Mayor in the eyes of the ecclesiastical authorities. M. de Valenod had, as it were, said to the grocers of the district: 'Pick me out the two stupidest men amongst you' – to the lawyers: 'Point me out your two greatest dunces' – to the medical officers of health: 'Tell me who are your two greatest quacks.' When he had collected the most shameless members of every calling, he said to them: 'Now let's govern together.'

The way these people behaved shocked M. de Rênal. M. Valenod's obtuse vulgarity took offence at nothing, not even when young Father Maslon unsparingly challenged the truth of his statements in public. All the same, in the midst of his success, M. Valenod found need to fortify himself by little casual acts of rudeness against the harsh home-truths that everybody, as he well knew, had a right to address to him. The fears M. Appert's visit had left behind him had caused a redoubling of his activities. He had made three journeys to Besançon; he wrote several letters by every post; he sent others by unknown persons who came to visit him after dark. He had possibly made a mistake in turning old M. Chélan, the curé, out of his living; for by this vindictive step he had come to be regarded by a number of devout persons as a thoroughly wicked man. The service rendered him here, moreover, had put him entirely in the power of the Vicar-general, M. de Frilair, who asked him to undertake certain very curious commissions.

His diplomacy had brought him to this pass when he yielded to the pleasure of writing an anonymous letter. To add to his embarrassment his wife declared that she wished to have Julien in the house, an idea that vanity had put into her head.

As he was now placed M. Valenod foresaw a decisive quarrel with his former associate M. de Rênal. The latter would speak to him harshly, a thing that did not disturb him much. But he might write to Besançon, or even to Paris. All at once some minister's cousin might descend on Verrières and take over the charge of the workhouse. M. Valenod thought he would get in closer touch with the Liberals, which was why he had invited several of them to the dinner at which Julien had been present. They would be a powerful support to him against the Mayor. But then the election might supervene and it was all too clear that keeping the workhouse was incompatible with a vote for the wrong party. The tale of these artful schemes, which Madame de Rênal had very clearly divined, had been related to Julien while he gave her his arm as they went from one shop to another, and had gradually led them on to the Cours de la Fidélité, where they passed several hours very nearly as peaceful as those they had spent at Vergy.

M. Valenod had all the while been trying his best to postpone a decisive quarrel with his old patron by adopting a bold line of approach himself. That day his system worked, but made the Mayor's ill-temper worse. Never had vanity at grips with the greediest, meanest feelings a narrow-minded love of money inspires reduced any man to a more pitiable state of mind than that in which the Mayor found himself as he entered the tavern. Never, on the contrary, had his children been in a gayer, merrier mood. This contrast put the finishing touch to his petulant anger.

'From what I can see,' he said as he came in, 'my family find my presence here unwelcome.' The tone of his voice was intended to impress them.

The only answer his wife made to this was to draw him aside and explain to him the necessity of sending Julien away. The hours of happiness she had just experienced had given her back the ease and strength of mind she needed for carrying out the plan of action she had been pondering over for the past fortnight.

What finally and thoroughly upset the poor Mayor of Ver-

rières was the knowledge that people in the town were making
fun of him in public because of his fondness for money. M.
Valenod's generosity was open-handed as a robber's and he had,
for his part, acquitted himself magnificently in the five or six
most recent collections on behalf of the Brotherhood of Saint
Joseph, the Congregation of the Virgin, the Congregation of the
Holy Sacrament, etc., etc. On the register of the friars who undertook these collections M. de Rênal's name had often been seen in
its place at the bottom of the list amongst the names of country
squires of Verrières and the neighbourhood, all cunningly ranged
in order according to the amount of their donation. It was no use
his saying that he himself *made no profits*. The clergy are not
accustomed to treat such things as a matter of jest.

The pleasure of carrying one's head high all
the year through is well paid for by certain
trying moments one needs must pass.

                                                    CASTI

LET us, however, leave this little man to his little fears. Why has
he taken a man of spirit into his house, when all he needed
was one with the soul of a lackey? Why doesn't he know how to
choose his people? In the nineteenth century when an influential
man of good family meets a man of spirit, in the ordinary course
of events he either has him put to death, condemned to exile or
imprisonment, or humiliates him in such a way that the fellow
is foolish enough to die of grief. In this instance, by chance, the
man of spirit is not the one to suffer.

The great misfortune of little towns in France or of governments voted into power, as in New York, is the impossibility of
forgetting that there are men like M. de Rênal alive in this world.
In the midst of a town of twenty thousand inhabitants such men
form public opinion, and public opinion is a fearful thing in a
country that has its *Charter*. A man endowed with a noble, generous heart and who would have been your friend had he not
lived a hundred leagues away judges you in the light of public
opinion in your town, which is formed by all those fools who
chance to be born noble, rich, and mediocre. Woe to the man who
stands out above the rest!

Immediately after dinner, the whole family set off again for
Vergy; but, two days later, Julien saw them all back once more in
Verrières. Not an hour had passed before, to his great surprise, he
found out that Madame de Rênal was hiding something from
him. Every time he appeared she broke off her conversation with
her husband, and almost seemed to wish him to go away. Julien
did not wait twice for this warning. He became cold and reserved; Madame de Rênal noticed it and did not attempt any
explanation.

Is she intending to give me a successor? thought Julien. And
only yesterday she was so friendly to me! But that, so they say,
is just how these noble ladies behave – like kings who are never
so full of friendly attentions as to the minister who, on reaching
home, will find a letter announcing his dismissal from office.

Julien remarked that in these conversations, so suddenly inter-rupted whenever he came near, there was frequent mention of a certain large house belonging to the commune of Verrières which stood facing the church in the best quarter of the town, and was old, but of enormous size and plentifully furnished with rooms. What can this house and a new lover have in common? Julien wondered. In his grief he kept on repeating those charming lines of Francis I, which seemed new to him just because Madame de Rênal had taught them to him less than a month ago. How many vows, how many caresses had at that time given the lie to each of these lines?

> Woman's fancy changeth ever;
> Fool, be wise – and trust her never.

M. de Rênal set off in haste for Besançon. This journey had been decided on within the space of two hours and he seemed very much perturbed. On his return he flung a large packet wrapped in grey paper on to the table.

'There's this silly business settled,' he said to his wife.

An hour later, Julien saw the bill-poster carrying this large packet away, and followed him eagerly. I'll know the secret of this at the first street corner, he thought.

He waited impatiently behind the bill-poster who was daubing the back of the bill with his big brush. No sooner was it in posi-tion than Julien's curiosity could see the very detailed advertise-ment of the letting by public auction of the large, old house so often mentioned by name in M. de Rênal's conversations with his wife. The assigning of the lease was announced for the following day at two o'clock in the assembly room at the Town Hall, the moment the third candle went out.

Julien was greatly disappointed; he thought it very short notice. How could there be time for all the prospective bidders to get to know of it? As for the rest, this bill, which was dated a fortnight back and which he read from top to bottom in three different parts of the town, taught him absolutely nothing.

He went to look at the house to let. The caretaker, unaware of his approach, was remarking in mysterious tones to a neighbour: 'What's the use! It's a waste of time, M. Maslon promised him he'd have it for three hundred francs; and as the Mayor jibbed at this, M. de Frilair, the Vicar-general, sent for him to go to the Bishop's palace.' Julien's arrival appeared to embarrass the two friends very much and they did not add another word.

Julien did not fail to be present at the assigning of the lease. The ill-lit room was crowded; but everyone was scanning his neighbours up and down in a most peculiar way. All eyes were glued to a table on which Julien noticed three lighted candle-ends on a pewter plate. The auctioneer's clerk was calling out: 'Three hundred francs, gentlemen!'

'Three hundred francs! That's a bit too thick!' one man said under his breath to his neighbour. Julien was standing between them. 'It's worth eight hundred or more. I'll raise the bid.'

'You'll only bring trouble on your head. What would you gain by turning M. Maslon and M. Valenod against you, not to mention the Bishop and his dreadful Vicar-general and the whole of their gang.'

'Three hundred and twenty francs!' shouted the other.

'You silly ass!' his neighbour replied. 'There's one of the Mayor's spies right beside you here,' he added, pointing to Julien.

Julien turned round quickly to snub him for his remark, but neither of these natives of Franche-Comté was paying him any attention. Their self-possession restored his own. At this moment, the last candle-end went out, and the auctioneer in his drawling voice assigned the house for the next nine years to M. de Saint-Giraud, senior clerk in the prefect's office at — for three hundred and thirty francs.

As soon as the Mayor had gone, people began to pass remarks. 'There's thirty francs the commune'll have to pay for Grugeot's folly,' said one. 'But M. de Saint-Giraud will take it out on Grugeot,' came the answer. 'He'll make him feel it.'

'What a filthy shame!' said a fat man on Julien's left. 'A house I'd have given eight hundred francs for myself to make a factory. And I'd have got a bargain, too.'

'What's the use of talking?' answered a young manufacturer on the Liberal side. 'Doesn't M. de Saint-Giraud belong to the *Congrégation*? Haven't all his four children got scholarships? Poor man! The commune of Verrières has to supplement his salary by five hundred francs. That's all.'

'And to think the Mayor couldn't stop it!' a third man remarked. 'He's an Ultra, for sure, but he doesn't pinch people's property.'

'Doesn't pinch things?' put in another. 'Oh no! only just as my new shoe pinches. Everything of that sort goes into one great common purse and it's all shared out at the end of the year. But there's young Sorel. Let's be off.'

Julien returned to the house in a very bad temper, and found Madame de Rênal very sad.

'You've come from the auction?' she said to him.

'Yes, madam, I have. And there I had the honour of being taken for a spy of his Worship the Mayor.'

'If he'd listened to me he'd have gone out of town.'

At this moment M. de Rênal appeared, looking very glum. Dinner passed without a word being said. M. de Rênal gave Julien orders to accompany the children to Vergy. The journey was a sad one; Madame de Rênal tried to comfort her husband.

'You should be used to it, my dear,' she said.

In the evening they all sat silent round the family hearth, with nothing to distract them but the sound of beechwood bursting into flame. It was one of those moments of sadness such as occur even in the most united families.

Suddenly one of the children cried joyfully : 'There's the bell ! Someone's ringing the bell !'

'Damn it !' cried the Mayor. 'If that's M. de Saint-Giraud coming to bother me on the pretext of thanking me for what I've done, I'll give him a piece of my mind. It's just too much ! That fellow Valenod's the man he should feel obliged to. I'm only the man who's been compromised. What can I possibly say if those blasted Jacobin papers get hold of the story and describe me as an old buffer out of the Ark?'

Just at that moment a very good-looking man with great black side-whiskers came into the room behind the footman.

'Your Worship the Mayor, I am il signore Geronimo. Here is a letter from the Chevalier de Beauvaisis, attaché at the embassy at Naples, which he gave me for you when I left. That's only nine days ago,' added Signor Geronimo cheerfully, looking at Madame de Rênal. 'The Signor de Beauvaisis, your cousin, and my good friend, madam, tells me you speak Italian.'

The Neapolitan's genial good-humour changed this sad evening into a very merry one. Madame de Rênal was absolutely determined to give him some supper. Wishing at all costs to make Julien forget the name of spy which twice that day had sounded in his ears, she put the whole house in a bustle.

Signor Geronimo was a celebrated singer, a very well-bred yet a very jolly man, two qualities hardly compatible any longer in France. After supper he sang a little duet with Madame de Rênal

and told the most delightful stories. At one o'clock in the morning
the children protested when it was suggested to them that they
should go to bed.

'Just one more story,' said the eldest boy.

'It's my own story, signorino,' Signor Geronimo replied. 'Eight
years ago I was a young pupil like you at the Naples Conservatoire – I mean I was your age, but I hadn't the honour to be the
son of the illustrious Mayor of that charming town of Verrières.'
This remark made M. de Rênal sigh and glance at his wife.

'Signor Zingarelli,' the young singer went on, slightly exaggerating his Italian accent and making the children roar with
laughter, 'he is a terribly strict master. He isn't liked at the Conservatoire but he always wants people to act as if they liked him.
I used to go out as often as I could. I would go to the San Carlino
theatre, where I listened to music fit for the gods. But, good
heavens! how could I manage to collect the eight sous it cost to
get into the pit? That's an enormous sum of money,' he said
with a glance at the children, who laughed aloud.

'Signor Giovannone, the manager of the theatre San Carlino,
heard me sing. I was thirteen. "This child", he said, "is a treasure."

' "Would you like me to offer you an engagement, my dear
young friend?" he said.

' "How much will you give me?"

' "Forty ducats a month," he said. That, young gentlemen, is
one hundred and sixty francs. I thought I saw the heavens open.

' "But how," said I to Giovannone, "can I get such a hard man
as Zingarelli to let me go?"

' "*Lascia fare a me*," he said.'

'Leave it to me!' the eldest child exclaimed.

'Quite right, my little Lord. Signor Giovannone said to me,
"First of all, my dear boy, there's this little matter of your contract." I sign: he gives me three ducats. I'd never seen so much
money before. Then he tells me what to do.

'The next morning I ask for an interview with this terrible
Signor Zingarelli. His old manservant shows me in. "What do
you want, you rascal?" says Zingarelli. "Maestro," said I, "I'm
sorry for my bad behaviour. I'll never get out of the Conservatoire
any more by climbing over the railings. I'm going to work twice
as hard."

' "If I weren't afraid of ruining the best bass I've ever heard,
I'd shut you up, you young rogue, for a fortnight on bread and
water!"

' "Maestro," I answered, "I'm going to be an example to the whole school, *credete a me*. But I've one favour to ask. If anyone comes and asks for me to sing outside the school, please refuse to let me. Please, please, say you can't."

' "And who the deuce d'you think would ask for a scamp like you? Are you trying to make fun of me? Be off with you now, be off !" he said to me, aiming a kick at the seat of my trousers, "or you'll be shut up on dry bread, I warn you."

'One hour later, Signor Giovannone arrives to see the Director. "I have come," he says to him, "to ask you to make my fortune by letting me have Geronimo. Let him sing for me in my theatre, and this very next winter I can get my daughter married."

' "What are you going to make of a scamp like that?" says Zingarelli. "I won't consent; you shan't have him. Besides, even if I did consent, he'd never want to leave the Conservatoire. He's just sworn to me he wouldn't."

' "If it's only a question of what he wants," says Giovannone gravely, pulling the contract out of his pocket, "see here, *carta canta!* Here's his signature."

'Thereupon Zingarelli, fuming with rage, clutches hold of the bell-pull and hangs on to it, boiling with anger, he shouts : "See to it that Geronimo's turned out from the Conservatoire." So they expelled me, and there I was roaring with laughter. That same evening I sang the *aria del Moltiplico*. Punchinello wants to get married, he counts on his fingers all the things he wants for his house and every second gets tangled up in his calculations.'

'Oh ! won't you please sing us that aria, sir ?' said Madame de Rênal.

Geronimo sang it and all the company laughted till they cried. Il signor Geronimo did not go off to bed until two o'clock. The next morning he left the family delighted with his charming manners, his obliging ways, and his gaiety. M. and Madame de Rênal gave him the necessary letters of introduction to the French court.

So there's deceit everywhere you look, thought Julien. Here's Signor Geronimo going off to London with sixty thousand francs' worth of fees. But for the shrewdness of the manager of the San Carlino, his heavenly voice would not have been known and admired until ten years later.... Upon my word, I'd rather be a Geronimo than a Rênal. Society doesn't pay him so much honour, but he isn't worried by having to make assignments like the one today, and his life is a merry one.

There was one thing that astonished Julien – the weeks of loneliness he had passed at Verrières had been a period of happiness for him. He had encountered disgust and melancholy nowhere save at the dinners to which he had been invited. Hadn't he been able to read and write and muse undisturbed in this deserted house? And without being dragged away from his dreams of glory every minute by the cruel necessity of studying the motions of a base mind and, in addition, of deceiving it by hypocritical words and actions.

Could happiness then be so close at hand, he thought.... The expenses of such a life are small. I can, if I like, marry Elisa or become Fouqué's partner.... But the traveller who has just climbed a mountain sits down on the summit and finds a perfect pleasure in resting there – would he be happy if he were obliged to rest all the time?

Madame de Rénal had come to a point when her mind was full of sinister thoughts. In spite of her resolve, she had confided to Julien the whole story of the assigning of the lease. Will he then make me forget every vow I've made? she thought.

Had she seen her husband in danger, she would without hesitation have sacrificed her own life to save his. She was one of those noble, romantic creatures for whom to see the possibility of a generous act and not perform it causes remorse almost equal to that which follows an act of crime. All the same there were dark, distressing days when she found it impossible to drive out of her mind the image of the too great happiness she would feel if, suddenly left a widow, she could marry Julien.

He loved her sons much more than their father loved them; and they adored him, in spite of his just severity. She knew very well that if she married Julien she would have to leave Vergy and its so dearly loved shade. She pictured herself living in Paris, continuing to educate her sons in a way that everyone admired. Her children, she herself, and Julien would all of them be completely happy.

Strange effect of marriage – or what the nineteenth century has made of it! The boredom of married life is inevitably the death of love whenever love has preceded marriage. Yet, at the same time, as a certain philosopher has pointed out, this boredom soon leads on, with people rich enough not to have to work, to a distaste for every kind of tranquil joy and creates, in all but those women who are cold and hard by nature, a predisposition to love.

This philosopher's dictum inclines me to excuse Madame de Rênal, but no one in Verrières made excuses for her, and the whole town, though she did not suspect it, was interested in nothing but her scandalous love-affair. On account of this important matter, people were much less bored than usual that autumn.

Autumn and part of the winter passed rapidly by. They had to leave the woods of Vergy behind. Those who belonged to the best society in Verrières began to grow indignant when their denunciations produced so little effect on M. de Rênal. In less than a week those serious-minded people who find compensation for their habitual gravity in the pleasure of carrying out commissions of this kind were imparting to him the cruellest suspicions while expressing themselves in the most measured terms.

M. Valenod, who was playing for caution, had found Elisa a place with a noble and highly respected family, which included five women. Elisa, fearing, so she said, that she would not find a situation for the winter, had only asked this family for about two-thirds of what she had received at the Mayor's. On her own initiative, this young woman conceived the excellent idea of making her confession to her former curé, M. Chélan, and at the same time to the new one, in order to give them both a detailed account of Julien's love-affair.

On the stroke of six on the morning after Julien's arrival, Father Chélan sent for him. 'I'm not asking you,' he said. 'I'm imploring, and if need be ordering you to say nothing. I insist on your going off in three days' time either to the seminary at Besançon, or to your friend Fouqué, who is still of a mind to arrange a splendid future for you. I've provided for everything, I've arranged everything; but you must leave Verrières and not came back for a year.'

Julien gave no reply – he was considering whether he ought not to feel offended at the care that M. Chélan, who after all was not his father, had shown on his behalf.

'Tomorrow, at the same time,' he said at length to the curé, 'I hope to have the honour of seeing you again.'

M. Chélan, who had been reckoning by such high-handed action to carry the day with so young a man, found a good many things to say to him. While showing complete humility in his expression and outward demeanour, Julien did not open his mouth.

He left the priest's house at last and ran to warn Madame de

Rênal, whom he found in a state of desperation. Her husband had just been speaking to her with a certain amount of frankness. The natural weakness of his character, supported by the prospect of the Besançon inheritance, had made him decide to consider her as perfectly innocent. He had just confided to her what he had discovered about the strange state of public opinion in Verrières. Public opinion was at fault, people had been led astray by envious minds, but, after all, what could one do?

For a moment Madame de Rênal entertained the illusion that Julien could accept M. Valenod's offer and remain in Verrières. But she was no longer the shy and simple woman she had been a year ago; her fatal passion and her remorse had opened her eyes. Soon, however, she experienced the pain of proving to herself, while at the same time listening to her husband, that a separation, at least for a short space of time, had become unavoidable.

Away from me, she thought, Julien will sink back again into those ambitious designs so natural to a man who has no money. And I, good God! I who am so rich! — so uselessly rich as far as my happiness is concerned! he'll forget me. A man so lovable as he is is sure to be loved and love in return. Ah, unhappy woman! ... What cause have I to complain? Heaven is just, I was not good enough to stop sinning, and heaven takes my power of judgement from me. I had only to win Elisa over by giving her money; nothing would have been easier. I did not trouble to give it a moment's thought. Mad dreams of love occupied all my time. And now I'm lost.

One thing struck Julien when he told Madame de Rênal the dreadful news that he was going away — he met with no sort of selfish objection. She was obviously making an effort to keep back her tears.

'Firmness is what we need, my dear.' She cut off a lock of his hair. 'I don't know what I shall do,' she said, 'but if I should die, promise me you'll never forget my children. Whether you're far away or close at hand, try to make them good and honourable men. If there's a fresh revolution, there'll be a massacre of all the nobles, their father may possibly have to emigrate on account of that peasant who was killed on a roof. Watch over my family. Give me your hand. Good-bye, my love! These are our last moments now. Once this great sacrifice is made, I shall have the courage, I hope, to think of my reputation.'

Julien had expected despair. He was touched by the simplicity of this farewell.

'No, I won't accept your saying good-bye to me like this. I'll go away – they want me to go – you want it yourself. But three days after I've gone, I'll come back by night and see you.'

Life had become transformed for Madame de Rênal. So Julien really loved her since, of his own accord, he had thought of the idea of seeing her again! Her frightful sorrow was changed into one of the keenest stirrings of joy she had ever felt in all her life. Everything became easy to her. The certainty of seeing her lover again relieved these last moments of all their heart-rending anguish. From that instant both Madame de Rênal's behaviour, and its outward expression on her face, became noble, resolute, and completely becoming.

M. de Rênal came in shortly after, beside himself with rage. Finally he spoke to his wife of the anonymous letter he had received two months before.

'I mean to take it along to the Casino and point out to everybody that it comes from that infamous wretch Valenod, whom I rescued from beggary and made one of the richest citizens of Verrières. I'll shame him publicly for it and then I'll fight a duel with him. This is really too much!'

Good gracious! I might become a widow, thought Madame de Rênal. Almost at the same moment she said to herself, if I don't prevent this duel, as I certainly can, I shall be guilty of murdering my husband.

Never had she soothed his vanity with greater skill. In less than two hours she had made him see – and all the time for reasons he had himself discovered – that he ought to show still more marked friendship towards M. Valenod and even take Elisa back into the house. It needed courage on Madame de Rênal's part to help her make up her mind to see this young woman, who was the cause of all her misfortunes, once again. But she had got the idea from Julien.

At length, after being put back three or four times on the right track, M. de Rênal arrived of his own accord at the idea – a most grievous one to him from the monetary point of view – that the worst disaster that could happen to him would be for Julien, in the midst of the hubbub and gossip now exciting the whole of Verrières, to remain there as tutor to M. Valenod's children. It was evidently in Julien's interest to accept the Superintendent's offer. On the other hand it was important for M. de Rênal's good repute that Julien should leave Verrières and enter a seminary at Besançon or Dijon. But how could he be persuaded, and what would he live on when he got there?

M. de Rênal, seeing the imminent approach of a monetary sacrifice, was even more sunk in despair than his wife. For her part this conversation had left her in the state of a man of spirit who, tired of life, had swallowed a dose of *stramonium*. He acts, so to speak, as if he were only worked by a spring, and no longer shows any interest in anything. Thus it happened to Louis XIV to say as he lay dying: 'When I was King.' A marvellous remark!

Very early on the following morning, M. de Rênal received an anonymous letter. This one was written in the most abusive language. The grossest terms applying to his situation appeared on every line. It was the work of some envious underling or other. This letter brought him round again to the idea of fighting with M. Valenod. Soon his courage led him on to the point of considering immediate action. He left the house alone, went into the gunsmith's shop to buy some pistols, and had them loaded.

The cold fury of her husband's temper alarmed Madame de Rênal – it summoned up once more the sinister idea of widowhood she had found so difficult to drive away. She shut herself up with him. For several hours she talked to him, but all in vain; this fresh anonymous letter had made up his mind for him. She finally managed to change the courage needed for boxing M. Valenod's ears into a resolve to offer Julien six hundred francs for a year's board and lodging at the seminary. M. de Rênal, cursing a thousand times over the day he had entertained the disastrous idea of taking a tutor into his house, forgot the anonymous letter.

He was slightly consoled by an idea he did not confide to his wife. With a little skilful management, and by taking advantage of this young man's romantic notions, he hoped to persuade him to refuse M. Valenod's offer for a lesser sum.

Madame de Rênal found much more difficulty in proving to Julien that if, to suit her husband's convenience, he sacrificed the post worth eight hundred francs which the Superintendent was offering him, he could accept some kind of compensation without feeling ashamed.

'But,' insisted Julien, 'I've never had any idea of accepting this offer, not even for a moment. You've made me too accustomed to delicate ways of living, the gross vulgarity of people like that would kill me.'

Cruel necessity with her iron hand made Julien's will give way. His pride suggested to him the illusion of accepting the sum the Mayor offered him merely as a loan, and giving him a note of hand in which he undertook to repay it with interest in five years' time.

Madame de Rênal had still a few thousand francs hidden away in the little cave in the mountains. She offered them to him trembling, feeling only too well they would be angrily refused.

'Do you want,' said Julien, 'to make the memory of our love seem odious to me?'

Julien at length left Verrières. M. de Rênal felt very happy when, the fateful moment for accepting some money from him having arrived, Julien found the sacrifice too great. He refused it bluntly. M. de Rênal fell on his neck, with tears in his eyes. On Julien's asking for a testimonial he could not, in his enthusiasm, find terms magnificent enough to praise his conduct. Our hero had five louis put by and counted on asking Fouqué for a similar sum.

He was greatly moved. But when only a league from Verrières, where he left so much love behind him, there was nothing in his mind but thoughts of the delight of seeing a capital town, a great military centre like Besançon.

During this brief three days' separation Madame de Rênal was the victim of one of love's cruellest deceptions. Life was just bearable, for between herself and extreme unhappiness there was her final meeting with Julien. She counted the hours, the minutes, even, that separated her from him. At length, on the night of the third day, she heard his appointed signal in the distance. After passing through innumerable dangers, Julien stood before her.

From that moment, one thought possessed her – I'm seeing him for the last time. Far from responding to her lover's eagerness, she was like a corpse with hardly a sign of life. If she forced herself to say she loved him, it was in an awkward way that almost proved the opposite. Nothing could take her mind off the cruel thought of endless separation. Julien's suspicious nature made him believe for a moment that he was already forgotten. His stinging words to this effect were only received with big tears falling silently down, and an almost convulsive clutching of his hand.

'But how, in heaven's name, can you expect me to believe you?' was Julien's reply to his mistress's frigid protestations. 'You'd show a hundred times more genuine friendliness to Madame Der-ville, to a mere acquaintance.'

Paralysed with fear and grief, Madame de Rênal could only say: 'Nobody could possibly feel unhappier ... I wish I could die ... I feel my heart turning to ice. ...' Such were the longest replies he could get from her.

When the approach of day came to make his departure neces-sary, Madame de Rênal's tears completely ceased. Without a word, without returning his kisses, she watched him fasten a knotted rope to the window. It was all in vain for Julien to say: 'Here we are in the situation you've so earnestly wished for. From now on you can live without remorse. You won't be seeing your children in their graves whenever they're the least bit out of sorts.' She answered coldly: 'I'm sorry you can't give Stanislas a good-bye kiss.'

In the long run the lack of warmth in the embraces of this living corpse made a deep impression on Julien; for several leagues he could think of nothing else. His heart was sorely wounded, and, before going over the mountain, he kept on turning round so long as he could see the steeple of the church in Verrières.

CHAPTER 24 : *A Provincial Capital*

> What noise, what a number of busy people!
> What plans for the future in a twenty-year-
> old head! What entertainment to divert the
> mind from love!
>
> BARNAVE

AT length, on the summit of a distant mountain, he caught a
glimpse of black walls; it was the citadel of Besançon. How
different it would be for me, he said sighing, if I were entering
this fortified town to become a second lieutenant in one of the
regiments in charge of its defence!

Besançon is not only one of the prettiest towns in France, it
also abounds with high-hearted and intelligent people. But Julien
was only a simple peasant and had no means of approach to distinguished men.

He had got a layman's suit from Fouqué, and was wearing it as
he passed over the drawbridge. His mind full of the story of the
siege of 1674, he wanted to look at the ramparts and the citadel
before shutting himself up in the seminary. Two or three times
he came near to being arrested by the sentry as he was making
his way into places where military acumen, intent on getting a
yearly sum of twelve or fifteen francs by selling hay, forbids the
public to enter.

The height of the walls, the depth of the moats, the terrible
aspect of the cannon had for several hours been absorbing his
attention when he happened to pass by the big café situated on
the public walk along the ramparts. He remained motionless
with admiration; it was no use his reading the word 'Café' in-
scribed in large letters above two enormous doors – he could not
believe his eyes. He made an effort to overcome his shyness, and,
venturing to go inside, found himself in a large room some thirty
or forty feet long, with a ceiling at least twenty feet high.
Everything seemed magic to him that day.

Two games of billiards were in progress. The waiters were
calling out the score; the players were running round the billiard-
tables in the midst of a crowd of spectators; floods of tobacco
smoke, surging out of everyone's mouth, enveloped them all in
a bluish cloud. The high stature of the men, their round shoulders, their ponderous way of walking, their enormous whiskers,
the long frock coats in which they were clad, all attracted Julien's

attention. These noble scions of ancient Vesontio never spoke without shouting; they affected the pose of formidable warriors. Julien stood still, admiring them, and musing on the vastness and magnificence of a great capital like Besançon. He did not by any manner of means feel brave enough to ask those gentlemen, looking so aloof as they called out the score at billiards, to bring him a cup of coffee.

The barmaid, however, had remarked the charming face of this respectable young countryman with a little bundle under his arm, who had stopped three feet away from the stove, and was gazing at the fine white plaster bust of His Majesty. This tall young woman of Franche-Comté, with a very good figure and dressed in a manner well suited to keep up the café's reputation, had already said, 'Yes, sir? Yes, sir?' twice in a low tone of voice intended only for Julien's ear. Julien's gaze met two big, blue, and very melting eyes and realized these words were addressed to him.

He stepped briskly towards the counter and the pretty girl as if he were marching to meet the enemy, but in carrying out this important manoeuvre, he dropped his bundle.

What pity will not be inspired by our provincial in the hearts of Parisian schoolboys, who already, at fifteen, can enter a café with such an air of distinction. These lads, however, although they have such good style at fifteen, tend at eighteen to become rather loutish. The impulsive shyness found in the provinces can sometimes be conquered, and then it teaches a man to have strength of will. As he approached this very beautiful young woman who had condescended to speak to him, Julien, gaining courage by victory over his shyness, was thinking, I must tell her the truth.

'Madam, I've just come to Besançon for the first time in my life. I'd very much like a roll and a cup of coffee. I'll pay for it, of course.'

The barmaid smiled slightly and then blushed; she feared, on this handsome young man's account, ironical attention and jocular remarks on the part of the billiards players. He would be frightened and would not come there again.

'Sit yourself down here, close to me,' she said to him, pointing to a marble table almost hidden from view by the huge mahogany counter jutting out into the room.

The barmaid leant over the counter, thus giving herself a chance to show off her superb figure. Julien remarked it; his ideas took a new direction. The handsome barmaid had just put a cup, some sugar, and a roll in front of him. She lingered over summoning a waiter to bring some coffee, realizing well that with this waiter's arrival her *tête-à-tête* with Julien would be at an end.

Julien, deep in thought, was comparing this lively, fair-haired beauty with certain memories of his that often troubled him. The thought of the passion of which he had been the object almost took all his shyness away. The handsome young lady had only a minute; she read the meaning in Julien's glances.

'The smoke from these pipes makes you cough. Come and have breakfast here tomorrow before eight o'clock. I'm almost always alone at that time.'

'What's your name?' said Julien, with an engaging smile of happy shyness.

'Amanda Binet.'

'Will you allow me to send you, in an hour from now, a little parcel the same size as this one?'

The fair Amanda paused to think for a moment.

'I'm watched. What you ask might get me into trouble. However I'll write my address on a card and you can put it on your little parcel. Don't be afraid to send it.'

'My name's Julien Sorel,' the young man said. 'I've neither relations nor friends in Besançon.'

'Ah! I understand,' she said joyfully. 'You've come to study law?'

'Alas, no!' Julien replied. 'I'm being sent to the seminary.'

The most utter despondency clouded Amanda's features. She called a waiter – she had the courage to do so now. The waiter poured out Julien's coffee, without looking at him.

Amanda was taking money at the counter; Julien felt proud of having dared to speak to her; over at one of the billiard-tables a quarrel started. The shouts of the players accusing each other of lying, resounding through this enormous room, made a din that astonished Julien. Amanda was in a dreamy mood and kept her eyes lowered.

'If you like, mademoiselle,' he said boldly to her all of a sudden, 'I'll say I'm your cousin.'

This slight air of authority pleased Amanda. He's not a mere nobody, she thought. She said to him very quickly, without looking at him: 'I'm from Genlis, myself, near Dijon. Say that you're from Genlis too and my mother's cousin.'

'I won't fail to.'

'Every Thursday in summer at five o'clock the young gentlemen from the seminary pass by this café.'

'If you're thinking of me have a bunch of violets in your hand when I pass.'

Amanda looked at him in amazement; her glance turned Julien's courage into boldness; all the same he blushed deeply as he said to her: 'I feel I've fallen most violently in love with you.'

'Please speak a little lower, then,' she said.

Julien thought of recalling some phrases from an odd volume of the *Nouvelle Héloïse* he had discovered at Vergy. His memory served him well. For the past ten minutes he had been quoting the *Nouvelle Héloïse* to Mademoiselle Amanda, who was thrilled; he was enjoying his own daring gallantry when all at once an icy expression came over the face of the fair native of Franche-Comté. One of her lovers was just coming in at the door of the café.

He slouched up to the counter whistling, and looked at Julien, whose imagination, ever given to extremes, was filled with nothing but the thought of a duel. He grew very pale, pushed his cup away, assumed an air of confidence, and studied his rival very attentively. As this rival's head was bent while he poured himself out a glass of brandy at the counter, Amanda with a glance ordered Julien to lower his eyes. He obeyed her, and for two minutes remained motionless where he was, pale and resolute, thinking only of what was going to happen; he really looked very fine at that moment.

The rival had been astonished by Julien's eyes. He swallowed his glass of brandy at a gulp, said a word or two to Amanda, thrust both his hands into the pockets of his capacious top-coat, and looking at Julien went towards the billiard-table whistling. Julien sprang up wild with anger, but he did not know how to set about being insulting. He put down his little bundle, and with the most jaunty air that he could manage walked up to the billiard-table.

In vain his more prudent self was saying: If you fight a duel the moment you arrive in Besançon, you wreck your career in the Church. What does that matter? he thought. Nobody shall say I overlooked insolence from anyone.

Amanda remarked his courage; it made a very pretty contrast with his artless manners. All in a moment she preferred him to the tall young man in a top-coat. She got up and, while seeming to follow with her eyes some passer-by in the street, she quickly interposed herself between Julien and the billiard-table.

'Be careful of looking down your nose at this gentleman. He's my brother-in-law.'

'What do I care about that? He looked at me.'

'Do you wish to make me miserable? For sure, he looked at you; maybe he'll even come and speak to you. I've told him you're a relation of my mother's and that you've just come from Genlis. He's from Franche-Comté and has never travelled any farther than Dôle, on the Burgundy road. So say just what you like to him and don't be afraid of anything.'

Julien still hesitated. Her barmaid's imagination providing her with an abundant store of lies, she added very quickly: 'For sure he looked at you, but that was just at the moment he was asking me who you were. The man's a bit of a bear with everyone. He didn't mean to insult you.'

Julien's eyes followed the alleged brother-in-law. He saw him buy a ticket for the game of pool they were playing on the farther side of the two tables. Julien heard his loud voice call out truculently: 'It's my turn!' He pushed briskly past Mademoiselle Amanda and took a step or two towards the billiard-table. Amanda seized hold of his arm. 'Come and pay me first,' she said.

She's quite right, thought Julien. She's afraid I'll go away without paying her. Amanda was just as upset as he was and very red; she gave him his change as slowly as she could, all the time saying to him under her breath: 'Get out of here at once, or I won't like you any more – and yet, I like you very much.'

Julien went out, indeed, but very slowly. Isn't it my duty, he kept on saying to himself, to go and take my turn at staring at that rude fellow? This uncertainty kept him standing there for an hour, on the rampart walk in front of the café, looking to see if his man came out. He did not appear, and Julien walked away.

He had only been for a few hours in Besançon, and he had already got the better of one of his qualms. The old army surgeon, in spite of his gout, had once given him a few lessons in fencing; such was all the skill Julien found to hand to serve his anger. But this would have been no embarrassment at all if he had known how to show his anger in any other way than by a box on the ear, and had been able to tell, supposing they came to blows, whether or no his huge rival would have beaten him and left him lying.

For a poor devil like myself, without patrons or money, thought Julien, there won't be any great difference between a seminary and a prison. I must leave my layman's clothes in some inn or other and put on my black suit. If ever I manage to get out of the seminary for a few hours I can very well, with my layman's suit at hand, go and see Mademoiselle Amanda again. This reasoning was all very fine, but Julien, though he passed in front of all the inns, did not dare to enter one of them.

At last, as he was passing for the second time in front of the Hôtel des Ambassadeurs, his anxious eyes encountered those of a big stout woman with a very high colour, still fairly young, who looked both happy and jolly. He went up to her and told her his story.

'Why, for sure, my handsome little abbé,' said the landlady of the Hôtel des Ambassadeurs, 'I'll look after your clothes for you and even give them a brush fairly often. It's not a good thing, in these days, to leave a coat of good cloth untouched.' She took a key and showed him into a room herself, recommending him to write down a note of what he was leaving.

'Bless my soul! You look fine like that, M. Sorel, your reverence,' the fat woman said to him when he came downstairs to the kitchen. 'And,' she added in a low voice, 'it'll only cost you twenty sous instead of the fifty everyone pays, for we really must be kind to your poor little pocket.'

'I've twenty louis,' Julien answered with a touch of pride.

'Ah! for heaven's sake!' the good landlady replied in alarm, 'don't talk so loud. There are plenty of rogues in Besançon. They'd steal all that from you in less than no time. And take special care you don't go into any cafés, they're full of bad characters.'

'Really?' said Julien, to whom her remark had given cause for thought.

'Never come anywhere except to my house. You'll always find a good friend here, mind you, and a good dinner, too, for twenty sous. That's saying something, I should hope. Now go and sit yourself down at table, and I'll serve you myself.'

'I couldn't eat anything,' said Julien, 'I'm too excited. When I leave your house I'm entering the seminary.'

The good woman would not let him go until she had filled his pockets with food. Julien at last went on his way towards this place of dread. The landlady, standing on the doorstep, pointed out the road he should take.

CHAPTER 25 : *The Seminary*

> Three hundred and thirty-six dinners at 85
> centimes a head, three hundred and thirty-six
> suppers at 38 centimes, a cup of chocolate for
> anyone with a right to it – How much can I
> make on my tender?
>
> *Besançon's Valenod*

FROM a long way off he saw the gilded iron cross above the door; he made his way slowly towards it; his knees seemed to be giving way under him. So there's this hell on earth, he thought, from which I shall never be able to get out! He finally made up his mind to ring. The noise of the bell resounded as in a deserted house.

At the end of ten minutes, a pale-faced man dressed in black came to let him in. This porter had a curious cast of face. The bulging green irises of his eyes were round as those of a cat; the rigid outline of his eyebrows announced him totally incapable of kindly feeling; his thin lips widened into a half-circle over protruding teeth. All the same no trace of crime was apparent on this visage, but rather that utter insensitivity which inspires so much more terror in the young. The only emotion Julien's rapid glance could dimly perceive on this long, sanctimonious face was a profound contempt for anything one might wish to talk to him about which was not concerned with heaven.

Julien raised his eyes with an effort and, in a voice that quavered in response to his beating heart, he explained that he wished to speak to M. Pirard, the Rector of the seminary. Without saying a word the man in black made a sign to him to follow. They went up two storeys by a broad staircase with wooden banisters; its warped steps slanted sharply on the side opposite the wall and looked as if they were about to come tumbling down. A little door, above which was a great funereal cross made of deal and painted black, was opened after some difficulty, and the porter showed him into a low and gloomy room with whitewashed walls, on which hung two large pictures time had blackened. There, Julien was left alone. He felt utterly discouraged; his heart was beating violently; he would have been glad to have dared to weep. A deathly silence reigned throughout the house.

At the end of a quarter of an hour, the porter with the sinister

face appeared again on the threshold of a door at the other end
of the room, and, without condescending to speak, beckoned to
him to come forward. He entered a room even larger than the
first and very badly lit. It also had whitewashed walls, but
was not furnished. Only in a corner near the door Julien noticed
in passing a deal bed, two straw-bottomed chairs, and a little un-
padded armchair of deal.

Right at the other end of the room, close to a little window
with yellowed panes, and garnished with one or two flower vases
in a very dirty condition, he saw a man in a tattered cassock
sitting at a table. He seemed to be angry and was picking up one
by one a crowd of little slips of paper which he arranged in order
on his table after writing a word or two on each. He did not
notice Julien's presence. The latter stood stockstill in the middle
of the room, where he had been left by the porter, who had gone
out shutting the door behind him.

Ten minutes passed in this way; the shabbily dressed man still
went on writing. Julien's terror and agitation were such that he
felt ready to sink to the floor. A philosopher might have said,
perhaps mistakenly : 'Such is the violent impression ugliness
makes on a nature formed to love what is beautiful.'

The man who was writing raised his head. Julien did not notice
this until a moment had passed, and even when he saw the terrifying glance directed at him he still stood there motionless, as if
struck dead by the sight. Julien's troubled eyes could barely distinguish a long, narrow face completely covered in red spots,
save on the forehead where a deathly pallor could be seen.
Between these reddened cheeks and this white forehead, two
little black eyes, of a kind to strike terror into the bravest heart,
were gleaming at him. The vast contours of this forehead were
framed in thick, lank tufts of jet-black hair.

'Will you or won't you come nearer?' said the man at last,
impatiently.

Julien advanced with faltering steps and at length, almost ready
to fall and pale as he never had been before in his life, he stopped
three feet away from the little deal table covered with slips of
paper.

'Nearer,' said the man.

Julien advanced once more, with his hand outstretched as if he
were looking for something on which he could lean for support.

'Your name?'

'Julien Sorel.'

'You've arrived very late,' he was told, as once again these terrible eyes were fixed on him.

Julien could not bear that glance, stretching out his hand as if trying to hold himself up, he fell full length on the floor. The man rang the bell. Julien had only lost the use of his eyes and the power to move; he heard steps approaching.

He was picked up and set down in the little deal armchair. He heard this terrifying man say to the porter: 'Apparently he's fallen down in an epileptic fit. That's the final touch!'

When Julien was able to open his eyes, the red-faced man was going on with his writing; the porter had vanished. I must be brave, our hero said to himself, and above all hide what I'm feeling. He felt violently sick. If something dreadful happens, he thought, heaven knows what they'll think of me! The man left off writing at last and with a sidelong glance at Julien said, 'Are you in a fit state to answer me?'

'Yes, sir,' Julien replied in a faint voice.

'Ah! that's fortunate.'

The man in black had half risen to his feet and was hunting impatiently for a letter in one of the drawers of his deal table. It creaked as it opened. He found the letter, sat slowly down, and looking at Julien again with a glance calculated to snatch from him what little life he had remaining, said to him: 'You have been recommended to me by M. Chélan. He was the best curé in the diocese, and upright man if anyone is, and a friend of mine for the last thirty years.'

'Ah! then it is M. Pirard to whom I have the honour of speaking,' said Julien in the very faintest voice.

'Obviously,' the Rector replied, looking at him crossly.

The gleam of his little eyes grew brighter, and this was followed by an involuntary movement of the muscles at the two corners of his mouth. It was the expression of a tiger enjoying a foretaste of the pleasure of devouring its prey.

'Chélan's letter is short,' he said as if to himself. '*Intelligenti pauca*. At the present time, one cannot write too little.'

He read the letter aloud. 'I am sending you,' wrote M. Chélan, 'Julien Sorel of this parish, whom I christened nearly twenty years ago. He is the son of a carpenter, who is rich but gives him nothing. Julien will be a notable worker in our Lord's vineyard. He is not lacking in memory or intelligence and he is thoughtful. But will his vocation last? Is it sincere?'

'*Sincere!*' repeated Father Pirard with an air of astonishment, as

he glanced at Julien; but his expression was already a little less
denuded of all human feeling. '*Sincere!*' he repeated, lowering his
voice and resuming his reading.

'I ask you' (the letter went on) 'for a scholarship for Julien Sorel;
he will earn it by undergoing the necessary tests. I have taught
him a little theology, the theology of the good, old school of men
like Bossuet, the two Arnaulds, and Fleury. If the young man in
question does not seem to you suitable, send him back to me. The
Superintendent of the workhouse, whom you know well, is offering him eight hundred francs as his children's tutor. I am at peace
in myself, thanks be to God. I am getting accustomed to that terrible shock. *Vale et me ama.*'

Father Pirard, slowing down his voice as he read the signature,
pronounced the word 'Chélan' with a sigh.

'He is at peace,' he said. 'His virtues indeed deserved this reward. God grant the same to me, if there be occasion for it!'
Looking heavenwards, he crossed himself. At the sight of this holy
sign Julien felt some lessening of the deep horror which had
chilled him to the marrow ever since he entered this house.

'I have here three hundred and twenty candidates for the most
holy of all callings,' Father Pirard said at last, in a tone of voice
which was severe, but not unkindly. 'Only some seven or eight
of them are recommended to me by men like Father Chélan. So,
out of three hundred and twenty-one, you will be the ninth. My
protection, however, implies neither favouritism nor indulgence,
but an increased care for you and more severity towards your
vices. Go over there and lock the door.'

Julien attempted to walk and succeeded in not falling. He
noticed, close to the door by which he had come in, a little window looking out towards the country. He gazed at the trees; the
sight of them did him good; it was just as if he had caught a
glimpse of old friends.

'*Loquerisne linguam latinam?* (Do you speak Latin?)' Father
Pirard said to him as he was coming back.

'*Ita, pater optime* (yes, most excellent Father),' Julien answered,
beginning to recover his senses a little. Certainly no one in the
world had seemed less excellent than Father Pirard during the last
half hour.

The conversation continued in Latin. The expression in the
abbé's eyes grew gentler; Julien was beginning to regain his self-
possession. How weak of me, he thought, to let myself be imposed
on by these outward signs of goodness! This man will turn out

quite simply to be a rogue like M. Maslon. Julien congratulated himself on having hidden almost all his money inside his boots.

Father Pirard examined Julien in theology, and was surprised at the extent of his knowledge. His astonishment increased when he concentrated his questions on the Holy Scriptures. But when he arrived at questions on patristic doctrine he saw that Julien did not know Saint Jerome, Saint Augustine, Saint Bonaventure, Saint Basil, etc., even by name.

In fact, thought Father Pirard, there's the fatal leaning towards Protestantism with which I've always reproached Chélan – a thorough, and indeed too thorough, knowledge of the Holy Scriptures. (Julien had just been speaking to him, without being questioned on the matter, about the *actual* date at which Genesis, the Pentateuch, etc., had been written.)

Where does all this endless argumentation concerning the Holy Scriptures lead us, thought Father Pirard, if it isn't to *examination of one's own conscience*, that is to say to the most fearful extreme of Protestantism? And, apart from such indiscreet learning, nothing touching the Fathers of the Church to balance such a tendency.

But the astonishment of the Rector of the seminary knew no bounds when, on questioning Julien about the authority of the Pope, in expectation of hearing maxims of the ancient Gallican Church, the young man recited to him the whole of M. de Maistre's book.

The man Chélan is a strange individual, thought Father Pirard. Has he shown him that book to teach him to take it as a joke?

He questioned Julien all in vain in the attempt to find out if he seriously believed in M. de Maistre's doctrines. The young man could only answer from what he remembered. From this moment Julien was really at his ease and felt master of himself. At the end of a long examination it seemed to him that M. Pirard's severity towards him was no longer anything but assumed. And indeed, but for that austere rule of gravity which for fifteen years he had imposed on himself in dealing with his pupils, the Rector of the seminary would, on behalf of logic, have embraced Julien; such perspicacity, such precision, and such clear-cut intelligence were to be found in his answers.

Here is a sane, courageous mind, he said to himself. But *corpus debile* (the body is weak).

'Do you often fall down like that?' he said to Julien in French as he pointed to the floor.

'It's the very first time in my life,' said Julien, blushing like a child. 'The sight of the porter's face froze me stiff.'

Father Pirard almost smiled. 'There you see the effect of the vain pomps and vanities of this world. You are accustomed to laughing faces which are, indeed, the theatres where falsehood plays it part. Truth, sir, is austere. But is it not our task here below to be austere ourselves? You must watch to keep your conscience on guard against this weakness – *too much sensibility to vain outward graces.*'

'If you had not been recommended to me,' Father Pirard said, reverting with marked pleasure to the Latin tongue, 'I repeat, if you'd not been recommended to me by such a man as Father Chélan, I would talk to you in the vain language of this world to which it seems you are too much accustomed. A scholarship such as you ask for, with all your expenses covered, is the most difficult thing in the world to obtain. But Father Chélan has deserved very little after fifty-six years of apostolic labours if he cannot dispose of one scholarship at the seminary.'

Having said this Father Pirard recommended Julien not to join any secret society or *congrégation* without his consent.

'I give you my word of honour,' said Julien with the open-hearted enthusiasm of a well-bred man.

For the first time the Rector of the seminary smiled. 'That expression,' he said, 'is not permissible here. It recalls too much the vain sense of honour of men of the world that leads them into so many errors and often into crime. Your obedience is due to me by virtue of the Bull *Unam Ecclesiam* of his Holiness the Pope, paragraph 17. I am your ecclesiastical superior. In this house, my very dear son, to hear is to obey. How much money have you?'

(Now we're getting to it! thought Julien. That's the reason for the 'very dear son'.)

'Thirty-five francs, father.'

'Write down very carefully what use you make of this money. You will have to account for it to me.'

This painful session had lasted three hours. Julien fetched the porter.

'Put Julien Sorel in cell 103,' said Father Pirard to the man. As a great mark of distinction he was allowing Julien a room to himself. 'Take his trunk there,' he added.

Julien, looking down, recognized the trunk directly in front of him. For three hours he had been looking at it and had not realized it was his.

When they arrived at number 103 it was a tiny little room, eight foot square, on the top floor of the house. Julien noticed that it looked out towards the ramparts, and beyond them could be seen the lovely plain which the Doubs cuts off from the city.

What a charming view! cried Julien; but while talking thus to himself he had no feeling of what his words expressed. The very violent sensations he had experienced in the little time he had been in Besançon had completely exhausted his strength. He sat down by the window on the single wooden chair in his cell and fell fast asleep. He did not hear the bell ring for supper nor for evensong; they had forgotten about him. When the first rays of sunlight woke him the following morning he found himself lying on the floor.

> I am all alone in the world, no one condescends to give me a thought. All those whom I see rising to success have an impudence and a hardness of heart I do not find in myself. They hate me because I am naturally disposed to kindness. Ah! I shall die soon, either of hunger, or of grief at finding men so stony-hearted.
> YOUNG*

H E hurriedly brushed his clothes and went downstairs. He was late and was severely scolded by one of the assistant masters. Instead of seeking to make excuses, Julien crossed his arms on his breast. '*Peccavi, pater optime*' (Father, I have sinned, I confess my fault), he said with an air of contrition.

This first appearance was a great success. The more knowing among the students saw that they had to do with a man who knew more than the elements of his profession. Julien saw himself the object of general curiosity, but they found nothing in him but silence and reserve. According to the rules of conduct he had drawn up for himself, he looked on his three hundred and twenty fellow-students as enemies – the most dangerous enemy of all in his eyes was Father Pirard.

A few days later Julien had to choose a confessor, and a list was handed to him. Good heavens! what do they take me for? he thought. Do they think I don't understand *what's what*? And he chose Father Pirard.

Although he had no idea of it, this was a decisive step. A young seminarist, quite a boy, who from the very first day had declared himself Julien's friend, told him that if he had chosen the Vice-Rector, M. Castanède, he would perhaps have acted more wisely.

'Father Castanède,' the young seminarist added, bending over towards his ear, 'is an enemy of M. Pirard, who's suspected of being a Jansenist.'

Every one of our hero's first steps, for all he thought himself so cautious, were, like his choice of a confessor, careless blunders. Led astray by all the overweening confidence natural to a man with imagination, he took the will for the deed, and thought him-

* Translated from the French. I cannot trace the original. [Tr.]

self past master in hypocrisy. His folly went to such lengths that he reproached himself for his success in this art of weaklings.

Alas! it's my only weapon! he said to himself. In another age the way I'd have *earned my bread* would have been by deeds that speak for themselves carried out in the face of the enemy.

Some nine or ten of the seminarists lived in an odour of sanctity and had visions like those of Saint Theresa or of Saint Francis on Mount Verna in the Apennines, at the time he received the imprint of the sacred wounds. This was, however, a great secret and kept hidden by their friends. The poor young visionaries themselves were nearly always in the infirmary. A hundred or so of the others combined robust faith with indefatigable industry. They worked until they made themselves ill, though without learning very much. Two or three others stood out among the rest on account of their genuine talent. Amongst these was a student named Chazel; but Julien felt a dislike for them and they for Julien.

The remainder of the three hundred and twenty-one students were merely uncouth fellows who could never be sure of understanding the Latin words they were repeating all day long. Almost all of them were peasants' sons, who preferred to earn their bread reciting a handful of Latin words rather than by hacking up the soil. It was after observing this that Julien, from the very first few days, promised himself a swift success. In every calling, he thought, intelligent minds are needed, for after all there is work to be done. Under Napoleon, I'd have been a sergeant; amongst all these future parish priests, I'll be a Vicar-general.

All these poor devils, compelled to work from childhood, he added, have lived up to the time of their arrival here on sour milk and black bread. In their cottages, they did not have meat to eat more than five or six times a year. Like those Roman soldiers who found war a period for rest, these uncouth peasants are enchanted with the delights the seminary has to offer.

Julien could never read in those lacklustre eyes of theirs anything more than the after-dinner sensation of bodily appetite appeased or the expectation of bodily pleasure preceding the meal. Such were the people amongst whom he had to make his mark. But what Julien did not know, and what no one thought of telling him, was that to take first place in the various courses on doctrine, Church history, etc., etc., attended by the seminarists was in their eyes nothing but the sin of *vainglory*.

Ever since the days of Voltaire, or since the introduction of government by two Chambers, which is at bottom nothing more or less than the bringing in of *suspicion and self-examination* and teaching the mind of a nation the bad habit of self-mistrust, the Church in France seems to have realized that its chief enemies are books. It is surrender of the heart that stands for everything in its eyes. To succeed in one's studies, even though they be sacred duties, is suspect – and rightly so. Who can prevent a man of superior intellect from going over to the other side as did Siéyès and Grégoire! The trembling Church clings to the Pope as to her only hope of salvation. The Pope alone can attempt to stifle self-examination and by means of the pious pomp and ceremony of his court make an impression on the sick and weary minds of worldly men and women.

Julien, half discerning these various truths which, nevertheless, every word uttered in a seminary tends to prove false, sank into a mood of the deepest melancholy. He worked hard, and quickly succeeded in learning a number of things very useful to a priest, but very false in his eyes, and in which he felt no sort of interest at all. He believed there was nothing else he could do.

Am I forgotten then by all the world? he thought. He did not know that Father Pirard had received and thrown into the fire one or two letters with the Dijon postmark in which, for all the extreme propriety of their language, the most ardent passion found an outlet. It seemed as if deepest remorse was striving with this love. So much the better, thought Father Pirard, at least the young man has not loved an irreligious woman.

One day Father Pirard opened a letter that seemed half effaced by tears; it was a letter of eternal farewell.

Heaven at last [so the writer told Julien] *has granted me grace, not to hate the author of my sin – he will always be what I hold most dear on earth – but to hate the sin itself. I have made my sacrifice, dearest – not without tears, as you can see. The salvation of those beings to whom I owe myself – and whom you have loved so fondly – has won the victory. A just, but terrible God can no longer take vengeance on them for their mother's crimes. Goodbye, Julien – be just in all your dealings with men.*

The end of this letter was almost illegible. It gave an address in Dijon, and yet it was hoped that Julien would never answer it, or at least would answer in words that a woman restored to virtue could hear without blushing.

Encouraged by the indifferent food provided by the man who contracted for dinners at the seminary at 83 centimes a head, Julien's melancholy was beginning to affect his health when one morning Fouqué suddenly appeared in his room.

'At last I've managed to get in,' he said. 'I've come five times to Besançon, honestly I have, just on purpose to see you. And always to find a closed door staring me in the face. I've posted someone to watch at the entrance to the seminary. Why the devil don't you ever go out?'

'It's a trial of strength I've imposed on myself.'

'I find you greatly changed, but anyhow I've seen you at last. Two fine silver crowns worth five francs apiece have taught me what a fool I was not to have offered them on my first trip here.'

Conversation between the two friends prolonged itself endlessly. Julien changed colour when Fouqué said to him: 'By the way, have you heard? Your pupils' mother has become remarkedly devout.' He spoke in the offhand way that makes such an extra-ordinary impression on passionate natures to whose dearest in-terests the speaker all unwittingly deals a devastating blow.

'Yes, my dear chap,' he added, 'most ardently devout. It's said she goes on pilgrimages. But to the everlasting shame of M. Maslon, who has been spying so long on Father Chélan, Madame de Rênal wouldn't have anything to do with him. She goes to confession at Dijon or Besançon.'

'She comes to Besançon?' cried Julien, blushing to the roots of his hair.

'Yes, very often,' replied Fouqué with a quizzical air.

'Have you any copies of the *Constitutionnel* on you?'

'What did you say?' asked Fouqué.

'I'm asking you if you have any copies of the *Constitutionnel*,' Julien answered. 'They cost thirty sous apiece here.'

'What! you've Liberals! Even in the seminary!' cried Fouqué. 'My poor France!' he added, imitating Father Maslon's hypo-critical, honeyed tones.

This visit would have made a deep impression on our hero, but that, the very next day, a remark addressed to him by the young seminarist from Verrières who seemed to him such a boy led him to make an important discovery. Ever since he had been in the seminary Julien's conduct had been nothing but a series of false steps. He laughed bitterly at himself.

Actually, he handled all the important actions in his life very skilfully, but he paid little attention to details, and details are all that the shrewdest minds in a seminary think about. His fellow-students, in consequence, already looked upon him as a *freethinker*. A host of little insignificant acts had given him away.

In their eyes he was convicted of the heinous vice of thinking for himself and of forming his own judgements instead of blindly following authority and example. Father Pirard had been of no help to him at all; he had not addressed a single word to him outside the confessional and even there he was more given to listening than speaking. It would have been a very different thing if he had chosen Father Castanède.

From the moment Julien became aware of his folly his boredom left him. He wanted to find out the full extent of the harm and, with this in view, he abandoned in some slight degree his proud and stubborn silence by means of which he was wont to keep his fellow-students at a distance. Then it was that they took their revenge. His advances were greeted with a contempt that amounted to derision. He realized that since his arrival in the seminary there had not been a single hour, particularly during recreation, which might not have led them to draw conclusions either for or against him, might not have increased the number of his enemies or won the goodwill of some seminarist or other who was genuinely good, or was a little less uncouth than the rest. The harm he had to undo was immense, the task of undoing it extremely arduous. Henceforth Julien was on his guard – he had to construct an entirely new character for himself.

He found it very difficult, for instance, to control the movement of his eyes. They were not without reason kept lowered in places such as this. How easily I took things for granted at Verrières, thought Julien. I thought I was living then, but I was only preparing myself for life. Here I am at last in the world as I shall find it till I have finished playing my part, with enemies all around me. How immensely difficult it is, he went on thinking, to play the part of hypocrite every minute – it's enough to make the labours of Hercules pale beside it. The Hercules of modern times would be a man like Sixtus V, whose humility, for fifteen consecutive years, deceived the forty cardinals who had known him impetuous and arrogant during the whole of his youth.

So learning is considered nothing here! he said with scornful regret. Progress in the knowledge of dogma, in Church history, etc. counts in appearance only. Everything said on such matters is only designed to entrap such fools as me. My only merit, alas! consisted in my rapid progress, in my ability to swallow such humbug. Do they at bottom value this nonsense at its true worth? Do they judge it as I do? And I was idiot enough to be proud of this! The fact that I always get first place has only served to make me bitter enemies. Chazel, who is a better scholar than myself, always chucks in a blunder or two in his essays to get himself put down fifth on the list. If he does come out top, it's merely out of absence of mind. Ah! how useful one word, just one little word, from M. Pirard would have been to me.

From the moment Julien was undeceived, the lengthy exercises ascetic piety enjoins, such as saying the rosary five times a week, intoning canticles to the Sacred Heart, etc., etc., which once had seemed to him such a deadly bore, became the most interesting and active moments of his life. After thinking seriously about himself and seeking above all things not to overestimate his own capabilities, Julien did not all at once aspire, as did the other seminarists who set an example to the others, to fill every minute with *significant* acts, in other words those that give proof of a kind of Christian perfection. There is, in seminaries, a way of eating a boiled egg that indicates the progress made in a life of piety. Will the reader, who possibly smiles at this, kindly remember the many mistakes made by the abbé Delille in eating an egg, when invited to dine with a great lady at the court of Louis XVI.

Julien attempted at first to reach the stage of *non culpa*, that is to say the position of the young seminarist whose way of walking and of moving his arms, his eyes, etc., although not indicative of worldly preoccupations, all the same shows as yet no sign that the whole of his being is absorbed in thoughts of the other world or the *utter nothingness* of this one.

Julien was constantly finding, written with a piece of charcoal on the walls of the corridors, such phrases as this – What are sixty years of trial, weighed in the balance against an eternity of bliss or an eternity of boiling oil in hell! He no longer treated such things with contempt; he understood he must keep them ceaselessly before his eyes. What shall I be doing my whole life long? he would say to himself – I shall be selling seats in heaven to the faithful. How will such a place be made visible before their eyes? – By the difference between my outside appearance and that of a layman.

After several months of incessant application, Julien still continued to look as if he *thought*. Neither his way of moving his eyes nor of controlling his mouth proclaimed the absolute faith that is ready to believe everything and uphold everything, even to the

point of martyrdom. It made Julien furious to find himself surpassed in a thing of this kind by the roughest, rudest peasants.
There were very good reasons why they should not wear a
thoughtful air.

What trouble did he not take to assume an expression denoting
blind and fervent faith prepared to believe and suffer anything,
such a cast of face as is frequently found in monasteries in Italy
and of which, for us who are laymen, Guercino has left such perfect examples in his religious pictures.

On high festivals, sausages and pickled cabbage were served out
to the seminarists. Julien's neighbours at table noticed that he was
insensitive to such delights. That was one of his first crimes; his
fellow-students saw in it an odious symptom of the most asinine
hypocrisy. 'Look at that proud, finicking fellow,' they would say,
'posing as if he despised his portion. Sausages and pickled cabbage! Shame on him, nasty uppish fellow! The devil's darling!'

Alas! the ignorance of these young peasants, who are my companions, is of immense advantage to them, so Julien would exclaim in moments of discouragement. No teacher has to rid them,
on their arrival at the seminary, of such a frightful number of
worldly notions as I brought with me and which, no matter what
I do, they contrive to read in my face.

Julien would study, with attentiveness bordering on envy, the
most uncouth among these young peasants on their arrival at the
seminary. At the moment they were stripped of their rateen
jackets and made to don black cassocks, all the education they
had was limited to a vast and boundless respect for cash, *hard or
soft*, as they say in Franche-Comté. Such is the consecrated, epic
term in that province for the sublime idea of ready money.

For such seminarists, as for the heroes of Voltaire's tales, happiness consists above all in a really good dinner. Julien discovered
in almost all of them an inborn respect for the man who wears
a broadcloth suit. A feeling like this appreciates at its worth, or
even below its worth, the system of *distributive justice*, as ad-
ministered in our courts of law. 'What can one gain,' they would
often say to each other, 'from going to law with one of those *big
pots*?' This is the term they use in the Jura valleys to describe a
wealthy man. You can judge of their respect for the wealthiest
concern of all – the Government! In the eyes of these peasants of
Franche-Comté, failure to smile respectfully at the mere mention
of the Prefect's name passes for rashness; and rashness in a poor
man is promptly punished by lack of bread.

After being at first as it were stifled by a feeling of contempt, Julien's heart was finally filled with pity. It had often happened that the fathers of his classmates had come home to their cottages on a winter's evening to find neither bread nor chestnuts nor potatoes there. What is surprising then, thought Julien, if in their eyes the happy man is first and foremost one who has just dined well, and next to him the man who owns a good suit of clothes? My companions have a settled vocation, that is to say they see in the ecclesiastical calling a prolongation of this sort of happiness – a good dinner and a warm suit for winter.

Julien happened to hear a young seminarist say to his friend: 'Why shouldn't I become Pope like Sixtus V, who was once a swineherd?'

'It's only the Italians who are chosen as Pope,' his friend replied. 'But certainly some amongst us will be chosen by lot for positions as Vicars-general, Canons, and, maybe, Bishops. M. P—, who's Bishop of Châlons, is a cooper's son. That's what my father is.'

One day, in the middle of a class on dogma, M. Pirard sent for Julien. The poor fellow was delighted to escape from the physical and moral atmosphere in which he was immersed.

Julien met with the same kind of welcome from the Rector as had so greatly terrified him on the day he entered the seminary.

'Pray explain to me what's written on this playing card,' he said to Julien, looking at him in such a way that he felt he would sink into the earth.

Julien read the words: 'Amanda Binet, Café de la Girafe, before eight o'clock. Say you're from Genlis and my mother's cousin.' He realized the immensity of his danger. Father Castanède's secret police had stolen this address from him.

'The day I entered here I was trembling,' he answered, looking at Father Pirard's forehead, for he could not face his terrible eye. 'M. Chélan had told me that this place was full of tale-telling and spitefulness of every kind; spying on one's companions and informing against them is encouraged here. Heaven wills it should be so, to let young priests see life as it is and inspire them with a disgust for this world and its pomps.'

'So you'd even try your eloquence on me,' said Father Pirard, in a rage. 'You young scoundrel!'

'At Verrières,' replied Julien coldly, 'my brothers beat me whenever they had reason to be jealous of me.'

'Keep to the point! To the point!' cried Father Pirard, almost beside himself.

Without allowing himself to be in the least intimidated, Julien resumed his tale.

'On the day I arrived in Besançon, round about midday I felt hungry and I went into a café. My heart was full of aversion for so profane a place, but I thought my lunch would cost me less than at an inn. A lady, who seemed to be the proprietress, took pity on me because I looked inexperienced. "Besançon is full of rogues," she told me. "I'm afraid for you, sir. If anything bad should happen to you, rely on me for help. Send to my house before eight o'clock. If the porters at the seminary refuse to take your message, say you're my cousin and born at Genlis. . . ." '

'The truth of all this foolish chatter will be checked,' cried Father Pirard, finding himself unable to keep still where he was and walking to and fro in the room. 'Go back to your cell !'

The abbé followed Julien in and locked the door. He then began to search his trunk, at the bottom of which he had hidden the fatal card. There was nothing missing from this trunk, but several things had been disarranged; and yet he always kept the key with him. What good luck, thought Julien, that during all the time of my blindness I never made use of M. Castanède's leave to go out, though he offered it me frequently and with a kindness I now understand. I might perhaps have been stupid enough to change my suit and go and see the fair Amanda. I'd have ruined myself. When they despaired of profiting from knowledge gained in this way they informed against me so as not to lose their advantage.

Two hours later, the Rector sent for him. 'You did not lie to me,' he said, looking less severe. 'But keeping this address is an act of imprudence the true seriousness of which you cannot grasp. Unhappy boy ! In ten years' time it may be used against you.'

CHAPTER 27 : *First Experience of Life*

> The present age, good God! It is the Ark of
> the Lord – woe to the man who lays his hand
> on it!
> DIDEROT

THE reader will, I hope, kindly allow us to give very few clear or precise details of this period in Julien's life. This does not mean that our knowledge of them is lacking, very much the opposite; but possibly what he saw in the seminary is too dark in tone for the gentler shades of colour we have tried to preserve in these pages. Our contemporaries, who are pained by certain things, are unable to call them to mind without a feeling of horror which nullifies any other kind of pleasure, even that of reading a story.

Julien had succeeded very ill in his attempts at a hypocritical demeanour; he experienced moments of disgust and even utter discouragement, knowing himself a failure, and a failure, moreover, in a most miserable profession. The least assistance from outside would have sufficed to give him new courage, for the obstacle to be overcome was not great; but he was all alone, like a derelict ship in the midst of the Atlantic.

And even if I were to succeed, he said to himself, I'd have to spend my life in such bad company! – gluttons with not an idea in their heads beyond the bacon omelette they'll gobble down at dinner, or men like Father Castanède, for whom no crime is too black! They will attain to power – but, heaven help us, at what a price!

Man's will is strong; I read it everywhere; but is it strong enough to overcome disgust like this? The task of great men was an easy one; however terrible the danger, they found some beauty in it – who but myself can understand the ugliness around me!

This was the most critical moment of his life. It would have been so easy for him to enlist in one of those fine regiments stationed at Besançon! He could become a teacher of Latin – he needed so little to live on! But then he would no longer have a career, no longer a future to stir his imagination – that would be death. Let me give you one of his melancholy days in detail.

In my presumption, he said to himself one morning, I have often congratulated myself on being different from other young peasants. Well, I've lived long enough to see that *difference en-*

genders hate. This great truth had been revealed to him by one of his most galling failures.

For a whole week long he had worked hard to make himself agreeable to a student who lived in the odour of sanctity. He was walking in the courtyard with him, submissively listening to the most tedious nonsense. All at once the weather turned stormy, the thunder growled and the saintly student, rudely pushing him aside, exclaimed: 'Listen now, it's each one for himself in this world. I don't want a thunderbolt to burn me. God may send lightning to strike you down as an infidel, as another Voltaire.'

His teeth clenched with rage and his eyes wide-open towards a sky furrowed with lightning, Julien cried in his heart: I'd deserve to be overwhelmed by it if I went to sleep in a storm! On to the conquest of another snivelling hypocrite!

The bell rang for Father Castenède's class on Church history. These young peasants, so frightened by the painful toils and poverty their fathers had endured, were taught that day by the abbé that the Government, which in their eyes was so terrible a thing, had no real or legitimate power save in virtue of what was delegated to it by God's representative on earth.

'Make yourselves worthy of the Pope's loving kindness by the holiness of your lives and by your obedience. Be *like a rod in his hands*,' he added, 'and you will attain to a proud position from which you will have supreme command, out of reach of all control; an impregnable position, of which the Government pays a third of the stipend, and the faithful, educated by your sermons, the other two-thirds.'

As he was going out of his lecture, M. Castanède stopped in the courtyard and spoke to the students grouped in a circle round him. 'It can be truly said of a parish priest,' he remarked, 'that the post is worth what the man himself is worth. I myself, who am speaking to you here, have known of parishes up in the mountains where the perquisites were worth much more than those of many curés in town. There was as much money, without counting the fat capons, the eggs, the fresh butter, and innumerable other agreeable trimmings. And up there the curé is unquestionably the first man in the place – not a single good meal to which he isn't invited and where he is not lavishly entertained, etc.'

M. Castanède had hardly gone to his room before the students separated into groups. Julien was not included in any one of them; he was left alone as the black sheep of the party. In every group he saw a student toss a halfpenny into the air; if he guessed heads or tails correctly, his companions concluded he would soon have a parish richly furnished with perquisites.

Anecdotes followed. A certain young priest, who had hardly been ordained a year, having offered a tame rabbit as a gift to an aged curé's maidservant, had managed to get asked for as curate, and the curé having died shortly after, he had a few months later taken his place in the comfortable living. Another had contrived to get himself chosen to succeed to a living in a very prosperous market town, just by being present at every meal at the table of a paralytic old priest and cutting up his chicken for him. Seminarists, like all young people in every profession, exaggerate the effect of any little circumstance out of the ordinary run that strikes the imagination.

I must get inured to these conversations, thought Julien. Whenever they were not talking of sausages or comfortable livings, the students would discuss with each other the worldly side of ecclesiastical doctrine, such as disputes between bishops and prefects, between mayors and parish priests. Julien saw the idea of a second God taking shape, but a God much more to be feared and much more powerful than the first – this second God was the Pope. The students said among themselves, but with bated breath and at times when they were quite sure of not being overheard by Father Pirard, that if the Pope did not put himself to the trouble of nominating every prefect and every mayor in France, it was because he had handed over this task to the King of France in naming him the eldest son of the Church.

It was round about this time that Julien got the idea of turning M. de Maistre's *Livre du Pape* to advantage and winning some esteem for himself. He certainly astonished his companions; but that was an added misfortune, for he offended them by expounding their own opinions better than they could do it themselves. M. Chélan had acted as unwisely in Julien's case as in his own. After accustoming him to reason correctly and not let himself be satisfied with words devoid of meaning, he had neglected to tell him that such a habit is a crime in an individual who commands little respect; for all competent reasoning gives offence.

Julien's eloquence, therefore, was accounted a fresh crime. His fellow-students, after long pondering over his case, finally summed up all the horror he made them feel for him in a single epithet. They nicknamed him Martin Luther, particularly so, they said, because of that infernal logic of which he was so proud.

Several of the young seminarists had fresher complexions and could pass for handsomer lads than Julien; but he had white hands and certain delicate habits of cleanliness he could not keep hidden. This advantage was not one at all in the drab and cheerless house into which fate had thrown him; the unwashed peasants amongst whom he lived declared that his morals were very lax.

We fear we may weary the reader with the recital of our hero's countless misfortunes. For example, one of the most lusty of his companions tried to make a habit of fighting him. He was obliged to arm himself with a steel compass and indicate by his gestures that he would make use of it. In a spy's report, gestures cannot figure so advantageously as words.

> All hearts were moved. God's presence seemed
> to have descended into these narrow, gothic
> streets, adorned on every side with draperies,
> and thickly strewn with sand by the loving
> care of the faithful.   YOUNG*

JULIEN tried in vain to make himself appear humble and dull-witted; he could please nobody – he was too different. Yet all the teachers here, he said to himself, are men with very keen minds and selected from scores of other men. How is it they don't find my humility to their liking? One man alone seemed to take even too much advantage of his readiness to believe anything and to let himself seem as if taken in by everything. This was Father Chas-Bernard, who was in charge of religious ceremonials at the cathedral, where, for fifteen years past, he had been kept in hopes of a Canonry. In the meantime, he gave instruction in the art of sacred oratory at the seminary.

In the days of his blindness, this course was one of those in which Julien found himself most frequently top of the class. Father Chas had taken this as an excuse for showing his friendship, and when they came out of his lectures would readily take his arm for a turn or two round the garden.

What's his idea? Julien would ask himself. He was surprised to find the abbé talking to him for hours on end about the vestments, etc., belonging to the cathedral. There were seventeen chasubles, trimmed with braid, not to mention the vestments worn at funerals. They had great hopes of the aged Madame de Rubempré, the President's widow. This lady, who was ninety years old, had, for the past seventy years at least, been carefully keeping the gowns that were made for her wedding, of magnificent Lyons silk, brocaded with gold.

'Just imagine it, my dear boy,' Father Chas would say, stopping short in his walk and opening his eyes very wide, 'these stuffs stand upright of themselves, there's so much gold in them. It's generally believed in Besançon that under Madame de Rubempré's will the cathedral treasure will be increased to the extent of more than ten chasubles, without counting in five or six copes for high festivals. I'll go even further,' Father Chas would add, lowering

* Translated from the French. I cannot trace the original. [Tr.]

his voice, 'I've reason to believe that Madame de Rubempré will leave eight magnificent silver-gilt candlesticks, said to have been bought in Italy by Charles the Bold, Duke of Burgundy, whose favourite minister was an ancestor of hers.'

What is this man up to, anyhow, with all this rigmarole about old clothes? thought Julien. He's been cleverly leading up to some point for absolute ages, and nothing to see for it yet. He must distrust me very much! He's more cunning than any of the others, whose secret can easily be guessed inside a fortnight. I've got it! this man's ambition has made him suffer for fifteen years.

One evening, in the middle of a fencing lesson, Julien was called away to see Father Pirard, who said to him: 'Tomorrow is the Feast of *Corpus Domini* (Corpus Christi). Father Chas-Bernard wants you to help him decorate the cathedral, go and do what he orders.' Father Pirard called him back and added, with a look of pity: 'I leave it to you to see if you want to take advantage of the chance to wander out into the town.'

'*Incedo per ignes* (I have secret enemies),' Julien answered.

Very early on the following morning, Julien went to the cathedral, keeping his eyes on the ground. It did him good to see the streets and note the stir and bustle beginning to spread itself through the town. Everywhere people were draping the fronts of their houses for the procession. The whole of the time he had spent in the seminary seemed to him no more than a moment. His thoughts were of Vergy and of the fair Amanda Binet also, whom he might happen to meet, for her café was not very far away. From some distance off he saw Father Chas-Bernard on the steps of his beloved cathedral. He was a stout man with a beaming face and a frank expression; that day he was exultant.

'I have been waiting for you, my dear son,' he exclaimed as soon as Julien was near enough to be seen. 'You're very welcome. This day's task will be long and strenuous, let's fortify ourselves by having our first breakfast. There'll be a second one at ten o'clock while they're celebrating High Mass.'

'I'm anxious, sir,' said Julien gravely, 'not to be left for a single instant alone. Be good enough to note, sir,' he added, pointing to the clock above their heads, 'that I've got here at one minute to five.'

'Ah! so you're frightened of those little wretches at the seminary! It's very foolish of you to think of them,' said Father Chas. 'Is a road any less beautiful because there are thorns in the hedges on either side? Travellers go their way and leave the spiteful thorns to wither away on their stems. Besides we must get to work, my dear boy, we must get to work!'

Father Chas was right in saying the task would be strenuous. The day before there had been a grand funeral ceremony in the church and it had not been possible to get anything ready. They had therefore, in a single morning, to drape every one of the gothic pillars outlining the nave and both the aisles with a kind of mantle of red damask cloth up to a height of thirty feet. The bishop had sent along four upholsterers by the mail-coach from Paris; but these gentlemen could not do everything themselves, and so far from encouraging the fumbling efforts of their fellow-workers from Besançon, they made them twice as clumsy by laughing at them.

Julien saw he would have to climb up the ladder himself; his nimbleness served him well. He made himself responsible for directing the work of the local upholsterers. Father Chas gazed delightedly at him as he flitted from one ladder to another.

When all the pillars were draped in damask, there was the business of fixing five enormous clumps of feathers on top of the great canopy above the high altar. Here eight tall, twisted columns of Italian marble support the weight of a gorgeous crowning of gilded wood; but to reach the centre of this canopy you have to walk along an old, wooden cornice, very possibly worm-eaten, and forty feet above the ground.

The sight of this steep ascent had quenched the exuberant gaiety hitherto shown by the upholsterers from Paris. They gazed at it from below, found much to say about it, but did not begin to climb. Julien snatched up one of the bunches of plumes and ran up the ladder. He arranged them very neatly on the ornament in the form of a crown in the centre of the canopy.

As he came down from the ladder, Father Chas-Bernard clasped him in his arms. 'Optime!' the good priest exclaimed, 'I'll tell his Lordship of this.'

Their ten o'clock meal was a very gay one. Father Chas had never seen his church so beautiful.

'My dear disciple,' he said to Julien, 'my mother used to hire out chairs in this venerable cathedral, so that in some sort of way I have been nurtured in this great building. Robespierre's reign of terror ruined us, but though I was only eight years old I was already helping the priest at masses held in secret, and food was given me on days when there was mass. No one knew how to fold a chasuble better than I did, the trimming never got frayed. Ever since Napoleon restored religious worship, I have had the joy of directing everything in this ancient edifice. Five times a year, my eyes behold it decked with these lovely trappings. But never has it been so resplendent, nor have the damask draperies been so neatly hung, nor have clung so trimly to the pillars as they do today.'

He's going to tell me his secret at last, thought Julien. Here he is, talking about himself and in a mood for confidences. But this man, although evidently worked up, said nothing indiscreet. And yet, thought Julien, he's worked very hard, he's happy and there's been no stint of wine. What a man! What an example for me! He deserves a medal (this was a slangy expression he had picked up from the old army surgeon).

As the *Sanctus* bell began to ring, Julien thought he would like to put on a surplice and follow the Bishop in the stately procession. 'But the thieves, my dear boy, the thieves!' cried Father Chas. 'You haven't thought of that. The procession will leave the church; but you and I will keep watch. We shall be very lucky if there's not an ell or two missing from that handsome braid round the base of the pillars. That's yet another gift from Madame de Rubempré; it comes from her great-grandfather, the famous count. It's pure gold, my dear boy,' Father Chas added, speaking in his ear and obviously very excited, 'and nothing sham about it! I'll put you to watch in the north aisle – mind you don't leave it. I'll take the south aisle and the nave myself. Keep an eye on the confessionals, that's where the women who spy for the thieves watch for the moment when our backs are turned.'

Just as he finished speaking, the clock struck a quarter to twelve. At the very same moment the great bell made itself heard. It rang a full peal; its deep, full, solemn tones stirred Julien's imagination and lifted it above the earth. The perfume of incense and of rose petals scattered in front of the altar by little children dressed like Saint John added a finishing touch to his ecstasy.

The deeply sonorous tones of this bell should not have awakened anything in Julien but the thought of twenty men working for fifty centimes apiece, aided, perhaps, by fifteen or twenty pious worshippers. He should have thought of the wear and tear on the bell-ropes and the wooden framework, of the risk to the bell itself which comes tumbling down every two hundred years. He should have reflected on some way of reducing the wages of these bell-ringers or of paying them by means of some indulgence or grace drawn from the rich resources of the Church, yet making her purse no leaner.

Instead of such sage reflections, Julien's spirit, borne upwards on the rich, bass tones of the bell, was wandering through worlds upon worlds of the imagination. He will never make a good priest, nor a good administrator. Natures yielding to emotion like this are good at most to make artists only.

Here Julien's presumption bursts into the full light of day. Some fifty, maybe, of his fellow-seminarists, made attentive to the real things in life on learning of the universal hatred of priests and the Jacobinism lurking in ambush behind every hedge, would have thought, on hearing the great bell of the cathedral, of nothing but the bell-ringers' wages. They would have studied, with all the mathematical accuracy of Barème, the question of whether the degree of emotion felt by the public was worth the money these bell-ringers were paid. Had Julien wished to consider the material interests of the cathedral his imagination, overstepping the mark, would have thought of how to save forty francs on the upkeep of the building, and let slip a chance of avoiding an outlay of twenty-five centimes.

All the while the procession was going on its way through the streets of Besançon on the sunniest day in the world and stopping in front of the glittering altars of repose, erected by people of influence, each seeking to outdo the other, the church was wrapped in deepest silence. Half-darkness reigned inside this place, and a delightful coolness; the air was still fragrant with the scent of flowers and incense.

The silence, the utter solitude, the coolness of the long aisles imparted still more sweetness to Julien's musing. He was not afraid of being disturbed by Father Chas, who was busy in another part of the church. His spirit had almost shaken itself free of its mortal husk, now pacing slowly up and down the north aisle over which he had been set to watch. He felt all the more at peace from having made sure there was no one in the confessionals but a few pious women. His eyes gazed round him blindly.

He was half roused out of his trance by the sight of two very well-dressed women who were kneeling, the one in a confessional and the other, close to the first, at a *prie-dieu*. He looked at them, seeing nothing; all the same, whether out of some vague sense of his duties, or admiration for the simple well-bred style in which these ladies were dressed, he noted that there was no priest in the confessional. It's odd, he thought, that these fine ladies, if they are devout, aren't on their knees before some altar of repose; or, seeing they belong to high society, haven't taken their places in the front row of one of the balconies. How well that dress is cut! How gracefully it hangs! He slackened his pace in an attempt to see them.

On hearing the sound of Julien's footsteps break in upon this solemn silence, the one who was kneeling in the confessional turned her head slightly. Suddenly she gave a loud cry and fainted. As her strength deserted her, this kneeling lady fell backwards; her friend, who was close by, rushed forward to help her. At that same moment Julien caught sight of the shoulders of the lady who was falling back. A twisted rope of large, real pearls, which was very familiar to him, caught his eye. What was his state of mind when he recognized Madame de Rênal's hair! It was she. The lady who was trying to support her head and prevent her from falling altogether was Madame Derville. Out of his mind, Julien darted forward; Madame de Rênal in falling would possibly have dragged her friend down with her if Julien had not supported them both. He saw Madame de Rênal's head, its pale face utterly devoid of feeling, drooping against his shoulder. He helped Madame Derville lay this lovely head on a straw-seated chair for support; he was on his knees.

Madame Derville turned round and recognized him. 'Go away, sir, go away!' she said to him in the sharpest tones of anger. 'And above all, don't let her see you again. The sight of you is bound to fill her with horror – she was so happy before you came! Your conduct is atrocious. Go away at once, remove yourself if you've any decency left.'

These words were spoken with so much authority, and Julien at the moment was feeling so weak, that he went away and left them. She's always hated me, he said to himself, referring to Madame Derville.

At that very moment, the nasal chant of the foremost priests in the procession rang through the church; they were coming back. Father Chas-Bernard called to Julien several times, but Julien did not hear him. Finally the abbé came up to the pillar behind which Julien, half dead, had taken refuge.

'You're feeling ill, my son,' said Father Chas on seeing him so pale and almost unable to walk. 'You've been working too hard.' The abbé offered him his arm. 'Come and sit down on this little seat put there for the giver of holy water. You'll be behind me, I'll hide you.' They were just standing by the great west door. 'Calm yourself. We have still a good twenty minutes before his Lordship arrives. Try to recover yourself; I'll help you up when he passes; for I'm strong and vigorous, in spite of my age.'

But when the Bishop passed, Julien was trembling so much that Father Chas gave up the idea of presenting him.

'Don't be too grieved about it,' he said. 'I'll find another opportunity.'

That evening, he had ten pounds' weight of candles sent to the seminary chapel, saved, so he said, by Julien's care and the promptness with which he had snuffed them out. Nothing could have been further from the truth. The poor boy was quite snuffed out himself. He had not had a single idea in his head since catching sight of Madame de Rênal.

> He knew the temper of his age, he knew his
> district – now he is a wealthy man.
> *The Forerunner*

JULIEN had not yet emerged from the depths of brooding thought into which he had been plunged by the incident in the cathedral when, one morning, stern Father Pirard sent for him.

'Father Chas-Bernard has just written me a letter in which he speaks well of you. I am fairly satisfied with your general conduct. You are extremely rash and thoughtless, though without seeming to be so. However, up till now, you have shown you have a kind, and even courageous heart. As for your intelligence, it's above the average. On the whole, I see in you a spark of something which should not be left to die out.

'After fifteen years' labour, I am about to leave this house. My crime is that I have left my seminarists their freedom of conscience and have neither supported nor hindered that secret society of which you spoke to me in the confessional. Before I go, I want to do something for you. But for the information laid against you on the strength of Amanda Binet's letter found in your possession, I would have acted two months sooner, for you deserve it. I'm making you assistant tutor in the Old and New Testament.'

Julien, in a transport of gratitude, had, indeed, some idea of flinging himself on his knees and giving thanks to God; but he yielded to a truer impulse. Going up to Father Pirard, he took his hand and pressed it to his lips.

'What are you thinking of?' cried the Rector angrily; but Julien's eyes said even more than his action.

Father Pirard looked at him in amazement, like a man who for many long years had grown unused to meeting with finer feelings. This attention made the Rector give himself away; his voice faltered.

'Yes, indeed, my son, I have grown fond of you. Heaven knows it is indeed against my will. I ought to be fair, and feel neither hatred nor love towards anyone. Your career will be a painful one; I see in you something that offends the common run of men. Jealousy and calumny will pursue you. In whatever place Providence chooses to put you, your colleagues will never see you without hating you; and if they pretend to love you it will only be to betray you all the more effectively. There is only one remedy for this – seek help only from God, who has given you in punishment for your presumption the unavoidable lot of being hated. Let your conduct be blameless – this is the only expedient I can see for you. If you hold fast to truth with unconquerable tenacity, sooner or later your enemies will be confounded.'

It was so long since Julien had listened to a friendly voice that one act of weakness must be forgiven him – he burst into tears. The abbé held out his arms to him; this moment was a very sweet one for them both.

Julien was wild with joy. This promotion was the first he had won; it had immense advantages. To realize what these were one would have to spend months on end without a moment's solitude, in close contact, too, with companions who were, to say the least, unwelcome and for the most part insufferable. Their shouting would have been enough in itself to unhinge a delicately balanced mind. These well-fed, well-clothed peasants did not know how to keep their rollicking joy to themselves, they did not feel such joy complete unless they were yelling as loud as their lungs would let them.

Julien now had his meals alone, or almost alone, an hour later than the other seminarists. He had a key to the garden and could walk there at times when no one was about.

To his great amazement, he found himself less hated. He had expected that, on the contrary, their hatred of him would have increased. His secret desire that no one should say a word to him, which had been all too plain and had earned him so many enemies, was no longer taken as an indication of ridiculous pride. In the eyes of those coarse-grained beings around him it became a proper sense of his own dignity. Their hatred grew noticeably less, especially among his younger companions, now become his pupils, and whom he treated with very great courtesy. By degrees, he even came to have some of them on his side; it became bad form to call him Martin Luther.

What is the use of naming his friends or his enemies, anyway? Such things are ugly, and all the uglier because the picture is true. Yet they are the only teachers of morals the people have, and what would become of the people without them? Can newspapers ever take the place of the parish priest?

Ever since Julien's new rise in status, the Rector of the seminary had made a point of never addressing a word to him except before witnesses. Such conduct showed discretion in the master's interest as well as the pupil's; but it was above all a trial of strength. Pirard, the austere Jansenist, held as a fixed principle that, if a man appears to have some merit in your eyes, you should put obstacles in the way of all his desires and all his undertakings; if this merit is real, he will easily finds means to upset or circumvent these obstacles.

It was the hunting season. Fouqué got the idea of sending a boar and a stag to the seminary as if they came from Julien's relations. The dead beasts were put down in the passage between the kitchen and the refectory, where all the seminarists saw them as they went into dinner. This gift occasioned much curiosity. The boar, dead as he was, made the younger students afraid; they put out a hand and touched his tusks. Nobody talked of anything else for a week.

This gift, by assigning Julien to that section of society which commands respect, dealt envy its death blow; Julien was now a superior being hallowed by wealth. Chazel and the more important of the students made advances to him and almost seemed as if they might complain because he had not warned them that his family was rich and had thus made them run the risk of failing to show respect for money.

There was a conscription for military service from which Julien, as a seminarist, was exempt. He was deeply affected by this circumstance. There's the moment for ever gone by, he thought, when, had it been twenty years earlier, a hero's life would have begun for me!

He was walking by himself in the seminary garden when he heard some stonemasons, busy at work in the cloister wall, talking to each other.

'Well! I've got to go!' said one. 'There's a new call-up.'

'In that *other man's* day, blow me if masons didn't become officers or even generals – that's been known to happen.'

'Just you go and look at them now! There's nought but beggars joining up. Anyone with a bit o' cash stays at home.'

'Who's born poor, stays poor – and that's that.'

'I say, is it true what they say that the *other's* dead?' a third mason chimed in.

'It's just the nobs who say so, mind you. They were afraid of the *other*.'

'Wasn't it different then! The way work thrived in his day!

And to think his own marshals did the dirty on him! There's treachery if you like!'

This conversation comforted Julien a little. As he moved away he quoted with a sigh:

The only king the common folk remember!

The period of examinations came round. Julien answered brilliantly; he saw that even Chazel was making efforts to display all his learning.

On the first day, the examiners appointed by M. de Frilair, the famous Vicar-general, were greatly upset at having to put that young Julien Sorel, who had been pointed out to them as Father Pirard's pet pupil, continually first, or at least second, on their list. Bets were made in the seminary that in the final list of the whole examination, Julien would take first place, a position that carried with it the honour of dining with his Lordship the Bishop.

At the end of one session, however, in which matters relating to the Fathers of the Church came up, an astute examiner, after questioning Julien on Saint Jerome and his passion for Cicero, went on to speak of Horace, Virgil, and other profane writers. Unknown to his companions, Julien had learnt a great number of passages from these authors off by heart. Carried away by his success, he forgot where he was, and, in response to reiterated requests from the examiner, recited several of Horace's odes and gave lively paraphrases of them. After letting him give himself away for twenty minutes, the examiner suddenly changed countenance and reproached him acidly for the time he had wasted on such profane studies and the vain or criminal ideas they had put into his head.

'You're right, sir, I've behaved very foolishly,' Julien admitted humbly, realizing he had been the victim of a clever ruse.

The trick this examiner played was thought a very dirty one, even in the seminary; but this did not prevent Father Frilair, that cunning individual who had so skilfully organized the whole network of the *Congrégation* in Besançon, and whose official reports to Paris made judges, prefects, and even the general officers of the garrison tremble, from writing down, with the hand that wielded such power, the number 198 against Julien's name. It gave him joy to mortify his enemy, the Jansenist Pirard, in this way.

For the past ten years his great concern had been to take the control of the seminary away from him. Father Pirard, following himself the principles of conduct he had outlined to Julien, was sincere, religious, innocent of all intrigue, and devoted to his duty. But heaven, in its wrath, had given him that choleric temper which is apt to take keen offence at affronts and to hate as keenly. None of the outrageous insults directed at him were lost on so fiery a nature. He would have handed in his resignation a hundred times already, but that he believed that he was of use in the position where Providence had placed him. I hinder the progress of Jesuitry and idolatry, he would say to himself.

At the time of the examinations, he had not spoken to Julien for possibly two months; yet he was ill for a week when, on receiving the official letter announcing the results of this competitive test, he saw the number 198 against the name of a pupil whom he regarded as the pride of his institution. The only consolation for this stern man was to concentrate on Julien all his machinery of supervision. He was delighted to find in him neither anger, nor plans for revenge, nor discouragement.

A few weeks later, Julien was startled by the receipt of a letter which bore the Paris postmark. At last, he thought, Madame de Rênal has remembered her promises. An individual, who signed himself 'Paul Sorel' and who claimed to be a relation, sent him a bill of exchange for five hundred francs. The letter went on to say that if Julien continued to study the best Latin authors and made successful progress in his studies a similar sum would be sent to him every year.

It must be she, it's just like her kindness! said Julien to himself, greatly touched. She wants to comfort me – but why not a single friendly word?

He was mistaken; Madame de Rênal, guided in her conduct by Madame Derville, was wholly taken up with her own deep remorse. In spite of herself, she often thought of the extraordinary being who had turned her whole life upside down, but she would not have had any idea of writing to him.

If we were to adopt the language of the seminary we might recognize a miracle in this sending of five hundred francs, and say they came from M. de Frilair himself, whom heaven was using to bestow this gift on Julien.

Twelve years before, the abbé de Frilair had arrived in Besançon with a very scantily furnished portmanteau containing, so the chronicle relates, the whole of his fortune. He now found himself one of the richest property owners in the district. In the course of his prosperous career he had bought one half of an estate, the other half of which had come to M. de la Mole as a legacy. This was the occasion of a serious lawsuit between these two influential people.

In spite of the distinction of his life in Paris and the posts he held at court, his Lordship the Marquis de la Mole felt it would be dangerous to engage in a contest with a Vicar-general who was reputed to make and unmake prefects. Yet instead of soliciting a gratuity of fifty thousand francs – to be entered in the budget under the name of anyone authorized to draw public money – and surrendering this miserable lawsuit for a similar sum to M. de Frilair, the Marquis grew obstinate. He thought he had right on his side – a fine right, indeed! If, by the way, it is permissible to say so, what judge is there who has not a son or a cousin whom he wishes to push into society?

Let me say, to open the eyes of the blindest among you, that a week after he had received a first judgement in his favour, the abbé de Frilair got into the Bishop's carriage and went off in it to take the cross of the Legion of Honour to his lawyer himself. M. de la Mole, a trifle astounded at his adversary's attitude, and feeling that his own lawyers were beginning to give way, asked M. Chélan for advice and was put by him in touch with M. Pirard.

At the time our story begins the Marquis's relations with M. Pirard were of several years' standing. Father Pirard brought all his characteristic vehemence to bear on this business. After visiting the Marquis's lawyers incessantly, making a study of his case, and judging his cause to be just, he came out openly as M. de la Mole's advocate against the all-powerful Vicar-general. The latter was outraged at the impertinence, and from an insignificant little Jansenist, too!

'Just look at these court nobles who claim to be so powerful!' the abbé de Frilair would say to his intimate friends. 'M. de la Mole hasn't sent a single wretched decoration to his agent in Besançon and now he's going to let him lose his post without lifting a finger. And yet, so my letters inform me, this noble peer never lets a week go by without going to display his blue ribbon in the drawing-room of the Keeper of the King's Seal, whoever he may be!'

In spite of all Father Pirard's diligence, and although M. de la Mole was always on the best of terms with the Minister of Justice, and above all with his officials, all that he had been able to do after six years' exertions was just not to lose his case completely.

Ceaselessly engaged in correspondence with Father Pirard over a business both of them pursued with such passionate concern, the Marquis came in the end to have a liking for the abbé's particular type of mind. Little by little, in spite of the immense difference in their social positions, their letters took on a friendly tone. The abbé would tell the Marquis how people wished to force him, by constant outrageous insults, to hand in his resignation. In the angry mood inspired by the infamous stratagem, as he called it, employed against Julien, he told the Marquis his story.

Although very rich, this Marquis was not in the least miserly. In all the time he had known him, he had never been able to get Father Pirard to accept even the repayment of postal expenses incurred on account of the lawsuit. He jumped at the idea of sending five hundred francs to the abbé's favourite pupil.

M. de la Mole put himself to the trouble of writing with his own hand the letter sending this money. This made him think about the abbé.

One day the latter received a short note inviting him to go without delay to an inn on the outskirts of Besançon on a matter of urgent business. There he found M. de la Mole's steward.

'His Lordship has ordered me to bring his carriage for you,' said the man. 'He hopes that after reading this letter you will find it convenient to set off for Paris in four or five days' time. I'm going to employ this interval, if you will be good enough to tell me how long it will be, in inspecting his Lordship's estates in Franche-Comté. After which, on any day that suits you, we will leave for Paris.'

The letter was very short.

Shake yourself free, my dear sir [it read], *of all these provincial worries, and come and breathe the peaceful air of Paris. I am sending you my carriage, which has orders to await your decision for four days. I will wait for you myself in Paris until Tuesday. You have only to say yes, my dear sir, for me to accept in your name one of the best livings in the neighbourhood of Paris. The richest of your future parishioners has never seen you, but he is more devoted to you than you may believe. He is the Marquis de la Mole.*

Without suspecting it, stern Father Pirard loved this seminary peopled with his enemies and to which for fifteen years he had devoted all his thoughts. M. de la Mole's letter was for him like the sudden appearance of a surgeon entrusted with the duty of performing a severely painful but necessary operation. His dismissal was certain. He arranged to meet the steward in three days' time.

For the next forty-eight hours he was in a fever of uncertainty. Finally, he wrote to M. de la Mole and composed a letter for the Bishop which was a masterpiece of clerical style, but a trifle long. It would have been difficult to find phrases more irreproachable or expressing more sincere respect. All the same this letter, destined to give M. de Frilair an uncomfortable hour or two with his patron, set forth every serious ground of complaint and even descended to details of petty, underhand acts of persecution, which were now, after six years' endurance of them, obliging Father Pirard to leave the diocese. Wood had been stolen from his woodpile, his dog had been poisoned, and so on.

Having finished the letter, he sent to wake Julien, who, at eight o'clock in the evening, was already asleep, like all the other seminarists.

'You know where the Bishop's palace is?' he said to him in the best classical Latin. 'Take this letter to his Lordship. I won't hide from you that I am sending you into the midst of wolves. Be all eyes and ears. No falsehoods, mind, in your answers; but remember that anyone who questions you might possibly take a real delight in doing you harm. I'm very glad, my son, to give you this experience before I leave; for I won't hide from you that the letter you're taking contains my resignation.'

Julien stood there without moving. He was fond of Father Pirard. In vain the voice of prudence warned him : When this man leaves the Jesuit faction here will take away my job, and maybe drive me out.

He could not think about himself. What was embarrassing him was trying to phrase something he wanted to say politely, and his mind was really not up to it.

'Well, my young friend, aren't you going?'

'It's just that I've heard people say, sir,' said Julien timidly, 'that during your long term of office you haven't saved anything. I've got a hundred francs.' His tears prevented him from saying anything more.

'That also will be noted,' the ex-Rector said coldly. 'Go off to the Bishop's. It's getting late.'

That evening, as chance would have it, M. de Frilair was on duty in the Bishop's drawing-room. His Lordship was dining with the Prefect. It was therefore to M. de Frilair that Julien handed the letter, though he did not recognize him.

Julien was surprised to see the abbé boldly opening the letter addressed to the Bishop. Soon the Vicar-general's handsome face expressed astonishment mingled with keen satisfaction, and then grew graver than before. While he was reading, Julien, struck with his good looks, had time to study him. His face would have had more gravity in it, but for the extreme astuteness apparent in certain of his features, which might even have indicated sly-ness had the owner of this handsome face ceased for a moment to think about his appearance. His very prominent nose pro-truded in a perfectly straight unbroken line and unfortunately gave to his profile otherwise very distinguished an irremediable likeness to a fox. For the rest, this abbé who appeared so deeply taken up with M. Pirard's resignation was dressed with an elegance Julien found very pleasing, and which he had not seen in any other priest.

Julien did not learn until later what the abbé de Frilair's special talent was. He knew how to amuse his Bishop, a pleasant old man who was just suited to life in Paris and looked on Besançon as a place of exile. The Bishop had very bad eyesight, and was passionately fond of fish. The abbé de Frilair would re-move the bones of any fish served at his Lordship's table.

Julien was gazing silently at the abbé as he read the letter for the second time, when suddenly the door burst open. A footman, in handsome livery, passed quickly through. Julien had just time to turn round towards the door, where he saw a little old man, wearing a pectoral cross. He fell on his knees; the Bishop looked at him with a kindly smile and passed on. The handsome abbé followed him, leaving Julien alone in the drawing-room to admire its pious splendour at his leisure.

The Bishop of Besançon, a man whose spirit had been tried, but not quenched, by the long drawn out hardships of the Emi-gration, was sixty-five years of age, and was worried exceedingly little by what might happen in ten years' time.

'Who is that seminarist with the keen, intelligent face, whom I thought I saw as I went by?' asked the Bishop. 'Shouldn't they, according to my regulations, be in bed at this hour?'

'This one is very wide-awake, I assure you, my Lord, and he brings great news – the resignation of the only remaining Jan-

senist in your district. That terrible Father Pirard understands
at last how to take a hint.'

'Well!' said the Bishop laughing, 'I defy you to find another
man as good in his stead. And to show you how I value this
man, I'm inviting him to dine with me tomorrow.'

The Vicar-general tried to slip in a word or two on the choice
of a successor; but the prelate, little in the mood to talk business,
said to him : 'Before we get another man in, let's find out a little
why this one's leaving. Call in that seminarist to see me – truth
is in the mouths of babes and sucklings.'

Julien was summoned. I'm about to find myself in the company
of two inquisitors, he thought. Never had he felt more courageous.

At the moment he entered, two valets, better dressed than M.
Valenod himself, were disrobing his Lordship. The prelate, before
coming to M. Pirard, thought he ought to question Julien about
his studies. He touched on dogma, and was astonished. Soon he
passed to the humanities, to Virgil, Horace, and Cicero. These
names, thought Julien, earned me 198th place on the list. I've
nothing to lose – let's try to shine. In this he succeeded, delighting
the Bishop, who was an excellent humanist himself.

At dinner at the prefect's, a young woman, justly celebrated,
had recited the poem on Mary Magdalene. The Bishop was all set
for a literary discussion, and very quickly forgot Father Pirard
and matters of business altogether, to discuss with the seminarist
whether Horace had been rich or poor. The Prelate cited several
odes, but at times his memory was caught napping, whereupon
Julien in a very unassuming way would recite the ode from
beginning to end. What struck the Bishop was that Julien's voice
never strayed beyond a conversational tone; he would repeat his
twenty or thirty Latin lines just as if he were talking about
things that went on in his seminary. They spoke at length of
Virgil and Cicero. Finally the prelate could not refrain from
complimenting the young seminarist.

'No one could possibly have studied to better advantage,' he
said.

'My lord,' said Julien, 'your seminary can offer you a hundred
and ninety-seven individuals much less undeserving of your high
praise.'

'How's that?' asked the prelate, astonished by this figure.

'I can support by official proof what I have the honour to tell
your lordship. At the annual examination at the seminary I was

given the hundred and ninety-eighth place for my answers on those very matters which have earned me your lordship's approval at this moment.'

'Ah! so it's Father Pirard's pet pupil,' exclaimed the Bishop laughing, with a glance at M. de Frilair. 'I might have expected as much; but all's fair in war. Isn't it true, my young friend,' he added, addressing Julien, 'that they had to wake you up to send you here?'

'Yes, my lord. I've only once in my life been outside the seminary alone, and that was to go and help Father Chas-Bernard decorate the cathedral on Corpus Christi day.'

'*Optime*,' said the Bishop. 'What, was it you who gave such a proof of courage in putting the tufts of feathers on top of the canopy? They make me shudder every year; I'm always afraid they'll cost me a man's life. You'll go far, my young friend; but I don't want to put an end to your career – which should be a brilliant one – by letting you die of hunger.'

On an order from the Bishop, biscuits and Malaga wine were brought, to which Julien did justice, and still more the abbé de Frilair, who knew his Lordship liked to see people eat merrily and with a good appetite.

The Prelate, more and more pleased with this end to his evening, touched on Church history for a moment, but noticing that Julien could not follow him, he went on to the state of morals under the emperors of the age of Constantine. The end of paganism was accompanied by the same state of doubt and disquietude which depresses the sad, world-weary minds of the nineteenth century.

The Bishop remarked that Julien did not even know Tacitus by name. To his Lordship's amazement, Julien replied to him candidly that this author was not to be found in the library at the seminary.

'I'm very glad of it,' the Bishop said brightly. 'You've got me out of a difficulty. For the last ten minutes I've been trying to find some way of thanking you for the pleasant evening you've given me, and in a very unexpected way indeed. I didn't look to find a finished scholar in one of the students at my seminary. Although such a gift is not strictly orthodox, I want to give you a copy of Tacitus.'

The prelate had eight handsomely bound volumes brought in, and was good enough to write in his own hand a complimentary dedication in Latin to Julien Sorel, on the title-page of the first volume. The Bishop prided himself on his fine knowledge of Latin. In conclusion he said to him in a serious tone of voice that contrasted sharply with his manner during the rest of the conversation : 'If you behave yourself, young man, you shall one day have the best living in my diocese, and that won't be a hundred leagues distant from my episcopal palace – *but you must behave yourself.*'

As the clock struck the hour of midnight, Julien, laden with his volumes and in a great state of amazement, left the palace; his Lordship had not said a single word to him about Father Pirard. What most amazed Julien were the Bishop's extremely polished manners. He had no idea there was such ceremonious urbanity combined with such natural dignity. Julien was particularly struck with the contrast on seeing Father Pirard again, waiting for him with glum impatience.

'*Quid tibi dixerunt?* (What did they say to you?)' the abbé shouted to him loudly as soon as he came near enough to be seen. As Julien was getting slightly muddled in his efforts to translate what the Bishop had said into Latin, the ex-Rector said to him, in his usual harsh voice and exceedingly graceless manner: 'Speak in French, and give me his Lordship's own words without adding or subtracting anything.'

He turned over the leaves of the magnificent Tacitus, seemingly horrified at their gilt edges. 'That's a strange kind of present from a Bishop to a young seminarist, isn't it?' he remarked.

Two o'clock was striking when, after hearing a very detailed report, he allowed his favourite pupil to return to his room.

'Leave me the first volume of your Tacitus, the one with the Bishop's dedication in it,' he said to him. 'This single line of Latin will act like a lightning conductor for you in this house after I've gone. *Erit tibi, fili mi, successor meus tanquam leo quaerens quem devoret.* (For my successor will be to you, my son, as a raging lion seeking whom he may devour.)'

The next morning Julien found something strange in the way his companions spoke to him. It made him all the more reserved. That's the effect of Father Pirard's resignation, he thought. Everyone in the house knows about it, and I'm considered his favourite pupil. There must be something insulting behind this behaviour. Yet he could not see that there was; on the contrary, hatred was absent from the eyes of those he met as he passed through the dormitories. Finally the little seminarist said to him laughing: '*Cornelii Taciti opera omnia* (The complete works of Tacitus).'

At these words, which were overheard, all the students, as if striving to outdo each other, congratulated Julien not only on the magnificent present he had received from his Lordship, but also on the two hours' conversation with which he had been honoured. Everything was known about it, down to the smallest detail. From that moment envy was at an end. Everyone paid the most servile court to him; Father Castanède, who the evening before had behaved to him with the utmost insolence, came and took him by the arm and invited him to lunch. A fatal trait in Julien's character had made him feel greatly pained by the rudeness of these coarse-minded fellows; their servility disgusted him and gave him no pleasure at all.

Round about midday, Father Pirard said good-bye to his students, but not without delivering a stern farewell speech. 'Do you wish for wordly honours,' he said to them, 'for every social advantage, for the pleasure of being in authority, of defying law and order and being rude with impunity to all men? Or do you desire your eternal salvation? the least intelligent amongst you have only to open your eyes to recognize the difference between these two paths.'

He had scarcely gone before the devout members of the Sacred Heart went off to chant a *Te Deum* in the chapel. Nobody in the seminary took the ex-Rector's address seriously. 'He's very sore about his dismissal,' was said on all sides. Not a single student was simple-hearted enough to believe in a voluntary resignation of a post which carried with it the opportunity of so many contacts with important contractors.

Father Pirard established himself in the finest hostelry in Besançon, and giving as his pretext some business affairs which did not exist, arranged to spend two days there. The Bishop had entertained him to dinner at which, to amuse himself at the Vicar-general's expense, he did his best to bring the abbé out to the best advantage. They were at dessert when the strange news arrived from Paris of Father Pirard's appointment to the magnificent living of N—, four leagues distant from that city. The kindly prelate congratulated him sincerely. He saw in all this affair an instance of *good play*, which put him in the best of humours, and gave him the highest opinion of the abbé's talents. He gave him a splendid testimonial in Latin and, on the abbé de Frilair's venturing to protest, commanded him to keep silence.

In the evening, his Lordship went with his marvellous tidings to the Marquis de Rubempré's house. It was a great surprise to the best society in Besançon; everyone was lost in conjectures concerning this extraordinary mark of favour. They already saw Father Pirard a bishop. The most subtle minds believed that M. de la Mole had been made a minister, and allowed themselves to smile that day at the imperious airs the abbé de Frilair gave himself in society.

The next morning Father Pirard had almost a following in the streets, and shopkeepers came to the door of their shops as he went to canvass the Marquis's judges; for the very first time, they received him politely. The stern Jansenist, enraged at everything he saw, put in a long spell of work with the lawyers he had chosen for M. de la Mole, and then left for Paris.

He very foolishly told two or three of his former schoolfellows who accompanied him as far as the carriage, where they admired its coats-of-arms, that after being in charge of the seminary for fifteen years he was leaving Besançon with saving amounting to five hundred francs. These friends embraced him with tears in their eyes, and afterwards said to each other: 'Our good Father might have spared himself this lie, it makes him too ridiculous.'

The common herd, blinded by love of money, were not capable of understanding that it was Father Pirard's sincerity that had given him the strength to stand up to a six years' struggle with Marie Alacoque, the Sacred Heart of Jesus, the Jesuits, and his Bishop.

> There is only one true patent of nobility – the
> title of Duke. Marquis is laughable; but say
> the word 'Duke', and every head turns round.
> *Edinburgh Review*

THE Marquis de la Mole's reception of Father Pirard was marked by none of those little, lordly mannerisms seemingly so polite, yet so impertinent to the man who understands them. This would have been a waste of time, and the Marquis was enough engrossed in high affairs of state to have no time to waste. For the last six months he had been manoeuvring to make both King and nation accept a certain ministry, which, out of gratitude, would make him a duke.

For many long years the Marquis had been asking his lawyer in Besançon for a clear, concise report on his lawsuits in Franche-Comté. How could this celebrated lawyer have explained these matters to him, if he did not understand them himself? The little sheet of paper Father Pirard handed to him made everything plain.

'My dear abbé,' said the Marquis after hurrying through all the conventional polite remarks and questions on personal matters in less than five minutes, 'in the midst of all my supposedly comfortable circumstances, I lack time to give serious attention to two little matters that are after all very important – my family and my own affairs. I pay great attention to the fortunes of my house, I can advance them considerably; I take care of my pleasures too, and that's a thing of the first importance – at least in my eyes,' he added, surprising a look of astonishment in Father Pirard's. Although a man with plenty of common sense, the abbé was amazed to find an old man talking so openly of his pleasures.

'No doubt there are industrious people in Paris,' the noble lord went on, 'but perched aloft on the fifth floor only. The moment I get in contact with a man, he selects a flat on the second floor and his wife selects an at-home day. Consequently, no more work, and no more efforts save to be, or appear to be, in society. That's their sole concern as soon as they get enough to live on.

'As for my lawsuits, and indeed for each lawsuit taken by itself; I've lawyers who are literally killing themselves; one of them died of consumption the day before yesterday. But as for my affairs in general, would you believe me, sir, if I told you that for the past three years I've given up trying to find a man who, while writing my letters, condescends to give a little serious thought to what he's doing? All this by the way, is only a kind of preface.

'I've great respect for you and would venture to say, although this is the first time I've seen you, that I've taken a liking to you. Will you be my secretary, with a salary of eight thousand francs – or even double as much? I shall still be the gainer, I assure you. And I'll make it my business to see your fine living is still kept open for you, in case the day arrives when we don't suit each other any longer.'

Father Pirard refused this offer, but towards the close of the conversation the very real difficulty in which the Marquis found himself suggested an idea to him.

'I left a poor young fellow behind in the seminary; if I'm not mistaken, he's in for a very hard time. If he were a monk pure and simple, he'd already be in solitary confinement. Up to the present this young man knows nothing but Latin and the Holy Scriptures; but it's not impossible that one of these days he'll display great ability, either as a preacher or a spiritual adviser. I don't know how he'll turn out, but there's a sacred fire within him, and he may go far. I had counted on handing him over to our Bishop if ever we had one with a little of your way of looking at men and things.'

'What is this young man's background?'

'He's said to be the son of a carpenter in our mountains, but I rather think he's the natural son of some rich man. I saw him receive an anonymous, or pseudonymous, letter containing a bill of exchange for five hundred francs.'

'Ah! it's Julien Sorel,' said the Marquis.

'How do you come to know his name?' Father Pirard asked in surprise.

And, as he was blushing at this question, the Marquis, looking as if the question embarrassed him, replied, 'That's something I'm not going to tell you.'

'Well,' continued Father Pirard, 'you might try to make a secretary of him; he's energetic, and he's sensible. In short, it's an experiment worth trying.'

'Why not?' said the Marquis. 'But would he be a man to let himself be bribed to spy on me by the prefect of the police, or any one else? That's my only objection.'

Father Pirard having given him favourable assurances on this point, the Marquis took out a thousand franc note and said: 'Send this to Julien Sorel for his travelling expenses, and get him to come.'

'It's easy to see you live in Paris,' said Father Pirard. 'You know nothing of the tyranny that lies heavy on us poor provincials, especially those priests who aren't on friendly terms with the Jesuits. They won't let Julien Sorel leave; they'll know how to take cover behind the most cunning pretexts, they'll tell me he's ill, letters will be lost in the post, etc., etc.'

'One of these days,' said the Marquis, 'I'll take a letter to the Bishop from the Minister.'

'I was forgetting to warn you of one thing,' said the abbé. 'This young man, though of low birth, has a high spirit. It won't be of any service to offend his pride – you'd only make him stupid.'

'I like that,' said the Marquis. 'I'll make him a companion to my son – will that be enough?'

Some time later, Julien received a letter in an unknown hand, with the Châlon postmark. In it he found a draft on a trades-man in Besançon and instructions to present himself in Paris without delay. The letter was signed with a fictitious name, but as Julien opened it he started; a great blot of ink had been dropped on the thirteenth word – it was the signal he had agreed on with Father Pirard.

Less than an hour later, Julien was summoned once more to the Bishop's palace, where he received a most fatherly welcome. In between quoting Horace, his Lordship paid him some very neat compliments on the high destiny awaiting him in Paris, all of which called for explanation before he could express his thanks. Julien could find nothing to say because, in the first place, he knew nothing. His Lordship was very considerate to him; one of the minor clerics at the palace wrote to the Mayor, who came hurrying up with a passport he had signed himself but on which the traveller's name was left blank.

That evening, before midnight, Julien was at Fouqué's house, to find this sagacious individual more astonished than delighted at the future awaiting his friend.

'It'll all end up for you,' said this member of the Liberal party, 'with a government post where you'll be forced to do something for which the newspapers will slang you. I shall have news of you by seeing you shamed. Mind you, it's better, even from a money point of view, to earn a hundred louis in a sound timber business, where one is one's own master, than to get five thousand francs from any government, even if it were that of King Solomon himself.'

Julien could see nothing in this but the narrow-minded views of a respectable countryman. He was at last to make his appearance in the theatre of great events. The happiness of going to Paris, which he pictured to himself as full of clever, scheming fellows, thorough hypocrites, but as polished in their manners as the Bishop of Besançon and the Bishop of Agde, shut out the sight of everything else. He represented himself to his friend as being deprived of freedom of choice by Father Pirard's letter.

Towards twelve o'clock the next day he arrived at Verrières, feeling himself the happiest of men, and counting on seeing Madame de Rênal again. He went first to visit his patron, good Father Chélan, where he met with a harsh reception.

'So you think you're under some obligation to me?' said M. Chélan without returning his greeting. 'You'll have lunch with me, and while you're having it someone will go and hire a horse for you, and you'll leave Verrières *without seeing anyone.*'

'To hear is to obey,' answered Julien with a seminarist's air; and they talked of nothing but theology and the humanities.

He mounted his horse and rode three miles, after which, catching sight of the wood with no one by to see him enter, he went right in. At sunset, he sent the horse home, and later, going into a peasant's house, he got him to agree to sell him a ladder and follow him, carrying the ladder as far as the little wood looking down on the Cours de la Fidélité at Verrières.

'So we're some miserable conscript who's deserted . . . or maybe a smuggler,' said the peasant as he took his leave. 'But what's the harm in that! My ladder's handsomely paid for, and I wouldn't say I haven't myself been up to high jinks now and then in my life.'

The night was very dark. Towards one o'clock in the morning Julien entered Verrières, carrying his ladder. He climbed down as quickly as he could into the bed of the stream which runs through M. de Rênal's magnificent gardens at a depth of ten feet, with a wall enclosing it on either side. Julien climbed up easily with the help of the ladder. What welcome can I expect from the watch-dogs? he thought. That's the whole question. The dogs barked and came rushing towards him; but he whistled softly and they crept up fawning.

Clambering up next from terrace to terrace he easily managed, although all the iron gates were locked, to get right under Madame de Rênal's bedroom window which, on the garden side, was only nine or ten feet above the ground. There was a little heart-shaped opening in the shutters which Julien knew well. To his great grief, the little opening was not lit up by the glow of a nightlight from within.

Good heavens! he said to himself, Madame de Rênal can't be in this room tonight! Where can she be sleeping? The family is in Verrières, for I found the dogs here; but in this room without a light I might come upon M. de Rênal himself, or some stranger, and then what a scandal there'd be!

His most prudent course was to withdraw; but such a choice filled Julien with horror. If it's someone I don't know, I'll take to my heels and leave my ladder behind; but if she's there – what sort of welcome awaits me? Remorse and deep religious devotion – that I can't doubt – have taken possession of her mind. But, after all, she still retains some memory of me, since she's just written me a letter. This argument decided him.

With trembling heart, but none the less determined to see her or die, he flung a handful of little pebbles against the shutter. No reply. He leant his ladder up against the side of the window and knocked on the shutters with his hand, at first softly and then more loudly. However dark it may be, thought Julien, someone might take a shot at me. The thought of this reduced his mad enterprise to a question of courage.

This room must be empty tonight, he thought, or whoever's sleeping in it would have woken up by now. No need to go carefully any longer; the only thing is to try and not be overheard by people in bed in the other rooms.

He got down, placed his ladder against one of the shutters, climbed up again, and putting his hand through the heart-shaped opening, was lucky enough to come fairly quickly on the wire attached to the hook that fastened the shutter. He tugged at the wire; to his inexpressible joy he found that the shutter was no longer fastened and yielded to his efforts. He opened it wide enough to put his head through, and said two or three times in a low voice: 'It's a friend.'

By straining his ears, he made sure that nothing disturbed the deep silence of the room; but certainly there was no lamp, even half turned down, in the fireplace. That was indeed a bad sign.

Beware of gunshots! For a brief space of time he reflected; then he tapped on the window with his finger. No answer. He knocked more loudly. Even if I have to smash the glass, he thought, I must put an end to this. Whilst he was knocking very loudly, he thought he could dimly see a white shadow moving through the darkness across the room. At last – there was no possible doubt about it – he saw a shadow that seemed to be coming towards him extremely slowly. Suddenly he caught sight of a cheek, pressed up against the windowpane through which he was looking.

He started and drew back a little. But the night was so dark that, even at this short distance, he could not make out if it was Madame de Rênal. He feared a first cry of alarm; he could hear the dogs faintly growling as they prowled about round the foot of the ladder. 'It's me, a friend,' he repeated fairly loudly. No answer, the white ghost had vanished. 'Be kind, and let me in. I must speak to you – I'm too unhappy !' He knocked in a way that threatened to break the glass.

A little sharp sound could be heard. The window latch yielded. He pushed back one side of the casement and jumped into the room. The white ghost drew away from him; he caught hold of its arms; it was a woman. All his courageous imaginings faded to nothing. If it's really she, what is she going to say? What was his state of mind when a faint cry told him it was Madame de Rênal !

He clasped her close in his arms. She was trembling and had barely strength enough to thrust him from her.

'Wretched man ! What are you doing?' she cried.

Her voice, quavering with emotion, could hardly articulate the words. Julien recognized the most genuine indignation in its tones.

'I'm come to see you after fourteen months' cruel separation.'

'Go out of this room at once and leave me. Ah ! M. Chélan, why did you keep me from writing to him? I could have prevented this horrible thing.' She pushed him away with really extraordinary force. 'I repent of my crime,' she said in a voice that broke with emotion. 'Heaven in its mercy has granted me pardon. Go out of this room. And quickly !'

'After fourteen months' unhappiness, I certainly won't leave you until I've talked to you. I want to know all you've done. Ah ! I've loved you fondly enough to deserve such confidences. ... I want to know everything.'

The note of authority in his voice had power over Madame de Rênal against her will. Julien, who had been clasping her pas-

sionately, resisting all her efforts to free herself, now loosened the
hold of his arms about her. This action slightly reassured Madame
de Rênal.

'I'm going to draw up the ladder,' he said, 'so that we shan't be
compromised if any of the servants, wakened by the noise, should
make a round of the house.'

'Ah! don't do that,' she said, in genuine anger, 'but, on the
contrary, leave this room. What do I care about men? It's God
who sees the frightful scene you're forcing on me, and will punish
me for it. You're taking a mean advantage of feelings I once had
for you, but have no longer. Are you listening to me, M. Julien?'
He was drawing the ladder slowly up so as not to make any noise.

'Is your husband in town, my dear?' he said, not with intent
to defy her, but absent-mindedly yielding to old habit.

'For pity's sake, don't speak to me like that, or I'll call my husband. Whatever the consequences, I'm only too guilty already for
not having driven you away. I pity you,' she said in an attempt
to wound his pride, so quick, as she knew, to take offence.

This rejection of all intimate forms of speech, this abrupt way
of severing ties so tender, and on which he still relied, drove
Julien's passionate frenzy of love to the verge of delirium.

'What! is it possible you no longer love me?' he said to her in
those heartfelt tones so difficult to hear and remain unmoved. She
did not answer. He, for his part, was weeping bitterly. He really
had no strength left to speak.

So I'm completely forgotten by the only being who's ever loved
me! he thought. What's the good of going on living any longer?
All his courage had left him as soon as he had no longer to fear
the risk of meeting a man. Everything had faded from his heart –
except love.

He wept for a long time silently. He took hold of her hand; she
tried to draw it away; yet after several convulsive movements
she let it stay in his. It was extremely dark; they found themselves both sitting on Madame de Rênal's bed.

How different things were fourteen months ago! thought
Julien; and his tears fell faster. Thus absence infallibly destroys
all human emotions!

'Be so kind as to tell me what has happened to you,' Julien
said at length, embarrassed by her silence and speaking in a voice
interrupted by his tears.

'There was no doubt,' Madame de Rênal replied in a hard voice
with a hint of severity and blame for Julien in its tones, 'that at

the time you went away the error of my ways was known to the town. Your behaviour had been so very indiscreet! Some time later, when I was in despair, that worthy man Father Chélan came to see me. For a long time he vainly tried to obtain a confession from me. One day he got the idea of taking me to the church in Dijon where I made my first communion; and there he dared to be the first to speak. ...' Madame de Rênal was interrupted by her tears. 'What a moment of shame! I confessed everything. This kindly man was good enough not to overwhelm me with the weight of his indignation; he shared my distress. Every day at that time I was writing letters which I did not dare to send you; I hid them carefully, and whenever I felt too miserable I would shut myself up in my room and read my letters all over again.

'Finally Father Chélan managed to get me to put them in his keeping. ... One or two, written rather more discreetly, had already been sent to you. – You didn't answer me.'

'But I never received any letter from you at the seminary – never, I swear it!'

'Good heavens! who could have intercepted them?'

'You can judge my grief – before the day I saw you in the cathedral, I didn't know if you were still alive.'

'God gave me grace,' replied Madame de Rênal, 'to understand how greatly I had sinned against him, against my children and my husband. Yet he has never loved me as I believed you loved me at that time. ...'

Without, indeed, any idea of what he was doing and quite beside himself, Julien rushed into her arms. But Madame de Rênal pushed him away and went on speaking with a fair amount of determination. 'My worthy friend M. Chélan made me understand that in marrying M. de Rênal I had pledged him all my affections, even those which I myself did not know of, and had never experienced before a certain fatal liaison. ... Ever since making the great sacrifice of those letters which were so dear to me, my life has run on, if not happily, at least sufficiently calmly. Don't disturb it; be a friend to me ... the best friend I have.' Julien covered her hand with kisses; she was conscious that he was still crying.

'Don't cry,' she said, 'you distress me so. ... Tell me in your turn what you've been doing.' Julien could not speak. 'I want to know what your life in the seminary was like,' she repeated, 'then you must go away.'

Without really thinking of what he was telling her, Julien spoke of the numberless intrigues and instances of jealousy he had met with at first, then of his more peaceful existence after his appointment as junior lecturer.

'It was then,' he added, 'that after a long period of silence, intended no doubt to make me realize what I see only too plainly today – that you didn't love me any more, that I'd become an object of indifference to you. . . .' Madame de Rênal pressed both his hands in hers. 'It was then you sent me the sum of five hundred francs.'

'I never sent it,' said Madame de Rênal.

'It was a letter with the Paris postmark, and signed Paul Sorel to disarm all suspicion.'

A short discussion then arose as to the origin of the letter. Psychologically, the situation changed. Madame de Rênal and Julien had, all unwittingly, abandoned their somewhat stilted tone, and had returned once more to that of intimate affection. So intense was the darkness that they could not see each other, but the sound of their voices said everything. Julien put his arm round his mistress's waist, a gesture fraught with danger. She tried to push Julien's arm away, but he distracted her attention rather cleverly at this moment by some interesting detail in his story. This arm remained, as if forgotten, in the position it occupied.

After many conjectures as to the origin of the letter containing five hundred francs, Julien had resumed his tale; he was gradually gaining a little more mastery over himself, as he spoke of his past life, which interested him so little compared with what was happening to him at this moment. His attention was wholly concentrated on the way in which his visit would end. The short, curt tones of the phrase, 'Go away !' still reached him at intervals.

What a disgrace for me if I'm shown the door ! he said to himself. The sting of it will be enough to poison my whole life. She will never write to me. God knows when I shall return to these parts again ! From that moment, whatever spiritual quality there had been in Julien's attitude promptly vanished from his heart. Seated beside a woman he adored in this room where he had been so happy, almost clasping her in his arms, discerning clearly in the intense darkness around him that for a moment past she had been weeping, conscious of her sobs from the convulsive heaving of her breast, he was so unfortunate as to become a cool, dispassionate schemer, as cold and calculating almost as when, in the courtyard of the seminary, he found himself the victim of some ill-mannered jest on the part of a fellow-student stronger than himself.

Julien spun out his story by talking of the unhappy life he had led since leaving Verrières. So, said Madame de Rênal to herself, after a year of absence and almost entirely deprived of any sign of remembrance, his only thought, whilst I was forgetting him, was of the happy days he had experienced at Vergy. Her sobs came faster; Julien saw his story had been successful. Realizing it was time to play his last card, he came abruptly to the letter he had received from Paris.

'I've said good-bye to the Bishop.'

'What! you're not coming back to Besançon again! You're leaving us for good?'

'Yes,' answered Julien firmly. 'Yes, I'm turning my back on a place where I'm forgotten even by the person I've loved most dearly in all my life, and I'm leaving it never to see it again. I'm going to Paris. . . .'

'Going to Paris!' Madame de Rênal exclaimed rather loudly. Her voice, almost stifled by tears, revealed her extreme distress. Julien had need of such encouragement; he was about to attempt a step which might decide everything against him; unable to see anything, he had known nothing of the effect his words had just produced until she uttered this cry. He hesitated no longer; fear of future regrets completely restored his self-control. Rising to his feet he added coldly : 'Yes, madam. I'm leaving you for good and all. I wish you happiness – good-bye.'

He took a few steps towards the window; he was already opening it. Madame de Rênal rushed up to him and fell into his arms.

Thus, after three hours' conversation, Julien obtained what he had so passionately longed for during the first two hours of it. Had a return to tenderness and a forgetfulness of remorse come sooner to Madame de Rênal it would have been the divinest happiness, but contrived in this way by artful means it was merely a pleasure. Julien was absolutely determined, against his mistress's express request, to light the lamp.

'Do you want then,' he said, 'to leave me with no memory of having seen you? Must the love in those charming eyes be lost to me? The whiteness of this pretty hand remain unseen? Just think, I may possibly be leaving you for a very long time.'

At this thought, which made her burst into tears, Madame de Rênal could refuse him nothing. But dawn was already beginning

to pick out in sharp relief the outline of the fir-trees on the mountain to the east of Verrières. Instead of leaving, Julien, off his
head with love and delight, asked Madame de Rènal to let him
spend the whole of the day hidden in her room, and not leave it
until the following night.

'Why not?' she said, 'this fatal relapse of mine robs me of self-
respect and makes me unhappy for ever.' She clasped him in her
arms. 'My husband,' she added, 'isn't the same to me any more –
he suspects something; he believes I've tricked him over all this
business and shows himself very annoyed with me. If he should
hear the slightest noise, I'm ruined; he'll turn me out of the house
like the miserable sinner I am.'

'Ah! that's a phrase of Father Chélan's,' said Julien. 'You
wouldn't have talked to me like that before my sad departure for
the seminary. You loved me then!'

Julien was rewarded for the self-possession with which he delivered these words; he found his mistress suddenly forgetting
the risk she ran from her husband's presence in the house to think
of the much more considerable danger of seeing Julien doubt her
love. Daylight was fast growing stronger and vividly lighting up
the room. Julien discovered anew all the exquisite pleasure pride
can afford in being allowed to see this charming woman, the only
one he had ever loved and who, but a few, short hours before,
had been wholly possessed by fear of God and love of duty, once
more in his arms and almost at his feet. Resolutions strengthened
by a year's unbroken fidelity had not been able to stand up to his
courage.

Soon they heard noises in the house and Madame de Rênal began to worry over something to which she had given no thought.

'That spiteful Elisa will be coming into this room,' she said to
her lover. 'What can we do with this enormous ladder? Where
can we hide it? Ah! I'll carry it up to the attic,' she suddenly
cried, with a kind of childish eagerness.

'But you'll have to go through the manservant's bedroom,' said
Julien in amazement.

'I'll leave the ladder in the corridor, call the servant, and send
him on some errand for me.'

'Think of something ready to say in case the man notices it in
the corridor as he's passing.'

'Yes, my angel,' said Madame de Rênal, giving him a kiss. 'And
mind you think of hiding quickly under the bed if Elisa comes in
while I'm away.'

Julien was surprised at this sudden gaiety. So the approach of real, solid danger, far from worrying her, he thought, makes her light-hearted again, since she forgets her remorse. What a really superior woman! Ah! there's a heart over which it's glorious to reign. Julien was enchanted.

Madame de Rênal took hold of the ladder; it was obviously too heavy for her. Julien went to her aid. He was admiring that dainty figure which gave so little promise of strength, when, all at once, she picked up the ladder without any assistance and bore it off as she would have done with a chair. She carried it quickly into the corridor where she laid it down alongside the wall. She called the servant and, to give him time to dress, went up to the top of the dovecote.

When she came back into the corridor five minutes later she found the ladder no longer there. What had become of it? If Julien had been out of the house she would have been hardly affected by his danger. But if, at this moment, her husband should see the ladder! This incident might have frightful consequences. She ran up and down through the whole of the house, and finally discovered the ladder up under the roof, where the servant had taken it – and even hidden it. This circumstance was strange; some time ago, it might have alarmed her.

What does it matter to me what happens in twenty-four hours' time, when Julien will have gone? Won't everything then mean nothing for me but horror and remorse? She had a kind of vague idea that she ought to take her own life – but what did that matter? After a cruel separation that she had believed to be for ever, he had been given back to her, she was seeing him once more, and what he had gone through to reach her showed so much love!

On telling Julien of the incident of the ladder, she asked: 'How shall I answer my husband if the servant tells him he's found this ladder?' She pondered for a moment. 'It will take them twenty-four hours to discover the peasant who sold it to you.' Then she flung herself into Julien's arms, holding him tight in a convulsive embrace. 'Ah! to die like this!' she cried, covering his face with her kisses. 'But I can't let you die of hunger,' she added, laughing.

'Come along,' she said, 'first of all, I'll hide you in Madame Derville's room, which is always kept locked.' She went to the end of the corridor to keep watch, and Julien ran past. 'Mind you don't open the door if anyone knocks,' she said as she locked him in. 'Anyhow it would only be the children having a game with each other.'

'Get them to come into the garden, under the window, so that I can have the pleasure of seeing them,' said Julien. 'And get them to talk.'

'Yes, I will,' cried Madame de Rênal as she was going away.

She came back very soon with oranges, biscuits, and a bottle of Malaga wine; she had not been able to steal any bread.

'What's your husband doing?' said Julien.

'He's with some peasants writing out contracts of sale.'

But eight o'clock had struck and there was a good deal of noise in the house. If Madame de Rênal were not seen about, they would look for her everywhere; she was obliged to leave him. She soon returned, contrary to all caution, and brought him a cup of coffee; she was trembling for fear he should die of hunger. After breakfast, she managed to bring the children along with her under the window of Madame Derville's room. He found them much taller, but either they had grown rather plain and uninteresting, or possibly his ideas had altered. Madame de Rênal talked to them about Julien. The eldest boy's answers were full of friendship and regret for their former tutor, but the two youngest ones appeared to have almost forgotten him.

M. de Rênal did not go out that morning. He was continually about the house, upstairs and down, busy concluding bargains with certain peasants to whom he was selling potatoes. Up till dinner time Madame de Rênal had not a moment to spare for her prisoner. When the bell had rung and dinner was served Madame de Rênal got the idea of taking a plate of hot soup to him secretly. As she was approaching his room very quietly, carrying the plate with the utmost care, she came face to face with the servant who had hidden the ladder that morning. At that moment he was also moving very quietly down the corridor and seemed to be listening. Probably Julien had been rashly walking about. The servant moved off a little abashed. Madame de Rênal walked boldly into Julien's room; this encounter made him shudder.

'You're frightened!' she said to him. 'For my part, I'd brave every danger in the world without turning a hair. There's only one thing I fear, and that's the moment after you've left me, when I'll be all alone.' And she ran off.

Ah! thought Julien enraptured, remorse is the only danger this sublime creature dreads!

Evening came round at last. M. de Rênal went off to the Casino.

Madame de Rênal had given out she had a frightful headache. She went up to bed, hastened to send Elisa away, and got up again to let Julien in.

It turned out he was really famished. Madame de Rênal went to the pantry to get him some bread. Julien heard a loud cry. Madame de Rênal came back and told him that as she went into the unlit pantry and was going up to the dresser in which the bread was kept, just as she put out her hand she touched a woman's arm. It was Elisa, who had uttered the cry Julien had heard.

'What was she doing there?'

'Stealing sweets — or possibly spying on us,' Madame de Rênal replied with complete indifference. 'But luckily I found a pie and a loaf of bread.'

'What have you got in there?' said Julien, pointing to her pockets. Madame de Rênal had forgotten that, ever since dinner-time, they had been filled with bread.

Julien clasped her eagerly, passionately in his arms; never before had she seemed to be so beautiful as now. Even in Paris, his bemused mind was thinking, I can't possibly meet anyone with a nobler nature. She showed all the awkward embarrassment of a woman little used to attentions of this kind, but she showed at the same time the true courage belonging to one who is only frightened by dangers of another, and very much more terrible, order.

While Julien was eating his supper with a keen appetite and his mistress was joking with him about the frugality of his meal, the door of the room was all at once violently shaken. It was M. de Rênal.

'Why have you locked yourself in?' he called out to her loudly. Julien had only just time to slip under the sofa.

'What! you're completely dressed,' said M. de Rênal as he entered, 'you're having supper and you've locked the door!'

On any ordinary day, such a question, addressed to her with all his usual conjugal curtness, would have made Madame de Rênal feel upset, but now she was conscious that her husband had only to stoop down a little to catch sight of Julien. M. de Rênal had flung himself into the chair on which Julien had been sitting a moment before and which was directly facing the sofa.

Her headache served as an excuse for everything. While M. de Rênal was giving her in his turn a long and detailed account of how he had won the pool at billiards in the Casino — 'A pool of

nineteen francs, by Jove,' he added — she noticed Julien's hat on
a chair three feet away. With formidable presence of mind, she
began to undress and at a given moment, passing rapidly behind
her husband, she flung a dress over the chair with the hat on it.

At last M. de Rênal went away. She begged Julien to repeat
the story of his life at the seminary. 'Yesterday, I wasn't listening
while you were talking to me — I was only thinking of persuading
myself to send you away.'

She was rashness itself. They were talking very loudly — it
might have been about two o'clock in the morning — when they
were interrupted by a violent knock on the door. It was M. de
Rênal again.

'Open the door very quickly, and let me in,' he said, 'there
are burglars in the house. Saint-Jean discovered their ladder this
morning.'

'This is the end of everything,' cried Madame de Rênal, flinging
herself into Julien's arms. 'He's coming to kill us both, he doesn't
believe there are burglars. I shall die in your arms, happier in my
death than I ever was in my life.' She made no reply to her husband, who was getting angry; she was clasping Julien in a passionate embrace.

'Save Stanislas's mother,' he said to her with a look of command. 'I'm going to jump down into the courtyard from the
dressing-room window and escape into the garden, the dogs know
me. Make my clothes into a bundle and throw it down into the
garden as soon as you can. Meanwhile, let him break the door in.
And mind particularly to make no admissions, I forbid it. It's
better for them to suspect than be certain.'

'You'll be killed if you jump,' was her only answer, her only
anxiety.

She accompanied him to the dressing-room; then gave herself
time to hide his clothes. Finally she opened the door to discover
her husband in a boiling rage. Without saying a word, he looked
round her room, then went into the dressing-room and disappeared. Julien's clothes were thrown out to him, he caught them
and then ran rapidly down to the lower end of the garden in the
direction of the Doubs. As he was running he heard the whistle
of a bullet, and simultaneously the sound of a gun being fired.

It isn't M. de Rênal, he thought, he's too bad a shot for that.
The dogs were running noiselessly at his side; a second shot
apparently broke one dog's paw, for it began to utter piteous
cries. Julien leapt over one of the terrace walls, ran about fifty

paces under cover, and then started to run off in another direction. He heard voices calling to each other, and distinctly saw his enemy, the valet, firing off his gun. A farmer came up as well and began firing blindly on the other side of the garden, but Julien had already reached the banks of the Doubs, where he put on his clothes.

An hour later, he was three miles out of Verrières on the road to Geneva. If they suspect anything, thought Julien, they'll look for me along the Paris road.

PART TWO

She is not pretty, she wears no rouge.

SAINTE-BEUVE

CHAPTER 1 : *The Pleasures of Country Life*

> O country scenes, when shall my eyes behold you !
> HORACE

'You've no doubt come, sir, to wait for the Paris mail,' remarked the landlord of the inn at which he had stopped for breakfast.

'Today's or tomorrow's – I don't much mind,' replied Julien.

The mail-coach arrived as he was making this show of indifference. There were two places free.

'What ! it's you, my poor Falcoz,' said the traveller arriving from the direction of Geneva to the one who was getting into the coach at the same time as Julien.

'I thought,' said Falcoz, 'you had settled down in the neighbourhood of Lyons, in a delightful valley beside the Rhône.'

'Finely settled ! I'm running away from it.'

'Indeed ! You're running away ? You, Saint-Giraud, with your air of respectability, have you gone and committed some crime?' said Falcoz, laughing.

'Upon my word, just as good as. I'm running away from the abominable life they lead in the provinces. I like cool woods and quiet fields, as you know – you've often accused me of being romantic. I didn't want to hear any talk of politics in my life, and it's politics that's driving me away.'

'But what's your party?'

'None at all – and that's my ruin. Here's the sum of my politics : I love music, I love pictures; a good book is a major event in my life. I'm just reaching forty-four. How much longer have I to live? Fifteen, twenty – thirty years at most. Well, in thirty years' time, I maintain, ministers'll be a trifle more astute, but just as decent fellows as they are today. English history serves me as a mirror of our future. There'll still be a king wishing to extend his prerogatives, still people ambitious to become Deputies – the renown and the thousands of francs Mirabeau gained will prevent the wealthy men of this province from sleeping – they'll call that holding Liberal views and being friends of the people. Extremists on the Right will still be possessed by a longing to become peers or gentlemen in waiting. Everyone will want to have a hand on the tiller of the Ship of State, for it's a paying job. Will there never then be even a tiny, humble place for a simple passenger?'

'Quite so, quite so. And that must be all very jolly for you with your peaceful disposition. Would it be the last elections that are driving you out of the province?'

'My troubles go further back. Four years ago I was forty, and had five hundred thousand francs — today I'm four years older and probably minus five hundred thousand francs, which I'm about to lose on the sale of my country house at Montfleury, near the Rhône — a marvellous position.

'In Paris, I got tired of that perpetual comedy in which what you call nineteenth-century civilization obliges one to play a part. I was thirsting for kindly, easy-going ways and the simple life. I bought an estate in the mountains near the Rhône — nothing finer under the sun.

'For six months the curate of the village and the clod-hopping country squires of the neighbourhood courted my favour; I invited them to dinner. "I've left Paris," I told them, "so that I'd never talk or hear talk of politics for the rest of my life. As you see, I don't subscribe to any paper. The fewer letters the postman brings me, the greater is my satisfaction."

'That wasn't what the curate had counted on. Soon I was the victim of a multitude of impertinent petitions, pesterings, and what-not. I wanted to give two or three hundred francs a year to the poor — I was asked to give them to various pious societies : the Guild of Saint Joseph, of the Virgin Mary, and so on. I refused; they then abused me in a hundred ways. I was stupid enough to get annoyed. I couldn't go out of a morning any longer to enjoy the beauty of the mountains, without coming upon some tiresome thing or other to snatch me from my dreams and remind me unpleasantly of men and their spiteful ways.

'In processions at Rogation time, for instance, with the special chant that pleased me — it's probably some Greek melody — my fields were no longer blessed, because, as the curate said, they were owned by an ungodly man. The cow belonging to a pious old peasant woman died — they said it was all on account of a neighbouring pond that belonged to me, the infidel, the freethinker from Paris. A week later I found my fish floating belly upwards, poisoned with lime. I was surrounded with bothers and annoyances of every kind and shape. The justice of the peace, a decent sort of fellow, but afraid of losing his job, always gave the verdict against me. The peaceful fields became my hell. Once it was discovered that the curate, who's head of the *Congrégation* in that village, had given me up as lost, and that the chief man among the Liberals, a retired army captain, didn't support me – everyone fell on me, down to the mason whom I'd helped to earn his bread for a year, and the wheelwright who tried to cheat me – and get away with it, too – whenever he mended one of my ploughs for me.

'To get some support and win at least some of my lawsuits, I became a Liberal. But, as you were saying, those blasted elections came on, and they asked me for my vote. . . .'

'For someone you didn't know.'

'Not at all, for someone I knew only too well. I refused, a frightful act of imprudence! From that moment, I had the Liberals too to contend with, my position became intolerable. I really believe that if the curate had taken it into his head to accuse me of murdering the maid, they'd have been twenty witnesses of both parties to swear they'd seen me commit the crime.'

'So you want to live in the country without pandering to your neighbours' passions, without even lending an ear to their tittle-tattle. What a mistake! . . .'

'Anyhow, I've corrected it. Montfleury's up for sale. If I have to, I'll lose fifty thousand francs, but I'm full of joy – I'm leaving this hell of hypocrisy and petty vexations. I'm going to seek solitude and rustic tranquillity in the only place where they exist in France – in a fourth-floor flat overlooking the Champs Elysées. And yet, I'm busy considering whether I shan't be beginning my political career all over again in the district of le Roule, by distributing consecrated bread to the parishioners.'

'Nothing of this would have happened to you in Bonaparte's day,' said Falcoz, his eyes bright with rage and regret.

'Maybe so, but why didn't that Bonaparte of yours manage to keep his position? Everything I have to put up with today is his fault.'

At this point Julien grew even more attentive. From the very first word spoken he had realized that this Bonapartist, Falcoz, was the onetime friend of M. de Rênal's boyhood, disowned by him in 1816; and that Saint-Giraud must be the brother of the senior clerk in the prefect's office in —, who knew how to get houses owned by the commune assigned to him cheap.

'And all that is your Bonaparte's doing,' Saint-Giraud continued. 'A decent sort of man, as inoffensive as you make them, who's forty years old and has five hundred thousand francs, can't settle down in the provinces and find peace there; that fellow's priests and nobles drive him out.'

'Ah! don't speak ill of him,' exclaimed Falcoz. 'France has never been so high in the esteem of other nations as during the thirteen years of his reign. There was some quality of greatness then in everything people did.'

'Your Emperor – devil take him!' replied the man of forty-four, 'was only great on the field of battle, and at the time he put finance on its feet round about 1802. What was the meaning of all his conduct after that? What with his chamberlains, his pomp, and his receptions at the Tuileries, he produced a new edition of all the senseless follies of monarchy. It was a revised version, it might still have done for a century or two. The nobles and the priests have tried to go back to the old edition, but they haven't the iron hand that's needed to make the public buy it.'

'There's the old printer talking!'

'Who is it who's hounding me out of my property?' put in the printer angrily. 'The priests, whom Napoleon recalled by his *Concordat*, instead of treating them as the State treats doctors, lawyers, and astronomers, by regarding them as citizens only, without worrying about the business by which they make their living. Would insolent noblemen exist today if your Bonaparte hadn't created barons and counts? No, all that had gone out of fashion. Next to the priests, it was these little, rustic lordlings who vexed me most and forced me to become a Liberal.'

The conversation was endless; this theme will occupy the minds of Frenchmen for another half-century more. As Saint-Giraud still went on repeating how impossible it was to live in the provinces, Julien timidly suggested M. de Rênal as an example.

'Good gracious, young man, you're a simple sort of fellow!' exclaimed Falcoz. 'He's made himself into a hammer – and a terrible one at that – to avoid being made an anvil. All the same, I see Valenod outstripping him. Do you know that rascal? He's the genuine article. What will your M. de Rênal say if one of these fine days he finds himself sacked and M. Valenod put in his place?'

'He'll be left alone with his crimes,' remarked Saint-Giraud. 'So you know Verrières, young man? Well then, Bonaparte – heaven confound him – he and all his imperial trumpery made possible the rule of the Rênals and the Chélans, which has brought about the reign of the Valenods and the Maslons.'

The gloomy political trend of this conversation astonished Julien and took his attention away from his voluptuous dreams. He was little impressed by his first view of Paris seen from a distance. Castles in Spain which his fancy constructed of what his future destiny would be had to battle against the still present memory of the twenty-four hours he had just spent in Verrières. He vowed to himself never to desert his mistress's children, and to forsake everything for them, if ever the tactless indiscretions of the clergy gave France a republic, bringing with it persecution of the nobles.

What would have happened, he wondered, if on the night of his arrival at Verrières he had found, at the moment of leaning his ladder up against the window of Madame de Rênal's room, that it was occupied by a stranger or by M. de Rênal? Yet all the same, what exquisite delight in those first two hours when his mistress had earnestly wanted to send him away and he had been sitting beside her in the darkness, pleading his cause! Memories such as these will haunt a heart like Julien's for a lifetime. The rest of this interview was already confused in his mind with memories of the first days of their love some fourteen months before.

Julien was startled out of his brown study by the stopping of the coach. They had just entered the mail-coach yard in the rue Jean-Jacques Rousseau. He hailed an approaching cab. 'I want to go to Malmaison,' he said.

'At this time of day, sir? And what's your business there?'

'That's no concern of yours. Drive on!'

All genuine passion thinks of nothing but itself. That is why, so it seems to me, passions are absurdly out of place in Paris, where your neighbours are always claiming a right to much of your attention. I will refrain from giving you an account of Julien's rapture at the sight of Malmaison. He was in tears. What! in spite of those hideous white walls just put up that year, and which cut the park up into sections? Yes, sir; for Julien, as for posterity, there was nothing to choose between Arcola, Saint Helena, and Malmaison.

That evening Julien wavered a long time before going into a theatre; he had curious notions concerning this place of perdition. Deep-rooted suspicions prevented his admiring Paris as it was in the living present; he was only moved by the monuments his hero had left behind. Here am I, he thought, in a city which is the centre of hypocrisy and intrigue! Here the patrons of the abbé de Frilair hold sway.

On the evening of his third day there, curiosity overcame his plans for seeing everything before visiting Father Pirard. In a cold tone of voice the abbé explained to him what kind of life awaited him in the house of the Marquis de la Mole.

'If at the end of a few months you don't prove yourself useful, you'll go back to the seminary, but through the front door. You are going to live in the Marquis's house; he's one of the noblest peers in France. You will wear black, but like a man who's in mourning, and not like a cleric. I insist on your going three times a week to continue your studies in theology at a seminary to which I will give you an introduction. Every day at twelve o'clock in the morning you will settle down in the Marquis's library, where he reckons to keep you occupied writing letters concerning lawsuits or other business. The Marquis writes a brief note in the margin of each letter he receives, indicating the kind of answer you must make to it. I have guaranteed that in three months' time you will be in a position to answer these letters in such a way that, out of the dozen or so you present to him for signature, the Marquis will be able to sign eight or nine of them. Every evening at eight o'clock you will put his writing-desk in order and at ten o'clock you will be free.

'It's possible,' Father Pirard went on, 'that some old lady or some soft-tongued man will hint to you of immense advantages, or quite bluntly offer you gold to show them the letters the Marquis receives . . .'

'Oh, sir !' exclaimed Julien, blushing.

'It's odd,' remarked Father Pirard, with a bitter smile, 'that, poor as you are, and after a year spent in the seminary, you have still some such virtuous indignation left. You must have been very blind !'

'Would it be in his blood?' said Father Pirard under his breath and as if talking to himself. 'What's strange about this,' he said, looking at Julien, 'is that the Marquis knows you . . . I don't know how. He's giving you, to begin with, a salary of one hundred louis. He's a man who only acts according to his fancy — that's his chief fault. He'll vie with you in childish follies. If he's satisfied with you, in course of time your salary may even be raised to eight thousand francs.

'But you are well aware,' the abbé went on tartly, 'that he isn't giving you all this money merely for love. It will be your business to make yourself useful. If I were in your place, I would say very little, and above all never talk of anything of which I was ignorant.

'Ah ! by the way,' said Father Pirard, 'I've been making some inquiries for you. I was forgetting M. de la Mole's family. He has two children, a daughter and a son of nineteen, a superlatively elegant young man and an utter madcap, who doesn't know from one hour to the next what he's going to do. He's intelligent and he's brave; he fought in the Spanish campaign. The Marquis hopes – I don't know why – that you'll make friends with young Count Norbert. I told him you were a fine Latin scholar – possibly he thinks you'll teach his son some ready-made phrases based on Cicero or Virgil.

'In your place, I would never allow this young man to make fun of me; before yielding to his overtures which, though marred by a touch of irony, will be perfectly polite, I would make him repeat them more than once.

'I won't hide from you the fact that the Comte de la Mole will certainly feel contempt for you at the outset, because you are merely one of the lower middle class. His ancestor was attached to the court and had the honour of being beheaded in the Place de Grève on the 26th of April 1574 for his part in a political intrigue. You yourself are the son of a carpenter of Verrières, and moreover in his father's employ. Weigh these differences well, and study the history of this family in Moreri; all the toadies who dine at this house make what they call delicate allusions to this work from time to time.

'Be careful how you answer Count Norbert's jesting; he's a major in the Hussars and a future peer of the realm – and don't come whining to me afterwards.'

'It seems to me,' said Julien, blushing deeply, 'that I mustn't even answer a man who feels contempt for me.'

'You've no idea of that sort of contempt; it will only show itself by exaggerated compliments. If you were a fool, it might take you in. If you want to get on in the world, you should let yourself be taken in.'

'The day I can't put up with that any more,' said Julien, 'shall I be thought ungrateful if I go back to my little cell, No. 108?'

'No doubt,' replied Father Pirard, 'all the grovelling nobodies in the house will slander you, but I'll intervene, myself. *Adsum qui feci*. I'll say your decision originates from me.'

Julien was deeply distressed by the bitter and almost spiteful tone of Father Pirard's voice; it altogether undid the effect of his last reply. The fact is that the abbé had conscientious scruples about his liking for Julien, and it was with a sort of religious dread that he interfered so directly in another man's fate.

'You will also,' he added in the same ungracious manner, and as if he were carrying out a painful duty, 'see her Ladyship the Marquise de la Mole. She is a tall, fair woman, pious, arrogant, extremely polite, and even more extremely insignificant. She is the daughter of the old duc de Chaulnes, so famous for his aristocratic prejudices. This great lady is a kind of epitome, in high relief, of the main characteristics of women of her rank. She, for her part, does not hide her opinion that the only kind of superiority she values is that of having ancestors who took part in the crusades. Money comes only a long way behind. Does that astonish you? We are no longer in the provinces, my friend.

'In her drawing-room you'll find a number of great nobles talking in a tone of singular levity about our princes. As for Madame de la Mole, she lowers her voice out of respect every time she pronounces the name of a prince and, more particularly, of a princess. I wouldn't advise you to say in front of her that Philip II or Henry VIII were monsters. They were KINGS – and that gives them an imprescriptible right to respect from lowborn creatures such as you and me. We are priests, however,' added M. Pirard, 'for she will take you for such; by virtue of this office, she regards us as a species of upper manservant necessary to her salvation.'

'It seems to me, sir,' said Julien, 'that I shan't be staying in Paris very long.'

'That's as it may be. But take good note that no man of our calling can make his way except with the help of these noble lords. With that something or other in your character which, for me at least, is indefinable, unless you do make your way you're in for persecution – there's no middle way for you. Don't deceive yourself. People can see you're not gratified when they address a remark to you; in a sociable country like this, you're bound for disaster if you don't attain to a position where men respect you.

'What would have become of you in Besançon, if it hadn't been for this whim of the Marquis de la Mole? One day you'll understand all the exceptional character of what he's doing for you; and if you're not an inhuman brute, you'll be eternally grateful to him and his family. How many priests as poor as yourself, and better scholars, have existed for years in Paris on the fifteen sous they got for masses said and the ten sous for lectures at the Sorbonne! ... Remember what I told you last winter about the early years of that scoundrel, Cardinal Dubois. Does your pride, perchance, allow you to believe that you're more gifted than he?

'I myself, for instance, who am a quiet, middling sort of man, thought to end my days in the seminary; I committed the childish folly of letting myself get attached to it. Well, I was just about to be dismissed when I sent in my resignation. Do you know what my whole fortune was? – I had a capital of five hundred and twenty francs, neither more nor less; not a single friend, and barely two or three acquaintances. M. de la Mole, whom I'd never seen, got me out of this quandary. He had only to say the word, and I was given a living where the parishioners are comfortably off and superior to all grosser vices, and I've a stipend that makes me ashamed, it's so disproportionate to what I do. I've only talked to you at such length to supply that head of yours with a little ballast.

'Just one word more – I'm unfortunately rather cantankerous; it's possible we might cease to be on speaking terms. Should the Marquise's haughty manners or her son's ill-natured chaff make this house really unbearable, I'd advise you to finish your studies in some seminary less than thirty leagues from Paris, and in the north rather than the south. There's more civilization in the north, and I must admit,' he added, lowering his voice, 'the proximity of the Paris newspapers puts some fear into petty tyrants.

'If we should go on finding pleasure in each other's society, and supposing M. de la Mole's house doesn't suit you, I can offer you a post as my curate, and give you half of what this living brings in. I owe you all this and more,' he added, cutting short Julien's thanks, 'for the remarkable offer you made me at Besançon. If, instead of five hundred and twenty francs, I had had nothing, you would have saved my life.'

The biting tone had disappeared from Father Pirard's voice. To his great embarrassment, Julien felt tears welling up in his eyes. He was dying to fling himself into his friend's arms; he could not keep from saying, with the manliest air he could assume: 'My father hated me from my cradle – that was one of my greatest misfortunes. But I'll never rail at chance any more, I've found a friend in you, sir.'

'All right, all right,' said Father Pirard, feeling embarrassed. Then, finding opportunely a phrase befitting the Rector of a seminary, he added: 'You must never speak of chance, my son, but always of Providence.'

The cab drew up. The driver lifted the brass knocker of an enor-

mous door. It was the Hôtel de la Mole; and to give passers-by no
chance of doubting this, its name was to be read on a black
marble tablet above the door.

Such pomposity displeased Julien. They're so afraid of Jacobins!
They see a Robespierre with his tumbril behind every hedge – so
often so much as to make one die of laughter. Yet they advertise
their dwelling like this for the rabble to pick them out and
pillage them, too, supposing there's a revolution. He communicated this idea to Father Pirard.

'Ah! my poor boy – I'll soon be having you as my curate. What
a frightful idea you've got hold of there.'

'I find nothing simpler,' said Julien.

The porter's gravity and, in particular, the cleanliness of the
courtyard left him wonderstruck. The sun was shining brightly.

'What marvellous architecture!' he remarked to his friend.

He was referring to one of those large private houses in the
Faubourg Saint-Germain, which have such insignificant façades
and were built round about the time of Voltaire's death. Never
have fashion and beauty been such poles apart from one another.

CHAPTER 2 : *Entry into Society*

> What a comical and affecting memory is that of the first drawing-room in which, at eighteen, one makes one's first appearance alone and without a friend! A glance from a woman was enough to terrify me; the more I wished to please, the more awkward I became. I had the most mistaken ideas about everything. Either I was expansive for no motive at all, or else I saw an enemy in every man who looked at me without smiling. But then, in the midst of this fearful unhappiness my shyness caused me, how really beautiful was a beautiful day!
>
> KANT

JULIEN stopped to gaze open-mouthed in the middle of the courtyard.

'Do try to look sensible,' said Father Pirard. 'First you think of the most horrible ideas, and next, you're just a child! Have you forgotten Horace's *nil mirari* (never show enthusiasm)? Just consider how all this tribe of lackeys, seeing you standing here, will make fun of you; they'll see in you one of their equals unjustly placed above them. Under cover of good-nature, of giving you sage advice and guiding you in the right direction, they'll be trying to trip you into making some gross blunder.'

'I defy them to do it,' said Julien biting his lip, all his old mistrust returning.

The reception-rooms on the first floor through which the two men passed before reaching the Marquis's study would have seemed to you, good reader, as gloomy as they were magnificent. One might offer them to you just as they are, yet you would refuse to live in them; they are the country of yawns and dreary argument. Julien was still more spellbound at the sight of them. How can anyone be unhappy, he thought, who lives in such a splendid dwelling!

They finally arrived at the most unprepossessing of the rooms in this superb suite, one into which daylight could hardly penetrate. There they found a lean little man with piercing eyes who was wearing a blond wig. Father Pirard turned towards Julien and introduced him. It was the Marquis. Julien had much difficulty in recognizing him, he appeared so urbane. He was no longer the noble lord of the Abbey of Bray-le-Haut, so haughty in his bearing. It seemed to Julien that there was much too much hair in his wig, and with the help of such an impression he did not feel at all abashed.

This descendant of the friend of Henry III seemed to him at first rather shabbily dressed. He was thin and fidgeted a good deal. Julien soon remarked, however, that the Marquis had a type of politeness even more agreeable to the man he was addressing than that of the Bishop of Besançon himself.

The interview lasted less than three minutes. As they were going out Father Pirard said to Julien : 'You stared at the Marquis as you would at a picture. I'm not very well versed in what these people here call manners – you will soon know more about it than I do – but certainly the boldness of your glances seemed to me a trifle impolite !'

They had got into the cab again; the driver pulled up near the ramparts. Father Pirard ushered Julien into a spacious suite of reception-rooms, where he noticed there was no furniture. He was looking at a magnificent clock, representing a subject which in his opinion was highly indecent, when a very elegant gentleman, with his face wreathed in smiles, came up to him. Julien bowed slightly.

The gentleman put his hand on his shoulder, smiling. Julien gave a start and jumped backwards, red with anger. Father Pirard, for all his gravity, laughed till the tears came into his eyes. The gentleman was a tailor.

'I'm giving you back your liberty for a couple of days,' said Father Pirard as they went out. 'You can't be presented to Madame de la Mole before then. In the first moments of your stay in this modern Babylon any other man would watch over you as if you were a girl. If you must get ruined, ruin yourself at once, and I shall be quit of the weakness I show in caring for you. The morning of the day after tomorrow, this tailor will bring you two suits; you will give five francs to the young fitter who tries them on. By the way, don't let these Parisians hear the sound of your voice. If you say a word they'll find out a way of making you look ridiculous. It's a special knack of theirs. Be at my house at noon on the day after tomorrow. Off with you now, and ruin yourself. . . . I was forgetting one thing – go and order yourself some boots, shirts, and a hat at these addresses.'

Julien looked at the handwriting of the addresses.

'They're in the Marquis's hand,' said Father Pirard. 'He's an active man who foresees everything and prefers doing things to giving orders. He's engaging you to spare him bothers of this kind. Will you have enough quickness of wit to carry out properly all the business this nimble-witted man will only hint at? That's what the future will show – be on your guard!'

Julien went to the tradesmen whose addresses he had been given, but did not utter a word. He remarked that he was treated with respect, and that the shoemaker, when writing his name in his account book, put down 'M. Julien de Sorel'.

In the cemetery of Père-Lachaise a very forthcoming individual, who was even more Liberal in his speech, offered his services in pointing out the tomb of Marshal Ney, whom the sagacity of statecraft had deprived of the honour of an epitaph. But when this Liberal, who had almost embraced him with tears in his eyes, had taken leave of him, Julien's watch had departed too. A couple of days later, all the richer for this experience, he presented himself to Father Pirard, who looked at him very hard.

'It seems you're on the way to becoming a coxcomb,' said Father Pirard severely. He was, in truth, very presentable, but the abbé was too much of a provincial himself to notice that Julien still retained the slouching gait considered both elegant and impressive in the provinces. When the Marquis saw Julien he judged these graces in such a different way from Father Pirard that he said to him : 'Would you have any objection if M. Sorel took dancing lessons?'

The abbé was paralysed with amazement.

'No,' he finally answered, 'Julien is not a priest.'

The Marquis, running up a little back staircase two steps at a time, went himself to install Julien in a comfortable little attic looking down on the huge garden belonging to the house. He asked him how many shirts he had got at the linen-draper's.

'Two,' answered Julien, abashed at finding so great a noble descend to such details.

'Very good!' the Marquis replied in a serious manner and a certain curt, commanding tone of voice, which gave Julien cause for thought. 'Very good! get twenty-two more. Here is your first quarter's salary.'

As they came down from the attic, the Marquis summoned an elderly man : 'Arsène,' he said to him, 'you will look after M. Sorel.' A few minutes later, Julien found himself in a magnificent library; this was a moment full of delight. To prevent himself being surprised in his emotion, he went and hid himself in a little dark corner, from whence he contemplated with rapture the resplendent backs of the books. I shall be able to read all those, he thought. How could I not like being here? M. de Rênal would have felt himself shamed for ever if he had done the hundredth part of what M. de la Mole has just done for me.

But let me see what letters I have to copy out. This task completed, Julien ventured to approach the books; he became almost mad with joy on looking into an edition of Voltaire. To avoid being taken by surprise, he ran to open the door, after which he gave himself the pleasure of opening each of the eighty volumes in turn. They were sumptuously bound, a masterpiece of work by the best bookbinder in London. It was more than enough to carry his admiration to its height.

An hour later, the Marquis came in, looked at the letters, and was surprised to see that Julien had written *cela* with a double 'l', *cella*. So all that the abbé told me about his learning was quite simply a fairy-tale! The Marquis, greatly disappointed, said to him gently: You're not quite sure of your spelling?'

'That's true,' said Julien, without thinking in the least of how he was injuring himself. He was feeling touched by the Marquis's goodness to him; it made him call to mind M. de Rênal's supercilious manner.

So my experiment with this young abbé from Franche-Comté is all a waste of time, thought the Marquis. And I so much needed a reliable man!

'*Cela* is written with one "l" only,' the Marquis told him. 'When you've finished copying your letters look up in the dictionary any words you are not sure of spelling rightly.'

At six o'clock the Marquis sent for him. He looked with evident pain at Julien's boots. 'I've one thing with which to reproach myself,' he said. 'I did not tell you that at half past five every day you are expected to dress.'

Julien looked at him without understanding what he meant.

'I mean you must change into shoes and stockings. Arsène will remind you. Today I will make your excuses for you.'

As he finished speaking, M. de la Mole ushered Julien into a drawing-room resplendent with gilding. On similar occasions M. de Rênal had never failed to quicken his pace so that he might have the advantage of passing first through the door. His former patron's petty vanity was the cause of Julien's treading on the Marquis's feet and making him suffer great pain on account of his gout. Ah! he's clumsy into the bargain, thought the Marquis.

He introduced him to a tall woman of imposing appearance. It was the Marquise. Julien thought she had a slightly insolent air, a little like that of Madame de Maugiron, wife of the sub-prefect of the district of Verrières, when she attended the official dinner on the feast of Saint-Charles. Somewhat disturbed by the extreme splendour of the drawing-room, Julien did not hear what M. de la Mole was saying. The Marquise hardly deigned to give him a glance. There were a few men present, amongst whom Julien, to his indescribable pleasure, recognized the Bishop of Agde who, a few months back, had condescended to talk to him at the ceremony of Bray-le-Haut. This young prelate was no doubt frightened by the melting glances Julien shyly cast his way, and was not at all anxious to recognize this visitor from the provinces.

The men assembled in the drawing-room seemed to Julien to have something glum and constrained in their manner; people converse in undertones in Paris, and do not lay stress on trifles.

A handsome young man with a moustache, who was very pale and very slender, came in towards half past six. He had a very small head.

'You always keep us waiting,' said the Marquise, whose hand he was kissing.

Julien realized it was the Comte de la Mole. He found him a charming person from the very first glance. Can that really be the man, he said to himself, whose offensive jokes would drive me out of this house?

After taking a good look at Count Norbert, Julien noticed that he was booted and spurred; and I, he thought, am obliged to wear shoes, apparently as an inferior. They sat down to table. Julien heard the Marquise pass a caustic remark, with her voice a little raised. Almost at the same time he noticed a young woman, with the palest golden hair and a shapely figure, who came and sat down opposite him. He did not, however, find her pleasing. As he looked attentively at her, he thought he had never seen such beautiful eyes; but they indicated an exceedingly cold disposition. Later on he decided that their expression was one of boredom, critical of everyone else, yet at the same time mindful of an obligation to impress other people.

Madame de Rênal, herself, had very beautiful eyes, he thought – everyone complimented her on them; but they had nothing in common with these. Julien knew too little of the world and its ways to discern that the fire that from time to time lit up the eyes of Mademoiselle Mathilde – for so he had heard her called – was a flash of wit. When Madame de Rênal's grew bright, it was with the fire of her emotions, or with generous indignation kindled by the tale of some base action.

Towards the end of the meal, Julien hit on a word to describe Mademoiselle de la Mole's type of beauty. They are scintillating eyes, he said to himself. Otherwise, she sadly resembled her mother, whom he was finding more and more unlikeable; and he left off looking at her. Count Norbert, on the other hand, seemed worthy of admiration from every point of view. Julien was so captivated by him that it did not enter his head to be jealous of him or hate him because he was richer and nobler than himself.

Julien thought the Marquis was looking bored. When they were reaching the second course, he said to his son : 'Norbert, I must ask you to look after M. Julien Sorel, whom I've just taken on my staff, and whom I hope to make a man of, if that (*cella*) is possible.'

'He's my secretary,' the Marquis remarked to his neighbour, 'and he writes *cela* with two *lls*.'

Everyone looked at Julien, who bowed to Norbert in a rather too exaggerated way; but on the whole, people approved of his appearance.

The Marquis must have mentioned the type of education Julien had received, for one of the guests began to tackle him on the subject of Horace. It was precisely by talking of Horace, thought Julien, that I managed to impress the Bishop of Besançon. Apparently these people don't know any other author.

From that moment, he became master of himself, a change made easier by his having just decided that Mademoiselle de la Mole would never count as a woman in his eyes. Since his time at the seminary he had defied men to do their worst and did not let himself be easily intimidated by any man. He would have enjoyed complete command over himself had the dining-room been less magnificently furnished. There were, in fact, two mirrors, each of them eight feet high, in which he glanced from time to time at the man who was questioning him on Horace and which still overawed him. His sentences, for a provincial, were not too long-winded. He had fine eyes, to which his eager, yet hesitant, shyness, turning to joy whenever he chanced to answer well, imparted still more fire. The company found him a likeable fellow. This sort of inquiry gave a touch of interest to a solemn dinner. The Marquis urged Julien's interrogator by a sign to press him hard. Can it really be possible, he was thinking, that the fellow knows something!

Julien went on answering, inventing his replies out of his head and losing enough of his timidity to show, not exactly wit — a thing impossible for a man who does not speak the language of Paris — but original ideas, although expressed with neither grace nor relevancy; and it was evident that he was completely at home with Latin.

Julien's opponent was a member of the Académie des Inscriptions who, by chance, knew Latin. He discovered a very good humanist in Julien, and being no longer afraid of making him blush, tried in good earnest to embarrass him. In the heat of the combat, Julien at last forgot the sumptuous furnishings of the dining-room and proceeded to develop ideas on the Latin poets which his interrogator had read nowhere. As a man of good breeding he gave the young secretary credit for them. By some happy chance discussion was opened on whether Horace was rich or poor — a genial, carefree, pleasure-loving man like Chapelle, the friend of Molière and La Fontaine; or some poor devil of a poet-laureate, attached to the court and writing odes for the king's birthday, as did Southey, the man who denounced Lord Byron. People talked of the state of society under Augustus and under George IV. At both these periods the aristocracy was all-powerful; but in Rome it saw its power being snatched away by a simple knight like Maecenas; while in England the nobility had reduced George IV to something almost like the position of a Venetian Doge. This discussion seemed to arouse the Marquis out of the state of torpor into which boredom had plunged him during the earlier part of dinner.

All these modern names such as Southey, Lord Byron, George IV, which Julien was hearing for the first time pronounced, meant nothing to him at all. But it escaped no one's notice that every time there was mention of things that had happened in Rome, a knowledge of which could be extracted from the works of Horace, Martial Tacitus, and so forth, there was no question of his superiority. Julien shamelessly annexed several ideas he had picked up from the Bishop of Besançon in the famous discussion he had had with this prelate — they were not among the least appreciated.

When they grew tired of talking about poets, the Marquise, who made it a rule to admire everything her husband found amusing, condescended to look at Julien. 'This young abbé's

awkward manners may possibly conceal a man of learning,' remarked an academician who happened to be sitting near to the
Marquise; and Julien caught something of what he was saying.
Stereotyped phrases rather suited the mentality of the mistress
of the house; she adopted this one about Julien, and was pleased
with herself for having invited the academician to dinner. M. de
la Mole finds him amusing, she thought.

This immense valley, full of brilliant lights
and so many thousands of men, dazzles my
eyes. Not one of them knows me, they are
all my superiors. My head grows dizzy.

REINA

V ERY early next morning Julien was copying out letters in
the library when Mademoiselle Mathilde came in by the
little private door very neatly disguised by backs of books. While
Julien was full of admiration at this contrivance, Mademoiselle
Mathilde seemed greatly surprised and rather put out at meeting
him there; with her hair in curl-papers, she seemed to Julien to
have a hard, arrogant, and almost masculine air. Mademoiselle de
la Mole had found out the secret of stealing books from her father's
library without its being noticed. Julien's presence in the library
made that morning's expedition useless, and this vexed her all
the more because she had come to get the second volume of
Voltaire's *Princess de Babylone* – a fitting complement to an education eminently royalist and religious in tone, the prime achieve-
ment of the Sacré-Cœur ! At nineteen, this poor girl already
needed something with a touch of spice and wit about it to
make her interested in a novel.

Towards three o'clock Count Norbert appeared in the library;
he came to consult a newspaper, so as to be able to talk politics
that evening, and seemed very glad to see Julien, whose existence
he had forgotten. His manners were perfect; he offered to take
Julien out riding.

'My father gives us leave of absence until dinner time.'

Julien noticed his use of 'us', and found it charming.

'Goodness me, my lord,' he said, 'if it were a question of cutting
down an eighty-foot tree, of lopping off its branches and sawing it
up into planks, I venture to say I'd make a pretty good job of it.
But as for getting astride a horse, that's a thing that hasn't
happened to me six times in my life.'

'Well, this will be the seventh,' said Norbert.

Underneath, Julien's mind was harking back to the entry of the
King of — and he really believed himself a tip-top rider. However, as they were coming back from the Bois de Boulogne, Julien,
trying to avoid a carriage, fell plumb into the middle of the rue

du Bac, and covered himself with mud. It was a very good thing he had two suits. At dinner, the Marquis, trying to make conversation, asked him for news of his ride. Norbert hastened to answer for him without giving particulars.

'His lordship is very good to me,' Julien put in, 'I'm very grateful to him and fully appreciate his kindness. He was good enough to let me have the gentlest and nicest-looking horse possible; but after all he could not tie me on to it, and, for lack of this precaution, I tumbled off right into the middle of that terribly long street near the bridge.' Mademoiselle Mathilde vainly tried to cover up a burst of laughter, and with tactless curiosity begged for details, Julien handled the situation with much simplicity and with a kind of unconscious grace.

'I have good hopes of this young priest,' the Marquis said to the academician. 'A provincial showing simplicity on such an occasion ! That's a thing that's never been seen before, and never will be again. And on top of it all he relates his misadventure in front of *the ladies* !'

Julien put those who listened so much at their ease about his mishap that by the end of dinner Mademoiselle Mathilde was questioning her brother on the details of this unlucky incident. As this went on for a very long time and Julien happened several times to catch her eye, he ventured to answer her directly, although she had not addressed any questions to him, and in the end all three of them were laughing together, like three young inhabitants of some village deep in the woods.

The following day, Julien attended a couple of lectures in theology and came back later to copy out a score of letters. He found ensconced close to his seat in the library a young man very neatly dressed, but whose general appearance was mean and whose countenance bore a look of envy.

The Marquis came in.

'What are you doing here, M. Tanbeau?' he said to the newcomer in a severe tone of voice.

'I thought . . .' the young man answered with a sneaking sort of smile.

'No, sir, you *did not think*. This is a tentative act on your part, but a very ill-judged one.'

Young Tanbeau got to his feet in a rage and disappeared. He was the nephew of the academician who was on friendly terms with Madame de la Mole, and was intending to become a writer. The academician had got the Marquis to take him on as his secretary. Tanbeau, who usually worked in an out-of-the-way room, learning of the favours granted to Julien, had wished to share them, and had come and taken up his quarters in the library that morning, complete with inkstand, pen, and papers.

At four o'clock Julien, after a little hesitation, ventured to make his appearance in Count Norbert's room. The latter was about to go out riding and, having perfect manners, felt somewhat embarrassed.

'I think,' he said to Julien, 'that you'll soon be going to the riding-school; and in a few weeks' time I shall be delighted to ride with you.'

'I wished to have the honour of thanking you for all the kindness you have shown me,' said Julien. 'Believe me, sir,' he added very gravely, 'I am conscious of all I owe you. If your horse was not hurt by my clumsiness yesterday, and if no one else is riding him, I should like to ride him today.'

'All right, my dear Sorel, but it's at your own risk. Just suppose I've put forward every objection prudence demands. But the fact is it's four o'clock, and we've no time to lose.'

Once he was on horseback Julien asked: 'What must I do to keep from falling off?'

'A great many things,' answered Norbert, roaring with laughter, 'such as, for instance – lean your body well back.'

Julien set off at a sharp trot. They reached the Place Louis XVI.

'Now then, young daredevil,' said Norbert, 'there are too many carriages here, and with careless drivers, too! Once you're on the ground, their gigs will run right over your body; they'll not risk spoiling their horses' mouths by pulling them up short.'

A score of times Norbert saw Julien on the point of falling off; but after all the ride ended without an accident. On their return the young count said to his sister: 'Allow me to introduce you to a bold and reckless rider.'

At dinner, speaking to his father down the whole length of the table, he did justice to Julien's daring. It was all there was to praise in his way of riding. That morning the young count had heard the men who were grooming the horses in the stable-yard take Julien's fall as an occasion for coarse and cruel fun at his expense.

In spite of all their kindness to him, Julien soon felt completely isolated in the midst of this family. All their ways and habits seemed strange to him, and he made every sort of mistake. His blunders were a source of delight to all the menservants.

Father Pirard had gone off to his living. If Julien is a feeble reed, let him perish, he thought; if he's a man of spirit, let him puzzle things out for himself.

> What is he doing here? Does he like the
> place? Does he think he will make other
> people like him?   RONSARD

IF everything in the lordly drawing-room of the Hôtel de la
Mole seemed strange to Julien, this pale young man in black
seemed in his turn a very strange individual to anyone who
condescended to notice him. Madame de la Mole suggested to her
husband that when they had certain imporant people to dine
they should send him out on some business or other.

'I'm anxious to carry on with my experiment to the very end,'
the Marquis replied. 'Father Pirard insists that we are wrong in
trying to crush the self-respect of people whom we admit to our
circle. *One can only lean on something that has resistance,* etc.
This fellow is only out of place because his appearance is unfamiliar; as for the rest, he's as good as deaf and dumb.'

If I want to get my bearings, said Julien to himself, I must
write down the names, and a word or two about the characters of
people I see visiting this drawing-room.

He put down first on his list some five or six friends of the
family who, thinking the Marquis for some capricious reason had
taken him under his wing, cultivated his acquaintance in and
out of season. They were rather miserable creatures, more or less
obsequious, though, it must be said in commendation of this type
of person, not equally obsequious to all and sundry. There were
those among them who would have allowed the Marquis to mis-
handle them, but were up in arms at a harsh word addressed to
them by Madame de la Mole.

As for the master and mistress of the house, the groundwork
of their characters consisted of too much boredom and too much
pride; they were too much given to seek escape from boredom
by wounding other people's feelings to hope to make a real friend
of anyone. All the same, except on rainy days and in rare
moments of exasperated boredom, they were always known to be
perfectly civil.

If the five or six toadies who expressed such fatherly regard for
Julien had deserted the Hôtel de la Mole, the Marquise would
have had to endure long periods of isolation; and isolation, in

the eyes of a woman of her rank, is a fearful thing—it is a mark of social disgrace.

The Marquis was absolutely correct in his behaviour to his wife; he took care to see that her drawing-room was adequately furnished with guests—not with peers, for he found his new-made associates insufficiently noble to be entertained at his house as friends, and not amusing enough to be received on an inferior footing.

It was not until very much later that Julien fathomed these mysteries. The policy of the government in power, which forms the main topic of conversation in middle-class houses, is never touched on in the houses of people of the Marquis's rank, except at moments of great emergency.

The need of amusement, even in this age of boredom, has still such hold over men that even on days when people were invited to dinner, the Marquis had scarcely left the drawing-room before every one of the guests was rushing away. Provided you did not treat God, the clergy, the King, or anyone holding public office as a matter for jest; provided you did not speak in praise of Béranger, the newspapers of the opposite party, Voltaire, Rousseau, or anyone allowing himself any freedom of speech; provided, above all, that you never mentioned politics—then you were free to discuss anything you pleased.

Neither an income of a hundred thousand crowns, nor the blue ribbon of the Saint-Esprit, could prevail against this drawing-room constitution. The least idea with any life in it was considered grossly out of place. In spite of good form, perfect manners, and an anxiety to please, boredom was written on every brow. Young people coming there to pay their respects, afraid of saying anything that might lay them under suspicion of having a thought of their own, or of having read some prohibited book, lapsed into silence after making a few very tasteful remarks on Rossini or the weather.

Julien observed that conversation was usually kept alive by two Viscounts and five Barons whom M. de la Mole had known at the time of the emigration. These gentlemen each possessed an income of six to eight hundred livres; four of them swore by the *Quotidienne* and three by the *Gazette de France*. Every day one of these persons had some story to tell of the Château in which the word 'admirable' was not sparingly used. He wore, so Julien noticed, five decorations, the others, as a rule, had only three.

As some compensation for this, ten footmen were to be seen in the antechamber, and the whole evening through ices and tea were handed round every quarter of a hour, and towards midnight there was a kind of supper with champagne.

This was the reason why Julien sometimes felt inclined to stay there till the end; for the rest, he almost failed to understand how anyone could listen seriously to the kind of conversation usual in this drawing-room with its magnificent gilding. Sometimes he watched the speakers to see if they themselves were finding their own words ridiculous. My M. de Maistre, whose works I know by heart, expresses himself a hundred times better, he thought, and yet I find him very boring.

Julien was not the only one to notice this atmosphere, so stifling to the mind. Some found consolation in eating a great number of ices, others in the pleasure of saying for the rest of the evening: 'I've just come from the Hôtel de la Mole, where I learnt that Russia, etc., etc.'

Julien found out from one of the family's obsequious friends that not six months before Madame de la Mole had rewarded more than twenty years' assiduous attentions by making a prefect out of poor Baron le Bourguignon, who had been a sub-prefect ever since the Restoration.

This great event had given fresh stimulus to the zeal of all these gentlemen. Before that time they would have taken offence at a very trifling matter; now they no longer took offence at anything. The lack of consideration shown them was rarely intentional, but two or three times at table already Julien had overheard a brief interchange of remarks between the Marquis and his wife which were cruelly cutting to those who were seated near them. These two lordly personages did not disguise their sincere contempt for everyone who was not descended from people *who rode in the royal coaches*. Julien remarked that the word *'crusade'* was the only one that gave to their faces an air of solemn gravity mixed with respect. At ordinary times their respect had always a shade of condescension about it.

Surrounded by all this magnificence and all this boredom, Julien was only interested in M. de la Mole; he was pleased to hear him one day protesting that he had had nothing whatever to do with poor Le Bourguignon's promotion. This was out of politeness for the Marquise; Julien had learnt the truth from Father Pirard.

One morning the abbé was working with Julien in the Mar-

quis's library, busy on the interminable lawsuit with M. de Frilair. 'Sir,' said Julien suddenly, 'is dining every day with her
ladyship the Marquise one of my duties, or is it a kindness on
their part?'

'It's a signal honour!' replied Father Pirard, deeply shocked.
'M. N——, the academician, who has been paying them assiduous
court for the past fifteen years, has never been able to obtain
such a thing for his nephew, M. Tanbeau.'

'For me, sir, it's the most painful part of my job. I found it less
boring in the seminary. I see even Mademoiselle de la Mole yawning now and then, and she ought to be accustomed to the amiable
attentions of friends of the family. I'm frightened I'll fall asleep.
Won't you kindly get permission for me to go and dine for forty
sous at some humble inn?'

The abbé, like a true *parvenu*, was very sensible of the honour
of dining with a great noble. As he was trying to make Julien
understand this feeling, a faint noise made them turn their heads.
Julien saw Mademoiselle de la Mole listening to them. He blushed.
She had come to look for a book and had overheard everything; it
made her feel some respect for Julien. There's a man, she thought,
who didn't come grovelling into this world like that old abbé.
Heavens! how ugly he is.

At dinner Julien did not venture to look at Mademoiselle de la
Mole, but she was kind enough to address some remarks to him.
They were expecting a good number of people that day and she
urged him to stay behind after dinner. Young Parisian women
are not very fond of people of a certain age, especially when
they do not dress very smartly. Julien did not need much sagacity
to perceive that the people of M. Le Bourguignon's group, who
had remained in the drawing-room, had the honour of being the
usual target of Mademoiselle de la Mole's caustic wit. That day,
whether or no it was a pose on her part, she was very sarcastic
on the subject of bores.

Mademoiselle de la Mole was the centre of a little group that
gathered every evening behind the Marquise's enormous easy
chair. Amongst them were the Marquis de Croisenois, the Comte
de Caylus, the Vicomte de Luz, and two or three other young
officers who were friends of Norbert or his sister. These gentlemen
sat on a big blue sofa. At the end of the sofa, facing that on
which the sparkling Mathilde was sitting, Julien sat silent on a
rather low, cane-bottomed chair. This modest seat was coveted
by all the company of toadies. Norbert gave his father's young

secretary a decent pretext for remaining there by addressing him directly, or mentioning him by name once or twice in the course of the evening.

That day Mademoiselle de la Mole asked him the height of the hill on which the citadel of Besançon stands. Julien found it impossible to say whether this hill was higher or less high than Montmartre. He frequently laughed very heartily at what this little group was saying; but he felt himself incapable of any such inventiveness as theirs. It was like a foreign language, which he understood but could not speak.

That day Mathilde's friends waged incessant war against the people who képt arriving in the drawing-room. The friends of the family were given first preference, as being better known. You can judge if Julien was attentive; everything interested him, both in the matter and the manner of their jesting.

'Ah! here's M. Descoulis,' said Mathilde. 'He's left off his wig. Does he hope to win a prefecture by his genius? He's displaying that bald forehead of his which he claims to be packed with lofty ideas.'

'He's a man with a world-wide acquaintance,' said the Marquis de Croisenois. 'He comes to my uncle the Cardinal's as well. He's capable of keeping a lie on foot for years on end about every one of his friends, and he has two or three hundred. He knows how to feed a friendship – that's his special gift. You'll see him, just as you see him now, already bespattered with mud, at the door of some friend's house on the stroke of seven in the morning – and in winter.

'He picks a quarrel with someone from time to time, and writes seven or eight letters just to keep it going. Then he effects a reconciliation and out come seven or eight letters more full of transports of goodwill. But it's when he unburdens himself with the frank sincerity of an honest man who keeps nothing hid in his heart that you find him at his best. Such are his usual tactics whenever he has some favour to ask. A vicar-general of my uncle's is marvellous at telling the story of M. Descoulis' life since the Restoration. I'll bring him along to see you.'

'Well, anyhow,' said the Comte de Caylus, 'you won't catch me believing such tales. It's merely professional jealousy between people of no importance.'

'M. Descoulis will be mentioned in history,' the Marquis replied. 'He brought about the Restoration in company with the Abbé de Pradt, M. de Talleyrand, and M. Pozzo di Borgo.'

'The man has handled millions,' said Norbert, 'and I can't understand why he comes here to pocket my father's insulting quips, which are often revolting. Only the other day he called out to him from the other end of the table: "How many times have you betrayed your friends, my dear Descoulis?"'

'But is it really true he has betrayed anybody?' said Mademoiselle de la Mole. 'Who hasn't betrayed someone or other?'

'What! you've got that infamous Liberal, M. Sainclair, here!' said the Comte de Caylus to Norbert. 'What the devil's he doing in this house? I must go over and speak to him, and get him to talk to me. They say he's such a clever fellow.'

'But what sort of welcome will he get from your mother?' said M. de Croisenois. 'He has such extravagant ideas, so generous, and so independent....'

'Look and see,' said Mademoiselle de la Mole, 'there's your independent man, bowing low to the ground in front of M. Descoulis and seizing hold of his hand. I almost thought he was going to raise it to his lips.'

'M. Descoulis must be on better terms with the government than we thought,' said M. de Croisenois.

'Sainclair's come here to get elected to the Academy,' said Norbert. 'Look, Croisenois, how he's bowing to Baron L—.'

'It would be less degrading if he went on his knees to him,' put in M. de Luz.

'My dear Sorel,' said Norbert, 'you who are such an intelligent chap, although you've just arrived from your mountains, must take good care you never bow before anyone as you see this great poet doing, not even before God himself.'

'Oh! there's the very paragon of wit, M. le Baron Bâton,' said Mademoiselle de la Mole in faint imitation of the footman's voice as he just announced him.

'Even your servants laugh at him, I believe,' said M. de Caylus. 'Baron Bâton — what a name!'

'"What's in a name!" as he was saying to us the other day,' replied Mathilde. 'Imagine the Duc de Bouillon announced for the first time. In the case I'm referring to all the public needs is to get a little used to it ...'

Julien moved away from the sofa. But little alive as yet to the subtle charms of such delicate raillery, he considered that raillery must be founded on reason for him to laugh at a joke. He saw nothing in these young people's remarks but a tendency to disparage everything, and he was shocked by it. His provincial — or perhaps English – prudery went so far as to see envy in it, but here he was certainly mistaken.

Count Norbert, he said to himself, whom I've seen making three rough copies before writing a letter of twenty lines to his colonel, could reckon himself very lucky if once in his life he had written a single page like those of M. Sainclair.

Moving about unnoticed on account of his little importance, Julien came close to several groups of people; he followed Baron Bâton from a distance, wishing to hear him speak. This very intelligent man looked worried, and Julien only saw him recover himself a little after he had hit on one or two pungent phrases. It seemed to Julien that a mind of this type needed room to expand.

The Baron could not express himself tersely; he required at least four sentences of six lines each for his wit to shine.

'*The fellow doesn't talk, he lectures,*' said someone behind Julien. Turning round, he blushed with joy on hearing Comte Chalvet, the keenest mind of his age, addressed by name. Julien had often come across his name in the *Mémorial de Saint-Hélène* and in fragments of history dictated by Napoleon. Comte Chalvet was very concise in his speech; his epigrams were lightning flashes, well-aimed, vigorous, and profound. If he spoke on any question, the discussion immediately advanced a stage. He brought facts to bear on it; it was a pleasure to hear him speak. As a politician, however, he was cynical and shameless.

'I keep an open mind, myself,' he was saying to a gentleman with three decorations, whom he was apparently ridiculing. 'Why would you have me today of the same opinion as I was six weeks ago? If that were so, then opinion would be my tyrant.'

Four serious-looking young men who were grouped around him scowled at this remark; such gentlemen do not like jocular ways. The Count saw he had gone too far. Luckily he caught sight of that outwardly honest but inwardly artful man, M. Balland, and engaged him in conversation. People gathered round, realizing that poor Balland was a lamb for the slaughter. Although hideously ugly, M. Balland, by sheer force of morale and morality, and after a first venture into society which defies description, had married a very rich woman, who died; then he married a second, also very rich, who did not appear in social circles. He enjoyed, in all humility, an income of sixty thousand livres, and had his own obsequious following. Comte Chalvet spoke to him of all this, without pity either. Soon there was a ring of thirty people round them, all of them smiling, even the serious young men, the hope of their day and generation.

Why does he come to M. de la Mole's, where he's obviously everyone's butt? thought Julien. He went up to M. Pirard to ask him the reason; M. Balland made his escape.

'Good,' said Norbert. 'There's one of my father's spies gone; only that little cripple Napier is left.'

Can that be the answer to the riddle, thought Julien. But, in that case, why does the Marquis have M. Balland here?

Stern Father Pirard stood scowling in a corner of the room, listening to the footmen announcing the guests.

'Why, it's just a den of thieves,' he said, like Basilio, 'I see no one arriving but people with damaged reputations.'

The fact was that Father Pirard did not know what appertains to good society. But, from his Jansenist friends, he had gained very accurate notions of those men who only make their way into drawing-rooms either by their extreme adroitness in the service of every party, or by reason of fortunes shamefully acquired. For a few minutes that evening he answered Julien's eager questions out of the abundance of his heart, and then stopped short, deeply grieved at having always to speak ill of everyone and imputing it to himself as a sin. A man of choleric temper and a Jansenist, yet holding charity to be a Christian duty, his life in society was a constant conflict.

'What a horrible face that Father Pirard has!' Mademoiselle de la Mole was saying as Julien returned to the sofa.

Julien felt annoyed; and yet she was right. M. Pirard was unquestionably the most honest man in the room, but his blotched face, contorted by the pangs of conscience, made him look hideous at that moment. Trust what faces tell you after that! thought Julien. It's precisely when Father Pirard's scrupulous conscience is reproaching him for some trifling sin that he appears horrible; whereas on that fellow Napier's face, for all he's a notorious spy, one reads a look of pure and tranquil bliss. All the same Father Pirard had acknowledged the claims of his present position in so far as to engage a valet, and he was now very properly dressed.

Julien noticed something very peculiar happening in the drawing-room; all eyes were turning round towards the door, voices sank to a murmur. The footman was announcing the famous Baron de Tolly, to whom the recent elections had drawn everyone's attention. Julien moved forward and got a very good view of him. The Baron was president of one of the voting colleges; he had the bright idea of juggling away the little slips of paper bearing the votes of one of the parties. By way of compensation, however, he had replaced them with a due proportion of other little slips of paper marked with a name that pleased him. This decisive manoeuvre was noted by some of the electors, who hastened to congratulate Baron de Tolly. The good man was still pale from this undertaking; certain ill-conditioned persons had pronounced the words 'penal servitude'. M. de la Mole received him coldly. The poor Baron made a hasty retreat.

'If he leaves us so quickly, it must be he's going to visit the famous conjuror, M. Comte,' said Comte Chalvet, whereupon everyone laughed.

In the midst of a group of great noblemen who never opened their mouths, and of scheming fellows, mostly of bad repute, but all of them men of intelligence, who swarmed one on top of the other into M. de la Mole's drawing-room (there was talk of appointing him to a Ministry), young Tanbeau entered upon his first campaign. If he had not as yet acquired any fineness of perception, he made up for it, as will be seen, by the vigorous tone of his conversation.

'Why don't they sentence this man to ten years' imprisonment?' he was saying at the moment when Julien approached his group. 'Reptiles should be kept shut up in the deepest underground dungeon; they ought to be left to die in the dark, otherwise their venom swells and becomes more dangerous. What's the use of sentencing him to a fine of a thousand crowns? He's poor, maybe, and that's all the better; but his party will pay for him. He should have had a fine of five hundred francs and ten years in a dungeon.'

Good God! who's the monster they're talking about? thought Julien, marvelling at his colleague's vehement tone and nervous gesticulations. The little, thin, worn face of the Academician's nephew was at that moment hideous. Julien soon ascertained that he was referring to Béranger, the greatest poet of the day.

'Ah, you wretch,' cried Julien, half aloud, and his eyes grew wet with generous tears. Ah! you nasty little beggar! he thought, I'll make you pay for those words.

Yet these, he thought, are the forlorn hope of the party which has the Marquis as one of its leaders. As for the illustrious man he's slandering, how many decorations, how many sinecures might he not have accumulated if he had sold himself, I won't say to M. de Nerval's sluggish Ministry, but to one of those passably honest ministers whom we've seen succeeding each other?

Father Pirard beckoned to Julien from across the room; M. de la Mole had just had a word with him. But when Julien, who had been listening, with downcast eyes, to a bishop's tale of woe, was free at last and could join his friend, he found him cornered by that abominable young Tanbeau. The little wretch detested him as the source of favours shown to Julien, and now came to pay court to him.

'When will death deliver us from that ancient body of corruption?' It was in such terms of Biblical vigour that the little man of letters was referring at this moment to that estimable man, Lord Holland. His special talent was a thorough knowledge of the biography of living men, and he had just been making a rapid survey of all the men who might aspire to some position of influence under the new King of England.

Father Pirard moved into an adjoining room, where Julien followed him.

'I must warn you the Marquis has no love for scribblers; it's his one antipathy. Have a knowledge of Latin, of Greek, if possible, the history of the Egyptians, of the Persians, etc; he will honour you and respect you as a scholar. But don't write a single page in French, especially on serious matters above your station; he would call you a scribbler and bear a grudge against you. How is it that, living in a great nobleman's house, you don't know what the duc de Castries said of D'Alembert and Rousseau: "Fellows like these want a say in everything, yet they haven't a thousand crowns a year"?'

Everything gets known, thought Julien, here as in the seminary. He had written nine or ten fairly emphatic pages as a sort of eulogy of the old army surgeon who, he said, had made a man of him. And this little notebook, said Julien to himself, has always been kept under lock and key. He went upstairs, burnt his manuscript, and returned to the drawing-room. The distinguished rogues had departed, only the men with decorations remained.

Round the table, which the servants had just brought in ready laid, were seated seven or eight ladies, very noble, very pious, and very prim, between thirty and thirty-five years of age. The distinguished Madame de Fervaques, a Marshal's widow, entered the room, full of apologies for the lateness of the hour. It was after midnight; she went and sat down next to the Marquise. Julien was deeply moved; her eyes and her expression were just like those of Madame de Rênal.

There were still a number of people in Mademoiselle de la Mole's group. She and her friends were busy making fun of the unfortunate Comte de Thaler. He was the only son of the famous Jew, renowned for the wealth he had acquired in lending money to kings to make war on the common people. The Jew had lately died, leaving his son an income of a hundred thousand crowns a month, and a name that, alas, was only too well known!

So peculiar a position called for simplicity of character or very great strength of mind. Unfortunately, the Comte was merely a puppet, stuffed with pretensions inspired in him by his flatterers.

M. de Caylus maintained that someone had implanted in him the will to ask for the hand of Mademoiselle de la Mole (to whom the Marquis de Croisenois, who would one day inherit a dukedom with an income of one hundred thousand livres, was paying his addresses).

'Oh, don't accuse him of having any will!' Norbert said in pitying tones.

What this poor Comte de Thaler most lacked, perhaps, was will-power. From this point of view, he would have made a worthy king. Yet while he took advice from everyone, he had not the courage to follow any course advised to the very end.

His face alone, as Mademoiselle de la Mole would say, was enough to fill one with unending delight. It presented a singular blend of nervousness and discontent; but from time to time it plainly displayed fleeting glimpses of self-importance, together with that air of authority which the wealthiest man in France ought to assume, especially when he is fairly good-looking, and is not yet thirty-six.

'There's a sort of timid insolence about the fellow,' M. de Croisenois would say. The Comte de Caylus, Norbert, and two or three other young men with moustaches chaffed him to their hearts' content without his suspecting it, and finally sent him away as one o'clock was striking.

'Is that your famous pair of Arabs you're keeping standing at the door in this weather?' Norbert asked him.

'No, it's a new pair that cost me very much less. The left-hand horse cost me five thousand francs and the one on the right is worth only a hundred louis. But I must assure you he is only taken out at night. And that's because his trot goes perfectly

with the other's.' He went away and the other gentlemen left a
minute or two later, laughing at him as they went.

So I've been allowed to see the opposite extreme to my condition, thought Julien as he heard them laughing on the stairs. I
haven't so much as twenty louis a year and I've found myself
side by side with a man who has an income of twenty louis an
hour, and they laughed at him. . . . Such a sight cures one of envy.

> They have grown so accustomed here to dull,
> drab tones of speech that any idea with the
> least touch of colour seems vulgar. Woe to the
> man who talks with a little originality!
>
> FAUBLAS

AFTER several months of trial, here is the point that Julien had reached on the day the family steward handed him his third quarter's salary. M. de la Mole had entrusted to him the task of supervising the administration of his estates in Normandy and Brittany. Julien made frequent journeys there. It was his particular duty to deal with correspondence relating to the famous lawsuit with M. de Frilair, a matter on which M. Pirard had given him instructions.

From short notes which the Marquis would scribble on the margin of every sort of document addressed to him, Julien composed letters which for the most part received the Marquis's signature. His teachers at the school of theology complained of his want of application, but regarded him none the less as one of their most brilliant pupils. These various tasks, which he attacked with all the energy of a thwarted ambition, had quickly robbed Julien of the fresh complexion he had brought with him from the provinces. His pale cheeks were a merit in the eyes of his companions at the seminary. He found them much less malicious, much less inclined to fall on their knees before a piece of money than the students at Besançon; as for them, they thought he was consumptive.

The Marquis had given him a horse, but, afraid lest one of the students should see him out riding, Julien had told them that this exercise had been ordered him by the doctors. Father Pirard had taken him to several Jansenist houses. Julien was astonished; the idea of religion was linked in his mind with that of hypocrisy and the hope of making money. He admired the austere piety of these men who were not continually thinking of ways and means. A new world opened before him. Among the Jansenists he made the acquaintance of a certain Count Altamira, a man nearly six foot tall, a Liberal, under sentence of death in his own country, and very pious. He was struck by this strangely contrasted love of God and love of freedom.

Julien was on rather cool terms with Count Norbert, who had found that he answered back too sharply when certain of the Count's friends were chaffing him. Having been guilty once or twice of a breach of manners, Julien had made it a rule never to say a single word to Mademoiselle de la Mole. Everyone in the house was perfectly civil to him, but he felt he had sunk in their estimation. His provincial good sense explained such a result by the popular proverb: *Familiarity breeds contempt*. Possibly he had clearer vision than at first, or perhaps the first enchantment worked by Parisian urbanity had lost its spell. As soon as he left off working he fell a prey to the deadliest boredom; such is the withering effect of that exquisite politeness, so measured, and so perfectly graduated according to the rank of the recipient, that characterizes good society. A heart ever so slightly sensitive sees through the trick.

No doubt the provinces deserve some censure for their vulgar and rather uncivil ways; but there people show a touch of warmth in their answers. Julien's self-respect was never wounded at the Hôtel de la Mole, but often, by the end of the day, he felt inclined to weep. In the provinces, if you meet with an accident on entering a café the waiter there takes some interest in you; but should this accident entail something galling to your pride, he will go on repeating ten times over the very word that makes you writhe. In Paris, people are civil enough to hide their laughter, but you always remain a stranger.

Let us pass over in silence a host of little misadventures which might have put Julien in a ridiculous light, if he had not been in some sort beneath ridicule. His absurd sensibility made him commit innumerable blunders. All his amusements were precautionary measures – he practised pistol shooting every day, and became one of the more promising pupils of the most celebrated fencing-masters. As soon as he had a moment to himself, instead of employing it in reading, as was once his custom, he would rush off to the riding-school and ask for the most vicious horse. When he went out with the riding-master he was almost invariably thrown off.

The Marquis found him useful because of his dogged application to work, his silence, and his intelligence, and by degrees put him in charge of all his little intricate business matters. In moments when his lofty ambitions left him respite, the Marquis handled his own affairs with a certain shrewdness; as he was in a position to know what was going on, he made some rather good speculations. He bought houses and woodlands; but he easily lost his temper. He was constantly giving hundreds of louis away, and going to law over hundreds of francs. High-spirited, wealthy men seek entertainment and not results from their business transactions. The Marquis had need of a chief of staff to order all his financial affairs in a way that was clear and easy to grasp.

Madame de la Mole, although by nature circumspect, would sometimes make fun of Julien. Great ladies have a particular horror of sudden reactions arising from sensibility; this seems to them the antithesis of good manners. Two or three times the Marquis spoke up for him: 'If he seems ridiculous in your drawing-room,' he would say, 'he's an excellent fellow at his desk.' Julien, for his part, thought he had grasped the Marquise's secret. She condescended to take an interest in everything the moment the Baron de la Joumate was shown in. He was a chilly individual, with a face that never showed any emotion. Small, thin, ugly, and very smartly turned out, he spent his days at the Château and, as a rule, had nothing to say about anything. That was his particular way of thinking. Madame de la Mole would have been wildly delighted, for the very first time in her life, if she could have secured him as a husband for her daughter.

CHAPTER 6: A Question of Accent

> If self-conceit is pardonable, it is in early youth, for then it is an exaggeration of some likeable trait. It needs a touch of love, of gaiety, of nonchalance. But as for pompous self-conceit! Self-conceit assuming an air of gravity and consequence! Such an excess of stupidity is reserved for the nineteenth century. And these are the people who hope to chain up that hydra-headed monster, *Revolution!*   *Le Johannisberg* (Pamphlet)

FOR a newcomer who, out of pride, never asked a single question, Julien did not stumble into too many serious blunders. One day, when he was driven into a café in the rue Saint-Honoré by a sudden downpour, a tall young man in a topcoat of beaver cloth, astonished by his glowering looks, began to stare back at him in his turn, in exactly the same way as Mademoiselle Amanda's lover had long ago stared at him, in Besançon.

Julien had too often taken himself to task for overlooking this first insult to tolerate such a glance. He demanded an explanation. The man in the topcoat retorted with the foulest insults. Everyone in the café gathered round; passers-by stopped short in front of the door. With true provincial caution, Julien always carried a brace of pocket pistols; his hand, thrust into his pocket, gripped them convulsively. He was wise enough, however, to confine himself to repeating at short intervals: 'Your address, sir. I find you contemptible.'

The persistency with which he clung to these seven words finally impressed the crowd. 'Damn it all! that other fellow, who's doing all the talking, really ought to give him his address.' The man in the topcoat, hearing this opinion reiterated, flung five or six visiting-cards right in Julien's face. Luckily none of them hit him, for he had promised himself not to use his pistols unless he was touched. The man made off, but not without turning round from time to time to shake his fist at him and utter more abuse.

Julien found himself dripping with sweat. So this vilest of

creatures has power to excite me to such an extent! he said to himself. How can I rid myself of this humiliating sensibility?

Where could he look for a second? He had not a single friend. He had had a few acquaintances, but all of these, after showing some interest in him for six weeks or so, had invariably cooled off. I'm an unsociable creature, he thought, and now I'm cruelly punished for it. Finally he thought of going to see a retired lieutenant of the 96th, named Liéven, a poor devil with whom he frequently practised fencing. Julien was frank with him.

'I'm very willing to act as your second,' said Liéven, 'but on one condition. If you don't wound your man, you must fight with me, there and then.'

'All right,' said Julien, overjoyed. And they went to seek out M. C. de Beauvoisis at the address shown on the cards, in the heart of the Faubourg Saint-Germain.

It was seven o'clock in the morning. Not until he was sending in his name did it occur to Julien that the man might be Madame de Rênal's young relative, formerly attaché to the Embassy at Rome or Naples, who had given the singer Geronimo a letter of introduction. Julien had handed to the tall footman one of the cards flung at him the day before, together with one of his own.

He and his second were kept waiting for a good three-quarters of an hour; finally they were shown into a marvellously stylish apartment, where they found a tall young man got up like a tailor's dummy. His features presented the perfection and the insipidity of the Greek idol of beauty. His head, which was remarkably narrow, was crowned with hair of most exquisite fairness, very carefully curled, with not a single hair standing out above the rest. It's just to have his hair curled like this, thought the lieutenant of the 96th, that this damned young puppy has kept us waiting. His striped dressing-gown, his morning trousers, everything in short, down to his embroidered slippers, was correct and marvellously well appointed. The vacuous, aristocratic cast of his features proclaimed that his ideas were few and always in good form; in fact, the ideal of the agreeable man, with a horror of the unexpected and of ridicule, and with plenty of gravity.

Julien, to whom his lieutenant of the 96th had explained that to keep a man waiting so long after rudely flinging his card in his face was an additional insult, marched boldly into M. de Beauvoisis's room. It was his intention to be insolent, but he wished at the same time to appear well-bred.

He was so much surprised by the gentleness of M. de Beauvoisis's manner, by his air of mingled formality, self-importance, and self-satisfaction, by the marvellous elegance of his surroundings, that in the twinkling of an eye he lost all idea of being insolent. This was not his man of the day before. So great was his astonishment at meeting so distinguished an individual instead of the rude fellow he had come to look for, that he could not find a single word to say. He handed him one of the cards that had been flung at him.

'That is my name,' said the man of fashion, in whom Julien's black coat, at seven o'clock in the morning, awakened little respect. 'But, upon my honour, I don't understand. . . .'

His way of pronouncing these last words made Julien feel some of his anger returning. 'I have come to fight with you, sir,' he said, and rapidly explained the situation.

M. Charles de Beauvoisis, after mature reflection, was rather pleased with the cut of Julien's coat. It's clearly one of Staub's, he said to himself as he listened to Julien. That waistcoat's in very good taste, the boots are all right; but, on the other hand, that black suit at this hour of the morning! It will be to give him a better chance of escaping a bullet, was his comment.

As soon as he had hit on this explanation, he reverted to a perfect politeness, and treated Julien almost as an equal. Their conversation was somewhat long, the matter in hand was delicate; but in the end Julien could not reject the evidence. The perfectly well-bred man he saw before him did not in the least resemble that unmannerly individual who, the day before, had insulted him.

Julien felt an insurmountable disinclination to take his leave; he lingered over the business of explaining, taking note, meanwhile, of the self-sufficiency of the Chevalier de Beauvoisis, for so he had described himself, rather shocked at Julien's addressing him as plain 'Monsieur'.

Julien admired his gravity, which was tinged with a certain modest self-conceit, but never laid aside for a single moment. He was astonished by his curious way of moving his tongue in enunciating his words. . . . But all said and done, there was nothing in all this to supply the slightest reason for provoking a quarrel.

The young diplomat very graciously offered to fight, but the lieutenant of the 96th, who for the past hour had been sitting with his legs apart, his hands on his thighs and his arms akimbo, decided that his friend M. Sorel was not the kind of man to pick a quarrel, in the German way, with another man, just because someone had stolen that man's visiting cards.

Julien left the house in a very bad temper. The Chevalier de Beauvoisis's carriage was waiting for him in the courtyard, in front of the steps. Happening to look up, Julien recognized his man of the day before in the coachman. Seeing him, catching hold of him by his thick coat, pulling him off his seat, and giving him a thorough hiding with his whip, were the work of a moment. Two lackeys tried to defend their fellow-servant. They hit out at Julien with their fists; he immediately drew out one of his pocket pistols and fired at them; they took to their heels. It was all over in a minute.

The Chevalier de Beauvoisis came downstairs with the most comical gravity, repeating in his aristocratic voice: 'What's this? What's this?' He was obviously full of curiosity, but diplomatic dignity did not allow him to show any greater interest. When he knew what it was all about, an air of cold disdain on his features contested still with the cool, yet faintly humorous, composure which should never be absent from a diplomat's face.

The lieutenant of the 96th realized that M. de Beauvoisis felt a desire to fight; diplomatically, he tried to keep all the advantages of the initiative on his friend's side. 'This time,' he exclaimed, 'there's matter for a duel!' 'I should rather think so,' replied the diplomat.

'I'm dismissing this rascal,' he said to his lackeys. 'One of you others get up on the box.' They opened the carriage door; the Chevalier insisted that Julien and his second should get in first. They went to find one of M. de Beauvoisis's friends, who suggested a quiet spot. The conversation on the way was most correct. The only thing out of the ordinary was the diplomat in his dressing-gown.

These gentlemen, thought Julien, although they're real nobles, aren't bores like the people who come to dine with M. de la Mole. And I can see why, he added a moment later, they admit a little indecency in their conversation. They were talking of dancers the public had singled out in a ballet performed on the previous evening. These gentlemen alluded to certain spicy stories about which Julien and his second, the lieutenant of the 96th, were completely ignorant. Julien was not so foolish as to pretend he had heard them; he confessed his ignorance with very good grace. This frankness pleased the Chevalier's friend; he told him the stories in the fullest detail, and in a very interesting way.

Julien could not get over his amazement at one thing. The carriage was held up for a moment by an altar of repose which was being erected in the middle of the street for the Corpus Christi procession. These gentlemen indulged in a number of jocular remarks. The curé, according to them, was the son of an Archbishop. Never would anyone have dared to say such a thing in the house of the Marquis de la Mole, who hoped to become a duke.

The duel was over in an instant; Julien got a bullet in his arm. They bound it up for him with handkerchiefs, which they soaked in brandy, and the Chevalier very politely begged Julien to let him see him home in the same carriage that had brought them. On Julien's naming the Hôtel de la Mole, the young diplomat and his friend exchanged glances. Julien's cab was waiting, but he found the conversation of these gentlemen infinitely more entertaining than that of the worthy lieutenant of the 96th.

Good God! thought Julien, is that all there is to a duel? How lucky I was to come across that coachman again! How unfortunate for me if I had had to endure such an insult a second time in a café! Their amusing conversation had hardly been interrupted. Julien realized that diplomatic affectations have their uses, after all.

So boredom isn't an integral part of aristocratic conversation! he thought. These men here can joke about the Corpus Christi procession, they venture to tell the most risqué stories and with picturesque details, too. Indeed the only thing they really lack is a sensible notion of politics, and this lack is more than made up for by their charming manners and the perfect aptness of their expressions. Julien felt strongly drawn towards them. How glad I should be, he thought, if I could see them often!

They had hardly taken leave of each other before the Chevalier de Beauvoisis rushed off to make inquiries; but with not very famous results. He was very curious to get to know this man; but would it be fitting to call on him? The little information he had obtained was hardly of a kind to encourage him.

'This is all quite frightful,' he said to his second. 'I can't possibly admit I've fought a duel with someone who's merely M. de la Mole's secretary, and that just because my coachman stole my visiting cards.'

'It's certain there's every possibility of one's being exposed to ridicule by this story.'

That very evening, the Chevalier de Beauvoisis and his friend spread it abroad that M. Sorel, who was, by the way, a perfectly charming young man, was the natural son of one of M. de la Mole's intimate friends. Once this was established, the young diplomat and his friend condescended to pay Julien one or two visits during the fortnight in which he was confined to his room. Julien confessed to them that he had only once in his life been to the Opera.

'But that's terrible,' they said. 'No one ever goes anywhere else. Your first outing must be to the Opera to hear *Comte Ory*.'

At the Opera, the Chevalier de Beauvoisis presented him to the famous singer Geronimo, who was having an immense success at the time.

Julien very nearly worshipped the Chevalier; this blend of self-respect, mysterious pomposity, and youthful silliness held him spellbound. For one thing, the Chevalier stammered slightly because he often had the honour to meet a great nobleman who suffered from this infirmity. Julien had never found such amusingly ridiculous ways, and the perfect manners which a poor fellow from the provinces should try to imitate, combined in one and the same human being.

He was seen at the Opera with the Chevalier de Beauvoisis; this association made people talk of him.

'Well!' said M. de la Mole to him one day, 'so now you are the natural son of a rich gentleman of Franche-Comté, who's an intimate friend of mine!'

The Marquis cut Julien short as he tried to protest that he had not helped in any way to set this rumour going.

'You see, sir, M. de Beauvoisis did not wish to have fought a duel with a carpenter's son.'

'I know, I know,' said M. de la Mole. 'It's up to me now to give some consistency to this story, which suits my convenience. But I've one favour to ask of you, which will not cost you more than a bare half-hour of your time. Every evening when there's an Opera on, go and stand in the vestibule when people of the best society are coming out. I still notice at times some provincial mannerisms in you. You must get rid of them; besides it's not a bad thing to know, at least by sight, certain people of importance to whom I may one day send you on some errand. Go to the box office and make yourself known: they have a pass ready for you.'

CHAPTER 7 : *An Attack of Gout*

> So I got promotion, not for any merit of mine,
> but because my master had the gout.
>
> BERTOLOTTI

THE reader may be surprised at this free and almost friendly tone; we have forgotten to say that for three weeks the Marquis had been kept at home by an attack of gout.

Mademoiselle de la Mole and her mother were at Hyères, staying with the Marquise's mother. Count Norbert only saw his father for an occasional moment or two; they were on very good terms, but had nothing to say to each other. M. de la Mole, reduced to Julien's society, was astonished to find he had ideas. He made him read him the daily papers, and soon the young secretary was able to pick out the interesting passages. There was a new paper which the Marquis abhorred; he had sworn never to read it, yet talked about it daily. This made Julien laugh. The Marquis, vexed with the present state of affairs, made Julien read him some Livy; he found the improvised translation very entertaining.

One day, in that tone of exaggerated politeness which often made Julien lose patience, the Marquis said to him : 'Allow me, my dear Sorel, to make you a present of a blue coat. When it pleases you to put it on and come to see me, you will be, in my eyes, the younger brother of the Comte de Retz, that is to say, the son of my old friend the Duke.'

Julien did not understand very clearly what it was all about; that same evening he ventured to pay a visit in the blue coat. The Marquis treated him as an equal. Julien had a noble enough heart to recognize true politeness, but he had no idea of its finer shades. He would have sworn, before this whim on the part of the Marquis, that it would be impossible to be received by him with more courteous respect. What a wonderful gift ! said Julien to himself; when he rose to go the Marquis apologized for not being able to see him to the door because of his gout.

A singular notion occupied Julien's mind : can he be making fun of me ? he thought. He went to seek counsel of Father Pirard, who, less courteous than the Marquis, only whistled by way of answer and went on to talk of other things. The next morning, Julien appeared before the Marquis, in his black coat, with a portfolio and letters for signing. He was received in the old way. In the evening, dressed in his blue coat, it was with an altogether different tone and one that was absolutely as polite as on the previous evening.

'Since you aren't too bored by the visits you are kind enough to pay to a poor, sick old man,' said the Marquis, 'you must talk to him of all the little incidents in your life, but frankly, and without thinking of anything but telling your tale clearly and in an amusing way. For one must have amusement,' the Marquis went on, 'that's the only real thing in life. A man can't save my life on the battle-field every day, nor every day make me the present of a million; but if I had Rivarol sitting here, beside my couch, he would relieve me of an hour's pain and boredom every day. I knew him well in Hamburg, during the Emigration.'

The Marquis went on to tell Julien anecdotes of Rivarol and the men of Hamburg, who had to put four of their heads together to understand the point of one single witty remark.

M. de la Mole, thrown back on the society of this young priestling, was anxious to tickle him into liveliness. He goaded Julien's pride to show its mettle. Since he was asked for the truth, Julien resolved to tell him the whole story, keeping silence on two things only – his fanatical admiration for a name that put the Marquis out of temper, and an utter lack of faith rather unbecoming in a future curé. His little affair with the Chevalier de Beauvoisis came in at a very opportune moment. The Marquis laughed till he cried over the scene in the café in the rue Saint-Honoré, with the coachman hurling foul abuse at him. This was a period of perfect frankness in the relations between employer and protégé.

M. de la Mole was interested in this strange personality. At first, he encouraged Julien's absurdities, with intent to get some enjoyment out of them; but soon he found it more interesting to correct, in the gentlest way, the young man's unsound notions of men and things. Other provincials who come to Paris admire everything, the Marquis reflected. This fellow hates everything. They have too much affectation, he hasn't enough, and fools therefore take him for a fool.

The intense cold of that winter prolonged this attack of gout, which lasted for several months.

People get fond of a fine spaniel, thought the Marquis; why am I so ashamed of my fondness for this young cleric? He's an original sort of fellow. I treat him like a son – well, what's the harm in that? This whim of mine, supposing it lasts, will cost me a diamond worth five hundred louis in my will.

Once the Marquis had realized the steadiness of his protégé's character, he entrusted him with some new piece of business every day. Julien noted with alarm that this noble lord sometimes happened to give him contradictory instructions about the same thing. This might seriously compromise him. After that Julien never did any work with the Marquis without bringing along a notebook in which he recorded all decisions arrived at, and the Marquis initialled them. Julien had engaged a clerk who copied out the instructions relating to each several bit of business in a special book, in which were also kept copies of all the letters.

The idea seemed at first the most ridiculously tedious thing possible. In less than two months, however, the Marquis realized its advantages. Julien suggested taking on a clerk from a bank, who would keep accounts in double entry of all the receipts and expenditure on properties Julien was asked to look after.

These measures opened the Marquis's eyes to such an extent that he was able to afford the pleasure of venturing on two or three fresh speculations without recourse to his broker, who had been robbing him.

'Take three thousand francs for yourself,' he said one day to his young minister.

'But, sir, people might take a wrong view of my conduct. '

'What do you want, then?' replied the Marquis crossly.

'I want you to be so kind as to make a formal agreement, and write it down in your own hand in the book; this agreement will grant me a sum of three thousand francs. All this book-keeping, anyhow, was Father Pirard's idea.' The Marquis, with an expression as bored as that of the Marquis de Moncade listening to his steward, M. Poisson, rendering his accounts, wrote out the agreement.

In the evening, when Julien appeared in his blue coat, business was never mentioned. The Marquis's favours so flattered our hero's continually wounded self-respect that soon, in spite of himself, he felt a certain fondness for this affable old man. Not that Julien had any sensibility, as Paris interprets this term; but he was not without human feeling, and nobody, since the death of the old army surgeon, had spoken to him so kindly. He noted with amazement that the Marquis showed a polite consideration for his self-esteem which he had never received from the old surgeon.

In the end he realized that the surgeon had been prouder of his Cross than the Marquis was of his Blue Ribbon. The Marquis was the son of a great nobleman.

One day, at the end of a morning interview, when he wore his black suit and came to talk on business, the Marquis found Julien so entertaining that he kept him there for two whole hours, and insisted on giving him a handful of banknotes his broker had just brought from the Bourse.

'I hope, M. le Marquis, I shall not be wanting in the profound respect I owe you if I beg you to let me say a few words.'

'Say what you will, my dear boy.'

'Will your Lordship graciously permit me to decline this gift. It is not addressed to the man in black, and it would entirely spoil the relations you have so kindly allowed to exist with the man in blue.' He bowed most respectfully, and left the room without a glance at the Marquis.

This incident amused the Marquis. He told Father Pirard about it that evening.

'I must indeed confess something to you, my dear Abbé. I know all about Julien's birth, and I authorize you not to keep this confidence secret.'

His behaviour this morning was noble, thought the Marquis, and I, for my part, shall treat him as nobly born.

Some time after this, the Marquis was at length able to leave his room.

'Go and spend a couple of months in London,' he said to Julien, 'special couriers and other messengers will bring you the letters I receive, with my notes. You will write the replies and send them back, enclosing each letter with its reply. I've reckoned out that the delay will not exceed five days.'

As he travelled post along the road to Calais, Julien was feeling full of amazement at the futility of this so-called business on which he was being sent.

We will not describe the feeling of horror, and almost of hatred, with which he set foot on English soil. His mad enthusiasm for Bonaparte is well known to you. In every officer he met he saw a Sir Hudson Lowe, in every nobleman a Lord Bathurst, ordering the shameful humiliations of Saint Helena, to be rewarded by ten years of office.

In London he came at last in touch with the extremist limits of dandyism and self-conceit. He had made friends with some young Russian noblemen who initiated him.

'You are predestined to it, my dear Sorel,' they told him. 'Nature has given you that air of cold aloofness, *as if a thousand leagues removed from everyday interests*, which we ourselves try so hard to acquire.'

'You have no idea of the age in which you are living,' Prince Korasoff said to him – '*always do the opposite of what people expect of you*. That, upon my honour, is the only religion of the day. Don't be either foolish or affected, for then people will expect foolishness and affectation, and you won't be obeying this precept.'

Julien covered himself with glory one day in the Duke of Fitz-Folke's drawing-room, where he and Prince Korasoff had been invited to dine. They were kept waiting for an hour. The way in which Julien behaved amongst the twenty people waiting is still quoted by young attachés to embassies in London. His demeanour was pricelessly entertaining.

For all his friends the dandies could do to dissuade him, he was keen on meeting the celebrated Philip Vane, the only philosopher England has had since Locke. He found him at the end of his seventh year in prison. There's no trifling with the aristocracy in this country, thought Julien; and on top of it all, Vane is disgraced, abused, etc.

Julien found him in the best of spirits; the rage of the aristocracy seemed to amuse him. There's the only merry fellow I've met in England, thought Julien, as he left the prison.

'*The most useful idea for tyrants*,' Vane had said to him, '*is the idea of God.*' ... We will suppress the rest of his philosophy as being too cynical.

On his return, M. de la Mole asked him : 'What amusing ideas have you brought me from England?' He remained silent. 'Well, what ideas have you brought, amusing or not?' the Marquis went on, sharply.

'First of all,' said Julien, 'the sanest Englishman is mad for one hour in the day. He's haunted by the demon of suicide, who is their national deity.

'Secondly, intelligence and genius lose twenty-five per cent of their value on landing in England.

'Thirdly, nothing in the world is so beautiful, so marvellous, and so appealing as an English landscape.'

'My turn now,' said the Marquis.

'First of all, why did you go and say, at the ball at the Russian Embassy, that there are three hundred thousand young men of twenty-five in France all passionately eager for war? Do you think that shows proper respect for kings?'

'One doesn't know what to say when speaking to our leading diplomats. They've a mania for starting serious discussions. If one confines oneself to commonplaces from the newspapers, one's taken for a fool. If one allows oneself to say something true and original, they're taken aback and don't know what to answer; and the very next morning, at seven o'clock, they send one a message by the First Secretary to say one's been impolite.'

'That's not bad,' said the Marquis laughing. 'All the same, I'd wager, my young wisehead, that you haven't guessed what you went to do in England.'

'Pardon me,' replied Julien. 'I went there to dine once a week with His Majesty's Ambassador, who is the politest of men.'

'You went to get this Cross you see here,' said the Marquis. 'I don't want you to discard your black coat and I've grown used to the more amusing tone I've adopted with the man in a blue one. Until further orders, understand this: when I see you wearing this Cross, you'll be my friend, the Duc de Retz's younger son who, without knowing it, has been for the past six months engaged in diplomatic business. Please note,' the Marquis added, looking very grave and cutting short Julien's expressions of gratitude, 'that I have no wish to raise you above your station. That's always a mistake, for patron as for protégé. When you begin to get tired of my lawsuits, or when you no longer suit me, I will ask for a good living for you, like the one our friend Father Pirard has – and *nothing more*,' the Marquis added, very drily.

This Cross set Julien's pride at its ease; he talked much more freely. He less frequently felt himself insulted or made the butt of those remarks into which one could very well read a somewhat uncivil meaning, and which in the course of a lively conversation may slip from anyone's lips.

He had his Cross to thank for a rather peculiar visit – this was from the Baron de Valenod, who came to Paris to thank the Minister for his Barony and establish good relations with him. He was about to be appointed Mayor of Verrières in place of M. de Rênal.

Julien was consumed with inward laughter when M. de Valenod gave him to understand that it had just been discovered that M. de Rênal was a Jacobin. The fact was that, in a new election which was about to take place, the newly made Baron was the candidate supported by the government, and at the central voting college of the Department, which in truth was strongly Ultra-Royalist, it was M. de Rênal who was being put forward by the Liberals.

Julien tried in vain to get news of Madame de Rênal; the Baron appeared to remember their former rivalry and remained impervious to hints. He ended by asking Julien for his father's vote at the coming election. Julien promised to write.

'You really ought, my dear Chevalier, to introduce me to his Lordship the Marquis de la Mole.'

I ought, indeed, thought Julien – but such a rogue!

'To tell you the truth,' he replied, 'I am too humble a person at the Hôtel de la Mole to take it upon myself to introduce anyone.'

Julien told the Marquis everything; that evening he informed him of Valenod's pretensions, and gave him an account of his actions and general behaviour since 1814.

'Not only,' replied the Marquis gravely, 'will you introduce this new Baron to me tomorrow, but I'll invite him to dinner the day after. He will be one of our new Prefects.'

'In that case,' Julien answered coldly, 'I ask for the post of Superintendent of the workhouse for my father.'

'Capital!' said the Marquis, recovering his gaiety. 'It's granted; I was expecting a sermon. You're shaping well.'

M. de Valenod informed Julien that the keeper of the lottery bureau at Verrières had just died. Julien thought it good fun to give this post to M. de Cholin, that old idiot whose petition he had once picked up in the room occupied by M. de la Mole. The Marquis laughed heartily over the petition, which Julien recited to him while getting him to sign the letter asking the Minister of Finance for this post.

M. de Cholin had hardly been appointed before Julien learnt that the Deputies of the Department had asked for this post for M. Gros, the celebrated mathematician. This noble-hearted man had an income of only fourteen hundred francs, and had been lending six hundred francs every year to the late holder of the post, to help him bring up his family.

Julien was amazed at what he had done. It's nothing really, he said to himself. I'll have to bring myself to commit many other acts of injustice if I want to get on, and know how to cover them up, moreover, with fine sentimental phrases. Poor M. Gros! It's he who deserved this Cross, it's I who have it, and I must conform to the wishes of the Government that gives it to me.

> 'Your water does not refresh me,' said the
> thirsty genie. 'Yet it is the coolest well in the
> whole of Diarbekir.'   PELLICO

JULIEN returned one day from the charming estate of Ville-quier, on the banks of the Seine, in which M. de la Mole took a special interest because, out of all his properties, it was the only one that had belonged to the celebrated Boniface de la Mole. He found the Marquise and her daughter at the Hôtel, having just returned from Hyères.

Julien was now a dandy, and understood the art of life in Paris. He behaved to Mademoiselle de la Mole with perfect coolness. He seemed to have kept no memories of the time when she asked him so gaily for details of his way of falling off a horse.

Mademoiselle de la Mole found him taller and paler. Nothing of the provincial remained, in his figure or in his dress; it was not the same with his conversation – there was still something pal-pably too serious, too dogmatic about it. In spite of these ultra-rational qualities, and thanks to his pride, it showed no trace of inferiority; it was only that he gave the impression of still re-garding too many things as important. It was evident, however, that he was a man who would stand by his word.

'He lacks lightness of touch, but not intelligence,' said Made-moiselle de la Mole to her father as she chaffed him over the Cross he had given Julien. 'My brother has been asking you for this for the past eighteen months, and he is a La Mole!'

'Yes, but Julien has a gift for doing unexpected things. That's never been the case with the La Mole you mention.'

The Duc de Retz was announced.

Mathilde felt seized by an irresistible fit of yawning; the sight of this man made her think of the antiquated gildings and the old familiar faces of her father's drawing-room. She drew for herself a wearisome picture of the life in Paris upon which she was entering anew. And yet, at Hyères, she had longed for Paris.

And yet I'm only nineteen ! she thought. The age of happiness, as all those gilt-edged idiots call it. She looked at nine or ten volumes of newly published poems which had accumulated on the drawing-room table during her absence in Provence. It was her misfortune to have more intelligence than MM. de Croisenois, de Caylus, de Luz, and the rest of her friends. She could imagine all they would say to her about the beautiful skies of Provence, poetry, the South, and so forth.

Those very lovely eyes, in which deepest boredom reigned, and, even worse, despair of ever finding pleasure, rested on Julien. At least, he was not exactly like anyone else.

'M. Sorel,' she said to him in that curt, sharp voice, with nothing feminine about it, which is affected by women of the highest rank, 'M. Sorel, are you coming to M. de Retz's ball tonight?'

'Mademoiselle, I haven't had the honour of being presented to his Grace the Duke.' (One would have said that these words and this title flayed the mouth of this proud provincial.)

'He has asked my brother to bring you; and, if you came, you could tell me all about our place at Villequier; there's some talk of our going there in the spring. I'd like to know if the house is habitable, and if the neighbourhood is as pretty as people say. There are so many reputations wrongly acquired!'

Julien made no reply.

'Come to the ball with my brother,' she added, very curtly.

Julien bowed low. So, even in the midst of a ball, I must make an account of myself to every single member of the family! Don't they pay me as their man of business? His ill-temper led him on to add: Heaven knows whether what I say to the daughter will not upset the plans of her father, brother, and mother! It's absolutely the court of a reigning monarch. One is expected to be a complete nonentity, and at the same time to give no one any right to complain.

How I dislike that great, tall girl! he thought as he looked at Mademoiselle de la Mole walking up to her mother, who had called her to introduce her to a number of her women friends. She overdoes every fashion, her gown is falling off her shoulders ... she's even paler than when she went away.... How colourless her hair ... is that because of its fairness? You'd say that the daylight shines through! ... What arrogance in her way of bowing, of looking at people! what queenly gestures! Mademoiselle had just beckoned to her brother as he was leaving the drawing-room.

Count Norbert came up to Julien. 'My dear Sorel,' he said, 'where would you like me to meet you to take you to M. de Retz's ball? He told me particularly to bring you.'

'I am well aware to whom I owe so much kindness,' answered Julien, bowing low to the ground.

His ill-temper, finding nothing to object to in the tone of politeness, and even of interest, in which Norbert had addressed him, began to vent itself on the answer he had made to this civil remark. He found a tinge of servility in it.

On his arrival at the ball that night, he was struck by the magnificence of the Hôtel de Retz. The entrance court was covered with an immense crimson awning studded with golden stars: nothing could have been more elegant. Underneath this awning the courtyard was transformed into a grove of orange trees and oleaners in bloom. As care had been taken to bury the tubs sufficiently deep, the oleanders and orange trees appeared to spring up out of the ground. Sand had been scattered over the path where the carriages had to pass.

The general effect of this seemed extraordinarily impressive to our provincial. He had no idea such magnificence could exist; in an instant his excited imagination had soared a thousand leagues above ill-temper. In the carriage, on their way to the ball, Norbert had been in the best of spirits, while he himself had seen nothing but the dark side of things; no sooner had they entered the courtyard than their roles were interchanged.

Norbert was only conscious of one or two details, to which, in the midst of all this splendour, it had not been possible to attend. He reckoned the cost of each item, and the higher the total mounted, the more, so Julien remarked, he showed an almost jealous irritation and, finally, became very glum.

As for Julien, spell-bound with admiration and almost timid from too strong emotion, he reached the first of the reception-rooms where dancing was going on. People were crowding through the door of the second room, and the concourse was so great that it was impossible for him to advance. This second room was decorated to represent the Alhambra in Granada.

'You must agree she's the queen of the ball,' remarked a young man with a moustache, whose shoulder was digging into Julien's chest.

'Mademoiselle Fourmont, who's been considered the prettiest of them all throughout the winter, is well aware she's gone down to second place,' replied his neighbour. 'Just look at the funny face she's making.'

'She's certainly putting all sails out to win admiration. Look, do you see her gracious smile the instant she's dancing alone in the quadrille? Upon my word, it's priceless!'

'Mademoiselle de la Mole would seem to have full command of the pleasure she gets from her triumph, of which she's very well aware. You'd say she's afraid of seeming attractive to anyone who speaks to her.'

'Why, of course! That's the whole art of seduction.'

Julien was trying in vain to catch a glimpse of this alluring woman; seven or eight men taller than himself prevented him from seeing her.

'There's a good deal of coquetry in that noble reserve,' replied the young man with the moustache.

'And those big blue eyes so slowly lowered at the moment you'd say they're about to give her away. By Jove! nothing could be cleverer.'

'Look how very ordinary the fair Fourmont appears beside her,' remarked a third.

'That air of reserve implies: "How charming I could show myself to you, were you the man who was worthy of me".'

'And who could be worthy of the sublime Mathilde?' the first man asked. 'Some reigning monarch, handsome, clever, well-made, a hero in battle, and, at the most, twenty years of age.'

'A natural son of the Emperor of Russia, for whom, in consideration of the marriage, a kingdom would be found: or, quite simply, the Comte de Thaler, who looks like a peasant in his Sunday best. . . .'

The door was clear of people, Julien could go through.

Since she appears so remarkable in the eyes of these dolled-up puppies, she's worth the trouble of studying, he thought. I shall understand what perfection means to such people.

As he was trying to catch her eye, Mathilde looked at him. Duty calls, said Julien to himself, but with no ill-temper left save in his expression. Curiosity urged him forward with a pleasure which Mathilde's gown, cut extremely low on the shoulders, rapidly heightened in a way that, in truth, was hardly flattering to his self-esteem. There's youth behind her beauty, he thought. Five or six young men, amongst whom Julien recognized those he had heard talking at the door, stood between her and him.

'You, sir,' she said, 'you've been here all the winter. Now tell me, isn't it true that this ball is the prettiest of the season?' He made no reply.

'I think this Coulon quadrille quite marvellous; and these ladies are dancing it beautifully.' The young men turned round to see who was the lucky man from whom she was absolutely determined to get an answer. It was not an encouraging one.

'I'd scarcely be a good judge of that, Mademoiselle. My life is taken up with writing. This is the first ball of such magnificence I've seen.'

The young men with moustaches were scandalized.

'You're a wise man, M. Sorel,' she went on with more marked interest, 'you look on all these balls, all these festivities, with the eye of a philosopher, just like Jean-Jacques Rousseau. Such follies astonish you, but don't tempt you.'

One thing she said checked Julien's soaring fancy, driving all illusions from his heart. His lips took on an expression of disdain which was, perhaps, a little overdone.

'Jean-Jacques Rousseau,' he answered, 'is nothing but a fool in my eyes when he constitutes himself a judge of good society; he didn't understand it, and viewed it with the heart of a lackey risen above his station.'

'He wrote the *Contrat Social*,' said Mathilde, with a note of reverence in her voice.

'And while he preaches a Republic and the overthrow of royal rights and privileges, this upstart goes off his head with joy if a Duke alters the course of his after-dinner constitutional to see one of his friends home.'

'Ah, yes! The Duc de Luxembourg at Montmorency accompanies a M. Coindet part of the way to Paris ...' replied Mademoiselle Mathilde with the whole-hearted delight of a first enjoyable taste of pedantry. She was intoxicated with her own learning, almost like the academician who discovered the existence of King Feretrius. Julien's glance remained piercing and stern. Mathilde had felt a momentary enthusiasm; her partner's coldness took her completely aback. She was all the more surprised because it was she who usually produced this effect upon other people.

The Marquis de Croisenois advanced eagerly towards Mademoiselle de la Mole. He stopped for a moment three feet away from her, unable to get through to her on account of the crowd. He looked at her, smiling at the obstacle between them. The young Marquise de Rouvray, Mathilde's cousin, was close beside them, leaning on the arm of her husband, who had only been married to her for a fortnight. The Marquis de Rouvray, who was also very young, showed all the love that takes possession of a man who,

having made a suitable match arranged entirely by his family
lawyers, finds he has married a perfectly adorable woman. M. de
Rouvray would be a Duke on the death of a very aged uncle.

While the Marquis de Croisenois, unable to make his way
through the crowd, was looking at Mathilde with a smiling face,
she let her big, heavenly blue eyes rest on him and his neighbours.
What could be more dreary, she thought, than all that group!
Look at Croisenois, who hopes to marry me; he's sweet-tempered
and polite, he has perfect manners like M. de Rouvray. But for
the fact that they bore me, these gentlemen would be very likeable. He, too, will accompany me to balls, with the same smug
look of contentment. A year after we're married, my carriage, my
horses, my gowns, my country house twenty leagues out of Paris,
will all be as good as they could possibly be, all that's needed in
short to make an upstart die of envy – a Comtesse de Roiville, for
instance. And after that? . . .

Mathilde grew bored in anticipation. The Marquis de Croisenois
managed to get near her, but she went on dreaming without
listening to him. The sound of his words mingled with the
throbbing murmur of the ball. Her eye mechanically followed
Julien, who had moved away with a respectful, but proud and
sullen air. Over in a corner, apart from the whirling throng, she
caught sight of Count Altamira, who was, as the reader knows,
under sentence of death in his own country. In the reign of Louis
XIV, one of his ancestors had married a Prince de Conti; the
memory of this afforded him a little protection against the secret
agents of the *Congrégation*.

I can see nothing conferring honour on a man except sentence
of death, thought Mathilde. It's the only thing that can't be
bought.

Ah! that's a witty remark I've just made to myself! What a
pity it didn't occur to me at a time when I could have got some
credit for it! Mathilde had too much taste to drag into her conversation any witticism made up beforehand; but she had also
too much vanity not to be delighted with her own wit. A look of
happiness replaced the boredom apparent on her features. The
Marquis de Croisenois, who was still talking to her, thought to see
in this a hint of success, and redoubled his eloquence.

What could any ill-natured person find fault with in my
epigram? Mathilde asked herself. I'd answer my critics thus: 'The
title of Baron or Viscount – that can be bought; a Cross – why,
that's given away; my brother's just had one, and what has he

done? Promotion in the Army, that can be contrived. Ten years of garrison duty, or a relative who's Minister of War, and you become a cavalry major, like Norbert. A great fortune! That is still the most difficult thing to get, and consequently the most meritorious. That's queer! it's just the opposite of all the books tell you. ... Well, then, to acquire a fortune, you just marry M. Rothschild's daughter.

That remark of mine is really rather profound. A death sentence still remains the only thing for which no one has ever thought of asking.

'Do you know Count Altamira?' she asked M. de Croisenois.

She had an air of returning from such a distance, and this question had so little connexion with all the poor Marquis had been saying to her for the past five minutes, that his affability was quite upset. All the same he was a man of quick intelligence, and very widely famed as such.

Mathilde's rather eccentric, he thought. That's a disadvantage – but she brings her husband such a fine position in society. I don't know how the Marquis does it; he's friends with all the best people in every party; he's a man who just can't go under. Besides, Mathilde's eccentricity may pass for genius. Combined with noble birth and a considerable fortune, genius is not looked on as ridiculous, and then, what distinction she has! She shows too, when she likes, a marvellous admixture of wit, character, and aptness in conversation which makes her a perfectly delightful companion. ...

As it is difficult to do two things well at the same time, the Marquis answered Mathilde with a vacant air and as if repeating a lesson. 'Who doesn't know poor Altamira?' he said. And he went on to give her the story of his fantastically absurd and unsuccessful conspiracy.

'Very absurd!' murmured Mathilde as if speaking to herself, 'but he has done something. I wish to see a man; bring him to me,' she said to the Marquis, who was deeply shocked.

Count Altamira was one of the most open admirers of the haughty and almost impertinent demeanour of Mademoiselle de la Mole; she was, according to him, one of the very loveliest women in all Paris.

'How beautiful she would look on a throne,' he said to M. de Croisenois, as he allowed himself to be led to her without any sign of reluctance. There are not wanting people in this world who would like to establish the principle that nothing is such bad form as a conspiracy in the nineteenth century; it reeks of Jaco-binism. And what is more repulsive than an unsuccessful Jaco-bin?

Mathilde glanced at M. de Croisenois as if she were faintly ridiculing Altamira, but she listened to him with pleasure. A conspirator at a ball, that's a pretty contrast, she thought. In this conspirator, with his black moustache, she thought to discover a likeness to a lion in repose; but she quickly found that his mind had room for only one point of view – an intense admiration for utilitarian principles.

The young Count considered nothing worthy of his attention except what might give his country a government by two Chambers. He gladly left Mathilde, the prettiest person at the ball, because he saw a Peruvian General enter the room. Despair-ing of Europe as Metternich had organized it, poor Altamira had fallen back on the idea that, when the States of South America became strong and powerful, they might restore to Europe the liberty that Mirabeau had sent over to them.

A surging mob of young men with moustaches had descended on Mathilde. She had clearly seen that Altamira had not fallen under her spell, and felt piqued by his departure. She saw his dark eyes sparkle as he talked to the Peruvian General. Mademoiselle de la Mole gazed at the young Frenchmen with that air of pro-found gravity which none of her rivals could imitate. Which of these, she thought, could manage to incur the death sentence, even supposing the chances were all on his side?

The peculiar way she looked at them flattered the less quick-witted, but made the rest uneasy. They feared the explosion of some lively quip which it would be difficult to parry.

Good birth, thought Mathilde, gives a man a hundred qualities the absence of which would offend me; I see this, for instance, in Julien – but it neutralizes those qualities of the spirit which pro-voke the death sentence.

Someone near-by remarked at that moment: 'This Count Alta-mira is the second son of the Prince of San Nazaro-Pimentel. It was a Pimentel who attempted to save Conradin, beheaded in 1268. They are one of the noblest families in Naples.'

There's a fine proof, thought Mathilde, of my maxim – Good birth robs a man of that high spirit without which men do not bring sentence of death on their heads! I'm fated, it seems, to talk nonsense tonight. Since I'm merely a woman like all the rest, well, I'd better dance. She yielded to the entreaties of M. de

Croisenois, who for the past hour had been begging her for a gallop. To take her mind off her misadventure in philosophy, Mathilde allowed herself to be perfectly enchanting; M. de Croisenois was in raptures.

But neither dancing, nor the wish to please one of the handsomest gentlemen of the court, nor anything else at all could distract Mathilde. She was the queen of the ball; she knew it, yet remained indifferent.

What a colourless life I shall lead with a creature like Croisenois, she said to herself, as he escorted her back to her seat an hour later. . . . Where does pleasure exist for me, she added sadly, if, after six months' absence, I can't find it in the midst of a ball which rouses the envy of all the women in Paris? And yet I'm surrounded by the homage of a company which couldn't, to my mind, be more select. There's not a single member of the middle-class present except a few peers and a Julien or two. All the same, she added with increasing sadness, what advantages have I not been given by fate ! A brilliant reputation, riches, youth – everything, in short, but happiness !

The most doubtful of my advantages, moreover, are precisely those of which people have been talking to me all the evening. I've wit, or so I believe, for obviously everyone's afraid of me. If anyone ventures to touch on a serious subject, at the end of five minutes' conversation he arrives all out of breath, and as if he had made a grand discovery, at something I've been repeating to him for the last hour. I'm beautiful, I've that advantage for which Madame de Stael would have sacrificed everything – and yet the fact remains that I'm bored to death. Is there any reason why I'd be less bored if I change my name to that of the Marquis de Croisenois?

But, heavens above ! she added, almost longing to cry, isn't he a model of perfection, the masterpiece of education in this present age? You can't even look at him without his thinking of something obliging, and even witty, to say to you. He's brave. . . . But that man Sorel's a curious creature, she reflected, and her eyes, lacklustre up till now, took on a look of anger. I told him I had something to say to him, and he hasn't condescended to reappear !

CHAPTER 9 : *The Ball*

> A lavish display of dress, a blaze of candle-
> light, perfumes; so many pretty arms, and
> lovely shoulders; bouquets, the entrancing
> melody of Rossini's music, Ciceri's paintings!
> I am carried right out of myself!
>
> UZERI'S *Travels*

'You look cross,' said the Marquise de la Mole. 'I warn you, that is unbecoming at a ball.'

'It's only a headache,' replied Mathilde, in a tone of disdain, 'it's too hot in here.'

At that moment, as if to justify Mademoiselle de la Mole, old Baron de Tolly fainted and fell to the floor; they had to carry him out. There was talk of apoplexy, it was a disagreeable thing to happen.

Mathilde paid no attention, it was a fixed habit of hers never to look at old men or at any persons noted for their gloomy conversation. She began dancing to avoid this chatter about apoplexy, which after all was no such thing, for two days later the Baron was about again.

But M. Sorel still doesn't appear, she said to herself again when she had stopped dancing. Her eyes were almost roaming round in search of him, when she caught sight of him in another room. Strangely enough, he seemed to have lost that air of cold impassibility so natural to him; he no longer looked like an Englishman.

Why, he's chatting to my condemned man, Count Altamira! said Mathilde to herself. His eyes are alight with gloomy fire; he looks like a Prince in disguise; his glance is prouder than ever.

Julien was coming up to where Mathilde was standing, still chatting with Altamira; she stared at him, scanning his features, seeking to find in them those high qualities which earn for a man the honour of being sentenced to death.

'Yes,' he was saying to Count Altamira, 'Danton really was a man!'

Good heavens! can he be another Danton, Mathilde said to herself. But he has such a noble face, and that man Danton was so frightfully ugly, a butcher, I believe. Julien was still fairly close to her; she did not hesitate to call out to him. She was consciously proud of asking a question that was rather extraordinary for a girl to ask.

'Wasn't Danton a butcher?' she asked him.

'Why, yes, in certain people's eyes,' Julien answered, with an expression of the most ill-disguised contempt, his eyes still ablaze from his conversation with Altamira, 'but unfortunately for people of good birth he happened to be a lawyer at Méry-sur-Seine; that is to say, Mademoiselle,' he added spitefully, 'he began his career like several peers I see here tonight. It's true that in beauty's eyes, Danton had a tremendous disadvantage – he was extremely ugly.'

These last words were uttered rapidly, in an extraordinary tone which was certainly far from polite.

Julien waited for a moment, the upper half of his body slightly inclined, his expression one of proud humility, which seemed to say : I am paid to answer you, and I live on my pay. He did not deign to raise his eyes to look at Mathilde. As for her, with her own lovely eyes extraordinarily wide open and fixed upon him, she looked as if she were his slave. At length, as this silence lasted, he looked at her as a servant looks at his master when awaiting orders. Although his eyes gazed straight into Mathilde's, still staring at him with a curious expression, he moved away with noticeably eager haste.

And to think that he, who is really so handsome, thought Mathilde at length, awakening from her dreams, should speak in such praise of ugliness ! Never a thought of himself ! He's not like Caylus or Croisenois. This man Sorel has something of the air my father adopts when he gives such a good imitation of Napoleon, at a ball. She had completely forgotten Danton. I'm certainly feeling bored tonight, she thought. She caught hold of her brother's arm and, to his great annoyance, forced him to take her round the ballroom. The idea had occurred to her of following the condemned man's conversation with Julien.

The crowd was enormous. She managed, all the same, to catch up with them at the moment when Altamira, who was two feet in front of her, was walking up to a tray of ices to help himself. He was talking to Julien, half turned towards him. He saw an arm in a braided sleeve stretched out to take the ice next to his. The gold lace apparently attracted his attention, for he turned completely round to the eminent person to whom this arm belonged. Immediately a look of slight contempt came into his noble, ingenuous eyes.

'You see that man,' he whispered to Julien. 'He's Prince d'Ara-celi, the — Ambassador. This morning he applied to M. de Nerval, your French Foreign Minister, for my extradition. Look, he's over there playing whist. M. de Nerval is rather inclined to hand me over, for we gave you back two or three conspirators in 1816. If they surrender me to my king, I shall be hanged within twenty-four hours. And it's one of those handsome gentlemen with moustaches who'll arrest me.'

'The vile brutes!' cried Julien, half aloud.

Mathilde did not lose a single syllable of their conversation. Her boredom had vanished.

'Not so vile after all,' Count Altamira answered. 'I spoke to you of myself to give you a vivid impression of the truth. Look at Prince d'Araceli. Every five minutes his eyes wander to his Golden Fleece; he cannot get over the pleasure of seeing this bauble on his chest. The poor man's really nothing but an anachronism. A century ago, the Golden Fleece was an outstanding mark of honour, but then it would have been well out of his reach. Today, any person of birth must be an Araceli to be thrilled by it. He would have had a whole town hanged to get hold of it.'

'Is that the price he paid for it?' asked Julien, earnestly.

'No, not exactly,' Altamira answered coldly. 'Possibly he had thirty or so rich landowners in his district, who were said to be Liberals, flung into the river.'

'What a brute!' repeated Julien.

Mademoiselle de la Mole, leaning forward with the keenest interest, came so close to him that her beautiful hair was almost touching his shoulder.

'You are very young!' replied Altamira. 'I told you I had a married sister in Provence. She's still pretty, kind, too, and gentle. She's an excellent mother to her family, faithful to all her duties, and religious without being excessively so.'

What is he driving at? thought Mademoiselle de la Mole.

'She is happy,' Comte Altamira went on, 'and so she was in 1815. I was hiding in her house at the time, on her estate near Antibes. Well, the moment she heard of Marshal Ney's execution, she began to dance!'

'I can't believe it!' said Julien, aghast.

'That's party spirit,' Altamira replied. 'There's no real true passion left in the nineteenth century. That's why people get so bored in France. The greatest cruelties are committed, yet not from motives of cruelty.'

'So much the worse!' said Julien. 'When people commit crimes they should at least find some pleasure in committing them. That's all that's good about them, and one can't find the slightest justification for them, except on such grounds.'

Mademoiselle de la Mole, entirely forgetting what she owed to herself, had thrust herself almost directly in between Altamira and Julien. Her brother, who, being used to obeying her, had given her his arm, had now turned his gaze towards some other part of the room, and to keep himself in countenance, was trying to appear as if held up by the crowd.

'Quite right,' said Altamira. 'People do everything without pleasure, without any remembrance of what they've done – even crimes. I could point out ten men, perhaps, in this ballroom, who will be damned as murderers. But they've forgotten it, and so has the world.

'Many of them are moved to tears if their dog breaks its paw. At Père-Lachaise, when, as you say so charmingly in Paris, flowers are strewn on their graves, we shall be told they combined all the virtues of the old paladins, and people will speak of the doughty deeds of their great-great-grandfather who lived in the days of Henri IV. If, despite the good offices of Prince d'Araceli, I don't get hanged and if ever I'm permitted to enjoy my fortune in Paris, I'd like to invite you to dine with nine or ten murderers, whom people honour and who feel no remorse.

'You and I will be the only ones at this dinner whose hands are not stained with blood, but I shall be despised as a bloody monster and a Jacobin, and you will merely be despised as a low-class fellow intruding upon good company.'

'Nothing could be truer,' remarked Mademoiselle de la Mole.

Altamira looked at her in amazement; Julien did not deign to look.

'Take note,' continued Altamira, 'that the revolution at the head of which I found myself was unsuccessful, but only because I did not want to let three men's heads be cut off, and distribute among our supporters some seven or eight millions which happened to be in a safe to which I held the key. My king, who today is all agog to have me hanged, and who before the revolution was on friendly, and even familiar, terms with me, would have given me the Grand Cordon of his Order if only I had let those three heads fall and distributed the money in that safe; for I should have won at least a partial success, and my country would have had some sort of Charter. . . . That's the way of the world – just a game of chess.'

'At that time,' replied Julien, 'you didn't know the game. . . . But now . . .'

'I'd have heads cut off, you mean? I'd not be a Girondin, as only the other day you gave me to understand I was? . . . I will give me an answer,' said Altamira sadly, 'when you've killed a man in a duel, which is, after all, a much less ugly thing than having him put to death by the executioner.'

'Upon my word,' said Julien, 'the end justifies the means. Now if I had any power, instead of being a mere nonentity, I'd have three men hanged to save the lives of four.'

In his eyes was manifest the fire of martyrdom, and contempt for the vanity of human judgement; they encountered those of Mademoiselle de la Mole who was standing close by him, and his contempt, far from changing to an air of gracious civility, seemed to grow all the greater. This shocked her intensely; but it was no longer in her power to put Julien out of her mind.

She moved away, hurt and resentful, making her brother go with her. I must have some punch, and dance a good deal, she said to herself. I intend to choose the best dancer I can, and make an impression at all costs. Good, here's the Comte de Fervaques, who's noted for his impertinence. She accepted his invitation, and they began dancing. It remains to be seen, she thought, which one of us two will be the ruder, but, to fool him to my heart's content, I'll have to get him talking. Presently, everyone else in the quadrille was merely making a show of dancing. No one wanted to lose a single one of Mathilde's piquant repartees. M. de Fervaques was disconcerted, and finding nothing but elegant phrases to put forward in place of ideas, began to scowl. Mathilde, who was feeling cross, treated him cruelly and made an enemy of him. She danced until daybreak and finally left the ballroom horribly tired. But, in the carriage, the little strength she had remaining was still employed in making her utterly sad and miserable. She had been scorned by Julien, and was unable to return his scorn.

Julien's happiness was at its height. All unconsciously carried away by the music, the flowers, the beautiful women, the general elegance, and most of all, by his own imagination, which was lost in dreams of glory for himself and liberty for all mankind, he said to Altamira : 'What a fine ball ! there's nothing lacking.'

'Thought is lacking,' replied Altamira. His face betrayed that scorn which is all the more stinging because it is plain to see that politeness imposes the duty of hiding it.

'You are here, my lord. Doesn't that count as thought, and what's more, thought conspiring?'

'I am here on account of my name. But thought is hated in your drawing-rooms. It must never rise above the level of a music-hall number; then it receives due credit. But as for the man who thinks, you call him a *cynic*, if there's any vigour or originality in his sallies. Isn't that the name that one of your judges bestowed on Courier? You put him in prison, and Béranger, too. Everyone among you, who has a mind worth anything, is bundled into the police court by the *Congrégation*; and the best people applaud.

'That's because your antiquated society esteems decorum above all else. . . . You will never rise higher than martial gallantry. You'll have many a Murat; but never a Washington. I can see nothing in France but vanity. A man who says original things may easily burst out with some rash sally, whereupon his host imagines himself insulted.'

Just as he was saying this, the Count's carriage, which was taking Julien home, arrived at the Hôtel de la Mole. Julien had taken a violent liking to his conspirator. Altamira had paid him a handsome compliment, springing evidently out of deep conviction. 'You haven't a Frenchman's frivolous mind,' he told him, 'and you understand the principle of *utility*.'

It so happened that, only two evenings before, Julien had seen *Marino Faliero*, a tragedy by M. Casimir Delavigne. Hasn't Israel Bertuccio, mused our rebellious plebeian, more character than all those Venetian nobles? And yet they are people of proved nobility going back to the year 700, a century before Charlemagne, whilst the noblest of those at M. de Retz's ball this evening only go back, and even then by fits and starts, to the thirteenth century. Anyhow, amongst these Venetian nobles, so great by birth, but so flabby, so anaemic in character, Israel Bertuccio is the man one remembers.

A conspiracy cancels every title conferred by social caprice. In circumstances such as these a man straightway assumes the rank assigned to him by his manner of facing death. Even the mind loses some of its supremacy. What would Danton be today, in this age of Valenods and Rênals? Not even deputy to the Public Prosecutor. What am I saying? he would have sold himself to the *Congrégation*; he'd have been a Minister, for after all this great man, Danton, stooped to stealing. Mirabeau, too, sold himself. Napoleon robbed Italy of millions, otherwise he would have been held up by poverty. Only La Fayette never stole. Must one steal? Must one sell oneself? Julien asked himself. This question pulled him up short. He spent the rest of the night reading the history of the Revolution.

The next morning, while he was copying his letters in the library, he could still think of nothing but Count Altamira's conversation.

As a matter of fact, he said to himself after a long fit of musing, if those Spanish Liberals had compromised the people by a few crimes, they wouldn't have been so easily swept away. They were boastful, chattering children. . . . Like myself! cried Julien all at once, as though waking up with a start.

What difficult things I ever done to give me the right to judge poor devils who once in their lives, after all, have dared to plan, to embark on action? I'm like a man who, on rising from table, exclaims: 'I'm not dining tomorrow, but that won't prevent me from feeling as energetic and lively as I do today.' Who knows what a man may feel in the middle of a great action? . . . These lofty thoughts were interrupted by the unexpected arrival of Mademoiselle de la Mole, who was just coming into the library. He was so excited by his admiration for the high qualities of Danton, Mirabeau, and Carnot, who had managed not to be defeated, that his eyes rested upon Mademoiselle de la Mole, but without his thinking of her, without his greeting her, almost without his seeing her. When at last his big, wide-open eyes became conscious of her presence, the light in them was quenched. Mademoiselle de la Mole remarked this with a feeling of bitterness.

It was all to no purpose her asking him for a volume of Vély's *Histoire de France*, which was up on the highest shelf, so that Julien was obliged to fetch the longer of the two ladders. He brought the ladder, looked for the volume, and handed it to her, without as yet being able to give her a thought. As he carried the ladder back, in his haste he bumped his elbow against one of the glass doors of the bookcase; the splinters, showering on to the floor, woke him up at last. He hastened to apologize to Mademoiselle de la Mole; he tried to be polite, but he was nothing more. Mademoiselle de la Mole saw quite clearly that she had disturbed him, and that he would have preferred to go on dreaming of what was occupying his mind, rather than talk to her.

After gazing at him intently, she went slowly out of the room. Julien watched her as she went, taking delight in the contrast between the simplicity of her present costume and the elegant splendour of her dress the night before. The difference in her expression was equally striking. This girl, so haughty at the Duc de Retz's ball, had at this moment almost a suppliant's look. As a matter of fact, said Julien to himself, that black gown sets off the beauty of her figure even better. But why is she in mourning?

If I ask the reason for this mourning, he thought, I may find I've committed a further blunder. Julien was completely roused out of his deep soul-stirring dreams. I must read over all the letters I've written this morning, he thought. Heaven knows how many words were left out and how many silly mistakes I'll find. As he was making an effort to read the first of these letters, he heard the rustle of a silk dress close by. He turned sharply round; Mademoiselle de la Mole was standing two feet away from his table, and laughing. This second interruption made Julien lose his temper.

As for Mathilde, she had just become acutely aware that she meant nothing to this young man; her laughter was intended to cover her embarrassment, and did so successfully.

'You're clearly thinking about something very interesting, M. Sorel. Can it be some curious tale connected with the conspiracy that has sent Count Altamira here to Paris? Tell me, please, what it's all about. I'm burning to know; I'll be discreet, I swear I will!' She was astonished at the words as she uttered them. What! pleading with an underling! Her embarrassment increased; she added with a touch of flippancy: 'What can have turned you, who are ordinarily so cold, into a creature inspired, a sort of man like one of Michael Angelo's prophets?'

This keen and somewhat impertinent questioning, wounding Julien deeply, roused all his mad enthusiasm again.

'Did Danton do well to steal?' he said to her gruffly and in a manner that every moment grew wilder. 'The revolutionaries of Piedmont, of Spain, should they have compromised the people by committing crimes? Should they have given away every post in the army, and every Cross, even to men who didn't deserve them? Wouldn't the men who wore these Crosses have dreaded the return of the monarchy? Ought they to have let the treasury in Turin be pillaged? In a word, Mademoiselle,' he said, coming towards her with a terrifying expression, 'must a man who wants to drive ignorance and crime off this earth pass through it like a whirlwind and do evil indiscriminately?'

Mathilde was frightened; she could not meet his gaze, and recoiled a pace or two. She looked at him for a moment; then, ashamed of her fear, she went with a light step out of the library.

> Love! in what follies do you not contrive to
> make us find delight?
>
> *Letters of a Portuguese Nun*

JULIEN read his letters over. As the sound of the dinner bell
came to his ears, he said to himself: How ridiculous I must
have appeared in the eyes of that Parisian doll! What folly to
have told her what was really in my mind! Yet, perhaps, it
wasn't so great a folly. Speaking the truth on this occasion was
worthy of me.

But why, by the way, did she come and question me on intimate matters! Such questions from her are impertinent. It's not
good manners. My thoughts about Danton are no part of the
service for which her father pays me.

As he entered the dining-room, the sight of Mademoiselle's
deep mourning, which impressed him all the more forcibly because no one else in the family wore black, made him forget his
ill-temper.

After dinner, he found his mind completely free of all those
enthusiastic fancies which had haunted him throughout the day.
By good luck, the academician who knew Latin was one of the
party at dinner. There's the man who's least likely to think me a
fool if, as I suppose, my question about Mademoiselle's mourning
is out of place.

Mathilde was looking at him with a curious expression. There
you plainly see, thought Julien, the coquetry of the women of
these parts, as Madame de Rênal depicted it. I wasn't pleasant
with her this morning, I didn't give in to her fancy for conversa-
sion. She values me all the more highly for that. No doubt there'll
be the devil to pay for it. Later on, her disdainful pride will know
very well how to take its revenge. Well, I defy her to do her
worst. How different from the woman I've lost! such unaffected
charm! such simplicity! I knew her thoughts before she knew
them herself; I saw them taking shape; my only antagonist in her
heart was fear lest her children should die; that was a natural,
reasonable kind of affection, which I found lovable even though
I suffered by it. I've been a fool. The ideas I had formed of Paris
prevented me from appreciating that sublime woman.

Good God! what a difference! And what do I find here? Cold,

arrogant vanity, every fine shade of self-esteem – and nothing else.

They were getting up from the table. I mustn't let anyone get hold of my academician, thought Julien. He went up to him as they were going out into the garden, and assuming a meek, insinuating air, he shared his rage at the success of *Hernani*.

'If we were only still in the days of *lettres de cachet*!' he said.

'Then he wouldn't have dared' cried the academician, with a gesture worthy of Talma.

While they were talking of a flower, Julien quoted a line or two from Virgil's *Georgics*, and decided that nothing could equal the poetry of the abbé Delille. In short, he flattered the academician in every possible way, after which he said to him, with an air of the utmost indifference: 'I suppose Mademoiselle de la Mole has had a legacy from some uncle, for whom she is in mourning.'

'What! You're one of the household,' said the academician, suddenly stopping still, 'and you don't know about this mad fancy of hers? As a matter of fact, it's strange her mother allows such things. But, between ourselves, it isn't strength of character that most distinguishes the people in this house. Mademoiselle de la Mole has enough for them all, and imposes her will on them. Today's the 30th of April!' The academician stopped talking, and looked at Julien with a knowing air. Julien smiled as intelligently as he could.

What connexion, he wondered, can there possibly be between imposing your will on a whole household, wearing black, and the 30th of April? I really must be even stupider than I thought.

'I must confess ...' he said to the academician, his eyes still asking questions.

'Let us take a turn round the garden,' said the academician, delighted at the hint of a chance to narrate a long and well-phrased story.

'What! do you really mean to say that you don't know what occurred on the 30 April 1574?'

'And where?' said Julien, in astonishment.

'On the Place de Grève.'

Julien was in such a state of amazement that this name did not enlighten him. Curiosity, and the expectation of hearing something of tragic import, gave to his eyes the brightness a storyteller so loves to see in his audience. The academician, thrilled to find a virgin ear, related at full length to Julien how, on the 30 April 1574, Boniface de la Mole, the handsomest young man of his age, together with his friend Annibal de Coconasso, a gentleman of Piedmont, had been beheaded on the Place de Grève. La Mole was the fondly idolized lover of Queen Marguerite of Navarre. 'And note,' the academician added, 'that Mademoiselle de la Mole's name is *Mathilde-Marguerite*.' La Mole was at the same time one one of the Duc d'Alençon's favourites and an intimate friend of his mistress's husband, the King of Navarre, afterwards Henri IV. On Shrove Tuesday in this year, 1574, the Court happened to be at Saint-Germain, with poor King Charles IX, who was at the point of death. La Mole wished to kidnap his friends, the Princes, whom Catherine de Medici was holding as prisoners at the Court. He brought up two hundred horsemen right under the walls of Saint-Germain, the Duc d'Alençon took fright, and La Mole was summarily handed over to the executioner.

'But what most touches Mademoiselle de la Mole, as she told me herself seven or eight years ago, when she was only twelve – for the girl's got a head, such a head! . . .' The academician raised his eyes to heaven. 'What impressed her in this political catastrophe was that Queen Marguerite of Navarre, who had waited in hiding in a house on the Place de Grève, boldly sent to the executioner for her lover's head. And the following night, at midnight, she took this head with her in her carriage, and went to bury it with her own hands in a chapel at the foot of the hill of Montmartre.'

'No, it's not possible,' cried Julien, deeply moved.

'Mademoiselle de la Mole despises her brother because, as you see, he is utterly unconcerned with all such ancient history, and does not wear mourning on the 30th of April. It is since this famous execution, and in memory of La Mole's close friendship with Coconasso – who being an Italian was called Annibal – that all the men of this family have borne this name. And this man Coconasso,' the academician added, lowering his voice, 'was, according to Charles IX himself, one of the most brutal assassins on the 24 August 1572. But how is it possible, my dear Sorel, that you are ignorant of such things, you, who are one of the household?'

'Then that must be why, during dinner, Mademoiselle de la Mole twice addressed her brother as Annibal. I thought I hadn't heard correctly.'

'It was a reproach. It's strange the Marquise allows such follies. . . . That tall girl's husband will have some pretty pranks to put up with!'

These words were followed by five or six sarcastic remarks. Julien was shocked at the gleam of spiteful joy in the academician's eyes. Look at us now, he thought, a couple of servants engaged in speaking ill of our masters. But nothing should really surprise me coming from this academician.

Julien had caught him on his knees one day before the Marquise, begging her for a tobacco licence for a nephew in the provinces. That evening, a little maid who waited on Mademoiselle de la Mole, and who was pursuing Julien with her attentions, as once Elisa had done, gave him the idea that her mistress's mourning was not in any way assumed for effect. She really loved this La Mole, the dearly cherished lover of the wittiest and most intelligent queen of her age, who had died because he had sought to free his friends. And what friends, too! The First Prince of the Blood and King Henri IV.

Accustomed to the entirely artless simplicity transparent in all Madame de Rênal's behaviour, Julien saw nothing but affectation in all the women in Paris, and if at any time he felt in the least disposed to melancholy, he could think of nothing at all to say to them. Mademoiselle de la Mole proved an exception.

He was beginning not to consider any longer as hardness of heart that species of beauty which belongs to a noble demeanour. He had long conversations with Mademoiselle de la Mole, who would sometimes walk up and down with him in front of the open windows of the drawing-room after dinner. She told him one day she was reading d'Aubigné's *Histoire Universelle* and Brantôme. Strange books to read, thought Julien, when her father doesn't allow her to read Walter Scott's novels!

One day, her eyes sparkling bright with the pleasure that is a proof of heartfelt admiration, she told him of the strange feat of a young woman in the reign of Henri III, of which she had just read in the *Mémoires de l'Étoile*. Discovering that her husband was unfaithful, she had stabbed him with a dagger.

This flattered Julien's vanity. A person surrounded by such deference, and who, according to the academician, ruled all the household, condescended to speak to him in a manner that might almost resemble friendship.

I was mistaken, said Julien, on second thoughts. It isn't friendship, I'm only like the confidant in a tragedy — it's just her need of someone to talk to. This family take me for a scholar. I'll go and read Brantôme, d'Aubigné, and l'Étoile. I shall then be able to challenge the truth of some of the anecdotes Mademoiselle de la Mole mentions to me. I mean to get out of playing the part of a passive confidant.

By degrees, his conversations with this girl, whose bearing was at once so dignified and easy, became more interesting. He forgot to play his sorry part of plebeian in revolt. He found her well-informed and even able to reason. Her opinions in the garden differed widely from those she openly expressed in the drawing-room. At times she showed with him an enthusiasm and a frank-ness which formed a perfect contrast to her usual manner, so haughty and so cold.

'The Wars of the League are the heroic age of France,' she said to him one day, her eyes alight with intelligence and enthusiasm. 'Then each man fought to achieve some particular aim, in the wish to make his party triumph, not merely to gain some paltry Cross, as in your Emperor's time. You must agree that there was less egotism and pettiness in that. I love that age.'

'And Boniface de la Mole was its hero,' he said to her.

'At least he was loved as maybe it's sweet to be loved. What woman alive today would not shrink with horror from touching a decapitated lover's head?'

Madame de la Mole called her daughter indoors. Hypocrisy, to be of service, must be kept hidden; and Julien, as you see, had taken Mademoiselle de la Mole partly into his confidence con-cerning his admiration for Napoleon.

There's the immense advantage they have over us, thought Julien, left alone in the garden. The history of their ancestors raises them above vulgar feelings, and they don't have to be for ever thinking of how to earn their bread! What a miserable position! he added bitterly. I'm unworthy to discuss such high concerns. My life is nothing but one hypocrisy after another, because I haven't an income of a thousand francs to buy my daily bread.

'What are you dreaming of now, sir?' asked Mathilde as she came running back to him.

Julien was weary of self-contempt. Out of pride, he told her frankly what he was thinking, blushing deeply at mentioning his poverty to someone who was so rich. He tried to make it clear by the haughtiness of his tone that he did not ask for anything. Never had Mathilde thought him so handsome; she discovered in his face an expression of sensibility and frankness which he often lacked.

Less than a month later, Julien was walking, lost in thought, in the garden of the Hôtel de la Mole; but his face no longer bore the hard imprint of a pride turned inwards on itself by a constant sense of inferiority. He had just come back from the drawing-room door, after escorting Mademoiselle de la Mole, who claimed she had hurt her foot when running with her brother.

She leant upon my arm in a most peculiar way, said Julien to himself. Am I a fatuous ass, or can it be true that she's taken a liking to me. She listens to me so gently even when I'm confiding to her all that my pride makes me suffer ! She, who's so haughty with everyone else ! They'd be greatly surprised in the drawing-room if they saw that look on her face. It's very certain she never adopts such a kind and gentle manner with anyone but myself.

Julien tried not to take an exaggerated view of this singular friendship. In his own mind he compared it to an armed truce. Each day, when they met, before resuming the almost intimate tone of the day before, they were on the verge of asking each other : 'Are we going to be friends or enemies today ?' Julien had realized that if he once allowed this very haughty girl to insult him with impunity, all would be lost. If I must quarrel with her, wouldn't it be better to do so from the outset, by standing up for the lawful rights of my pride, rather than by repelling the marks of contempt which would quickly follow the least neglect of what I owe to my personal dignity ?

Several times, on days when they were in a fractious mood, Mathilde would try to adopt the manner of a great lady with him; she showed a rare skill in these attempts, but Julien rudely repulsed them.

One day he interrupted her abruptly. 'Has Mademoiselle de la Mole,' he said to her, 'any orders to give to her father's secretary ? He must give heed to such orders and carry them out respectfully; but apart from that, he has nothing whatever to say to her. He is not paid to tell her his thoughts.'

This state of affairs, and the singular doubts in Julien's mind, drove away the boredom he habitually found in this drawing-room which, although so magnificent, was a place where one felt afraid of everything and where it was thought improper to treat anything as a joke.

It would be amusing if she were in love with me, thought Julien. But whether she loves me or not, he went on, I've made a close confidant of an intelligent girl, before whom I see the whole household tremble, and the Marquis de Croisenois more than any-one. That very polished young man, who's so gentle and so brave, who combines in himself all the advantages of birth and fortune, a single one of which would make my heart so glad! He is madly in love with her, he is going to marry her. Look at all the letters M. de la Mole has made me write to the two lawyers arranging the terms of the contract! And I who find myself, pen in hand, in such a subordinate position, triumph two hours later, here in the garden, over this very agreeable young man; for after all, her preference for me is strikingly plain. Perhaps, too, she hates him as a future husband. She's proud enough for that. The favours she shows me then are only accorded to me as to a confidential servant.

But no, either I'm mad, or she's making love to me; the more I show myself cold and deferential with her the more she seeks me out. That might be obstinacy, or merely a pose; but I see her eyes light up when I appear unexpectedly. Are the women of Paris able to pretend to such an extent? What do I care! I have appearances on my side, let me make the most of them. Heavens, how lovely she is! How I delight in those big blue eyes, seen at close range, and gazing at me as they so often do. How different is this year's spring from the last, when I was living in misery, keeping up my spirits only by my strength of character, in the midst of three hundred dirty, evil-minded hypocrites. I was almost as evil as they.

In moments of doubt and distrust, Julien would think: This girl is making a fool of me; she and her brother have leagued together to play some trick at my expense. Yet she appears to be so scornful of her brother's lack of energy! He's brave, and that's all, she tells me. He hasn't a single idea that ventures to run counter to the fashion. I'm the one who's always obliged to stand up for him. A girl of nineteen! Can a girl of this age be faithful at every minute of the day to a self-prescribed code of hypocrisy?

On the other hand, when Mademoiselle de la Mole's big blue eyes gaze fixedly at me with a certain curious expression, Count Norbert always moves away. That seems to me suspicious; oughtn't he to be furious at his sister's singling out a *servant* of their household? For so I've heard the Duc de Chaulnes refer to me. At this memory anger replaced all other feelings. Is it just a love for old-fashioned ways of speech in this crotchety old duke?

Anyhow, she's a pretty creature! Julien added, with a tigerish glare. I'll get her, and then be off — and bad luck to the man who hinders me in my flight!

This idea became Julien's sole preoccupation; he could no longer think of anything else. His days sped by like hours.

At every moment of the day, while trying to keep his attention on some serious matter, his mind would let everything slide, and he would wake up a quarter of an hour later, his heart beating fast, his head confused, still dreaming of this one idea : Does she love me?

I admire her beauty, but I fear her mind.
                                                    MÉRIMÉE

HAD Julien employed in studying what went on in the draw-ing room the time he spent in exaggerating Mathilde's beauty, or in working himself up into a fury against a haughti-ness, natural in her family, but which she was forgetting on his account, he would have understood the essential constituents of her power to dominate everyone around her. The moment any-one displeased Mademoiselle de la Mole, she knew how to punish the offender by a witty thrust so quietly delivered, so well-chosen, so apparently courteous, so nicely timed, that the more its victim pondered it, the more painfully it hurt. Little by little she became unbearably cruel to those whose vanity she had wounded.

As she attached no value to many things that were earnestly sought after by her family she always seemed in their eyes to be cool and self-possessed. Aristocratic drawing-rooms are pleasant to refer to after one has left them, but that is all; mere politeness is worth nothing save on first acquaintance. Julien experienced this after the first thrill of delight, the first shock of surprise. Politeness, he reflected, is nothing more than the absence of the irritability that comes from ill-breeding. Mathilde was often bored, perhaps she would have been bored anywhere. At such times it became a distraction and a genuine pleasure for her to give sharper point to some witty, sarcastic remark.

It was possibly in order to have victims slightly more amusing than her distinguished relatives, or the academician and the five or six other inferior persons who paid court to her, that she had given grounds for hope to the Marquis de Croisenois, the Comte de Caylus and two or three other young men of the highest distinction. They were nothing more to her than fresh targets for her pointed wit.

We must confess with pain, for we are fond of Mathilde, that she had received letters from several of these young men, and had occasionally answered them. We hasten to add that this young person provides an exception to the manners of the age. The pupils of the noble Convent of the Sacred Heart cannot, generally speaking, be accused of a lack of discretion.

One day the Marquis de Croisenois handed back to Mathilde a

rather compromising letter she had written him the day before. He thought to further his cause to a great degree by this signal mark of discretion. But indiscretion was what Mathilde liked in her correspondence; she took a pleasure in running risks. She did not speak to him again for the next six weeks.

She was amused by these young men's letters; but, according to her, they were all alike. It was always the most profound, the most melancholy passion.

'Every one of them,' she would say to her cousin, 'is the same perfect gentleman, ready to set off for the Holy Land. Can you think of anything more insipid? And this is the sort of letter I shall be receiving for the rest of my life! Such letters as these can only change every twenty years, to suit with the occupation then in vogue. They must have been less colourless in the days of the Empire. Then all these young men of the world had seen or done one or two things that *really* had something of greatness about them. My uncle, the Duc de N—, fought at Wagram.'

'What intelligence is needed in giving a sabre thrust?' said Mademoiselle de Saint Hérédité, Mathilde's cousin. 'Yet whenever such a thing has happened to them, how often they talk about it!'

'Oh, well, those stories amuse me. To have been in a *real* battle, one of Napoleon's battles, in which ten thousand soldiers were killed, that's a proof of courage. Exposing oneself to danger elevates the soul and preserves it from the boredom in which all my poor adorers seem to be plunged; and it's catching, this boredom. Which of them ever has any idea of doing something out of the ordinary? They seek to win my hand – a fine exploit! I'm rich and my father will help his son-in-law to get on. Ah! if only he could discover one who'd be a little entertaining!'

Mathilde's lively, crisp, and picturesque way of looking at things had, as you can see, a bad effect on her speech. A remark of hers would often seem wanting in taste in the eyes of her extremely well-mannered friends. Had she been less in vogue, they would often have come near to admitting that her language had something too highly coloured about it for feminine delicacy.

She, for her part, was most unjust to the handsome riders who throng the Bois de Boulogne. She envisaged the future, not with terror, that would have been too violent an emotion, but with a feeling of distaste very rare at her age.

What had she left to wish for? Fortune, high birth, intelligence, and beauty, all these, so people said, and so she believed, had been heaped upon her by the hand of fate.

Such were the thoughts of the most envied heiress in the Faubourg Saint-Germain, when she began to find pleasure in walking with Julien. She was amazed at his pride; she admired the ingenuity of this humble commoner. He will manage to get himself made a Bishop, she thought, just like Father Maury.

Soon the sincere, unfeigned resistance, with which our hero greeted a number of her ideas, began to occupy her mind; she pondered over it; she handed on to her cousin the tiniest detail of these conversations, only to discover that she could not manage to convey their character in full.

A sudden thought enlightened her – I've had the good fortune to fall in love, she said to herself one day, in an ecstasy of joy past believing. I'm in love, I'm in love, that's clear ! Where can a girl of my age, young and beautiful and intelligent, find a thrill, if not in love? Try as I may, I shall never feel any love for Croisenois, Caylus, or anyone of their sort. They're perfect, perhaps too perfect; in short, they bore me.

She ran over in her mind all the descriptions of passion she had read of in *Manon Lescaut*, the *Nouvelle Héloïse*, the *Lettres d'une Réligieuse Portugaise*, and so forth. There was no question, of course, of anything but a *grande passion*; a trivial love affair would have been unworthy of a girl of her age and birth. She gave the name of love only to that heroic feeling which was to be met with in France in the days of Henri III and Bassompierre. A love of this sort never basely succumbed to obstacles; far from that, it made one do great deeds. What a misfortune for me, she thought, that there's no real Court like that of Catherine de Medici or Louis XIII. I feel myself equal to everything that is most daring and most great. What couldn't I do with a king who was a man of spirit, like Louis XIII, sighing at my feet ! I'd lead him into the Vendée, as Baron de Tolly so frequently remarks, and from there he'd win back his kingdom; then there'd be an end to the Charter ... and Julien would help me. What's lacking in him? Name and fortune. He'd make a name for himself, he'd acquire a fortune.

Croisenois lacks nothing; and all his life long he'll never be anything more than a Duke, half Ultra, half Liberal, a creature who can't make up his mind, who always avoids extremes and *in consequence always finds himself in the second rank*.

What great enterprise is there that is not an *extreme* at the moment of undertaking it? It's after it's accomplished that it seems possible to the ordinary run of men. Yes, it is love with all

its miracles that is taking possession of my heart; I feel it by the
fire that stirs in my veins. Heaven owed me this favour. It will
not have showered all its benefits on a single human being in
vain. My happiness will be worthy of me. Not one of my days
will bear a cold resemblance to the day before. It already shows
a high heart and a daring spirit to love a man so far beneath me
in social position. Let me see; will he continue to deserve me? At
the first sign of weakness I see in him, I'll give him up. A girl of
my birth, and with the chivalrous spirit people are good enough
to attribute to me (this was one of her father's expressions) ought
not to behave like a foolish, silly creature.

Isn't that the part I'd be playing if I let myself love the Marquis
de Croisenois? It would be just a new edition of the happiness
of my cousins, whom I despise so utterly. I know beforehand
everything the poor Marquis would say to me, and all that I'd
have to say to him in reply. What sort of love is that which makes
one yawn? One might as well take to religion. I'd have the same
sort of show for the signing of my marriage contract as my
youngest cousin, with my noble relations getting sentimental, if
they didn't, by the way, lose their tempers over a final clause in-
serted the day before in the contract by the solicitor to the other
party.

CHAPTER 12 : Is he a Second Danton?

> An *itch or excitement*, such was the character
> of my aunt, the beautiful Marguerite de
> Valois, who shortly after this was married to
> the King of Navarre, whom we see at present
> reigning in France under the name of Henri
> IV. A need for hazardous sport was the whole
> secret of this amiable princess's character;
> from thence came her quarrels and her recon-
> ciliations with her brothers, from the age of
> sixteen. Now what can a young woman
> hazard? All that she has most precious: her
> honour, her lifelong reputation.
>
> *Mémoires du duc d'Angoulême,*
> *fils naturel de Charles IX*

BETWEEN Julien and myself there's no contract to be signed, no family solicitor needed; everything here is on a heroic scale, everything springs from chance. But for nobility, which he lacks, it's the love of Marguerite de Valois for young La Mole, the most distinguished man of his day. Is it my particular fault if the young men of the Court are such staunch upholders of convention, and grow pale at the mere idea of any adventure slightly out of the ordinary run? For them a little expedition to Greece or Africa is the height of audacity, and even then they can't move a step except in a troop. As soon as they find them-selves on their own, they're frightened, not of Bedouin spears, but of ridicule, and this fear drives them crazy.

My dear Julien, on the contrary, only likes to act alone. There's never the slightest thought, in this privileged human being, of seeking support or help from other people! He despises other people, and that's why I don't despise him.

If, while still poor, Julien had been noble, my loving him would be nothing more than a vulgar act of folly, a commonplace mis-alliance; I wouldn't want such a thing; it would have nothing of what characterizes a grand passion – the enormous obstacles to override, the dark uncertainty of the outcome.

Mademoiselle de la Mole was so taken up with this fine line of argument that the following day, without realizing what she was doing, she sang Julien's praises to the Marquis de Croisenois and her brother. Her eloquence rose to such heights that she made them annoyed.

'Beware of that young man with so much energy !' exclaimed her brother. 'If a Revolution breaks out again, he'll have us all guillotined.'

Avoiding a direct answer, she hastened to chaff her brother and the Marquis de Croisenois over the fear they had of energy, which was, indeed, nothing more than the fear of meeting the unexpected, the dread of finding oneself at a loss in the face of unforeseen events.

'Always, gentlemen, always this same fear of ridicule, a monster which, unfortunately, gave up the ghost in 1816.'

'Ridicule,' so M. de la Mole would say, 'does not exist any more in a country where there are two Parties.' His daughter had understood what he meant.

'And so, gentlemen,' she remarked to Julien's enemies, 'you'll have lived in fear all your lives, and afterwards you'll be told :

It wasn't a wolf, it was only its shadow.'

Soon after this Mathilde left them. Her brother's remark had filled her with horror; it made her very uneasy; but when she woke up the next morning, she saw in it the very highest praise.

In this age, in which all energy is dead, she thought, his energy makes them afraid. I'll tell him what my brother said. I want to see what answer he makes; but I'll choose a moment when his eyes are shining. Then he can't lie to me.

Can he be a second Danton ? she added after a long, vague fit of musing. Well, suppose a Revolution did break out again. What parts would Croisenois and my brother play then ? It's already prescribed for them – sublime resignation. They'd be heroic sheep, allowing their throats to be cut without a word. Their only fear when dying would still be the fear of showing bad form. My dear Julien would blow out the brains of the Jacobin who came to arrest him, if he had the slightest hope of escaping. He, at any rate, has no fear of bad form.

This last idea left her pensive; it revived painful memories and took away all her courage. It reminded her of the chaffing remarks of MM. de Caylus, de Croisenois, de Luz, and her brother. These gentlemen were unanimous in accusing Julien of a *priestly air* of hypocritical meekness.

But, she went on suddenly, her eyes agleam with joy, the bitterness and the frequency of their cruel banter proves that, for all they can say, he's the most distinguished man we've seen this winter. What do his faults matter, or his ridiculous ways? There's greatness in him and they are shocked by it, they are otherwise so good-natured and so indulgent. Certainly he's poor, and has studied to become a priest; they are officers, and have no need to study; it's much easier for them.

In spite of all the drawbacks of his everlasting black suit, and his clerical cast of face, which he needs must assume, poor boy, if he is not to die of hunger, nothing could be plainer than that they're afraid of his ability. As for this priestly expression, he no longer wears it when we've been a few minutes alone together. Whenever, too, these gentlemen utter any remark which they consider subtle or original, isn't their first glance always at Julien? I've noticed that very plainly. And yet they know very well that he never speaks to them, unless he's asked a question. I'm the only one to whom he addresses a word. He thinks me high-minded. He only answers their objections just as fully as politeness demands, and then immediately keeps them at a respectful distance. With me, he'll argue for hours on end, not feeling sure of his ideas so long as I put forward the least objection. Anyhow, this winter there've been no duels; his only way of attracting attention has been by words. Now my father, a man of superior intelligence, who will greatly advance the fortunes of our house, has a great respect for Julien. Everyone else hates him, but no one despises him, except my mother's saintly friends.

The Comte de Caylus had, or feigned to have, a great passion for horses; he spent all his time in the stable, and frequently lunched there. This great passion, combined with his habit of never laughing, had won him great esteem from all his friends. He was the shining light of their little circle.

The following day, as soon as they had assembled behind Madame de la Mole's easy chair, Julien being absent, M. de Caylus, backed up by Croisenois and Norbert, made a lively attack on Mathilde's good opinion of Julien, without any pertinent reason, and almost as soon as he saw Mademoiselle de la Mole. She scented this subtle manoeuvre a mile off and was delighted by it.

There they are, she thought, all of them banded together against a man who doesn't get ten louis a year, and who can't answer them except when he's questioned. They're afraid of him in his black coat. What would it be if he wore epaulettes?

She had never been more brilliant. From the very first onslaught she covered Caylus and his allies with volleys of sarcastic wit. When the fire of chaff from these distinguished officers had been forced to die down, she spoke to M. Caylus.

'Were some clod-hopping country gentleman from the mountains of Franche-Comté,' she said, 'to discover tomorrow that Julien is his natural son, and give him a name and a few thousand francs, within six weeks, gentlemen, he'd have a moustache like yours; in six months he'd be an officer of Hussars like you yourselves. And then the greatness of his character will no longer be a subject for jest. I can see you obliged to fall back, my Lord Duke-to-be, on that old, bad line of argument; the superiority of the Court nobility to provincial nobles. But what reserves will you have left, if I choose to drive you into a corner and am so unkind as to make Julien's father a Spanish Duke, a prisoner of war in Besançon in Napoleon's time, and who, from qualms of conscience, acknowledges him on his deathbed?'

All these assumptions of illegitimacy were considered in rather bad taste by MM. de Caylus and de Croisenois, and that was all they saw in Mathilde's argument.

However much Norbert was under his sister's influence, the meaning of her words was so plain that he assumed an air of gravity, little suited, we must admit, to his smiling, good-natured face. He ventured to say a few words to her.

'Are you feeling ill, my dear?' Mathilde answered him, assuming a slightly grave expression. 'You must be feeling very ill indeed to answer chaffing by preaching morals. Moralizing, from you! Are you seeking a post as Prefect?'

Mathilde very soon forgot the Comte de Caylus' vexed expression, Norbert's sulks, and M. de Croisenois' dumb despair. She had to make up her mind about an ominous idea which had taken complete possession of her.

Julien is sincere enough with me, she told herself; at his age, in a position of inferiority and wretched as an astounding ambition can make him, he needs a woman to love him. I am perhaps that woman, but I see no sign of love in him. Being by nature so bold and daring he would have spoken to me of love.

This uncertainty, this parleying within herself, which, from that time onwards, occupied every moment of Mathilde's time, and for which, each time Julien spoke to her, she found fresh arguments, completely banished those periods of boredom to which she was so continually liable.

The daughter of an able, intelligent man who might well become a Minister, and give the clergy back their woodlands, Mademoiselle de la Mole had been the object of the most extravagant flatteries at the Convent of the Sacred Heart. There is no compensation for such a misfortune. People had persuaded her that, in view of her advantages of birth, fortune, etc. she ought to be happier than other girls. This is the origin of boredom in princes, and of all their follies.

Mathilde had not escaped the disastrous influence of such an idea. However intelligent a girl may be, she is not, at ten years of age, on her guard against the flatteries of a whole convent, especially when they appear to be so well founded.

From the moment she made up her mind that she was in love with Julien, she no longer felt bored. Every day she congratulated herself on the decision she had made to indulge in a grand passion. This kind of amusement has many dangers, she thought. All the better! A thousand times better!

Without this grand passion, I'd have pined away with boredom at the finest moment in a girl's life, from sixteen to twenty. I've already lost the best years, forced, as my only pleasure, to listen to the senseless chatter of my mother's friends, who at Coblentz, in 1792, were not, so I'm told, quite so strict in their conduct as they are in their conversation today.

It was while Mathilde was troubled with these grave doubts that Julien was at a loss to understand the lingering glances that came his way. He was indeed plainly aware of an increasing coldness in Comte Norbert's manner, an extreme haughtiness in that of MM. de Caylus, de Luz, and de Croisenois. He was used to it. He sometimes suffered this calamity after an evening in which he had shone more brightly than befitted his station. But for the special welcome Mathilde gave him, and the curiosity aroused in him by everything to do with this circle, he would have held back from following these brilliant young men with moustaches into the garden, when they went there after dinner in Mathilde's company.

Yes, it's impossible to hide it from myself, thought Julien, Mademoiselle de la Mole does look at me in a peculiar way. But even when her beautiful blue eyes seem to be staring at me with least restraint, deep down in them I can always read cool self-possession, criticism, and malice. Can this by any possibility be love? How different was the look in Madame de Rênal's eyes.

One evening after dinner, Julien, who had gone with M. de la Mole to his study, was hastening back into the garden. As he was

walking boldly up to Mathilde's group, he overheard a few words
spoken in a loud tone of voice. She was teasing her brother. Julien
distinctly heard his own name uttered twice. He made his appearance; immediately deep silence fell, and useless attempts were
made to break it. Mademoiselle de la Mole and her brother were
too much excited to think of another topic of conversation. MM.
de Caylus, de Croisenois, de Luz, and another of their friends
showed themselves icily cold to Julien. He left them and went
away.

> Disconnected remarks, chance meetings are transformed to incontrovertible proofs in the eyes of a man with imagination, provided there is a little fire in his heart. SCHILLER

THE next day he again surprised Norbert and his sister as they were talking about him. On his arrival, a deathly silence fell, as on the previous evening. His suspicions knew no bounds. Can these charming young people be planning to make a fool of me? he thought. This is far more likely, I must admit, than a pretended passion on the part of Mademoiselle de la Mole for a poor devil of a secretary. In the first place, do people of this sort have passions? Hoaxing is a speciality of theirs. They are jealous of my wretched little superiority in conversation. Jealousy, that's another of their foibles. Everything's transparently plain with this set. Mademoiselle de la Mole wants to persuade me that she has singled me out, simply to present me as a spectacle to her future husband.

This cruel suspicion completely altered Julien's attitude of mind. Such an idea found in his heart a dawning love which it had no difficulty in destroying. This love was founded only on Mathilde's rare beauty, or rather on her queenly ways and her marvellous taste in dress. In this respect Julien was still an upstart. A pretty woman of the world is, so people affirm, what most astonishes a clever peasant when he pushes his way into the higher rank of society. It was by no means Mathilde's character that for days past had set Julien dreaming. He had sense enough to realize that he had no knowledge of her character. All that he saw of it might only be an outward show.

For instance, Mathilde would not for anything in the world have missed attending mass on a Sunday; almost every day she went to church with her mother. If, in the drawing-room of the Hôtel de la Mole, some incautious fellow, forgetting where he was, allowed himself to make the remotest allusion to some jest against the real or supposed interests of the Monarchy or the Church, Mathilde at once became frigidly severe. Her face, which was usually so provokingly lively, took on the impassive haughtiness of an old family portrait.

Yet Julien had ascertained that she always kept one or two

of Voltaire's most philosophical works in her room. He himself would often remove by stealth a volume or two of that handsome sumptuously bound edition. By slightly separating each volume from its neighbour, he concealed the absence of the volume he was taking away; but he soon perceived that someone else was reading Voltaire. He had recourse to a seminarist's trick: he placed a few strands of horsehair across the volumes which he supposed might interest Mademoiselle de la Mole. They disappeared for weeks at a time.

M. de la Mole, losing patience with his bookseller, who kept sending him all the sham *Mémoires*, instructed Julien to buy any new book that was at all sensational. But, to prevent the poison from spreading through the household, the secretary had orders to put these books in a little bookcase that stood in the Marquis's own room. Julien was soon certain that if any of these new books were in the least way hostile to the interests of the Monarchy and the Church they were not slow to disappear. It was not Norbert who was reading them.

Julien, exaggerating the importance of this discovery, credited Mademoiselle de la Mole with all Machiavelli's duplicity. This supposed villainy was in his eyes a charm, almost the only charm of mind she possessed. An overdose of hypocrisy and virtuous conversation drove him to such extremes. He rather inflamed his imagination than let himself be carried away by love.

It was after losing himself in dreams of the elegance of Mademoiselle de la Mole's figure, of her excellent taste in dress, the whiteness of her hand, the beauty of her arms, the easy nonchalance of all her movements, that he found himself in love. Then, to complete the spell, he imagined her to be a Catherine de Medici. Nothing was too deep or too criminal for the character he ascribed to her. It was the ideal of the Maslons, the Frilairs, the Castanèdes whom he had admired as a boy. In a word, it was, for him, the ideal of Paris.

Has anything funnier ever been known than the belief that there is depth or criminality in the Parisian character?

It's possible that this trio may be making a fool of me, thought Julien. The reader is but little acquainted with his character if he has not already seen the sombre, chilly expression on his face in response to Mathilde's glances. A bitter irony repulsed the assurances of friendship which Mademoiselle de la Mole, astonished by his conduct, ventured to risk on two or three occasions.

Stung by this sudden odd behaviour, this girl's heart, naturally cold, bored, and responsive only to things of the mind, became as passionate as it was in its nature to be. But there was a great deal of pride in Mathilde as well, and the birth of a feeling which made all her happiness dependent on another was accompanied by sombre melancholy.

Julien had made sufficient progress since his arrival in Paris to discern that this was not the barren melancholy of boredom. Instead of being eager, as once she had been, for evening parties, plays, and every kind of distraction, she avoided them.

Music, when sung by Frenchmen, bored Mathilde to death, yet Julien, who made it his duty to be present at the close of the Opera, noticed that she let herself be taken there as often as she could. He thought to observe that she had lost a little of the perfect poise which once distinguished all her actions. She would sometimes reply to her friends with jests that in their pointed vigour amounted to insults. It seemed to him that she had taken a dislike to M. de Croisenois. That young man must be tremendously fond of money, thought Julien, not to turn his back on a girl like that, however rich she may be! As for himself, indignant at these insults offered to masculine dignity, he grew increasingly colder towards her, and sometimes went so far as to answer her rather discourteously.

However much he had resolved not to be taken in by Mathilde's marks of interest, they were so very evident on certain days, and Julien, who was beginning to use his eyes, found her so pretty to look at, that at times he was almost ensnared by them.

The skill and forbearance of these young men and women of the world will end by triumphing over my want of experience, he said to himself. I must go away and put an end to all this. The Marquis had just entrusted him with the management of a number of small estates and houses he owned in lower Languedoc. A journey there was necessary; M. de la Mole reluctantly consented. Except in matters of high ambition, Julien had become his second self.

After all, thought Julien as he made ready for his journey, they haven't managed to trick me. Whether the jokes that Mademoiselle de la Mole makes at the expense of these gentlemen are real, or only intended to give me confidence, I've had some fun out of them. If there's no conspiracy against the carpenter's son, Mademoiselle de la Mole is a mystery to me, but she's just as much so for M. de Croisenois as for me. Yesterday, for instance, her ill temper was certainly real, and I had the pleasure of seeing

a young man as rich and noble as I am penniless and plebeian
made to knuckle under in my favour. That's my finest triumph;
it will make me merry as I speed in my post-chaise over the plains
of Languedoc.

He had kept his departure secret, but Mathilde knew better
than he that he was leaving Paris the next day, and for a very
long time. She pleaded a splitting headache, which was made
worse by the stuffy atmosphere of the drawing-room. She walked
for some little time in the garden and so tormented Norbert, the
Marquis de Croisenois, Caylus, de Luz, and a few other young
men who had dined at the Hôtel de la Mole, with her biting
sarcasm, that she obliged them to take their leave. She looked at
Julien in a curious way.

This look is possibly just a piece of play-acting, thought Julien
– but that hurried breathing, all that agitation! Nonsense! he
said to himself, who am I to judge of all such things? This is just
part of that most exquisite subtlety practised by Parisian women.
This hurried breathing, which so nearly moved me, she'll have
picked up from Léontine Fay, whom she's so fond of.

They were left alone; conversation was plainly languishing.
No! Julien feels nothing for me, said Mathilde to herself, in a
really miserable frame of mind.

As he was taking leave of her, she clutched his arm tightly.
'You will receive a letter from me this evening,' she said to him
in a voice so faltering that he could scarcely hear her. Julien was
quickly touched by this.

'My father,' she went on, 'has a proper regard for the services
you render him. You *must not* go away tomorrow; find some excuse.' And she ran off.

Her figure was entrancing. It would not have been possible to
have a prettier foot, she ran with a grace that left Julien spell-
bound; but who would guess what his second thought was after
she was completely out of sight? He was offended by the imperious tone in which she had uttered the words, *you must*. Louis
XV, too, at the point of death, had been deeply vexed by the word
must, clumsily used by his chief physician, and Louis XV was no
upstart.

An hour later a footman handed Julien a letter; it was purely
and simply a declaration of love.

The style is not too affected, said Julien to himself, seeking by
literary comments to restrain the joy that made his cheeks contract and obliged him to laugh in spite of himself.

'And so I,' he suddenly exclaimed, with a passion too strong to be restrained, 'I, a poor peasant, have received a declaration of love from a great lady !

'As for myself, I've not done so badly,' he added, reining in his joy as much as he could. 'I've managed to preserve the dignity of my character. I have never said I was in love.' He began to study her handwriting; Mademoiselle de la Mole wrote in a pretty little English hand. He needed to have some physical occupation to take his mind off a joy that was almost delirium.

Your going away forces me to speak. . . . It would be more than I could endure not to see you any more. . . .

A sudden thought struck Julien forcibly as a discovery, interrupting his scrutiny of Mathilde's letter, and increasing his joy. 'I'm preferred to M. de Croisenois,' he cried, 'I, who say nothing but serious things ! And he's such a handsome fellow ! He wears a moustache, and attractive uniform; he always finds some witty, ingenious thing to say, exactly at the right time, too.'

It was a delightful moment for Julien; he wandered round the garden, madly happy.

Later, he went upstairs to his office, and had himself shown in to the Marquis de la Mole, who luckily had not gone out. He proved to him with ease, by showing him a few stamped documents which had come from Normandy, that his attention to certain lawsuits in that province obliged him to postpone his departure for Languedoc.

'I'm very glad you're not going away,' said the Marquis when they had finished talking business. '*I like seeing you about.*' Julien left the room; this remark made him feel embarrassed.

And I am going to seduce his daughter ! Perhaps make impossible that marriage with the Marquis de Croisenois on which all his hopes for the future are centred. If he is not made a duke, at least his daughter will be entitled to a duchess's stool at Court. Julien thought of setting off for Languedoc in spite of Mathilde's letter, in spite of the explanation he had given the Marquis. This lightning flash of virtue died out very quickly.

How good of me, a mere commoner, he said to himself, to take pity on a family of this rank. I, whom the Duc de Chaulnes calls a domestic servant ! How does the Marquis add to his enormous fortune? By selling some of his securities whenever he hears at the Château there's a likelihood of a *coup d'état* the following day ! And, I, cast down to the lowest rank by a stepmotherly

Providence, I, to whom she has given a noble heart and less than a thousand francs of income, which means not enough for my daily bread, *yes, precisely speaking, not enough for my daily bread* – am I to refuse a pleasure offered to me! A cool, clear spring welling up to quench my thirst in the burning desert of mediocrity I struggle across with such pain! Upon my word, I'm not such an ass. Each man for himself in this desert of egoism men call life.

And he remembered certain disdainful glances cast his way by Mademoiselle de la Mole, and particularly by the *ladies* amongst her friends. The pleasure of triumphing over the Marquis de Croisenois completed the rout of this recall of virtue.

How I would love to make him angry, thought Julien. With what assurance would I now slash at him with my sword. He made a gesture as if he were giving a thrust in *seconde*. Before this, I was a snivelling pedant, basely taking advantage of a little courage. After this letter I'm his equal.

'Yes,' he said aloud with infinite delight, speaking slowly and deliberately, 'the respective merits of the Marquis and myself have been weighed, and the poor carpenter from the Juras carries the day.'

'Good!' he cried. 'There's my signature to my answer ready to hand. Don't go and imagine, Mademoiselle de la Mole, that I'm forgetting my position. I'll make you realize and feel clearly that it's the son of the carpenter for whom you are betraying a descendant of the renowned Guy de Croisenois, who followed Saint Louis on his Crusade.'

Julien could not contain his joy. He was obliged to go down into the garden. His room, where he had locked himself in, seemed too narrow a space for him to breathe in.

'I, a poor peasant from the Jura,' he kept on repeating. 'I, who am condemned to wear this dreary black coat year in, year out! Alas, twenty years earlier I'd have been in uniform like them! In those days a man of my sort was either killed, or *a General at thirty-six*.' This letter, which he kept tightly clutched in his hand, gave him the stature and the bearing of a hero. Nowadays, it's true, with this black coat, one can get at forty a stipend of a hundred thousand francs and the Blue Ribbon, like his Lordship the Bishop of Beauvais.

'Well, anyhow,' he said to himself, laughing like Mephistopheles, 'I've more intelligence than they; I know how to choose the uniform of my day.' And he felt an increased attachment to his ambition and his clerical habit. How many Cardinals have been of humbler birth than myself and yet have attained to positions of authority! My fellow-countryman, Granvelle, for example.

Gradually Julien's excitement died down; prudence rose to the surface. He said to himself, like his master Tartuffe, whose part he knew by heart:

> *'I might believe these words an honest trick. . . .*
> *Yet I'll not trust such soft, beguiling speech*
> *Unless her favours, after which I sigh,*
> *Come to assure me that she does not lie.*

'Tartuffe, too, was ruined by a woman, and he was as good a man as any. . . . My answer may be shown. . . . Well, here's the remedy to that,' he added, pronouncing his words slowly and with an accent of suppressed ferocity, 'we'll begin it with the most piquant phrases of the sublime Mathilde's letter.

'Yes, but four of M. de Croisenois's lackeys dart out at me, and snatch the original away. No! for I am well armed and accustomed, as they know, to open fire on lackeys.

'Well, then, one of them has courage; he rushes at me. He has been promised a hundred napoleons. I am flung into prison with all the proper legal procedure; I appear in the police court and they sentence me, with every appearance of justice and equity on the judges' part, to keep MM. Fontan and Magalon company at Poissy. There I sleep hugger-mugger with four hundred beggarly rogues. . . . And I am to feel pity for such people!' he cried, springing impetuously to his feet. 'Have they any for the Third Estate when they have them in their clutches?' These words were the last dying gasp of his gratitude towards M. de la Mole which, in spite of himself, had been tormenting him up till then.

'Softly, my honourable gentlemen, I understand this little piece of Machiavellianism; Father Maslon or M. Castanède at the seminary would not have done better. You will take away the letter *that incited me*, and I become the second volume of Colonel Caron at Colmar.

'Just a moment, gentlemen, I'm going to send the fatal letter in a well-sealed packet to be in Father Pirard's keeping. He is an honest man, a Jansenist, and as such secure against all temptations money can offer. Yes, but he opens letters. . . . I must send this one to Fouqué.'

It must be admitted that the look in Julien's eyes was horrible, the expression of his features hideous; it spoke of nothing but pure and simple criminality. He was the type of the unhappy wretch at war with the whole of society.

'To arms!' cried Julien, leaping at one bound down the steps in front of the house. He went into the letter-writer's booth down the street; the man was terrified. 'Copy this,' he said, giving him Mademoiselle de la Mole's letter.

While the writer was at his task, he himself wrote to Fouqué, begging him to keep a precious trust for him. But, he interrupted himself to remark, the secret agents at the Post Office will open my letter and hand over to you the one you're looking for – no, gentlemen. He went and bought an enormous Bible from a Protestant bookseller, skilfully concealed Mathilde's letter inside the binding, had the whole thing packed up, and his parcel went off by mail coach addressed to one of Fouqué's workmen, whose name was unknown to anyone in Paris.

When this was done, he went back, nimble and light-hearted, to the Hôtel de la Mole. 'Now for our part!' he cried, locking himself in his room and flinging off his coat.

What, Mademoiselle [he wrote to Mathilde], so it is Mademoiselle de la Mole who sends by Arsène, her father's servant, a too seductive letter to a poor carpenter from the Jura, no doubt to make fun of his simplicity.

And he copied down from the letter he had just received the phrases which bore the clearest meaning.

His own letter would have done credit to the diplomatic circumspection of the Chevalier de Beauvoisis. It was still only ten o'clock; Julien, drunk with happiness and with the sense of his own power, so novel to a poor devil like himself, went off to the Italian Opera. He heard his friend Geronimo sing. Never had music so exalted him. He was a god.

CHAPTER 14 : A Girl's Thoughts

> What bewilderment! What sleepless nights!
> Good God! shall I make myself an object of
> scorn! He himself will despise me. But he is
> leaving, he is going far away.
>
> ALFRED DE MUSSET

MATHILDE had not written to him without an inward struggle. Whatever had been the beginning of her interest in Julien, it very soon mastered the pride which, ever since she was conscious of her own self, had been sole ruler of her heart. This cold, disdainful spirit was for the first time carried away by passionate feelings. But if this passion mastered her pride, it still remained faithful to habits pride had formed. Two months of conflict and of novel sensations reshaped so to speak the whole of her moral being anew.

Mathilde believed she saw happiness before her eyes. This vision, all-powerful over a courageous heart when linked with a superior intelligence, had to wrestle long against a sense of dignity and all ordinary ideas of duty. One day, she went into her mother's room, on the stroke of seven in the morning, and begged her to allow her to retire to Villequier. The Marquise did not even deign to answer her request, and advised her to go back to bed. This was the last effort made by worldly wisdom and deference to accepted ideas.

The fear of behaving badly and of running counter to the ideas held sacred by people such as Caylus, Luz, and Croisenois, had fairly little power over her mind; such creatures as they did not seem to be made to understand her. She would have consulted them had it been a question of buying a carriage or an estate. Her real terror was lest Julien should be displeased with her.

Is it possible, she wondered, that he too has only the outward appearance of a superior being? She had a horror of want of character; that was her sole objection to the handsome young men around her. The more gracefully they made fun of everything that departs from fashion, or thinking to follow it, does so badly, the more they lost favour in her eyes.

They were brave, and that was all. And in what way are they brave, by the by? she would ask herself. In a duel – but a duel is now nothing more than a formality. Everything is known beforehand, even what a man should say as he falls. Stretched on the turf, his hand on his heart, there must be a generous pardon for his opponent, and a message for some fair lady, often an imaginary one, or one who goes to a ball on the day of his death for fear of arousing suspicion.

A man will brave danger at the head of a cavalry squadron all glittering with steel – but solitary danger, strange, unforeseen, and really hideous?

Alas! said Mathilde, it was at the Court of Henri III that one found men as great in character as by birth! Ah! if Julien had served at Jarnac or at Moncontour, I should no longer have any doubts. In those days of vigour and forceful action Frenchmen were not mere tailor's dummies. The day of battle was almost the day of least perplexities.

Their life was not confined like an Egyptian mummy inside wrappings always common to all alike, always the same. Yes, there was more true courage in going home alone, after leaving the Hôtel de Soissons, inhabited by Catherine de Medici, than in rushing off to Algiers today. A man's life was a succession of hazards. Now that civilization and the Chief of Police have driven hazard off the field, it's good-bye to the unexpected. If it crops up in our ideas, people can't find epigrams enough against it; if it crops up in events, no baseness is too low for our fears. Whatever act of madness our fear drives us to commit, excuses are found for it. Degenerate and tedious age! What would Boniface de la Mole have said if, raising his severed head from the tomb, he had seen, in 1793, seventeen of his descendants letting themselves be taken like sheep, to be guillotined two days later? Death was a certainty, but it would have been bad form for them to defend themselves and kill at least a Jacobin or two. Ah! in the heroic age of France in the days of Boniface de la Mole, Julien would have been the major, and my brother the young priest, a model of proprietory, with prudence in his eyes and discretion on his lips.

A few months before, Mathilde had despaired of meeting any human being who differed a little from the common pattern. She had found a certain happiness in allowing herself to write to a few young men in society. This unseemly boldness, so indiscreet in a young woman, might disgrace her in the eyes of M. de Croisenois, of his father, the Duc de Chaulnes, and all his household who, seeing the projected marriage broken off, would wish to know why. At that time, on occasions when she had written one of these letters, Mathilde passed a sleepless night. Yet these letters were only replies.

And now she was daring to say she was in love. She was writing *first* (what a terrible word) to a man in the lowest rank of society.

This circumstance, were it discovered, ensured her everlasting disgrace. Which of the women who came to see her mother would dare to take her side? What tactful phrase could be found for them to say to soften the blow inflicted by the frightful contempt of the drawing-rooms?

And even to speak to a man was shocking – but to write! '*There are things one does not write!*' Napoleon cried when he heard of the surrender of Baylen. And it was Julien who had told her of this saying! As if he were giving her a lesson in advance.

But all this was still nothing; Mathilde's anguish had other causes. Unmindful of the terrible effect on society, of the ineradicable stain entailing universal scorn, for she was outraging her caste, Mathilde was about to write to a being of a very different sort from men like Croisenois, Luz, and Caylus.

The depth, the unfathomed mystery of Julien's character would have been frightening, even if she were entering upon ordinary, conventional relations with him. But she was going to make him her lover, perhaps her master!

What claims will he not make upon me, if ever he has me completely in his power? Very well, I shall say to myself like Medea: '*Amidst all these perils I have still MYSELF.*'

Julien, she believed, had no reverence for noble birth. Worse than that, perhaps, he felt no love for her!

In those last moments of fearful doubt, ideas of feminine pride asserted themselves. Everything, cried Mathilde impatiently, should be out of ordinary in the lot of a girl like myself. Then the pride that had been instilled into her from her cradle strove against her virtue. It was just at this moment that Julien's departure precipitated everything. (Such characters are fortunately very rare.)

Late that night, Julien was malicious enough to have an extremely heavy trunk taken down to the porter's lodge; he summoned the footman who was courting Mademoiselle de la Mole's maid to carry it down. This manoeuvre may have no result, he said to himself, but if it's successful, she'll think I've gone. He went to sleep, highly delighted with this trick. Mathilde did not close her eyes.

The next day, very early in the morning, Julien left the house without being seen, but came back before eight o'clock.

Hardly had he entered the library before Mademoiselle de la Mole appeared at the door. He handed her his reply. He thought it his duty to speak to her; he could not have found a more convenient occasion, anyhow, but Mademoiselle de la Mole would not listen to him, and disappeared. Julien was delighted at this; he had not known what to say to her.

If all this, he thought, is not a game agreed on with Count Norbert, then clearly it must be that my cold glances have kindled this odd kind of love which this girl of noble birth imagines she feels for me. I'd be rather more of a fool than I ought if ever I let myself be drawn to feel any liking for that great flaxen doll. This consideration left him more cold and calculating than he had ever been before.

In the battle about to take place, he went on thinking, pride of birth will be like a high hill, forming a point of vantage between herself and me. It's on that ground we'll have to manoeuvre. I made a very great mistake in remaining in Paris; this postponement of my departure puts me in a worse position and exposes me to danger if all this is only a game. What risk was there in my going away? I should have been fooling them, if they were trying to make a fool of me. If her interest in me is in any way real, I'd have been increasing that interest a hundred times over.

Mademoiselle de la Mole's letter had afforded Julien's vanity such keen pleasure, that all the while he was exulting over what was happening, he had forgotten to give serious thought to the expediency of going away.

It was a fatal trait in his character to be acutely conscious of his mistakes. He was greatly vexed with himself over this one, and had almost given up thinking of the incredible victory that had preceded this slight reverse when, about nine o'clock, Mademoiselle de la Mole appeared on the threshold of the library door, flung him a letter, and rushed away.

It seems this is going to be a novel in letter-form, he said as he picked this one up. The enemy is making a false move; I, on my side, will bring coldness and virtue into play.

The letter asked for a definite answer in a tone of arrogance that gave fuel to his inward gaiety. He indulged himself in the pleasure of mystifying, for two pages on end, those persons who might wish to make a fool of him, introducing, with a last face-

tious thrust towards the close, the announcement of his decision
to leave Paris the following morning.

His letter written, he said to himself : The garden will do for
handing it to her, and out he went. He looked up at the window
of Mademoiselle de la Mole's room. It was on the first floor, but
there was a large entresol in between. This first floor was so high
up that as he walked, letter in hand, along the avenue of lime trees
Julien could not be seen from Mademoiselle de la Mole's window.
The arched vault formed by the very neatly trimmed limes intercepted the view. What ! said Julien angrily to himself, another
imprudence ! If they've undertaken to make fun of me, to let
myself be seen with a letter in my hand is just playing the
enemy's game.

Norbert's room was immediately above his sister's, and if
Julien came out from under the alley formed by the trimmed
branches of the limes the Count and his friends could follow all
his movements.

Mademoiselle de la Mole appeared behind the window panes; he
let her have a glimpse of his letter; she inclined her head. Immediately Julien ran back to his room, and happened to meet on the
staircase the fair Mathilde, who snatched the letter from him
with perfect ease of manner and with laughter in her eyes.

What passion there was in poor Madame de Rênal's eyes,
thought Julien, when, even after six months' intimacy, she ventured to receive a letter from me ! Never once, I believe, did she
look at me with laughter in her eyes.

He did not explain the rest of his reaction so clearly to himself; was he ashamed of something frivolous in his motives? But
what a difference, too, he went on to think, in the elegance of
her morning gown, in the general elegance of her appearance.
Any man of taste, catching sight of Mademoiselle de la Mole
thirty feet away, could tell at a glance the rank she occupies in
society. That is what may be accounted a patent merit.

While jesting with himself, Julien did not bring himself to the
point of admitting all that was in his thoughts. Madame de Rênal
had had no Marquis de Croisenois to sacrifice to him; he had had
no rival there except that low fellow the sub-prefect M. Charcot,
who called himself M. de Maugiron, because there were no
genuine Maugirons left.

At five o'clock, Julien received a third letter; it was thrown to
him through the library door. Mademoiselle de la Mole rushed
off again. What a mania for writing, he said to himself with a

laugh, when it's so easy for us to talk! The enemy is anxious to have my letters, and plenty of them, that's clear! He was in no hurry to open this one. More elegant phrases, he thought; but he grew pale as he read it. There were only eight lines:

I want to speak to you: I must speak to you, tonight. The moment one o'clock strikes, see that you are in the garden. Take the gardener's long ladder which is near the well; put it up against my window and climb up to my room. There is a moon tonight; but that doesn't matter.

> Ah! how cruel is the interval between the
> conception of a high enterprise and its execu-
> tion! What vain terrors! What hesitancies!
> Life is at stake. But far more than life –
> honour!   SCHILLER

THIS is becoming serious, thought Julien ... and a little too
plain, he added, after thinking it over. What! this fair and
noble lady can speak to me in the library with a freedom which,
heaven be praised, is unconfined; the Marquis never comes there
for fear I should show him my accounts. What! M. de la Mole
and Count Norbert, the only people who come in here, are out of
the house nearly all day. It's easy to note the moment of their return, and the sublime Mathilde, for whose hand a reigning
monarch would not be too noble, wishes me to commit an act of
appalling rashness!

It's clear they want to ruin me, or, at least, make a fool of me.
First of all, they tried to ruin me through my letters; these turn
out to be discreet; all right, they must have some act that's clear
as daylight. These pretty little gentlemen think me either too
stupid or too conceited. Hang it all! to climb in the brightest
moonlight ever seen, up a ladder like this to a first floor, five and
twenty feet above the ground! People will have plenty of time to
see me, even from the neighbouring houses. Shan't I look fine on
my ladder! Julien went up to his room and began to pack his
trunk, whistling as he did so. He had made up his mind to go,
without even answering the letter.

But this wise resolution gave him no peace of heart. If by
chance, he said to himself suddenly, when his trunk was shut,
Mathilde should be acting in good faith! Then, in her eyes, I
should be playing the part of an utter coward. I'm a man of base
extraction, I must show sterling qualities, ready on demand, without any easy counterfeit, and well attested by deeds that speak
for themselves. ...

He spent a quarter of an hour thinking the matter over. What's
the good of denying it? he said to himself. I shall be a coward in
her eyes. I lose not only the most distinguished person in high
society, as everyone was remarking at the Duc de Retz's ball, but
also the divine delight of seeing M. de Croisenois, a duke's son

and a future duke himself, sacrificed for me. A charming young man who has all the qualities I lack – a ready wit, birth, fortune. ...

Regret for this will haunt me all my life, not on her account, there are plenty of mistresses, but, as old Don Diego says, 'only one honour,' and here am I, clearly and plainly, drawing back in face of the very first danger that offers; for that duel with M. de Beauvoisis came merely as a joke. This is altogether different. A servant may shoot point-blank at me, but that's a lesser danger; I may forfeit my honour.

'This is getting serious, my lad,' he added aloud with a Gascon gaiety and accent. 'Honour is at stake. Never will a poor devil, whom chance has flung into so lowly a station as mine, find such an opportunity again; I shall have other successes with women, but they'll be minor affairs.'

For a long time he pondered, pacing up and down his room with hurried steps, stopping short from time to time. A magnificent marble bust of Cardinal Richelieu stood in his room, and his eyes were involuntarily drawn towards it. This bust seemed to be looking at him sternly as if reproaching him for the want of that boldness which ought to come so naturally to a Frenchman. In your time, great man, should I have hesitated?

Supposing, thought Julien finally, that at the worst this is all a plot, it's a very sinister one and very compromising for a young woman. They know I'm not the kind of man to keep silent. So they'll have to kill me. That was all very well in 1574, in the days of Boniface de la Mole, but the la Mole of today would never dare. These people are not the same any longer. Mademoiselle de la Mole is so envied! Tomorrow four hundred drawing-rooms would echo with her shame, and with what pleasure, too!

The servants chatter among themselves of the marked preference that is shown me. I know it, I've heard them. ...

On the other hand, her letters! ... They may believe I have them on me. If they surprise me in her room, they'll seize them. I'll have to deal with two, three, four men, who knows how many? But where will they get hold of these men? Where in Paris can one find underlings who'll be discreet? They are all afraid of the law. ... By Jove! it will be Caylus, Luz, Croisenois, and all that lot. The occasion, and the foolish figure I'll cut, will be what tempts them. Beware, Master Secretary, of Abelard's fate!

All right then, damn it! You'll bear some marks of mine, I'll strike at your faces, like Caesar's soldiers at Pharsalia. .... As for the letters, I can put them in a safe place.

Julien made copies of the two last, hid them inside one of the handsome volumes of the Voltaire in the library, and took the originals to the post himself.

On his return, he exclaimed with surprise and consternation: 'What madness am I rushing into now?' He had spent a whole quarter of an hour without giving serious thought to what he was about to do in the coming night.

But, if I back out of it, I can't fail to despise myself afterwards. All my life long, this action will remain a serious matter for doubt, and for me such doubt means the bitterest anguish of heart. Didn't I feel it over Amanda's lover? I believe I could forgive myself more easily for an open crime; once I'd confessed it, I'd put it out of my mind.

What! an incredible stroke of luck lifts me out of the crowd to make me the rival of a man who bears one of the finest names in France, and shall I light-heartedly declare myself his inferior! After all, it's cowardly not to go. 'That one word settles everything,' cried Julien, springing to his feet ... 'besides, she's such a pretty creature!'

If there's no treachery in this, what folly is she not committing for my sake! ... If it's a practical joke, by Jove! It's up to me, gentlemen, to turn jest into earnest, and that's what I'll do.

But what if they seize me and tie my arms the moment I enter the room? They may have prepared some ingenious booby trap!

It's like a duel, he laughed to himself, to every thrust there's a counterstroke, as my fencing master says, but God, who wills that the end should come, makes one of the two forget to parry. Besides, there's something here to answer them with; he drew out his pocket pistols; then, although they were fully charged, he renewed the priming.

There were still many hours to wait; in order to have something to do, Julien wrote to Fouqué:

My friend, open the enclosed letter only in case of accident, if you hear it said that something strange has happened to me. Then, strike out the proper names from the manuscript I send you, and make eight copies which you will send to the news-papers in Marseilles, Bordeaux, Lyons, Brussels, etc. Ten days later, have the manuscript printed, send the first copy to his

Lordship the Marquis de la Mole; and a fortnight after that, scatter the remaining copies about the streets of Verrières.

This short memorandum, justifying himself, and written in narrative form, which Fouqué was not to open except in case of accident, was made by Julien as little compromising as possible to Mademoiselle de la Mole, but, all the same, it defined his position very precisely.

Julien was just sealing his little packet, when the dinner bell rang; it made his heart beat fast. His imagination, engrossed in the story he had just composed, was entirely taken up with tragic presentiments. He had seen himself seized by the servants, throttled, and carried down into a cellar with a gag in his mouth. There, one of them kept an eye on him, and supposing the honour of this noble family demanded a tragic conclusion, it was easy to end everything with one of those poisons that leave no trace. Then they would say his death was due to some illness, and carry his dead body back to his room.

Moved, like a writer of plays, by his own story, Julien was feeling really afraid as he entered the dining-room. He looked at all the servants in their full livery, studying the cast of their faces. Which of them have been chosen for this night's enterprise? he wondered. In this family, memories of the Court of Henri III are so present, so often called to mind, that, if they think themselves outraged, they will act more resolutely than other people of their rank. He looked at Mademoiselle de la Mole, seeking to read in her eyes what her family was planning; she was pale, and had, so he thought, an expression on her face that was quite medieval. Never had he remarked such an air of grandeur about her, she was indeed beautiful and imposing. *Pallida morte futura*, he said to himself (her pallor proclaims her deep designs).

After dinner he made a point of lingering in the garden, but all to no purpose, Mademoiselle de la Mole did not appear. To talk to her at that moment would have lifted a heavy weight off his heart.

Why not confess it? He was afraid. As he had made up his mind to act, he gave way to this feeling without shame. Provided that at the moment of action I find in myself the necessary courage, what does it matter what I may be feeling at this moment? He went off to reconnoitre the position and to try the weight of the ladder.

This is an instrument, he said to himself, laughing, which I seem to be fated to make use of! – here as at Verrières. What a difference! Then, he added sighing, I was not obliged to feel suspicious of the person for whose sake I was exposing myself to danger. And what a difference, too, in the danger!

I might have been killed in M. de Rênal's gardens without risk of dishonour. It would have been easy to make my death seem inexplicable. Here, what foul tales will they not make up in the drawing-rooms of the Hôtel de Chaulnes, the Hôtel de Caylus, the Hôtel de Retz, etc. – in short, everywhere! Future generations will hold me as a monster for years to come.

Or for two or three years, he added, laughing at himself. But the thought of this overwhelmed him. As for me, where shall I find anyone to justify me? Even if Fouqué prints my pamphlet after my death, it will only be a further act of infamy. What! I am received into a house, and in payment for the hospitality I find, for the kindnesses they shower upon me, I print a pamphlet about what happens there! I attack a woman's honour! Ah! let me be the dupe – a thousand times rather.

That evening was a terrible one.

> This garden was very large, and had been laid
> out with the most perfect taste a few years
> before. But the trees were over a century old.
> It had something of a rustic air about it.
>
> MASSINGER

H E was on the point of writing to Fouqué to countermand his instructions when the clock struck eleven. He turned the key noisily in the lock of his door, as though he were locking himself in. Then he crept stealthily round the house to see what was happening everywhere, especially on the fourth floor, where the servants had their quarters. Nothing unusual was going on. One of Madame de la Mole's maids was giving a party, the servants were merrily drinking punch. People laughing like that, thought Julien, can't have been chosen to take part in this night's expedition, they would be more serious.

Finally he went and took up his post in a dark corner of the garden. If their plan is to keep what they're doing hidden from the servants in the house, they'll make the men whose task it is to surprise me come in over the garden wall.

If M. de Croisenois is tackling all this with any coolness and common sense, he's bound to find it less compromising for the young person he hopes to marry to have me surprised before the moment I enter her room.

He carried out a reconnaissance with thorough military precision. My honour's at stake, he thought. If I happen to make a slip, it won't excuse me in my own eyes to say to myself : I didn't think of that.

The weather was dishearteningly clear and calm. The moon had risen round about eleven o'clock and at half past twelve it completely lit up the whole side of the house facing on to the garden.

She's crazy, said Julien to himself. As one o'clock struck, there was still a light in Count Norbert's windows. Julien had never been so afraid in all his life, he saw only the dangers of the enterprise and did not feel the least enthusiasm.

He went to fetch the enormous ladder, waited five minutes, to leave time for her instructions to be countermanded, and at five past one placed the ladder up against Mathilde's window. He climbed quietly up, pistol in hand, astonished at not being attacked. As he approached the window it opened noiselessly.

'So you're here, sir,' Mathilde said to him with deep emotion. 'I've been following your movements for the last hour.'

Julien was greatly embarrassed, he did not know how to behave, his heart was quite empty of love. Thinking, in his perplexity, that he must be daring, he tried to embrace Mathilde.

'No, no!' she cried, thrusting him from her.

Greatly relieved at being repulsed, he took a quick glance round him; the moonlight was so brilliant that the shadows it formed in Mademoiselle de la Mole's room were quite black. There may very well be men hiding there without my seeing them, he thought.

'What have you got in the side pocket of your coat?' asked Mathilde, delighted at finding a topic for conversation. She was strangely distressed; all those feelings of reserve and shyness, so natural in a young girl of good family, had resumed their sway, and were torturing her.

'I've all sorts of weapons and pistols,' answered Julien, no less relieved at having something to say.

'You must remove the ladder,' said Mathilde.

'It's terribly big, and may break the windows of the drawing-room below, or of the entresol.'

'You mustn't break the windows,' Mathilde answered, trying in vain to adopt the tone of ordinary conversation. 'You could possibly lower the ladder, I think, by tying a rope to the top rung. I've always plenty of ropes in my room.'

And that's a woman in love! thought Julien. She dares to say she's in love! So much presence of mind and common sense in her precautions show me plainly enough that I'm not triumphing over M. de Croisenois, as I stupidly thought, but merely becoming his successor. Actually, what does it matter? It isn't as if I loved her. I'm triumphing over the Marquis in this sense, that he will be greatly annoyed at having a successor, and still more annoyed that his successor should be me. How arrogantly he looked at me yesterday evening in the Café Tortoni, pretending not to know me! How rudely he bowed to me later when he could no longer avoid it!

Julien had fastened the rope to the top rung of the ladder and was letting it down gently, leaning very far out over the balcony to prevent its touching the windows. A good time to kill me, he thought, if anyone's hidden in Mathilde's room. But deep silence still reigned everywhere.

The ladder reached the ground. Julien managed to lay it down flat in the bed of exotic plants that ran alongside the wall.

'What will my mother say,' said Mathilde, 'when she sees her beautiful plants all crushed ! . . . You must throw down the rope,' she added, perfectly coolly. 'If anyone saw it leading up to the balcony it would be a difficult circumstance to explain.'

'And how me gwine get away?' said Julien, in a playful tone, imitating the Creole form of speech. (One of the maids in the house was a native of San Domingo.)

'You get away by door,' said Mathilde, delighted with his idea. Ah ! how worthy this man is of all my love, she thought.

Julien had just let the rope drop down into the garden. Mathilde clutched his arm. He thought an enemy had seized hold of him, and turned round sharply, drawing his dagger. She thought she had heard a window open. They stood there motionless, without breathing. The moon shone full upon them. As the sound was not repeated, they felt no further cause for alarm.

Then there was fresh embarrassment, very great on both sides. Julien made sure that the door was fastened with all its bolts. He had a good mind to look under the bed, but did not dare; a footman or two might have been posted there.

Mathilde was plunged in all the agony of extreme shyness. She was horrified at her position.

'What have you done with my letters?' she said, at length.

What a fine opportunity of foiling these gentlemen's schemes if they're listening, and so avoiding a fight ! thought Julien.

'The first is hidden in a bulky Protestant Bible,' he said, 'which last night's mail is carrying off a long way from here.'

He spoke very distinctly as he entered on these details, and in such a way as to be overheard by any persons who might be concealed in two large mahogany wardrobes he had not dared to examine.

'The other two are in the post, and are following the same route as the first.'

'Good gracious ! but why all these precautions?' asked Mathilde in consternation.

Is there any reason I should tell her a lie? thought Julien; and he confessed to her all his suspicions.

'So that accounts for the coldness of your letters, my dear !'

cried Mathilde, in a tone of wild excitement rather than of tenderness.

Julien did not notice this fine distinction. Her use of the words *my dear* made him lose his head, or at least his suspicions vanished. He ventured to clasp in his arms this girl who was so beautiful and inspired such respect in him. This time he was only half repulsed.

He had recourse to his memory, as once, a good while ago, with Amanda Binet in Besançon, and quoted several of the finest phrases from the *Nouvelle Héloïse*.

'You have a man's heart, my love,' she replied, without paying very much attention to what he was saying. 'I wished to test your courage, I confess. Your first suspicions and your determination prove you even more fearless than I thought.'

Mathilde was forcing herself to adopt an intimate tone; she was evidently more attentive to this unfamiliar way of addressing him than to what she was actually saying. Such endearments, utterly bare of any note of tenderness, gave Julien no pleasure after the first moment. He was amazed at his lack of happiness; finally, in order to feel it, he appealed to reason. He saw himself esteemed by this very proud girl, who never bestowed unrestricted praise, and, with the help of this argument, he attained to a happiness based on self-esteem.

This was not, it is true, that ecstasy of the spirit he had experienced at times in Madame de Rênal's company. There was not a trace of tenderness in his feelings at this first moment of love. It was the keen happiness of gratified ambition, and Julien was above all things ambitious. He spoke again of the people he had suspected and of the precautions he had devised. As he spoke he was thinking how best to take advantage of his victory.

Mathilde, who was still deeply embarrassed, and had the look of one astounded by what she had done, seemed overjoyed at finding a topic of conversation. They talked of ways and means of seeing each other again. Julien took an exquisite pleasure in his own intelligence and bravery, of which he gave fresh proofs in the course of the discussion. They had to deal with extremely sharp-sighted people. Young Tanbeau was certainly a spy, but all the same Mathilde and he were not devoid of cunning themselves. What could be easier than for them to meet in the library, and make all·arrangements?

'I can put in an appearance, without rousing suspicion, in any part of the house,' added Julien, 'and almost in Madame de la

Mole's bedroom itself.' It was absolutely necessary to pass through this room to reach her daughter's. If Mathilde thought it better for him to arrive always by ladder, he would expose himself to this negligible danger with wild, delirious joy of heart.

As she listened to him speaking, Mathilde was shocked by his air of triumph. So he's now my master ! she said to herself, already consumed by remorse. Her reason was horrified at the signal act of folly she had just committed. Had it been possible, she would have annihilated both Julien and herself. Whenever, from time to time, her strength of will imposed silence on remorse, feelings of shyness and wounded modesty made her extremely miserable. She had not for a moment anticipated the dreadful state of mind in which she now found herself.

I must speak to him, though, she finally said to herself. That's an ordinary convention, one does speak to one's lover. And then, to carry out this duty, and with a tenderness far more evident in the words she used than in the tone of her voice, she told him of the various decisions to which she had come with regard to him in the course of the last few days.

She had decided that if he ventured to come to her room with the aid of the gardener's ladder, as she had told him to do, she would be wholly his. Yet never had things so tender been said in a colder and more formal tone. It was enough to make one hate the very idea of love. What a moral lesson for a rash young woman ! Is it worth while ruining one's future for a moment like this?

After long wavering, which, to a superficial observer, might have seemed the effect of the most unquestionable hatred, so greatly does a woman's consciousness of what she owes to herself find difficulty in yielding to so determined a will, Mathilde at length became for him a loving and a lovable mistress.

To tell the truth, their transports were somewhat forced. Passionate love was still rather more of a model they were imitating than the real thing.

Mademoiselle de la Mole believed that she was fulfilling a duty towards both herself and her lover. The poor boy, she said to herself, has shown consummate courage, I must make him happy, or I shall be the one who shows lack of character. Yet she could have wished to redeem at the cost of an eternity of sorrow the cruel necessity imposed upon her.

In spite of the frightful violence to her feelings, she retained perfect control of her tongue. No regret, no reproach came to mar this night which seemed to Julien a strange, rather than a happy, one. Good God! what a difference from his last stay of twenty-four hours at Verrières! These fine Parisian ways, he said to himself with extreme injustice, have discovered the secret of spoiling everything – even love.

He abandoned himself to these reflections while standing upright inside one of the great mahogany wardrobes into which he had been thrust at the first sound heard from the room next door, which was Madame de la Mole's. Mathilde accompanied her mother to Mass, the maids soon left the room, and Julien easily made his escape before they came back to finish their tasks.

He mounted his horse and made for the most solitary recesses of one of the forests in the neighbourhood of Paris. He was feeling much more astonished than happy. The happiness which, from time to time, came to take possession of his heart, was similar to that of a young Second Lieutenant, who as a result of some astonishing exploit has just been made a Colonel, on the field, by his Commander in Chief. He felt himself transported to a terrific height; all that had been above him the day before was now on his level or very far beneath him. Little by little Julien's happiness increased as he drew farther away from Paris.

If there was no trace of tenderness in his heart, it was because, however strange it may seem to say so, Mathilde, in all her behaviour towards him, had been fulfilling a duty. There was nothing unforeseen for her in all the events of that night except the unhappiness and the shame she had experienced in place of the perfect bliss of which novels tell us.

Can I have been mistaken? she said to herself. Can it be that I don't love him?

CHAPTER 17 : An Old Sword

> I now mean to be serious; – it is time,
> Since laughter nowadays is deemed too serious,
> A jeer at vice by virtue's called a crime.
>
> *Don Juan*

SHE did not appear at dinner. In the evening she came to the drawing-room for a moment, but did not look at Julien. This behaviour seemed to him strange. But, he thought, I don't know the ways of these society people; she'll give me some good reason for all this. None the less, driven by the most intense curiosity, he studied the expression of Mathilde's features, and could not conceal from himself that she looked cold and cruel. Evidently this was not the same woman who, the night before, had felt, or pretended to feel, transports of joy too excessive to be genuine.

The next day, and the day after, the same coldness on her side; she never once looked at him, she did not seem to be aware of his existence. Julien, consumed by the keenest anxiety, was a thousand leagues removed from the feeling of triumph which had animated him on the first day. Can it, by any chance, he wondered, be a return to virtue? But that was a very middle-class term for so haughty a person as Mathilde.

In the ordinary situations of life, thought Julien, she has hardly any belief in religion. She appreciates it as useful to the interests of her caste. But mayn't it be simply feminine delicacy that makes her reproach herself keenly for the fault she has committed? Julien believed he was her first lover.

Yet, one must admit, he would say to himself at other moments, that there's nothing artless, simple, or tender at all in her attitude; I've never seen her haughtier. Can it be that she despises me? It would be just like her to reproach herself with what she has done for me, merely because of my humble birth.

While Julien, full of prejudices drawn from books and from memories of Verrières, was pursuing his fantastic dream of a tender mistress who, from the moment she has made her lover happy, never gives a thought to her own existence, Mathilde's vanity was furiously incensed against him.

Since, for the past two months, she had ceased to be bored, she no longer dreaded boredom. Thus, without in the least suspecting it, Julien had lost his greatest advantage.

I've given myself a master, so Mademoiselle de la Mole was saying to herself, plunged in the most doleful grief. He may be the soul of honour, well and good; but if I provoke his vanity to extremes, he will revenge himself by making the nature of our relations known. Mathilde had never had a lover before, and at that moment in life which gives even the hardest hearts some soft illusions, she was tormented by the most bitter reflections.

He has tremendous power over me, since he rules by terror and can inflict a frightful punishment on me if I try him too far. This idea was enough of itself to incline Mathilde to insult him, for courage was the prime quality of her character. Nothing could stir her in any way or cure her of an underlying feeling of boredom constantly springing to life again, except the idea that she was putting her whole existence at hazard.

On the third day, as Mademoiselle de la Mole obstinately refused to look at him, Julien followed her after dinner, obviously against her will, into the billiard-room.

'Well, sir,' she said to him with hardly controlled anger, 'you must believe you have acquired very strong rights over me, since, against my very clearly expressed wishes, you attempt to speak to me. . . . Do you know that nobody in the world has ever dared so much?'

Nothing could have been more entertaining than the conversation between these two lovers, unconsciously animated with feelings of the keenest hatred towards each other. As neither of them had a patient temper, and as moreover they were used to the ways of polite society, it was not long before they both began to inform each other quite plainly that they had broken off friendly relations for good and all.

'I swear to you I will for ever keep your secret,' said Julien. 'I would even add that I'd never address a word to you again, if it weren't that your reputation might suffer from so marked a change.' He bowed respectfully and went away.

He was performing without difficulty what he regarded as a duty; he was very far from believing himself to be in love with Mademoiselle de la Mole. Certainly he had not been in love with her three days earlier, when he had been hiding in the great mahogany wardrobe. But everything changed rapidly in his heart from the moment he found he had quarrelled with her for ever.

His pitiless memory began to retrace for him the least events of that night which had, in reality, left him so cold. On the second night after this declaration of an eternal breach, Julien was driven almost mad by being forced to admit to himself that he was in love with Mademoiselle de la Mole. A terrible conflict followed this discovery; all his feelings were turned upside down. Two days later, instead of being haughty with M. de Croisenois, he could almost have embraced him with tears in his eyes.

Constant acquaintance with unhappiness gave him a glimmer of common sense; he decided to set off for Languedoc, packed his trunk and went to the post-house.

He felt his heart sink when on arriving at the stage-coach office he was informed that, by a strange chance, there was a seat vacant next day in the Toulouse mail. He booked it and came back to the Hôtel de la Mole to announce his departure to the Marquis.

M. de la Mole had gone out. More dead than alive, Julien went into the library to wait for him. What were his feelings on finding Mademoiselle de la Mole there?

On seeing him appear she assumed a disagreeable expression which it was impossible for him to misunderstand. Carried away by his misery, bewildered with surprise, Julien was weak enough to say to her, in the tenderest of tones, springing straight from the heart : 'Then you no longer love me?'

'I am horrified at having given myself to the first-comer,' said Mathilde, weeping with rage against herself.

'To the first-comer!' cried Julien, and he darted towards an old sword of the Middle Ages which was kept in the library as a curiosity.

His grief, which he believed extreme at the moment of his speaking to Mademoiselle de la Mole, had just been increased a hundredfold by the tears of shame he saw her shedding. He would have been the happiest of men if he could have killed her.

Just as he had drawn the sword, with some difficulty, from its antiquated sheath, Mathilde, delighted by so novel a sensation, advanced towards him proudly; her tears had ceased to flow.

The thought of M. de la Mole, his benefactor, came vividly before Julien's eyes. And I would kill his daughter ! he said to himself. How horrible ! He made a gesture as though to fling away the sword. Certainly, he thought, she's bound to burst out laughing at such a melodramatic action ! To this idea he owed the return of his self-possession. He glanced curiously at the blade of this old sword, as though he were looking for some spot of rust, then put it back into its sheath, and with the greatest calmness hung it up again on the nail of gilded bronze which supported it.

The whole of this action, very slow towards the end, lasted for quite a minute. Mademoiselle de la Mole gazed at him in astonishment. So I've just been on the point of being killed by my lover! she thought. This idea carried her back to the finest days of the age of Charles IX and Henri III.

She stood motionless in front of Julien, who had just replaced the sword, gazing at him with eyes in which there was no longer any hatred. It must be admitted that she looked very bewitching at that moment; certainly no woman had ever looked less like a Parisian doll (this term expressed Julien's chief objection to the women of this city).

I'm about to sink back into affection for him, thought Mathilde; and then he'd immediately think himself my master, after he'd left off thinking it, too, and at the very moment when I've just spoken to him so firmly. She rushed away.

Good God! how lovely she is, thought Julien as he saw her running away. And there's the creature who rushed with such eager passion into my arms not a week ago.... And those moments will never return! And it's all my fault! And at the moment of so extraordinary an action, and one that so deeply concerned me, I was insensitive to it!... I must confess I was born with a singularly dull and unhappy disposition.

The Marquis appeared; Julien hastened to inform him of his departure.

'Where to?' said M. de la Mole.

'To Languedoc.'

'No, you won't, if you please, you are reserved for a higher destiny; if you go away it will be to the North ... to use a military term, I even confine you to quarters at the Hôtel. You will oblige me by not being absent from it for more than two or three hours, I may need you at any moment.'

Julien bowed, and withdrew without uttering a word, leaving the Marquis greatly astonished; he was incapable of speech, and shut himself up in his room. There he was free to exaggerate all the atrocious cruelty of his lot.

So I can't even go away! he thought. Heaven knows how many days the Marquis is going to keep me here in Paris. Good God! what will become of me? And not a single friend I can ask for advice. Father Pirard wouldn't let me finish my first sentence, Count Altamira would offer to make me a member of some conspiracy.

And meanwhile, I'm going mad, I feel it. I'm quite mad! Who can guide me, what is to become of me?

CHAPTER 18: *Bitter Moments*

> And she admits it to me! She goes into the
> minutest details! Her very lovely eyes, gazing
> straight into mine, portray the love she feels
> for another!   SCHILLER

MADEMOISELLE DE LA MOLE, in an ecstasy of joy, could think of nothing but the bliss of having been at the point of death. She went so far as to say to herself: He is worthy to be my master, since he was just about to kill me. How many good-looking young men of the world would have to be melted into one to arrive at such an impulse of passion?

He looked very handsome, I must confess, at the moment he climbed on the chair, to replace the sword in exactly the same picturesque position as that to which the decorators had assigned it! After all, it wasn't so mad of me to love him.

If, at that moment, some honourable way of reconciliation had presented itself, she would have seized it gladly. Julien, securely locked in his room, was a prey to the most violent despair. In his raving, he thought of flinging himself at her feet. If, instead of hiding himself in an out-of-the-way corner, he had wandered through the house and out into the garden, so as to be at hand for any opportunity, he might perhaps in a single instant have changed his bitter misery into the keenest joy.

But that sharpness of wit for the absence of which we are blaming him would have ruled out that sublime gesture of his in seizing the sword which, at that moment, made him appear so handsome in the eyes of Mademoiselle de la Mole. This capricious fancy, working in Julien's favour, lasted the whole day through; Mathilde drew for herself a charming picture of those brief moments in which she had loved him, and looked back on them with regret.

Actually, she said to herself, my passion for that poor boy only lasted, in his eyes, from one hour after midnight, when I saw him arrive by his ladder, with all his pistols in the side pocket of his coat, up till eight o'clock in the morning. It was a quarter of an hour later, as I was hearing Mass at Saint Valère's, that I began to think he would imagine himself my master and might well try to make me obey him out of terror.

After dinner, Mademoiselle de la Mole, far from avoiding

Julien, spoke to him, and almost compelled him to accompany
her into the garden; he obeyed her. This was a test which so far
had been wanting. Mathilde was unconsciously yielding to the
love she was beginning to feel for him again; she found an
extreme pleasure in walking by his side, casting curious glances
at those hands which that morning had snatched up the sword
to kill her.

After such an action, after all that had happened, there could
no longer be any question of returning to old topics of conversation.

Gradually Mathilde began to speak to him in confidential, intimate terms of the state of her heart. She found a strangely exquisite delight in a conversation of this kind; she went so far as to
tell him of the momentary inclination she had felt towards M. de
Croisenois, M. de Caylus. . . .

'What! M. de Caylus too!' cried Julien, all the bitter jealousy
of a forsaken lover bursting through the words. Mathilde judged
this to be the case, and was not offended.

She went on torturing Julien by giving him a detailed and
most graphic description of her feelings in the past, in tones that
revealed their innermost truth. He saw she was describing what
was present before her eyes, and experienced the pain of noting
that, as she spoke, she was discovering for herself what was in her
own heart.

Jealous grief can go to no further extremes. To suspect that a
rival is loved is already a very bitter thing, but to find the love
this rival inspires confessed in every detail by the woman you
adore is undoubtedly the height of sorrow.

Oh, how greatly was Julien punished at that moment for the
impulse of pride which had led him to set himself above Caylus
and Croisenois, and all their sort! With what intense and heartfelt grief he now exaggerated their least little advantages! In
what ardent good faith he now despised himself!

Mathilde seemed to him adorable; words are too weak to express the intensity of his admiration. As he walked beside her,
casting stolen glances at her hands, her arms, her queenly bearing, he was on the point of falling at her feet, overcome with love
and sorrow, and crying to her: 'Have pity on me!'

And this creature, he thought, who's so lovely, so far above all
the rest, and who once loved me, will doubtless soon be in love
with that M. de Caylus.

Julien could not doubt Mademoiselle de la Mole's sincerity: the accent of truth was all too evident in everything she said. That absolutely nothing might be wanting to complete his misery, there were moments when, by dint of concentrating on feelings she had once experienced for M. de Caylus, Mathilde came to speak of him as if she loved him at that moment. Certainly there was love in the tones of her voice; Julien realized it clearly.

Had all inside his breast been flooded with molten lead, he would have suffered less. How could this poor boy, having reached such a pitch of misery, guess that it was because Mademoiselle de la Mole was talking to him that she found so much pleasure in recalling the faint stirrings of love she had formerly felt for M. de Caylus or M. de Luz?

No words could express Julien's anguish. He was listening to detailed confidences of love felt for others in that same avenue of limes where, so few days since, he had been waiting for one o'clock to strike before entering her room. No human being can endure a higher degree of unhappiness.

This cruel kind of intimacy lasted for a whole, long week. Mathilde sometimes appeared to seek, and sometimes not to avoid, opportunities of speaking to him; and the subject of conversation to which they both seemed to revert with a sort of painful delight was the recital of feelings she had experienced for other men. She told him of the letters she had written; she recalled for his benefit even the words she had used, she quoted whole sentences to him. On the last days of this week, she seemed to be studying Julien with a kind of malignant pleasure. His sufferings afforded her intense enjoyment.

It can be seen that Julien had no experience of life; he had not even read any novels. Had he only been a little less clumsily shy, and coolly remarked to this girl, whom he so adored and who offered him such curious confidences: 'Admit that although I am not so worthy as these gentlemen, yet all the same I am the one you love . . .', perhaps she would have been glad to have had him read her mind; success at least would have depended entirely upon the grace with which Julien had expressed this idea, and the moment he had chosen. Anyhow, he came out well, and with advantage to himself, from a situation which was on the way to becoming monotonous in Mathilde's eyes.

'So you no longer love me, while I adore you !' Julien said to her one day, beside himself with love and grief. This was almost the worst blunder he could have made.

His remark destroyed in the twinkling of an eye all the pleasure

Mademoiselle de la Mole was finding in talking to him about the state of her heart. She was beginning to feel astonished that after what had happened he did not take offence at what she told him; she was on the point of imagining, at the moment he made this foolish remark, that perhaps he no longer loved her. Pride has doubtless quenched his love, she was thinking. He is not the man to see creatures like Caylus, Luz, and Croisenois preferred to him with impunity. No, I shall never see him at my feet again!

On the preceding days, in his artless grief, Julien had often spoken in sincere praise of the outstanding qualities of these gentlemen; he went so far as to over-estimate them. This delicate shade had not escaped the notice of Mademoiselle de la Mole, she was astonished by it, but did not guess its cause. Julien's mad, bewildered heart, in praising a rival whom he believed to be loved, participated in that rival's happiness.

His very frank, but very stupid, remark altered the whole situation in a moment. Mathilde, sure of being loved, felt utter contempt for him.

She was walking with him at the moment of this ill-timed outburst; she left him there; her last glance expressed the most fearful scorn. When she was back in the drawing-room, she did not look at him again for the rest of the evening. The following day, this feeling of scorn for him took entire possession of her heart; there was no longer any question of the impulse which, for the past week, had led her to find such pleasure in treating Julien as her most intimate friend; the very sight of him was unpleasing to her. Mathilde's sensations even amounted to disgust; no words could express the utter contempt she felt whenever her eyes chanced to fall on him.

Julien had understood nothing of all that, for the space of a week, had been going on in Mathilde's heart; but he was conscious of her scorn. He had the good sense to appear before her as rarely as possible, and he never looked at her.

But it was not without a feeling of mortal anguish that he deprived himself in some sort of her company. He thought he could feel his misery still more increased by this. Courage can reach no further limits in a man's heart, he said to himself. He spent his days sitting at a little window right up in the attics of the house; the shutters were kept carefully closed, and from there, at least, he could catch a glimpse of Mademoiselle de la Mole whenever she appeared in the garden.

What were his feelings when, after dinner, he saw her walking there with M. de Caylus, M. de Luz, or some other man for whom she had confessed some slight inclination in the past?

Julien had had no idea of such an intensity of unhappiness; he was on the point of crying out; that resolute heart was at last shocked and bewildered beyond believing.

Every thought that was not concerned with Mademoiselle de la Mole had become hateful to him; he was incapable of writing the simplest letters.

'You've lost your wits,' the Marquis said to him.

Julien, trembling lest he should be found out, said he was feeling ill and managed to make himself believed. Luckily for him, the Marquis chaffed him at dinner over his coming journey. Mathilde realized that it might be a very long one. Julien had been avoiding her for several days already, and those brilliant young men who had everything that was lacking in this exceedingly pale and gloomy individual, whom once she had loved, had no longer any power to distract her from her dreams.

Any ordinary girl, she said to herself, would have sought for the man of her choice among the young men who attract all eyes in a drawing-room; but one of the characteristics of genius is not to let its thoughts trail along in the rut traced out by the common herd.

As the companion of a man like Julien, who lacks nothing but the fortune I possess, I shall continually attract attention, I shall by no means pass through life unnoticed. So far from ceaselessly dreading a revolution like my cousins, who, out of fear of the people, dare not scold a postillion who drives them badly, I shall be sure of playing a part, and a great part, too, for the man of my choice has character and boundless ambition. What does he lack? Friends? Money? I can give him that. But in her thoughts she was treating Julien rather as an inferior being, who can be made to love one as one wishes.

CHAPTER 19 : *The Italian Opera*

> O how this spring of love resembleth
> The uncertain glory of an April day;
> Which now shows all the beauty of the sun,
> And by and by a cloud takes all away!
>
> SHAKESPEARE

INTENT on thoughts of the future and of the singular part she hoped to play, Mathilde soon came to look back with regret on the dry, metaphysical discussions she had so often had with Julien. Wearied with such high thoughts, she sometimes regretted also the moments of happiness she had experienced in his company. These last memories did not rise before her without exciting remorse, which at certain moments overwhelmed her.

But if one feels fondness, she said to herself, it's fitting for a girl like me not to forget her duties except for a man of merit. No one will say it's his handsome moustache or his graceful seat on a horse that seduced me, but his profound discussions on the future awaiting France, his ideas on the possible resemblance between the events about to swoop down upon us and the Revolution of 1688 in England. I've been seduced, she said to quiet her remorse, I'm a weak woman, but at least I haven't been led astray like a flibbertigibbet by external advantages.

If there should be a Revolution, why should not Julien Sorel play Roland's part, and I the part of Madame Roland? I prefer that part to Madame de Staël's : immoral conduct will be a hindrance in our time. Certainly no one shall reproach me for a second act of weakness; I'd die of shame.

Mathilde's musings were not all so serious, it must be admitted, as the thoughts we have just written down. She would look at Julien, finding a charming grace in his most insignificant actions.

There's no doubt, she said to herself, that I've managed to destroy any idea in his mind that he has the slightest rights. The unhappy and profoundly passionate way in which the poor boy spoke to me of love a week ago proves it, anyhow. I must agree it was very extraordinary of me to get angry over a remark so alight with respect and passion. Am I not his wife? This remark was very natural, and, I must confess, very endearing. Julien still loved me after endless conversations, in which I had spoken to him, and very unkindly, too, of nothing but frivolous inclinations for those young society men of whom he's so jealous, which the boredom of the life I lead had inspired in me. Ah! if he but knew how little danger there is for me in such people! How in comparison with him they seem to me such pale and sickly copies, all cut to the same pattern.

As she made these reflections, Mathilde's pencil was tracing lines at random on a page of her album. One of the profiles she had just completed amazed and delighted her; it was strikingly like Julien. It's the voice of heaven! Here's one of the miracles of love! she cried in rapture. Quite unconsciously I've drawn his portrait.

She rushed off to her room, locked herself in, applied herself to her task, and tried hard to draw a portrait of Julien. But she could not do it; the profile sketched by accident still remained the best likeness. Mathilde was enchanted by this; she saw in it clear proof of a grand passion.

She did not lay aside her album until very late, when the Marquise sent for her to go to the Italian Opera. She had one idea only, to catch Julien's eye, so as to make her mother invite him to accompany them.

He did not appear; the ladies had only a few very dull people in their box. During the first act of the opera, Mathilde sat dreaming of the man she loved with keen and passionate ecstasy. But in the second act, an axiom of love sung, it must be admitted, to a melody worthy of Cimarosa, found its way into her heart. The heroine of the opera was saying: 'I deserve to be punished for the too great adoration I feel for him, I love him too much!'

The moment she heard this sublime *cantilena*, everything else in the world faded from Mathilde's consciousness. She was spoken to, she did not answer; her mother scolded her, she could hardly manage to look at her. Her ecstasy reached a point of passionate exaltation comparable to the most violent emotions that Julien, during the last few days, had been feeling for her. The *cantilena*, full of celestial grace, to which was sung the axiom that seemed so strikingly appropriate to her own situation, occupied every moment in which she was not thinking directly of Julien. Thanks to her love of music, she became that evening what Madame de Rênal invariably was when thinking of him. Love that originates in the brain has doubtless a more subtle wit than heartfelt love, but it has only rare moments of enthusiasm; it knows itself too well, it criticizes itself incessantly; so far from leading the mind astray; it is built up entirely upon reasoned thought.

On her return to the house, in spite of all that Madame de la Mole could say, Mathilde pretended she had an attack of fever, and spent part of the night playing the *cantilena* over and over again on her piano, and singing the words of the famous air that had charmed her :

> *Devo punirmi, devo punirmi,*
> *Se troppo amai.*

The result of this night of madness was that she imagined she had succeeded in conquering her love.

(This page will damage its author in more ways than one. Ice-cold hearts will accuse him of impropriety. He does not attempt to insult those young persons who shine in Parisian drawing-rooms by supposing a single one of them to be susceptible to mad impulses such as degrade Mathilde's character. This character is wholly drawn from imagination, and conceived as being well outside those social habits which will assure the nineteenth century so distinguished a place amongst all other centuries.

It is certainly not prudence that is lacking in the young society misses who have adorned this winter's ballrooms.

Nor do I think one can accuse them either of turning their noses up too markedly at a brilliant fortune, horses, fine estates, or anything that ensures an agreeable position in society. So far from looking upon such advantages as merely boring, they generally make them the object of their constant desires, and if there is any passion in their hearts it is for such things as these.

It is not love either that has a chief hand in the career of young men who, like Julien, are endowed with a certain degree of talent; these attach themselves with obstinate tenacity to some particular set, and if that set 'makes good', all the best things society can give are showered upon them. Woe to the studious man who does not belong to any set; even his minor, doubtful successes will be held against him, and superior virtue will triumph over him by robbing him of these.

Why, my good sir, a novel is a mirror journeying down the high road. Sometimes it reflects to your view the azure blue of heaven, sometimes the mire in the puddles on the road below. And the man who carries the mirror in his pack will be accused by you of being immoral ! His mirror reflects the mire, and you blame the mirror ! Blame rather the high road on which the puddle lies, and still more the inspector of roads and highways who lets the water stand there and the puddle form.

Now that we are quite agreed that a character like Mathilde's is impossible in our virtuous, and no less prudent age, I am less afraid of vexing you by continuing my account of the follies of this charming girl.)

For the whole of the next day she watched for opportunities of assuring herself of her triumph over her crazy passion. Her chief aim was to make herself as unpleasant as possible to Julien; but not one of her movements escaped his notice.

Julien was feeling too miserable and, above all, too greatly agitated to guess what so complex an operation of passion really meant, still less was he able to understand all that was favourable in it for himself. He fell a victim to it; never, perhaps, had his unhappiness been so intense. His actions were so little under the control of his mind that if some cantankerous philosopher had said to him : 'Try to take swift advantage of conditions tending to be in your favour; in this highbrow kind of love one finds in Paris, the same sort of mood cannot last for more than a couple of days,' he would not have understood him. But however excited he might be, Julien had a sense of honour. His first duty was discretion; this much he understood. To ask for advice, to tell of his anguish to the first man he met would have been happiness comparable to that of the poor wretch who, as he crosses a burning desert, receives from the sky a drop of ice-cold water. He realized his danger, he was afraid of answering with a torrent of tears any busybody who questioned him; he shut himself up in his room.

He saw Mathilde walking for a long time in the garden. When at length she had left it, he went down there; he walked across to a rose-tree from which she had plucked a flower.

The night was dark, he could give himself up to his misery without restraint, without fear of being seen. It was plain to him that Mademoiselle de la Mole was in love with one of those young officers with whom she had just been chatting so gaily. He himself had once been loved by her, but she had recognized his little worth.

And indeed, said Julien to himself with full conviction, I'm worth very little. All said and done, I'm a very dull fellow, very commonplace and very boring to other people, and quite insupportable to myself. He was sick to death of all his own good qualities, of all the things he had once enthusiastically loved, and in this state of *inverted imagination*, he attempted, in the light of his imagination, to interpret life. This is the error of a man of superior quality.

Several times the idea of suicide presented itself to him; this image was full of charm; it was like a vision of a blissful rest, of the ice-cold glass of water offered to the poor wretch who is dying of thirst and heat in the desert.

My death will increase the contempt she feels for me! he cried. What a memory I shall leave behind!

Sunk in the deepest abyss of misery, a human being has no resource but courage. Julien had not enough intelligence to say to himself: I must be bold. But as he looked up at the window of Mathilde's room, he could see through the shutters that she was putting out her light. He pictured to himself that charming room he had seen, alas, but once in his life. His imagination went no further!

The clock struck one; from hearing the sound of its striking to telling himself: I am going up by the ladder, was the work of a moment.

This was a flash of genius; solid reasons came crowding after. Could I be in a worse plight than now! he said to himself. He ran to fetch the ladder; the gardener had fastened it with a chain. With the hammer of one of his pocket pistols, which he broke, Julien, animated at that moment by a superhuman strength, wrenched open one of the links of the chain that held the ladder. In a very few minutes he had mastered the obstacle and had placed the ladder up against Mathilde's window.

She'll be angry, she'll overwhelm me with her scorn, what of that? I'll give her a kiss, a last kiss, and then go up to my room and kill myself.... My lips will have touched her cheeks before I die!

He flew up the ladder, he tapped at the shutter; a second or two later Mathilde heard him; she tried to open the shutter, but the ladder was in the way. Julien clung to the iron hook placed there to keep the window open, and, at the risk of coming hurtling down time and again, gave the ladder a violent shake and shifted it a little. Mathilde was able to open the shutter.

He flung himself into the room more dead than alive.

'So it's you, my dear!' she said, rushing into his arms.

Who can describe the intensity of Julien's happiness? Mathilde's joy almost equalled his.

She spoke to him against herself, she accused herself to him.

'Punish me for my appalling pride,' she said to him, hugging him so tightly that she almost suffocated him. 'You are my master, I am your slave. I must beg you, on my knees, to forgive me for having tried to rebel.'

She slipped from his arms to fall at his feet. 'Yes, dearest, you are my master,' she repeated, in a frenzy of love and joy. 'Reign over me for ever, punish your slave severely, whenever she seeks to rebel.'

In another moment, she had torn herself from his embraces and lit a candle. Julien had all the difficulty in the world to prevent her from cutting off all one side of her hair.

'I want to remind myself,' she said, 'that I am your handmaid. If ever my detestable pride should lead me astray, show me this hair, and say : "It's no longer a question of love, it doesn't matter what emotion your heart may be feeling at this moment, you have sworn to obey me, I put you on your honour to obey".'

But it is wiser to suppress the description of such a degree of wild and wayward bliss.

Julien's self-command was equal to his happiness. 'I must go down the ladder,' he said to Mathilde, when he saw the dawn appear above the distant chimneys to the east, beyond the gardens. 'The sacrifice I am imposing on myself is worthy of you. I am depriving myself of some hours of the most astounding happiness a human soul can enjoy. It's a sacrifice I am making to your reputation; if you know my heart you understand what violence I am doing to my feelings. Will you always be to me what you are at this moment? But the voice of honour speaks, and that is enough. I must tell you that, since our first meeting, suspicion has not been directed only against thieves. M. de la Mole has set a watch in the garden. M. de Croisenois is surrounded by spies, everything he is doing each night is known. . . .'

At the thought of this, Mathilde shrieked with laughter. Her mother and one of the maids were woken up; all at once she heard voices speaking to her through the door. Julien looked at her; she turned pale as she scolded the maid, and did not deign to say a word to her mother.

'But if it should occur to them to open the window, they'll see the ladder !' said Julien.

He embraced her once more, swung himself on to the ladder, and slid rather than climbed down it; in a moment he was on the ground.

Three seconds later the ladder was under the avenue of limes and Mathilde's honour was safe. When Julien recovered his senses, he found himself covered with blood and half naked; he had cut himself in his precipitate descent.

The intensity of his happiness had restored all the energy of his character; had a score of men confronted him, to attack them single-handed would, at that moment, have been but one pleasure the more. Luckily for him his martial valour was not put to the test; he laid the ladder down in its usual place, put the chain that fastened it back in its place; and did not forget to come back and obliterate the mark left by the ladder in the bed of exotic flowers underneath Mathilde's window.

As in the darkness he passed his hand over the soft earth to make sure that the mark was effaced, he felt something drop on his hand; it was a whole side of Mathilde's hair which she had cut off and thrown down to him.

She was at the window. 'Look what your servant sends you,' she said fairly loudly, 'It's the token of my eternal obedience. I renounce the exercise of my own reason; be my master, dearest.'

Julien, overcome, was on the point of fetching back the ladder, and climbing up again to her room, but in the end reason prevailed.

To enter the house from the garden was not an easy thing. He succeeded in forcing the door of a cellar; once in the house; he was obliged to break open, as silently as possible, the door of his own room. In his agitation he had left everything behind in the little room from which he had fled so quickly, including his key, which was in the pocket of his coat. If only she thinks of hiding all this tell-tale clothing ! he thought.

At length weariness prevailed over happiness, and, as the sun was rising, he fell into a deep sleep. The luncheon bell had great difficulty in waking him. He made his appearance in the dining-room. A short while after, Mathilde came in. It was a happy moment for Julien's pride when he saw the lovelight gleaming in the eyes of this very beautiful creature, who was the object of so much homage; but soon his prudence found occasion for alarm.

Under pretext of having had little time to do her hair, Mathilde had purposely dressed it in such a way that Julien could see at a glance the whole extent of the sacrifice she had made for him in cutting some of it off the night before. If anything could have spoilt so lovely a face, Mathilde would have managed it; the whole of one side of that beautiful ash-gold hair was cut to within half an inch of her head.

The whole of Mathilde's behaviour during lunch was in keeping with this first act of imprudence. You would have said that she was making it her duty to let everyone know of her crazy passion for Julien. Fortunately, M. de la Mole and the Marquise were greatly taken up that day with a list of promotions to the Blue Ribbon, shortly to be made, and in which the name of M. de Chaulnes had not been included. Towards the end of the meal, Mathilde, in talking to Julien, chanced to address him as her 'master'. He blushed to the very roots of his hair.

Whether by chance or by Madame de la Mole's express design, Mathilde was not left for a minute alone throughout the day. That evening, however, as she was going from the dining-room into the drawing-room, she found an opportunity to say to him: 'Don't think it's my doing, but Mamma has just decided that one of her maids is to sleep every night in my room.'

The day sped by like lightning; Julien was at the height of his happiness. The following day, from seven o'clock in the morning, he installed himself in the library, hoping that Mademoiselle de la Mole would deign to put in an appearance. He had written her a letter of interminable length.

He did not see her until a few hours later, at lunch. Her hair was dressed that day with the greatest care; a marvellous art had contrived to hide the place where the hair had been cut off. She looked once or twice at Julien, but with a calm, polite expression in her eyes; there was no longer any question of her calling him 'master'.

Julien's amazement cut short his breath ... Mathilde was reproaching herself for almost all she had done for him.

On mature reflection, she had decided that he was an individual who, if not altogether ordinary, at any rate did not stand out sufficiently from the common run of men to deserve all the strange follies she had dared to commit for him. On the whole, she was hardly thinking of love; she was weary of loving that day.

As for Julien, the reactions of his heart were those of a boy of sixteen. Terrible doubts, amazement, and despair, turn by turn seized hold upon him during this meal which seemed to be everlasting.

As soon as he could decently leave the table, he rushed headlong rather than ran to the stable, saddled his horse himself, and went off at a gallop. He was afraid of disgracing himself by some act of weakness. I must kill my heart by tiring out my body, he said to himself as he galloped through the Meudon woods. What have I done, what have I said, to merit such disgrace?

I must do nothing, say nothing today, he thought on his return to the house, be dead in body as I am in spirit. Julien is no longer alive, it is his corpse that still stirs restlessly.

CHAPTER 20: *The Japanese Vase*

> His heart does not at first take in the whole
> grave extent of this disaster; he is more dis-
> turbed than moved by it. But as his power of
> reason gradually returns, he feels the depth of
> his misfortune. Every pleasure in life is as
> nothing to him, he can only feel the sharp
> claws of the despair that is rending him. But
> what is the use of speaking of physical pain?
> What pain felt by the body alone can com-
> pare with this?
>
> JEAN-PAUL

THE dinner bell was ringing, Julien had only just time to
dress. He found Mathilde in the drawing-room, urgently
pleading with her brother and M. de Croisenois not to go and
spend the evening with Madame de Fervaques, the Marshal's
widow.

She could hardly have been more alluring and more charming
towards them. After dinner M. de Luz, M. de Caylus, and several
of their friends came in. One would have said that Mademoiselle
de la Mole had resumed, along with the cult of sisterly affection,
that of the strictest conventions. Although the weather was
lovely that evening, she insisted on not going out into the
garden; she was determined not to let anyone move away from
the easy chair in which Madame de la Mole was sitting. The blue
sofa was the centre of the group, as in winter.

Mathilde had taken a dislike to the garden, or at any rate it
seemed to her utterly devoid of interest – it was associated with
memories of Julien.

Unhappiness dulls the mind. Our hero made the foolish mistake of settling down on that little cane chair which had
formerly witnessed such brilliant triumphs. That evening, nobody
said a word to him; his presence there seemed to pass unnoticed,
or even worse. Those of Mademoiselle de la Mole's friends who
were sitting close to him on the sofa made as though they were
turning their backs on him, or at least he fancied they were.

I'm out of favour at court, he reflected. He decided to watch
those people who were trying to humiliate him with their disdain.

M. de Luz's uncle held an important post in the King's Household, as a result of which this handsome officer started every

conversation with each fresh arrival with the following interesting piece of news: his uncle had set off at seven o'clock for Saint-Cloud, and expected to spend the night there. This item was introduced in the most seemingly artless way, but it never failed to appear.

Considering M. de Croisenois with the stern eye of grief, Julien noted the tremendous influence this pleasant, good-natured young man attributed to occult causes. So much so that he became moody and ill-tempered on seeing any event of the least importance ascribed to a simple and quite natural cause. There's a streak of insanity there, thought Julien. This character is remarkably akin to that of the Emperor Alexander, as Prince Korasoff described him to me. During the first year of his stay in Paris, poor Julien, only just out of the seminary, dazzled by the graces, so new to him, of these agreeable young men, could feel nothing but admiration for them. Their true character was only just beginning to outline itself before his eyes.

I'm playing an undignified part here, he suddenly thought. The question was how to get up from his little cane chair in not too awkward a way. He tried to think of one, calling on an imagination already too much occupied elsewhere to invent something altogether new. He had to fall back on his memory, and this, it must be confessed, was not at all rich in resources of this type. The poor boy was still little used to the ways of the world, and was therefore completely and noticeably awkward when at last he got up to leave the drawing-room. Unhappiness was all too evident in his manner. For three-quarters of an hour he had been playing the part of an importunate inferior from whom people take no care to hide what they think.

The critical observations he had just been making on his rival saved him, however, from taking too tragic a view of his misfortunes. He had still, to uphold his pride, the memory of what had happened two evenings before. Whatever advantages they may have over me, he thought as he went out into the garden alone, Mathilde has never been to anyone of them what, twice in my life, she has been to me.

His wisdom went no further. He completely failed to understand anything of the character of that extraordinary creature whom chance had recently made absolute mistress of all his happiness.

He confined himself the next day to tiring himself and his horse to death. He made no further attempt, that evening, to go near

the blue sofa to which Mathilde clung. He noticed that Count
Norbert did not even vouchsafe him a glance when he met him in
the house. He must be doing particular violence to himself, he
thought, when he's so naturally polite.

Sleep would have been a happiness to Julien. In spite of physical fatigue, memories of a too alluring sort began to invade his
whole imagination. He had not the wit to see that by his long
excursions on horseback through the woods around Paris, which
had an effect only on himself and in no way on Mathilde's heart
or mind, he was leaving the disposal of his fate to chance.

It seemed to him that one thing would be of infinite solace to
his grief, and that would be to speak to Mathilde. But what,
indeed, could he venture to say to her?

That was the question upon which one morning at seven
o'clock he was deep in thought when he saw her coming into the
library.

'I know, sir, that you wish to speak to me.'

'Good God! who told you that?'

'I know it, does it matter how? If you have no sense of honour,
you can ruin me, or at least attempt to do so. But such a danger,
which I don't believe to be real, certainly won't prevent me from
being sincere. I no longer love you, sir; my crazy fancy deceived
me.'

At this terrible blow, Julien, distracted with love and misery,
tried to vindicate himself. Nothing could have been more absurd.
Can one offer any vindication for failing to please? But reason
had no longer any control over his actions. Blind instinct impelled
him to delay the decision of his fate. It seemed to him that so long
as he went on talking, everything could not be at an end.
Mathilde did not listen to his words, the sound of them irritated
her, she could not conceive how he could have the audacity to
interrupt her.

Remorseful virtue and resentful pride made her, that morning,
equally unhappy. She was in some sort shattered by the dreadful
idea of having given certain rights over herself to a mere humble
priest, who was a peasant's son. It's almost, she said to herself at
moments when she exaggerated her misfortune, as if I had to
reproach myself with a partiality for one of the footmen.

With proud and daring characters, there is only one step from
anger against oneself to fury with other people; transports of
rage afford one intense delight in such circumstances.

In a moment, Mademoiselle de la Mole reached the pitch of

heaping on Julien marks of the most supreme contempt. She had infinite ingenuity, and this ingenuity revelled in the art of torturing other people's self-esteem and wounding it most cruelly.

For the first time in his life, Julien found himself subjected to the action of a superior mind provoked by the most violent hatred against him. So far from having at that moment the least thought of defending himself, he reached the point of self-contempt. Hearing her heap upon him such cruel marks of scorn, so skilfully calculated to destroy any good opinion he might have of himself, it seemed to him that Mathilde was right, and that she was not saying enough.

Mathilde, for her part, found it an exquisite satisfaction for her pride in punishing in this way both herself and him for the adoration she had felt a few days before.

She had no need to invent or to think for the first time of the cruel things she was saying to him with so much pleasure. She was only repeating what the counsel for the prosecution had been saying for a week past in her heart. Each word increased Julien's frightful misery a hundredfold. He tried to escape; Mademoiselle de la Mole gripped his arm with a grasp of authority.

'Kindly mark,' he said to her, 'that you are speaking very loud. You'll be heard in the next room.'

'What does that matter!' Mademoiselle de la Mole replied proudly, 'who will dare to tell me I've been overheard? I wish to cure your petty self-conceit for ever of any notions it may have formed about me.'

When Julien was able to leave the library, he was so amazed that he felt his unhappiness less keenly : 'So that's that ! she no longer loves me,' he said to himself repeatedly, speaking out loud as though to inform himself of his position. It appears that she has loved me for a week or ten days, and I shall love her all my life long. Can it really be that, only a few short days ago, she meant nothing, nothing at all, to my heart !

Mathilde's heart was full to overflowing with the joys of gratified pride – so she had managed to break with him for ever ! The idea of winning so complete a victory over so strong an inclination made her absolutely happy. So this little gentleman will realize, once and for all, she thought, that he has not, and never will have, any power over me. She was so happy that, at that moment, she actually felt she had ceased to love him.

After so frightful, so humiliating a scene, love would have

become an impossibility with any human being less passionate than Julien. Without departing for a single instant from what she owed to herself, Mademoiselle de la Mole had said to him certain of those unpleasant things which are so well calculated as to appear to be true, even when one remembers them in cold blood.

The conclusion that Julien drew first of all from so amazing a scene was that there were no limits to Mathilde's pride. He firmly believed that all was over for ever between them and yet, the next day, at lunch, he was shy and awkward in her presence. This was a fault with which, up till then, nobody could have reproached him. In little things as in great, he knew clearly what he ought and what he wanted to do, and carried it out.

That day, after lunch, when Madame de la Mole asked him for a seditious yet rather rare pamphlet, which her parish priest had brought to her secretly that morning, Julien, as he took it off the side table, overturned an old blue porcelain vase, the ugliest thing imaginable.

Madame de la Mole rose to her feet with a cry of distress and came over to examine the fragments of her cherished vase. 'It was old Japan porcelain,' she said, 'it came to me from my great-aunt the Abbess of Chelles. It was a present from the Dutch to the Duke of Orleans when he was Regent, and he gave it to his daughter....'

Mathilde had followed her mother, overjoyed to see the destruction of this blue vase which she thought so hideously ugly. Julien remained silent and not too greatly upset; he saw Mademoiselle de la Mole standing quite close to him.

'This vase,' he said to her, 'is destroyed for ever, and so it is with a feeling which once was master of my heart. Pray accept my apologies for all the follies it has made me commit.' And he went out of the room.

'One would really think,' said Madame de la Mole, as he was going, 'that this M. Sorel is proud and pleased with what he has done.'

Her words sank straight into Mathilde's heart. It's true, she told herself, my mother has guessed rightly; that is indeed what he feels. Then only did her joy in the scene she had made with him the day before fade from her mind. Ah, well, all is over, she said to herself with apparent calm. I am left with a great example. My mistake has been frightful, humiliating. It will serve to make me wise for the rest of my life.

Why didn't I speak the truth? thought Julien. Why does the love I felt for this crazy girl continue to torment me?

This love, far from dying down as he hoped, made rapid progress. She is crazy, that's true, he said to himself – but is she any less adorable for that? Could anyone possibly be lovelier? Is not every keen delight the most refined civilization can offer combined in full measure in Mademoiselle de la Mole? These memories of past happiness took possession of Julien's mind, and quickly destroyed all the work of reason. For reason fights in vain against memories of this sort; its stern endeavours only increase their charm.

Twenty-four hours after the breaking of the old Japanese vase, Julien was decidedly one of the unhappiest of men.

CHAPTER 21 : *The Secret Note*

For everything I relate, I have seen; and although I may have been deceived in what I
saw, I shall certainly not deceive you in the
telling of it. *From a Letter to the Author*

THE Marquis sent for him. M. de la Mole seemed rejuvenated,
his eyes were very bright.

'Let us talk a little about your memory,' he said to Julien. 'I
hear it is phenomenal! Could you learn four pages by heart and
go and repeat them in London? But without altering a word?'

The Marquis was peevishly fidgeting with the pages of that
day's *Quotidienne*, and trying in vain to dissimulate a very
serious expression which Julien had never before seen him display, even when they were discussing the Frilair lawsuit.

Julien was already sufficiently used to the way of polite society
to know that he must appear to be completely taken in by the
light tone adopted with him.

'This number of the *Quotidienne* is not perhaps very amusing,
but if your Lordship will allow me, tomorrow I shall have the
honour of reciting it to you from beginning to end.'

'What! even the advertisements?'

'Absolutely correctly, and without missing a word.'

'Do you give me your word for that?' went on the Marquis,
suddenly becoming grave.

'Yes, sir. Only the fear of failing to keep it might cloud my
memory.'

'It's just that I forgot to ask you this question yesterday. I am
not asking you to swear never to repeat what you are about to
hear; I know you too well to insult you in that way. I have
answered for you, and I am going to take you into a room where
twelve persons will be assembled. You will take notes of what
each man says.

'Don't be alarmed, it won't be a muddled sort of conversation.
Each man will speak in his turn, I won't say in a formal order,'
the Marquis went on with a return to that shrewdly witty
manner which came so naturally to him. 'While we are talking
you will be writing down a score or so of pages. You'll come
back here with me, we'll reduce those twenty pages to four. Those
four pages are the ones which you will repeat to me tomorrow

morning instead of the whole number of the *Quotidienne*. You will set off immediately after. You must travel post like a young man travelling for his own amusement. Your aim will be to pass unnoticed by anyone. You'll find yourself in the presence of a very important person. There, you'll need more skill. It will be your business to deceive everyone around him; for among his secretaries, or his servants, there are men in the pay of our enemies who lie in wait for our agents, to intercept them.

'You shall have a letter of introduction, which will not be noticeable. When his Excellency looks at you, you will take out this watch of mine you see here, which I am lending you for the journey. Put it on now, that's always so much done, and give me yours.

'The Duke himself will condescend to write down at your dictation the four pages you will have learnt by heart. When that is done, but mind you not before, you may, if his Excellency questions you, give him an account of the meeting at which you are going to be present.

'One thing that will prevent you from getting bored during the journey is that, between Paris and the Minister's house, there are people who would ask for nothing better than to fire a shot at M. Sorel. Then his mission is at an end and I foresee great delay; for, my dear fellow, how shall we learn of your death? Your zeal cannot go so far as to send us notice of it.

'Now run off quickly and buy yourself a complete outfit,' the Marquis went on, looking grave. 'Dress yourself in the style of two years ago. This evening you must look a little shabby. On the contrary, when you're travelling, you will dress as usual. Does that surprise you, do your suspicions make you guess the reason? Yes, my young friend, one of these revered personages whom you are going to meet tonight is quite capable of sending information about you, as a consequence of which someone may quite probably give you at least a dose of opium, in some comfortable inn where you will have ordered supper.'

'It would be better,' said Julien, 'to go some thirty leagues farther on, and not take the direct route. We're talking of Rome, I suppose. . . .'

The Marquis assumed an air of haughty displeasure which Julien had not seen him wear so markedly since Bray-le-Haut.

'You shall learn that, sir, when I find fit to tell you. I don't like questions.'

'That was not a question,' Julien answered effusively. 'I swear to you, sir, I was thinking aloud, I was seeking in my own mind the safest route.'

'Yes, it seems your mind was very far away. Never forget that an ambassador, especially one of your age, should not appear as if forcing confidences.'

Julien was greatly mortified, he was in the wrong. His self-esteem sought for an excuse but found none.

'Learn to realize,' M. de la Mole added, 'that a man always appeals to his heart when he has done something foolish.'

An hour later, Julien was in the antechamber of the Marquis's room in a very inferior turnout, an ancient suit of clothes, a doubtfully white neckcloth, and something of a hangdog air about his whole appearance. At the sight of him, the Marquis burst out laughing, and it was only then that Julien was completely vindicated.

If this young man betrays me, thought M. de la Mole, whom can I trust? And yet, when it comes to action, one must trust someone. My son and his brilliant friends of a similar stamp have courage and loyalty enough for a hundred thousand. If it came to fighting, they would perish on the steps of the throne. They know how to do everything ... except what is required at this moment. Devil take me if I can think of one of them who could learn four whole, long pages by heart and travel a hundred leagues without someone getting on his trail. Norbert would know how to get himself killed like his ancestors, but a conscript knows as much. . . .'

The Marquis pondered, lost in thought: And even if it came to getting killed, perhaps this fellow Sorel would be as capable there as he. . . .

'Let us get into the carriage,' said the Marquis as if seeking to drive away some thought that worried him.

'Sir,' said Julien, 'while they were altering this coat for me, I learnt the first page of today's *Quotidienne* by heart.'

The Marquis took the paper and Julien said his piece without getting a single word wrong. Good, thought the Marquis, who was in a very diplomatic mood that evening, during all this time the young man is not noticing the streets through which we are passing.

They came at last into a large and rather dismal-looking room, partly panelled and partly hung with green velvet. In the middle of the room a scowling footman had just set up a large dinner table, which he subsequently converted into a conference table by means of an immense green cloth covered with inkstains, the relic of some Ministry or other.

The master of the house was an enormously stout man, whose name was not given. Julien gathered from his expression and his expansive way of talking that he was not the kind of man to take offence easily.

At a sign from the Marquis, Julien had remained at the lower end of the table, where, to keep himself in countenance, he began to sharpen some quills. Out of the corner of his eye, he counted some seven speakers, but he could see nothing of them but their backs. Two of them appeared to him to be addressing M. de la Mole on terms of equality, the others seemed more or less deferential.

Another person came into the room unannounced. That's strange, thought Julien, no one is announced in this room. Can this precaution have been taken in my honour? Everyone rose to welcome the newcomer. He was wearing the same extremely distinguished decoration as three of the men who were already in the room. Everyone spoke rather low. To form an opinion of the newcomer Julien was reduced to what he could learn from his features and general appearance. He was short and thickset, with a florid complexion and gleaming eyes without any expression save the vicious ferocity of a wild boar.

Julien's attention was sharply attracted from him by the almost immediate arrival of a wholly different type of person. He was a tall man, very thin and wearing three or four waistcoats. His eyes were kind, his gestures polished.

That is just the face of the old Bishop of Besançon, thought Julien. This man was evidently a cleric, he did not appear to be more than fifty or fifty-five. No one could have looked more fatherly.

The young Bishop of Agde appeared, and looked greatly surprised when, on gazing round at the company, his eyes alighted on Julien. He had not spoken to him since the ceremony at Bray-le-Haut. His look of surprise embarrassed and annoyed Julien. What! thought the latter, will my knowing a man always be to my disadvantage? All these noble lords whom I've never seen before don't intimidate me in the least, and this young Bishop's glance turns me cold as ice. It must be admitted I'm a very peculiar and a very unfortunate individual.

An extremely dark little man came in with a great deal of fuss and bustle shortly after, and started to speak from the moment he reached the door. He had a sallow complexion and looked a trifle mad. From the time this relentless chatterbox arrived, people broke up into groups, apparently to avoid the boredom of listening to him.

As they moved farther and farther away from the fireplace, they came nearer to the bottom end of the table, where Julien was installed. He became more and more embarrassed in his manner, for, after all, however hard he tried, he could not avoid hearing them, and however slight his experience might be, he understood the full importance of things they were talking about without any attempt at concealment; and yet how greatly these apparently exalted personages whom he had under his eyes must care that such things should remain a secret.

Already, working as slowly as he could, Julien had sharpened a score of quills; this resource would soon fail him. He looked in vain for an order in M. de la Mole's eyes; the Marquis had forgotten him.

What I'm doing here is quite ridiculous, Julien said to himself as he cut away at his pens. But people who have such insignificant faces, and yet are entrusted by others or by themselves with such high interests, must needs be very sensitive. My unfortunate way of looking at people has something inquisitive and hardly respectful about it, which would doubtless annoy them. If I lower my eyes too obviously, I shall look as if I were storing what they say in my mind.

His embarrassment was intense, he was hearing some extraordinary things.

The Republic! – For one who would sacrifice
everything to the common weal, there are
thousands – nay, millions – who recognize no
claim but that of their pleasures and their
vanity. In Paris, a man wins respect on
account of his horse and carriage, and not for
his virtue.   NAPOLEON: *Mémorial*

THE footman came in hurriedly, announcing: 'His Grace the
Duc de —.'

'Hold your tongue, you fool,' said the Duke as he entered. He
delivered these words so well and with such regal dignity that
Julien could not help thinking that knowing how to lose his
temper with a footman was the sum total of this great personage's
knowledge. Julien raised his eyes and lowered them immediately.
He had so accurately guessed the importance of this new arrival
that he trembled lest his glance might seem impertinent.

The Duke was a man of fifty, dressed like a dandy, and walking
as if on springs. He had a narrow head with a large nose, and a
face that jutted forward in prominent curves. It would have been
difficult for anyone to look at once so noble and so insignificant.
His arrival determined the opening of the meeting.

Julien was abruptly interrupted in his physiognomical scrutiny
by M. de la Mole's voice. 'May I present to you the Abbé Sorel,'
the Marquis was saying. 'He is endowed with an astonishing
memory. It was only an hour ago that I spoke to him of the
mission with which he might be honoured, and in order to give
us a proof of his memory, he learnt the first page of the *Quotidienne* by heart.'

'Ah! the news from abroad about that poor fellow N—,' said
the master of the house. He picked up the paper quickly, and
looking at Julien with an air that was comical in its attempt to
appear important: 'Go ahead, sir,' he said.

There was deep silence, all eyes were fixed on Julien; he repeated his lesson so well that at the end of twenty lines the Duke
said: 'That will do.' The little man with the wild boar's eyes sat
down. He was the chairman, for he was no sooner seated, than he
pointed out a card table to Julien, and signed to him to bring it
up beside him. Julien settled himself there with all the necessary

writing materials. He counted twelve people seated round the green cloth.

'M. Sorel,' said the Duke, 'please go into the next room. We shall send for you.'

The master of the house assumed a very anxious expression. 'The shutters are not closed,' he half whispered to his neighbour. 'It's no good your looking out of the window,' he cried to Julien in a stupid sort of way. Here am I shoved into the thick of a conspiracy, to say the least, thought Julien. Fortunately, it's not one of those that lead to the Place de Grève. Even if there were danger in it, I owe that much to the Marquis, and more. I should be happy, if it were granted to me to atone for the sorrows my follies may one day cause him.

While still thinking of his follies and of his unhappiness, he gazed at his surroundings in a way that would make him never forget them. Only then he remembered that he had not heard the Marquis tell his footman the name of the street, and that the Marquis had sent for a cab, a thing he never did.

Julien was left for a long time to his reflections. He was in a drawing-room hung in red velvet with broad stripes of gold braid. On the side-table there was a great ivory crucifix, and on the mantelpiece M. de Maistre's book, *Du Pape*, with gilt edges, and magnificently bound. Julien opened it so that he might not appear to be listening. From time to time voices rose very loud in the next room. At last the door opened, his name was called.

'Remember, gentlemen,' the chairman was saying, 'that from this moment we are speaking in the presence of the Duc de —. This, gentlemen,' he said, pointing to Julien, 'is a young candidate for the priesthood, devoted to our sacred cause, and who, with the help of his astonishing memory, will have no difficulty in repeating even our least important remarks.

'It is this gentleman's turn to speak,' he said, indicating the man with the fatherly expression, who was wearing three or four waistcoats. Julien felt it would have been quite natural to refer to him as the gentleman with the waistcoats. He took some paper and wrote at great length.

(Here the author would have liked to introduce a page of asterisks. 'That will not look elegant,' says the publisher, 'and for such a frivolous book a want of elegance means death.'

'Politics,' the author retorts, 'are like a stone tied to the neck of literature which, in less than six months, will drown it. Politics in the middle of things that concern the imagination are like a pistol-shot in the middle of a concert. The noise is ear-splitting and yet lacks point. It does not harmonize with the sound of any instrument. This talk of politics will mortally offend half my readers, and bore the other half, who have already come across far more vigorous and detailed politics in their morning paper.'

'If your characters don't talk politics,' my publisher replies, 'then they're no longer Frenchmen of 1830, and your book is no longer a mirror, as you claim. . . .')

Julien's written report covered twenty-six pages. Here is a very colourless digest of it, for I have been obliged, as usual, to suppress all those absurdities, the over-frequency of which would have appeared shocking, or hardly probable. (See the *Gazette des Tribunaux*.)

The man with the waistcoats and the fatherly expression (he was, perhaps, a Bishop) smiled frequently, and then his eyes, within the frame of their fluttering lids, took on an extraordinary brightness, and an expression less vague than usual. This personage, who was asked to speak first, in the presence of the Duke – but what Duke? Julien wondered – apparently to state the views of the meeting and to perform the functions of Solicitor General, seemed to Julien to fall into the uncertainty and the lack of clear conclusions with which these magistrates are so often reproached. In the course of the discussion the Duke even went so far as to twit him with it.

After several phrases of moralizing and benign philosophy, the man with the waistcoats said: 'That noble country, England, guided by a great man, the immortal Pitt, spent forty thousand million francs to wreck the Revolution. If this assembly will permit me to allude with some frankness to a melancholy subject, England does not sufficiently understand that with a man like Bonaparte, more particularly when one had nothing with which to oppose him but a handful of good intentions, there was no sure way but that of personal approach. . . .'

'Ah! another speech in praise of assassination!' said the master of the house, looking worried.

'Spare us your sentimental homilies,' cried the chairman angrily, his wild boar's eye alight with a savage gleam. 'Pray continue,' he said to the man with the waistcoats. The chairman's cheek and brow grew purple with rage.

'That noble country, England,' the speaker went on, 'is crushed today. For every Englishman, before paying for his daily bread, is obliged to pay the interest on the forty thousand million francs

which were employed against the Jacobins. And she has no longer
a Pitt. . . .'

'She has the Duke of Wellington,' said a military personage,
assuming an air of great importance.

'Pray silence, gentlemen,' cried the chairman. 'If we are still in
disagreement, there will have been no use our asking M. Sorel
to come in.'

'Everyone knows that our honoured friend is full of ideas,' the
Duke remarked with an air of annoyance and a glance at the
interrupter, formerly one of Napoleon's generals. Julien saw that
this was an allusion to something personal and highly offensive.
Everyone smiled; the renegade General seemed beside himself
with rage.

'There is no longer a Pitt, gentlemen,' the speaker went on with
the disheartened air of a man who despairs of making his hearers
listen to reason. 'And even if there were a new Pitt in England,
a nation is not hoodwinked twice by the same means. . . .'

'That is why a conquering general, another Bonaparte, is
henceforth impossible in France,' the military interrupter broke
in.

On this occasion, neither the chairman nor the Duke ventured
to show annoyance, though Julien thought he could read in their
eyes a strong desire to do so. They lowered their eyes, and the
Duke contented himself with sighing in such a way as to be
heard by all.

But the speaker had lost his temper.

'You are in a hurry for me to finish,' he said heatedly, completely laying aside that smiling affability and moderation of
speech which Julien had imagined to be the natural expression
of his character. 'You are in a hurry for me to finish; you give me
no credit for the efforts I am making not to offend the ears of
anyone present, however long they may be. Well then, gentlemen, I will be brief.

'And I will tell you very bluntly : England has not a halfpenny
to spare for the service of the good cause. Were Pitt himself to
return, he would not succeed, with all his genius, in throwing
dust in the eyes of the small landowners of England, for they
know that the short campaign of Waterloo alone cost them one
thousand million francs. Since you wish for plain, outspoken
phrases,' the speaker went on, growing more and more excited,
'I will say to you : *Help yourselves*, for England has not a single
guinea at your service, and if England does not pay you, Austria,

Russia, Prussia, who have only courage and no money, cannot undertake more than one campaign or two against France.

'One can hope that the young soldiers collected together by the Jacobins will be beaten in the first campaign; but in the third (even though I should pass for a revolutionary in your prejudiced eyes) you will have the soldiers of 1794, who were no longer the peasant battalions of 1792.'

Here there were volleys of interruptions from three or four points at once.

'Sir,' said the chairman to Julien, 'go into the next room' and make a fair copy of the first part of the report you have written.' Very regretfully, Julien left the room. The speaker had just embarked on probabilities which formed the usual subject of his meditations. They're afraid I might laugh at them, he thought.

When he was recalled, M. de la Mole was speaking, in an earnest manner which, to Julien, who knew him, seemed highly amusing.

'... Yes, gentlemen,' he was saying, 'it is above all of this unhappy race that one can say: "Shall it become a god, a table, or a basin?"

' "It shall be a god!" cries the fabulist. It is to you, gentlemen, that so profound and noble a saying seems to apply. Act for yourselves, and our noble land of France will once more appear almost as our ancestors made her, and as our eyes have seen her still, before the death of Louis XVI.

'England, or at least her noble Lords, abhor this vile Jacobinism as much as we do ourselves. Without English gold, neither Austria, Prussia, nor Russia can engage in more than two or three battles. Will that suffice to bring about a happy occupation, such as that which M. de Richelieu so idiotically frittered away in 1817? I do not think so.'

At this point an interruption occurred, but it was drowned in a cry of 'silence!' from the whole company. It originated once more from the former General of the Empire, who was anxious to obtain the Blue Ribbon, and wished to occupy a prominent place among those who were drawing up the secret note.

'I do not think so,' repeated M. de la Mole when the tumult had died down. He emphasized the 'I' with an insolence that charmed Julien. That's a good stroke, he said to himself as he let his pen fly on almost as fast as the Marquis's words. With one well-placed word the Marquis wiped out the renegade General's twenty campaigns.

'It is not to foreigners alone,' the Marquis went on in the most measured tones, 'that we can owe a fresh military occupation. That group of young hopefuls who write incendiary articles for the *Globe* will provide you with three or four thousand young captains amongst whom may be found a Kléber, a Hoche, a Jourdan, a Pichegru, though not so zealous.'

'We failed to keep his glorious memory alive,' said the chairman. 'We ought to have made him immortal.'

'There must be two parties in France,' M. de la Mole went on, 'but two parties, not in name only, but clearly defined, sharply divided. Let us know whom we have to crush. On the one hand, the journalists, the electorate, public opinion; in short, the younger generation and all those who admire it. While it is dazed by the sound of its own vain babbling, we ourselves have the certain advantage of handling the Budget.'

Here there was another interruption.

'You, sir,' said M. de la Mole to the interrupter with a disdainful ease of manner, 'you don't handle, since the term offends you, you squander the forty thousand francs granted you in the Budget and the eighty thousand you receive from the Civil List.

'Well, sir, since you force me to it, I take you boldly as an example. Like your noble ancestors who followed Saint Louis to the Crusade, you ought, for those hundred and twenty thousand francs, to show us at least a regiment, a company, say half a company, were it only made up of fifty men ready to fight, and devoted to the good cause, living or dying. You have merely hired menservants, of whom, in the event of an uprising, you yourself would be afraid.

'The Throne, the Altar, the Nobility, may perish any day, so long as you yourselves have not created in each Department a force of five hundred *devoted* men; but devoted, I would say, not only with all the gallant courage of Frenchmen, but with the constancy also of Spaniards.

'One half of this troop must consist of our sons, our nephews, in short of gentlemen by birth. Each of them will have at his side, not some glib little townsman ready to hoist the tricolour cockade if 1815 should come round again, but a good, honest peasant, simple and frank like Cathelineau. Our gentlemen will have trained him in our principles; he should be, if possible, his foster-brother. Let each of us sacrifice the fifth part of his income to form this loyal little troop of five hundred men in each Department. Then you may count on a foreign occupation. No foreign

soldier will ever penetrate even as far as Dijon, unless he is sure
of finding five hundred comrades-in-arms in each Department.

'Kings of other countries will listen to you only when you give
them news of twenty thousand gentlemen ready to take up arms
and open the gates of France to them. This service, you will say,
is arduous. Gentlemen, this is the price we pay for our lives. Between the liberty of the Press and our existence as gentlemen
there is war to the death. Become manufacturers, peasants – or
take up your guns. Be timorous if you will, but do not be stupid.
Open your eyes.

'*Line up in your battalions*, I say to you in the words of the
Jacobin song. Then there will be found some noble Gustavus
Adolphus who, moved by the imminent peril to monarchical principles, will rush to your aid three hundred leagues away from his
own country, and do for you what Gustavus Adolphus did for
the Protestant princes. Will you forever be talking without
acting? In fifty years' time there will be nothing in Europe but
Presidents of Republics and not a single King. And with these
four letters, K, I, N, G, the priest and the gentleman too will disappear. I see nothing any more but *candidates* paying court to
unwashed *majorities*.

'It is no use your saying that France at this moment has not
one General of high repute, known and loved by all, that the Army
is organized only to serve the interests of the Monarchy and the
Church, that all its old campaigners have been discharged, whilst
each of the Prussian and Austrian regiments have fifty non-com-
missioned officers who have been under fire.

'Two hundred thousand young men of the lower middle classes
are passionately eager for war....'

'Let us have done with unpleasant truths,' was said in a tone
of importance by a grave personage, apparently high up on the
scale of ecclesiastical preferment, for M. de la Mole smiled
pleasantly instead of showing annoyance, which was a clear sign
to Julien.

'Let us have done with unpleasant truths, and let us sum up,
gentlemen. The man who has to have his gangrened leg ampu-
tated would be ill-advised to say to his surgeon : "This bad leg is
perfectly sound." Forgive me the expression, gentlemen, the noble
Duke of — is our surgeon.'

There, thought Julien, the cat's out of the bag at last. It's towards — that I shall be galloping tonight.

> The first law for every creature is that of self-preservation, of keeping alive. You sow hemlock, and expect to see the ripening ears of corn!
>
> MACHIAVELLI

THE grave personage went on speaking; it was obvious he knew his subject. With a gentle, measured eloquence, which pleased Julien immensely, he propounded the following great truths:

'(1) England has not a single guinea at our service; economy and Hume are fashion there. Even the *Saints* will not give us money and Mr Brougham will laugh in our faces.

'(2) Without English gold, it is impossible to get more than two campaigns out of the Monarchs of Europe; and two campaigns will not be enough against the middle classes.

'(3) The necessity of forming an armed party in France, without which the upholders of the monarchical principle in Europe will not risk even those two campaigns.

'The fourth point which I venture to put before you is this: *The impossibility of forming an armed party in France without the Clergy.* I say it to you boldly, gentlemen, because I am going to prove it to you. We must give the Clergy everything:

'(1) Because, pursuing their own business day and night, and guided by men of high capacity established far from the reach of storms, three hundred leagues away from your frontiers. . . .'

'Ah! Rome! Rome!' cried the master of the house.

'Yes, sir, *Rome!*' the Cardinal answered proudly. 'Whatever more or less ingenious jests were current when you were young, I will say boldly, in 1830, that the Clergy, guided by Rome, are the only people in touch with the lower orders. Fifty thousand priests repeat the same words on the day appointed by their leaders, and the common people, who, after all, provide the soldiers, will be more moved by the voice of their priests than by all the little poems in the world.' (This personal allusion provoked some murmurs.)

'The Clergy have an intellect superior to yours,' the Cardinal went on, raising his voice. 'All the steps you have taken towards this capital issue, *having an armed party in France*, have already been taken by us.' Here he brought forward facts.... 'Who sent eighty thousand muskets to the Vendée,' etc., etc.?

'So long as the Clergy are deprived of their woodlands, they possess nothing, yet, at the first onset of war, the Minister of Finance writes to his agents that no one has any money except the priests. At heart, France is without religion, and loves war. Whoever gives her a war will be doubly popular, for making war means starving out the Jesuits, to use a vulgar expression. Making war means freeing that monstrously proud race, the French, from the threat of foreign intervention.'

The Cardinal secured a favourable hearing. ... 'It would be essential,' he said, 'that M. de Nerval should leave the Ministry, his name is a source of needless irritation.'

At these words, everyone got up and began speaking at once. They'll be sending me away again, thought Julien. But even the sagacious chairman himself had forgotten Julien's presence, and indeed his existence. All eyes were turned towards a man whom Julien recognized. It was M. de Nerval, the Chief Minister, whom he had noticed at the Duc de Retz's ball.

The tumult was at its height, as the newspapers say in talking of the Chamber, but at the end of a good quarter of an hour there was comparative silence once more.

Then M. de Nerval rose to his feet, and adopting an apostolic manner, began to speak : 'I have no intention of declaring to you,' he said in a peculiar tone of voice, 'that I am not attached to my office. It has been pointed out to me, gentlemen, that my name doubles the strength of the Jacobins by turning against us many people of moderate views. I would therefore willingly retire from office; but the ways of the Lord are plain only to the few. And, gentlemen,' he added, looking the Cardinal in the face, 'I have a mission. Heaven has told me : "Either you shall bring your head to the scaffold, or re-establish absolute Monarchy in France, and reduce the two Chambers to what Parliament was under Louis XV – and that, gentlemen, I will do.' He stopped speaking, sat down, and there was deep silence.

What a good actor ! thought Julien. He made the mistake, as he almost always did, of attributing too much cleverness to other people. Excited by the debates of so lively an evening, and above all by the sincerity of the discussion, M. de Nerval at that moment believed in his mission. Though he had great courage, he had little common sense.

Midnight struck during the silence that followed the fine

phrase, 'I will do it.' It seemed to Julien that the sound of the clock had something of a funereal solemnity. He was deeply moved.

The discussion soon began again with increasing energy, and, more particularly, with incredible naïvety. These men will have me poisoned, thought Julien at certain moments. How can they say such things in front of a mere commoner?

Two o'clock struck, and they were still talking. The master of the house had long been asleep, and M. de la Mole was obliged to ring and have fresh candles brought in. M. de Nerval, the Minister, had left at a quarter to two, not without having frequently studied Julien's face in a mirror which hung beside him. His departure seemed to put everyone at his ease.

While fresh candles were being brought, the man with the waistcoats whispered to his neighbour: 'Heaven knows what that fellow will say to the King. He can make us look very foolish, and spoil our plans for the future.

'You must admit he shows a rare sort of conceit, and even impudence, in showing himself here. He used to come here before he rose to be a Minister; but a portfolio alters everything, swamps all a man's other interests. He ought to have felt that.'

The instant the Minister had gone, Bonaparte's General had shut his eyes. He now began talking of his health, his wounds, looked at his watch, and left.

'I wouldn't mind betting,' remarked the man with the waistcoats, 'that the General is running after the Minister. He'll find excuses for being found here, and pretend he can do what he likes with us.'

When the servants, who were half asleep, had finished changing the candles, the chairman said: 'Let us now discuss things seriously, gentlemen, and not go on trying to persuade one another. Let us consider the tenor of the note that in forty-eight hours will be before the eyes of our friends from abroad. There has been some mention of Ministers. We can say, now that M. de Nerval has left us, what do we care for Ministers? We will bend them to our will.'

The Cardinal showed his approval by smiling in a subtle way. 'Nothing is easier, it seems to me, than to sum up our position,' remarked the young Bishop of Agde in tones that revealed the repressed and inward fire of the most ardent fanaticism. Up till then he had remained silent, but his eyes, which Julien had been watching, though at first calm and gentle, had blazed into flame during the first hour's discussion. Now his heart overflowed like lava from Vesuvius.

'From 1806 to 1814,' he said, 'England made only one mistake – that of not dealing directly and personally with Napoleon. As soon as that man had created Dukes and Chamberlains, as soon as he had restored the Throne, the mission God had entrusted to him was at an end; he was ripe only for destruction. The Holy Scriptures teach us in more than one passage the way to make an end of tyrants.' (Here followed several Latin quotations.)

'Today, gentlemen, it is not a man that we must destroy – it is Paris. The whole of France copies Paris. What is the use of arming your five hundred men in each Department? A risky enterprise and one that will never end. What is the use of involving France in a matter which is peculiar to Paris? Paris alone, with her newspapers and her drawing-rooms, has done the damage; let this modern Babylon perish.

'There must be an end of this rivalry between the Church and Paris. Such a dramatic conclusion is actually in the worldly interests of the Monarchy. Why did not Paris dare to breathe a word under Bonaparte? Ask the artillery of Saint-Roch.'

* * *

It was not until three o'clock in the morning that Julien left the house with M. de la Mole. The Marquis was shamefaced and weary. For the first time, in speaking to Julien, there was a note of pleading in his voice. He asked him to give him his word never to disclose these excesses of zeal – that was his name for them – which he had chanced to witness. 'Do not mention it to our friend from abroad, unless he seriously insists on it to gain knowledge of our young hotheads. What does it matter to them if the Government be overthrown? They will become Cardinals and take refuge in Rome. We, in our country houses, shall be massacred by the peasants.'

The secret note which the Marquis drafted from the long report of six and twenty pages written by Julien was not ready until a quarter to five.

'I'm tired to death,' said the Marquis, 'as you can easily see from this note, which is far from clear at the end. I am more dissatisfied with it than with anything I ever did in my life. Look here, my boy,' he added, 'go and lie down for a few hours, and for fear of your being kidnapped, I'll lock you up in your room.'

Next day, the Marquis took Julien to an isolated country house,

at some distance from Paris. They found there some curious in-
mates, whom Julien took to be priests. He was given a passport
bearing an assumed name, but indicating the real destination of
his journey, which he had always pretended not to know. He set
off by himself in a carriage.

The Marquis had no misgivings as to his memory, Julien had
repeated the contents of the note several times; but he was greatly
afraid of his being intercepted.

'Take special care not to look like anyone but some fashionable
fool who's travelling to kill time,' he said to him in a friendly
way, just as Julien was leaving the drawing-room. 'There may
perhaps have been two or three false brethren in our gathering
last night.'

The journey was swift, but a very sad one. Julien was hardly
out of sight of the Marquis before he had forgotten both the secret
note and his mission, and was thinking only of Mathilde's scorn.

In a village a few leagues beyond Metz, the postmaster came
and told him that there were no horses left. It was ten o'clock
at night. Feeling intensely annoyed, Julien ordered supper. He
walked along in front of the door, and gradually slipped unnoticed into the stableyard. He saw no horses there.

All the same, that man's manner was very strange, thought
Julien. His churlish eyes were studying me closely.

He was beginning, as you see, not to believe exactly everything
he was told. He thought of making his escape after supper, and, to
find out at any rate something of the lie of the land, he left his
room and came to warm himself by the kitchen fire. What was
his joy upon finding there Signor Geronimo, the famous singer !

Ensconced in an armchair he had made them push up close to
the fire, the Neapolitan was uttering loud groans and talking
more, by himself alone, than the score of German peasants
grouped, open-mouthed, around him.

'These people here are ruining me,' he cried to Julien. 'I have
promised to sing tomorrow at Mayence. Seven reigning Princes
have gathered there to hear me. But let's go out and get some air,'
he said with a meaning look.

When he had gone about thirty yards down the road, and was
well out of earshot, he said to Julien : 'Do you know what's going
on ? This postmaster is a rogue. While I was strolling about, I gave
a franc to a little rascal who told me everything. There are more
than a dozen horses in a stable right at the other end of the
village. They're out to delay some courier or other.'

'Really?' said Julien, with an air of innocence.

The discovery of this sly trick was not everything; they must get away. But that is what Julien and his friend could not manage to do. 'Let's wait until it's daylight,' said the singer finally; 'they're suspicious of us. Tomorrow morning we'll order a good breakfast, and while they're preparing it, we'll go for a stroll, make our escape, hire some horses, and get to the next posthouse.'

'And your luggage?' said Julien, who was thinking that perhaps Geronimo himself might have been sent to intercept him. They had to have supper and retire to bed. Julien was in his first sleep when he was woken with a start by the voices of two people talking quite unconcernedly in his room.

He recognized the postmaster, equipped with a dark lantern. The light was directed towards the carriage-trunk which Julien had had brought up to his room. Beside the postmaster was another man who was calmly rummaging in the open trunk. Julien could only make out the sleeves of his coat, which were black and very close-fitting.

It's a cassock, he said to himself, quietly seizing hold of his pocket pistols which he had placed under his pillow.

'Don't be afraid of him waking up, your reverence,' said the postmaster. 'The wine we gave them was some of what you prepared yourself.'

'I can't find any trace of papers,' the curé replied. 'A good quantity of linen, oils, pomades, and other useless trifles. It's some young man of the world, intent on his own pleasures. The messenger is more likely to be the other one, who puts on an Italian accent.'

The men came close up to Julien to search the pockets of his travelling coat. He was greatly tempted to kill them as thieves. He very much longed to do it. . . . I should be an utter fool, he said to himself, I should compromise my mission. After searching his coat the priest remarked: 'This is no diplomat.' He moved away, and wisely too.

If he touches me as I lie in bed, said Julien to himself, he'll regret it! He may quite well come and stab me, and I won't allow that.

The priest turned his head, Julien half-opened his eyes. What was his amazement! It was Father Castanède! And indeed, although the two men had tried to lower their voices, it had seemed to him, from the very first, that he recognized the sound of one of them. Julien was seized with an inordinate desire to rid the world of one of its vilest rogues. . . .

But my mission! he reminded himself.

The priest and his acolyte went out. A quarter of an hour later, Julien pretended to wake up. He called out and woke up the whole house.

'I've been poisoned,' he exclaimed. 'I'm in horrible pain!' He wanted a pretext for going to Geronimo's aid. He found him half asphyxiated by the laudanum that had been put in his wine.

Fearing some funny trick of this kind, Julien had drunk for supper some chocolate which he had brought with him from Paris. He could not succeed in getting Geronimo sufficiently wide-awake to make him agree to leave the place.

'Though I were given the whole kingdom of Naples,' said the singer, 'I would not give up the exquisite pleasure of sleep at this moment.'

'But the seven reigning Princes!'

'Let them wait.'

Julien set off alone and arrived without further incident at the house of the very important personage. He wasted a whole morning in unsuccessfully soliciting an interview. By good luck, towards four o'clock, the Duke decided to take the air. Julien saw him leave the house on foot, and did not hesitate to ask him for alms. When he was within two feet of the great man, he pulled out the Marquis's watch, and made great play of showing it. '*Follow me at a distance,*' he was told without a glance his way.

About a quarter of a league farther on, the Duke turned sharply into a little coffee-house. It was in a bedroom of this third-rate inn that Julien had the honour of reciting his four pages to the Duke. When he had finished, he was told: '*Begin again and go more slowly.*'

The Prince took notes. '*Go on foot to the next posthouse. Leave your luggage and your carriage here. Get to Strasbourg as best you can, and on the twenty-second of this month* (it was then the tenth) *be here in this same coffee-house at half past twelve. Do not leave here until after half an hour. Keep silence!*'

Such were the only words that Julien heard. They were enough to fill him with the deepest admiration. So that's how one handles affairs, he thought. What would this great statesman say if he had heard those hot-headed chatterboxes three days ago?

Julien took two days to get to Strasbourg. He felt that there was nothing for him to do there, and took a long way round. If that devil, Father Castanède, has recognized me, he's not the man to be easily put off the scent. . . . And what pleasure it would give him to make a fool of me and a failure of my mission!

Father Castanède, the head of the secret agents of the *Congrégation* along the whole of the northern frontier, had fortunately not recognized him. And the Jesuits of Strasbourg, although very full of zeal, never thought of keeping an eye on Julien, who, with his Cross and his blue greatcoat, looked like a young soldier greatly preoccupied with his personal appearance.

CHAPTER 24 : *Strasbourg*

Infatuation! Thou hast all love's driving force,
all its capacity for feeling sorrow. Its enchanting pleasures, its mild delights are alone beyond thy sphere. I could not say, as I watched
her sleeping: She is all mine with her angelic
beauty and her sweet frailties! There she lies,
delivered into my power, as heaven in its
gracious mercy made her to enchant man's
heart.   SCHILLER

OBLIGED to spend a week in Strasbourg, Julien sought distraction in thoughts of military glory and devotion to his
country. Was he in love, then? He had not the slightest idea, but
in his tortured heart he found Mathilde the absolute mistress of
his happiness as of his imagination. He had need of all his strength
of mind to keep himself from sinking into despair. To think of
any subject that had nothing to do with Mademoiselle de la Mole
was beyond his power. Ambition, and the minor triumphs of
vanity had in the past taken his mind off those feelings Madame
de Rênal had inspired in him. Mathilde had absorbed all; he found
her everywhere in his future.

On every hand, in this future, Julien foresaw failure. This individual whom you have seen at Verrières so full of presumption,
so full of pride, had fallen into an absurd extreme of self-deprecia-
tion.

Three days earlier, it would have given him pleasure to kill
Father Castanède; at Strasbourg, if a child had started to quarrel
with him he would have sided with the child. As he looked back
on the past considering those opponents and open enemies whom
he had encountered in the course of his life, he found that he himself, Julien, had always been in the wrong.

It was just that he had now an implacable enemy in that powerful imagination, which once had been constantly employed in
depicting such brilliant successes for him in the future.

The utter solitude of a traveller's life made the power of this
dark imagination all the greater. What a treasure a friend would
have been! But, thought Julien, is there anywhere in the world
a heart that beats for me? And even if I had a friend, would not
honour command my eternal silence?

He was riding in a melancholy mood through the country round Kehl, a little market town on the banks of the Rhine, immortalized by Desaix and Gouvion Saint-Cyr. A German peasant pointed out to him the little streams, the roads, and the tiny islands of the Rhine which the valour of these great Generals has made famous. Julien, holding the reins in his left hand, was carrying, spread out in his right, the magnificent map which adorns the *Mémoires du Maréchal Saint-Cyr*. A merry shout made him raise his head.

It was Prince Korasoff, his London friend, who some few months before had expounded to him the first principles of elegant fatuity. Faithful to this great art, Korasoff, who had just arrived in Strasbourg, had spent the last hour at Kehl, and had never in his life read a single line about the siege of 1796, began to explain it all to Julien. The German peasant gazed at him in astonishment; for he knew enough to make out the enormous blunders into which the Prince was falling. Julien, with his mind a thousand leagues away from what the peasant was thinking, was looking with amazement at this handsome young man, and admiring his grace in the saddle.

A happy nature! he said to himself. How well his riding breeches fit; how elegantly his hair is cut! Alas! If I had been like that, perhaps after loving me for three days she wouldn't have taken a dislike to me.

When the Prince had ended his siege of Kehl, he said to Julien: 'Why, you look like a Trappist, you're overdoing the principle of gravity I gave you in London. A melancholy air can never be good form; what you want is to look bored. If you're melancholy, it means you want something you haven't got, or there's something in which you haven't succeeded. *That's an admission of inferiority*. On the other hand, if you're bored, it means that the person who has vainly tried to please you is your inferior. Realize, my dear fellow, what a grave mistake you are making.'

Julien flung a crown to the peasant who was listening to them open-mouthed.

'Good!' said the Prince. 'There's grace in that, and a noble disdain! Very good indeed!' And he put his horse into a gallop. Julien followed him, senseless with admiration.

Ah! If I had been like that, he thought, she would not have preferred Croisenois to me! The more his reason was shocked by the Prince's absurdities, the more he despised himself for not admiring them, and considered himself unfortunate in not sharing them. Self-contempt can go no further.

The Prince found him decidedly melancholy. 'Look here, my dear fellow,' he said to him, 'have you lost all your money, or are you possibly in love with some little actress?'

The Russians imitate French ways, but are always fifty years behind. They have just reached the days of Louis XV.

This jesting about love brought tears to Julien's eyes. Why shouldn't I consult this very agreeable fellow? he asked himself suddenly.

'Why, yes, my dear man,' he said to the Prince, 'you find me in Strasbourg very much in love, indeed, a rejected lover. A charming woman, who lives in a neighbouring town, has jilted me after three days of passion, and the change is killing me.'

He described to the Prince, under an assumed name, Mathilde's character and actions.

'You needn't go on,' said the Prince. 'To give you confidence in your physician, I'll finish the story. This young woman's husband possesses an enormous fortune, or, what is more likely, she herself belongs to one of the noblest families in the district. She must have some reason for being proud.'

Julien nodded his head; he had no longer the heart to speak.

'Very good,' said the Prince, 'here are three rather bitter pills for you to swallow without delay:

'First: Every day you must go and see Madame —. What's her name?'

'Madame de Dubois.'

'What a name!' said the Prince roaring with laughter. 'But forgive me, to you it is sublime. You absolutely must see Madame de Dubois every day, and above all be careful not to let her think you cold and offended; remember the great principle of this age – be the opposite to what people expect. Show yourself to her precisely as you were a week before she honoured you with her favours.'

'Ah! but I was calm, then,' cried Julien in despair, 'I thought I was taking pity on her. . . .'

'The moth gets burnt by the candle,' the Prince went on, 'a comparison as old as the world.

'First of all: you will see her every day.

'Secondly: you will pay court to a woman of her circle, but without any appearance of passion in your behaviour, you understand? I won't hide it from you, yours is a difficult part to play.

You have to pretend, and if your pretence is found out, why then you're lost!'

'She has so much intelligence, and I've so little. I'm lost,' said Julien sadly.

'No, you are only more in love than I thought. Madame de Dubois is profoundly interested in herself, like all those women who have received from heaven either too high a rank or too much money. She looks at herself instead of looking at you, and so doesn't know you. During the two or three little outbursts of passion she has allowed herself in your favour, she has, by a great effort of imagination, seen in you the hero of her dreams and not yourself as you really are. ... But what the devil, these are mere elements, my dear Sorel – are you an utter schoolboy?

'By Jove! Let's go into this shop! Here's a charming black cravat. You would say it was made by John Anderson of Burlington Street. Do me the pleasure of taking it and throwing that vile black string you've got round your neck as far away as you can.

'And now,' the Prince went on as they left the shop of the best haberdasher in Strasbourg, 'what sort of friends has Madame de Dubois? Good God! what a name! Don't get cross, my dear Sorel, I can't help it. ... To whom will you pay court?'

'To an unrivalled prude, the daughter of an immensely rich stocking-merchant. She has the loveliest eyes in the world, which I find infinitely attractive. She is certainly the most important person in the district; but amid all her grandeur, she blushes deeply and is quite overcome with confusion if any one happens to mention trade or shops. And unfortunately for her, her father was one of the best-known tradesmen in Strasbourg.'

'So that if one mentions *industry*,' said the Prince, laughing, 'you can be sure that your fair one is thinking of herself and not of you. This ridiculous trait is really divine and most useful, it will prevent you from losing your head for a single moment in the presence of her lovely eyes. Your success is sure.'

Julien was thinking of Madame de Fervaques, the Marshal's widow, who often came to the Hôtel de la Mole. She was a beautiful foreigner who had married the Marshal a year before his death. Her whole life seemed to have no other object than to make people forget that she was the daughter of a tradesman, and in order to count as someone in Paris she had become a leading light among the virtuous.

Julien sincerely admired the Prince. What would he not have given to have his absurd ways! The conversation between the two friends was endless; Korasoff was in raptures; never had a Frenchman listened to him for so long. So at last, thought the Prince with delight, I've managed to get a hearing by giving lessons to my masters.

'So we're quite agreed,' he repeated to Julien for the tenth time, 'not the faintest shadow of passion when you're talking to your young beauty, the stocking-merchant's daughter, in front of Madame de Dubois. On the other hand, burning passion when you write to her. Reading a well-written love letter is a supreme delight to a prude; it's a momentary relaxation. She's not playacting, she dares to listen to her heart; therefore, two letters daily.'

'Never, never!' said Julien, losing courage. 'I'd rather let myself be pounded to pieces in a mortar than compose three sentences. I'm a corpse, my dear fellow, don't hope for anything more from me. Let me die by the roadside.'

'And who said anything about composing sentences? I've six volumes of love letters in manuscript in my bag. There are ones for every type of feminine character. I have some for the most unassailable virtue. Didn't Kalisky make love on the Terrace at Richmond – you know the place, about ten miles out of London – to the prettiest Quakeress in all England?'

Julien was feeling less miserable when he parted from his friend at two o'clock in the morning.

Next day the Prince sent for a copyist, and two days later Julien had fifty-three love letters all properly numbered, designed to appeal to the most sublime and most sober virtue.

'There aren't fifty-four,' said the Prince, 'because Kalisky was sent about his business. But what does it matter to you if this stocking-merchant's daughter treats you ill, since you only wish to make an impression on the heart of Madame de Dubois?'

They went out riding together every day; the Prince had taken a violent liking to Julien. Not knowing how to give him proof of his sudden friendship, he ended by offering him the hand of one of his cousins, a wealthy heiress in Moscow. 'And once you are married,' he added, 'my influence and that Cross you are wearing will get you made a Colonel inside two years.'

'But this Cross was not given me by Napoleon – quite the contrary.'

'What does that matter,' said the Prince, 'didn't he invent it? It's still the highest decoration by far in Europe.'

Julien was on the point of accepting; but duty recalled him to see the important personage; on parting from Korasoff he promised to write to him. He received the reply to the secret note and hastened back to Paris. But he had hardly been there for more than two consecutive days, before leaving France and Mathilde seemed to him a worse agony than death itself. I won't marry the millions Korasoff offers me, he said to himself, but I will follow his advice.

After all, he went on thinking, the art of seduction is his profession; he has thought of nothing else for fifteen years, since he's thirty now. It can't be said he's lacking in intelligence; he is shrewd and cautious; enthusiasm and poetry are impossibilities for such a temperament. He's a practised go-between – one reason the more why he shouldn't make mistakes.

I must, and I will make love to Madame de Fervaques. She will possibly bore me a little, but I'll gaze into those lovely eyes which are so like the eyes that loved me best in all the world. She's a foreigner; that's a fresh character to study.

I'm off my head, I'm a drowning man, I must follow some friend's advice and not trust to my own judgement.

> But if I partake of this pleasure so prudently
> and so gingerly it will no longer be a pleasure
> for me.   LOPE DE VEGA

IMMEDIATELY on his return to Paris, and on leaving the study of the Marquis de la Mole, who seemed greatly upset by the despatches presented to him, our hero hurried off to visit Count Altamira. This handsome foreigner, in addition to his distinction of being under sentence of death, was also a man of considerable gravity and had the good fortune to be very religious. These two good qualities, and, more than all the rest, the Count's high birth, were entirely to the taste of Madame de Fervaques, who saw him frequently.

Julien confessed to him gravely that he was deeply in love with her.

'She is a woman of the purest and highest virtue,' Altamira answered, 'only it is a little too Jesuitical and over-emphatic. There are days when I understand every single word she uses, but can't catch the meaning of the sentence as a whole. She often gives me the idea that I don't know French as well as people say. This acquaintance will make you talked about; it will give you importance in the eyes of the world. But let us go and see Bustos,' said the Count, who had an orderly mind. 'He has paid court to Madame de Fervaques.'

Don Diego Bustos made them explain the matter to him at considerable length, without saying a word, just like a lawyer in his office. He had a round, fat monkish face, with a black moustache, and an air of inimitable gravity; in fact, a good *Carbonaro*.

'I understand,' he said at length to Julien. 'Has Madame de Fervaques had lovers, or hasn't she? Have you, therefore, any hope of success? That is the question. This amounts to saying that, for my own part, I had no success. Now that I am no longer resentful, I argue in this way with myself: she is often in a temper, and as I will show you shortly, she is pretty vindictive.

'I don't consider she has that choleric temperament which is a mark of genius, and which casts over every action a sort of gloss of passion. On the contrary, she derives her rare beauty and extremely fresh complexion from the calm and phlegmatic temperament of the Dutch.'

Julien was growing impatient with the Spaniard's stolid slowness and imperturbable phlegm. From time to time, for all he could do, a monosyllable or two escaped his lips.

'Do you intend to listen to me?' asked Don Diego Bustos gravely.

'Forgive my *furia francese*. I am all ears,' said Julien.

'The Maréchale de Fervaques, then, is much given to hatred; she is pitiless in her pursuit of people she has never seen – lawyers, poor devils of literary men who have written songs like Collé's, you know this one:

> ' *'Tis my folly*
> *To love Polly.* ...'

And Julien had to endure the whole song from beginning to end. The Spaniard was very glad of a chance to sing in French.

This exquisite little ditty had never been listened to with greater impatience. When it was over, Don Diego Bustos said to Julien: 'Madame de Fervaques made the author of the song "One day Cupid in a tavern" lose his job.'

Julien shuddered for fear lest he should want to sing this one, but Don Diego contented himself with analysing it. It was actually blasphemous and hardly decent.

'When the Maréchale flew into a rage over this song,' said Don Diego, 'I pointed out to her that a woman of her rank really should not read all the silly things that were published. However much progress piety and decorum make, there will always be a literature of tavern life in France. When Madame de Fervaques had the author, a poor devil on half pay, deprived of a post worth eight hundred francs, I said to her, "Take care, you've attacked this wretched versifier with your own weapons, he may reply to you with his rhymes. He will make a song upon virtue. The gilded drawing-rooms will be on your side; people who like to laugh will repeat his scurrilous jests." Do you know, sir, what Madame de Fervaques said to me in reply? "In the service of our Lord all Paris would see me walk to my martyrdom. It will be a novel spectacle in France. The common people will learn to respect true nobility. It would be the finest hour of my life." Her eyes had never looked more beautiful.'

'And she has marvellous eyes,' exclaimed Julien.

'It's obvious you're in love. ... So,' Don Diego Bustos went on gravely, 'she hasn't the choleric temper that inclines to vengeance. If all the same she likes injuring people, it is because she is unhappy. I suspect some kind of inward sorrow. Isn't it possible that she is a prude who has grown tired of her profession?'

The Spaniard gazed at him in silence for fully a minute.

'That is the whole question,' he added gravely, 'and this is something from which you can derive some hope. I thought about it a great deal during the two years in which I professed myself her most humble servant. All your future, my young lover, hangs on this great problem. Is she a prude grown tired of her vocation, or is she cruel to others because she is unhappy herself?'

'Or rather,' said Altamira, emerging at last from his profound silence, 'could it be what I have said to you a score of times already? Purely and simply a Frenchwoman's vanity. It's the memory of her father, the famous cloth merchant, that causes unhappiness in this naturally hard and sullen heart. There could only be one way of happiness for her, that of living in Toledo, and being tormented by a confessor, who every day would show her the yawning jaws of hell.'

As Julien was leaving, Don Diego said to him : 'Altamira tells me that you are one of us. One day you will help us to win back our freedom, so I am ready to help you in this little diversion. It would be a good thing for you to be acquainted with the Maréchale's style. Here are four letters in her own hand.'

'I'll copy them,' cried Julien, 'and bring them back to you.'

'And no one will ever learn from you a word of what we have been saying?'

'Never, upon my honour !' cried Julien.

'Then, may God be your help !' the Spaniard added; and he escorted Julien and Altamira in silence to the head of the stairs.

This scene cheered our hero a little; he almost smiled. So here's the pious Altamira, he said to himself, helping me in an adulterous adventure.

Throughout the whole of Don Diego Bustos' grave conversation Julien had been attentive to the striking of the hours on the clock of the Hôtel d'Aligre.

It was getting near to dinner time; he was going to see Mathilde again ! He went home, and dressed himself with great care.

My first blunder, he said to himself as he was going downstairs. I must carry out the Prince's prescription to the letter. He went upstairs again, and put on the simplest possible travelling costume.

Now, he said to himself, there's the question of how I shall look at her. It was only half past five, and dinner was at six. He decided to go down to the drawing-room and found it deserted. At the sight of the blue sofa he was moved to tears. Soon his cheeks began to burn. I must tire out this foolish sensibility, he said to himself angrily, it might betray me. He took up a newspaper to keep himself in countenance and strolled three or four times from the drawing-room to the garden.

It was only in fear and trembling, and safely hidden behind a large oak tree, that he ventured to raise his eyes to Mademoiselle de la Mole's window. It was tight shut; he nearly fell to the ground, and remained for a long time leaning up against the oak. Then, with faltering steps, he went to look once more at the gardener's ladder.

The link of the chain, forced open by him in circumstances, alas, so different, had not been mended. Carried away by a mad impulse, Julien pressed it to his lips.

After wandering to and fro for a long time between the drawing-room and the garden, Julien found himself horribly tired; this was an initial success of which he was keenly conscious. My eyes will be lifeless, and will not betray me, he thought. One after the other the guests arrived in the drawing-room. The door never opened without causing a deadly shock to Julien's heart.

They sat down to table. Mademoiselle de la Mole appeared at last, still faithful to her habit of keeping people waiting. On catching sight of Julien she blushed deeply; she had not been told of his arrival. Following Prince Korasoff's recommendation, Julien looked at her hands; they were trembling. Disturbed himself, beyond all power of expression, by this discovery, he was lucky enough only to appear tired.

M. de la Mole sang his praises. The Marquise spoke to him shortly afterwards, and kindly remarked on his look of fatigue. Julien kept on saying to himself : I must not look at Mademoiselle de la Mole too much, neither must my eyes seem to avoid her. I must appear to be as I really was a week before my unhappy reverse. He had occasion to be satisfied with his success, and remained in the drawing-room. Attentive for the first time to the mistress of the house, he made every effort to get the men of the company to talk, and to keep the conversation alive.

His politeness was rewarded; towards eight o'clock, Madame de Fervaques was announced. Julien slipped away and presently reappeared, dressed with the utmost care. Madame de la Mole was infinitely obliged to him for this mark of respect, and wishing to show her satisfaction, mentioned his journey to Madame de

Fervaques. Julien installed himself beside the Marshal's widow, in such a way that Mathilde should not be able to see his eyes. Seated thus, in accordance with all the rules of art, Madame de Fervaques became the supreme object of his awestruck admiration. It was with a burst of eloquence on this sentiment that the first of the fifty-three letters Prince Korasoff had presented to him began.

The Maréchale announced that she was going on to the Italian Opera. Julien hastened there, and came across the Chevalier de Beauvoisis, who took him to a box reserved for the Gentlemen of the Household, just next to that of Madame de Fervaques. Julien gazed at her incessantly. I must keep a diary of the siege, he said to himself, as he returned home, otherwise I might lose count of some of my attacks. He forced himself to write down two or three pages on this tedious subject and thus succeeded – marvellous to relate – in almost forgetting to think of Mademoiselle de la Mole.

Mathilde herself had almost forgotten him while he was away. After all, he is only a very common sort of creature, she thought, his name will always remind me of the greatest mistake of my life. I must return in all sincerity to conventional standards of decorum and honour; a woman has everything to lose in forgetting them. She showed herself inclined at last to allow the conclusion of the contract with the Marquis de Croisenois, agreed on such a long while back. He was mad with joy. He would have been greatly astonished if anyone had told him that resignation was the underlying cause of that state of mind on Mathilde's part which made him so proud.

All Mademoiselle de la Mole's ideas were changed at the sight of Julien. Really and truly, she said to herself, that man is my husband. If I sincerely return to the paths of virtue, he is obviously the man I ought to marry.

She was looking for importunate entreaties, for an air of misery on Julien's part; she prepared her answers, for there was little doubt that on rising from table he would attempt to say a few words to her. Far from it, he remained obstinately in the drawing-room, his eyes did not even turn towards the garden – heaven knows with what difficulty! It would be better to get our explanation over at once, thought Mademoiselle de la Mole. She went out into the garden alone; but Julien did not appear. Mathilde came and strolled past the drawing-room windows. She saw him busily engaged in describing to Madame de Fervaques the old ruined castles that crown the slopes that border the Rhine and give them so much character. He was beginning to hold his own not too badly in the sentimental, picturesque style of speech which passes for wit in certain drawing-rooms.

Prince Korasoff would have felt really proud, had he found himself in Paris; this evening was exactly as he had foretold. He would have approved, too, of the way Julien behaved on the following days.

An intrigue among members of the power behind the throne was about to dispose of a few Blue Ribbons. Madame de Fervaques insisted that her great-uncle should be made a Knight of the Order; the Marquis de la Mole was making a similar claim for his father-in-law. They joined forces, and the Maréchale came nearly every day to the Hôtel de la Mole. It was from her that Julien learnt that the Marquis was about to become a Minister; he was putting forward to the *Camarilla* a highly ingenious plan for rescinding the Charter without any fuss in three years' time.

If M. de la Mole became a Minister, Julien might expect a bishopric; but to his eyes all such great interests were hidden as though behind a veil. His imagination now perceived them only vaguely, and as it were in the far distance. The frightful unhappiness that had become a mania with him made him see all the interests of his life confined to his relations with Mademoiselle de la Mole. He calculated that after five or six years of constant effort, he might succeed in making her love him once more.

That exceedingly cool head of his, as you see, was reduced to a state of utter unreason. Of all the qualities that had distinguished him in the past, only a hint of firmness remained. Substantially faithful to the plan of behaviour dictated to him by Prince Korasoff, he took up his position every evening close beside Madame de Fervaques's armchair, but found it impossible to think of a single word to say to her.

The constraint he was imposing on himself to appear in Mathilde's eyes as if cured of his love absorbed all his strength of heart and mind; he remained at the Maréchale's side like a creature hardly alive. Even his eyes, as happens in the extremity of physical anguish, had lost all their fire.

Since Madame de la Mole's point of view was never anything but an imitation of the opinions of that husband who might one day make her a Duchess, for a few days past she had been lauding Julien's merits to the skies.

CHAPTER 26 : *Platonic Love*

> There also was of course in Adeline
> That calm patrician polish in the address,
> That ne'er can pass the equinoctial line
> Of anything which Nature would express:
> Just as a Mandarin finds nothing fine,
> At least his manner suffers not to guess
> That anything he views can greatly please.
>
> *Don Juan*, xiii. 84

THERE is a touch of madness in the way that all this family looks at things, thought Madame de Fervaques. They are infatuated with their little abbé, who can do nothing but look and listen, though with rather attractive eyes, it's true.

Julien, for his part, found in the Maréchale's manner an almost perfect example of that patrician calm which bespeaks a scrupulous politeness and still more the impossibility of feeling any keen emotion. Any unexpected gesture or impulse, any lack of self-control, would have shocked Madame de Fervaques almost as much as a want of queenly dignity towards one's inferiors. The least sign of sensibility would have seemed in her eyes a sort of *moral intoxication* for which one ought to blush, and which was highly detrimental to what a person of exalted rank owed to herself. Her great delight was to speak about the last royal hunting party, and her favourite book the *Mémoires du Duc de Saint-Simon*, particularly the genealogical part.

Julien knew the position which, from the way the lights were placed, was best suited to Madame de Fervaques's type of beauty. He would get there before her, taking great care, however, to turn his chair so that he should not be able to see Mathilde. Astonished by these constant efforts to avoid her, she left the blue sofa one evening and came to work at a little table close beside the Marquise's armchair. Julien could see her at close range from under the brim of Madame de Fervaques's hat. Those eyes, which held his fate in their power, seen from so near, made him at first afraid, then startled him violently out of his normal apathy. He talked, and talked very well.

He addressed himself to the Maréchale, but his sole aim was to react upon Mathilde's heart. He grew so excited that in the end Madame de Fervaques could not understand what he was saying.

This was a first point in his favour. Had Julien taken it into his head to round off his success by a phrase or two full of German mysticism, of high piety, or Jesuitical sentiments, the Maréchale would have ranged him there and then amongst those men of superior quality called to regenerate their age.

Since he has enough bad taste, said Mademoiselle de la Mole to herself, to talk so long and so fervently to Madame de Fervaques, I won't listen to him any longer. For the rest of the evening she kept her word, although with difficulty.

At midnight, as Mathilde was taking her mother's candlestick to escort her to her room, Madame de la Mole stopped on the stairs to utter an out-and-out panegyric of Julien. Mathilde's temper gave way completely; she found it impossible to sleep. One thought soothed her: The man I despise can all the same pass for a man of great worth in the Maréchale's eyes.

As for Julien, he had now taken action; he felt less miserable. His eyes happened to fall on the portfolio of Russian leather in which Prince Korasoff had enclosed the fifty-three love letters he had presented to him. Julien saw a note at the bottom of the first page: *Send No. 1 a week after the first meeting.*

I'm late! exclaimed Julien, for it's ever so long since I first met Madame de Fervaques. He set to work at once to copy out this first love letter; it was a homily packed with phrases about virtue, and deadly dull. Julien was lucky enough to fall asleep over the second page.

A few hours later the sun, already fully risen, surprised him with his head leaning on the table. One of the most painful moments of his life was that in which, each morning, as he awoke, he realized his misery anew. That day, he was almost laughing as he finished copying his letter. Is it possible, he asked himself, that any young man exists who could write like this? He counted several sentences of nine lines each. At the foot of the original he found a note in pencil: *Deliver this letter yourself, on horseback, in a black cravat and a blue greatcoat. Hand the letter to the porter with a shamefaced air; a look of profound melancholy in your eyes. If you catch sight of any one of the maids, wipe your eyes furtively and address a few words to her.* All this was faithfully carried out.

What I'm doing is very bold, thought Julien as he left the Hôtel de Fervaques, but so much the worse for Korasoff. Daring to write to a woman so famed for her virtue! I shall be treated with the utmost contempt, and nothing will amuse me more. This is, after all, the only kind of comedy I appreciate. Yes, indeed, covering that hateful creature whom I call myself with ridicule will amuse me. If I consulted myself, I'd commit some crime by way of distraction.

For a month past, the happiest moment in the day for Julien had been the one in which he brought his horse back to the stables. Korasoff had expressly forbidden him to look, upon any pretext whatsoever, at the mistress who had forsaken him. But this horse's step, which she knew so well, and Julien's way of rapping with his whip at the stable door to summon one of the men, sometimes drew Mathilde to stand behind her window curtain. The muslin was so fine that Julien could see through it. By looking up in a certain way from under the brim of his hat, he could catch a glimpse of Mathilde's form without seeing her eyes. Consequently, he told himself, she can't see mine, and that doesn't amount to looking at her.

That evening, Madame de Fervaques behaved to him exactly as though she had not received the philosophical, mystico-religious dissertation he had handed with such an air of melancholy to the porter in the morning. The evening before, chance had revealed to Julien how to become eloquent; he settled down in such a way as to see Mathilde's eyes. She, for her part, left the blue sofa a moment after the Maréchale's arrival; this meant deserting her usual circle. M. de Croisenois seemed greatly dismayed at this new caprice; his evident grief relieved Julien's suffering of its keenest pangs.

This unexpected turn in his fortunes made him talk divinely; and as self-conceit can steal even into those hearts that serve as temples of the most august virtue, Madame de Fervaques said to herself as she stepped into her carriage: Madame de la Mole is right, that young priest has distinction. My presence must have frightened him in the first few days. As a matter of fact, all those one meets in this house are very frivolous-minded. All the virtue I find there is due to age, and has had very great need of the icy hand of time. This young man will have been able to see the difference. He writes well; but I very much fear his request to be enlightened by my counsels, which he makes in his letter, may be really only a feeling unconscious of its own nature.

All the same, how many conversions have begun in this way? What makes me augur well of this one is the difference in his style from that of the young men whose letters I have had occasion to see. It is impossible not to recognize a certain eloquent fervour, a serious depth of mind, and much conviction in the prose of this young aspirant to the priesthood. He has surely Massillon's benign virtue.

CHAPTER 27 : *The Best Positions in the Church*

Services ! talents ! merit ! bah ! — join a clique.
Télémaque

THUS the idea of a bishopric was for the first time associated with thoughts of Julien in the head of a woman who sooner or later would be distributing the best positions in the Church. This happy circumstance would hardly have interested him; his own thoughts at this moment did not rise above anything alien to his present state of unhappiness. Everything made it worse; the sight of his room, for instance, had become unbearable. At night, when he came back to it with his candle, each piece of furniture, each little ornament seemed to take on a voice to inform him harshly of some new detail of his misery.

That evening, as he entered it with a buoyancy he had not known for a very long time, he said to himself : I'm condemned to hard labour, let's hope the second letter will be as boring as the first.

It was even more so. What he was copying seemed to him so absurd that he came to transcribing it line by line, without thinking of the meaning.

It's even more pompous, he thought, than the official documents of the Treaty of Munster, which my master in diplomacy made me copy out in London.

It was only then that he remembered the letters from Madame de Fervaques, the originals of which he had forgotten to return to that grave Spanish gentleman, Don Diego Bustos. He hunted them out. They were really almost as full of rigmarole as those of the young Russian noble. They were utterly and entirely vague. They tried to say everything, and yet say nothing. It's the Aeolian harp of style, thought Julien. In the midst of the loftiest reflections on the nothingness of things, on death, infinity, and so on, I find nothing real except a horrible fear of being laughed at.

The monologue we have summarized here was repeated over and over for the space of a fortnight. Falling asleep while transcribing a kind of commentary on the Apocalypse, going the next day with a melancholy air to deliver a letter, putting his horse back in the stables in the hope of catching sight of Mathilde's gown, working, putting in an appearance at the Opera on evenings when Madame de Fervaques did not come to the Hôtel de la

Mole – such were the momentous events of Julien's life. There was more interest in it when Madame de Fervaques came to see the Marquise. Then he could catch a glimpse of Mathilde's eyes from under the side brim of the Maréchale's hat, and would wax eloquent. His picturesque and sentimental phrases were beginning to assume a more striking and more elegant shape.

He was acutely conscious that what he was saying must seem absurd in Mathilde's eyes, but he tried to impress her by his elegant choice of words. The more I say what is false, he thought, the more I ought to please her. And then, with shocking boldness, he began to exaggerate certain aspects of nature. He very quickly perceived that, if he were not to appear a mere common creature in the Maréchale's eyes, he must above all steer clear of simple and rational ideas. He continued on these lines, or cut short his flights of fancy according as he read success or indifference in the eyes of the two noble ladies whom he was out to please.

On the whole, he found life less dreadful than when his days had been spent in doing nothing.

But, here am I, he said to himself one evening, copying out the fifteenth of these odious dissertations. The first fourteen have been faithfully handed over to Madame de Fervaques's porter. I shall soon have the honour of filling all the pigeonholes in her desk. And yet she treats me exactly as though I were not writing ! What can be the end of all this ? Can my constancy bore her as much as it does me ? I must say this Russian friend of Korasoff's must have been a dreadful fellow in his day; no one could be more deadly dull.

Like everyone of limited intelligence whom chance brings face to face with the operations of a great commander, Julien understood nothing of the attack the young Russian had launched against the heart of the young Englishwoman. The first forty letters were intended only to make her pardon him for his boldness in writing. The point was to make this sweet and gentle person, who possibly was bored to death, acquire the habit of receiving letters which were perhaps a trifle less insipid than her ordinary, everyday life.

One morning, a letter was handed to Julien. He recognized Madame de Fervaques's coat of arms and broke the seal with an eagerness that would have seemed to him quite impossible a few days before. It was merely an invitation to dinner.

He rushed to consult Prince Korasoff's instructions. Unfortunately the young Russian had chosen to be as frivolous as Dorat, just where he ought to have been simple and intelligible. Julien could not guess what moral attitude he ought to adopt when dining with the Marshal's widow.

The drawing-room was extremely magnificent, with gildings like those of the Galerie de Diane at the Tuileries and oil paintings in the panelled woodwork. There were daubs of light paint here and there on these pictures; Julien learnt later on that the subjects had seemed rather indecent to the lady of the house and she had had the pictures amended. Our moral age! he thought.

In the drawing-room he remarked three of the eminent personages who had been present at the drafting of the secret note. One of them, His Grace the Bishop of —, the Maréchale's uncle, had the patronage of benefices, and, so it was said, could refuse his niece nothing. What an immense step forward I have made, thought Julien, with a melancholy smile, and how cold it leaves me! Here am I dining at the same table as the famous Bishop of —.

The dinner was indifferent and the conversation of a kind to try one's patience. It's like the table of contents of a badly written book, thought Julien. All the most important subjects of human thought are boldly embarked upon. But listen to it for three minutes, and you'll ask yourself which is the greater, the dogmatic assurance of the speaker or his atrocious ignorance.

The reader has doubtless forgotten that little man of letters, named Tanbeau, the nephew of the academician and a budding professor, who with his vile slanders, seemed to have taken upon himself to poison the minds of everyone in the drawing-room of the Hôtel de la Mole.

It was from this little man that Julien first got the idea that Madame de Fervaques, while not answering his letters, might very possibly look with indulgence on the feeling that dictated them. M. Tanbeau's black heart was torn asunder by the thought of Julien's successes; but on the other hand, a man of worth cannot, any more than a fool, be in two places at once. If M. Sorel, thought Tanbeau, becomes the lover of the sublime Madame de Fervaques, she will give him some sort of advantageous position in the Church, and I shall be rid of him at the Hôtel de la Mole.

Father Pirard also addressed lengthy sermons to Julien on his successes at the Hôtel de Fervaques. There was a sort of *sectarian rivalry* between the austere Jansenist and the drawing-room of the virtuous Madame de Fervaques, with its Jesuitical, monarchical principles and its plans for reforming society.

> Now once he was really convinced of the
> Prior's asinine stupidity he fairly usually suc-
> ceeded in calling what was white, black, and
> what was black, white. LICHTEMBERGER

THE Russian instructions gave stringent orders that one must
never contradict in conversation the person to whom one was
writing. One must never lay aside, on any pretext whatsoever,
the role of the most ecstatic admirer. Every one of the letters was
based on this supposition.

One evening, in Madame de Fervaques's box at the Opera,
Julien was praising to the skies the ballet in *Manon Lescaut*. His
sole reason for doing so was that he found it dull. The Maréchale
remarked that this ballet was very inferior to the Abbé Prévost's
novel.

What! thought Julien, surprised and amused, a person of such
exalted virtue praising a novel! It was Madame de Fervaques's
custom to profess, two or three times a week, the most utter contempt for these writers who, by means of such vulgar works,
seek to corrupt a younger generation, only too prone, alas, to
sensual errors.

'In its immoral and pernicious class, *Manon Lescaut*,' continued
Madame de Fervaques, 'occupies, so I am told, one of the highest
places. The frailties and well deserved afflictions of a guilty heart
are, so people say, depicted there with a truth that is in some
way profound; which did not prevent your Bonaparte on Saint
Helena from pronouncing it to be a novel written for lackeys.'

This remark restored Julien's mind to all its former alertness.
Someone has been trying to ruin me with the Maréchale; she
must have been told of my enthusiasm for Napoleon. This fact
has annoyed her enough for her to yield to the temptation of
making me feel her anger. This discovery kept him amused for
the rest of the evening, and made him amusing too. As he was
taking leave of the Maréchale in the vestibule of the Opera, she
said to him: 'Remember, sir, that people who love me must not
love Bonaparte; they may at most accept him as a necessity imposed on us by Providence. Anyhow, the man had not a supple
enough mind to appreciate great masterpieces.'

People who love me! Julien repeated to himself. Either that

means nothing, or means everything. These are secrets of
language we poor provincials don't possess. And he thought very
deeply of Madame de Rênal, as he copied an immensely long
letter intended for the Maréchale.

'How is it,' she said to him the next day with an air of indifference he thought badly feigned, 'that you mentioned *London*
and *Richmond* to me in a letter you wrote last night, it appears,
after leaving the Opera?'

Julien was greatly embarrassed. He had copied the letter line by
line without thinking of what he was writing, and apparently
had forgotten to replace the words *London* and *Richmond*, which
occurred in the original, with *Paris* and *Saint-Cloud*. He started
two or three times to say something, but could not finish his
sentence; he felt himself on the point of giving way to a fit of
helpless laughter. Finally, in his search for words, he hit upon
this idea: 'Excited by the discussion of the most sublime, the
most lofty interests of the human mind, my own, in writing to
you, may perhaps have become distracted.'

I'm creating an impression, he said to himself, therefore I can
spare myself further boredom this evening. He left the Hôtel de
Fervaques in haste. That evening, taking another look at the
original of the letter which he had copied the night before, he
came very quickly to the fatal passage in which the young
Russian spoke of London and Richmond. Julien was quite surprised to find this letter almost tender.

It was the contrast between the apparent frivolity of his talk
and the sublime and almost apocalyptic profundity of his letters
that had led to his being singled out. The length of his sentences
was especially pleasing to the Maréchale; this was not the erratic,
desultory style brought into fashion by that monster of iniquity,
Voltaire. Although our hero did everything in the world to
banish all traces of common sense from his conversation, it still
retained a flavour of something anti-monarchical and irreligious
which did not escape the notice of Madame de Fervaques. Surrounded by persons who were pre-eminently moral, but who often
did not have one idea in the course of an evening, this lady was
deeply impressed by everything that seemed to be something of a
novelty; but, at the same time, she felt she owed it to herself to
be shocked by it. She called this failing 'bearing the imprint of this
frivolous age'.

But drawing-rooms like this are only worth a visit when one
has some favour to beg. All the boredom of this life devoid of

interests which Julien was leading is doubtless shared by the reader. These are the barren tracts of our journey.

Throughout all the encroachments of the Fervaques episode on Julien's time, Mademoiselle de la Mole had to make determined efforts not to think of him. Her heart was torn by violent conflicts. Sometimes she flattered herself that she despised this very glum young man; yet, against her will, she found his conversation captivating. What astonished her most of all was his utter insincerity. He did not say a word to the Maréchale which was not either a downright lie, or at any rate the most shocking travesty of his own point of view, which Mathilde knew so perfectly upon almost every subject. This Machiavellian behaviour impressed her. What depths of subtlety ! she thought ! How different from those pompous idiots or common rogues like M. Tanbeau, who speak the same language !

All the same, he passed through some frightful days. Appearing each evening in the Maréchale's drawing-room was for him the accomplishment of the most painful of his duties. His efforts to play a part ended by robbing his spirit of all its strength. Often, at night, as he crossed the huge courtyard of the Hôtel de Fervaques, it was only by force of character and by reasoning with himself that he managed to keep his mind a little above the level of despair.

I conquered despair in the seminary, he would say to himself, and yet what a frightful prospect lay before me then ! Whether I made or marred my fortune, I saw myself obliged, in either case, to spend my whole life in close company with all that is most contemptible and most revolting under the sun. The following spring, only eleven short months later, I was the happiest of all the young men of my age.

But often enough all these fine arguments were of no effect against the dreadful reality. Every day he saw Mathilde at lunch and at dinner. From the numerous letters dictated to him by M. de la Mole, he knew her to be on the eve of marrying M. de Croisenois. Already that agreeable young man was appearing twice a day at the Hôtel de la Mole; the jealous eye of a forsaken lover did not miss a single one of his actions.

Whenever he thought he had seen Mademoiselle de la Mole treating her suitor kindly, on going back to his room, Julien could not help looking lovingly at his pistols.

Ah, how much wiser I should be, he said to himself, to cut the marks off my linen, and go off into some lonely forest, twenty

leagues out of Paris, there to end this hateful life. A stranger to
the district, my death would remain hidden for a fortnight, and
who, when a fortnight had passed, would give a thought to me!

This was very sensible reasoning. But next day, a glimpse of
Mathilde's arm between her sleeve and her glove was enough to
plunge our young philosopher deep into cruel memories, yet
which, all the same, made him cling to life. All right, he would
then say to himself, I'll follow this Russian policy to the very
end. But what will that end be?

As for the Maréchale, after I've copied out these fifty-three
letters, I'll certainly write no more. As for Mathilde, these last
six weeks of such painful play-acting will either make no impression at all on her anger, or will win me a moment's reconciliation. Good God! I should die of joy! And he could not
follow his thought any further.

When, after a long fit of musing, he succeeded in resuming the
argument with himself: Then, he said to himself, I should gain
one day's happiness, after which a fresh beginning of her harshness, founded, alas, on my insufficient power to please her; and I
should be left without resources, I should be ruined, lost for ever.

What guarantee can she give me with a character like hers?
Alas! my manners will be found wanting in elegance, my way of
speaking heavy and monotonous. Good God! Why am I what I
am?

CHAPTER 29 : *Boredom*

> Sacrificing oneself to one's passions, well and
> good – but to passions one does not feel! O
> wretched nineteenth century!   GIRODET

AFTER having read Julien's first letters without any pleasure,
Madame de Fervaques was beginning to be absorbed by them.
One thing, however, grieved her. What a pity, she thought, that
M. Sorel is not really a priest! One could admit him to a sort of
intimacy. With that Cross and his almost layman's clothes, one
lays oneself open to unkind questions, and how is one to answer
them? She did not finish her thought. Some malicious friend, it
would have run, may suppose and even spread it abroad that he is
some young cousin of inferior rank on my father's side, some
tradesman decorated for services in the National Guard.

Until the moment of her first meeting Julien, it had been
Madame de Fervaques's greatest pleasure to write the word *Maréchale* before her name. From that time onwards an upstart's
vanity, morbid and quick to take offence, had to fight against a
budding interest.

It would be so easy, the Maréchale said to herself, for me to
make a Vicar-general of him in some diocese not far from Paris!
But plain M. Sorel, and, what is more, a mere secretary to M.
de la Mole! It's too distressing!

For the very first time, this spirit *afraid of everything* was
moved by an interest outside its own pretensions to rank and to
social superiority. Her old porter noticed that, whenever he
brought her a letter from that handsome young man who had
such a sad expression, he was sure to see the absent-minded, dis-
contented look that the Maréchale always took care to assume
when any of her servants entered the room vanish immediately
from her face.

The boredom of a mode of life the sole ambition of which was
to impress the outside world, without her feeling in her inmost
heart any real delight in this kind of success, had become so intolerable since she had begun to think of Julien, that the fact of
having spent an hour on the previous evening with that strange
young man was enough to ensure that her maids would not be ill-
treated for one whole day. His growing credit was proof against
certain very cleverly written anonymous letters. It was all in

vain for little Tanbeau to supply MM. de Luz, de Croisenois, de Caylus with two or three cunning bits of scandal which these gentlemen took pleasure in spreading abroad, without paying too much attention to the truth of these accusations. Madame de Fervaques, whose mind was not made to withstand such vulgar methods, would tell Mathilde of her doubts and was always comforted.

One day, after having inquired three times if there were any letters, Madame de Fervaques suddenly decided to write and answer Julien. This was a victory gained by boredom. At the second letter the Maréchale was almost brought to a standstill by the impropriety of writing in her own hand such a vulgar address as : M. Sorel, c/o M. le Marquis de la Mole.

'You must bring me some envelopes with your address on them,' she said to Julien very curtly one evening.

So now I'm appointed as a sort of footman-lover, thought Julien, bowing, and wrinkling up his face in secret amusement to look like Arsène, the Marquis's aged valet.

That same evening he brought a few envelopes with him, and very early the next morning he received a third letter. He read five or six lines at the beginning and two or three towards the end. It covered four pages in a small and very cramped handwriting.

Gradually it became her pleasant custom to write every day. Julien answered her with faithful copies of the Russian letters, and such is the advantage of a bombastic style, that Madame de Fervaques was not at all surprised at the want of connexion between the replies and her own letters.

How it would have vexed her pride if little Tanbeau, who had appointed himself a voluntary spy on Julien's actions, had been able to tell her that all these letters, with their seals unbroken, were flung pell-mell into Julien's drawer.

One morning, the porter came into the library to bring him a letter from the Maréchale. Mathilde met the man, and caught sight of the letter with the address in Julien's writing. She went into the library as the porter was coming out. The letter was still lying on the edge of the table, for Julien, who was very busy writing, had not put it into his drawer.

'This is what I cannot endure,' cried Mathilde, seizing the letter, 'you are forgetting me completely, me, your wife. Your behaviour, sir, is shocking.'

At these words, her pride, amazed at the frightful impropriety of her action, choked her, and she burst into tears; a moment later it seemed to Julien that she was unable to breathe.

Surprised, bewildered, Julien did not clearly grasp all the wonder and the happiness this scene held for him. He helped Mathilde to sit down; she all but surrendered herself to his arms.

The first instant he realized the meaning of this gesture was one of utter joy. The second was filled with thoughts of Korasoff — I can ruin everything by a single word.

His arms grew rigid, so painful was the constraint imposed on him by policy. I must not even allow myself to press this lovely, yielding body to my heart, or she will despise me and treat me harshly. What a frightful character!

And while he cursed Mathilde's character, he loved her a hundred times more on that account; it seemed to him he was holding a queen in his arms.

Julien's unfeeling coldness gave a sharper edge to the pangs of wounded pride that rent Mathilde's heart. She was far from having the necessary self-command to try and read in his eyes what he felt for her at that moment. She could not bring herself to look at him; she trembled to meet the expression of his scorn.

Sitting motionless on the couch in the library, with her head turned away from Julien, she was suffering the keenest anguish pride and love can force a human heart to undergo. Into what a frightful act of indiscretion had she not blindly rushed!

It was reserved for me, unhappy creature that I am, to see the most indelicate advances repulsed. And repulsed by whom? interjected a pride maddened by suffering — by one of my father's servants.

'That is what I will not endure,' she cried out. And springing to her feet in fury, she opened the drawer of Julien's table, which stood just two feet away. She remained frozen with horror at the sight of nine or ten letters exactly like the one the porter had just brought in. On all the envelopes she recognized Julien's writing, more or less disguised.

'And so,' she cried, beside herself with rage, 'not only are you in favour with her but you despise her. You, a mere nobody, despising the Maréchale de Fervaques!

'Ah, forgive me, my dear,' she went on, flinging herself at his feet, 'despise me if you will, but love me. I can no longer live deprived of your love.' And she fell down in a dead faint.

So there she lies, thought Julien, that proud creature — there at my feet!

> As the blackest sky
> Foretells the heaviest tempest.
> *Don Juan,* i. 75

IN the midst of this highly emotional scene, Julien was more amazed than happy. Mathilde's insulting remarks showed him how wise the Russian policy had been. *Say little, do little,* there lies my one way of salvation.

He lifted Mathilde up and without saying a word laid her down again on the couch. Gradually she was overcome by tears.

To keep herself in countenance, she took Madame de Fervaques's letters in her hands, and slowly broke the seals. She gave a nervous start on recognizing the Maréchale's handwriting. She turned over the sheets of these letters without reading them; most of them were six pages long.

'Give me some answer, at least,' said Mathilde at length in a most beseeching tone of voice, but without venturing to look at Julien. 'You know very well I'm proud. It's an unfortunate consequence of my position, and even, I must confess, of my character. So Madame de Fervaques has stolen your heart from me.... Has she made for you all the sacrifices to which that fatal passion has led me?'

A gloomy silence was Julien's only answer. By what right, he thought, does she ask me for a betrayal of confidence unworthy of an honourable man?

Mathilde tried to read the letters, but her tear-filled eyes made this impossible. For a month past, she had been miserable, but so proud a spirit was far from confessing its feelings to itself. Chance alone had occasioned this outburst; for a moment jealousy and love had proved too strong for pride. She was seated on the couch and quite close to him. He saw her hair, and her neck white as alabaster; for a moment he forgot all duty to himself and, slipping his arm round her, he almost clasped her to his breast.

She turned her head towards him slowly. He was astonished at the sorrow in her eyes, which was so intense as to make it impossible for him to recognize their usual expression. Julien felt his strength beginning to fail him, so stupendously difficult was the act of courage he was forcing upon himself.

Those eyes will quickly express nothing but the coldest disdain, thought Julien, if I allow myself to be drawn into the happiness of showing my love for her. Meanwhile, in a faint voice and in words she had hardly strength enough to utter, she was repeating to him at that moment her assurance of all her regret for actions which an overweening pride might have counselled her to take.

'I too have my pride,' Julien said to her in hardly articulate speech, while his features revealed an extreme point of physical exhaustion.

Mathilde turned sharply round towards him. To hear his voice was a joy she had almost ceased to hope for. At that moment, she recalled her disdainful behaviour only to upbraid it; she would gladly have discovered some unusual, incredible act by which she could prove to him how greatly she adored him and loathed herself.

'It is probably on account of that pride,' Julien went on, 'that, for an instant, you singled me out. It is certainly because of that courageous strength of mind, which is fitting in a man, that you respect me at this moment. I may be in love with the Maréchale. . . .'

Mathilde started; her eyes took on a strange expression, she was about to hear her sentence pronounced. This movement did not escape Julien's notice; he felt his courage weaken.

Ah! he thought, listening to the sound of the meaningless words his mouth was uttering, as he might have listened to a noise from outside, if I could only cover those pale cheeks with kisses without your feeling them, my love! . . .

'I may be in love with the Maréchale,' he went on, his voice growing all the time fainter and fainter, 'but I certainly have no positive proof of her interest in me.'

Mathilde gazed at him; he bore up under her gaze, or at least he hoped his face had not betrayed him. He felt himself filled with love for her right to the innermost recesses of his heart. Never had he adored her so intensely; he was almost as mad with love as Mathilde. Had she had enough coolness and courage to handle the situation adroitly, he would have fallen at her feet and vowed to give up all this silly pretence.

He had strength enough to manage to go on talking. Ah! Korasoff, his inward self exclaimed, why aren't you here? How I need a word from you to guide my conduct!

Meanwhile his voice was saying aloud: 'In default of any other feeling, gratitude would suffice to attach me to the Maréchale. She has shown me indulgence, she has comforted me when I was despised. I may perhaps not place unbounded faith in certain manifestations, which are doubtless flattering, but possibly also of somewhat brief duration.'

'Ah! gracious heavens!' cried Mathilde.

'Very well! What guarantee will you give me?' Julien went on in alert and vigorous tones, in which for the moment the cautious methods of diplomacy were seemingly abandoned. 'What guarantee, what deity will answer to me for it that the position to which you seem for the moment disposed to restore me will last for more than a couple of days?'

'The intensity of my love and of my unhappiness if you no longer love me,' she said to him, taking hold of his hands and turning round towards him....

The violent movement she had just made had disarranged her pelerine a little; Julien caught sight of her lovely shoulders. The slight disorder of her hair recalled to him an exquisite memory.

He was about to yield. One rash word, he said to himself, and I'll bring round again that long succession of days spent in despair. Madame de Rênal found reasons for doing as her heart dictated; this young girl of high society only lets her heart be moved when she has proved to herself by very good reasons that it ought to feel emotion.

He grasped this truth in the twinkling of an eye, and in the twinkling of an eye regained his courage. He freed his hands, which Mathilde was clasping in hers, and with every mark of deference drew a little way away from her. Human courage can go no further. He then busied himself in gathering together all Madame de Fervaques's letters which were scattered over the couch, and with a show of extreme, and at that moment cruel, politeness added: 'If Mademoiselle de la Mole will kindly permit me to reflect upon all this.'

He moved quickly away and left the library; she heard him shutting all the doors in turn.

The brute is not in the least perturbed, she said to herself. But what am I saying! A brute! he's wise, and discreet, and kind. It's I who am more in the wrong than could be imagined.

This point of view persisted. Mathilde was almost happy that day, for she was wholly and completely in love. You would have said that this heart had never been troubled by pride – and such pride too.

She started with horror when, that evening in the drawing-room, a footman announced Madame de Fervaques; the man's voice seemed to her to have a sinister ring. She could not endure the sight of the Maréchale, and quickly left the room. Julien, feeling little pride in his hard-won victory, had been afraid of what his own eyes might reveal, and had not dined at the Hôtel de la Mole.

His love and his happiness increased rapidly as the moment of battle receded; he had already begun to find fault with himself. How could I have resisted her? he thought. What if she should cease to love me! A single moment may work changes in that proud spirit, and I must confess I've treated her abominably.

In the evening he felt that he absolutely must put in an appearance in Madame de Fervaques's box at the Italian Opera. She had expressly invited him; Mathilde would not fail to hear of his presence there, or of his discourteous absence. Despite the obvious soundness of this argument, he had not the strength, in the earlier part of the evening, to plunge into company. If he talked, half his happiness would be taken from him.

Ten o'clock struck: he absolutely had to appear. Luckily he found the Maréchale's box full of women, and was relegated to a seat by the door, entirely hidden by their hats. This position saved him from a ridiculous situation; the divine tones of Carolina's despair in *Il matrimonio segreto* made him burst into tears. Madame de Fervaques saw these tears; they were in so marked a contrast to the usual manly firmness of his features, that this noble lady's spirit, for so long steeped in all the most corrosive elements of an upstart's pride, was moved to pity by them. The little she had left of a woman's heart led her to speak. She wished to enjoy the sound of her own voice at that moment.

'Have you seen the la Mole ladies?' she asked him. 'They are in the third tier.' Julien immediately craned his head forward into the house, leaning somewhat rudely over the ledge of the box. He saw Mathilde; her eyes were bright with tears.

And yet, thought Julien, it isn't their day for the Opera. What eagerness!

Mathilde had persuaded her mother to come to the Opera, despite the unsuitable position of the box which a humble hanger-on of the family had eagerly offered them. She wished to see whether Julien would spend that evening with the Maréchale.

CHAPTER 31 : *'Make her Afraid'*

> So this is the wondrous miracle of your civili-
> zation! You have turned love into a mere
> humdrum affair.
>
> BARNAVE

JULIEN hurried off to Madame de la Mole's box, where the
first thing that met his eyes was the sight of Mathilde's, wet
with tears. She was weeping without restraint; there was no one
there but people of little importance, the friend who had lent the
box, and one or two men of her acquaintance. Mathilde laid her
hand on Julien's; she seemed to have forgotten all fear of her
mother. Almost choked by tears, she said nothing to him but the
one word : 'Guarantees !'

Whatever happens, I must not speak to her, thought Julien,
deeply moved himself, and covering his eyes with his hand as
though to shade them from the glare of the chandelier that shone
dazzlingly into the boxes on the third row. If I speak, she can no
longer doubt the depth of my emotion, the tone of my voice will
betray me, all may still be lost.

His inward struggles were far more painful than in the morning, his heart had had time to feel emotion. He was afraid of
giving Mathilde's vanity a chance to exult. Though dizzy with
love and passionate desire, he grimly forced himself not to speak
to her.

This is, to my mind, one of the finest traits in his character; a
human being capable of putting such constraint on himself may
go far, *si fata sinant.*

Mademoiselle de la Mole insisted upon taking Julien home with
them. Fortunately it was raining hard. But the Marquise made
him sit facing herself, talked to him without stopping, and
prevented his saying a word to her daughter. One would have
thought that the Marquise was taking thought for Julien's
happiness. No longer afraid of ruining everything by showing
overmuch emotion, he surrendered himself to it without restraint.

Dare I tell you that when he got back to his room Julien threw
himself on his knees and covered with kisses the love letters given
him by Prince Korasoff?

Oh marvellous man ! he cried in his frenzy. What do I not owe
to you?

By degrees he recovered a little self-possession. He compared himself to a general at the moment of winning the first half of a great battle. The advantage is a real, a tremendous one, he said to himself. But what is going to happen tomorrow? A single instant may ruin everything.

A passionate impulse moved him to open the *Mémoires* dictated by Napoleon at Saint Helena, and for two whole hours he forced himself to read them; his eyes alone were reading, but what did that matter, he forced himself to read. All the while he was so strangely occupied, his head and his heart, soaring to the plane of the very highest actions, were all unknown to him busy at work. This heart of hers is very unlike Madame de Rênal's, he said to himself, but his thoughts went no further.

Make her afraid, he cried all of a sudden, flinging his book right away. An enemy will only obey me in so far as I make him fear me, then he will not dare to despise me. He paced up and down his little room, wild with joy, though his happiness, in truth, was rather one of pride than of love.

Make her afraid! he repeated proudly to himself, and he had reason to be proud. Even in moments of greatest happiness, he thought, Madame de Rênal always doubted whether my love was equal to her own. Here, I have a demon to subdue, therefore subduing must be my task.

He knew quite well that next morning, by eight o'clock, Mathilde would be in the library. He did not appear there until nine, burning with love, but his head controlled his heart. Not a single minute went by, perhaps, without his repeating to himself: Keep her mind occupied all the time with this grave doubt: Does he love me? Her distinguished rank, and the flatteries of all those who speak to her, make her a *little too much* inclined to self-assurance.

He found her seated on the couch, pale and calm, but apparently incapable of making a single movement. She held out her hand to him. 'I've offended you, it's true, my dear. Are you possibly angry with me?'

Julien was not expecting so simple a tone. He was on the point of giving himself away.

'You wish for guarantees, my dear,' she went on after a silence she had hoped to see broken; 'that's only right. Elope with me, let's go off to London. I shall be ruined for ever, disgraced. . . .' She found courage enough to withdraw her hand from Julien's so as to cover her eyes with it. All feelings of modesty and womanly virtue had returned to her heart.... 'All right!' she said at length with a sigh, 'disgrace me. That is a guarantee.'

Yesterday I was happy, thought Julien, because I had the courage to be severe with myself. After a short moment's silence, he managed to control his heart enough to say in an icy tone: 'Once we are on the way to London, once you are disgraced, to use your own expression, who will answer for it that you will love me? That my presence in the post-chaise will not seem unwelcome to you? I'm not a heartless brute; to have ruined your reputation will seem to me only a further cause for grief. It's not your position in society that's the obstacle, but unfortunately your own character. Can you promise yourself that you will love me for a week?'

(Ah! let her love me for a week, a week only, Julien murmured to himself, and I shall die of joy. What do I care for the future, what do I care for life itself? And this divine happiness can begin at this very instant if I will, it depends entirely on me.)

Mathilde saw he was thinking deeply.

'Then I'm altogether unworthy of you,' she said, taking hold of his hand.

Julien embraced her, but at once the iron hand of duty gripped his heart. If she sees how much I adore her, I shall lose her, he thought. And, before he withdrew himself from her arms, he had resumed all the dignity that befits a man.

On that day and the days that followed it, he managed to conceal the intensity of his bliss. There were moments in which he denied himself even the pleasure of clasping her in his arms. At other times, a wild access of joy prevailed over counsels of prudence.

It was beside a bower of honeysuckle in the garden, arranged so as to hide the ladder, that he was once accustomed to take his place to gaze from afar at the shutters of Mathilde's window and lament her lack of constancy. Close by, there stood a very big oak, and the trunk of this tree prevented his being seen by prying eyes.

As he passed with Mathilde by this spot which recalled to him so vividly the intensity of his grief, the contrast between past despair and present bliss was too strong for a temperament like his. Tears came flooding into his eyes, and carrying his mistress's hand to his lips, he told her: 'Here I passed my life thinking of you; from here I gazed at that shutter, waiting for hours on end for the happy moment when I should see this hand push it open.'

He gave way completely. He painted for her, in those true colours which no one can invent, the depths of his despair at that time. Brief phrases interspersed here and there bore witness to this present happiness of his, which had put an end to that terrible pain.

Good God, what am I doing! thought Julien, suddenly recovering his wits. I'm ruining everything.

In his intense alarm, he thought he already saw less love in Mademoiselle de la Mole's eyes. This was an illusion; but Julien's expression suddenly changed and his whole face grew pale as death. His eyes for a moment lost their light, and a look of arrogance not devoid of malice quickly succeeded that of the most sincere and most wholehearted love.

'What is the matter with you, dearest?' Mathilde anxiously and tenderly inquired.

'I'm lying,' said Julien crossly, 'and I'm lying to you. I reproach myself for it, and yet God knows that I respect you sufficiently not to lie. You love me, you are devoted to me, and I have no need to make up fine speeches in order to please you.'

'Good heavens! Were they only fine speeches, all those enchanting things you've been saying to me for the last ten minutes?'

'And I reproach myself keenly for them, my dear. I made them up long ago for a woman who loved me and used to bore me. . . . That's the worst trait in my character. I denounce myself to you. Please forgive me.'

Bitter tears streamed down Mathilde's cheeks.

'Whenever,' continued Julien, 'a mere hint of something that's shocked me drives me into a fit of absent-mindedness for the moment, my accursed memory, which here and now I deplore, offers me something to fall back on, and I take a mean advantage of it.'

'So I've unconsciously happened to stumble on something that has displeased you?' said Mathilde with charming simplicity.

'I remember one day, as you passed by these honeysuckles, you plucked a sprig of their flowers. M. de Luz took it from you and you let him keep it. I was only a step or two away.'

'M. de Luz? But that's impossible,' replied Mathilde with the haughtiness that came so naturally to her. 'I don't do things like that.'

'I'm certain you did,' Julien retorted sharply.

'Well then, my dear, it must be true,' said Mathilde sadly

lowering her eyes. She was positive that for many months past she had not allowed M. de Luz to behave in any such way.

Julien gazed at her with inexpressible tenderness. No, he said to himself, she does not love me *any the less.*

That evening she took him laughingly to task for his liking for Madame de Fervaques — a commoner in love with a new-made lady of title ! 'Hearts of that species are perhaps the only ones my Julien cannot inflame. She's made a real dandy of you,' she said, toying with his hair.

During the period in which he believed himself to be scorned by Mathilde, Julien had become one of the best-dressed men in Paris. Yet he still had one advantage over other men of this type; once he had finished his dressing, he gave his clothes no further thought.

One thing vexed Mathilde. Julien still went on copying out the Russian letters and sending them to the Maréchale.

CHAPTER 32 : *The Tiger*

Alas! why these things and not others!
BEAUMARCHAIS

An English traveller relates how he lived on friendly terms with a tiger; he had reared it and would fondle it, but always kept a loaded pistol on his table.

Julien never abandoned himself utterly to his happiness except at moments when Mathilde could not read the expression in his eyes. He was exact in carrying out the duty of addressing a few harsh words to her from time to time.

When Mathilde's gentleness, which he remarked with amazement, and her absolute devotion to him came near to robbing him of all mastery over himself, he had the courage to leave her abruptly.

For the very first time Mathilde was in love. Life, which had always trailed along for her at a snail's pace, now took wings.

As her pride, however, had always to find some outlet, she sought to expose herself boldly to all the risks that her love could make her run. It was Julien who was cautious; and it was only when there was any question of danger that she did not yield to his will. Yet, while submissive and humble with him, she showed all the more arrogance towards anyone else in the house who came near, whether relations or servants.

In the drawing-room in the evening, with sixty people around, she would call Julien to her side and talk with him for a long time in private.

One day when little Tanbeau installed himself beside them, she begged him to go to the library and fetch her the volume of Smollett's works containing the Revolution of 1688. As he was hesitating: 'There is no need to hurry,' she added with a glance of insulting disdain which was like balm to Julien's heart.

'Did you see the little brute's expression?' he asked her.

'His uncle has put in ten or twelve years' service in this drawing-room, otherwise I'd have packed him off at once.'

Her behaviour towards MM. de Croisenois, de Luz, and the rest, although outwardly polite, was none the less provoking in reality. Mathilde reproached herself keenly for all the confidences she had made to Julien in the past, and all the more because she dared not confess to him that she had exaggerated the almost entirely innocent marks of interest she had shown these gentlemen.

In spite of her finest resolves, her woman's pride prevented her every day from saying to Julien : 'It was just because I was talking to you that I found pleasure in describing my weakness in not taking my hand away when M. Croisenois, as he laid his hand down on a marble table beside mine, happened to touch it lightly.'

Nowadays, hardly had one of these gentlemen been speaking to her for a moment or two, before she discovered she had a question to put to Julien, and this made a pretext for keeping him by her side.

She found that she was pregnant, and joyfully told Julien the news.

'Do you doubt me now? Isn't this a guarantee? Now I'm your wife for ever.'

This announcement struck Julien with deep amazement. He nearly forgot the principle that guided his behaviour. How can I be wilfully cold and insulting to this poor girl who is ruining herself for me? Did she look at all unwell, even on those days when the awe-inspiring voice of wisdom made itself heard, he could no longer find the heart to address to her a single one of those cruel remarks, so indispensable, in his experience, to the continuance of their love.

'I intend to write to my father,' Mathilde said to him one day. 'He is more than a father to me – he is a friend. And as such I should feel it unworthy of you and of myself to try to deceive him, even for a moment.'

'Good God ! what are you going to do?' said Julien in alarm.

'My duty,' she replied, her eyes gleaming with joy.

She felt she was showing a braver spirit than her lover.

'But he'll turn me out of the house in disgrace !'

'He's within his rights, we must respect them. I'll give you my arm, and we'll go out by the front door, in the full light of day.'

Julien in amazement begged her to put it off for a week. 'I can't,' was her answer. 'Honour calls, I know my duty. I must carry it out, and at once.'

'Well then, I order you to wait,' said Julien firmly. 'Your honour's safe, I'm your husband. This grave step is bound to alter both our positions. I am also within my rights. Today is Tuesday; next Tuesday is the day of the Duc de Retz's reception. In the evening, when M. de la Mole comes home, the porter shall hand him the fatal letter.... His only thought is of making you a Duchess, I know it for sure – think what his grief will be!'

'Do you mean – think of his vengeance?'

'I may feel pity for my benefactor, deep distress at the thought of injuring him. But I'm not afraid and never will be afraid of any man.'

Mathilde gave way. Since she had told Julien of her condition, this was the first time he had spoken to her with authority. Never had he loved her so dearly. The tender side of his nature glady seized on the pretext afforded by Mathilde's condition to excuse himself from addressing a few unkind remarks to her. He was greatly worried by the idea of a confession to M. de la Mole. Was he going to be parted from Mathilde? And however great her sorrow at seeing him go, would she, a month after his departure, be thinking of him still?

He felt an almost equal horror of the just reproaches the Marquis might address to him.

That evening he confessed to Mathilde this second cause for grief and then, carried away by love, admitted the other also.

Mathilde grew pale.

'Would six months spent away from me,' she said, 'really mean unhappiness to you?'

'Immense unhappiness, the only one in the world I view with terror.'

Mathilde was overjoyed. Julien had persevered so well in playing his part that he had succeeded in making her think that of the two she was the more in love.

The fatal Tuesday came round. At midnight, on returning home, the Marquis found a letter with instructions on the envelope to open it himself and only when there were no witnesses present.

Father [the letter ran],
Every social tie is broken between us, only natural ties remain. After my husband, you are and always will be the dearest person in the world to me. My eyes fill with tears, I think of the pain I am causing you, but for my shame not to be made public, and to give you time to think things over and to act, I have been unable to postpone any longer the confession that I owe you. If your affection for me, which I know to be very great, will consent to allow me a small annual allowance, I will go and settle anywhere you please, in Switzerland, for instance, with my husband. His

name is so obscure that no one will recognize your daughter in Madame Sorel, the daughter-in-law of a carpenter of Verrières. There is the name I have found it so hard to write. I dread, for Julien, your so evidently just anger. I shall not be a Duchess, Father; but I knew it when I fell in love with him; for I was the first to fall in love, it was I who seduced him. I inherit from you too high a spirit to let my attention dwell on what is or seems to me to be vulgar. It is all to no purpose that, in the intention of pleasing you, I have considered M. de Croisenois. Why did you place real merit under my eyes? You told me yourself on my return from Hyères: 'This young Sorel is the only man I find amusing.' The poor boy is, if possible, as greatly distressed as I am at the pain this letter will cause you. I cannot prevent your being angry with me as a father; but love me as a friend.

Julien respected me. If now and then he spoke to me, it was solely because of his deep gratitude to you; for the natural pride of his character leads him never to reply, except in his official capacity, to anyone above his station. He has a keen, innate sense of differences in social position. It was I myself, I blush to admit it to my best friend, and never will make such a confession to any other, it was I who one day in the garden clung tightly to his arm.

In twenty-four hours from now why should you feel vexed with him? My fault is irreparable. If you require it, I will be the one to hand on to you the assurances of his profound respect and of his despair at having displeased you. You need never set eyes on him; but I shall go and join him wherever he chooses. It is his right, it is my duty; he is the father of my child. If in your kindness you are pleased to allow us six thousand francs to live on, I shall accept them with gratitude. If not, Julien intends to settle at Besançon, where he will take up the profession of teacher of Latin and Literature. However low the position at which he starts, I am certain that he will rise higher. With him, I have no fear of obscurity. Should there be a Revolution, I am sure of a leading part for him. Could you say as much of any of those who have asked for my hand? They have fine estates? I cannot find in that single circumstance any reason for admiration. My Julien will attain to a high position even under the present régime – if he had a million francs and my father's protection. . . .

Mathilde, who knew the Marquis to be a man who acted entirely on first impulses, had written eight pages.

What should I do? Julien was asking himself while M. de la Mole was reading this letter. Where, first of all, lies my duty, and secondly my interest? What I owe him is tremendous. But for him I'd be some poor rogue of an underling, and not enough of a rogue not to be hated and persecuted by all the rest. He's made me a man of the world. My *necessary* acts of roguery will be firstly less frequent, and secondly, less mean. That's more than if he'd given me a million. I owe him this Cross and a semblance of diplomatic services which have raised me above my equals.

If he took up his pen to prescribe how I should behave, what would he write? ...

Julien was abruptly interrupted by M. de la Mole's old valet.

'The Marquis asks you to come at once, whether you are dressed or not.' As he walked beside Julien the valet added under his breath: 'His Lordship is mad with rage. You'd better be careful.'

> In cutting this diamond an unskilful diamond cutter has robbed it of some of its liveliest sparkle. In the Middle Ages, nay, even in Richelieu's day, a Frenchman had the *strength to will.*
>
> MIRABEAU

JULIEN found the Marquis in a furious rage. For the first time in his life, perhaps, this noble lord was guilty of bad form; he hurled at Julien all the insults that came to his lips. Our hero was astonished, inwardly fuming, but through it all his sense of gratitude remained unshaken. How many fine projects, long cherished in his inmost thoughts, he said to himself, does this poor man see crumbling to nothing in a moment? But I owe him an answer, my silence would increase his anger. The part of Tartuffe provided him with a reply.

'I am no angel. . . . I have served you well, you have paid me generously. . . . I did feel grateful, but I am only twenty-two. In this house, no one understood my mind, except yourself, and that lovable creature.'

'You miserable wretch!' cried the Marquis. 'Lovable! lovable! the day you found her lovable you ought to have fled.'

'I tried to; I asked you at the time if I might go to Languedoc.'

Tired of pacing furiously up and down, the Marquis, overcome with grief, flung himself into an armchair. Julien heard him murmur to himself: 'The fellow's not really a scoundrel.'

'No, I'm not one to you,' cried Julien, falling at his feet. But he felt extremely ashamed of this impulse and got up again very quickly.

The Marquis was really out of his mind. At the sight of this action he began once more to pour on Julien atrocious insults worthy of a cab-driver. The novelty of these oaths was possibly a distraction.

What! my daughter is to be called Madame Sorel! What! my daughter is not to be a Duchess! Every time these two ideas presented themselves to him in such sharp relief, M. de la Mole was in torment, and the reactions of his mind were no longer under control. Julien feared he would get a thrashing.

During lucid intervals, and as the Marquis began to get

accustomed to his misfortune, the reproaches he addressed to Julien became fairly reasonable.

'You ought to have gone away, sir,' he said. 'It was your duty to go.... You are the lowest of mankind....'

Julien went to the table and wrote:

For a long time my life has been insupportable, I am putting an end to it. I beg his Lordship the Marquis to accept, together with the expression of my boundless gratitude, my apologies for any embarrassment which my death in his house may cause.

'Will your Lordship deign to read over this paper.... Kill me,' said Julien, 'or have me killed by your valet. It is one o'clock in the morning, I am going to stroll in the garden near the wall at the far end.'

'Go to the devil!' the Marquis shouted after him as he was leaving the room.

I understand, thought Julien. He wouldn't be sorry to see me spare his valet the trouble of causing my death. All right, let him kill me, I'm offering him this satisfaction.... But, by Jove, I'm in love with life. I owe myself to my son.

This idea, which for the first time appeared thus clearly defined to his imagination, entirely occupied his thoughts after the first few minutes of walking had been taken up with a sense of his own danger.

This entirely fresh interest made a prudent man of him. I need advice, he thought, to help me in dealing with this fiery-tempered man. He can't see reason, he's capable of anything. Fouqué is too far off, besides he wouldn't understand the feelings of a heart like the Marquis's.

Count Altamira.... Can I be sure of eternal silence? My request for advice must not be a definite act, which might complicate the situation for me. Alas! there is no one left but that grim Father Pirard.... His mind is narrowed by Jansenism. Some rogue of a Jesuit would know more of the world, and be more what I want.... M. Pirard's quite capable of thrashing me, at the mere mention of my crime.

Tartuffe's ingenuity came to Julien's aid. Very well, he said. I'll go and confess to him. Such was the final decision he came to in the garden, after walking about there for two whole hours. He no longer thought that he might be surprised by a gunshot; he was nearly dropping with sleep.

Next morning, very early indeed, Julien was several leagues

from Paris, knocking at the austere Jansenist's door. He found, to his great astonishment, that Father Pirard was not unduly surprised by his confidences.

'I ought perhaps to blame myself a little,' said Father Pirard with more uneasiness than anger. 'I had thought that I guessed this love affair. My friendship for you, you little wretch, prevented me from warning her father....'

'What is he going to do?' said Julien eagerly.

(He felt an affection for the abbé at that moment, and a quarrel with him would have been most painful.)

'I can see three courses of action,' said Julien. 'In the first place, M. de la Mole can have me killed.' And he told the abbé of the letter announcing his suicide which he had left with the Marquis. 'Secondly, he can have me shot down by Count Norbert, who will challenge me to a duel.'

'Would you accept?' said the abbé, getting to his feet in a fury.

'You're not letting me finish. I'd certainly never fire on the son of my benefactor.

'Thirdly, he can send me away. If he says to me: "Go to Edinburgh, go to New York," I shall obey. Then they can conceal Mademoiselle de la Mole's condition; but I'll never allow them to do away with my child.'

'That, you need not doubt, will be the first thought of that corrupt man.'

In Paris, Mathilde was in despair. She had seen her father about seven o'clock. He had shown her Julien's letter, she was trembling lest he should have thought it a noble thing to put an end to his life. And without my permission! she said to herself with a grief that was partly anger.

'If he's dead, then I'll die too,' she said to her father. 'And it's you who'll be the cause of his death.... Possibly you'll rejoice at it.... But I swear to his departed spirit that I'll put on mourning at once, and be publicly known as his widow, Madame Sorel. I'll send out funeral cards, you may count on that. ... You won't find me either faint-hearted or a coward.'

Love drove her to a frenzy. In his turn, M. de la Mole was left speechless.

He began to take a somewhat reasonable view of what had happened. Mathilde did not appear at lunch. The Marquis felt an immense weight lifted off his mind, and was particularly flattered on discovering that she had said nothing to her mother.

About midday Julien returned; the courtyard rang with the

clatter of his horse's hoofs. He dismounted. Mathilde sent for him and flung herself into his arms almost under the eyes of her maid. Julien was not very grateful for these transports, he had come from his long conference with Father Pirard in a diplomatic and very calculating frame of mind. Reckoning up possibilities had somewhat dulled his imagination. Mathilde, with tears in her eyes, informed him that she had read the letter in which he spoke of suicide.

'My father may change his mind; if you want to please me, set off at once for Villequier. Mount your horse and leave the Hôtel before they get up from table.'

As Julien's air of frigid astonishment remained unchanged, she burst into a flood of tears.

'Let me look after our affairs,' she cried excitedly, clasping him in her arms. 'You know very well that I don't part from you of my own free will. Write to me under cover to my maid, and see that the address is in a strange hand. As for me, I shall write you volumes. Good-bye. And now be off.'

Her last words wounded Julien, but he obeyed. It's fated, he thought, that even in their best moments, these people find out how to offend me.

Mathilde set herself firmly against all her father's *prudent* plans. She obstinately refused to negotiate on any other basis than this : She would become Madame Sorel, and either live in poverty with her husband in Switzerland, or with her father in Paris. She thrust aside the suggestion of a secret confinement.... 'That would open the way to possibilities of slander and disgrace. Two months after our marriage I shall travel abroad with my husband and it will be easy for us to pretend that my child was born at a suitable date.'

Received at first with outbursts of rage, this firmness ended by making the Marquis feel uncertain.

In one of his softer moods he said to his daughter : 'Look, here's a certificate for shares bringing in ten thousand livres a year. Send it off to your Julien, and see that he very quickly makes it impossible for me to take it back.'

In *obedience* to Mathilde, whose love of giving orders he knew well, Julien had made an unnecessary journey of forty leagues. He was at Villequier, looking into the farmers' accounts; the Marquis's gift occasioned his return. He went to seek shelter with Father Pirard, who, during his absence, had become Mathilde's most useful ally. Every time the Marquis questioned him, he proved that any other course than a public marriage would be a sin in the sight of God.

'And fortunately,' the abbé added, 'the wisdom of this world is here in accordance with religion. Could you rely for a single instant on Mademoiselle de la Mole, with her impetuous nature, to keep a secret she had not imposed on herself? If you do not allow the straightforward course of a public marriage, society will busy itself for very much longer about this curious misalliance. Everything must be said straightway, without the least mystery, real or apparent.'

'That is true,' the Marquis reflected gravely. 'By such a method, any talk of the marriage after a lapse of three days will be merely the gossip of idle minds. We must take advantage of some important measure against the Jacobins to slip through unnoticed in its train.'

Two or three of M. de la Mole's friends were of Father Pirard's opinion. The great obstacle in their eyes was Mathilde's determined character. But in spite of all such fine arguments, the Marquis could not accustom his mind to giving up all hope of a *Duchess's stool* for his daughter.

His memory and his imagination were filled with all sorts of tricks and deceptions which had still been possible when he was young. Yielding to necessity, going in fear of the law, seemed to him a thing both absurd and dishonouring for a man of his rank. He was paying dearly now for those enchanting dreams concerning his daughter's future in which he had been indulging for the past ten years.

Who could have foreseen it? he said to himself. A girl of such a haughty character, such high intelligence, prouder than myself of the name she bears! One whose hand had been asked of me, long before she was old enough to marry, by all the most illustrious names in France!

All thoughts of prudence must be abandoned. This age is destined to bring everything to nought! We are marching towards chaos.

> The Prefect as he rode along was saying to
> himself: Why should not I become a Minister,
> the President of the Privy Council, or a Duke?
> This is how I would make war. ... By this
> means I would bind all innovators in chains.
>
> *The Globe*

No argument avails to destroy the empire of ten years of pleasant day-dreams over the mind. The Marquis thought it unreasonable to be angry, but he could not bring himself to forgive. If that fellow Julien could only die by accident, he would sometimes say to himself. ... In this way his downcast imagination found some solace in pursuing the absurdest fantasies, which nullified the influence of Father Pirard's sage advice. Thus a month passed by without the slightest advance in the negotiations.

In this family affair, as in matters political, the Marquis had sudden bright ideas over which he waxed enthusiastic for the space of three days. During that time no plan of conduct would please him on account of its being supported by sound arguments, but such arguments found favour in his sight only for the measure of support they gave to his pet scheme. For three whole days he would labour with all the fiery enthusiasm of a poet to bring matters to a certain pitch; on the fourth, he no longer gave it a thought.

Julien was at first bewildered by the Marquis's dilatory methods; but after some weeks, he began to surmise that M. de la Mole, in dealing with this affair, had no settled plan of action.

Madame de la Mole and the rest of the household believed that Julien was travelling in the provinces to see to the administration of the estates; actually, he was in hiding in Father Pirard's house, and saw Mathilde almost every day. As for her, she went to spend an hour each morning with her father, but sometimes they went for weeks on end without mentioning the matter that occupied all their thoughts.

'I don't want to know where that man is,' the Marquis said to her one day, 'just send him this letter.'

Mathilde looked at it and saw:

My estates in Languedoc bring in 20,600 francs. I give 10,600 to my daughter, and 10,000 to M. Julien Sorel. I am handing over the property itself, that goes without saying. Tell the notary to draft two separate deeds of gift and bring them to me tomorrow; after which, no further relations between us. Ah! sir, ought I to have expected anything like this?

The Marquis de la Mole

'Thank you very much,' said Mathilde gaily. 'We'll go and settle in the Château d'Aiguillon, between Agen and Marmande. They say the country there is as beautiful as in Italy.'

This gift came as a great surprise to Julien. He was no longer the severe, cold man we knew. The destiny of his child absorbed all his thoughts in advance. This unexpected fortune, a fairly considerable one for so poor a man, made him ambitious. He saw himself, with what he and his wife would have, with an income of 36,000 francs. As for Mathilde, all her feelings were absorbed in adoration of her husband, for such was the name her pride always gave to Julien. Her great, her sole ambition was to have her marriage recognized. She spent her whole time in exaggerating the extreme discretion she had shown in linking her destiny with that of a man of superior quality. Personal merit was very much to the fore in her mind.

This almost continual separation, the numberless matters of business, the little time they had for talking of love, combined to complete the good effect of the sensible policy Julien had devised some time before. In the end Mathilde began to grow impatient at seeing so little of the man she had now really come to love.

In a momentary fit of temper she wrote to her father, beginning her letter like Othello:

That I have preferred Julien to the pleasures society offered to the daughter of the Marquis de la Mole, is sufficiently proved by my choice. These pleasures of social prestige and petty vanity mean nothing to me. Soon it will be six weeks that I have been living apart from my husband. Before next Thursday, I shall leave my father's house. Your kind gifts have made us rich. No one except the estimable Father Pirard knows my secret. I shall go to him; he will marry us, and an hour after the ceremony we shall be on our way to Languedoc, and never appear again in Paris save by your orders. But what grieves me to the heart is that all this will provide a savoury bit of gossip at my expense and

*yours. May not the pointed remarks of a foolish public oblige our
excellent Norbert to pick a quarrel with Julien? In such an event,
I know him, I should have no power to control him. We should
find in his heart something of plebeian up in arms. On my knees,
dearest father, I implore you, come and attend our wedding in
M. Pirard's church, next Thursday. The point of any malicious
tale will be blunted, and the life of your only son, the life of my
husband made safe, etc. etc.*

The Marquis found himself peculiarly embarrassed by this
letter. He had now at last to *make up his mind*. All his little
accustomed ways of thought, all the opinions of coarse-minded
friends ceased to have any weight with him.

In these strange circumstances, the most strongly marked
features of his character, imprinted there by incidents of his
youth, regained full control of his mind. Unhappy experiences
of life as an *emigré* had made him a man of imagination. After
enjoying for two years an immense fortune and the highest
honours at court, he had been thrust forth in 1793 into the midst
of the frightful miseries of the Emigration. This hard school had
wrought changes in a twenty-two-year-old heart. In reality he
was encamped amid his present wealth rather than dominated
by it. But this same imagination which had saved his soul from
the deadly canker of gold had made him the helpless victim of a
mad desire to see his daughter honoured with a high-sounding
title.

During the six weeks just past, the Marquis, impelled at one
moment by caprice, had decided to make Julien rich. Poverty
seemed to him ignoble, dishonouring to himself, M. de la Mole,
impossible for the husband of his daughter; he scattered his money
freely. Next day, his imagination pursuing another course, it
seemed to him that Julien would understand the dumb language
of this bestowal of money, change his name, go off to exile in
America, and write to tell Mathilde he was dead to her. M. de la
Mole took this letter for granted, and went on to consider its effect
on his daughter's character. . . .

On the day on which he was roused out of such youthful
dreams by Mathilde's *real* letter, after having pondered for a long
time over the idea of killing Julien, he was dreaming of building up
a brilliant career for him. He was making him take the name of
one of his estates; and why should he not get his own peerage
passed down to him? His father-in-law, the Duc de Chaulnes,

had several times, since his only son had been killed in Spain, spoken to him of his desire to hand on his title to Norbert. . . .

It cannot be denied, the Marquis said to himself, that Julien shows a singular aptitude for business, a daring spirit, even *brilliance* perhaps. . . . But deep down in his character, I find something alarming. That is the impression he produces on everyone, so there must be something real in it. (The more difficult this reality was to grasp, the more it alarmed the old Marquis's imaginative mind.)

My daughter expressed it to me very aptly the other day (in a letter that has been suppressed): 'Julien doesn't belong to any drawing-room or any particular set.' He has not provided himself with any backing against me, not the least resource if I throw him over. . . . But does that imply ignorance of the present state of society? . . . Two or three times I have told him: 'There is no real advantage in applying for membership of any society but that of the drawing-rooms. . . .'

No, his particular genius is not that of the cunning, pettifogging lawyer who never loses a minute nor an opportunity. . . . It is nothing like a temperament after the style of Louis XI. On the other hand, I find his mind full of the most ungenerous maxims. I'm completely baffled. . . . Can it be that he repeats those maxims to himself to serve as a *dam* against his own passions?

Anyhow, one thing is plain as daylight: he cannot abide contempt. That gives me some hold over him.

He does not worship high birth, it is true; he has no instinctive respect for us. . . . That's a fault; but, after all, the heart of a seminarist should be out of patience only with a lack of pleasures and of money. He himself, a very different type of man, cannot put up with contempt at any price.

Urged on by his daughter's letter, M. de la Mole realized the necessity of making up his mind. Here, in short, is the great question: has Julien's impudence gone so far as to put him on to making love to my daughter, because he knows that I love her more than anything in the world, and that I have an income of a hundred thousand crowns?

Mathilde protests the opposite. . . . No, Master Julien, this is a point on which I desire to be under no illusion.

Has this been a case of instantaneous, heartfelt love? Or rather a vulgar desire of raising oneself to a high position? Mathilde is sharp as a needle, she realized from the first that any suspicion of this kind might ruin him with me. Hence her admission that she was the first to make up her mind to love. ...

Imagine a girl of so lofty a character so far forgetting herself as to stoop to physical advances ! ... To cling to his arm in the garden, one evening, how frightful ! As if she had not a hundred less indelicate ways of letting him know of her regard. *Who makes excuses, accuses himself.* I don't trust Mathilde. ...

That day, the Marquis's deliberations were more conclusive than usual. All the same, habit prevailed; he resolved to gain time by writing to his daughter; for letters were passing between them from one part of the house to the other. M. de la Mole did not dare to stand up to Mathilde in a discussion. He was afraid of bringing the whole matter to an end by sudden concession.

Take care [he wrote] *of committing any fresh act of folly. Here is a commission as Lieutenant of Hussars for M. le Chevalier Julien Sorel de la Vernaye. You see what I am doing for him. Do not oppose my wishes, nor question me. See that he sets off within twenty-four hours to report himself at Strasbourg where his regiment is stationed. Here is a draft on my bankers; see that I am obeyed.*

Mathilde's love and joy knew no bounds. Wishing to take advantage of her victory, she replied at once :

M. de la Vernaye would be at your feet, overwhelmed with gratitude, if he knew all that you are condescending to do for him. But, in the midst of this generosity, my father has forgotten me. Your daughter's honour is endangered. A single indiscretion may leave an everlasting stain, which an income of twenty thousand crowns would not efface. I will not send this commission to M. de la Vernaye unless you give me your word that in the course of the next month, my marriage shall be celebrated in public, at Villequier. Shortly after this period, which I implore you not to exceed, your daughter will be unable to appear in public except under the name of Madame de la Vernaye. Let me thank you, dear papa, for having saved me from the name of Sorel, etc. etc.

The reply was unexpected.

Obey me, or I take everything back. Tremble, rash girl. I do not yet know what sort of man your Julien is, and you yourself know even less than I do. Let him start for Strasbourg and be careful to

*behave himself. I will let you know my wishes in a fortnight's
time.*

This very firm reply astonished Mathilde. The words, *I do not
know Julien* plunged her into a day-dream, which quickly ended
in the most enchanting suppositions; but she believed them to be
the truth. My Julien's mind does not wear the shoddy little
uniform of the drawing-rooms, and my father disbelieves in his
superiority precisely on account of the fact that proves it. . . .

All the same, if I don't obey this characteristic whim of his, I
see the possibility of a public scene; a scandal would lower my
standing in society, and might make me less attractive in Julien's
eyes. After the scandal . . . ten years of poverty; and the folly of
choosing a husband for his merits alone can only be saved from
ridicule by the most dazzling wealth. If I live at a distance from
my father, at his age, he may forget me. . . . Norbert will marry
some attractive, cunning woman; Louis XIV in his old age was
bewitched by the Duchesse de Bourgogne. . . .

She decided to obey, but was careful not to let Julien know
the contents of her father's letter; his intractable character might
have led him to commit some act of folly.

That evening, when she told Julien that he was a Lieutenant
of Hussars, his joy was unbounded. It can be imagined from what
one knows of his lifelong ambition, and from the passionate love
he now felt for his child. He was struck with astonishment at
the change of name.

At last, he said to himself, my romantic story reaches its conclusion, and the credit is in the end all mine. I have managed to
win the love of this monstrously proud creature, he said, looking
at Mathilde. Her father cannot live without her, nor she without
me.

CHAPTER 35 : A Storm

O God, grant me mediocrity !

MIRABEAU

His mind was absorbed in thought; he made only a half-hearted response to her eager expression of affection. He remained silent and moody. Never had he appeared so great, so adorable in Mathilde's eyes. She dreaded some subtle working of his pride which would come to upset the whole position.

Almost every morning, she had seen Father Pirard arriving at the house. Might not Julien with his help have fathomed something of her father's intentions? Might not the Marquis, moved by some momentary whim, have written to Julien? After such great good fortune, how explain Julien's air of severity? She did not dare to question him.

She *did not dare!* She, Mathilde! There was, from that moment, in her feeling for Julien, something vague, inexplicable, almost bordering on terror. That hard heart felt all the passion that is possible in one brought up amid the superabundance of civilization Paris admires.

Early next morning Julien was at Father Pirard's presbytery. A pair of post horses arrived in the courtyard drawing a dilapidated chaise, hired from the neighbouring post.

'Such a conveyance is no longer in keeping,' the stern abbé told him gruffly. 'Here are twenty thousand francs M. de la Mole sends you as a present; he expects you to spend them within the year, taking care, however, to make yourself as little ridiculous as possible.' (In so large a sum, lavished on a young man, the priest saw nothing but an occasion of sin.)

'The Marquis adds: "M. Julien de la Vernaye will have received this money from his father, whom there is no need to describe more fully. M. de la Vernaye may possibly think it proper to make some present to M. Sorel, a carpenter of Verrières, who took care of him in his childhood." ... I can undertake this part of the commission,' the abbé went on. 'I have at last made M. de la Mole make up his mind to come to terms with that M. de Frilair, who is such a Jesuit. His influence is decidedly too strong for us. The tacit recognition of your noble birth by that man who rules in Besançon will be one of the conditions implied in the agreement.'

Julien could no longer control his excitement; he embraced the abbé, he saw himself recognized.

'What are you thinking of?' said the abbé, thrusting him away. 'What is the meaning of this worldly vanity? As for Sorel and his sons, I shall offer them, in my name, an annual allowance of five hundred francs, to be paid to each of them separately, so long as I am satisfied with them.'

Julien had already become cold and distant. He thanked the abbé, but in the vaguest terms, and without binding himself to anything. Can it indeed be possible that I am the natural son of some great noble exiled among our mountains by that terrible Napoleon? Every moment this idea seemed to him less improbable. ... My hatred for my father would be a proof. ... I should no longer be a monster !

A few days after this monologue, the Fifteenth Regiment of Hussars, one of the most distinguished in the army, was drawn up in battle-formation on the parade ground in Strasbourg. The Chevalier de la Vernaye was mounted on the finest horse in Alsace, which had cost him six thousand francs. He had joined as Lieutenant, without having ever been a Second Lieutenant, save on the muster-roll of a regiment of which he had never heard.

His impassive air, his severe and almost cruel eyes, his pallor, his unalterable self-possession had begun to win a reputation for him from the very first. In a short time, his perfect, unassuming politeness, his skill with the pistol and his swordsmanship, which he made known without undue affectation, banished all idea of joking audibly at his expense. After wavering for five or six days, the general opinion of the Regiment declared itself in his favour. 'This young man,' said the older officers who were given to chaffing, 'has everything except youth.'

From Strasbourg, Julien wrote to M. Chélan, the former curé of Verrières, who was now approaching the farthest limits of old age:

You will have learnt, with a joy of which I have no doubt, of the events that have led my family to make me rich. Here are five hundred francs which I beg you to distribute quietly, and without mentioning my name, to those unhappy souls who are poor as once I was myself, and whom, without doubt, you are helping as once you helped me.

Julien was intoxicated with ambition and not with vanity; all the same he gave a great deal of attention to his outward appearance. His horses, his uniforms, the liveries of his servants were all maintained with a nicety that would have done honour to the punctiliousness of a great English noble. Though only just a Lieutenant, promoted by favour and of two days' standing, he was already beginning to reckon that in order to be, like all the great Generals, Commander-in-Chief at thirty at the latest, he would need to be at twenty-three something more than a mere Lieutenant. He could think of nothing but of glory and of his son.

It was in the midst of transports of the most unbridled ambition that he was surprised by a young footman from the Hôtel de la Mole, who arrived with a letter.

All is lost [wrote Mathilde]. *Hasten here as quickly as possible, sacrifice everything, if need be, desert. As soon as you arrive, wait for me in a cab, near the little door into the garden, just by No. — rue —. I will come out to speak to you. I may perhaps be able to let you into the garden. All is lost, and, I fear irretrievably. Count on me, you will find me loyal and steadfast in adversity. I love you.*

Within a few minutes, Julien obtained leave from his Colonel and rode full speed out of Strasbourg; but the frightful anxiety which consumed him did not permit him to continue this mode of travel farther tnan Metz. He jumped into a post-chaise and with almost incredible rapidity arrived at the appointed place outside the little door of the garden of the Hôtel de la Mole. This door opened, and in a moment Mathilde, forgetting all respect for public opinion, rushed into his arms. Fortunately, it was only five o'clock in the morning and the street was still deserted.

'All is lost! My father, dreading my tears, went away on Thursday night. Where to? No one knows. Here is his letter; read it.' And she got into the cab with Julien.

I could forgive everything [the letter ran] *except the plan of seducing you because you are rich. That, unhappy girl, is the frightful truth. I give you my word of honour that I will never consent to a marriage with that man. I promise him an income of ten thousand francs if he will consent to live abroad, beyond the French frontier, or better still in America. Read the letter which I have received in reply to information I asked for. The shameless fellow had even urged me himself to write to Madame de Rênal. I will never read a single line from you about this man.*

I have a horror both of Paris and of you. I urge you to keep the strictest secrecy about what must shortly happen. Give up this vile fellow freely and frankly, and you will regain a father.

'Where is Madame de Rênal's letter?' asked Julien coldly.
'Here it is. I didn't want to show it to you until I had broken the news.'
The letter ran as follows:

What I owe to the sacred cause of religion and morality obliges me, Sir, to the painful step which I take in approaching you. An infallible principle commands me at this moment to do ill to my neighbour, but in order to prevent a more shameful offence. The sorrow I feel must be overborne by a sense of duty. It is only too true, Sir, that the conduct of the person with regard to whom you ask me to tell the whole truth may have seemed hard to explain or even admitted of honourable explanation. I might have thought it fitting to conceal or to disguise a part of the truth, discretion called for this as well as religion. But that conduct, about which you desire to know, has been in fact extremely reprehensible, and more so than I can say. Poor, grasping creature, it was with the help of the most consummate hypocrisy, and by seducing a weak and unhappy woman, that he sought to make a position for himself and to become somebody. It is part of my painful duty to add that I believe that M. J— has no religious principles. I am bound in conscience to believe that one of his methods of success in a household is to seek to seduce the woman who has most influence there. Under cover of a show of disinterestedness and by making use of phrases from novels, his great and only object is to arrive at securing control over the master of the house and his fortune. He leaves behind him unhappiness and everlasting regret, etc., etc., etc.

This letter, extremely long and half effaced by tears, was certainly in Madame de Rênal's hand; it was even written with greater care than usual.
'I cannot blame M. de la Mole,' said Julien when he had finished reading it. 'He is right and wise. What father would want to give his dearly loved daughter to such a man! Good-bye!'
Julien jumped out of the cab and ran to his post-chaise which had drawn up at the end of the street. Mathilde, whom he seemed to have forgotten, made a few steps forward as if to follow him; but the stares of the tradesmen who were coming to peer out of

the doors of their shops, and to whom she was known, forced her to retreat in haste into the garden.

Julien had set off for Verrières. On this rapid journey he was unable to write to Mathilde as he had intended; his hand made nothing but illegible scrawls on the paper.

He arrived at Verrières on a Sunday morning. He went into the local gunsmith's shop, where he was overwhelmed with congratulation on his recent fortune. It was the talk of the district.

Julien found much difficulty in making him understand that he wanted a brace of pocket-pistols. At his request, the gunsmith loaded them.

The *three bells* were just sounding; this is a signal well known in French villages, which, after the various peals of the morning, announces that Mass is about to begin.

Julien entered the newly built church of Verrières. All the tall windows of the building were veiled with crimson curtains. He found himself standing a few feet behind Madame de Rênal's pew. It seemed to him that she was praying fervently. The sight of this woman who had loved him so dearly made Julien's arm tremble in such a way that he could not at first carry out his design. I can't do it, he said to himself, I'm physically incapable of it.

At that moment, the young clerk who was serving at Mass rang the bell for the Elevation of the Host. Madame de Rênal bowed her head, which for an instant was almost entirely hidden by the folds of her shawl. Julien was no longer able to see her so plainly. He fired a shot at her with one pistol and missed her. He fired a second shot; she fell.

> Do not look for any weakness on my part. I
> have avenged myself. I have deserved death
> and here I am. Pray for my soul.
>
> SCHILLER

JULIEN stood there motionless, deprived of sight. When he
came to himself a little, he noticed all the congregation rushing out of the church; the priest had left the altar. Julien began
to walk at a fairly slow pace in the wake of some women who
were screaming as they went out. One woman, who was trying
to escape more quickly than the rest, gave him a violent push; he
fell down. His feet were entangled in a chair overturned by the
crowd; as he got up again, he felt a tight grip on his neck, it was
a gendarme in full uniform who was arresting him. Mechanically
Julien tried to get hold of his pocket-pistols, but a second gendarme
seized him by the arms.

He was led off to prison. They took him into a room; they
handcuffed him, and left him by himself; the door was shut on
him with a double turn of the key. All this was carried out very
quickly, and he was unconscious of it.

Yes, indeed, all is over, he said to himself on recovering his
senses. Yes, it's the guillotine in a fortnight ... unless I kill myself
in the meantime.

His reasoning went no further. His head felt as if it had been
violently squeezed. He looked round to see if anyone had hold
of it. After a few moments, he fell sound asleep.

Madame de Rênal was not mortally wounded. The first bullet
had passed through her hat; as she turned round the second shot
had been fired. This bullet had struck her on the shoulder, and
by some surprising chance, had been deflected by the shoulder-
blade, which all the same it shattered, on to a gothic pillar, from
which it broke off an enormous splinter of stone.

When, after a long and painful dressing, the surgeon, a grave
sort of man, said to Madame de Rênal : 'I answer for your life as
for my own,' she was deeply distressed.

For a good while past she had sincerely longed for death. The
letter, which her confessor for the time being had ordered her to
write, and which she had written to M. de la Mole, had dealt the
finishing stroke to this creature weakened by too long continued

grief. This grief came from Julien's absence; she herself called it *remorse*. Her spiritual director, a virtuous and fervently religious young cleric, newly come from Dijon, was under no misapprehension.

To die thus, but not by my own hand, is not a sin, thought Madame de Rênal. God will pardon me, perhaps, for rejoicing in my death. She did not dare to add: And to die by Julien's hand, that is the very height of bliss.

She was hardly rid of the surgeon's presence and of all the friends who had flocked to see her, when she sent for her maid Elisa.

'The gaoler,' she said to her, blushing deeply, 'is a cruel man. He will no doubt treat him harshly, thinking by that to do something that will please me. ... I cannot bear that idea. Couldn't you go yourself, as if on your own, and hand the gaoler this little packet containing a few louis? You will tell him that religion does not permit his ill-treating him. ... But he must be particularly careful not to go and talk about this gift of money.'

It was to this circumstance which we have just mentioned that Julien was indebted for the gaoler's humane behaviour. This gaoler was that M. Noiroud, the perfect government official, who, as we have seen, was so finely frightened by M. Appert's visit.

A magistrate made his appearance at the prison. 'I am guilty of premeditated murder,' Julien said to him. 'I bought the pistols and had them loaded by so-and-so, the gunsmith. Article 1342 of the Penal Code is quite clear, I deserve death, and I expect it.' The magistrate, astonished at this manner of answering, tried to multiply his questions in such a way that the accused might contradict himself in his replies.

'But don't you see,' said Julien, smiling, 'that I am making myself out as guilty as you could wish? Come now, sir, you won't fail to get the prey you're after. You shall have the pleasure of passing sentence on me. Pray spare me your presence.'

I have still one tiresome duty to perform, thought Julien. I must write to Mademoiselle de la Mole.

I have taken my revenge [he told her]. *Unfortunately my name will appear in the papers, and I cannot escape from this world incognito. I shall die within two months. My revenge has been terrible, so too is the grief of being parted from you. From this moment, I forbid myself either to write or to utter your name.*

*Never speak of me, not even to my son; silence is the only way
of honouring my memory. To the ordinary run of men I shall be
a common murderer. . . . At this supreme moment you must allow
me to tell you the truth — you will forget me. This great catastrophe, concerning which I recommend you never to open your
lips to any living soul, will for several years to come have exhausted all those romantic and too adventurous tendencies I saw
in your nature. You were made to live with the heroes of the
Middle Ages; show their firmness of character. Let what must
happen, happen in secret, and without compromising you. You
will take an assumed name and confide in no one. If you absolutely must have some friend to help you, I bequeath you Father
Pirard.*

*Don't speak to anyone else, especially not to men of your own
class, such as Luz or Caylus.*

*A year after my death, marry M. de Croisenois; I command it as
your husband. Don't write to me, I shouldn't answer. Although
far less of a villain than Iago, or so it seems to me, I will say as he
did: 'From this time forth I never will speak word.'*

*No one shall see me either speak or write. You will have had my
last words as also my last adoring thoughts.*

                                                            J. S.

It was after sending off this letter that Julien, having slightly
recovered his senses, felt for the first time very unhappy. One
after the other, all the hopes ambition had planted had to be
rooted up out of his heart by the fatal words: 'I am to die.'
Death, in itself, did not seem *horrible* in his eyes. His whole life
had been nothing but a long preparation for misfortune, and he
had been careful not to overlook that event which is considered
the greatest misfortune of all.

Good heavens! he said to himself, why, if in sixty days from
now I had to fight a duel with a man who was an exceedingly
skilful fencer, should I be so weak as to think of it day and night,
and with terror in my heart?

He spent over an hour endeavouring to find out exactly where
he stood from this point of view.

When he had seen clearly what was in his heart, and the truth
appeared as plainly before his eyes as one of the pillars of his
prison, he began to think of remorse.

Why should I feel any? I have been injured in the most
frightful way; I have taken life, I deserve to die, but that is all.

I die after having settled my accounts with mankind. I leave behind me no obligation unfulfilled, I owe no man anything; there is nothing shameful in my death but the instrument of it. That alone, it is true, richly suffices to shame me in the eyes of the townsfolk of Verrières; but, from an intellectual point of view, what opinion could be more contemptible? I've one way left of making myself important in their eyes : that's by scattering gold among the crowd as I go to my doom. The memory of me, linked with the thought of gold, will be a bright and splendid one for them.

After this argument, which at the end of a minute seemed to him self-evident, Julien said to himself; I've nothing more to do on this earth. Whereupon he fell sound asleep.

Towards nine o'clock in the evening, the gaoler woke him up by bringing in his supper.

'What are they saying in Verrières?'

'M. Julien, the oath I took before the Crucifix, in the King's court, on the day I was installed in my post, obliges me to hold my tongue.'

He said nothing more, but still lingered. The spectacle of this vulgar hypocrisy amused Julien. I must keep him waiting a long time, he thought, for the five francs he wants as the price of his conscience.

When the gaoler saw the meal coming to an end without any attempt at bribery, he said in a smooth, deceitful way : 'The friendship I feel for you, M. Julien, obliges me to speak, although people may say it's against the interests of justice, since it might help you in drawing up your defence. ... M. Julien, who is a kind young gentleman, will be glad if I tell him that Madame de Rênal is getting better.'

'What! she's not dead?' cried Julien, beside himself with amazement.

'What! You didn't know anything about it?' said the gaoler with an air of stupidity which quickly changed to one of joyful greed. 'It would be very proper of your Honour to give something to the surgeon who, according to law and justice, should say nothing. But to please your Honour I went to his house, and he told me everything. ...'

'In short, it's not a fatal injury,' said Julien, losing patience. 'You answer for that with your life?'

The gaoler, a gigantic fellow six foot tall, took fright and drew back towards the door. Julien saw he was going the wrong way to arrive at the truth; he sat down again and tossed a napoleon to M. Noiroud.

As the man's story began to prove to Julien that Madame de Rênal's wound was not mortal, he felt himself overcome by tears. 'Get out!' he said abruptly.

The gaoler obeyed. No sooner was the door shut than Julien cried, Good God! she is not dead! And sinking to his knees, he wept hot tears.

In this supreme moment he believed in God. What matter the hypocrisies of the priests? Can they detract in any way from the truth and sublime majesty of God?

Only then did Julien begin to repent of the crime he had committed. By a coincidence that saved him from despair, at that instant only was he delivered from the state of physical irritation and semi-insanity in which he had been plunged since leaving Paris for Verrières.

His tears sprang from a generous source, he had no doubt as to the sentence that was in store for him.

And so she will live! he said to himself. ... She will live to pardon me and to love me. ...

Very late the next morning the gaoler woke him. 'You must have a marvellously stout heart, M. Julien,' the man said to him. 'Here's twice I've come in and didn't feel inclined to wake you. Here are two bottles of excellent wine which M. Maslon, our curé, sends you.'

'What! is that rascal still here?' said Julien.

'Yes, sir,' replied the gaoler, lowering his voice. 'But don't talk so loud, it might do you harm.'

Julien laughed heartily.

'At the point I have reached, my good man, you alone could harm me by ceasing to be gentle and humane. ... You shall be well paid,' said Julien, stopping short and resuming his imperious manner, a procedure which he justified immediately by the gift of a small coin.

M. Noiroud told him once more, and in the fullest detail, all he had heard about Madame de Rênal, but he did not mention Mademoiselle Elisa's visit.

The man was as servile and compliant as it is possible to be. An idea crossed Julien's mind : This sort of misshapen giant may possibly earn three or four hundred francs, for his prison is hardly crowded. I can guarantee him ten thousand if he will agree to escape to Switzerland with me. The difficulty will be to persuade

him of my good faith. The idea of the long discussion he would
have to hold with so vile a creature filled Julien with disgust, and
he fell to thinking of other things.

That evening, there was no longer time. A post-chaise came to
fetch him at midnight. He was very well pleased with the gendarmes who were his travelling companions. In the morning,
when he arrived at the prison of Besançon, they were good enough
to give him lodging on the upper floor of a gothic keep. He
guessed the architecture to date from the beginning of the four-
teenth cenury; he admired its grace and its pleasingly delicate
beauty. Through a narrow gap between two walls on the farther
side of a deep courtyard, there was a glimpse of a magnificent view.

The next morning he was formally questioned, after which he
was left in peace for several days. His mind was calm. He could
find nothing but what was simple in his case: I attempted to
kill, I deserve to be killed myself.

He did not pause to think any further on this matter. The trial,
the annoyance of appearing in public, his defence, all these he
considered as so many trifling embarrassments, tedious ceremonies
about which it would be time to think on the day itself. The
moment of death had scarcely greater power to hold his attention. I'll think about that after the sentence, he said to himself.
He did not find life at all tedious, he was considering everything
from a new point of view; he had done with ambition, he very
seldom thought of Mademoiselle de la Mole. Remorse was very
much in his mind, often bringing before his eyes the image of
Madame de Rênal, above all in the silence of the night, broken
only, in this lofty keep, by the cry of the sea-eagle!

He thanked heaven that he had not wounded her mortally.
What an amazing thing! he said to himself. I thought that by
her letter to M. de la Mole she had forever destroyed my future
happiness, and less than a fortnight after the date of that letter,
I no longer give a thought to what at that time occupied my
mind. ... Two or three thousand livres a year to live quietly in a
mountain village like Vergy ... I was happy then ... I did not
realize my own happiness.

At other moments, he would start up out of his chair. If I had
wounded Madame de Rênal mortally, I would have killed myself. ... I need to feel certain of this, not to regard myself with
horror.

Shall I kill myself? that is the all-important question, he
thought. Those judges so wedded to formalities, so hot in their

pursuit of a poor wretch who's accused, and who'd have the
worthiest citizen strung up to hang a decoration on their own
chests. . . . I should withdraw myself from their power, from their
insults couched in ungrammatical French, which the local newspaper will call eloquence. . . .

I may live for five or six weeks still, more or less. Kill myself!
Good heavens, no! he said to himself a few days later, Napoleon
lived on. . . .

Besides, I find life pleasant; this abode of mine is quiet. I've no
bores here, he added, laughing; and he set to work to make a list
of the books he wished to have sent to him from Paris.

The tomb of a friend.

STERNE

HE heard a very loud noise in the corridor; it was not the hour for visiting his cell. The sea-eagle flew away screaming, the door opened, and the venerable curé Chélan, trembling all over and clutching his cane, flung himself into his arms.

'Ah! gracious God, is it possible, my son. ... Monster, I ought to say.'

And the good old man could not add another word. Julien was afraid he would fall. He was obliged to lead him to a chair. The hand of time weighed heavily upon this man, in former days so full of energy. He seemed to Julien to be no longer anything but the shadow of his former self.

When he had recovered his breath, he said: 'Only the day before yesterday I received your letter from Strasbourg with the five hundred francs for the poor of Verrières. It was brought to me up in the mountains at Liveru, where I have gone to live with my nephew Jean. Yesterday, I learnt of the catastrophe. ... Oh, heavens! Is it really possible!' The old man was no longer weeping, he looked as if his mind was a blank, and added mechanically: 'You'll need your five hundred francs, I have brought them back to you.'

'I need to see you, Father!' cried Julien, deeply touched. 'And anyhow, I have some money.'

But he could no longer get a sensible answer. From time to time M. Chélan shed a few tears, which stole silently down his cheeks; then he would gaze at Julien, and seeming as if dazed at seeing him, take his hands and raise them to his lips. That countenance, once so full of life, and on which the noblest sentiments found such vigorous expression, now wore a settled look of apathy. Some peasant fellow came very soon to look for the old man. 'We mustn't let him get tired,' he said to Julien, who realized that this was the nephew. This short visit left Julien plunged in grief so bitter that it kept him from tears. Everything seemed to him sad and void of comfort; he felt his heart frozen to ice in his breast.

This was the bitterest moment of all he had passed through since his crime. He had just seen death before him, in all its ugliness. All illusions of high-souled courage and nobility had scattered like a cloud before the storm.

This dreadful state lasted for several hours. After the mind has been poisoned, one needs physical antidotes and a glass of champagne. Julien would have thought himself a coward had he resorted to such things. Towards the end of a frightful day, the whole of which he had spent in pacing up and down in his narrow prison, he exclaimed, What a fool I am! It's only if I were fated to die in my bed that I ought to let myself be plunged in the depths of misery by the sight of this poor old man; but a swift death in the flower of youth is precisely what saves me from such sad decay.

Whatever arguments he brought forward, Julien found himself moved to self-pity like any other faint-hearted human being, and was in consequence made miserable by this visit.

No longer was there any trace of rugged grandeur about him, no longer any Roman virtue; death appeared to him as something looming high above him, and a very much less easy thing.

This shall serve as my thermometer, he said to himself. This evening I am ten degrees below the courage which must raise me to the level of the guillotine. This morning, I had that courage. Anyhow, what does it matter? If only it comes back again at the moment when I need it. This idea of a thermometer amused him, and finally succeeded in diverting his thoughts.

On waking up next morning, he was ashamed of himself as he had been the day before. My happiness, my peace of mind are at stake, he thought. He almost made up his mind to write to the District Attorney to ask that nobody should be allowed in to see him. What about Fouqué? he thought. If he makes a violent effort to come to Besançon, how distressed he will be.

It was possibly two months since he had given Fouqué a thought. I made a fine fool of myself at Strasbourg, he said to himself. I had no ideas beyond the cut of my collar. Memories of Fouqué were very much in his mind, and left him in a softer mood. He strode up and down in his agitation. I'm now decidedly twenty degrees below the level of death. ... If this weakness increases, it would be better for me to kill myself. What a joy it would be to the Maslons and the Valenods if I died like a snivelling cur!

Fouqué arrived; this simple, kindly soul was distracted with grief. His sole idea, if he had one at all, was to sell all that he possessed in order to suborn the gaoler and so save Julien's life. He dilated at length upon M. de Lavalette's escape from captivity.

'You're causing me pain,' Julien said to him. 'M. de Lavalette was innocent, I am guilty. Without intending it, you make me think of the difference. . . . But is it really true?' he went on, suddenly becoming critical and suspicious once more. 'What! would you sell all you have?'

Fouqué, overjoyed to find his friend at last responsive to his dominant idea, gave him a long and detailed account, to the nearest hundred francs, of what he would make from each of his properties.

What a sublime effort in a small country landowner! thought Julien. How much thrift, how many petty acts of cheese-paring which made me blush for him when I saw them, is he sacrificing for me! Not one of those fine young fellows I've met at the Hôtel de la Mole would have any of his absurd little ways; but excepting those who are very young and have also inherited fortunes, and know nothing of the value of money, which of those fine Parisians would be capable of such a sacrifice?

All Fouqué's slips in grammar, all his vulgar mannerisms were lost to sight; he flung himself into his arms. Never have the provinces, contrasted with Paris, received a finer tribute of homage. Fouqué, overjoyed at the gleam of enthusiasm he read in his friend's eyes, took it as a sign of his consent to the plan for escape.

This vision of the *sublime* restored to Julien all the strength which M. Chélan's sudden visit had taken from him. He was still very young, but, to my mind, he was a healthy sapling. Instead of growing, like the majority of men, from a tender shoot into a crooked tree, age would have given him a heart quick to feel pity, he would have been cured of his insane distrust. . . . But what is the use of such vain predictions?

Interrogations were becoming more frequent in spite of all the efforts made by Julien, whose answers were all framed to bring the whole business more quickly to an end. 'I have committed murder, or at least tried to commit it, and with premeditation,' so he went on repeating day after day. But the magistrate was above all else a formalist. Julien's statements by no means curtailed the examination; the magistrate's vanity was stimulated by them. Julien did not know that they had intended to move him into a horrible underground cell, and that it was thanks to Fouqué's efforts that they let him remain in his charming room one hundred and eighty steps above the ground.

The Abbé de Frilair was one of a number of important people who contracted with Fouqué for the supply of their firewood. The worthy timber merchant had access even to the all-powerful Vicar-general. To his inexpressible delight, M. de Frilair informed him that, moved to pity by the fine qualities of Julien's character and by the services he had rendered in the past to the seminary, he intended to speak to the magistrate on his behalf. Fouqué saw a faint hope of saving his friend, and bowing to the ground as he went out, he begged the Vicar-general to expend a sum of ten louis in masses imploring the acquittal of the accused.

Fouqué was strangely mistaken. M. de Frilair was not at all a man of Valenod's stamp. He refused the offer and even tried to make the worthy peasant understand that he would do better to keep his money. Seeing that it was impossible to make himself clear without being indiscreet, he advised him to distribute this sum in alms for the poor prisoners, who, as a matter of fact, were in need of everything.

This fellow Julien is an odd creature, thought M. de Frilair, his action is inexplicable, and nothing ought to be inexplicable to me. Perhaps it will be possible to make a martyr of him. In any case, I'll find out what lies behind this affair, and perhaps find an opportunity of putting some fear into that woman, Madame de Rênal, who has no respect for us, and in her heart detests me. ... Possibly I might even discover in all this some striking means of effecting a reconciliation with M. de la Mole, who has a weakness for this young seminarist.

The documents relating to his lawsuit had been signed some weeks before, and Father Pirard had left Besançon, not without having made mention of the mystery surrounding Julien's birth, on the very day on which that unhappy young man had tried to kill Madame de Rênal in the church of Verrières.

Julien saw only one disagreeable incident between himself and death, and that was a visit from his father. He consulted Fouqué about his idea of writing to the District Attorney, asking to be excused from having visitors. This horror of seeing his father, and at such a moment, profoundly shocked the timber-merchant's simple, honest heart.

He thought he understood why so many people felt a passionate hatred of his friend. Out of respect for that friend's sorrow, he concealed what he felt.

'In any case,' he answered coldly, 'this order of solitary confinement would not apply to your father.'

> But there is so much mystery in her move-
> ments, such elegance in her figure! Who can
> she be?   SCHILLER

THE doors of the keep were flung open at a very early hour
the next morning. Julien woke up with a start.

Oh, good God, he thought. Here comes my father. What an
unpleasant scene!

At that very moment, a woman dressed as a peasant flung herself into his arms; he had some difficulty in recognizing her. It
was Mademoiselle de la Mole.

'Unkind wretch, I learnt nothing from your letter but where
you were. As for what you call your crime, and which is really
nothing but a noble revenge that shows me all the high quality
of the heart that beats in your breast, I heard of it only in Verrières. . . .'

Despite his suspicions of Mademoiselle de la Mole, which by
the way he did not definitely admit to himself, Julien found her
extremely attractive. How was it possible not to see in this way
of speaking and behaving a noble, disinterested emotion, far
above anything that a mean and vulgar spirit would have dared
to show? It seemed to him that he was still loving a queen, and
a few moments later there was a rare nobility in his thoughts
and his speech as he said to her; 'I was seeing the image of the
future clearly outlined before my eyes. After my death, I wedded
you to M. de Croisenois, who would have been marrying a widow.
The noble, but slightly romantic spirit of this young widow,
struck with amazement and won over to the worship of common,
everyday prudence by an event which for her was singular, tragic,
and sublime, would have condescended to recognize the very
real worth of this young Marquis. You would have resigned yourself to being happy in what the world calls happiness – reputation, riches, high position. But, my dear Mathilde, your arrival
here in Besançon, if it is suspected, will be a mortal blow to M.
de la Mole, and that is what I will never forgive myself. I have
already caused him so much sorrow! The academician will say he
has been warming a serpent in his bosom!'

'I must confess,' said Mademoiselle de la Mole, half angrily,
'that I little expected so much cold reasoning, so much concern

for the future. My maid, who is almost as cautious as you are, procured a passport for herself, and it is under the name of Madame Michelet that I have travelled here post-haste.'

'And did Madame Michelet find it so easy to make her way in here to me?'

'Ah! you're still the same superior man who won my favour. First of all, I offered a hundred francs to a magistrate's secretary who claimed that my entry into this prison was impossible. But once he had taken the money, this polite gentleman kept me waiting, and raised objections. I thought he was thinking of robbing me. . . .' She broke off.

'Well?' said Julien.

'Don't be angry with me, my darling Julien,' she said as she embraced him, 'I was obliged to give my name to this secretary, who took me for some young needlewoman from Paris, in love with the handsome Julien. . . . Indeed, those are his very words. I swore to him that I was your wife, and I shall have a permit to see you every day.'

That's the final act of folly, thought Julien, I couldn't prevent it. After all, M. de la Mole is so great a nobleman that public opinion will easily find an excuse for the young Colonel who marries this charming widow. My death will cover everything. He abandoned himself in ecstasy to Mathilde's love; there was madness in it, greatness of soul, all the wildest, strangest things. She seriously proposed to him that they should die together.

After these first moments of rapture, when her longing for the happiness of seeing Julien was satisfied, her mind was suddenly possessed with keen curiosity. She gazed attentively at her lover, and found him far superior to anything she had imagined. He seemed to her the reincarnation of Boniface de la Mole, but in a more heroic guise.

Mathilde went to see the leading lawyers of the place, whom she offended by offering them gold too crudely; but they ended by accepting.

She quickly came to the conclusion that in any kind of shady transaction concerning matters of high importance, everything in Besançon depended upon the Abbé de Frilair.

Under the humble name of Madame Michelet she at first found insuperable obstacles in the way of securing an interview with the all-powerful Jesuit. But rumours of the beauty of a young needlewoman, madly in love, who had come from Paris to Besançon to comfort the young Abbé Julien Sorel, spread through the town.

Mathilde sped through the streets of Besançon alone and on foot; she hoped she would not be recognized. . . . In any event, she thought it would not be without service to her cause to make a great impression on the common people. In her folly she dreamt of provoking them to riot in order to save Julien on the way to his death. Mademoiselle de la Mole imagined that she was simply dressed and in a fashion befitting a woman in sorrow; she was really dressed in a way to attract everyone's eye.

She had become the object of general attention in Besançon, when, after a week of solicitations, she obtained an audience of M. de Frilair.

However great her courage might be, the idea of an influential member of the *Congrégation* and that of profoundly sly and cautious villainy were so closely associated in her mind that she was trembling as she rang the bell at the door of the Bishop's palace. She was barely able to totter up the stairs that led to the Vicar-general's rooms. The loneliness of the episcopal palace chilled her with fear. I may sit down in an armchair, she thought, and the armchair grip me by the arms, and I shall have vanished. To whom can my maid go to ask for news of me? The Captain of Police will take good care not to interfere. . . . I'm all alone in this great town !

Her first glance at the apartment restored Mathilde's confidence. First of all, there was a footman in very smart livery to open the door. The drawing-room where she was asked to wait displayed that refined and tasteful luxury, so different from vulgar magnificence, which one meets in Paris only in the best houses. As soon as she caught sight of M. de Frilair's benign expression as he came towards her, all thoughts of a horrible crime faded from her mind. She did not find on this handsome face any imprint of that energetic and somewhat ferocious virtue so distasteful to Parisian society. The faint suspicion of a smile lighting up the features of the priest who was in supreme control in Besançon proclaimed the man accustomed to good society, the cultured prelate, the able administrator. Mathilde imagined herself in Paris.

It took M. de Frilair a few minutes only to lead Mathilde on to admit that she was the daughter of his powerful adversary, the Marquis de la Mole.

'As a matter of fact, I am not Madame Michelet,' she said, resuming all her haughtiness of manner, 'and this admission costs

me little, for I have come, sir, to consult you on the possibility
of procuring M. de la Vernaye's escape. In the first place he is
guilty of nothing more than an act of folly; the woman at whom
he fired is going on well. In the second place, to suborn the minor
officials, I can put down here and now fifty thousand francs, and
pledge myself to pay double that sum. Lastly, my own gratitude
and the gratitude of my family will find nothing impossible to do
for the man who has saved M. de la Vernaye.'

M. de Frilair appeared to be surprised at this name. Mathilde
showed him several letters from the Ministry of War, addressed
to M. Julien Sorel de la Vernaye.

'You see, sir, that my father had assumed responsibility for
his career. I married him secretly, my father wished him to become
a senior officer before consenting to a marriage which is a little
unusual for a la Mole.'

Mathilde remarked that M. de Frilair's expression of kindness
and mild amusement faded rapidly as he began to arrive at important discoveries. An air of astuteness mingled with profound
insincerity was portrayed on his features.

The abbé was beginning to have doubts; he read the official
documents over again slowly.

What advantage, he was wondering, can I gain from these
strange confidences? Here I am all of a sudden on intimate terms
with a friend of the famous Madame de Fervaques, the all-powerful niece of his Lordship the Bishop of —, through whom one
becomes a Bishop in France. What I have been used to think of as
something in the far-distant future offers itself to me unexpectedly. This may lead me to the goal of all my hopes.

Mathilde was at first alarmed by the sudden change in the expression of this very influential man, with whom she found herself alone in a remote room. But, good heavens, she said to herself
a moment later, wouldn't it have been the worst of misfortunes
if I had made no impression at all on the cold self-centred heart of
a priest who is sated with power and self-indulgence?

Dazzled by this rapid and unexpected path to the episcopacy
that was opening before his eyes, astonished at Mathilde's intelligence, for an instant M. de Frilair was off his guard. Mademoiselle
de la Mole saw him almost at her feet, so moved by eager ambition that he actually trembled with excitement.

Everything becomes clear, she thought. Nothing will be impossible here for a friend of Madame de Fervaques. Despite a still
very painful sense of jealousy, she found courage to explain that

Julien was an intimate friend of the Maréchale, and used to meet the Lord Bishop of — at her house almost every evening.

'Even if a list of thirty-six jurymen were to be drawn by lot four or five times in succession from among the most important inhabitants of this Department,' said the Vicar-general with the harsh light of ambition in his eyes, and stressing each of his words, 'I should consider myself most unfortunate if in each list I did not find eight or nine friends, and those the most intelligent of the lot. I should almost invariably have a majority, even more than that required for a verdict. You see, mademoiselle, it's so easy for me to grant absolution. . . .'

The Abbé de Frilair broke off suddenly, as if astonished at the sound of his own words; he was admitting things that are never uttered to the profane.

But Mathilde in her turn was struck dumb with amazement when he informed her that what most astonished and interested Besançon society in Julien's strange adventure, was that in the past he had inspired a grand passion in Madame de Rênal, and had for a long time shared her feelings. M. de Frilair easily perceived the extreme distress which his story provoked.

I have my revenge! he thought. Here, at last, is a way of managing this very determined young person; I was trembling lest I should not succeed in finding one. Her distinguished and somewhat intractable air increased in his eyes the charm of this rare beauty whom he saw almost suppliant before him. He recovered all his self-possession and did not hesitate to twist the dagger in her heart.

'I should not be surprised after all,' he remarked to her airily, 'if we were to learn that it was out of jealousy that M. Sorel fired his pistol twice at the woman whom once he loved so dearly. She is far from being unattractive, and for some time past she has been seeing a great deal of a certain Father Marquinot of Dijon, one of those Jansenist fellows, utterly without morals, like all of his kind.'

Leisurely and with a sort of sensual pleasure M. de Frilair went on torturing the heart of this lovely girl, whose weak side he had discovered.

'Why,' he asked, fixing a pair of burning eyes on Mathilde, 'should M. Sorel have chosen the church, if not because, at that very moment, his rival was there celebrating mass? Everyone agrees in granting marvellous intelligence and even greater discretion to the man who is so happy as to have your protection.

What would have been simpler than to hide himself in M. de Rênal's garden, which he knows so well? There, almost certain of not being seen, nor caught, nor suspected, he could have killed the woman who had made him jealous.'

These arguments, so apparently sensible, drove Mathilde completely frantic. That spirit, so proud and aloof, yet steeped in all that barren prudence which high society takes for a faithful representation of the human heart, was not made to comprehend in a flash the joy of utterly flouting prudence, which can be so keen a delight to an eager, fiery spirit. In the upper ranks of Parisian society, passion can very rarely divest itself of prudence, and it is from the fifth floor only that people throw themselves out of windows.

At last, the Abbé de Frilair was certain of his power. He gave Mathilde to understand (he was doubtless lying) that he could do what he liked with the particular Public Prosecutor who would conduct the case against Julien. After the names of the thirty-six jurors for the assizes had been chosen by ballot, he would make a direct and personal appeal to at least thirty of them.

If M. de Frilair had not thought Mathilde such a pretty creature, he would not have spoken to her so plainly until their fifth or sixth interview.

> March 31, 1676 – He that endeavoured to kill
> his sister in our house, had before killed a
> man, and it had cost his father five hundred
> écus to get him off; by their secret distribu-
> tion, gaining the favour of the counsellors.
>
> LOCKE

ON leaving the Bishop's palace, Mathilde did not hesitate to
send a messenger to Madame de Fervaques; the fear of compromising herself did not stop her for a second. She implored her
rival to obtain a letter for M. de Frilair written entirely in the
hand of the Lord Bishop of —. She even went so far as to beg
her to hasten to Besançon herself. This was a heroic gesture
from someone with so proud and jealous a temper.

Acting on Fouqué's advice, she had prudently refrained from
saying anything to Julien about what she was doing. Her presence caused him enough anxiety without that. More sensitive to moral issues at the approach of death than he had been
in the whole of his life, he was feeling twinges of conscience
not only about M. de la Mole but on Mathilde's account as
well.

Why is it, he asked himself, that when she is with me I find
myself absent-minded at times and even bored? She is ruining
herself for me, and this is how I repay her. Does it mean that I'm
really unkind and heartless? This question would have troubled
him little at the time when he was ambitious; for then the only
disgrace in his eyes was failure to make his way.

The uneasiness of mind he felt in Mathilde's presence was
all the more marked because at the moment he was inspiring
in her the strangest, wildest passion. She talked of nothing
but the extraordinary sacrifices she wanted to make to save
him.

Carried away by a feeling of which she was proud and which
was stronger than all her pride, she would have liked to let no
moment of her life go by that was not filled with some extraordinary action. The strangest schemes, the most fraught with
danger for herself, took up all her long conversations with Julien.
The gaolers, who had been well paid, allowed her to order every-

thing in the prison. Mathilde's ideas were not limited to the sacrifice of her reputation; she cared very little whether she let the whole of society know of her condition. Flinging herself on her knees in front of the King's carriage as it came galloping by, to ask for Julien's pardon, attracting His Majesty's attention at the risk of a thousand deaths, was one of the least fantastic dreams that haunted this feverishly courageous imagination. Through her friends in the King's household, she could count on obtaining admission to those parts of the Parc de Saint-Cloud closed to the public.

Julien felt himself hardly worthy of such devotion; to tell the truth he was tired of heroism. It was simple, artless, and almost timid affection that would have found him responsive, whereas, on the contrary, Mathilde's proud spirit must always include the idea of an audience, whether of common people or of *the other sort*.

In the midst of all her anguish, all her fears for the life of this lover, whom she was determined not to survive, she felt a secret longing to astonish the world by the extravagance of her love and the sublimity of her ventures.

Julien grew fretful over his inability to be moved by all this heroism. What would his anger have been if he had known of all the mad schemes with which Mathilde pestered the devoted, but eminently sensible and limited mind of the worthy Fouqué?

This good man did not quite know what to find fault with in Mathilde's devotion; he too would have sacrificed his whole fortune and exposed his life to the greatest risks to save Julien. He was stupefied by the amount of gold Mathilde scattered abroad. Fouqué, who had all a provincial's veneration for money, was at first impressed by the sums spent in this way.

Finally he discovered that Mademoiselle de la Mole's plans often varied, and to his great relief, he hit upon a word with which to express his blame of a character that he found so exhausting; she was *changeable*. From this epithet to that of *wrongheaded*, the direst anathema in the provinces, was but a step.

It's strange, said Julien to himself one day as Mathilde was leaving his prison, that so warm a passion, and one of which I am the object, should leave me so unmoved! And two months ago I adored her! I have certainly read that at the approach of death a man feels detached from everything; but it's frightful to feel oneself ungrateful and not be able to change. Am I an egoist, then? He addressed the most humiliating reproaches to himself on this point.

Ambition was dead in his heart, another passion had risen from its ashes; he called it remorse for having attempted to murder Madame de Rênal.

In point of fact, he was hopelessly in love with her. He found a curious kind of happiness, whenever, left absolutely alone and without any fear of interruption, he could abandon himself wholeheartedly to the memory of far-off, happy days spent at Verrières or Vergy. The tiniest little incident of that time, which had all too quickly taken wing, held for him an irresistible freshness and a charm. His successes in Paris never entered his mind; he had grown weary of them.

This tendency, which day by day grew stronger, was partly visible to Mathilde's jealous eyes. She saw quite clearly that she had to contend with a love of solitude. At times, with a feeling of terror in her heart, she uttered Madame de Rênal's name. She saw Julien shudder. From that moment, her passion knew neither bounds nor measure.

If he dies, I die after him, she would say to herself with the utmost sincerity. What would the drawing-rooms of Paris say to see a girl of my rank carry to such a point the adoration of a lover condemned to death? To discover such sentiments we must go back to the days of the heroes; it was love of this kind that made hearts beat in the age of Charles IX and Henri III.

In moments of keenest ecstasy, when she was clasping Julien's head to her heart, she would say to herself in horror: What! can this darling head be doomed to fall? Well, then, she would add, afire with a heroism not devoid of happiness, my lips, now pressed against these dear curls, will be cold as ice less than twenty-four hours after.

Memories of these moments of heroism and of wild, horrific transports held her in their iron grip. The idea of suicide, so absorbing in itself, and until then so foreign to that proud spirit, now made its entry there and soon established an absolute sway. No, Mathilde told herself proudly, the blood of my ancestors has not grown lukewarm in its descent to me.

'I have a favour to ask you,' her lover said to her one day. 'Put your child out to nurse at Verrières. Madame de Rênal will keep an eye on the nurse.'

'That's a very hard thing to say to me …' Mathilde turned pale.

'That's true, and I ask your pardon a thousand times,' cried Julien, waking out of his dreams, and clasping her in his arms.

After drying her tears, he came back to what was in his mind, but with more subtlety. He had given the conversation a melancholy philosophic turn, and now spoke of the future which was so soon to close for him. 'You must agree, my love, that passion is an accident in our lives, but an accident which happens only to natures of superior calibre. . . . My son's death would really be a welcome thing for your family's pride, and that is what menials will guess. Neglect will be the lot of this child of sorrow and shame. . . . I hope that at a date which I am not anxious to fix, but which all the same I have the courage to foresee, you will obey the last advice I give you : You will marry the Marquis de Croisenois.'

'What, when I'm dishonoured !'

'Dishonour cannot touch such a name as yours. You will be a widow, and the widow of a madman, that is all. I will go further: my crime, being free of any money motive, will be no dishonour. Perhaps, by that time, some wise, far-seeing legislator, taking advantage of contemporary bias, will have secured the suppression of the death penalty. Then, some friendly voice will quote as an example : "Why, there was Mademoiselle de la Mole's first husband – he was mad, but he wasn't wicked, not really a scoundrel. It was absurd to cut his head off. . . ." Then my memory will no longer be a shameful one; at least, after a certain time. . . . Your position in society, your fortune, and, let me add, your genius, will enable M. de Croisenois, once he is your husband, to play a part which, by himself, he never could hope to play. He has nothing but his birth and his gallant courage, and these qualities by themselves, though they were sufficient to make a man perfect in 1729, are an anachronism a century later, and only encourage false claims to greatness. A man must have other things besides if he is to become a leader of the younger generation in France.

'You will bring a resolute and adventurous character to the support of the political party into which you will thrust your husband. You can be the successor of women like Madame de Chevreuse and Madame de Longueville of the Fronde. . . . But by then, my love, the divine fire which inspires you at this moment will have become a little cooler.

'Allow me to tell you,' he said, after many preparatory remarks, 'in fifteen years from now you will regard the love you felt for me as a pardonable act of folly, but an act of folly all the same. . . .'

He broke off suddenly and returned to his dreams. He found himself once again confronted by that idea which had so deeply shocked Mathilde: In fifteen years' time Madame de Rênal will adore my son and you will have forgotten him.

CHAPTER 40 : *Peace of Mind*

> It is because I was once a fool that now I am
> wise. O philosopher, you who see nothing
> save things of the moment, how limited is
> your vision! Your eyes are not made to fol-
> low the underground workings of passion.
> FRAU VON GOETHE

THIS conversation was interrupted by a judicial inquiry,
followed by a conference with the lawyer conducting his
defence. These were the only absolutely disagreeable moments in
a life free from cares and anxieties and filled with tender dreams.

'It was murder, and premeditated murder,' said Julien to
magistrate and counsel alike. 'I'm sorry, gentlemen,' he added
smiling, 'but this reduces your task to a very small matter.'

After all, thought Julien, when he had managed to get rid of
these two persons, I must be brave, and apparently braver than
these two men. They regard as the worst of ills, as the *king of
terrors*, this duel with an unhappy ending, with which I shall
only concern myself seriously on the day itself.

It is just that I've known greater ills, Julien went on, philoso-
phizing to himself. I suffered very much more during my first
visit to Strasbourg, when I thought Mathilde had deserted me
. . . and to think that I once longed so passionately for that perfect intimacy which today leaves me so cold. . . . Actually, I am
happier by myself than when that lovely girl shares my solitude. . . .

The lawyer, a man of rules and formalities, thought him mad,
and agreed with public opinion in believing that it was jealousy
that had put the pistol into his hand. One day, he ventured to
suggest to Julien that this allegation, whether true or false, would
be an excellent line of defence. But the prisoner changed in the
twinkling of an eye to a creature full of vehement and caustic
rage.

'On your life, sir,' cried Julien, mad with anger, 'pray remember never again to put forward this abominable lie.' The
prudent lawyer was for the moment afraid of being murdered
himself.

He prepared his defence, for the decisive moment was drawing
near. In Besançon and throughout the whole of the Department

there was talk of nothing but this famous trial. Julien was in ignorance of this particular detail, having begged that no one should ever mention to him things of this sort.

That day, when Fouqué and Mathilde had tried to tell him of certain public rumours, which seemed to them of a nature to afford some grounds for hope, Julien had cut them short at the very first word.

'Leave me to enjoy my ideal life of dreams. Your petty fusses and worries, your details of material existence, all more or less wounding to my feelings, would drag me down from heaven. A man dies as best he can; I myself wish to think of death only in my own way. What do I care for *other people*? My relations with *other people* are soon to be abruptly severed. For pity's sake, don't speak to me of such people any more; it's quite enough to have to see the magistrate and my lawyer.'

Really, he said to himself, it seems I am fated to die a dreamer. A nobody like myself, sure of being forgotten in a fortnight, would, I must confess, be fooling himself completely, if he tried to play a part. It's strange, all the same, that I've only learnt the art of living now that I see the end of life so near.

He spent these last days pacing the narrow platform at the very top of the keep, smoking some excellent cigars which Mathilde had sent a courier to fetch from Holland, and with no suspicion that his appearance was daily awaited by all the telescopes in the town. His thoughts were away in Vergy. He never spoke to Fouqué of Madame de Rênal, but on two or three occasions this friend told him that she was rapidly getting better, and the words found an echo in his heart.

While Julien's mind was almost always completely absorbed in the realm of ideas, Mathilde, occupied with realities, as befits an aristocratic heart, had managed to advance the intimacy of the personal correspondence between Madame de Fervaques and M. de Frilair to such a point that already the magic word *Bishopric* had been written down.

The venerable prelate entrusted with the list of benefices added by way of postscript to his letter: 'That poor fellow Sorel is merely a hot-headed lunatic. I hope that he will be restored to us.'

At the sight of these lines, M. de Frilair was almost crazy with joy. He no longer doubted that he would save Julien.

'But for that Jacobin law which ordains the drawing-up of an endless list of jurors,' he said to Mathilde on the eve of the ballot for thirty-six jurymen for the assizes, 'and which has no other real object than to take all influence out of the hands of well-born people, I could have answered for the verdict. I certainly secured Father N—'s acquittal.'

It was with a feeling of pleasure that, next day, among the names drawn from the urn, M. de Frilair found those of five members of the *Congrégation* of Besançon, and, among those who were strangers to the town, the names of MM. de Valenod, de Moirod, and de Cholin. 'I can answer at once for these eight jurors,' he said to Mathilde. 'The first five are mere *machines*. Valenod is my agent, Moirod owes everything to me, and Cholin's a nincompoop who's afraid of everything.'

The newspapers broadcast throughout the Department the names of the jurors, and Madame de Rênal, to her husband's inexpressibly dismay, made up her mind to come to Besançon. All that M. de Rênal could obtain from her was that she would not leave her bed, so that she might avoid the unpleasantness of being summoned to give evidence. 'You don't understand my position,' said the former Mayor of Verrières. 'I'm now a Liberal renegade, or so they call me. There's no doubt but that rascal Valenod and M. de Frilair will persuade the District Attorney and the judges to do everything they can to make things unpleasant for me.'

Madame de Rênal yielded without difficulty to her husband's commands. If I were to appear at the Assize Court, she said to herself, I should seem to be demanding vengeance.

Despite all the promises of prudence made to her spiritual director and to her husband, she had no sooner arrived in Besançon that she wrote in her own hand to each of the thirty-six jurors:

I shall not appear on the day of the trial, Sir, because my presence in Court might prejudice M. Sorel's case. I desire only one thing in the world, and that passionately – that he should be acquitted. Pray have no doubts about it, the horrible thought that an innocent man has been sent to his death on my account would poison the rest of my life and undoubtedly shorten it. How could you condemn him to death while I myself remain alive? No, there is no possible doubt, society has not the right to snatch any man's life from him, especially from such a man as Julien Sorel. Everyone in Verrières has known him to be occasionally misguided. This poor young man has powerful enemies; but even among his enemies (and how many they are) who is there who calls in question his marvellous talents and his profound learning? You are not about to sit in judgement, Sir, upon an ordinary person. For close on eighteen months we have all known him to be pious, well-behaved, and devoted to his task; but, two or three times a year, he was subject to fits of melancholy that almost amounted to madness. The whole town of Verrières, all our neighbours at Vergy where we spend the summer, my entire family, and the Sub-Prefect himself, will render justice to his exemplary piety; he knows the Holy Bible from end to end by heart. Would a man without religious principles have applied himself for so many years to learning the Holy Scriptures? My sons will have the honour of presenting this letter to you themselves. They are children; be good enough to question them, Sir, they will give you all the details about this young man that may still be necessary to convince you of the barbarity of condemning him. Far from avenging me, you would be sentencing me to death.

What can his enemies put forward against this fact? The injury that resulted from one of those momentary fits of madness which my children themselves have sometimes noticed in their tutor is so far from dangerous that less than two months later it has allowed me to travel by coach from Verrières to Besançon. If I have reason to expect, Sir, that you will feel the least hesitation in the world about saving from the barbarity of the law a person who is so little guilty, I shall leave my bed, to which my husband's orders alone confine me, and come and fling myself at your feet.

Declare, Sir, that the fact of premeditation is not established, and you will not have to reproach yourself with the blood of an innocent man, etc. etc.

CHAPTER 41 : *The Trial*

> The district will long remember this famous
> case. Interest in the prisoner increased to
> excitement and anxiety, for his crime was
> astounding, yet not atrocious. Even had it
> been, this young man was so good-looking!
> His brilliant career so soon at an end, stirred
> them to keener pity. Will they sentence him
> to death? the women asked the men of their
> company, growing visibly pale as they waited
> for the answer.   SAINTE-BEUVE

At length the day so dreaded by Madame de Rênal and Mathilde
came round.

The unusual appearance of the town increased their terror, and
did not leave even Fouqué's stout heart unmoved. The whole
province had flocked to Besançon to see the trial of this romantic
case.

For several days there had been no room at the inns. The President of the Assize Court was assailed with requests for cards of
admission; every lady in the town wished to be present at the
trial; Julien's portrait was being hawked about the streets, etc.,
etc.

Mathilde was holding in reserve for this supreme moment a
letter written entirely in the hand of the Lord Bishop of —. This
Prelate, who governed the Church in France and appointed
Bishops, had deigned to ask for Julien's acquittal. On the eve of
the trial Mathilde took this letter to the all-powerful Vicar-
general.

At the end of the interview, as she was leaving the room in a
flood of tears, M. de Frilair spoke to her. 'I can answer for the
verdict of the jury,' he said, throwing off at last his diplomatic reserve, and almost appeared moved himself. 'Among the twelve
persons entrusted with the task of finding whether your protégé's
crime is clearly established, and in particular whether there was
premeditation, I can count six friends who have my success at
heart, and I have given them to understand that my promotion
to a Bishopric depends on them.

'Baron de Valenod, whom I have made Mayor of Verrières,
can do what he likes with two of his subordinates, MM. de Moirod

and de Cholin. True, fate has given us, for handling this affair, two jurors with extremely unsound opinions; but, although Ultra-Liberal, they obey my orders faithfully on important occasions, and I have sent to ask them to vote with M. de Valenod. I have been told that a sixth juror, a manufacturer who is immensely rich and a very loquacious Liberal, is secretly hoping for a contract from the Ministry of War, and no doubt would not wish to displease me. I have let him know that M. de Valenod has my final orders.'

'And who is this M. de Valenod?' asked Mathilde anxiously.

'If you knew him you would have no doubt of your success. He is a man with a bold tongue in his head, impudent, coarse, a born leader of fools. The year 1814 rescued him from beggary, and I am about to make him a Prefect. He is quite capable of thrashing the other jurors if they refuse to vote as he wishes.'

Mathilde felt a little reassured.

Another discussion awaited her that evening. To avoid prolonging a painful scene, the outcome of which was in his opinion certain, Julien was determined not to state his case at the trial.

'My counsel will do all the talking,' he said to Mathilde. 'Anyhow, I shall be only too long exposed as a spectacle for all my enemies. These provincials have been shocked by the rapid success which I owe to you, and, believe me, there's not one of them that doesn't long for my conviction, while reserving the right to shed crocodile tears when I am led out to die.'

'They wish to see you humiliated, that is only too true,' said Mathilde, 'but I don't believe they are cruel. My presence here in Besançon and the spectacle of my grief have interested all the women; your handsome face will do the rest. If you say but a single word before your judges, all the people in court will be on your side.' She went on in the same strain.

The following morning at nine o'clock, when Julien came down from his prison to enter the Great Hall of the Law Courts, it was with the utmost difficulty that the gendarmes succeeded in pushing aside the huge crowd of people pressed against each other in the courtyard. Julien had slept well, he was very calm, and felt no other emotion but a sort of philosophic compassion for that crowd of envious individuals who, without any feeling of cruelty, would soon be applauding his sentence of death. He was greatly surprised when, on being detained for more than a quarter of an hour in the midst of the crowd, he was obliged to recognize that his presence inspired these onlookers with tender pity. He did not hear a single unpleasant remark. These provincials are less ill-natured than I supposed, he said to himself.

On entering the court, he was struck by the graceful beauty of its architecture. It was a pure type of Gothic, with numbers of charming little pillars cut into the stonework with the utmost skill. He imagined himself in England.

But very soon his whole attention was absorbed by some twelve or fifteen pretty women who, seated directly opposite the dock, filled the three small galleries above the Judge's bench and the jury-box. On turning round towards the crowd of spectators, he saw that the circular gallery overhanging the main amphitheatre was filled with women; most of them were young and seemed to him extremely pretty; their eyes were bright and full of interest. In the rest of the court the crowd was enormous; people were jostling each other at the doors, and the attendants on guard were unable to obtain silence.

When every eye on the look-out for Julien became aware of his presence, on seeing him take his place on the slightly raised bench reserved for the prisoner, he was greeted with a murmur of astonishment and tender interest.

One would have said that day that he was under twenty; he was very simply dressed, but with perfect grace; his hair and brow were charming; Mathilde had chosen to preside over his toilet herself. Julien was extremely pale. Hardly had he taken his seat in the dock than he heard on all sides people saying: 'Gracious, how young he is ! . . .' 'But he's only a boy.' 'He's much better-looking than his portrait.'

'Prisoner,' said the gendarme seated on his right, 'do you see those six ladies seated up there in that gallery?' The gendarme pointed to a little gallery jutting out above that part of the amphitheatre where the jurymen were placed. 'That's the Prefect's lady,' the gendarme went on, 'just beside her Ladyship the Marquise de M——. That lady's a great friend of yours, I heard her talking to the examining magistrate. That's Madame Derville next to her.'

'Madame Derville !' exclaimed Julien, and a deep blush covered his forehead. When she leaves here, he thought, she will write to Madame de Rênal. He did not know of Madame de Rênal's arrival in Besançon.

The witnesses were examined; this took up several hours. At the opening words of the Public Prosecutor's speech, two of the ladies seated in the little gallery facing Julien burst into tears. Madame Derville doesn't show the same emotion, thought Julien. He noticed, however, that her cheeks were deeply flushed.

The Public Prosecutor dilated in flowery but incorrect French on the barbarous nature of the crime that had been committed. Julien noticed that Madame Derville's neighbours showed signs of keen disapproval. Several of the jury, apparently friends of these ladies, spoke to them and seemed to reassure them. That can only be a good omen, thought Julien.

Until then he had felt himself filled with unmixed contempt for all those men who were taking part in this trial. The Public Prosecutor's banal rhetoric increased this feeling of disgust. But by degrees his ice-bound heart was melted in face of the marks of interest of which he was clearly the object.

He was pleased with his Counsel's cool, collected manner. 'No fine phrases,' he said to him under his breath as the barrister was about to address the court.

'All that rhetoric pilfered from Bossuet and paraded against you has done you good service,' said his Counsel. And indeed, he had not been speaking for five minutes before almost all the women had their handkerchiefs in their hands. Encouraged by this, the Counsel addressed the jury in very strong language. Julien was quaking, he felt himself on the point of bursting into tears. Good God! he thought, what will my enemies say?

He was about to give way to the emotion that was gaining hold of him when, luckily for himself, he caught an insolent glance from Baron de Valenod.

That blackguard's eyes are blazing, he said to himself. What a triumph for that mean little soul! Even if my crime had entailed only this one consequence, I should be bound to rue it. Heaven knows what he will say of me to Madame de Rênal!

This thought effaced all others. Shortly afterwards, Julien was recalled to himself by sounds of approval from the public. His Counsel had just concluded his speech for the defence. Julien remembered that it was the correct thing to shake hands with him. The time had passed quickly.

Refreshments were brought in for Counsel and the accused. It was only then that Julien was struck by a particular circumstance; not one of the women had left the court to have dinner.

'Upon my word, I'm dying of hunger,' said his counsel, 'and you?'

'I am too,' said Julien.

'Look,' said his counsel pointing to the little gallery, 'there's the Prefect's wife having her dinner brought to her too. Keep up your courage, everything's going well.' The trial was resumed.

As the President was summing up, midnight struck, and he was obliged to break off. In the midst of the silence, of the universal suspense, the echoing strokes of the clock filled the court.

Here begins the last day of my life, thought Julien. Soon he felt himself inflamed by the idea of duty. Up till then he had controlled his emotion, and kept to his resolve not to say a word; but when the President of the Assizes asked him if he had any- thing to add, he stood up. Facing him he saw the eyes of Madame Derville which, in the lamplight, seemed to him to sparkle strangely. Can she by any chance be crying? he wondered, as he began to speak.

'Gentlemen of the Jury,' he said, 'a horror of contempt, which I thought I could defy at the hour of death, obliges me to speak. Gentlemen, I have not the honour to belong to the same class as yourselves, you see in me a peasant urged to revolt against the lowliness of his lot.

'I ask no mercy of you,' Julien went on, his voice growing stronger, 'I am under no illusion; death awaits me; the penalty will be just. I have been guilty of an attempt on the life of a woman most worthy of all respect, of all homage. My crime is atrocious, and it was *premeditated*. I have therefore, Gentlemen of the Jury, deserved death. But, even were I less guilty, I see before me men who, without pausing to consider what pity my youth may deserve, will wish to punish in my person and forever discourage that body of young men who, born in an inferior station, and in some degree oppressed by poverty, have the good fortune to secure for themselves a sound education, and the audacity to mingle with what the pride of rich men calls society.

'That is my crime, Gentlemen, and it will be punished with all the more severity in that, in point of fact, I am not being tried by my peers. In the jury-box I see not a single peasant who has grown rich, but simply and solely men of the middle-class en- raged against me....'

For twenty minutes Julien went on speaking in this strain; he said everything that was in his heart. The Public Prosecutor, who aspired to win the favour of the aristocracy, kept on springing up out of his seat; but in spite of the slightly abstract turn which Julien had given to the discussion, all the women were in floods of tears. Madame Derville herself had her handkerchief pressed to her eyes. Before concluding, Julien touched once more on the question of premeditation, on his repentance, on the respect, the filial and unbounded adoration which, in happier times, he had felt for Madame de Rênal.... Madame Derville uttered a cry and fainted.

One o'clock struck as the jury retired to their room. None of the women had left their seats; several of the men had tears in their eyes. Conversation was very lively at first; but by degrees, as the verdict of the jury was a long time coming, general weariness began to spread a calm over the assembled crowd. It was a solemn moment; the lamps cast a less brilliant light. Julien, who was utterly worn out, heard people around him discussing whether this delay was a good or a bad sign. He was pleased to see that everyone wished him well; the jury did not return, and yet not a woman left the court.

Just as two o'clock had struck, a great stir was heard. The little door of the jury-room opened. Baron de Valenod advanced with a solemn theatrical gait, followed by all the other jurymen. He coughed, then declared that on his soul and conscience the unanimous verdict of the jury was that Julien Sorel was guilty of murder, and of murder with premeditation. This verdict entailed the death sentence; it was pronounced a moment later. Julien looked at his watch; it was a quarter past two. Today is Friday, he thought.

Yes, but it's a lucky day for Valenod, who is sentencing me to death.... I'm too closely watched for Mathilde to save me, like Madame de Lavalette.... So in three days' time, at this same hour, I shall know the truth about the *great unknown*.

At that moment he heard a cry and was recalled to things of this world. The women round him were sobbing; he saw all faces turned towards a little gallery constructed behind the capital of a Gothic pilaster. He learnt afterwards that Mathilde had been hidden there. As the cry was not repeated, everyone turned round again to look at Julien, for whom the gendarmes were trying to clear a passage through the crowd.

Let's try not to give that rascal Valenod any chance to laugh, thought Julien. With what a sly, cajoling air of grief he uttered the verdict that brings with it the death penalty ! While that poor President of the Assizes, though he's been a judge for so many years, had tears in his eyes as he pronounced my sentence. What joy for that fellow Valenod to have his revenge for our old rivalry over Madame de Rênal ! . . . And so I shall never see her again ! It's all over. . . . A last farewell is impossible for us, I can feel it. . . . How happy I would have been to tell her all the horror I feel for my crime !

These words only : I consider that I am justly condemned.

CHAPTER 42 : *The Condemned Cell*

WHEN Julien was led back to prison he had been put into a cell reserved for those under sentence of death. He, who usually noticed even the tiniest details, had not remarked that he was not being taken up to his old room in the keep. He was pondering what he should say to Madame de Rênal, if, before the final moment, he should have the happiness of seeing her. He felt that she would interrupt him quickly, and was trying to find some way of expressing his repentance in the very first words he would say to her. How am I to convince her, after such an action, that I love her and her only? For after all I did try to kill her, either out of ambition or for love of Mathilde.

On getting into bed he found his sheets were made of some coarse material. His eyes were opened. Ah! I'm in the condemned cell, he thought. It's only right. . . .

Count Altamira once told me how, on the eve of his death, Danton remarked in his booming voice: 'It's a curious thing, the verb "to guillotine" cannot be conjugated in all its tenses. One can say: I shall be guillotined, thou wilt be guillotined, but one does not say: I have been guillotined.'

And why not, Julien went on, if there is another life? Good heavens! if I meet the God of the Christians – I'm lost! He is a tyrant, and, as such, is full of ideas of vengeance; his Bible speaks of nothing but horrible punishments. I have never loved him. I have never even allowed myself to believe that anyone could love him sincerely. He is without pity. (Here Julien called to mind several passages from the Bible.) He will punish me in some abominable way.

But if I meet the God of Fénelon! He will say to me perhaps: 'Much shall be forgiven thee, for thou hast loved much. . . .'

Have I loved much? Ah! I did love Madame de Rênal, but I behaved to her atrociously. There, as in other instances, I turned away from simple, unassuming worth after something that glitters. . . .

But then, what a prospect! Colonel of Hussars, should we go to war; Secretary of Legation in time of peace; after that Ambassador – for I should quickly have had a knowledge of affairs . . . and had I been utterly brainless, would the son-in-law of the Marquis de la Mole have any rivalry to fear? All my foolish blunders would have been forgiven me, or rather have ranked as merits. A man of excellent repute, enjoying life to the full in Vienna or London.

Not precisely that, sir — due for the guillotine in three days' time.

Julien laughed heartily over this sally of his own wit. Man, in truth, he reflected, has two separate beings inside himself. Who the devil hit upon that malicious idea?

All right, quite so, my friend, he replied to this interrupting voice, due for the guillotine in three days' time. M. de Cholin will hire a window, sharing expenses with Father Maslon. Well, then to pay for the cost of hiring that window, which of these two worthy gentlemen will rob the other?

A passage from Rotrou's Venceslas suddenly came into his head:

Ladislas: *My soul stands ready.*
The King (his father): *So does the scaffold; lay your head upon it.*

A fine reply, he thought and fell asleep. In the morning someone woke him up by a tight grip on his shoulder.

'What, already!' said Julien, opening his haggard eyes. He imagined himself to be in the executioner's clutches.

It was Mathilde. Luckily she didn't understand me, he thought. The reflection restored all his presence of mind. He found Mathilde changed as by a six months' illness; she was really unrecognizable.

'That wretch Frilair has played me false,' she said to him, wringing her hands; rage held her tears in check.

'Wasn't I fine yesterday when I stood up to speak?' was Julien's reply. 'I was improvising, and for the first time in my life! It's true there's reason to fear it may also be the last.'

Julien at that moment was playing upon Mathilde's character with all the poise of a virtuoso fingering the keys of a piano. 'It's true,' he went on, 'that I lack the advantage of noble birth, but Mathilde's high spirit has raised her lover to her own level. Do you think Boniface de la Mole would have borne himself better in front of his judges?'

Mathilde, that morning, was as unaffectedly tender as any poor girl living high up in an attic; but she could not get him to speak more simply. All unconsciously, he was paying her back for the torments she had so often inflicted on him.

We know nothing about the source of the Nile, thought Julien. It has been given to no man's eye to see the king of rivers in the form of a humble streamlet. In the same way no human eye shall ever see Julien weak, and particularly since he does not happen to be so. But I have a heart that is easily moved; the most common-place things, when uttered with an accent of truth, can make my voice tremble with emotion and even bring tears to my eyes. How many times have stony hearts not despised me for this weakness! They imagined that I was asking for pity, and that is what I will never endure.

They say that Danton, at the foot of the scaffold, was moved by the memory of his wife; but Danton had given strength to a nation of frivolous weaklings, and prevented the enemy from reaching Paris.... I alone know what I myself might have managed to do.... To others, I am at best a *might-have-been*.

If Madame de Rênal had been here, in my cell, instead of Mathilde, could I have answered for myself? The extravagance of my despair and of my repentance would have seemed in the eyes of the Valenods, and of all the patricians of the neighbourhood, a mere ignoble fear of death. They are so proud, those faint-hearted creatures whom their financial position places out of reach of temptation. 'See what it means to be born a carpenter's son!' so M. de Moirod and M. de Cholin who have just condemned me to death would have said. A man may become learned, or skilful, but as for courage! ... Courage is not a thing that can be taught. Not even to my poor Mathilde, who is weeping at this moment, or rather can weep no longer, he said to himself as he looked at her red eyes.... And he clasped her tight in his arms; the sight of genuine grief made him forget his syllogizing. She's possibly been crying all night, he said to himself, but how ashamed she will be one day to recall this memory! She will look on herself as a girl who was led astray, in early youth, by some low fellow's plebeian way of thinking.... That man Croisenois is weak enough to marry her, and upon my word, he'll do well. She will make him play a part,

> By virtue of the right
> A resolute spirit big with vast designs
> Holds o'er the duller minds of common men.

Really now, that's rather funny. Ever since I've been doomed to die all the lines I've ever known in my life are coming back to my mind. It must be a sign of mental decay....

Mathilde kept on saying to him in a faint voice: 'He's there, in the next room.' At length he began to pay attention to what she was saying. Her voice is weak, he thought, but all her imperious character still shows in its accents. She is lowering her voice so as not to lose her temper.

'Who is there?' he asked her gently.

'The lawyer, to get you to sign your appeal.'

'I shall not appeal.'

'What! You won't appeal?' she said raising her voice, her eyes ablaze with anger, 'and why not, if you please?'

'Because at this moment I feel that I have the courage to die without exciting undue derision. And who will assure me that in two months' time, after a long period of confinement in this damp cell, I shall be in an equally good frame of mind? I foresee interviews with priests, with my father.... I can imagine nothing in the world more disagreeable.... Let me die.'

This unlooked-for clash of opinions roused all the arrogant side of Mathilde's nature. She had not been able to see the Abbé de Frilair before the hour at which the cells in the Besançon jail were open to visitors; her rage rebounded on Julien's head. She adored him, yet, for the next quarter of an hour, he found once again in her violent abuse of his character, and her regrets that she had ever loved him, all that haughtiness of spirit which in the past had led her to heap scathing insults upon him in the library of the Hôtel de la Mole.

'Heaven owed it to the glory of your race,' he told her, 'to have let you be born a man.'

But as for me, he thought, I'd be an utter idiot to go on living for another two months, in this filthy place, the butt of all the infamous and humiliating reports that the patrician faction can devise against me, with this mad girl's curses for my only comfort.... All right then, the day after tomorrow I shall fight a duel with a man who is noted for his remarkable skill.... (Very remarkable, said his Mephistophelian counterpart, he never misses his stroke.)

Very well, that's settled, and a good thing, too. (Mathilde's eloquence was still flowing on.) No, good heavens, no, he said to himself, I will not appeal.

Having made this decision, he lapsed into dreaming once again. The postman on his rounds will bring the newspaper at six o'clock, as usual; at eight, after M. de Rênal has read it, Elisa, entering the room on tiptoe, will lay it down on her bed. Later, she will wake up; suddenly, as she reads, she will be troubled; her pretty hand will tremble; she will read till she comes to these words ... *At five minutes past ten he had ceased to live.*

She will shed hot tears, I know her; my attempt to murder her will have no weight, all will be forgotten, and the woman whose life I tried to take will be the only one who will weep sincerely for my death.

Ah ! this is a paradox ! he thought, and for the next quarter of an hour, during which Mathilde continued to make a scene, he thought only of Madame de Rênal. In spite of himself, and although frequently replying to what Mathilde said to him, he could not take his mind off the memory of that bedroom at Verrières. He saw the *Gazette de France* lying on the orange taffeta counterpane. He saw that snow-white hand clutching it convulsively; he saw Madame de Rênal weep. ... He followed the course of each tear down that charming face.

Mademoiselle de la Mole, having failed to get anything out of Julien, called the lawyer in. By a happy chance he was a former Captain of the Army in Italy, of 1796, when he had fought side by side with Manuel. For form's sake, he opposed the condemned man's decision. Julien, wishing to treat him with respect, explained all his reasons to him.

'I must admit, a man may think as you do,' M. Felix Vaneau (this was the lawyer's name) said to him in the end. 'But you have three clear days in which to appeal, and it is my duty to come back here each day. If, in the course of the next two months, a volcano opened beneath the prison, you would be saved. You may after all die of some disease,' he said, looking at Julien.

Julien shook his head. 'Thanks,' he said, 'you're a decent chap. I'll think it over.'

And when at last Mathilde went away with the lawyer, he had a far greater feeling of friendliness for the lawyer than for her.

CHAPTER 43 : *Old Love Renewed*

An hour later, when he was fast asleep, he was woken up by the feeling of tears dropping fast on his hand. Ah, it's Mathilde again, he thought to himself, half awake. She's coming, faithful to her promise, to attack my resolve with tender appeals to sentiment. Vexed at the prospect of a fresh scene in the pathetic manner, he did not open his eyes. The lines of Belphegor fleeing from his wife came into his head.

He heard a strange sigh; he opened his eyes – it was Madame de Rênal.

'Ah! So I see you again before my death. Is it an illusion?' he cried, flinging himself at her feet.

'But forgive me, madam,' he added immediately, coming to his senses, 'I am nothing but a murderer in your eyes.'

'Julien, I have come to implore you to appeal. I know you do not wish to. . . .' Her sobs choked her, she was unable to speak.

'Will you deign to forgive me?'

'If you want me to forgive you, dearest,' she said to him, rising and throwing herself into his arms, 'appeal at once against your death sentence.'

Julien covered her with kisses.

'Will you come and see me every day during the next two months?'

'I swear to you I will. Every day, unless my husband forbids it.'

'Then I'll sign!' cried Julien. 'What! you forgive me! Is it really possible?'

He clasped her in his arms; he was out of his mind. She uttered a faint cry.

'It's nothing,' she told him. 'You hurt me.'

'It's your shoulder,' cried Julien, bursting into tears. He drew back a little and covered her hand with burning kisses. 'Who would have foreseen this the last time I saw you, in your bedroom at Verrières?'

'Who would ever have said that I'd write that shameful letter to M. de la Mole?'

'Let me tell you that I have always loved you, that I have never loved anyone but you.'

'Is that really possible?' cried Madame de Rênal, in her turn overjoyed. She bent over Julien, who was on his knees before her, and for a long time they wept together in silence.

At no other time in his life had Julien experienced a moment like this.

After a long interval, when they were able to speak, Madame de Rênal said to him: 'And that young Madame Michelet, or rather Mademoiselle de la Mole – for I'm really beginning to believe this strangely romantic tale!'

'It's only true in appearance,' replied Julien. 'She is my wife, but she is not the mistress of my heart....'

And so, each interrupting the other a hundred times, they managed with much difficulty to tell each other of things they did not know. The letter written to M. de la Mole was the work of the young priest who guided Madame de Rênal's conscience, and had later been copied out by her. 'What a horrible action religion has made me commit!' she said to him, 'and even so I toned down the most frightful passages in the letter....'

Julien's rapturous joy proved to her how completely he forgave her. Never before had he been so madly in love.

'And yet I regard myself as religious,' said Madame de Rênal in the course of their conversation. 'I sincerely believe in God; I believe equally, and indeed it has been proved to me, that the sin I am committing is a dreadful one. Yet, the moment I see you, even after you have twice fired at me with your pistol....' Here, in spite of all she could do to stop him, Julien covered her with kisses.

'Let me alone,' she said. 'I want to talk seriously with you before I forget.... The moment I see you, all sense of duty vanishes, there's nothing left of me but love for you, or rather love is too weak a word. I feel for you what I should feel for God alone – respect, love, and obedience intermingled.... To tell the truth, I don't know what feelings you inspire in me.... If you asked me to stick a knife into your gaoler, the crime would be committed before I had had time to think. Explain this to me very precisely before I leave you, I want to see clearly into my own heart; for in two months' time we must say good-bye to each other.... But, by the way,' she said to him smiling, 'need we say good-bye?'

'I take back my word,' cried Julien springing to his feet. 'I will not appeal against sentence of death, if by poison, knife, pistol, charcoal, or any other means whatsoever, you attempt to put an end to your life or otherwise endanger it.'

Madame de Rênal's expression changed all at once; the keenest affection gave way to a look of pensive abstraction.

'If we were to die here and now?' she said at last.

'Who knows what we shall find in another life?' answered Julien. 'Torments perhaps, perhaps nothing at all. Why can't we spend two months in the most delightful way together? Two months, that's a good many days. I shall never have been so happy.'

'Never been so happy?'

'Never,' repeated Julien in raptures, 'and I'm speaking to you as I speak to myself. Heaven preserve me from exaggerating.'

'To speak in that way is to command me,' she said with a timid, melancholy smile.

'Very well! Then swear, on the love you bear for me, not to attempt your life by any means, direct or indirect. . . . Remember,' he added, 'that you have to live for the sake of my son, whom Mathilde will abandon to hirelings as soon as she becomes the Marquise de Croisenois.'

'I swear it,' she answered coldly, 'but I'm determined to take away with me your appeal written and signed by your own hand. I shall go myself to the District Attorney.'

'Take care, you will compromise yourself.'

'After the step I've taken in coming to see you in prison,' she said with an air of deep distress, 'I am for good and all, in Besançon and throughout Franche-Comté, the heroine of gossip-monger's tales. I have overstepped the bounds of strict modesty. . . . I am a woman who has forfeited her honour – it's true that it was for your sake. . . .'

There was such a note of sadness in her voice that Julien embraced her with a happiness quite new to him. It was no longer a frenzied ecstasy of love, it was the deepest gratitude. He had just realized, for the first time, the whole extent of the sacrifice she had made for him.

Some charitable soul no doubt informed M. de Rênal of the long visits which his wife was paying to Julien's prison; for at the end of three days he sent his carriage for her, with express orders for her to return at once to Verrières.

This cruel parting had been a bad beginning to the day for Julien. Two or three hours later, he was told that a certain designing priest, who had not, however, managed to impose himself upon the Jesuits in Besançon, had taken up his post that morning in the street, just outside the gate of the prison. It was raining hard, and the man was there, trying to pose as a martyr. Julien was little in the mood for such tomfoolery, it annoyed him extremely.

That morning he had already refused a visit from the priest, but the man had made up his mind to hear Julien's confession, and to make a name for himself among the young women of Besançon on the strength of all the confidences he would claim to have received.

This fellow kept on affirming at the top of his voice that he would remain a whole day and night at the prison gates. 'God has sent me to touch the heart of this second Apostate.' And the rabble, ever agog for a scene, were beginning to flock round him.

'Yes, my brethren,' he said to them. 'I shall spend the day here, and the night, and also every day and night that follows. The Holy Spirit has spoken to me. I have a mission from on high; I am the man appointed to save young Sorel's soul. Join your prayers with mine, etc. etc.'

Julien had a horror of scandal and of anything that might draw attention to himself. He pondered whether to seize the opportunity of slipping unnoticed out of the world; but he had still some hopes of seeing Madame de Rênal again, and he was desperately in love.

The prison gates faced on to one of the most frequented streets. The thought of this mud-bespattered priest attracting a crowd and creating a scandal was torture to his mind. And without a doubt every instant he's repeating my name! This moment was harder for him than death itself.

Two or three times, at intervals of an hour, he called one of the turnkeys who was devoted to him and sent him to see if the priest was still at the prison gates.

'He's on his two knees in the mud, sir,' the turnkey told him every time. 'He's praying at the top of his voice, and saying Litanies for your soul.' The impertinent rascal! thought Julien. At that moment, in fact, he heard a dull booming sound, it was the crowd reciting the responses in the Litany. As a last straw to his impatience, he saw the turnkey's own lips moving as he repeated the Latin phrases. 'People are beginning to say,' the turnkey added, 'that your heart must indeed be hardened to refuse this holy man's help.'

'O my country! In what a state of barbarism are you still!' cried Julien in a frenzy of rage. And he continued his reasoning aloud, without a thought of the turnkey's presence.

'The man wants an article in the paper, and now he's certain of obtaining it. Oh, these damned provincials! In Paris, I shouldn't have been subjected to all these vexations. Their kind of charlatanism is more subtle.

'Let this holy priest come in,' he said at last to the turnkey, while the sweat was pouring in torrents down his face. The turnkey crossed himself, and went out full of joy.

The holy priest turned out to be frightfully ugly, and even more frightfully befouled with mud. The cold rain that was falling increased the gloom and the dampness of his cell. The priest tried to embrace Julien and began to snivel pitifully as he spoke to him. This was plainly the most abject hypocrisy; Julien had never been so furious in his life.

A quarter of an hour after the priest's entry, Julien found himself an utter coward. For the first time death appeared horrible to him. He thought of the state of putrefaction in which his body would be two days after his execution, etc. etc.

He was on the point of betraying himself by some sign of weakness, or of flinging himself upon the priest and strangling him with his chain when he hit on the idea of begging the holy man to go and say a good forty-franc mass for him that very day. As it happened to be midday by then, the priest scurried off.

As soon as he had gone, Julien began to weep bitterly, and his tears were for his death. Gradually the thought came to him that if Madame de Rênal had been at Besançon, he would have confessed his weakness to her. . . .

At the very moment when he was most regretting the absence of this woman he adored, he heard Mathilde's step.

The worst evil of being in prison, he thought, is that one can never bar one's door. Everything that Mathilde said to him served only to irritate him.

She told him how, on the day of the trial, M. de Valenod, having his nomination as Prefect already in his pocket, had dared to snap his fingers at M. de Frilair and give himself the pleasure of condemning Julien to death.

' "What was your friend's idea," M. de Frilair was saying to me just now, "in arousing and attacking the petty vanity of that *middle-class aristocracy*? Why speak of *caste*? He pointed out to them what they ought to do in the interest of their own political party; these boobies hadn't given it a thought, and were quite prepared to shed tears. This interest of caste came in to blind their eyes to the horror of condemning a man to death. M. Sorel, you must admit, is very much of a novice in such matters. If we don't manage to save him by petitioning for his reprieve, his death will be a sort of *suicide* . . .".'

Mathilde could not tell Julien of something which she herself did not as yet suspect; namely, that M. de Frilair, seeing Julien's cause completely lost, thought it would serve his own ambitions if he aspired to become his successor.

Almost out of his mind with helpless rage and vexation, Julien said to Mathilde: 'Go and hear a mass on my behalf, and leave me a moment's peace.' Mathilde, who was already extremely jealous of Madame de Rênal's visits, and had just learnt of her departure, realized the cause of Julien's ill-temper and burst into tears.

Her grief was real and sincere; Julien saw this was so, and was only all the more irritated. He felt an urgent need of solitude, and how was he to secure it?

Finally, after trying every possible argument to soften him, Mathilde left him to himself; almost at the same moment Fouqué appeared.

'I really need to be alone,' he said to this faithful friend, and as he saw him hesitate, he added : 'I am composing a memorandum for my petition for reprieve ... and by the way ... if you want to please me, never speak to me of death. If I need any special services on that day, let me be the first to mention them to you.'

When Julien had at last secured solitude, he found himself more dejected and more of a coward than before. What little strength remained to his enfeebled spirit had been exhausted in the effort to conceal his state of mind from Mademoiselle de la Mole and from Fouqué.

Towards evening, one thought came to comfort him. If this morning, at the moment when death seemed so hideous, I had been warned to prepare myself for execution, *the eye of the public would have acted as a spur to my pride.* My bearing might perhaps have been a trifle pompous, like that of some bashful coxcomb on entering a drawing-room. A few clear-sighted people, if there be any such amongst these provincials, might have guessed my weakness ... *but no one would have seen it.*

And he felt himself relieved of a part of his unhappiness. I am a coward at this moment, he repeated to himself in a sing-song sort of way, but no one will know it.

An almost more disagreeable incident was in store for him the next morning. For a long time past, his father had been promising him a visit; that morning, before Julien was awake, the old white-haired carpenter appeared in his cell.

Julien felt utterly weak, he expected the most unpleasant reproaches. As a final touch to these painful sensations, he was feeling keen remorse that morning at not loving his father.

Chance has placed us close to each other on this earth, he said to himself as the turnkey was tidying up the cell a little, and we have done each other almost all the harm we could. He comes at the moment of my death to deal me the final blow.

The old man began his stern reproaches as soon as they were left without a witness. Julien could not hold back his tears. What shameful weakness ! he said to himself in a rage. He will go round everywhere exaggerating my lack of courage. What a triumph for the Valenods and all those dreary hypocrites who reign supreme in Verrières. They are very important people in France, they combine all the social advantages. Money falls into their hands, it's true, every honour is piled upon them, but I have a title of nobility in my heart.

And here is a witness whom everyone will believe, and who will assure the whole of Verrières, with a certain amount of exaggeration too, that I was weak in face of death! I shall seem to them to have shown myself a coward in a trial of courage well within everyone's grasp.

Julien was almost in despair. He did not know how to get rid of his father; and to find some subterfuge of a kind to deceive this very shrewd old man was, at this moment, altogether beyond his strength.

His mind ran rapidly over all the possibilities.

'I've some money put by!' he suddenly exclaimed.

This stroke of genius altered at once the look on the old man's face and Julien's own position.

'How ought I to dispose of it?' went on Julien, feeling calmer. The effect produced by his words had completely taken away his sense of inferiority.

The old carpenter was burning with a desire not to miss the chance of getting hold of this money, a part of which, so it seemed, Julien wanted to leave to his brothers. He spoke at great length and with some heat. Julien felt able to chaff him.

'Well now, the Lord has given me an inspiration about my will. I'll give a thousand francs to my brothers and the remainder to you.'

'That's very good,' said the old man, 'this remainder is my due. But since God in his mercy has touched your heart, if you wish to die like a good Christian, it's right you should pay your debts. There's still the cost of your keep and your schooling, which I advanced and which you haven't considered. . . .'

So that is a father's love! Julien repeated, in deep distress of heart, when at last he found himself alone. Soon the gaoler appeared.

'After a visit from the family, sir, I always bring my lodgers a bottle of good champagne. It's a little dear, six francs the bottle, but it cheers the heart.'

'Bring me three glasses,' said Julien, eager as a child, 'and get in two of the prisoners I hear walking in the corridor.'

The gaoler brought in two gaolbirds sentenced for some fresh crime, who were waiting to be sent back to the hulks. They were very jolly rogues and really quite remarkable for their cunning, courage, and coolness.

'If ye give me twenty francs,' said one of them to Julien, 'I'll tell ye the story of me life. It's a regular snorter.'

'But you'll tell me lies?' said Julien.

'Not on your life,' he answered. 'Me friend 'ere, oo's itchin' to 'ave me twenty francs, will tell on me if I don't give ye the truth.'

His story was revolting. It showed a brave heart in which there was only one passion – the greed of gold.

After they had gone, Julien was no longer the same man. All his anger against himself had vanished. The frightful grief, poisoned by cowardice, which had dug its fangs into him since the departure of Madame de Rênal, had turned to melancholy.

As I gradually became less and less fooled by appearances, he said to himself, I should have seen that Paris drawing-rooms are peopled with honest folk like my father, or clever rogues like these gaolbirds. They are right; these drawing-room fellows never get up of a morning with the poignant question in their minds : 'How shall I get my dinner?' And they boast of their probity ! And, when called to sit on a jury, they proudly condemn the man who has stolen a silver fork because he felt faint with hunger !

But when there's a Court, or when it's a question of securing or losing a ministerial portfolio, my honest drawing-room folk fall into crimes precisely the same as those the need for a meal has inspired in these two hardened offenders. . . .

There is no such thing as *natural law*; this term is merely an ancient piece of tommy-rot quite worthy of the Public Prosecutor who hunted me down the other day, and whose ancestor was enriched by property confiscated by Louis XIV. There is no *law*, save when some particular law exists forbidding a man to commit a certain act on pain of punishment. Before law comes into being, there is nothing *natural*, except a lion's strength, or the needs of the creature who suffers from hunger, from cold – in a word, from *want*. . . . No, the men whom people honour are only rogues who have had the good fortune not to be caught red-handed. The Prosecutor whom society sets on my track obtained his wealth by a shameful act. . . . I have attempted to take life, and I am justly condemned, but, apart from this single act, that man Valenod who condemned me is a hundred times more harmful to society.

And indeed, added Julien sadly, but without anger, for all his avarice, my father is worth more than any of those men. He has never loved me. I am now about to exceed all bounds by dishonouring him by my shameful death. That fear of being in want of money, that exaggerated view of the wickedness of human nature men call *avarice*, makes him see a prodigious source of consolation and security in the sum of three or four hundred louis I may leave him. On Sundays after dinner, he'll show his gold to all his envious neighbours in Verrières. 'Which of you,' his glance will say to them, 'would not, at this price, be delighted to have a son guillotined?'

This might be sound philosophy, but it was of a nature to make a man long for death. In this way, five long days passed by. He was polite and gentle to Mathilde, who was, as he saw, provoked by the most violent jealousy. One evening Julien thought seriously of taking his life. His spirit was unnerved by the deep dejection into which he had been cast by Madame de Rênal's departure. Nothing pleased him any more, either in real life or in the life of imagination. Lack of exercise was beginning to affect his health and to give him the weak and excitable character of a German student. He was losing that manly pride which rejects with a forcible oath certain unworthy ideas that assail the hearts of unhappy men.

I have loved truth . . . where can I find it? . . . Everywhere I see hypocrisy, or at least charlatanism, even among the most virtuous, even among the greatest men. His lips curled in disgust. No, man cannot place any trust in man.

Madame de —, when making a collection for her poor orphans, told me that such and such a Prince had just given her ten louis — a lie. But what am I saying? Napoleon at Saint-Helena ! . . . Pure charlatanism, a proclamation in favour of the King of Rome.

Good God ! If such a man, and still more at a time when misfortune should recall him sharply to a sense of duty, can stoop to charlatanism, what can one expect of the rest of his species?

Where lies Truth? . . . In religion? . . . Yes, he added, with the bitter smile of supreme contempt, in the mouths of the Maslons, the Frilairs, the Castanèdes. . . . Perhaps in true Christianity, whose priests are possibly paid no more than were the Apostles ! But Saint Paul was repaid by the pleasure of laying down the law, of holding forth, and of hearing people talk about him. . . .

Ah ! if there were a true religion. . . . Fool that I am ! I see a Gothic cathedral, stained glass windows centuries old. My fainting heart dreams of the priest who is pictured in those windows. . . . My soul would understand him, my soul has need of him. . . . I find only a conceited fool with greasy hair, a Chevalier de Beauvoisis, in fact, without his charm.

But a true priest, a Massillon, a Fénelon . . . Massillon made Dubois a bishop. The *Mémoires* of Saint-Simon have spoiled Fénelon for me. But a true priest, after all. . . . Then loving hearts would have some common meeting-place on earth. ... We should not be isolated. This good priest would speak to us of God. But what God? Not the God of the Bible, a petty despot, cruel and athirst for vengeance ... but Voltaire's God, just, kind, and infinite. ...

He was troubled by all his memories of that Bible which he knew by heart. ... But how, he thought, as soon as 'two or three are gathered together' can one believe in this great name of GOD, after the frightful abuse that our priests make of it?

To live in isolation. ... What torment!

I am becoming foolish and unjust, said Julien, beating his brow. I'm isolated here in this cell; but I haven't *lived in isolation* on this earth; I always had the compelling thought of *duty* with me. That duty, that, rightly or wrongly, I had prescribed for myself, has been like the solid trunk of a tree against which I could lean during the storm. I swayed to and fro, I was shaken. After all, I was only a man ... but I was not carried away.

It's the damp air of this cell that's making me think of isolation. ...

And why be a hypocrite still when cursing hypocrisy? It isn't death, nor the cell, nor the damp air, that's depressing me – it's the absence of Madame de Rênal. If I were at Verrières and were obliged, in order to see her, to live for whole weeks in hiding in the cellars of her house, should I complain?

The influence of my contemporaries is too strong for me, he said to himself aloud, laughing bitterly. Talking to myself all alone, with death two steps ahead, I'm still a hypocrite. ...

A hunter fires his gun in the forest, his quarry falls, he darts forward to seize it. His boot strikes an anthill two feet high, destroys the ants' dwelling-place, scatters the ants and their eggs far and wide. ... The most philosophical among the ants will never be able to understand that huge, black, fearful body – the hunter's boot – which all of a sudden has burst with incredible speed into their dwelling, preceded by a terrifying noise, accompanied by flashes of reddish fire. ...

So it is with life, death, and eternity, things that would be quite simple to anyone who had organs vast enough to comprehend them.

A mayfly is born at nine o'clock on the morning of a long summer day, to die at five that very afternoon – how should it understand the word *night*? Give it five more hours of life, it will see and understand what night means.

WHERE LIES TRUTH? 503

And so with me, I shall die at twenty-three. Give me five more years of life, to live with Madame de Rênal.

He began laughing like Mephistopheles. What folly to discuss these great problems!

Firstly, I am as much of a hypocrite as if there was someone there to hear me.

Secondly, I am forgetting to live and love, when I have so few days left to live. ... Alas! Madame de Rênal is absent from me; perhaps her husband will not allow her to return to Besançon any more, to disgrace herself still further.

That is what makes me isolated, and not the absence of a just, kind, and all-powerful God, who is neither malicious, nor greedy for vengeance. ...

Ah! if he existed. ... Alas! I would fall at his feet. I have deserved death, I would say to him, but great God, kind God, indulgent God, give me back the woman I love!

The night was by then far advanced. After an hour or two of peaceful sleep, Fouqué arrived.

Julien felt strong and resolute as a man who sees clearly into his own heart.

'I REALLY cannot play such a shabby trick on poor Father Chas-Bernard as to send for him,' he said to Fouqué, 'he wouldn't be able to eat his dinner for three days after. But try to find me some Jansenist, a friend of M. Pirard and proof against intrigue.'

Fouqué had been waiting impatiently for this opening. Julien discharged with fitting decorum all that is due to public opinion in the provinces. Thanks to the Abbé de Frilair, and in spite of his unfortunate choice of a confessor, Julien, in his cell, was under the protection of the Jesuits; if he had handled things better, he might have made his escape. But, as the bad air of the cell produced its effect, his powers of reasoning grew less. He was only all the happier for Madame de Rênal's return.

'My first duty is to you,' she said as she embraced him. 'I've run away from Verrières.'

There was no trace of petty vanity in Julien's feelings towards her, he told her of all his moments of weakness. She was kind and charming to him.

That evening, the moment she left the prison, she sent for the priest who had attached himself to Julien as to a prey to come to her aunt's house. As he wished only to win the good opinion of the young women belonging to the best society in Besançon, Madame de Rênal easily persuaded him to go and perform a novena at the abbey of Bray-le-Haut.

No words could express the wild extravagance of Julien's love.

By a liberal use of money, and by using and abusing what influence her aunt, a lady well known for her piety and her riches, possessed in the right quarter, Madame de Rênal obtained permission to see him twice a day.

On hearing this, Mathilde's jealousy was roused to frenzy. M. de Frilair had admitted to her that his prestige was not great enough for him to defy all convention so far as to get her permission to see her friend more than once a day. Mathilde had Madame de Rênal followed so as to be kept informed of the least step she took. M. de Frilair exhausted all the resources of an extremely cunning mind in trying to prove to her that Julien was unworthy of her. In the midst of all these torments, she only loved him all the more, and, almost every day, subjected him to a frightful scene.

Julien wished at all costs to behave to the very end as an honourable man towards this poor girl whom he had compromised so terribly; but, at every moment, the unbridled passion he felt for Madame de Rênal proved too strong for him. – When, because of the flimsiness of his arguments, he failed to convince Mathilde of the innocence of her rival's visits, he said to himself : At this moment, the end of the drama is inevitably very near; that gives me some excuse if I can't put up a better pretence.

Mademoiselle de la Mole had news of the death of the Marquis de Croisenois. The plutocratic M. de Thaler had ventured to make some unpleasant remarks about Mathilde's disappearance. M. de Croisenois called on him to request him to withdraw them. M. de Thaler produced some anonymous letters addressed to him, full of details so artfully placed side by side that it was impossible for the poor Marquis not to guess the truth.

M. de Thaler took the liberty of making some rather crude jokes. Mad with rage and grief, M. de Croisenois demanded such drastic apologies that the millionaire preferred a duel. Folly triumphed; and one of the men most worthy of a woman's love met his death while not yet twenty-four. This death made a strange, unhealthy impression on Julien in his weak state of mind.

'Poor Croisenois,' he said to Mathilde, 'really behaved very reasonably and honourably towards us. He might very well have hated me after your indiscreet behaviour in your mother's drawing-room, and have picked a quarrel with me; for the hatred that follows on contempt is usually very passionate.'

The death of M. de Croisenois altered all Julien's plans for Mathilde's future. He spent several days trying to prove to her that she ought to marry M. de Luz. 'He's a shy sort of fellow,' he told her, 'not too much of a Jesuit, and will no doubt put himself forward as a candidate for your hand. With less spectacular and more stable ambitions than poor Croisenois, he will make no difficulty about marrying Julien Sorel's widow.'

'And a widow,' Mathilde answered coldly, 'who has a contempt for grand passions; for she has lived long enough to see her lover, at the end of six months, prefer another woman, and one who is the origin of all their misfortunes.'

'You're being unjust. Madame de Rênal's visits will provide the barrister from Paris, who is undertaking my appeal, with some striking things to say. He will paint a picture of the murderer honoured by the kind attentions of his victim. That may create an impression, and one day, perhaps, you will see me the hero of some melodrama,' etc. etc.

Furious jealousy without prospect of vengeance, hopeless

sorrow endlessly prolonged (for even supposing Julien were saved, how could she manage to win back his heart?), the shame and grief of loving this faithless lover more than ever, had combined to force Mathilde into a sullen silence from which neither M. de Frilair's assiduous attentions, nor even Fouqué's honest bluntness of speech, could rouse her.

As for Julien, save in the moments stolen from him by Mathilde's presence, he was living upon love and with scarcely a thought of the future. As a curious result of this passion, when it is absolute and unfeigned, Madame de Rênal almost shared his light-hearted indifference and his playful gaiety.

'In the past,' Julien said to her, 'when I might have been so happy during our walks in the woods of Vergy, my fiery ambition carried my mind away into imaginary countries. Instead of clasping to my heart this lovely arm which was so close to my lips, I let the future bear me away from you. I was deep in the countless battles I should have to fight to carve for myself a glorious career.... No, I should have died without knowing what happiness meant, if you had not come to see me in this prison.'

Two incidents occurred to disturb this peaceful existence. Julien's confessor, for all that he was a Jansenist, was not proof against a Jesuit intrigue, and quite unconsciously became their tool.

He came one day to tell Julien that if he were not to fall into the dreadful sin of suicide, he must take every possible step to obtain his reprieve. Now, since the clergy had great influence with the Ministry of Justice in Paris, an easy way was offered to him – he must declare his conversion in a way to catch the public eye.

'To catch the public eye!' Julien repeated. 'Ah, I see your game – you, too, Father, trotting out the same old tricks as a missioner!'

'Your youth,' the Jansenist continued gravely, 'the attractive face with which Providence has endowed you, the motive itself of your crime, which remains a mystery, the heroic efforts Mademoiselle de la Mole has not spared on your behalf – everything, in short, including the amazing friendship your victim shows for you, have all combined to make you the hero of the young women of Bensançon. They have forgotten everything for you – even politics.

'Your conversion would find an echo in their hearts and would leave a deep impression there. You can be of the greatest service, to religion, and should I hesitate for the trivial reason that the

Jesuits would adopt the same course on a similar occasion! Thus, even in this particular case which escapes their clutches, they would still be doing harm! Don't let this be the case . . . the tears your conversion will cause to flow will undo the poisonous effect of ten editions of Voltaire.'

'And what shall I have left,' Julien answered coldly, 'if I despise myself? I have been ambitious, I am not going to blame myself for that; I acted then in accordance with the demands of the time. Now I live for the day, without thought of the morrow. But, as far as I can see, I should be making myself extremely unhappy if I allowed myself to slide into any act of cowardice. . . .'

The other incident, which affected Julien far more keenly, was connnected with Madame de Rênal. Some scheming friend or other had managed to persuade this timid, artless creature that it was her duty to go to Saint-Cloud and throw herself at the feet of King Charles X.

She had made the sacrifice of parting from Julien, and after such an effort, the unpleasantness of making a public spectacle of herself, which would formerly have seemed to her a worse evil than death, was no longer anything in her eyes.

'I'll go to the King, I'll openly confess that you are my lover; the life of a man, and of such a man as Julien, must override all other considerations. I shall say it was out of jealousy that you attempted my life. There are numberless instances of unfortunate young men who have been saved in such cases by the humanity of a jury or of the King.'

'I shall stop seeing you,' cried Julien, 'I shall have my prison door barred against you, and certainly kill myself in despair the day after, unless you swear to me not to take any step that will make a public spectacle of us both. This idea of going to Paris isn't your own. Tell me the name of that scheming woman who suggested it to you. . . .

'Do let us be happy for the very few days left of this short life. Let's keep our very existence hidden; my crime is only too conspicuous. Mademoiselle de la Mole has every influence in Paris, just try to believe she's doing all that's humanly possible. Here in the provinces I have all the rich and influential people against me. Your action would still further embitter these wealthy men who set discretion above everything and for whom life is such an easy matter. . . . Don't let's give any cause for laughter to the Maslons, the Valenods, and a host of other men more worthy than they are.'

Julien was beginning to find the foul air in his cell unbearable. Fortunately, on the day on which he was told he had to die, bright sunlight was making all nature gay, and he himself was in a mood for courage. To step out into the open air was a delightful sensation for him, as treading on dry land is for the sailor who has been long at sea. There now, he said to himself, everything is going well. ... My courage isn't failing me.

Never had that head such poetic beauty as at the moment when it was about to fall. The sweetest moments he had known in the past in the woods of Vergy came thronging back into his mind with the most eager insistence.

Everything passed off simply and decently, with no trace of affectation on his part.

Two days before, he had said to Fouqué: 'As to what my feelings will be, I cannot answer for them. This very damp, ugly cell brings on short bouts of fever in which I am not myself. But as for fear, no; not a soul shall see my cheeks grow pale.'

He had made arrangements in advance for Fouqué to carry off Mathilde and Madame de Rênal on the morning of his last day. 'Take them away with you in the same carriage,' he had told him. 'Arrange to keep the post-horses continually at the gallop. Either they'll fall into each other's arms, or express a deadly hatred for each other. In either case the poor women will have their minds slightly taken off their terrible grief.'

Julien had extracted a solemn promise from Madame de Rênal that *she* would live to watch over Mathilde's child.

'Who knows?' he said one day to Fouqué. 'Perhaps we still have sensations after our death. I should rather like to rest, since rest is the right word, in that little cave up on the high mountain overlooking Verrières. Many a time, as I've told you, after retiring for the night into this cave, and gazing into the distance over the richest provinces of France, I have felt my heart on fire with ambition: that was my passion then. ... In short, that cave is dear to me, and no one can deny that its situation is such as a philosopher's soul might envy. ... Well now, these worthy Jesuits in Besançon make money out of everything. If you know how to set about it, they'll sell you my mortal remains. ...'

Fouqué was successful in this sad bargain. He was spending the night alone in his room, beside the body of his friend, when, to his great surprise, he saw Mathilde appear. A few hours earlier he had left her ten leagues from Besançon. Her face was wild, her eyes distraught.

'I want to see him,' she said.

Fouqué had not the courage either to speak or to rise from his chair. He pointed with his finger to a great blue cloak on the floor; in it was wrapped all that remained of Julien.

She flung herself on her knees. The memory of Boniface de la Mole and of Marguerite de Navarre doubtless gave her super-human courage. With trembling hands she drew aside the cloak. Fouqué turned his eyes away.

He heard Mathilde walking hurriedly about the room. She was lighting a number of candles. When Fouqué had summoned up enough strength to look at her, she had placed Julien's head in front of her on a little marble table and was kissing his fore-head. . . .

Mathilde followed her lover to the tomb he had chosen for him-self. A great number of priests escorted the bier, and sitting all alone in her carriage draped in black, she bore on her knees, un-known to everyone, the head of the man she had loved so dearly.

Coming thus near to the highest point of one of the lofty moun-tains of the Jura, in the middle of the night, inside that little cave magnificently illuminated with countless candles, a score of priests celebrated the Office for the Dead. All the inhabitants of the little mountain villages through which the procession had passed had followed after, drawn by the extraordinary character of this strange ceremony.

Mathilde appeared in their midst in mourning garments that fell to her feet, and at the close of the service had several thou-sands of francs scattered amongst them.

Left alone with Fouqué, she insisted on burying her lover's head with her own hands. Fouqué went nearly mad with grief.

Mathilde's loving care had this rude cave adorned with marbles sculptured at great cost in Italy.

Madame de Rênal was faithful to her promise. She did not attempt in any way to take her own life; but, three days after Julien's death, she gave her children a last embrace, and died.

MORE ABOUT PENGUINS, PELICANS
AND PUFFINS

For further information about books available from Penguins please write to Dept EP, Penguin Books Ltd, Harmondsworth, Middlesex UB7 ODA.

In the U.S.A.: For a complete list of books available from Penguins in the United States write to Dept DG, Penguin Books, 299 Murray Hill Parkway, East Rutherford, New Jersey 07073.

In Canada: For a complete list of books available from Penguins in Canada write to Penguin Books Canada Ltd, 2801 John Street, Markham, Ontario L3R 1B4.

In Australia: For a complete list of books available from Penguins in Australia write to the Marketing Department, Penguin Books Australia Ltd, P.O. Box 257, Ringwood, Victoria 3134.

In New Zealand: For a complete list of books available from Penguins in New Zealand write to the Marketing Department, Penguin Books (N.Z.) Ltd, P.O. Box 4019, Auckland 10.

In India: For a complete list of books available from Penguins in India write to Penguin Overseas Ltd, 706 Eros Apartments, 56 Nehru Place, New Delhi 110019.